The
Gates to
Witch World

The Gates to Witch World

∞

Comprising
Witch World, Web of the Witch World,
and *Year of the Unicorn*

ANDRE NORTON

With an Introduction by C. J. Cherryh

TOR®

A Tom Doherty Associates Book
New York

THE GATES TO WITCH WORLD
Omnibus Copyright © 2001 by Andre Norton, LTD.

WITCH WORLD
Copyright © 1963 by Andre Norton

WEB OF THE WITCH WORLD
Copyright © 1964 by Andre Norton

YEAR OF THE UNICORN
Copyright © 1965 by Andre Norton

INTRODUCTION
Copyright © 2001 by C. J. Cherryh

Edited by James Frenkel

Design by Jane Adele Regina

Map of the Witch World by Jack Gaughan

A Tor Book
Published by Tom Doherty Associates, LLC
175 Fifth Avenue
New York, NY 10010

www.tor.com

Tor® is a registered trademark of Tom Doherty Associates, LLC.

Library of Congress Cataloging-in-Publication Data

Norton, Andre.
       The gates to the witch world / Andre Norton.—1st ed.
         p. cm.
       "A Tom Doherty Associates book."
       Contents: Witch world—Web of the witch world—Year of the unicorn.
       ISBN 0-765-30050-8
       1. Witch World (Imaginary place)—Fiction.   2. Fantasy fiction,
   American.   I. Title.

   PS3527.O632 A6 2001
   813'.52—dc21

                                                              2001041532

First Edition: December 2001

Printed in the United States of America

0   9   8   7   6   5   4   3   2   1

Contents

INTRODUCTION:
Andre Norton's Witch World

Once not so long ago, a handful of men and women wrote for a handful of magazines, the only magazines that would buy imaginative fiction. Understand, in that decade, personal defeatism and antiromance defined intellectual respectability among the literati. Those that bucked the tide were labeled pulp writers, genre writers, writers who might appeal only to unsophisticates and disaffected children. The machine age, they said, had killed romance. There were no new frontiers. There never, ever would be frontiers again.

Some writers didn't buy that bill of goods. These few writers wrote what they believed, wrote their optimism and laid out their view of a wider universe for anyone with the same views.

They could have gotten far richer in any other field.

They could have become literarily respectable.

They had two things on their side: integrity and a universe-view that reached backward and forward and sideways through time and space. And they knew they were right. The science they gathered out of small pulp magazines and the history everyone else thought was cut and dried was about to expand in all directions.

They defined what they wrote as science fiction—not fantasy, mind, since genres are really more about marketing than about reality, and the marketing department hadn't figured out there might be a viable distinction between the two.

Certainly the writers involved didn't see any hard and fast line they ought to be observing, and there were no few crossovers of type. Readers knew "the good stuff" when they found it and didn't quibble about what genre they read.

Book publishers that began to bring out "the good stuff" didn't make any distinction, either. The main marketing trick was to get "planet" or "star" somewhere into the title to cue the searching book-buyer that, yes, this book was one of that sort, and to get some sort of spaceship or extraordinary menace on the cover—a cover which, as like as not, bore only casual relationship to the content.

So a handful of brave writers and a dedicated readership kept "the good stuff" alive, and crossed lines between what was and what might be with no particular rule that said sf and fantasy couldn't mix. They were freethinkers, experimenters, people who'd kicked over one set of barriers and who were too busy writing to worry about defining themselves or what they did. Andre Norton wasn't one of the very first, but she was in the game way early.

And she's one of the longest practicing writers in the field, fortunately for us.

That period before there were rules gave us the usual mix of good and bad, and occasionally, by virtue of what the field was, gave us something truly wonderful.

I wasn't there, understand. But books cross time and space, and I read. I read everything I could get my hands on, and despite the best efforts of my local library to protect a young girl from "that stuff," I found it. I was entranced. Certain books I checked out so often the library had to install new slips. The supply of more such books was limited, but I read and reread and re-reread, oh, twenty and thirty times.

I hadn't yet met the Witchworld books. But I was on my way.

And meanwhile the real world, the world of stars and planets and science, was still going on, and more and more people were waking up to a conviction that the future mattered and that the past itself wasn't fixed and stable.

At the right time, and just when I needed them, I found these wonderful books. I was enthralled. I'd come a long way from my early convictions. I'd gotten involved in study, and gotten so wrapped up in data I'd forgotten to look around me—a mistake, you'll find, when you're dealing with Andre Norton's books. You begin in such an ordinary way, and then things begin to slip sideways on you.

Change happens. And the world shifts, not improbably, but inexorably. Andre Norton has a simple, elegant way of carrying a reader into a world; and of making that world so credible it seems it has to exist.

She has a rare gift, besides. She tells true stories. It doesn't matter that her worlds can't be located in any particular atlas. What does matter, what's always true in her stories, is her people. And the things you share with them— those are true. You become acquainted with the most remarkable individuals, like old friends that go on talking to you across a lifetime of distances and separations. You know what your own uncle Harry would say. You can hear him saying it. It's the same way with Andre Norton's characters.

And mind, the worlds themselves widen your way of thinking. Andre Norton still doesn't draw hard and fast lines between classifications. She has a spare, elegant style that builds worlds, describes aliens, describes personalities, and defines interactions so true to life a reader gets swept along in her reality faster than the reader realizes can happen.

Is the Witch World science fiction or fantasy? It's both, in that magical/ scientific way that still works in the hands of a master of the first order. A scientist says, thoughtfully, well, maybe . . . and wonders what sort of math underlies her shifts in time and space. And readers that appreciate myth and magic sit back in astonishment, because the Witch World has that true, deep gloss of legend. The rules are ours, but not ours, and the world, though not our world, is a place solid and real, populated by people of old-fashioned nobility and very credible threat.

It was years and years before I had the pleasure of a personal meeting with Andre Norton, bringing her an award she'd won, quite justly so. I had a few books to my credit. I was feeling pretty happy with my career. I looked up at her library and saw an absolutely amazing expanse of books with her name on the spine. So much for any new writer's claim to immortality. Her creative output includes titles among the most famous in the history of science fiction and fantasy—books absolutely seminal to the field.

And generation after generation has come into a field shaped and defined by those books.

Those of us who come into the field by certain portals have things in common: we know a certain route toward wonder. We have books to rec- ommend to each other. Books to buy for nieces and nephews. Books distinguished by good writing and solid story that are absolutely accessible for the newcomer to the field and productive of that "good-stuff" feeling for the old hands.

If you're replacing your tattered, often-read copies of the Witchworld books, I don't have to tell you a thing more than that.

If you read the Witch World ages ago and have somehow strayed away from that marvelous sense of wonder—read them again. Some books of your youth may not be as good as you remember—but in this case, classic means what classic ought to mean. The Witch World just gets better and better with rereading. It's so far ahead of the science of the age that it still works its magic.

And if you've never met the Witch World before, and it's all new to you, you have it all to find. Norton's much copied, much imitated, but you have the absolute original in your hands. Enjoy!

—C. J. Cherryh

Witch World

Contents

1. Venture of Sulcarkeep

$$\infty$$

I
Siege Perilous

T he rain was a slantwise curtain across the dingy street, washing soot from city walls, the taste of it metallic on the lips of the tall, thin man who walked with a loping stride close to the buildings, watching the mouths of doorways, the gaps of alleys with a narrow-eyed intentness.

Simon Tregarth had left the railroad station two—or was it three hours ago? He had no reason to mark the passing of time any longer. It had ceased to have any meaning, and he had no destination. As the hunted, the runner, the hider—no, he was not in hiding. He walked in the open, alert, ready, his shoulders as straight, his head as erect as ever.

In those first frantic days when he had retained a wisp of hope, when he had used every scrap of animal cunning, every trick and dodge he had learned, when he had twisted and back-trailed, and befogged his tracks, then he had been governed by hours and minutes, he had run. Now he walked, and he would continue to walk until the death lurking in one of those doorways, in ambush in some alley would confront him. And even then he would go down using his fangs. His right hand, thrust deep into the soggy pocket of his top coat, caressed those fangs—smooth, sleek, deadly, a weapon which fitted as neatly into his palm as if it were a part of his finely trained body.

Tawdry red-and-yellow neon lights made wavering patterns across the water-slick pavement; his acquaintance with this town was centered about a hotel or two located at its center section, a handful of restaurants, some stores, all that a casual traveler learned in two visits half a dozen years apart. And he was driven by the urge to remain in the open, for he was convinced that the end to the chase would come that night or early tomorrow.

Simon realized that he was tiring. No sleep, the need for constant sentry go. He slackened pace before a lighted doorway, read the legend on the rain-limp awning above it. A doorman swung open the inner portal and the man in the rain accepted that tacit invitation, stepping into warmth and the fragrance of food.

The bad weather must have discouraged patrons. Maybe that was why the headwaiter welcomed him so quickly. Or perhaps the cut of the still present-able suit protected from the damp by the coat he shed, his faint but unmistak-able natural arrogance—the mark left upon a man who has commanded his kind and been readily obeyed—insured for him the well-placed table and the speedily attentive waiter.

Simon grinned wryly as his eye sped down the lines of the menu, and there was a ghost of true humor in that grin. The condemned man would eat a hearty meal anyway. His reflection, distorted by the curving side of the polished sugar bowl, smiled back at him. A long face, fine-drawn, with lines at the corners of the eyes, and deeper-set brackets at the lips, a brown face, well weathered, but in its way an ageless face. It had looked much the same at twenty-five, it would continue to look so at sixty.

Tregarth ate slowly, savoring each bite, letting the comforting warmth of the room, of the carefully chosen wine, relax his body if not mind and nerves. But that relaxation nurtured no false courage. This was *the* end, he knew it—had come to accept it.

"Pardon . . ."

The fork he had raised with its thick bite of steak impaled did not pause before his lips. But in spite of Simon's iron control a muscle twitched in his lower eyelid. He chewed, and then he answered, his voice even.

"Yes?"

The man standing politely at his table might be a broker, a corporation lawyer, a doctor. He had a professional air designed to inspire confidence in his fellows. But he was not what Simon had expected at all, he was too respectable, too polite and correct to be—death! Though the organization had many servants in widely separated fields.

"Colonel Simon Tregarth, I believe?"

Simon broke a muffin apart and buttered it. "Simon Tregarth, but not 'Colonel,' " he corrected, and then added with a counterthrust on his own, "As you well know."

The other seemed a little surprised, and then he smiled, that smooth, soothing, professional smile.

"How maladroit of me, Tregarth. But let me say at once—I am not a member of the organization. I am, instead—if you wish it, of course—a friend of yours. Permit me to introduce myself. I am Dr. Jorge Petronius. Very much at your service, may I add."

Simon blinked. He had thought the scrap of future remaining to him well accounted for, but he had not reckoned on this meeting. For the first time in bitter days he felt, far inside him, the stir of something remotely akin to hope.

It did not occur to him to doubt the identification offered by this small man watching him narrowly now through the curiously thick lenses, supported by such heavy and broad black plastic frames that Petronius appeared to wear the half-mask of eighteenth-century disguise. Dr. Jorge Petronius was very well known throughout that half-world where Tregarth had lived for several violent years. If you were "hot" and you were also lucky enough to be in funds you went to Petronius. Those who did were never found thereafter, either by the law, or the vengeance of their fellows.

"Sammy is in town," that precise, slightly accented voice continued.

Simon sipped appreciatively at his wine. "Sammy?" he matched the other's detachment. "I am flattered."

"Oh, you have something of a reputation, Tregarth. For you the organization unleashed their best hounds. But after the efficient way you dealt with Kotchev and Lampson, there remained only Sammy. However, he is slightly different metal from the others. And you have, if you will forgive my prying into your personal affairs, been on the run for some time. A situation which does not exactly strengthen the sword arm."

Simon laughed. He was enjoying this, the good food and drink, even the sly needling of Dr. Jorge Petronius. But he did not lower his guard.

"So, my sword arm needs strengthening? Well, Doctor, what do you suggest as the remedy?"

"There is—my own."

Simon put down his wineglass. A red drop trickled down its side to be absorbed by the cloth.

"I have been told your services come high, Petronius."

The small man shrugged. "Naturally. But in return I can promise complete escape. Those who trust me receive the worth of their dollars. I have had no complaints."

"Unfortunately I am not one who can afford your services."

"Your recent activities having so eaten into your cash reserve? But, of course. However, you left San Pedro with twenty thousand. You could not have completely exhausted such a sum in this short interval. And if you meet Sammy what remains shall only be returned to Hanson."

Simon's lips tightened. For an instant he looked as dangerous as he was, as Sammy would see him if they had a fair, face-to-face meeting.

"Why hunt me up—and how?" he asked.

"Why?" Again Petronius shrugged. "That you shall understand later. I am, in my way, a scientist, an explorer, an experimenter. As for how I knew you were in town and in need of my service—Tregarth, you should be aware by now how rumor spreads. You are a marked man and a dangerous one. Your coming and going is noted. It is a pity for your sake that you are honest."

Simon's right hand balled into a fist. "After my activities of the past seven years you apply that label to me?"

It was Petronius who laughed now, a small chuckle, inviting the other to enjoy the humor of the situation. "But honesty sometimes has very little to do with the pronouncements of the law, Tregarth. If you had not been an essentially honest man—as well as one with ideals—you would never have stood up to Hanson. It is because you are what you are that I know you are ripe for me. Shall we go?"

Somehow Simon found himself paying his check, following Dr. Jorge Petronius. A car waited at the curb, but the doctor did not address its driver as the machine carried them into the night and the rain.

"Simon Tregarth." Petronius' voice was as impersonal now as if he recited data important only to himself. "Of Cornish descent. Enlisted in the U.S. Army on March tenth, 1939. Promoted on the field from sergeant to lieutenant, and climbed to rank of lieutenant colonel. Served in the occupation forces until stripped of his commission and imprisoned for—for what, Colonel? Ah, yes, for flagrant black market dealing. Only, most unfortunately the brave colonel did not know he had been drawn into a criminal deal until too late. That was the point, was it not, Tregarth, which put you on the other side of the law? Since you had been given the name you thought you might as well play the game.

"Since Berlin you have been busy in quite a few dubious exploits, until you were unwise enough to cross Hanson. Another affair into which you were pushed unknowingly? You seem to be an unlucky man, Tregarth. Let us hope that your fortunes change tonight."

"Where are we going—to the docks?"

Again he heard that rich chuckle. "We head downtown, but not to the harbor. My clients travel, but not by sea, air, or land. How much do you know of the traditions of your fatherland, Colonel?"

"Matacham, Pennsylvania, has no traditions I ever heard of—"

"I am not concerned with a crude mining town on this continent. I am speaking of Cornwall, which is older than time—our time."

"My grandparents were Cornish. But I don't know any more than that."

"Your family was of the pure blood, and Cornwall is old, so very old. It is associated with Wales in legends. Arthur was known there, and the Romans of Britain huddled within its borders when the axes of the Saxons swept them to limbo. Before the Romans there were others, many, many others, some of them bearing with them scraps of strange knowledge. You are going to make me very happy, Tregarth." There was a pause as if inviting comment; when Simon did not answer, the other continued.

"I am about to introduce you to one of your native traditions, Colonel. A most interesting experiment. Ah, here we are!"

The car had stopped before the mouth of a dark alley. Petronius opened the door.

"You now behold the single drawback of my establishment, Tregarth. This lane is too narrow to accommodate the car; we must walk."

For a moment Simon stared up the black mouth, wondering if the doctor had brought him to some appointed slaughterhouse. Did Sammy wait here? But Petronius had snapped on a torch and was waving its beam ahead in invitation.

"Only a yard or two, I assure you. Just follow me."

The alley was indeed a short one and they came out into an empty space between towering buildings. Squatting in a hollow ringed about by these giants was a small house.

"You see here an anachronism, Tregarth." The doctor set a key in the door lock. "This is a late seventeenth-century farmhouse in the heart of a twentieth-century city. Because its title is in doubt, it exists, a very substantial ghost of the past to haunt the present. Enter, please."

Later, as he steamed in front of an open fire, a mixture his host had pressed upon him in his hand, Simon thought that Petronius' description of a ghost house was very apt. It needed only a steeple-crowned hat for the doctor's head, a sword at his own side, to complete the illusion that he had stepped from one era into another.

"Where do I go from here?" he asked.

Petronius prodded the fire with a poker. "You shall go at dawn, Colonel, free and clear, as I promise. As to where," he smiled, "that we shall see."

"Why wait until dawn?"

As if being forced into telling more than he wished, Petronius put down the poker and wiped his hands on a handkerchief before he faced his client squarely.

"Because only at dawn does your door open—the proper one for you. This is a story at which you may scoff, Tregarth, until you see the proof before your eyes. What do you know of menhirs?"

Simon felt absurdly pleased that he could supply an answer the other obviously did not expect.

"They were stones—set in circles by prehistoric men—Stonehenge."

"Set up in circles, sometimes. But they had other uses also." Petronius was all unsuppressed eagerness now, begging for serious attention from his listener. "There were certain stones of great power mentioned in the old legends. The Lia Fail of the Tuatha De Danann of Ireland. When the rightful king trod upon it, it shouted aloud in his honor. It was the coronation stone of that race, one of their three great treasures. And do not the kings of England to this day still cherish the Stone of Scone beneath their throne?

"But in Cornwall there was another stone of power—the Siege Perilous. It was one rumored to be able to judge a man, determine his worth, and then deliver him to his fate. Arthur was supposed to have discovered its power through the Seer Merlin and incorporated it among the seats of the Round Table. Six of his knights tried it—and disappeared. Then came two who knew its secret and stayed: Percival and Galahad."

"Look here." Simon was bitterly disappointed, the more so because he had almost dared to hope again. Petronius was cracked, there was no escape after all. "Arthur and the Round Table—that's a fairy tale for kids. You're talking as if—"

"As if it were true history?" Petronius caught him up. "Ah, but who is to say what is history and what is not? Every word of the past which comes to us is colored and influenced by the learning, the prejudices, even the physical condition of the historian who has recorded it for later generations. Tradition fathers history and what is tradition but word of mouth? How distorted may such accounts become in a single generation? You yourself had your entire life changed by perjured testimony. Yet that testimony has been inserted in records, has now become history, untrue as it is. How can anyone say that this story is legend but that one a fact, and know that he is correct? History is made, is recorded by human beings, and it is larded with all the errors our species is subject to. There are scraps of truth in legend and many lies in accepted history. I know—for the Siege Perilous does exist!

"There are also theories of history alien to the conventional ones we learn as children. Have you ever heard of the alternate worlds which may stem from momentous decisions? In one of those worlds, Colonel Tregarth, perhaps you did not turn aside your eyes on that night in Berlin. In another you did not meet with me an hour ago, but went on to keep your rendezvous with Sammy!"

The doctor rocked back and forth on his heels, as if set teetering by the force of his words and belief. And in spite of himself Simon caught a bit of that fiery enthusiasm.

"Which of these theories do you intend to apply to my problem?"

Petronius laughed, once again at ease. "Just have the patience to hear me out without believing that you are listening to a madman, and I shall explain." He glanced from the watch on his wrist to the wall clock behind him. "We have some hours yet. So, it is like this—"

As the little man began mouthing what sounded like wild nonsense, Simon obediently listened. The warmth, the drink, the chance to rest were payment enough. He might have to leave to face Sammy later, but that chance he pushed to the back of his mind as he concentrated on what Petronius was saying.

The mellow chime of the ancient clock struck the hour three times before the doctor was done. Tregarth sighed, perhaps he had only been battered into submission by that flood of words, but if it *were* true—And there was Petronius' reputation. Simon unbuttoned his shirt and drew out his money belt.

"I know that Sacarsi and Wolverstein haven't been heard of since they contacted you," he conceded.

"No, for they went through their doors; they found the worlds they had always unconsciously sought. It is as I have told you. One takes his seat upon

the Siege and before him opens that existence in which his spirit, his mind—
his soul if you wish to call it that—is at home. And he goes forth to seek his
fortune there."

"Why haven't you tried it yourself?" That was to Simon the weak point in
the other's story. If Petronius possessed the key to such a door, why had he
not used it himself?

"Why?" The doctor stared down at the two plump hands resting on his
knees. "Because there is no return—and only a desperate man chooses an
irrevocable future. In this world we always cling to the belief that we can
control our lives, make our own decisions. But through there, we have made
a choice which cannot be canceled. I use words, many words, but at this
moment I cannot seem to choose them rightly to express what I feel. There
have been many Guardians of the Siege—only a few of them have used it for
themselves. Perhaps . . . someday . . . but as yet I have not the courage."

"So you sell your services to the hunted? Well, that is one way of making
a living. A list of your clients might make interesting reading."

"Correct! I have had some very famous men apply for assistance. Especially
at the close of the war. You might not believe the identity of some who sought
me out then, after fortune's wheel spun against them."

Simon nodded. "There *were* some notable gaps in the war criminal cap-
tures," he remarked. "And some odd worlds your stone must have opened if
your tale is true." He arose and stretched. Then went to the table and counted
out the money he took from his belt. Old bills, most of them, dirty, with a
greasy film as if the business they had been used for had translated some of
its slime to their creased surfaces. There remained in his hand a single coin.
Simon spun it in the air and let it ring down on the polished wood. The
engraved eagle lay up. He looked at it for a moment and then picked it up
again.

"This I take."

"A luck piece?" The doctor was busy with the bills, stacking them into a
tidy pile. "By all means retain it, then; a man can never have too much luck.
And now, I dislike speeding the parting guest, but the power of the Siege is
limited. And the proper moment is all-important. This way, please."

He might have been ushering one into a dentist's office, or to a board
meeting, Simon thought. And perhaps he was a fool to follow.

The rain had stopped, but it was still dark in the square box of yard behind
the old house. Petronius pushed a switch and a light fanned out from the back
door. Three gray stones formed an arch which topped Simon's head by a few
scant inches. And before that lay a fourth stone, as unpolished, unshaped and
angular as the others. Beyond that arch was a wooden fence, high, unpainted,
rotted with age, grimed with city dirt, and a foot or two of sour slum soil,
nothing else.

Simon stood for a long moment, inwardly sneering at his half-belief of a few moments earlier. Now was the time for Sammy to appear and Petronius to earn his real fee.

But the doctor had taken his stand to one side of the clock on the ground. He indicated it with a forefinger.

"The Siege Perilous. If you will just take your seat there, Colonel—it is almost time."

A grin, without humor, to underline his own folly, twisted Simon's thin-lipped mouth, as he straddled the stone and then stood for an instant partly under that arch before he sat down. There was a rounded depression to fit his hips. Curiously, with a sense of foreboding, he put out his hands. Yes, there were two other, smaller hollows to hold his palms, as Petronius had promised.

Nothing happened. The wooden fence, the strip of musty earth remained. He was about to stand up when—

"Now!" Petronius' voice fluted in a word which was half call.

There was a swirling within the stone arch, a melting.

Simon looked out across a stretch of moorland which lay under a gray dawn sky. A fresh wind laden with a strange, invigorating scent fingered his hair. Something within him straightened like a leashed hound to trace that wind to its source, run across that moorland.

"Your world, Colonel, and I wish you the best of it!"

He nodded absently, no longer interested in the little man who called to him. This might be an illusion, but it drew him as nothing else ever had in his life. Without a word of farewell Simon arose and strode beneath the arch.

There was an instant of extreme panic—such fear as he had never imagined could exist, worse than any physical pain—as if the universe had been wrenched brutally apart and he had been spilled out into an awful nothingness. Then he sprawled facedown on thick wiry turf.

II
Moor Hunt

*T*he dawn light did not mean sun to come, for there was a thick mist filling the air. Simon got to his feet and glanced back over his shoulder. Two rough pillars of reddish rock stood there, between them no city yard but a stretch of the same gray-green moor running on and on into a wall of fog. Petronius had been right: this was no world he knew.

He was shivering. Though he had brought his topcoat with him, he did not have his hat, and the moisture plastered his hair to his skull, trickled from scalp to neck and cheek. He needed shelter—some goal. Slowly Simon made a complete turn. No building showed within the rim of the horizon. With a shrug he chose to walk straight away from the rock pillars; one direction was as good as another.

As he plodded across the soggy turf the sky grew lighter, the mist lifted, and the character of the land changed slowly. There were more outcrops of the red stone, the rolling ground held more sharp rises and descents. Before him, how many miles away he could not judge, a broken line cut the sky, suggesting heights to come. And the meal he had treated himself to was many hours in the past. He twisted a leaf from a bush, chewed it absently, finding the flavor pungent but not unpleasant. Then he heard the noise of the hunt.

A horn called in a series of ascending notes, to be answered by a yapping and a single muffled shout. Simon began to trot. When he came out on the lip of a ravine he was certain that the clamor came from the other side of that cut, and was heading in his direction. With the caution of past commando training, he went to earth between two boulders.

The woman was the first to break from the cover of the scrub brush on the opposite bank. She sprinted, her long legs holding to the steady, dogged pace of one who has had a long chase behind, an even more distant goal ahead. At the edge of the narrow valley she hesitated to look back.

Against the grayish green of the vegetation her slim ivory body, hardly concealed by the tatters which were her only covering, seemed to be spotlighted by the wan light of the dawn. With an impatient gesture she pushed back strands of her long black hair, ran her hands across her face. Then she began to work her way along the crest of the slope, hunting for a path down.

The horn pealed and the yapping answered it. She started convulsively and Simon half arose out of his hiding place as he suddenly realized that in that grim hunt she must be the quarry.

He dropped to one knee again as she jerked one of her rags free from a thorn bush. The force of that impatient tug sent her skidding over the rim. Even then she did not scream, but her hands grabbed for a bush as she went forward, and its branches held. As she struggled for footing the hounds burst into view.

They were thin, white animals, their lanky bodies turning with almost boneless fluidity as they came to the edge of the valley wall. With sharp noses pointed down at the woman, they gave triumphant tongue in wailing howls.

The woman writhed, flinging out her legs in a frenzied fight to reach some toehold on a narrow ledge to her right, a ledge which might afford her a path to the valley floor. Perhaps she might have made it had the hunters not arrived.

They were on horseback, and he who wore the horn cord over his shoulder remained in the saddle, while his companion dismounted and walked briskly to look over, kicking and slapping the hounds from his path. When he saw the woman his hand went to a holster at his belt.

Seeing him in turn the woman stopped her vain efforts to reach the ledge, hanging from her bush, her blank face, impassive, up to his. He grinned as he unsheathed his weapon, obviously savoring the helplessness of his prey.

Then the slug from Simon's gun caught him dead center. With a scream he tottered forward and fell into the gully.

Before echo of shot and scream had died away, the other huntsman took cover, which told Simon a little of the caliber of those he faced. And the hounds went mad, racing wildly up and down, filling the air with their yapping.

But the woman made a last effort and found foothold on the ledge. She sped down that path to the floor of the gully, taking cover among the rocks and brush which choked it. Simon saw a flash in the air. Point deep in the earth, not two inches away from where he had crouched to make his shot, a small dart quivered back and forth and then stood still. The other hunter had given battle.

Ten years ago Simon had played such games almost daily, relished them. And, he discovered, some actions once learned by muscles and body are not quickly forgotten. He wriggled into denser cover to wait. The hounds were tiring, several had flung themselves down, to lie panting. It was now a matter of patience, and Simon had that in abundance. He saw that tremor of vegetation and fired for the second time—to be answered by a cry.

A few moments later, alerted by a crackling of brush, he crept to the edge of the valley, and so came face-to-face with the woman. Those dark eyes, set at a provocative slant in her triangular face, searched his with a keen intentness Simon found a little disconcerting. Then, as his hand closed about her shoulder to draw her into deeper cover, he gained a sharp impression of danger, of a desperate need to keep moving across the moor. There was only safety beyond the edge of the moor, back in the direction from which he had come.

So strong was that warning that Simon found himself crawling back among the rocks before getting to his feet and running, matching his stride to hers, the yammering of the hounds growing fainter behind them.

Although she must have already been running for weary miles, his companion held to a pace which he had to stretch to match. At last they came to a place where the moor began to give way to boggy ponds edged with waist-high weeds. It was then that a down wind brought them again the faint call of a horn. And at that echo the woman laughed, glancing at Simon as if to ask him to share some jest. She indicated the bog patches with a gesture which suggested that here lay their safety.

About a quarter of a mile before them a mist curled and curdled, thickening, spreading to cut across their path, and Simon studied it. In such a curtain they might be safe, but also they might be lost. And, oddly enough, that mist appeared to rise from a single source.

The woman raised her right arm. From a broad metal band about her wrist shot a flash of light, aimed at the mist. She waved with her other hand for him to be still, and Simon squinted into that curtain, almost certain he saw dark shapes moving about there.

A shout, the words of the cry incomprehensible, but the tone of challenge unmistakable, came from ahead. His companion answered that with a lilting sentence or two. But when the reply came she staggered. Then she drew herself together and looked to Simon, putting out her hand in half appeal. He caught it, enfolding it in his own warm fist, guessing they must have been refused aid.

"What now?" he asked. She might not be able to understand the words but he was certain she knew their meaning.

Delicately she licked a fingertip and held it into that wind rising to whip her hair back from a face on which a purple bruise swelled at jawline and dark shadows deepened the hollows beneath her high cheekbones. Then, still hand in hand with Simon, she pulled to the left; wading out into evil-smelling pools where green scum was broken by their passing and clung in slimy patches to her legs and his sodden slacks.

So they made their way about the edge of the bog, and that fog which sealed its interior traveled on a parallel course with them, walling them out. Simon's hunger was a gnawing ache, his soaked shoes rubbed blisters on his feet. But the sounds of the horn were lost. Perhaps their present path had baffled the hounds.

His guide fought her way through a reed thicket and brought them out on a ridge of higher ground where there was a road of sorts, hardened by usage, but no wider than a footpath. With it to follow they made better time.

It must have been late afternoon, though in that gray neutral light hours could not be marked, when the road began to climb. Ahead were the escarpments of the red rock, rising almost as a crudely constructed wall, pierced by a gap which cradled the road.

They were almost to this barrier when their luck failed. Out of the grass beside the trail burst a small dark animal to run between the woman's feet, throwing her off balance, sprawling on the beaten clay. She uttered her first sound, a cry of pain, and caught at her right ankle. Simon hastened to push her hands aside and used knowledge learned on the battlefield to assess the damage. Not a break, but under his manipulation she caught her breath sharply, and it was plain she could not go on. Then, once more, came the call of the horn.

"This tears it!" Simon said to himself rather than to the woman. He ran ahead to the gap. The trace of road wound on to a river in a plain, with no cover. Save for the rock pinnacles which guarded the pass, there was no other break in the flat surface of the ground for miles. He turned to the escarpment and examined it with attention. Dropping his coat, he kicked off his soggy shoes and tested handholds. Seconds later he reached a ledge which could be seen from road level only as a shadow. But its width promised shelter and it would have to do for their stand.

When Simon descended the woman came creeping toward him on her hands and knees. With his strength and determination added to hers they gained that shallow refuge, crouching so closely together in that pocket of wind-worn rock that he could feel the warmth of her hurried breath on his cheek as he turned his head to watch their back trail.

Simon also became aware of her trembling, half-clothed body as shudders shook her from head to foot when the wind licked at them. Clumsily he wrapped his coat, damp as it was, about her and saw her smile, though the natural curve of her lips was distorted by a torn lip marked by a recent blow. She was not beautiful, he decided; she was far too thin, too pale, too worn. In fact, though her body was frankly revealed by the disarray of her rags, he was conscious of no male interest at all. And as that thought crossed his mind Simon was also aware that she did in some way understand his appraisal and that it amused her.

She hitched forward to the edge of the hollow so that they were shoulder to shoulder, and now she pulled back the sleeve of his coat, resting her wrist, with its wide bracelet, on her knee. From time to time she rubbed her fingers across an oval crystal set in that band.

Through the keening of the wind they could hear the horn, the reply of the hounds. Simon drew his automatic. His companion's fingers flashed from the bracelet to touch the weapon briefly, as if by that she could devine the nature of the arm. Then she nodded as those white dots which were hounds came from the trees down the road. Four riders followed and Simon studied them.

The open method of their approach argued that they did not expect trouble. Perhaps they did not yet know the fate of their two comrades by the ravine; they might believe that they still trailed one fugitive instead of two. He hoped that that was the truth.

Metal helmets with ragged crests covered their heads and curious eye-pieces were snapped down to mask the upper halves of their faces. They wore garments which seemed to be both shirt and jacket laced from waist to throat. The belts about their waists were a good twenty inches wide and supported bolstered side arms, as well as sheathed knives, and various pouches and accoutrements he could not identify. Their breeches were tight fitting and their boots arose in high peaks on the outside of the leg. The whole effect was a uniform one, for all were cut alike of a blue-green stuff, and a common symbol was on the right breast of the shirt jackets.

The lean, snake-headed hounds swirled up the road and dashed to the foot of the rock, some standing on hind legs to paw at the surface below the ledge. Simon, remembering that silent dart, shot first.

With a cough the leader of the hunters reeled and slipped from his saddle, his boot wedging in the stirrups so that the racing horse jerked a limp body along the road. There was a shout as Simon snapped a second shot. A man caught at his arm as he took to cover, while the horse, still dragging the dead man, bore through the gap and down into the river plain.

The hounds ceased to cry. Panting, they flung themselves down at the foot of the pinnacle, their eyes like sparks of yellow fire. Simon studied them with a growing discomfort. He knew war dogs, had seen them used as camp guards. These were large beasts and they were killers, that was to be read in their stance as they watched and waited. He could pick them off one by one, but he dared not waste his ammunition.

Although the day had been so lowering, he knew that night would be worse with its full darkness, and it was coming fast. The wind sweeping wetly from the bogs was searching out their shelter with its chill.

Simon moved and one of the hounds jumped to alert, putting its forepaws on the rock and lifting a moaning howl of threat. Firm fingers closed about Simon's upper arm, drawing him back to his former position. Again through touch he received a message. As hopeless as their case appeared, the woman was not daunted. He gathered that she was waiting for something.

Could they hope to climb to the top of the escarpment? In the dusk he caught the shake of her unkempt head as if she had read that thought.

Once again the hounds were quiet, lying at the foot of the crag, their attention for the prey above. Somewhere—Simon strained to see through the dusk—somewhere their masters must be on the move, planning to close in about the fugitives. He knew his skill as a marksman, but conditions were now rapidly changing to the other's favor.

He nursed the automatic tensely, alert to the slightest sound. The woman stirred with a bitten-off exclamation, a gasp of breath. He did not need the urgent tug at his arm to make him look at her.

In the dusky quarter light a shadow moved up the end of the ledge. And she snatched his gun, gaining it by surprise, to bring down its butt with a vicious deadliness upon that creeping thing.

There was a thin squeal cut sharply in the middle. Simon grabbed the weapon and only when it was back safely in his grasp did he look at that broken-backed, squirming creature. Needle teeth, white and curved in a flat head, a narrow head mounted on a furred body, red eyes alive with something which startled him—intelligence in an animal's skull! It was dying, but still it wriggled to reach the woman, a faint hissing trilling between those fangs, malignant purpose in every line of its broken body.

With squeamish distaste Simon lashed out with his foot, catching the thing on its side, sending it over to plop among the hounds.

He saw them scatter, separate and draw back as if he had tossed a live grenade into the gathering. Above their complaint he heard a more heartening sound, the laughter of the woman beside him. And he saw her eyes were alight with triumph. She nodded and laughed again as he leaned forward to survey that pool of shadow which now lapped about the base of the pinnacle, concealing the body of the thing.

Had it been another form of hunter loosed upon them by the hidden men below? Yet the uneasiness, the swift departure of the dogs that now milled yards away, seemed to argue otherwise. If they coursed with the dead creature it was not by choice. Accepting this as just another of the mysteries he had walked into—of his own free will—Simon prepared for a night on sentry-go. If the silent attack of the small animal had been some move on the part of the besiegers, they might now come into the open to follow it up.

But, as the darkness thickened, there were no more sounds from below which Simon could interpret as attack. Again the hounds lay down in a half circle about the foot of the pinnacle, dimly visible because of their white hides. Once more Tregarth thought of climbing to the top of the outcrop—they might even cross it if the woman's lameness abated.

When it was almost totally dark she moved. Her fingers rested for a moment on his wrist and then slipped down to lie cool in his palm. Through his own watchfulness, through his listening for any sound, a picture formed in his mind. Knife—she wanted a knife! He loosened her hold and took out his penknife, to have it snatched from him eagerly.

What followed Simon did not understand, but he had sense enough not to interfere. The cloudy crystal strapped to her wrist gave off a faint graveside radiance. By that he watched the point of the knife stab into the ball of her thumb. A drop of blood gathered on the skin, was rubbed across the crystal, so for a moment the thick liquid obscured the scrap of light.

Then up from that oval shown a brighter glow, a shaft of flame. Again his companion laughed, the low chuckle of satisfaction. Within seconds the crystal was dim once again. She laid her hand across his gun and he read in that gesture another message. The weapon was no longer necessary, aid would come.

The swampland wind with its puffs of rottenness moaned around and between the tongues of rock. She was shivering again and he put his arm about her hunched shoulders drawing her to him so that the warmth of their bodies could be joined. Along the arch of the sky flashed a jagged sword of purple lightning.

III
Simon Takes Service

*A*nother vivid bolt of lightning rent the sky, just above the pinnacle. And that was the opening shot of such a wild battle of sky, earth, wind and storm as Simon had never seen before. He had crawled over battlefields under the lash of man-made terrors of war, but this was worse somehow—perhaps because he knew that there was no control over those flashes, gusts, blasts.

The rock shook and pitched under them as they clung like frightened little animals to each other, closing their eyes to the shock of each strike. There was a continuous roar of sound, not the normal rumble of thunder, but the throb of a giant drum beaten to a rhythm which sang angrily in one's blood and set the brain to spinning dizzily. The woman's face was pressed tight against him and Simon enfolded her shaking body as he would the last promise of safety in a reeling world.

It went on and on, beat, crash, lick of light, beat, wind—but as yet no rain. A tremor in the rock under them began to echo the thud of the thunderblasts.

A final spectacular blast left Simon both deaf and blind for a space. But as the seconds lengthened into minutes and there was nothing more, when even the wind appeared to have exhausted itself, sinking into small, fitful puffs, he raised his head.

The stench of burned animal matter poisoned the air. A wavering glow not too far away marked a brushfire. But the blessed quiet held and the woman stirred in his arms, pushing free. Once again he had an impression of confidence, a confidence mixed with triumph, some game had come to a victorious end and to the woman's satisfaction.

He longed for a light with which to survey the scene below. Had the hunter or hound survived the storm? Orange-red light lapped out from the fire toward the escarpment. Against the foot of the pinnacle lay a tangle of stiff white bodies. There was a dead horse in the road, a man's arm resting on its neck.

The woman pushed forward, searching with eager eyes. Then, before Simon could stop her, she had swung over the ledge and he followed, alert for attack, but seeing only the bodies in the firelight.

Warmth of flame reached them and it was good. His companion held out both arms to the glow. Simon skirted the dead hounds, scorched and twisted by the bolt which had killed them. He came to the dead horse with the idea of taking its rider's weapons. Then he saw the fingers in the animal's coarse mane move.

The hunter must be mortally injured, and certainly Simon had little feeling for him since that harrying chase across the moor and bog. But neither could he leave a helpless man so trapped. He struggled with the weight of the dead mount, got that broken body free where the light of the fire could show him who and what he had rescued.

Those strained, bloodstained, harshly marked features held no sign of life, yet the broken chest rose and fell laboriously and he moaned now and then. Simon could not have named his race. The close-cropped hair was very fair, silver-white almost. He had a boldly hooked nose between wide cheekbones, an odd combination. And Simon guessed that he was young though there was little of the unformed boy in that drawn face.

Still on its cord about his shoulder was a dented horn. And the rich ornamentation of his habit, the gem-set brooch at his throat, suggested that he was no common soldier. Simon, unable to do anything for those extensive hurts, turned his attention to the wide belt and its arms.

The knife he tucked into his own belt. The strange sidearm he took from its holster to examine carefully. It had a barrel, and something which could only be a trigger. But in his hand the balance felt wrong, the grip awkwardly shaped. He pushed it inside his shirt.

He was about to loosen the next item, a narrow cylinder, when a white hand flashed across his shoulder and took it.

The hunter stirred as if that touch, rather than Simon's handling, had reached his dazed brain. His eyes opened, feral eyes, with a gleam of light within their depths such as a beast's holds in the darkness. And there was that in those eyes which made Simon recoil.

He had met men who were dangerous, men who wanted his death and who would go about the business of securing it with a businesslike dispatch. He had stood face-to-face with men in whom some trait of character worked upon him until he hated them on sight. But never before had he seen any such emotion as lay at the back of those shining green eyes in the battered face of the hunter.

But Simon realized that those eyes were not turned upon him. The woman stood there, a little crookedly for she favored her injured ankle, turning over in her hands the rod she had stripped from the hunter's belt. Almost Simon expected to see in her expression some answer to that burning, corrosive rage with which the wounded man faced her.

She was watching the hunter steadily, without any sign of emotion. The man's mouth worked, twisted. He raised his head with a tortured, visible effort which racked his whole body and spat at her. Then his head cracked back against the roadway and he lay still as if that last gesture of detestation had drained all his reserves of energy. And in the light of the now dying fire his face went queerly slack, his mouth fell open. Simon did not need to note the end of that laboring rise and fall of the crushed chest to know that he was dead.

"Alizon—" The woman shaped the word carefully, looking to Simon and then to the body. Stopping she indicated the emblem on the dead man's jacket. "Alizon."

"Alizon," Simon echoed as he got to his feet, having no desire to plunder further.

Now she swung to face the gap through which the road ran on into the river plain.

"Estcarp—" Once more that careful pronouncement of a name, but her finger indicated the river plain. "Estcarp." She repeated that, but now touched her own breast.

And, as if by that name she had evoked an answer, there was a shrilling pipe from the other side of the gap. No demanding call such as the hunter's horns had given, but rather a whistling such as a man might make between his teeth as he waited for action. The woman replied with a shouted sentence which was taken up by the wind, echoed from the sides of the rock barrier.

Simon heard the thud of hooves, the jangle of metal against metal. But since his companion faced the gap welcomingly, he was content to wait before going into action. Only his hand closed about the automatic in his pocket and its blunt muzzle pointed to that space between the pinnacles.

They came one at a time, those horsemen. Skimming between the peaks, the first two fanning out, weapons ready. When they sighted the woman they called eagerly; plainly they were friends. The fourth man rode straight ahead to where Simon and the woman waited. His mount was tall, heavy through the barrel as if the animal had been selected to carry weight. But the figure in the high peaked saddle was so short of stature Simon thought him a young boy—until he swung to earth.

In the light of the fire his body glistened, and points of glitter sparkled on helm, belt, throat and wrist. Short he was, but his breadth of shoulder made that lack of height the more apparent, for his arms and chest were those intended for a man a third again his size. He wore armor of some sort with the apparent texture of chainmail, yet it clothed him so snugly that it might have been wrought of cloth, yielding to every movement of his limbs with the pliability of woven stuff. His helmet was crested with the representation of a bird, wings outstretched. Or was it a real bird charmed to unnatural immobility? For the eyes which glinted in its upheld head appeared to watch Simon with a sullen ferocity. The smooth metal cap on which it perched ended in a kind of scarf of the mail, looped about the wearer's neck and throat. He tugged at this impatiently as he walked forward, freeing his face from its half veiling. And Simon saw that he had not been so wrong in his first guess after all. The hawk-helmed warrior was young.

Young, yes, but also tough. His attention was divided between the woman and Simon, and he asked her a question as he surveyed Tregarth measuringly. She answered with a rush of words, her hand sketching some sign in the air between Simon and the warrior. Seeing that, the newcomer touched his helm in what was clearly a salute to the outlander. But it was the woman who commanded the situation.

Pointing to the warrior she continued her language lesson: "Koris."

It could be nothing but a personal name, Simon decided quickly. He jerked his thumb at his own chest:

"Tregarth, Simon Tregarth." He waited for her to name herself.

But she only repeated what he had said. "Tregarth, Simon Tregarth," as if to set the syllables deep in her mind. When she did not answer otherwise he made his own demand.

"Who?" he pointed straight at her.

The warrior Koris started, his hand going to the side arm at his belt. And the woman frowned, before her expression became so remote and cold that Simon knew he had blundered badly.

"Sorry," he spread his hands in a gesture which he hoped she would take for apology. In some way he had offended, but it was through ignorance. And the woman must have understood that, for she made some explanation to the young officer, though he did not look at Simon with any great friendliness during the hours which followed.

Koris, showing a deference which did not match the woman's ragged clothing, but did accord with her air of command, mounted her behind him on the big black horse. Simon rode behind one of the other guardsmen, linking his fingers in the rider's belt and clinging tight, as they headed back into the river plain at a pace which even the dark of the night did not keep from approaching a gallop.

A long time later Simon lay still in a nest of bed coverings and stared with unseeing eyes up at the curve of the carved wood canopy overhead. Save for those wide-open eyes he might have been deemed as suddenly asleep as he had been minutes earlier. But an old talent for passing from sleep into instant alertness had not been lost with his entrance into this new world. And now he was busy sorting out impressions, classifying knowledge, trying to add one fact to another to piece together a concrete picture of what lay about him beyond the confines of the massive bed, the stone walls of the room.

Estcarp was more than the river plain; it was a series of forts, stubborn defensive holds along a road marking a frontier. Forts where they had changed horses, had fed, and then swept on again, driven by some need for haste Simon had not understood. And at last it was a city of round towers, green-gray as the soil in which they were rooted under the pale sun of a new day, towers to guard, a wall to encircle, and then other buildings of a tall, proud-walking race with dark eyes and hair as black as his own, a race with the carriage of rulers and an odd weight of years upon them.

But by the time they had entered that Estcarp Simon had been so bemused by fatigue, so dulled by the demands of his own aching body, that there were only snatches of pictures to be remembered. And overlaying them all the sensation of age, of a past so ancient that the towers and the walls could have been part of the mountain bones of this world. He had walked old cities in Europe, seen roadways which had known the tramp of Roman legions. Yet the alien aura of age resting here was far more overpowering, and Simon fought against it when he marshaled his facts.

He was quartered in the middle pile of the city, a massive stone structure which had both the solemnity of a temple and the safety-promise of a fort. He could just barely remember the squat officer, Koris, bringing him to this room, pointing to the bed. And then—nothing.

Or was it nothing?

Simon's brows drew together in a faint frown. Koris, this room, the bed— Yet now as he stared up into the mingled pattern of intricate carving arching over him, he found things there which were familiar, oddly familiar, as if the symbols woven back and forth had a meaning which he would unravel at any moment now.

Estcarp—old, old, a country and a city, and a way of life! Simon tensed. How had he known that? Yet it was true, as real as the bed on which his saddle-sore body rested, as the carvings over him. The woman who had been hunted—she was of this race, of Estcarp—just as the dead hunter by the barrier had been of another and hostile people.

The Guardsmen in the frontier posts were all of the same mold, tall, dark, aloof in manner. Only Koris, with his misshapen body, had differed from the men he led. Yet Koris' orders were obeyed; only the woman who rode behind him had appeared to have more authority.

Simon blinked, his hands moved beneath the covers, and he sat up, his eyes on the curtains to his left. Soft as it had been, he had caught that whisper of footfall, and he was not surprised when the rings of the curtains clicked, and the thick blue fabric parted, so that he looked at the very man who had been in his thoughts.

Freed of his armor Koris was even more of a physical oddity. His too-wide shoulders, those dangling, overlong arms outweighed the rest of him. He was not tall and his narrow waist, his slender legs were doubly small in contrast to the upper part of his body. But set on those shoulders was the head of the man Koris might have been had nature not played such a cruel trick. Under a thick cap of wheat yellow hair was the face of a boy who had only recently come to manhood, but also the face of one who had had no pleasure in that development. Strikingly handsome, apart from those shoulders, jarring with them, the head of a hero partnered to the body of an ape!

Simon slid his legs down the mound of the high bed and stood up, sorry at that moment that he must force the other to look up to him. But Koris had moved back with the quickness of a cat and perched on a broad stone ledge running beneath a slit window, so that his eyes were still on a level with Tregarth's. He gestured with a grace foreign to his long arm to a nearby chest, indicating a pile of clothing there.

Those were not the tweeds he had crawled out of before seeking bed, Simon noted. But he also saw something else, a subtle reassurance of his present status there. His automatic, the other contents of his pockets, had been laid out with scrupulous neatness to one side of that new clothing. He was no prisoner, whatever other standing he might have in that hold.

He pulled on breeches of soft leather, resembling those Koris now wore. Supple as a glove, they were colored a dark blue. And with them were a pair of calf-high boots of a silvery gray substance he thought might be reptile hide. Having dressed so far he turned to the other and made gestures of washing.

For the first time a ghost of smile touched the Guardsman's well-cut mouth and he pointed to an alcove. Medieval the hold of Estcarp might be superficially, Simon discovered, but the dwellers therein had some modern views on sanitation. He found himself introduced to water which flowed, warm, from a wall pipe when a simple lever was turned, to a jar of cream, faintly fragrant, which applied and then wiped off erased all itch of beard. And with his discoveries came a language lesson, until he had a growing vocabulary of words Koris patiently repeated until Simon had them right.

The officer's attitude was one of studied neutrality. He neither made friendly overtures, save for his language instructions, nor accepted Simon's attempts at more personal conversation. In fact, as Tregarth pulled on a garment intended to serve as both shirt and jacket, Koris shifted halfway around on the window ledge to stare out into the day sky.

Simon weighed the automatic in his hand. The Escarpian officer appeared to be indifferent as to whether this stranger went armed or not. At length Tregarth slipped it into his belt above his lean and now empty middle, and signed that he was ready to go.

The room gave on a corridor and that, within a few paces, upon a stair down. Simon's impression of immeasurable age was confirmed by the hollows worn in those same stone steps, a groove running along the left wall where fingers must have passed for eons. Light came palely from globes set far above their heads in metal baskets, but the nature of that light remained a mystery.

A wider hall lay at the foot and men passed there. Some in the scaled mail were guards on duty, others had the easier dress Simon now wore. They saluted Koris and eyed his companion with a somber curiosity he found vaguely disconcerting, but none of them spoke. Koris touched Tregarth's arm, motioned to a curtained doorway, holding back a loop of the cloth in a way which suggested an order.

Beyond stretched another hall. But here the bare stone of the walls were covered with hangings bearing the patterns of the same symbols he had seen on the bed canopy, half-familiar, half-alien. A sentry stood to attention at the far end of that way, raising the hilt of his sword to his lips. Koris looped back a second curtain, but this time he waved Simon by him.

The room seemed larger than it was because of the vault of the ceiling which pointed up far overhead. Here the light globes were stronger, and their beams, while not reaching into those lofty shadows, did show clearly the gathering below.

There were two women waiting him—the first he had seen within the pile of the keep. But he had to look a second time to recognize in the one standing, her right hand on the back of a tall chair which held her companion, the woman who had fled before the hunters of Alizon. That hair which had hung in lank soaked strings about her then was coiled rather severely into a silver net, and she was covered primly from throat to ankle by a robe of a similar misty color. Her only ornament was an oval of the same cloudy crystal such as she had worn then in a wristband, but this hung from a chain so that the stone rested between the small mounds of her breasts.

"Simon Tregarth!" It was the seated woman who summoned him, so his eyes passed to her, and he found that he could not take them away again.

She had the same triangular face, the same seeking eyes, the same black coils of netted hair. But the power which emanated from her was like a blow. He could not have told her age, in some ways she might have seen the first stones of Estcarp laid one upon another. But to him she seemed ageless. Her hand flashed up and she tossed a ball toward him, a ball seemingly of the same cloudy crystal as the gem she and her lieutenant wore as jewels.

Simon caught it. Against his flesh it was not cold as he had expected, but warm. And as he instinctively cupped it in both hands, her own closed over her jewel, a gesture echoed by her companion.

Tregarth could never afterwards explain, even to himself, what followed. In some weird fashion he pictured in his mind the series of actions which had brought him to the world of Estcarp, sensing as he did so that those two silent women saw what he had seen and in a measure shared his emotions. When he had done that a current of information flowed in his direction.

He stood in the main fortress of a threatened, perhaps a doomed land. The age-old land of Estcarp was menaced from the north and from the south, and also from the sea to the west. Only because they were the heirs of age-old knowledge were the dark people of her fields, her towns and cities, able to hold back the press. Theirs might be a losing cause, but they would go down fighting to the last blow of sword from the last living Guardsman, the last blasting weapon man or woman could lay hand upon.

And that same hunger which had drawn Simon under the rough arch in Petronius' yard into this land, was alive and avid in him once more. They made no appeal to him, their pride was unbending. But he gave his allegiance to the woman who had questioned him, chose sides in that moment with a rush of a boy's openhearted enthusiasm. Without a spoken word passing between them, Simon took service in Estcarp.

IV
The Call Out of Sulcarkeep

Simon raised the heavy tankard to his lips. Over the rim of the vessel he watched the scene alertly. On his first acquaintance he had thought the people of Estcarp somber, overshadowed by a crushing weight of years, the last remnants of a dying race who had forgotten all but dreams of the past. But during the past weeks he had learned bit by bit how surface and superficial that judgment had been. Now in the mess of the Guards his attention flickered from face to face, reappraising, not for the first time, these men with whom he shared a daily round of duties and leisure.

To be sure their weapons were strange. He had had to learn the swing of a sword for use in close melee, but their dart guns were enough like his automatic to cause him little trouble. He could never match Koris as a warrior—his respect for that young man's skill was unbounded. However Simon knew the tactics of other armies, other wars, well enough to make suggestions even that aloof commander came to appreciate.

Simon had wondered how he would be received among the Guards—after all they were making a stand against high odds and to them any stranger might represent an enemy, a breach in the wall of defense. Only he had not reckoned with the ways of Estcarp. Alone in the nations of this continent, Estcarp was willing to welcome one coming with a story as wild as his own. Because the power of that ancient holding was founded upon—magic!

Tregarth rolled the wine about his tongue before he swallowed, considering objectively the matter of magic. That word could mean sleight-of-hand tricks, it could cover superstitious mumbo jumbo—or it could stand for something far more powerful. Will, imagination, and faith were the weapons of magic as Estcarp used it. Of course, they had certain methods of focusing or intensifying that will, imagination, and faith. But the end result was that they were extremely open-minded about things which could not be seen, felt, or given visible existence.

And the hatred and fear of their neighbors was founded upon just that basis—magic. To Alizon in the north, Karsten in the south, the power of the Witches of Estcarp was evil. "You shall not suffer a witch to live." How many times had that been mouthed in his own world as a curse against innocent and guilty alike, and with far less cause.

For the matriachate of Estcarp did have powers beyond any human explanation, and they used them ruthlessly when necessary. He had helped to bring a witch out of Alizon where she had ventured to be eyes and ears for her people.

A witch—Simon drank again. Not every woman of Estcarp had the Power. It was a talent which skipped willfully from family to family, generation to generation. Those who tested out as children were brought to the central city for their schooling and became dedicated to their order. Even their names were gone, for to give another one's name was to give a part of one's identity, so that thereafter the receiver had power over the giver. Simon could understand now the enormity of his request when he had asked the name of the woman in whose company he had fled over the moor.

Also the Power was not steady. To use it past a certain point wore hardly upon the witch. Nor could it always be summoned at will. Sometimes it was apt to fail at some crucial moment. So, in spite of her witches and her learnings, Estcarp had also her mail-clad Guards, her lines of forts along her borders, her swords loose in many sheaths.

"Sa . . ." The stool beside him was jerked back from the table as a newcomer swung leg across to sit. "It is hot for the season." A helm banged down on the board and a long arm swept out to reach the jug of wine.

The hawk on the discarded helm stared at Simon glassily, its beautifully wrought metallic plumage resembling true feathers. Koris drank while questions were shot at him from about the table, as men might aim darts for more deadly purpose. There was discipline in the forces of Estcarp but off duty there was no caste and the men about that board were avid for news. Their commander banged his tankard down with some force and answered briskly:

"You'll hear the muster horn before the hour of gate closing, in my opinion. That was Magnis Osberic who prayed safe passage from the west road. And he had a tail in full war gear. It is to my mind that Gorm makes trouble."

His words fell into a silence at the end. All of them, now including Simon, knew what Gorm meant to the Guards' Captain. For rightfully the lordship of Gorm should have rested in Koris' powerful hands. His personal tragedy had not begun there, but it had ended on that island when, wounded and alone, he had drifted from its shore, facedown in a leaking fishing boat.

Hilder, Lord Defender of Gorm, had been storm-stayed on those moors which were a no-man's-land between Alizon and the plains of Estcarp. There, separated from his men, he had fallen from a floundered horse and broken an arm, to blunder on in a half daze of pain and fever into the lands of the Tormen, that strange race who held the bogs against all comers, allowing no encroachment upon their soggy domain by any race or man.

Why Hilder had not been slain or driven forth again remained ever a mystery. But his story was untold even after he returned to Gorm some months later, healed again of body and bearing with him a new-made wife. And the men of Gorm—more straightly, the women of Gorm—would have none of that marriage, whispering that it had been forced upon their lord in return for his life. For the woman he had brought with him was mishapen of body, stranger yet of mind, being of the true blood of Tor. She bore him Koris in due time, and then she was gone. Perhaps she died, perhaps she fled again to her kin. Hilder must have known, but he never spoke of her again, and Gorm was so glad to be rid of such a liege lady that there were no questions asked.

Only Koris remained, with the head of a Gorm noble and the body of a bog loper, as he was never allowed to forget. And in time when Hilder took a second wife, Orna, the well-dowered daughter of a far-sailing sea master, Gorm again whispered and hoped. So they were only too willing to accept the second son, Uryan, who, it was plain to see, had not a drop of suspect outland blood in the veins of his straight young body.

In time Hilder died. But he was a long time in dying and those who whispered had a chance to make ready against that day. Those who thought to use Orna and Uryan for their purposes were mistaken, for the Lady Orna, of trading stock and shrewd, was no easily befooled female of the inner courts. Uryan was still a child, and she would be his regnant—though there were those who would say no to that unless she made a display of strength.

She was not a fool when she played one lord of Gorm against another, weakening each and keeping her own forces intact. But she was the worst befooled mortal in the world when she turned elsewhere for support. For it was Orna who brought black ruin to Gorm when she secretly summoned the fleet of Kolder to back her rule.

Kolder lay over the rim of the sea world, just where you could find only one man in ten thousand among the seafarers who could tell you. For honest men, or human men, kept aloof from that grim port and did not tie at its quays. It was accepted everywhere that those of Kolder were not as other men, and it was damnation to have any contact with them.

The death day of Hilder was followed by a night of red terror. And only one of Koris' superhuman strength could have broken from the net cast for him. Then there was only death, for when the Kolder came to Gorm, Gorm ceased to be. If any now lived there who had known life under Hilder, they had no hope. For Kolder was now Gorm, yes, and more than just the island of Gorm, for within the year stark towers had risen in another place on the coast and a city called Yle had come into being. Though no man of Estcarp went to Yle—willingly.

This Yle lay like a spreading stain of foulness between Estcarp and their one strong ally to the west—the sea wanderers of Sulcarkeep. These fighter-traders who knew wild places and different lands had built their stronghold by Estcarp favor on a finger of land which pointed into the sea, their road to encircle the world. Master Traders were the seamen of Sulcarkeep, but also they were fighting men who walked unchallenged in a thousand ports. No trooper of Alizon or shieldman of Karsten spoke to a Sulcarman except in a mild voice, and they were esteemed as swordbrothers by the Guardsmen of Estcarp.

"Magnis Osberic is not one to ride forth with the summoning arrow unless he must have already manned his walls," remarked Tunston, senior under officer who kept the forces of Estcarp to the mark. He arose and stretched. "We'd best see to our gear. If Sulcarkeep cries aid, then we loosen swords."

Koris gave only a preoccupied nod to that. He had dipped finger into his tankard and was drawing lines on the scrubbed board before him, chewing absentmindedly the while at a fist-sized hunk of brown bread. Those lines made sense to Simon, looking over the other's hunched shoulder, for they duplicated maps he had seen in the muster room of the city keep.

That finger which ended with Sulcarkeep on its tip formed one arm to encircle a wide bay, so that across the expanse of water the city of the traders faced—although many miles lay between them—Aliz, the main port of Alizon. In the confines of the bay itself was cupped the island of Gorm. And on that Koris carefully made the dot to signify Sippar, the main city.

Strangely enough Yle did not lie on the bayside section of the peninsula coast, but on the southwest portion of the shoreline, facing the open sea. Then there was a sweep of broken line southward, extending well into the Duchy of Karsten, all rock cliff with no safe anchorage for any ship. The bay of Gorm had been of old Estcarp's best outlet to the western ocean.

The Guards' Captain studied his work for a long instant or two and then with an impatient exclamation, rubbed his hand across it, smearing the lines.

"There is only one road to Sulcarkeep?" asked Simon. With Yle to the south and Gorm to the north, parties from each Kolder post could easily slice in two a peninsula road without greatly bestirring themselves.

Koris laughed. "There is one road, as old as the ages. Our ancestors did not foresee Kolder in Gorm—who in their sane minds could? To make safe that road," he put his thumb on the dot he had made for Sippar and pressed it against the age-hardened wood as if he were remorselessly crushing an insect, "we would have to do so here. You cure a disease by treating its source, not the fever, the wasting which are the signs of its residence in the body.

And in this case," he looked bleakly up at Tregarth, "we have no knowledge upon which to work."

"A spy—"

Again the Guards' officer laughed. "Twenty men have gone forth from Estcarp to Gorm. Men who suffered shape-changing without knowing whether they would ever again look upon their own faces in a mirror, but suffering that gladly, men who were fortified with every spell the learning here could summon for their arming. And there has come back out of Sippar—nothing! For these Kolder are not as other men and we know nothing of their devices of detection, save that they appear to be infallible. At last the Guardian forbade any further such ventures, since the drain of Power was too great to have only failure always as an answer. I myself have tried to go, but they had set a boundary spell which I cannot break. To land on Gorm would mean my death, and I can serve Estcarp better alive. No, we shall not tear out this sore until Sippar falls, and not yet have we any hopes of bringing that about."

"But if Sulcarkeep is threatened?"

Koris reached for his helm. "Then, friend Simon, we ride! For this is the strangeness of the Kolder: when they fight upon their own land or their own ships, the victory is always theirs. But when they assail clean territory where their shadow has not yet fallen, then there is still a chance to blood them, to swing swords which bite deep. And with the Sulcarmen the war ravens feed well. I would mark my Kolders when and while I can."

"I ride with you." That was a statement more than a question. Simon had been content to wait, to learn. He had set himself to school with the patience he had so painfully learned in the past seven years, knowing that until he mastered the skills which meant life or death here he could not hope for independence. And once or twice in the night watches he wondered whether the vaunted Power of Estcarp had not been used to bring about his acceptance of the status quo without question or rebellion. If so, that spell was wearing thin now; he was determined to see more of this world than just the city, and he knew that either he rode now with the Guard or he would go alone.

The Captain studied him. "We go for no quick foray."

Simon remained seated, knowing the other's dislike of being towered over and willing to propitiate him by that costless courtesy.

"When have I seemed to you one who expects only easy victories!" He got a caustic bite into that.

"See that you depend upon the darts, then. As a swordsman you are still scarcely better than a stall keeper of Karsten!"

Simon did not fire at that jibe, knowing that it was only too true. As a marksman with the dart guns he could match the best in the hold and come off a shade the winner. Wrestling and unarmed combat to which he brought the tricks of Judo, had given him a reputation with the men now reaching to the border forts. But in sword use he was still hardly better than the gawky recruits with only boy-down to be scrubbed from their cheeks. And he swung a mace which Koris handled with cat-ease as if it were a shoulder-breaking burden.

"Dart gun it is," he returned readily. "But still I ride."

"So be it. But first we see whether or no any of us are to take the road."

That was decided in the conclave into which the officers under Koris, the witches on duty in the hold, were summoned. Though Simon had no official standing in that company, he ventured to follow the Captain and was not refused entrance, taking his place on the ledge of one of the window embrasures to study the company with speculation.

The Guardian who ruled the keep and Estcarp beyond, the woman without a name who had questioned him on his first coming, presided. And behind her chair stood that witch who had fled before the hounds of Alizon. There were five more of the covenanted ones, ageless—in a way sexless—but all keen-eyed and watchful. He would far rather fight with them behind him than standing in opposition, Simon decided. Never had he known any like them, or seen such power of personality.

Yet facing them now was a man who tended to dwarf his surroundings. In any other company he might well have dominated the scene. The men of Estcarp were lean and tall, but this was a bronze bull of a man beside whom they were boys not yet come to their full growth. The armor plate which hooped his chest could have furnished close to two shields for the Guard, his shoulders and arms were a match for Koris' but the rest of his body was in keeping.

His chin was shaven, but on his broad upper lip a mustache bristled, stretching out across his weathered cheeks. And eyebrows furnished a second bar of hair on the upper part of his face. The helm on his head was surmounted with the skillfully modeled head of a bear, its muzzle wrinkled in a warning snarl. And a huge bearhide, tanned and lined with saffron yellow cloth, formed his cloak, gold-clawed forepaws clasped together under his square chin.

"We of Sulcarkeep keep traders' peace." Manifestly he was trying to tutor his voice to a tone more in keeping with the small chamber, but it boomed through the room. "And we keep it with our blades, if the need arises. But against wizards of the night of what use is good steel? I do not quarrel with the old learning," he addressed the Guardian directly, as if they faced each other across a trading counter. "To each man his own gods and powers, and never has Estcarp pushed upon others their own beliefs. But Kolder does not so. It laps out and its enemies are gone! I tell you, lady, our world dies, unless we rise to stem a tide together."

"And have you, Master Trader," asked the woman, "ever seen a man born of woman who can control the tides?"

"Control them, no, ride them, yes! That is my magic." He thumped his corselet with a gesture which might have been theatrical, save that for him it was right. "But there is no riding with Kolder, and now they plan to strike at Sulcarkeep! Let the stupid wits of Alizon think to hold aloof, they shall be served in turn as Gorm was. But Sulcarmen man their walls—they fight! And when our port goes, those sea tides sweep close to you, lady. Rumor says that you have the magic of wind and storm, as well as those spells which twist a man's shape and wits. Can your magic stand against Kolder?"

Her hands went to the jewel on her breast and she smoothed it.

"It is the truth I speak now, Magnis Osberic—I do not know. Kolder is unknown, we have not been able to breach its walls. For the rest—I agree. The time has come when we must take a stand. Captain," she hailed Koris, "what is your thought upon the matter?"

His handsome face did not lose its bitter shadow, but his eyes were alight.

"I say that while we can use swords, then let us! With your permission, Estcarp will ride to Sulcarkeep."

"The swords of Estcarp shall ride, if that is your decision, Captain, for yours is the way of arms and you speak accordingly. But also shall that other Power ride in company, so what force we have shall be given."

She made no summoning gesture, but the witch who had spied in Alizon moved from behind the chair to stand upon the Guardian's right hand. And her dark, slanted eyes moved over the company until they found Simon sitting apart. Had a shadow of a smile, gone in an instant, spread from her eyes to her lips? He could not have sworn to it, but he thought that was so. He did not understand why, but in that moment Simon was aware of a very fragile thread spun between them, and he did not know whether he chafed against the thinnest of bonds or not.

When they rode out of the city in the midafternoon Simon discovered by some chance his mount matched pace with hers. Like the men of the Guard she wore mail, the scarfed helmet. There was no outward difference between her and the rest, for a sword hung at her hip, and the same side arm at her belt as Simon carried.

"So, man of war from another world," her voice was low and he thought it for his hearing alone, "we travel the same trail once again."

Something in her serene composure irked him. "Let us hope this time to hunt instead of being hunted."

"To each his day," she sounded indifferent. "I was betrayed in Alizon, and unarmed."

"And now you ride with sword and gun."

She glanced down at her own equipment and laughed. "Yes, Simon Tregarth, with sword and gun—and other things. But you are right in one thought, we hasten to a dark meeting."

"Foretelling, lady?" His impatience ripened. For that moment he was an unbeliever. It was far easier to trust in steel which fitted into the hand than in hints, looks, feelings.

"Foretelling, Simon." Her narrow eyes regarded him still with that shadow smile somewhere in their depths. "I am laying no geas, nor quest upon you, outland man. But this I know: our two strands of life stuff have been caught up together by the Hand of the Over Guardian. What we wish and what will come of it may be two very different things. This I shall say, not only to you, but to all this company—beware the place where rocks arch high and the scream of the sea eagle sounds!"

Simon forced an answering smile. "Believe me, lady, in this land I watch as if I had eyes set around my head in a circlet. This is not my first raiding party."

"As has been known. Else you would not ride with the Hawk," she pointed with a lift of her chin to Koris. "Were you not of the proper metal he would have none of you. Koris is warrior bred, and a leader born—to Estcarp's gain!"

"And you foresee this danger at Sulcarkeep?" he pressed.

She shook her head. "You have heard how it is with the Gift. Bits and patches are granted us—never the whole pattern. But there are no city walls in my mind picture. And I think it lies closer than the sea rim. Loose your dart gun, Simon, or bare those knowledgeable fists of yours." She was amused again, but her laughter did not jeer—rather it was the open good humor of comradeship. He knew that he must accept her on her own proffered terms.

V
Demon Battle

*T*he troop from Estcarp pushed the pace but they had still a day's journey before them when they rode out of the last of the frontier posts and headed along the curve of the seaport highway. They had changed mounts regularly at the series of Guard installations and spent the night at the last fort, keeping to a steady trot that ate up the miles.

Although the Sulcarmen did not ride with the same ease as the Guard, they clung grimly to saddles which seemed too small for their bulk—Magnis Osberic not being unique in his stature—and kept up, riding with the fixed purpose of men to whom time itself was a threatening enemy.

But the morning was bright, and patches of purple flowering bush caught radiance from the sun. The air carried the promise of salt waves ahead and Simon knew a lift of heart which he had thought lost long ago. He did not realize that he was humming until a familiar husky voice cut from his left.

"Birds sing before the hawk strikes."

He met that mockery good-naturedly. "I refuse to listen to the croaking of ill—it is too fine a day."

She plucked at the mail scarf wreathing her shoulders and throat, as if its supple folds were a kind of imprisonment. "The sea—it is in the wind here—" Her gaze roamed ahead where the road rippled to the horizon. "We have a portion of the sea in our veins, we of Estcarp. That is why Sulcar blood can mingle with ours, as it has of times. Someday I would take to the sea as a venture. There is a pull in the very surge of the waves as they retreat from the shore."

Her words were a singing murmur, but Simon was suddenly alert, the tune he had hummed dried in his throat. He might not have the gifts of the Estcarp witches, but deep within him something crawled, stirred into life, and before he reasoned it through, his hand flashed up in a signal from his own past as he reined in his horse.

"Yes!" Her hand was flung to echo his and the men behind them halted. Koris' head whipped about; he made his own signal and the whole company came to a stop.

The Captain passed the lead momentarily to Tunston and rode back. They had their flankers out; nothing could be charged to lack of vigilance.

"What is it?" Koris demanded.

"We are running into something." Simon surveyed the terrain ahead, lying innocently open under the sun. Nothing moved except a bird spiraling high. The wind had died so that even its puffs did not disturb the patches of brush. Yet he would stake all his experience and judgment upon the fact that before them a trap was waiting to snap jaws.

Koris' surprise was fleeting. He had already glanced from Simon to the witch. She sat forward in the saddle, her nostrils expanded as she breathed deeply. She might have been trying the scent as does a hound. Dropping the reins she moved her fingers in certain signs, and then she nodded sharply with complete conviction.

"He is right. There is a blank space ahead, one I cannot penetrate. It may be a force barrier—or hide an attack."

"But how did he—the gift is not his!" Koris' protest was quick and harsh. He flashed a glance at Simon which the other could not read, but it was not of confidence. Then he issued orders, spurring forward himself to lead one of those circling sweeps which were intended to draw an overanxious enemy into the open.

Simon drew his dart gun. How had he known—how did he know they were advancing into danger? He had had traces of such foreknowldege in the past— as on the night he had met Petronius—but never had it been so sharp and clear, with a strength which increased as he rode.

The witch kept beside him, just behind the first line of Guards, and now she chanted. From inside her mail shirt she had brought out that clouded jewel which was both a weapon and the badge of her calling. Then she held it above her head at arm's length and cried aloud some command which was not in the tongue Simon had painstakingly learned.

There came into view a natural formation of rocks pointing into the sky like fangs from some giant jawbone, and, the road ran between two which met in the semblance of an arch. About the foot of the standing stones was a mass of brush, dead and brown, or living and green, to form a screen.

From the gem a spearpoint of light struck upon the tallest of those tooth-stones, and from that juncture of beam and rock spread a curling mist which thickened into a cottony fog, blanketing out the pillars and the vegetation.

Out of that clot of gray-white stuff burst the attack, a wave of armed and armored men coming forward at a run in utter silence. Their helms were head-enveloping and visored, giving them the unearthly look of beaked birds of prey. And the fact they advanced without any calls or orders along their ranks added to the weirdness of the sudden sortie.

"Sul . . . Sul . . . Sul . . . !" The sea rovers had their swords out, and swung them in time to that thunderous shout as they drew into a line which sharpened into a wedge, Magnis Osberic forming its point.

The Guard raised no shout, nor did Koris issue any orders. But marksmen picked their men and shot, swordsmen rode ahead, their blades ready. And they had the advantage of being mounted, while the silent enemy ran afoot.

Simon had studied the body armor of Estcarp and knew where the weak points existed. Whether the same was true of Kolder armor he could not tell. But he aimed for the armpit of one man who was striking at the first Guard to reach the cresting wave of the enemy forces. The Kolder spun around and crashed, his pointed visor digging into the earth.

"Sul . . . Sul . . . Sul . . . !" The war shouts of the Sulcarmen were a surf roar as the two bands of fighters met, mingled, and swirled in a vicious hand-to-hand combat. In the first few moments of the melee Simon was aware of nothing but his own part in the affair, the necessity for finding a mark. And then he began to note the quality of the men they battled.

For the Kolder force made no attempt at self-preservation. Man after man went blindly to his death because he did not turn from attack to defense in time. There was no dodging, no raising of shield or blade to ward off blows. The foot soldiers fought with a dull ferocity, but it was almost mechanical. Clockwork toys, Simon thought, wound up and set marching.

Yet these were supposed to be the most formidable foemen known to this world! And now they were being cut down easily, as a child might push over a line of toy soldiers.

Simon lowered his gun. Something within him revolted against picking off the blind fighters. He spurred his mount to the right in time to see one of the beaked heads turn in his direction. The Kolder came forward at a brisk trot. But he did not engage Simon as the other had expected. Instead he leaped tigerishly at the rider just beyond—the witch.

Her mastery of her horse saved her from the full force of that dash and her sword swung down. But the blow was not clean, catching on the pointed visor of the Kolder and so being deflected over his shoulder.

Blind as he might be in some respects the fellow was well schooled in blade work. The blue length of steel in his hand flashed in and out, in its passing sweeping aside the witch's weapon, tearing it from her hand. Then he cast aside his own weapon and his mail-backed glove grabbed for her belt, tearing her from the saddle in spite of her struggles, with an ease which Koris might have displayed.

Simon was on him now and that curious fault which was losing his comrades their battle possessed this Kolder as well. The witch was fighting so desperately in his hold that Simon dared not use his sword. He drew his foot from the stirrups as he urged his horse closer, and kicked out with all the force he could put behind that blow.

The toe of his boot met the back of the Kolder's round helmet, and the impact of that meeting numbed Simon's foot. The man lost his balance and sprawled forward, bearing the witch with him. Simon swung from the saddle, stumbling, with fear that his jarred leg would give under him. His groping hands slid over the Kolder's plated shoulders, but he was able to pull the fellow away from the gasping woman and send him over on his back, where he lay beetle-wise, his hands and legs still moving feebly, the blankness of his beaked visor pointing up.

Shedding her mailed gloves the woman knelt by the Kolder, busy with the buckles of his helm. Simon caught at her shoulder.

"Mount!" He ordered, drawing his own horse forward for her.

She shook her head, intent upon what she was doing. The stubborn strap gave and she wrenched off the helm. Simon did not know what he had expected to see. His imagination, more vivid than he would admit, had conjured up several mental pictures of the hated aliens—but none of them matched this face.

"Herlwin!"

The hawk crown helmet of Koris cut between Simon and that face as the Captain of the Guard knelt beside the witch, his hands going out to the fallen man's shoulders as if to draw him into the embrace of close friends.

Eyes as green-blue as the Captain's, in a face as regularly handsome, opened, but they did not focus either on the man who called, or the other two bending over him. It was the witch who loosened Koris' grip. She cupped the man's chin, holding still his rolling head, peering into those unseeing eyes.

Then she loosed him and pulled away, wiping her hands vigorously on the coarse grass. Koris watched her.

"Herlwin?" It was more a question addressed to the witch than an appeal to the man in Kolder's trappings.

"Kill!" she ordered between set teeth. Koris' hand went out to the sword he had dropped on the grass.

"You can't!" Simon protested. The fellow was harmless now, knocked partly unconscious by the blow. They could not just run him through in cold blood. The woman's gaze crossed his, steel cold. Then she pointed to that head, rolling back and forth again.

"Look, outworld man!" She jerked him down beside her.

With an odd reluctance Simon did as she had done, took the man's head between his hands. And on that moment of contact he nearly recoiled. There was no human warmth in that flesh; it did not have the chill of metal nor of stone, but of some unclean, flabby stuff, firm as it looked to the eye. When he stared down into those unblinking eyes, he sensed rather than saw a complete nothingness which could not be the result of any blow, no matter how hard or straightly delivered. What lay there was not anything he had ever chanced upon before—an insane man still has the cloak of humanity, a mutilated or mangled body could awaken pity to soften horror. Here was the negation of all which was right, a thing so loathsomely apart from the world that Simon could not believe it was meant to see sun or walk upon wholesome earth.

As the witch had done before him, he scrubbed his hands on the grass trying to rub from them the contamination he felt. He scrambled to his feet and turned his back as Koris swung the sword. Whatever the Captain struck was dead already—long dead—and damned.

There were only dead men to mark the Kolder force, and two slain Guardsmen, one Sulcar corpse being lashed across his horse. The attack had been so strikingly inept that Simon could only wonder why it had been made. He feel in step with the Captain and discovered that he was in search of knowledge.

"Unhelm them!" The order passed from one group of Guardsmen to the next. And beneath each of those beak helms they saw the same pale faces with heads of cropped blond hair, those features which argued they were akin to Koris.

"Midir!" He paused beside another body. A hand twitched, there was the rattle of death in the man's throat. "Kill!" The Captain's order was dispassionate, and it was obeyed with quick efficiency.

He looked upon every one of the fallen, and three more times he ordered the death stroke. A small muscle twitched at the corner of his well-cut mouth, and what lay in his eyes was far from the nothingness which had been mirrored in the enemies'. The Captain, having made the rounds of the bodies, came back to Magnis and the Witch.

"They are all of Gorm!"

"They *were* of Gorm," the woman corrected him. "Gorm died when it opened its sea gates to Kolder. Those who lie here are not the men you remember, Koris. They have not been men for a long time—a long, long time! They are hands and feet, fighting machines to serve their masters, but true life they did not have. When the Power drove them out of hiding they could only obey the one order they had been given—find and kill. Kolder can well use these things they have made to fight for them, to wear down our strength before they aim their greater blows."

That lip twitch pulled the Captain's mouth into something which curved but in no way resembled a smile.

"So in a measure do they betray a weakness of their own. Can it be that they lack manpower?" Then he corrected himself, slamming his sword back into its sheath with a small rasp of sound. "But who knows what lies in a Kolder mind—if they can do this, then perhaps they have other surprises."

Simon was well in the van as they rode on from that trampled strip of field where they had met the forces of Kolder. He had not been able to aid in the final task the witch urged on them, nor did he like to think now of those bodies left headless. It was hard to accept what he knew to be true.

"Dead men do not fight!" He did not realize he had protested that aloud until Koris answered him.

"Herlwin was like one born in the sea. I have watched him hunt the spear fish with only a knife for his defense. Midir was a recruit in the bodyguard, still stumbling over his feet when the assembly trumpet blew on the day Kolder came to Gorm. Both of them I knew well. Yet those things which lie behind us, they were neither Herlwin nor Midir."

"A man is three things." It was the witch who spoke now. "He is a body to act, a mind to think, a spirit to feel. Or are men constructed differently in your world, Simon? I cannot think so, for you act, you think and you feel! Kill the body and you free the spirit; kill the mind and ofttimes the body must live on in sorry bondage for a space, which is a thing to arouse man's compassion. But kill the spirit and allow the body, and perhaps the mind to live—" her voice shook, "that is a sin beyond all comprehension of our kind. And that is what has happened to these men of Gorm. What walks in their guise is not meant for earthborn life to see! Only an unholy meddling with things utterly forbidden could produce such a death."

"And you cry aloud the manner of our deaths, lady, should Kolder come into Sulcarkeep as it did to Gorm." The Master Trader pushed his heavy-boned mount up level with them.

"We have bested them here, but what if they muster legions of these half-dead to assault our walls? There are only a few men within the keep, for this is the trading season and nine-tenths of our ships are at sea. We needs must spread thinly in the fortress. A man may clip heads with a will, but his arm tires at the business. And if the enemy keeps coming they can overwhelm us by sheer weight of numbers. For they have no fear for themselves and will go forward where one of us might have a second thought, or a third!"

Neither Koris nor the witch had a ready answer for that. Only Simon's first sight of the trading port, hours later, was in a manner reassuring. Seamen though the Sulcarmen might be by first choice, they were also builders, using every natural advantage of the point they had selected as an asset in the erection of the keep. From the land side it was mainly wall with watch towers and firing slits in plenty. And it was only when Magnis Osberic escorted them within that they saw the full strength of the place.

Two arms of rock curved out to the sea—a crab's open claws—and between them was the harbor. But each of those claws had been reinforced with blocks of masonry, walls, watch points, miniature forts, connected to the main body with a maze of underground ways. Wherever possible the outer walls ran down straight to the pound of the waves, providing no possible hold for climbers.

"It would seem," Simon commented, "that this Sulcarkeep was built with the thought of war in mind."

Magnis Osberic laughed shortly. "Master Tregarth, the Peace of the Highways may hold for our blood within Estcarp, and to a measure within Alizon and Karsten—providing we clink gold in the hearing of the right ears. But elsewhere in the world we show swords along with our trade goods, and this is the heart of our kingdom. Down in those warehouses lies our life blood—for the goods that we barter is the flow of our life. To loot Sulcarkeep is the dream of every lordling and every pirate in this world!

"The Kolder may be the demon spawn rumor names them, but they do not disdain the good things of this earth. They would like to paddle their paws in our takings as well as the next. That is why we also have a last defense here—if Sulcarkeep falls her conquerors will not profit!" He brought his big fist down upon the parapet before them in a giant's crushing blow. "Sulcarkeep was built in my great-grandfather's day to provide all our race with a safe port in time of storm—storm of war as well as storm of wind and wave. And it would seem that we now need it."

"Three ships in the harbor," Koris had been counting. "A cargo bottom and two armed runners."

"The cargo is for Karsten in the dawning. Since it carries the Duke's bargainings it can go under his flag and her crew need not stand to arms in the port faring," remarked Osberic.

" 'Tis tongued about that the Duke is to wed. But there is a necklet of Samian fashioning lying in a chest down there intended for the white neck of Aldis. It would appear that Yvian may put the bracelet on some other's wrist, but he intends not to wear it on his own."

The witch shrugged and Koris appeared far more interested in the ships than in any gossip concerning the neighboring court. "And the runners?" he prompted.

"Those remain for a space." The Master Trader was evasive, "They shall patrol. I am better pleased to know what approaches from the sea."

A bomber might reduce the outer shell of Sulcarkeep to rubble in a run or two; heavy artillery could breach its massive walls within hours, Simon decided, as he continued on the inspection round with Koris. But there was a warren of passages and chambers in the rock beneath the foundations of the buildings, some giving on the sea—those having barred doors; unless the Kolder had weapons beyond any arms he had seen in this world, the traders would appear to be unnecessarily nervous. One could think that, until one remembered the empty-eyed foemen from Gorm.

He also noted that while there were guardrooms in plenty and well-filled racks of weapons, stands of the heavy mace-axes, there were few men, widely spread through those rooms, patrols stretched over area of wall. Sulcarkeep was prepared to equip and house thousands of men and a scant hundred or so stood to arms there.

The three of them, Koris, the witch, and Simon drew together on a sea tower where the evening wind strove against their mail.

"I dare not strip Estcarp," Koris spoke angrily, as if in reply to some argument neither of his companions heard, "to center all our manpower here. Such foolishness would be open invitation to Alizon or the Duchy to invade north and south. Osberic has an outer shell which I do not believe even the jaws of the Kolder can crack, but the meat within it is missing. He waited too long; with all his men in port he might hold, yes. With only this handful, I doubt it."

"You doubt, Koris, but you will fight," the woman said. There was neither encouragement nor discouragement in her tone. "Because that is what must be done. And it may well be that this hold will break the Kolder's jaws. But Kolder does come—that Magnis has foreseen truly."

The Captain looked at her eagerly. "You have a foretelling for us, lady?"

She shook her head. "Expect nothing from me that I cannot give, Captain. When we rode into that ambush I could see nothing but a blank ahead. By that very negative sign I recognized the Kolder. But better than that I cannot do. And you, Simon?"

He started. "I? But I have no pretense to your Power—" he began and then added more honestly, "I can say nothing—except as a soldier I think this is an able fort, and now I feel as one trapped within it." He had added that last almost without thinking, but he knew it for the truth.

"But that we shall not say to Osberic," Koris decided. Together they continued to watch the harbor as the sun set, and more and more the city beneath lost the form of a refuge and took on the outline of a cage.

VI
Fog Doom

*I*t began a little after midnight—that creeping line across the sea, blotting out both stars and waves, sending before it a chill which was born of neither wind nor rain, but which bit insidiously into a man's bones, slimed his mail with oily beads, tasted salty and yet faintly corrupt upon his lips.

The line of light globes which followed each curve of the claw fortifications was caught. One by one those pools of light were muffled into vague smears of yellow. To watch that creeping was to watch a world being blotted out inch by inch, foot by foot.

Simon strode back and forth across the small sentry platform on the central watch tower. Half the claw fortifications were swallowed, lost. One of the slim raiders in the harbor was sliced in two by that curtain. It resembled no natural fog he had ever seen, unlike the famous blackouts of London, the poisoned industrial smogs of his own world. The way it crept in from the west as a steady curtain suggested only one thing—a screen behind which an attack might be gathering.

Deadened and hollow, he caught the clamor of the wall alarms, those brazen gongs stationed every so many feet along the claws. Attack! He reached the door of the tower and met the witch.

"They're attacking!" Simon cried.

"Not yet. Those are storm calls, to guide any ship which might be seeking port."

"A Kolder ship!"

"Perhaps so. But you cannot overturn the customs of centuries in an hour. In fog Sulcarkeep's gongs serve seamen, only Osberic's orders can mute them."

"Then such fogs as this one *are* known?"

"Fogs are known. Such as this—that is another matter."

She brushed past him to come out into the open, facing seaward as he had done moments earlier, studying the fast-disappearing harbor.

"We of the Power have a certain measure of control over the natural elements, though like all else that is subject to failure or success beyond our forereckoning. It is within the province of any of my sisterhood to produce a mist which will not only confuse the eyes of the unwary, but also their minds—for a space. But this is different."

"It is natural?" Simon persisted, sure somehow that it was not. Though why he was so certain of that he could not explain.

"When a potter creates a vase he lays clay upon the wheel and molds it with the skill of his hands to match the plan which is in his brain. Clay is a product of the earth, but that which changes its shape is the product of intelligence and training. It is in my mind that someone—or something—has gathered up that which is a part of the sea, of the air, and has molded it into another shape to serve a purpose."

"And what do you in return, lady?" Koris had come out behind them. He strode straight to the parapet and slapped his hands down upon the water-pearled stone. "We are like to be blind men in this!"

She did not look away from the fog, watching it with the intentness of a laboratory assistant engaged in a crucial experiment.

"Blindness they may seek, but blindness can enfold two ways. If they will play at illusion—then let them be countered with their own trick!"

"Fight fog with fog?" the Captain demanded.

"You do not fight one trick with the same. They are calling upon air and water. Therefore we must use water and air in return, but in another fashion." She tapped her thumbnail against her teeth. "Yes, that might be a confusing move," she murmured as she swung around. "We must get down to the harbor level. Ask of Magnis a supply of wood, dry chips will be excellent. But, if he has them not, get knives that we may cut them. Also some cloth. And bring it to the center quay."

The choked clamor of the gongs echoed hollowly across the heart of the harbor as the small knot of Sulcarmen and Guards came out on the quay. An armload of board lengths appeared and the witch took the smallest. Her hands plied the knife clumsily as she strove to whittle out the rude outline of a boat, pointed at bow, rounded at stern. Simon took it from her, peeling off the white strips easily, the others following his example as the woman approved.

They had a fleet of ten, of twenty, of thirty chip boats, palm-size, each fitted with a stick mast and a cloth sail the witch tied into place. She went down on her knees before that line, and, stooping very low, blew carefully into each of the tiny sails, pressed her finger for a moment on the prow of each of the whittled chips.

"Wind and water, wind and water," she singsonged. "Wind to hasten, water to bear, sea to carry, fog to ensnare!"

Swiftly her hands moved, tossing one and another of the crude representations of a sea fleet out into the water of the harbor. The fog was almost upon them, but it was still not too thick for Simon to miss an amazing sight. The tiny boats had formed into a wedge-shaped line pointing straight for the now hidden sea. And, as the first dipped across the line of the fog curtain it was no hastily chipped toy, but a swift, gleaming ship, finer than the slim raiders Osberic had displayed with pride.

The witch caught at Simon's dangling wrist to draw herself to her feet again. "Do not believe all that you see, outworld man. We deal in illusion, we of the Power. But let us hope that this illusion will be as effective as their fog, frightening off any invaders."

"They can't be real ships!" Stubbornly he protested the evidence of his eyes.

"We depend too strongly upon our outer senses. If one can befool the eyes, the fingers, the nose—then the magic is concrete for a space. Tell me, Simon, should you be planning to enter this harbor for attack and then saw out of the fog about your ships a fleet you had not suspected was there, would you not think twice of offering battle? I have only tried to buy us time, for illusion breaks when it is put to any real test. A Kolder ship which would try to lock sides and board one of that fleet could prove it to be what it is. But sometimes time bought is a precious thing."

She was in a measure right. At least, if the enemy had planned to use the blanket of mist to cover an attack on the harbor, they did not follow through. There was no invasion alarm that night, neither was there any lifting of the thick cover over the city as the hour of dawn passed.

The masters of the three ships in the harbor waited upon Osberic for orders, and he could give none, save to wait out the life of the fog. Simon made the rounds of the Guards in Koris' wake, and sometimes it was necessary for one man to link fingers in the other's belt lest they lose touch, upon the outer stations of the sea wall. Orders were given that the gongs continue to beat at regular intervals, not now for the protection of those at sea, but merely that one sentry post keep in touch with the next. And men turned strained, drawn faces, half drew weapons as their reliefs came upon them, until one shouted the pass word or some identification ahead lest he be spitted upon the steel of a jumpy outpost.

"At this rate," Tregarth commented as he sidestepped one rush from a Sulcarman they came upon suddenly, and so saved himself from a crippling blow, if not worse, "they will not need to send any attack force, for we shall be flying out upon each other. Let a man seem to wear a beaked helm in this murk and he will speedily be short a head."

"So I have thought," the Captain answered shortly. "They play with illusion, too, born of our nerves and fears. But what answer can we give except what we had already done?"

"Anyone with good ears could pick up our pass words." Simon determined to face the worst. "A whole section of wall could fall to their control, post by post."

"Can we even be sure that this *is* an attack?" counter-questioned the other bitterly. "Outworlder, if you can give better orders here, then do so and I shall accept them gladly! I am a man of war, and the ways of war I know—or thought I knew—well. Also I believed that I knew the ways of wizards, since I serve Estcarp with a whole heart. But this is something I have never met before; I can only do my best."

"And never have I seen this manner of fighting either," Simon admitted readily. "It would baffle anyone. But this I think now—they will not come by sea."

"Because that is the way we look to have them creep upon us?" Koris caught him up quickly. "I do not think that the keep can be assaulted from land. These searovers have built shrewdly. It would need siege machinery such as would take weeks to assemble."

"Sea and land—which leaves?"

"Earth and air," Koris replied. "Earth! Those under passages!"

"But we cannot spread men too thinly to watch all the underground ways."

Koris' sea green eyes glowed with the same feral battle light Simon had seen in them at their first meeting.

"There is a watch which can be put upon them, needing no men. A trick I know. Let us get to Magnis." He began to run, the point of his sheathed sword clinking now and again against the stone walls as he rounded the turns in the keep corridors.

Basins were lined up on a table, of all sizes and several shapes, but they were uniformly of copper and the balls Koris was carefully apportioning, one to a bowl, were also of metal. One of the bowl-and-ball combinations, installed in the portion of wall overhanging an underground way, would betray any attempt to force the door far below by the oscillation of ball within basin.

Earth was safeguarded as best they could. Which left—the air. Was it because he was familiar with air warfare that Simon found himself listening, watching, at the cost of a crick in the neck, the murk encasing the towers of the port? Yet a civilization which depended upon the relatively primitive dart guns, the sword, the shield, and a mailed body for offense and defense—no matter what subtle tricks of the mind they called in bolstering aids—could not produce airborne attack as well.

Thanks to Koris' device of the bowls they had a few moments of warning when the Kolder thrust came. But from all five points where the bowls had been placed that alarm arose at nearly the same instant. The halls leading to each doorway had been stuffed during frenzied hours of labor with all the burnable stuff in the warehouses of the port. Mats of sheep wool and cowhair soaked in oil and tar, which the shipwrights used for the calking, were woven in around torn bales of fine fabrics, bags of dried grain and seeds, and oil and wine poured in rivulets to soak into these giant plugs.

When the bowls warned, torches were applied and other portals closed, sealing off from the central core those flame-filled ways.

"Let them run their cold dog noses into that!" Magnis Osberic thumped his war ax exultingly on the table in the central hall of the main keep. For the first time since the fog had imprisoned his domain the Master Trader appeared to lose his air of harassment. As a seafarer he hated and feared fog, be it born of nature or the meddling of powers. With a chance for direct action, he was all force and drive again.

"Ahhhhhh!" Across the hubbub in the hall that scream cut like a sword slice. Torture of body was not all of it, for only some supreme fear could have torn it from a human throat.

Magnis, his bull's head lowering as if he would charge the enemy, Koris, sword ready, a little crouched so that his dwarfish body gathered strength from the earth, the rest of the men in that chamber were frozen for a long second.

Perhaps because during all this period of waiting he had been half expecting it, Simon identified the source first, and sped for the stair which, three floors higher, gave upon the sentry go of the roof.

He did not reach that level. Screams and cries from above, the clash of metal against metal was warning enough. Slowing his pace, Simon drew his gun. And it was good he was cautious for he was midway to the second level when a body rolled down, missing him by a scant inch. It was a Sulcarman, his throat a ragged wound still pumping blood to spatter wall and stair. Simon looked up into a wild confusion.

Two Guardsmen and three of the seafarers still fought, their backs against the wall on the landing of the next level, keeping at bay invaders who attacked with the single-minded ferocity their kin had displayed at the road ambush. Simon snapped a shot, and then another. But a wave of beaked helms poured unceasingly from above. He could only guess that in some way the enemy had come by air and now held the top floors of the keep.

There was no time to speculate upon their method of getting there—it was enough that they had managed to break through. Two more of the seafarers, one of the Guard were down. The dead and wounded, friends and foe alike were disregarded by the beaked helms. Bodies slipped downstairs—they could not be stopped there. The plug must come below.

Simon leaped for the first landing, kicking open the two doors fronting on it. The furniture favored by Sulcar was heavy stuff. But the smaller pieces could be moved. In that moment Simon summoned up strength he did not know he possessed, jerking and pushing articles out to choke the stairwell.

A beaked head faced him through the upraised legs of a chair used to top his efforts, and a sword point struck for his face. Simon crashed the chair over on that helm. There was a smarting cut on his cheek but the attacker was not a part of the barricade.

"Sul! Sul!"

Simon was elbowed to one side and he saw Magnis' face, as red as its tawny bristle of mustache, loom up as the trader chopped down, smashed up at the first wave of invaders to reach the stair barrier and claw at the stuff which formed it.

Aim, fire, aim again. Throw away an empty dart clip, reload to fire anew. Straddle a Guardsman down moaning, until the man could be dragged back into whatever safety anyone could find in the keep now. Fire—Fire!

Somehow Simon had come back into the hall, then the party of which he was one were on another stairway, selling each flight dearly as they descended. There was a thin smoke here—tendrils of fog? No, for when it wreathed them its acrid bite stung nose and throat setting them coughing. Aim—fire—grab dart packs from the belt of a fallen Guardsman who could no longer use any weapon.

The steps were behind now. Men shouted hoarsely, and the smoke was worse. Simon smeared his hand across his watering eyes and pulled at the throat scarf of his helmet. His breath came in shallow gasps.

Blindly he followed after his companions. Doors of five-inch thickness swung after them, were barred and locked. One . . . two . . . three . . . four of such barriers. Then they stumbled into a room facing an installation housed in a casing taller than the giant of a man who leaned against it, dull-eyed. The Guardsmen and the seafarers who had made it rimmed the room, leaving the strange machine to the master of the city.

Magnis Osberic had lost his bear-crested helm, his fur cloak was a tattered string trailing from one shoulder. His ax lay across the top of the casing, and from its blade a red line dripped sluggishly to the stone pavement. The ruddiness of his coloring had faded, leaving his skin with a withered look. His eyes were wide, staring at men and not seeing them—Simon guessed that the man was in a state of shock.

"Gone!" He picked up the ax, slipped its long haft back and forth in his rope-callused hand. "From the air like winged demons! No man can fight against demons." Then he laughed softly, warmly, as a man might laugh when he took a willing woman into his arms. "But there is also an answer to demons. Sulcarkeep shall not serve that spawn for a nesting place!"

His bull head lowered for the charge once more, swung slowly as he singled out the Estcarp men from among his own followers. "You have fought well, you of the witch blood. But this last is no doom laid upon you. We shall loose the energy which feeds the city powers and blast the port. Get you forth that you may perhaps settle the accounting in a way those air-flying wizards can understand. Be sure we shall take with us such a number of them that they shall have thinned ranks against that day! Go your way, witch men, and leave us of Sulcarkeep to *our* final reckoning!"

Urged by his eyes and his voice, as if he had caught each of them in a bear's grip and thrust them away from him and his, the remnant of the Guard gathered together. Koris was still with them, his hawk helm lacking a wing. And the witch, her face serene, but her lips moving as she walked quietly across the chamber. Twenty more men and Simon.

As one the Guards drew to attention, their stained swords swinging up in salute to those they left. Magnis grunted.

"Pretty, pretty, witchmen. But this is no time for parade. Get out!"

They filed through a small door he indicated, Koris through last to slam and bar it. At a dead run they took that passage. Luckily there were globe lights set in the roof at intervals and the floor was smooth, for the need for haste burned in them.

The sound of sea and surf grew stronger and they came out in a cave where small boats swung at anchor.

"Down!" Simon was pushed aboard with others, and Koris' hand slapped between his shoulders, sending him facedown. Men landed on him and about him, pinning him flat to the rocking bottom. There was the slam of another door—or was it a deck shutting over them? Light was gone and with it air. Simon lay quiet, having no idea of what would happen next.

Under him the boat moved, men's bodies rolled, he was kicked, prodded, and he buried his face in the crook of his arm. The craft which held them swung about and his stomach fought against that motion. He had never been too good a sailor. Mainly occupied with his fight against sickness, he was not prepared for a blast which seemed to end the world with one blow of sound and pressure.

They were still rolling in the waves, but when Simon lifted his head he gulped clean air. He wriggled and strove, paying no attention to the grunts and protests of those about him. No more fog was his first dazed thought—and then—it was day! The sky, the sea about them, the coast behind were clear and bright.

But when did the sun rise from the shore, leap up in sky-touching flames from a land base? He had been deafened by the blast, but not blinded. They were heading out to sea, leaving the source of that heat and light behind them.

One . . . two . . . three cockshells of boats he counted. There were no sails, they must be motored in some way. A man sat erect in the stern of theirs, his shoulders identifying him. Koris held that tiller. They were free of the inferno which had been the port of Sulcarkeep, but where did they head?

Fog gone, and the fire on shore giving them light. But the waves which swept them along were not born of any calm sea. Perhaps the shock of that blast with which Magnis had destroyed the keep had been communicated to the ocean. For a wind drove down upon them as if a hand strove to press them beneath the surface, and those on board the featherweight ships began to realize that they had gained perhaps only a few minutes of life rather than full escape.

2. Venture of Verlaine

∞

I
Ax Marriage

*T*he sea was dull and gray, the color of an ax blade which would never take on a sheen no matter how much one polished, or a steel mirror misted by moisture one could not rub away. And above it the sky was as flat, until it was hard to distinguish the meeting line between air and water.

Loyse huddled on the ledge beneath the arrow-split window. She dreaded the depths, for this turret, bulging roundly from its parent wall, hung directly over the wicked, surf collared rocks of the shoreline, and she had no head for heights. Yet she was often drawn to this very seat because when one stared straight out into the emptiness, which was seldom troubled save by a diving bird, one could see freedom.

Her hands, long fingered, narrow of palm, pressed flat against the stone on either side of the window as she did lean forward an inch or so, making herself eye what she feared, as she made herself do many things her body, her mind shrank from. To be Fulk's daughter one must grow an inner casing of ice and iron which no blow to the flesh, no taunt to the spirit could crack. And she had been intent upon that fashioning of an interior citadel for more than half the years of her short life.

There had been many women at Verlaine, for Fulk was a man of lusty appetite. And Loyse had watched them come and go from her babyhood, cold-eyed and measuring herself. To none had he given wifehood, by none had he sired other offspring—which was Fulk's great dissatisfaction and so far her own gain. For Verlaine was not Fulk's by blood, but by his one and only marriage with her mother, and only as long as Loyse lived could he continue to hold it and its rich rights of pillage and wreckage, ashore and afield. There were kinsmen of her mother's in Karsten who would be quick enough to claim lordship here were she to die.

But, had Fulk sired a son by any of the willing—and unwilling—women he had brought to the huge bed in the lord's chamber, then he could have claimed more than just his own life tenancy for the male heir under the new laws of the Duke. By the old customs mother-right was for inheritance; now one took a father's holding, and only in cases where there was no male heir did the old law prevail.

Loyse cherished her tiny thread of power and safety, held to it as her one hope. Let Fulk be chopped down in one of his border raids, let him be sought out by some vengeful male of a family despoiled, and she and Verlaine would be free together! Ah, then they would see what a woman could do! They would learn that she had not been moping in secret all these years as most of them believed.

She drew back from the ledge, walked across the room. It was chill with the breath of the sea, gloomy with lack of sun. But she was used to cold and dusk, some of both were a fast part of her now.

Beyond the curtained bed she came to stand in front of a mirror. It was no soft lady's looking glass, but a shield, diamond-shaped, polished through patient hours until it gave back to the room a slightly distorted reflection. And to stand so, facing squarely what it told her, was another part of Loyse's strict self-discipline.

She was small, but that was the only feminine characteristic she shared with the blowsy women who satisfied her father's men, or with the richer fare he kept for his own enjoyment. Her body was as straight and slender as a boy's, with only shadow curves to hint she was not a lad. The hair which lay in braids across her shoulders, and then fell below waist level, was thick enough. But it was lank and of so pale a yellow that except in direct sunlight it was white as a beldame's, while lashes and brows of the same colorless tint made her face seem strangely blank and without intelligence. The skin pulled tightly across the fine bones of her face and chest was smooth and also lacking in any real color. Even the line of her lips was of the palest rose. She was a bleached thing, grown in the dark, but a vitality within her was as strong as the supple blade a wise swordsman chooses over the heavier hacking weapon of the inexperienced.

Suddenly her hands flew together, gripped tightly for an instant. Then she as quickly snapped them apart and to her sides, though under her hanging sleeves they were still balled into fists, nails biting palms. Loyse did not turn to the door, nor give any other outward hint that she had heard that rattling of the latch. She knew just how far she dared go in her subtle defiance of Fulk, and from that limit she never retreated. Sometimes, she thought despairingly, her father never recognized her rebellion at all.

The door slammed back against the wall. Verlaine's lord always treated any barrier as if he were storming an enemy fortress. And he tramped in now with the tread of a man who has just lifted the city keys from the sword point of a vanquished commander.

If Loyse was the colorless creature of the dark, Fulk was lord of sun and flamboyant light. His good body was beginning to show traces of his rough living, but he was still more than handsome, his red-gold head carried with the arrogance of a prince, his well-cut features only a little blurred. Most of

Verlaine worshiped their lord. He had an openhanded if uneven generosity when he was pleased, and his vices were all ones which his men understood and shared.

Loyse caught his reflection in the mirror, brave, bright, turning her even more into a night taper. But she did not face about.

"Greetings, Lord Fulk." Her voice was toneless.

"Lord Fulk, is it? Is that the way you speak to your father, wench? Come show a little more than ice in your veins for once, girl!"

His hand slid under one of the braids on her shoulder, and he forced her around, gripping with strength which would leave her bruised for a week. He did it deliberately, she knew, but she would give no sign of feeling.

"Here I come with news as would send any proper wench leaping with joy, and you turn me that cold fish face of yours with no pleasure," he contemplated jovially. But that which looked out of his eyes was not born of good humor.

"You have not yet voiced this news, my lord."

His fingers kneaded into her flesh as if seeking to find and crush the bones hidden there.

"To be sure I have not! Yet it is news as will set any maid's heart to pounding in her. Wedding and bedding, my girl, wedding and bedding!"

Purposely Loyse chose, but with a fear she had not known before, to misunderstand him.

"You take a lady for Verlaine, my lord? Fortune grant you a fair face for such an occurrence."

His grip on her did not loosen, and now he shook her, with the outward appearance of one playfully admonishing, but with a force which brought pain.

"You may be a wry-faced nothing of a woman, but you are not stupid of wit, no matter how you may think to befool others. You should be properly a female at your age. At least you will now have a lord to make trial of that. And I'd advise you not to play your tricks with him. By all accounts he likes his bedfellows biddable!"

What she had long feared most had come upon her and it brought with it a betrayal of feeling she could not bite back in time.

"A wedding needs free consent—" She stopped then, knowing shame for her momentary breaking.

He was laughing, relishing having torn that protest out of her. His hand moved across her shoulder to vise upon the back of her neck in a pinch which brought an involuntary gasp out of her. Then, as one moves a lifeless puppet, he whirled her about, pushing her face toward the mirror shield, holding her helpless there while he pelted her with words he believed would hurt worse than any beating his hands could inflict.

"Look upon that curdled mass of nothing you call a face! Do you think any man could set his lips to it without closing his eyes and wishing himself elsewhere? Be glad, wench, that you have something besides your face and that bone of a body to lure a suitor. You'll consent freely to anyone who'll take you. And be glad that you have a father who can make a bargain as good as I have for you. Yes, girl, you'd better crawl on those stiff knees of yours and thank any gods you have that Fulk looks after his own."

His words were a mutter of thunder; she saw no reflection in the mirror, save certain misty horrors of her own imagining. Which one of the brutes who rode in Fulk's train would she be thrown to—for some advantage for his lord?

"Karsten himself—" There was a sort of wonder underlying Fulk's rising exultation. "Karsten, mind you, and this lump of unbaked dough squeaks of consent! You *are* lacking in wits!" He released her with a sudden push which sent her flying against the shield and the metal rang against the wall. She fought for her balance, kept her feet, and turned to face him.

· "The Duke!" That she could not believe. Why should the ruler of the duchy ask for the daughter of a shore baron, old and proud as her maternal lineage might be?

"Yes, the Duke!" Fulk seated himself on the end of the bed, swinging his booted feet. "Talk of fortune! Some good providence winked at your birth, my girl. Karsten's herald rode in this morning with an offer of ax marriage for you."

"Why?"

Fulk's feet stopped moving. He did not scowl, but his face was sober.

"There are a bristle of reasons like darts at his back!" He held up his hands and began to tell off the fingers of one with the forefinger of the other.

"Item: The Duke, for all his might, was a rider of mercenaries before he set his seal on Karsten, and I doubt if he can rightly name his dam, let alone his sire. He crushed those of the lords who tried to face him down. But that was a good half-score of years ago and he no longer wants to ride in mail and smoke rebels out of their castles. Having won his duchy he wishes now some easy years in which to enjoy it. A wife taken from the ranks of those he opposed is a gift offering for peace. And while Verlaine may not be the richest hold in Karsten yet the blood of its lords is very high—was not that often made very plain to me when I came a-wooing? And I was no blank shield, but the younger son of Farthom in the northern hills." His lips twisted as if he remembered certain slights out of the past.

"And since you are the heiress of Verlaine you are very suitable."

Loyse laughed. "It cannot be true, lord, that I am the only marriageable maid of gentle birth in all Karsten."

"How right. And he could do very well elsewhere. But as I have said, my dearest of daughters, you have certain other advantages. Verlaine is a coast holding with age-old rights, and the Duke has ambitions which run in more peaceful lines now than sword conquest. What say you, Loyse, if there was to be a port here to attract the northern trade?"

"And what would Sulcarkeep be doing while such a port came into being? Those who swear by Sul are jealous of their holdings."

"Those who swear by Sul may soon be able to swear by nothing at all," he returned with a calm certainty which carried a note of conviction. "They have troublesome neighbors who are growing more troublesome yet. And Estcarp, where they might look for aid, is a hollow shell eaten out by its preoccupation with witchery. One push and the whole land will fall into the filthy dust which should have buried it long ago."

"So, for my blood and a plan for a port, Lord Yvian offers marriage," she persisted, unable yet to believe that this was true. "Yet is the mighty lord free to send his ax hither for a wedding? I am a maid close kept in a hold far from Kars, yet have I heard of a certain Aldis who issues orders, to have them promptly obeyed by all who wear the Duke's sign."

"Yvian will have Aldis, and, yes, half a hundred of her ilk, and it is no concern of yours, girl. Give him a son—if your thin blood can form a man, the which I doubt! Give him a son and hold up your head at the high table, but trouble him not with any mewling calls upon him for more than company courtesy. Be glad for your honors and if you are wise you'll speak Aldis and the others fair in their time. Yvian is not said to be a patient or easily forgiving man." He slid down the slope of the bed and stood up, ready to be gone. But before he went he detached a small key from the chain at his belt and tossed it to her.

"For all your ghost face, girl, you'll not go to your wedding without your due or gauds. I'll send Bettris to you; she has an eye for pretties and can help you pull out enough for robes. And veils for your face, you'll need them! And keep an eye to Bettris, don't let her take more than she can carry in her two hands—for herself."

Loyse caught up the key so eagerly that he laughed. "So that much of you is female—you want gauds as much as any wench. Give us another storm or two and we can make up what you drag out of the storehouse anyway."

He strode out, leaving the door wide open. As Loyse followed him to shut it once again, she treasured that key tight in her hand. For months, years, she had schemed to get that same bit of metal into her holding. Now she had been given it openly and none would dispute her rummaging for what she truly wanted in the storehouse of Verlaine.

Rights of wreckage and plunder over wave and shore! Since Verlaine Keep had risen on the heights between two treacherous capes, the sea had brought its lords a rich harvest. And the storehouse of the pile was indeed a treasure room, only opened upon its lord's orders. Fulk must believe that he had far the best of the bargain with Yvian to allow her unsupervised plundering there. For the company of Bettris she did not fear. Fulk's latest bedfellow was as greedy as she was fair, and she would not cast any eye on Loyse's choices, given a chance to hunt on her own.

She tossed the key from right hand to left, and for the first time a thin smile curved her pale lips. Well might Fulk be surprised at her choices from the treasure of Verlaine! Also he might be astounded at other things she knew about these walls which he accepted as such safe barriers. Her gaze flickered for a moment to the one where the shield mirror hung.

There was a hurried rap at her door. Loyse smiled again, this time with contempt. It had not taken Bettris long to act upon Fulk's orders. But at least the woman dared not intrude upon her lover's daughter uninvited. Loyse went to the door.

"The Lord Fulk—" began the girl who stood without, her plump beauty as full and vivid as Fulk's virility.

Loyse held up the key. "I have it." She named no name, gave no title to the other, but glanced at those well-rounded shoulders bursting out of the robe which strained over every luxuriant curve the other advertised. Behind Bettris were two of the serving men, a chest between them. Loyse raised her eyebrows and the other laughed nervously.

"Lord Fulk would have you select your brideclothes, lady. He said there was no need to be timid in the storehouse."

"The Lord Fulk is generous," returned Loyse tonelessly. "Shall we go?"

The women avoided the great hall and the outer chambers of the hold, for the treasure room lay at the foot of the tower in which were the private quarters of the family. For that Loyse was glad; she kept well away from the central life of her father's house. And when they came at last to the door opened by the key she bore, she was very pleased that only Bettris dared follow her within. The serving men pushed the chest in after them and left.

Three globes set in the ceiling gave light to show chests and boxes, bales and bags. Bettris smoothed the robe over her hips in the gesture of a keeper of a market stall settling down to a spate of bargaining. Her dark eyes darted from pile to pile, and Loyse, putting the key into her belt purse, added fuel to that avid hunger.

"I do not think that the Lord Fulk would deny you some selections for yourself. In fact he said as much to me. But I would warn you to be discreet and not too greedy."

Those plump hands fluttered from hips to full, only half-covered breasts. Loyse crossed to a table cutting down the center of the room, lifted the lid of a casket resting there. Even she blinked at the massed wealth within. She had not truly realized until that moment that Verlaine's rapine over the years had yielded so well. From a tangle of chains and necklets she freed a great brooch, gaudy with red stones and much chasing, a bauble not to her taste, but one which in a manner matched the overblown comeliness of her companion.

"Such a piece as this," she suggested and held it out.

Bettris' hands crooked to hold it, then she snatched them back. The point of her tongue showed between her wet red lips as she glanced from the brooch to Loyse and back again. Conquering her repugnance, the girl held the massive gem-set thing to the deep V-throat of the other's robe, mastering the impulse to jerk back when she felt the softness of Bettris' flesh.

"It becomes you, take it!" In spite of her wish Loyse's words were a sharp order. But the bait was taken. With attention only for the gems, the woman moved to the table, and Loyse was, for that moment and perhaps others, free to do as she pleased.

She knew what to look for, but how it might be stored she was unsure. Slowly the girl moved between piles of goods. Some were stained with salt rime and from one or two came a faint exotic scent. Having put a small barrier of boxes between herself and Bettris, she chanced upon a chest which looked promising.

Loyse's fragile appearance was deceiving. Just as she had disciplined her emotions and her mind against this day, so had she trained her body. The lid was heavy, but she had it up. And knew by the smell of oil, the sight of the discolored cloths on top, she was hot on the scent. She pawed aside those cloths gingerly, fearing to stain her hands and so reveal the nature of her search. Then she lifted out a shirt of mail, holding it to measure against her shoulders. Too large—perhaps she could find nothing fitted to her slight frame.

She delved deeper. A second shirt—a third—this must have been part of the stock in trade of a master smith. At the bottom was one which must have been made to order for the stripling son of some overlord. For against her it needed very little change at all. The rest were bundled back into the chest while she folded her find as small as possible.

Bettris was trapped by the casket of jewels and Loyse did not doubt that more than one piece from that coffer was now hidden about her person. But it gave her a chance to make her own raids, moving almost openly now between the box she had brought with her and her sources of supply, adding lengths of silk and velvet, a cape of fur, as topping concealment.

To please Bettris and forestall suspicion, Loyse chose from the jewelry also and then summoned the men to carry the chest back to her chamber. She was afraid Bettris might urge unpacking on her, but the bribe had worked well, the woman was in a fever to examine her own spoils privately and did not linger.

In a fury of speed, tempered by caution and the precision of careful fore-planning, Loyse set to work. Those hastily selected lengths of fabric, those packets of lace and embroidery, were dumped on her bed. Then she was on her knees clearing the coffer where her present wardrobe lay. Some things were long ready, fashioned long ago. But here were all the rest. With a care she had not granted the fine stuffs Loyse placed together the dower she intended to take from Verlaine, on her back, in her purse, in the saddle bags which were all she dared carry.

Mail shirt, leather underclothing, weapons, helm, gold trade tokens, a handful of jewels. Over those she threw once more her own garments, patting them smooth, with the care of a good housekeeper. She was breathing a little fast, but she had the coffer closed and was spreading out the other loot when she heard that tread outside—Fulk returning for his key.

Impulsively she caught up a veil bordered in silver thread, a dew-hung cobweb of a thing, and pulled it about her head and shoulders, seeing that it became her vilely, but generous enough now that her purpose was gained to allow her father his chance for a jeer or two. With it on she stepped once more to pose before the shield mirror.

II
Sea Wrack

*T*he very circumstances which she hoped would set her free worked against Loyse during the next few days. For while Yvian of Karsten did not ride himself to Verlaine either to inspect the bride he had bargained for or the heritage which would come with her, he sent a train proper enough to do her honor. And she was called upon to be on show, so that underneath her outer shell she seethed with impatience and growing desperation.

At last she pinned her hopes to the wedding feast, for then, if ever, there would be muddled heads within the keep. Fulk wanted to impress the Duke's lords with his lavish open-handedness. He would produce the liquid treasures of the hold and it would be her best chance to follow her plans.

The storm struck first, such a wild blast of wind and raging sea water as Loyse, familiar with that coast since her birth, had never seen before. For the spray reached high enough to spatter the windows of her tower room with its salt foam. And Bettris, and the maid Fulk had sent to help with the sewing of her robes, shivered and shrank with each bat of the wind's fist ringing through the stones of the walls.

Bettris stood up, a roll of fine green silk tumbling to the floor, her dark eyes wide. Her fingers moved in the sacred sign of her forgotten village childhood.

"Witch storm," her voice came small, overridden by the scream of the gale until Loyse heard only a thin whisper.

"This is not Estcarp," Loyse matched a length of embroidery to satin and set even stitches. "We do not have power over wind and wave. And Estcarp does not move beyond her own borders. It is a storm, that is all. And if you wish to please Lord Fulk you will not tremble at sea storms for Verlaine knows them often. How else," she paused to draw a new length of thread through a needle eye, "do you think our treasure is gathered?"

Bettris turned on her, lips strained over her sharp little teeth in a vixen's snarl. "I am coast born, I have seen storms in plenty. Yes, I have coursed the shore with the gleaners afterwards. Which is more than you have ever deigned to do, my lady! But this is like no storm I have seen or heard tell of in all my life! There is evil in it, I tell you—great evil!"

"Evil for those who must trust to the waves." Loyse put down her sewing. She crossed to the windows, but there was nothing to be seen through the lace of spume which blotted out the dark of the day.

The maid made no pretense at work. She was drawn in upon herself close to the hearth where sea coral burned fitfully, rocking back and forth, her hands pressed against her breast as if she would ease some pain there. Loyse went to her. She had little of pity or interest in the wenches of the castle—from Bettris and her countless predecessors to the slatterns in the kitchen. Now against her own inclination she asked:

"You ail, wench?"

The girl was cleaner than most. Perhaps she had been ordered to tidy herself before being sent hither. Now the face she turned to Loyse drew the attention of Fulk's daughter. This was no village girl, no peasant dragged in to pleasure a retainer and then become a work drudge. Her face was a mask of fear which had been so long a part of her that it had shaped her as a potter shapes clay. Yet under that something else struggled.

Bettris laughed shrilly. " 'Tis no pain in her belly that eats at her, only memories. She was a sea wrack herself once. Weren't you, slut!" Her soft leather shoe struck the girl's haunch, nearly turning her into the fire.

"Leave her alone!" For the first time Loyse flashed her hidden fire. She had always kept aloof from the strand after a storm, since there was nothing she could do to dispute Fulk's rule—or rather Fulk's license there—she would not harrow herself with sights she could not forget.

Bettris simpered uneasily. With Loyse she was uncertain of her ground, so she did not rise to the challenge.

"Send the muling idiot away. You will get no work from her as long as the storm rages—nor afterwards for a while. 'Tis a pity for she is clever with her needle, else she would have been sent to fatten the shore eels long ago."

Loyse went to the wide expanse of the bed where much of her gear had been spread about. There was a shawl there, plain in the welter of brilliant silks and fine fabrics. Catching it up she took it back to the fireside and threw it about the shuddering maid. Disregarding Bettris' amazement, Loyse dropped on her knees, put her hands to cover those of the girl, and looking into that drawn face, tried to will away from them both the grisly customs of Verlaine which had warped them in different ways.

Bettris pulled at her sleeve.

"How dare you?" Loyse blazed.

The other stood her ground, a sly grin now on her full lips. "The hour grows late, lady. Would Lord Fulk take it well that you nurse this slut when he meets with the Duke's lords to sign the marriage contract? Shall I tell him why you do not come?"

Loyse regarded her levelly. "I shall do my lord's biding in this, as in other things, wench. Do not think to lesson *me!*"

She broke hold with the girl's hands reluctantly, saying:

"Stay here. No one shall come near you. Understand—no one!"

Did the other understand? She was rocking back and forth again, racked by old pain cut into her dulled mind even after the scars had faded from her body.

"I do not need you to robe me," Loyse turned on Bettris, and the other flushed. She could not face the younger girl down and she knew it.

"You would be the better for some knowledge of the kind of sorcery any woman knows, lady," she replied sharply. "I could show you how to make a man look at you full faced as you pass. If you would but put a little dark stain upon your brows and lashes, some of the rose salve on your lips—" Her annoyance was forgotten, as her creative instinct aroused. She surveyed Loyse critically and impersonally and the other found herself listening in spite of her scorn for Bettris and all she represented. "Yes, if you would listen to me, lady, you could perhaps draw your lord's eyes away from that Aldis long enough for him to see another face. There are other ways, also, for the charming of a man." Her tongue tip worked along her lips. "There is much I could teach you, lady, which would give you weapons to use for yourself." She drew nearer, some of the glitter of the storm flashing in her eyes.

"Yvian has bargained for me as I stand," Loyse replied, rejecting Bettris' offer, all that Bettris stood for, "and so must be satisfied with what he gets!" And that is more true than Bettris can guess, she added silently.

The woman shrugged. "It is your life, lady. And before you are out of it, you shall discover that you cannot order it to your liking."

"Have I ever?" asked Loyse quietly. "Now go. As you have said, it grows late and I have much to do."

She sat through the ceremonies of the contract signing with her usual calm acceptance. The men the Duke had sent to fetch his bride to Kars were three very different types, and she found it interesting to study them.

Hunold was a comrade from Yvian's old mercenary days. He had a reputation as a soldier which reached even into such a backwater as Verlaine. Oddly enough his appearance did not match either his occupation, nor his reputation. Where Loyse had expected to see a man such as her father's seneschal—though perhaps slicked over with some polish—she found herself fronting a silk-clad, drawling, languid courtier, who might never have felt the weight of mail on his back. His rounded chin, long-lashed eyes, smooth cheeks, gave him a deceptive youth, as well as the seeming of untried softness. And Loyse, trying to match the man to the things she had heard concerning him, wondered and was a little afraid.

Siric, who represented the Temple of Fortune, who tomorrow would say the words while her hands rested on the war ax, thus making her as much Yvian's as if he clasped her in truth, was old. He had a red face and there was a swelling blue vein in the middle of his low forehead. As he listened or spoke in a soft bumble, he munched continually on small sweetmeats from a comfit box his servant kept ever in reach, and his yellow priest's robe strained over a paunch of notable dimensions.

The Lord Duarte was of the old nobility. But in turn he did not suit his role very well. Small and thin, with a twitching tic which pulled at his lower lip, the harassed air of a man constrained to some task he loathed, he spoke only when an answer was demanded of him. And alone of the three he paid some attention to Loyse. She discovered him watching her broodingly, but there was nothing in his manner which hinted of pity or promise of aid. It was rather that she was the symbol of trouble he would like to sweep from his path.

Loyse was grateful that custom allowed her to escape that night's feasting. Tomorrow she must sit through the start of the wedding banquet, but as soon as the wine began to pass—yes—then! Holding to that thought she hurried back to her room.

She had forgotten the sewing wench, and it was with a start that she saw a figure outlined against the window. The wind was dying now as if the worst of the storm had blown out. But there was another sound, the keening of one who has been hopelessly bereaved. And salt air bit at her from the opened pane.

Angry because of her own worries, tense over what was to come and to what she must nerve herself during the next twenty-four hours, Loyse sprang across the room and seized the swinging window frame, pulling at the girl that she might slam it shut. Though the wind had ceased, the clouds were still slashed by lightning. And in one such revelation Loyse saw what the other must have watched for long moments.

Driving in upon the waiting fangs of the cape were ships: two . . . three of them. And such ships as dwarfed the coastwise traders she had seen pulled to their deaths there before by that treacherous onshore current which enriched and damned Verlaine. These could only be part of a proud fleet of some great seafaring lord. Yet in the continued flashes of light which gave only seconds' viewing, Loyse could sight no activity on board any of the vessels, no attempts being made to ward off fate. They were ghost ships sailing on to their deaths and apparently their crews did not care.

The lights of the wreckers, of the shoreline scavengers, were already moving in clusters from the high gate of Verlaine. For a man on the spot might just conceal some rich picking for himself in the general confusion, though Fulk's weighty hand and a quick noose for those caught had cut down such thievery to a shadow. They would cast nets to bring in the flotsam, turn to tasks they had long practice in. And for any who went ashore still living! Loyse exerted her strength and dragged the girl away, shut and barred the window.

But to her surprise the face the other now turned to her was no longer troubled by ancient terrors. There was intelligence in the depths of the girl's dark eyes, excitement, a gathering strength.

She held her head slightly to one side as if she listened for some sound she must sort out of the brazen clamor of the storm. More and more it was apparent that whatever had been her place in the world before the sea brought her to Verlaine, she was no common soldier's wench.

"That which has been long in the building," the girl's tone was remote, she spoke as if from the core of some experience Loyse could never know. "Choose, choose well. For this night is the fate of countries, as well as that of men, to be made and unmade!"

"Who are you?" Loyse demanded as the girl continued to change before her eyes. She was no monster, put on no shape of beast or bird as rumor whispered could be done by the witches of Estcarp. But that which had lain dormant, wounded almost to death, within her struggled once again for life, showed through her scarred body.

"Who am I? Nobody . . . nothing. But one comes who is greater than the I who once lived. Choose well, Loyse of Verlaine—and live. Choose ill—and die, as I have died, bit by bit, day by day."

"That fleet—" Loyse half turned to the windows. Could it possibly be that some invader, reckless enough to sacrifice his ships to win foothold on the cape and so a path to Verlaine, sailed out there? That was a mad thought. The ships were doomed; few if any of their crewmen could win the shore alive, and there they would find the men of Verlaine had prepared the grimmest of welcomes.

"Fleet?" echoed the girl. "There is no fleet—only life—or death. You have something of us within you, Loyse. Prove yourself now and win!"

"Something of you? Who are you—or what?"

"I am nobody and nothing. Ask me rather what I was, Loyse of Verlaine, before your people pulled me from the sea."

"What were you?" the other asked obediently as might a child at an elder's command.

"I was one of Estcarp, woman of the sea coast. Now do you understand? Yes, I had the Power—until it was rift from me in the hall below us here, while men laughed and cheered the deed. For the gift is ours—sealed to our women—only while our bodies remain inviolate. To Verlaine I was a female body and no more. So I lost what made me live and breathe—I lost myself.

"Can you understand what it means to lose yourself?" She studied Loyse. "Yes, I almost believe that you do, since you move now to protect what you have. My gift is gone, crushed out as one crushes out the last coal of an unwanted fire, but the ashes of it remain. So do I now know that one greater than I had ever hoped to be comes in on the drive of the storm. And she shall determine more than one of our futures!"

"A witch!" Loyse did not shrink; instead excitement flared. The power of the women of Estcarp was legendary. She had fed upon every tale which had come out of the north concerning them and their gifts. And she smarted now with the realization of opportunity lost. Why had she not known of this woman before—learned of her—

"Yes, a witch. So they name us when they understand us but little. But do not think to have anything of me now, Loyse. I am only the charred brands of a long-quenched fire. Bend your will and wit to aid the other who comes."

"Will and wit!" Loyse laughed harshly. "Wit I have and will, but no power here, ever. Not one soldier will obey me, nor stay his hand at my bidding. Better appeal to Bettris. When my father is in humor with her, she has some slight recognition from his people."

"You have only to seize opportunity when it comes." The other allowed the shawl to slip from her shoulders, folded it neatly, and laid it on the bed as she passed it on her way to the door. "Take your opportunity and use it well, Loyse of Verlaine. And tonight sleep sound for your hour has not yet come."

She was out of the door before Loyse could move to stop her. And then the room was curiously empty, as if the girl had drawn after her some pulsing life which had watched and waited in shadowed corners.

Slowly Loyse put off her robe of ceremony, replaited her hair by touch, rather than with the aid of the mirror. Somehow she did not wish to look into that mirror now, for a pricking thought that something else might stand behind to peer over her shoulder lurked in her mind. Many foul deeds had been done in the great hall of Verlaine since Fulk became master there. But now she believed that perhaps the one which would bring him to judgment had been wrought with the woman of Estcarp for its victim.

And so intent was she upon her thoughts that she did not remember this was her wedding eve. For the first time since she had hidden them there, she did not bring out the garments resting at the bottom of her chest, to examine them and gloat over the promise they held.

Along the shore the wind whined, though it did not toss the spray mountain high as it had earlier. And those who sheltered, waiting for the harvest of waves and rocks were eager. The fleet which had looked so fine from the tower of Loyse's chamber, was even more imposing from the shore.

Hunold gripped his cloak tight at his throat and stared through the gloom. No ships of Karsten were those, and this wrecking could only serve the duchy. He was firm in the private belief that they were about to witness the last moments of an enemy raiding force. And it was equally good that he could keep an eye upon Fulk under these circumstances. Rumor had built very high the harvest of plunder Verlaine took. And when Yvian wedded that pale nothing of a wench, he could demand an accounting of all treasure in his wife's name. Yes, Fortune smiled when she set Hunold on the shore this night to watch, and list, and gather a report for the Duke.

Certain now that the doomed ships could not possibly claw off the cape, the wreckers from the hold boldly set out their lanterns along the strand. If fools from the vessels tried to come ashore at those beacons, so much the better, they would only save the plunderers the time and bother of hunting them down.

So it was that those beams, reaching out over the heaving of the waves, caught upon the first prow swinging inward. It loomed high, buoyed up by the combers, and there were shouts from the watchers, wagers hurriedly offered and accepted as to the place of its crashing. High it lifted and then slammed forward, the rocks under the forepart of its keel. Then—it was gone!

Those on the shore were men confronted by the impossible. At first some of the more imaginative were certain they sighted the wreckage of a broken-backed ship, sure that it was tossing near to their nets. But there was nothing but the froth of wind-beaten water. No ship nor wreckage.

None of them stirred. At that moment they were held by their disbelief in the evidence of their own eyes. Another of the proud ships was coming. This one pointed to the patch of rock upon which Hunold stood with Fulk as straightly as if some unseen helmsman set that course. In it came stoutly. No men clung to its rigging, no living thing could be sighted on deck.

Once again the waves raised up their burden to smash the vessel down upon the teeth of the reef. And this time it was so close to shore that Hunold thought a man could leap to where he himself stood from the deserted deck. Up and up the prow rose, its fantastically carved figurehead showing open jaws to the sky. Then down—the water swirling.

And it was gone!

Hunold threw out a hand, seized upon Fulk, only to see in the shocked paleness of the other's face the same incredulous terror. And when a third ship came in, boring straight for the reef, the men of Verlaine fled, some of them screaming in panic. Deserted lanterns lit a shore where nets trailed into foaming water empty of even one floating board.

Later a hand caught such a net, caught and held with a grip which was a last desperate clutch for life. A body rolled in the surf, but net held, and hand held. Then there was a long crawl for shore, until a beaten, half-dead swimmer lay prone on the sand and slept.

III
Captive Witch

*J*t was generally conceded among the commoners of Verlaine that the vanishing fleet they had gathered to plunder was an illusion sent by demons. And Fulk could not have flogged any man to the strand side the next morning. Nor did he try his leadership so high as to give such an order.

The affair of the marriage must still be pushed before any hint of this tale get back to Kars and give a legitimate reason for refusing the heiress of Verlaine. To counter any superstitious fears which the three ducal agents might harbor, Fulk reluctantly took them to the treasurehouse, presenting each with a valuable souvenir, setting aside a gem-set sword as a token of his admiration for the Duke's battle prowess. But throughout he sweated under his tunic, and fought in himself a new tendency to inspect dark corners of staircase and corridor a little too intently.

He also noted that none of his guests made any allusion to the happenings on the reef, and wondered whether that was a good or bad sign. It was not until they were in his private council chamber an hour before the wedding that Hunold took from the front of his furred overrobe a small object he set with some care in a patch of watery sunlight from the largest window.

Siric pushed his paunch against his knees and puffed once or twice as he leaned forward curiously to inspect it.

"What is this, Lord Commander? What is this? Have you despoiled some village brat of his toy?"

Hunold balanced his find on the palm of his hand. Clumsily fashioned as it was, the shape of the carved chip was clear enough—that of a boat. And a broken stick stood for a mast.

"This, Reverend Voice," he returned softly, "is the mighty ship, or one of the mighty ships, we saw come in to their end just outside these walls last night. Yes, it is a toy, but such a toy as we do not play with hereabouts. And for the safety of Karsten I must ask of you, Lord Fulk, what dealing do you have with that spawn of the outer darkness—the witches of Estcarp?"

Fulk, stung, stared at the chip boat. His face paled, and then grew dark as the blood tide arose. But he fought furiously to control his temper. If he played ill now he would lose the whole game.

"Would I have sent the gleaners to the reefs, prepared to receive a chip fleet to loot it?" He managed a reasonable counterfeit of serenity. "I take it that you fished that from the sea this morning, Lord Commander? But what leads you to believe that it was a part of any Estcarp magic, or that the ships we saw were born of such trickery?"

"This was plucked from the sand this morning, yes," Hunold agreed. "And I know of old the illusions of the witches. To make it certain, we found something else on the shore this morning, my men and I, and this is a very great treasure, one to rival any you have shown us as being wave-brought to your keep. Marc, Jothen!" He raised his voice and two of the Duke's shield-men came in, a roped prisoner between them, though they seemed uneasy to handle that captive.

"I give you part of the fleet," Hunold tossed the chip to Fulk. "And now, Lord Fulk, I show you one who had the making of it, if I mistake not, and I do not think that I do!"

Fulk was used to salt-stained captives dragged from the sea's maw and his dealing with such was swift, designed mostly to one end. Also once before he had handled the self-same problem and handled it well. Hunold might have shaken him for a space, only a very small space. He was fully confident again.

"So," he settled back in his seat with the smile of one watching the amusement of the less sophisticated, "you have taken you a witch." Boldly he surveyed the woman. She was a thin piece, but there was spirit in her—she would furnish good sport. Perhaps Hunold would like to undertake her taming. None of these witches were ever beauties, and this one was as washed out as if she had been fighting waves for a month. He studied the clothing covering her straight limbs more closely.

That was leather—garments such as one wore under mail! She had gone armed, then. Fulk stirred. A mail-clad witch and that phantom fleet! Was Estcarp on the move and did that move head toward Verlaine? Estcarp had several scores she might mark up against his hold, though hitherto no north-erner appeared to be aware of his activities. Put that to the back of the mind to be considered later; now one must think of Hunold and what could be done to keep Karsten an ally.

Carefully he avoided meeting the captive's eyes. But he asserted a measure of his old superiority.

"Has it not yet come to common knowledge in Kars, Lord Commander, that these witches may bend a man to their will by the power of their eyes? I see your shieldmen have taken no precautions against such an attack."

"It would seem you know something of these witches."

Careful now, thought Fulk. This Hunold did not keep his place at Yvian's right hand through the weight of his sword arm alone. He must not be provoked too far, only shown that Verlaine was neither traitor nor dolt.

"Estcarp has yielded tribute to our cape before." Fulk smiled.

Hunold seeing that smile, shot an order at his men. "You, Marc, your cloak over her head!"

The woman had not moved, nor had she uttered any sound since they had brought her in. They might have been dealing with a souless, mindless body. Perhaps she had been dazed by her close escape from the sea, rendered only half-conscious by some blow from a reef rock. However, none of the men within Verlaine would relax vigilance because their prisoner did not scream, or beg, or struggle uselessly. As the folds of the cloak settled about her head and shoulders Fulk leaned forward in his chair once more and spoke, his words aimed at her rather than the men he seemed to address—hoping to wring some response from her that he might judge her state of awareness.

"Have they not told you either, Lord Commander, how one disarms these witches? It is a very simple—and sometimes enjoyable—process." Deliberately he went into obscene detail.

Siric laughed, his hands curved to support his jerking paunch. Hunold smiled.

"You of Verlaine do indeed have your more subtle pleasures," he agreed.

Only the Lord Duarte remained quiet, his eyes bent upon the hands resting on his knees as he built and felled towers with his fingers. A slow, red-brown flush spread up his thin cheeks beneath the close-clipped old man's beard.

There was no movement from the half-shrouded figure, no sound of protest.

"Take her away," Fulk gave the order, a small test of power. "Give her to the seneschal; he will keep her safe against our further pleasure. For to all pleasures there is a proper season." He was now all the courteous host, secure in his position. "And now we have before us our Lord Duke's pleasure—the claiming of his bride."

Fulk waited. No one could have guessed the tension with which he listened for Hunold's next words. Until Loyse stood before the altar in the seldom-used chapel, her hands safely on the ax, the right words wheezed out by Siric, Hunold could cry off in his master's name. But once Loyse was Lady Duchess of Karsten, if only in name, then Fulk was free to move along a path of his own, one carefully foremapped and long anticipated.

"Yes, yes," Siric puffed and labored to his feet, his attention hastening to pull out the folds of his overcape. "The wedding—Must not keep the lady waiting, eh, Lord Duarte—young blood, impatient blood. Come, come, my lords—the wedding!" This was his part of the venture and for once that young, ice-eyed upstart of a soldier could have no leading role. Far more fit and proper for Lord Duarte of the oldest noble line in Karsten to bear the ax and stand

proxy for their overlord. That had been his own wise suggestion, and Yvian
had thanked him for it warmly before they had ridden out of Kars. Yes, Yvian
would discover . . . was discovering, that with the power of the Temple Broth-
erhood and the support of the old families, he would no longer have to listen
to such rufflers as Hunold. Let this marriage be solemnized and Hunold's sun
would approach its setting!

It was cold. Loyse sped along the balcony of the great hall which was the
heart of the keep. She had stood while the toasts were drunk, but she had not
given lip service to their pious sentiments for happiness in her new life—
happiness! Loyse had no conception of that. She wanted only her freedom.

When she slammed her door behind her, put in place the three bars which
could withstand even a battering ram, she went to work. Jewels were stripped
from throat, head, ear, finger, and thrown into a heap. Her long furred robe
kicked aside. Until at last she stood before the mirror on a shawl, too excited
to feel the cold seeping from the walls about her, her unbraided hair heavy
on her shoulders, falling in a curtain cloak to her bare flanks.

Lock by lock she slashed at it ruthlessly with her shears, letting the long
strands fall to the shawl. First to neck length, and then more slowly and
awkwardly, to the cropped head one might naturally expect to see beneath a
mail coif and helm. The tricks she had disdained to use at Bettris' urging, she
applied with careful concentration. A mixture of soot rubbed delicately into
her pale brows, more used upon her short, thick lashes. She had been so intent
upon the parts that she had not considered the whole. Now, stepping back a
little from the shield mirror, she studied her reflection critically, more than a
little startled at what she saw.

Her spirits soared; she was almost sure she could tramp into the great hall
below and have Fulk unable to set name to her. The girl ran to the bed, began
to dress in each garment she had prepared so well. Her weapon belt hitched
smoothly around her waist and she was reaching for the saddle bags. But her
hand moved slowly. Why was she so reluctant to see the last of Verlaine? She
had walked through the ceremonies of the day hiding her purpose, holding it
to her as a most precious possession. And she knew very well that the feast
was the best screen she could hope to find to cover her flight. Loyse doubted
if any sentry within or without the keep tonight would be overzealous on his
guard duty—in addition she had a secret exit.

Yet something held her there, wasting important moments. And she had
such a strong desire to return to the balcony overlooking the hall, to spy upon
the feasters there, that she moved to the door without conscious volition.

What had the wench said? Someone was coming in on the wings of the
storm—take your opportunity and use it well, Loyse of Verlaine! Well, this
was her opportunity and she was prepared to use it with all the wisdom her
life in Fulk's house had forced her to develop.

Yet when she moved it was not to her private ways, of which Fulk and his men knew nothing, but to that door. And even while she fought impulse and such senseless recklessness, her hand slid back the bars and she was in the hall, the heels of her boots clicking on the steps which would take her to the balcony.

Just as the heat of the keep's heart did not appear to rise to warm these upper regions, so did the noise below make only a clamor in which no voice, no stave of song, reached her as separate words. Men drank, they ate, and soon they would think of other amusements. Loyse shivered, yet she still lingered, her gaze for the high table and those who sat there, as if it were necessary to keep some close check upon their movements.

Siric, who in the chapel of Verlaine had actually achieved a short measure of dignity—or perhaps it was his robes of office which had conferred that momentary presence upon his bloated body—was all belly once more, cramming into his mouth the contents of an endless line of dishes, though his tablemates had long since turned to their wine.

Bettris, who had no right to any seat there until Loyse had left—as well she knew—for Fulk capriciously insisted upon some observances of proper conduct, had been watching for her chance. Now, bedecked with that garish brooch from the treasure house, she leaned against the carved arm of her lover's high seat ready for his attention. But, Loyse noted, her awareness of the whole scene heightened because she was a spectator only, Bettris also gave a sidewise, calculating glance now and again to Lord Commander Hunold. Just as she allowed a curved and dimpled white shoulder, artfully framed in the deep wine of her robe, to accent that surreptitous bid for regard.

Lord Duarte sat huddled in upon himself, occupying less than two-thirds of his chair of state, staring into a goblet he held as if he read in its depths some message he would rather not know. The plain lines of his plum robe, the pinched meagerness of his old features, gave him the aspect of a mendicant in that lavish assembly, and he put on no pretense of one enjoying the festivities.

She must go—now! With leather and mail, and over it all the cloak of a traveler, making her a dusky shadow among many shadows past the discerning of wine-bleared eyes, she was safe for a space. And it was so cold, colder than when the rime of winter patterned walls, yet it was well into spring! Loyse took one step and then another before that voiceless order which had brought her there drove her back to the railing.

Hunold leaned forward to speak to her father. He was a well-favored man; Bettris' interest was to be expected. His fox face with a fox brush of hair was as vivid as Fulk's for virile coloring. He made a quick gesture with his hands and Fulk voiced one of his great roars of laughter, the faint echoes of it reaching to Loyse's ears.

But there was a sudden sharp dismay on Bettris' face. She caught at Fulk's oversleeve which lay across the chair arm, and her lips shaped some words Loyse could not guess. He did not even turn his head to look at her. His hand flailed up in a cuff to sweep her from his side, back from the table, so that she sprawled awkwardly into the dust behind their chairs.

Lord Duarte arose, putting down his goblet. His thin white hands with their ropy blue veins pulled at the wide fur collar of his robe, drawing it closer about his throat, as if he alone in that company felt the same chill which benumbed Loyse. He spoke slowly, and it was clear that he made some protest. Also, from the way he turned aside from the table, it was apparent that he did not expect any polite reply or agreement from his companions.

Hunold laughed and Fulk drummed his fist upon the table in a signal to the wine steward, as the oldest of the Duke's deputies made his way among the tables of the lesser men on the floor below the dais to climb the stairs leading to his own apartment.

There was a flurry at the outer door of the hall. Men still fully armed and armored came in, and a path parted before them, leading to the dais. Some of the clamor died, fading as the guards tramped on, a prisoner in their midst. To Loyse it appeared that they hustled along a man, his hands bound behind his back. Though why they had also chosen to hide his head in a bag so that he staggered blindly in answer to their jerks at him, she could not guess.

Fulk threw out his arm, clearing a stretch of table between him and Hunold, sending flying Duarte's goblet so that its dregs of contents splashed Siric, whose hot protests neither man chose to heed. From a pocket the Lord of Verlaine brought a pair of wager discs, tossing them into the air and letting them spin on the board before they flattened so their uppermost legend might be read. He pushed them to Hunold, offering the right of first throw.

The Lord Commander gathered them up, examined them with a laughing remark, and then threw. Both men's heads bent and then Fulk took them up in turn to spin. Bettris, in spite of her rough rebuff, had crept forward, her eyes as fixed upon the spinning discs as were the men's. When they flattened, she resumed her grasp on Fulk's chair, as if the result of that throw had given her new courage, while Fulk laughed and made a mock salute to his guest.

Hunold arose from his seat and moved about the end of the table. Those about the prisoner widened their circle as he came down to front the blinded captive. He made no move to pull away the bag over the other's head, but his fingers caught at the stained leather jerkin, busy with the latches holding it. With a pull he ripped it open to the waist and there was a shout from the company.

The Lord Commander transferred his grip to the captive woman's shoulder as he faced the grins of the men. Then he displayed a strength surprising for his spare figure, and swung her over his shoulder, starting for the staircase.

Fulk was not the only one to protest missing the planned amusement, but Hunold shook his head and went on.

Would Fulk follow? Loyse did not wait to see. How could she stand against Fulk—even against Hunold? And why out of all those who had been unwilling prey of Fulk and his men in the past should Loyse be moved to help this particular one? Though she fought against the knowledge that she must take a hand in this, her feet bore her on, constrained to act against her better judgment.

She sped to her own chamber once more, finding it far easier to run in her new guise than in the robes of her sex. Once more the triple door bars thudded into place, and she was shedding her cloak, paying no attention to the reflection in the mirror of a slight youth in mail. Then the reflection was distorted as the mirror became a door.

Only dark lay beyond. Loyse must depend upon her memory, upon the many explorations she had made since three years before she had chanced upon this inner Verlaine which no other else within the pile seemed to suspect.

Steps; she counted aloud as she raced down them. One passage at the bottom, a sharp turn into a second. She brushed her hand along the wall as a guide as she hurried, trying to picture the proper ways to her goal.

Once more steps, upward this time. Then a round of light on one wall, marking one of the spy holes—this must give on an occupied room. Loyse stood on tiptoe to peer within. Yes, this was one of the state bedchambers.

Lord Duarte, looking even more shrunken and withered without his over-robe with its wide fur collar, passed about the foot of the bed and stood before the fire, his hands held out to the blaze, his small mouth working as he chewed upon some bitter word or thought he could not spit away.

Loyse went on. The next spyhole was dark, the room where Siric was housed no doubt. She quickened pace to reach the last where a second circle of gold showed light. So sure was she of this that she fumbled for the catch of the secret entrance without looking.

Mutterings—the sound of a scuffle. Loyse pushed her full weight on the concealed spring. But here there had been no careful oiling, no reason to keep it workable. It stuck. Loyse backed around and put her shoulder against it, bracing her hands flat against the wall on the other side of the narrow passage and then exerting her strength, saving herself from falling as it burst open by catching at the edges of the opening.

She whirled about, her sword out with the snap of one who had practiced in secret and steadily. Hunold's startled face fronted her from the bed where he fought to pin down his writhing victim. With the quick recovery and menace of a cat, he slid to the opposite side, abandoning his hold upon the woman, and sprang for the weapon belt hanging on the back of the nearest chair.

IV
The Inner Ways

*L*oyse had forgotten her new trappings and that Hunold might see in her another male come to spoil his sport. He had whipped out his dart gun, although she had sword in hand, his move being against age-old custom. But his aim wavered ever so slightly between the invader and the woman on the bed, who, in spite of her bound hands, was wriggling her way toward him across the rumpled covers.

Moved by instinct more than plan, Loyse seized upon the outer robe he had discarded and tossed it at him, thus perhaps saving her life. For the thick cloth folds deflected his aim and the dart quivered in the bedpost and not in her breast.

With a spate of oaths Hunold kicked at the tangle of cloth and swung upon the woman. She made no move to escape. Rather now she stood facing him with an odd calm. Her lips parted and an oval object dropped from between them, to swing on a short length of chain still gripped in her teeth.

The Lord Commander did not move. Instead his eyes traveled from one side to the other beneath his half-closed lids, following the slow pendulous passage of that dull gem.

Loyse was around the foot of the bed now, only to pause at a scene which might have been part of a nightmare. The woman edged around, and Hunold, his eyes fast on the gem at her chin level moved after her. Now her bound arms were presented to Loyse, her body formed a partial barrier between girl and man.

Hunold's eyes went left to right, and back, then, as the jewel quieted, he stood very still. His mouth opened slackly. There were beads of moisture forming along the edge of his hair line.

That drive which had brought her there, moving her about as a playing piece in some other's game, still held Loyse. She drew the cutting edge of the sword across the cords binding the woman's wrists, sawing through their cruel loops, freeing flesh which was ridged and purple. And when the last bit fell away the woman's arms dropped heavily to her sides as if they could not obey her will.

Hunold moved at last. The hand which gripped the dart gun circled, but slowly as if great pressure bent it. His skin glistened with sweat, a pendulous drop gathered upon his loose lower lip, spun a thread as it fell to his heaving chest.

His eyes were alive, fiery with hate and rising panic. Yet, still that hand continued to turn, and he could not tear his gaze away from the dull jewel. His shoulder quivered. Loyse across the few feet of space which separated them could sense the agony of his fruitless struggle. He no longer wanted to slay; he wanted only escape. But for the Lord Commander of Kars there was no escape.

The end of that barrel touched the soft, unweathered white of his upper breast where his throat met the arch of his chest. He was moaning, very faintly, as might a trapped animal, before the trigger clicked.

Coughing out a spume of blood, released from the vise of will which had forced him to his death, Hunold staggered forward. The woman slipped lithely aside, pushing Loyse with her. He fell up against the bed and collapsed half upon it, his head and shoulders down, his knees upon the floor as one might kneel in petition, as his hands tore spasmodically at the covers.

For the first time the woman looked directly at Loyse. She made an effort to raise one of those puffed and horribly swollen hands to her mouth, perhaps to hold the stone. And when she could not, she sucked the jewel back between her lips, nodding imperatively at the opening in the wall.

Loyse was no longer so assured. All of her life she had heard of the magic of Estcarp. But those had been tales of far-off things which did not demand full belief from the listener. The disappearance of the fleet along the reef the night before had been described to her by Bettris while she had been dressing for her bridal. But she had been so absorbed by her plans and fears at that moment that she had dismissed it all as a piece of great exaggeration.

What she had seen here was something which transcended all her ideas and she shrank from contact with the witch, stumbling ahead into the cavity of the ways, only wishing that she could or dared shut the other out with a safe wall between them. But the woman came readily after her with an agility which argued that she still had reserves of energy in spite of the rough handling she had known.

Loyse had no desire to linger with Hunold's body. Nor was she sure that Fulk, cheated of his sport, might not burst in at any moment. But she snapped shut the hidden panel with the greatest reluctance. And shivered throughout her body as the other pawed at her with one of those useless hands for a guide. She looped her fingers in the belt which still held the witch's ripped clothing to her body and drew her along.

They headed for her own chamber. There was so little time left. If Fulk followed the Lord Commander—if Hunold's body servant chanced into that room—or if for some reason her father would seek her out—! She must be out of Verlaine before dawn, witch or no witch! And setting her mind firm upon that, she towed the stranger along the dark ways.

Only, when she stood once more in the light, Loyse could not be as callous as her sense of urgency dictated. She found soft cloth to wash and bind the raw grooves cut in the other's wrists. And from her stores of clothing offered a selection to the other.

At last the witch mastered her body to the point where she was able to cup her hands beneath her pointed chin. She allowed the jewel to fall from her lips into that hold. Manifestly she did not want Loyse to touch it, nor would the girl have done so for less than her freedom.

"This about my neck please." For the first time the other spoke.

Loyse caught the jewel's chain, pulled open the catch and fastened it again beneath the ragged ends of hair which must have been cut as hastily and as inexpertly as her own—and perhaps for the same reason.

"Thank you, lady of Verlaine. And now, if you please," her voice was husky as if it rasped through a dry throat, "a drink of water."

Loyse held the cup to the other's mouth. "Thanks from you to me are hardly necessary," she returned with what boldness she could muster. "It would appear that you carry with you a weapon as potent as any steel!"

Over the rim of the cup the witch's eyes were smiling. Loyse, meeting that kindliness, lost some of her awe. But she was still young, awkward, unsure of herself, sensations she resented bitterly.

"It was a weapon I could not use until you distracted the attention of my would-be bedfellow, the noble Lord Commander. For it is one I dare not risk falling into other hands, even to save my own life. Enough of that—" She lifted her hands, examined the bandages about her wrists. Then she surveyed the disordered room, noting the shawl on the floor with its burden of sheared hair, the saddlebags on the coffer.

"It is not to your mind to travel to your bridegroom, my lady duchess?"

Perhaps it was the tone of her voice, perhaps it was her power compelling something within Loyse. But she answered directly with the truth.

"I am no duchess in Karsten, lady. Oh, they said the words over me this morning before Yvian's lords, and afterwards they paid me homage on their knees." She smiled faintly remembered what an ordeal that had been for Siric. "Yvian was none of my choosing. I welcome this wedding only to cover my escape."

"Yet you came to my aid," the other prompted, watching her with those great, dark eyes which measured until Loyse smarted under their gaze.

"Because I could not do otherwise!" she flared. "Something bound me here. Your sorcery, lady?"

"In a way, in a way. I appealed in my fashion to any within these walls who had the ability to hear me. It would appear that we share more than a common danger, lady of Verlaine, or," she smiled openly now, "seeing that you have changed your guise for this outfaring, lord of Verlaine."

"Call me Briant, a mercenary of blank shield," Loyse supplied, having prepared for that days ago.

"And where do you go, Briant? To seek employment in Kars? Or in the north? There will be a demand for blank shields in the north."

"Estcarp wars?"

"Say rather that war is carried to her. But that is another matter." She stood up. "One which can be discussed at length once we are without these walls. For I am sure you know a road out."

Loyse draped the saddlebags across her shoulder, drew the hood of her cloak over her uncrested helm. As she moved to turn off the light globes, the witch jerked at the shawl on the floor. Vexed at her own forgetfulness, the girl caught it and threw the strands of hair into the dying fire.

"That is well done," the other commanded. "Leave nothing which could be used to draw you back—hair has power." She glanced to the middle window. "Does that give on the sea?"

"Yes."

"Then lay a false trail, Briant. Let Loyse of Verlaine die to cover it!"

It was the work of a moment to throw open that casement, to drop her fine bride robe just below. But it was the witch who bade her fasten a scrap of undergarment to the rough edge of the stone still.

"With such open door to face them," she commanded, "I do not think they will seek too assiduously for other ways out of this chamber."

Back they went through the mirror door, and now their path led down through the dark where Loyse urged that they hug the wall to the right and take the descent slowly. Under their hands that wall grew moist, and dank smells of the sea, tainted with an ancient rottenness, were thick in the air. Down and down, and now the murmur of the waves came faintly thrumming through the wall. Loyse counted step after step.

"Here! Now there is the passage leading to the strange place."

"The strange place?"

"Yes. I do not like to linger there, but we shall have little choice. We must wait for the dawn light to guide us out."

She crept on, fighting the building reluctance within her. Three times had she come that way in the past, and each time she had carried on this silent warfare with her own body as the field of battle. Again she knew that rise of brooding apprehension, that threat out of the dark promising more and worse than just bodily harm. But still she shuffled on, her fingers hooked in her companion's belt, drawing her also.

Out of the blackness Loyse heard the heavy breathing, a catch of breath. And then the other spoke, in a faint whisper, as if there crouched near that which might overhear her words.

"This is a Place of Power."

"It is a strange place," Loyse repeated stubbornly. "I do not like it, but it holds our gate out of Verlaine."

Though they could not see, they sensed they had come out of the passage into a wider area. Loyse caught a glimpse of a bright point of light over head— the beacon of a star hung far above some rock crevice.

But now there was another faint gleam which brightened suddenly, as if some muffling curtain had been withdrawn. It moved through the air well above ground level—a round gray spot. Loyse heard a sing-song chant, words she did not know. And that sound vibrated in the curiously charged air of the space. As the light grew stronger she knew that it came from the witch's jewel.

Her skin tingled, the air about them was charged with energy. Loyse knew an avid hunger—for what she could not have told. In her other visits to this place, the girl had been afraid and had made herself linger to control that fear. Now she left fear behind, this new sensation was one she could not put name to.

The witch, revealed in the light of the gem on her breast, was swaying from side to side, her face set and rapt. The stream of words still poured from her lips—petition, argument, protective incantation—Loyse could not have said which. Only the girl knew that they were both caught up in a vast wave of some energizing substance drawn from the sand and rock under their feet, from the walls about them, something which had remained asleep through long centuries to come instantly awake and aware now.

Why? What? Slowly Loyse made a complete turn, staring out into the gloom she could not pierce by eyepower. What lurked just beyond the faint pool of light the jewel granted them?

"We must go!" That came urgently from the witch. Her dark eyes were widely open, her hand moved clumsily to Loyse. "I cannot control forces greater than my own! This place is old, also it is apart from humankind and from the powers we know. Gods were worshiped here once, such gods as altars have not been raised to these thousand years. And there is a residue of their old magic rising! Where is your outer gate? We must try it while yet we can."

"The light of your jewel—" Loyse shut her own eyes, pulling forth her memory of this place, as earlier she had used her memory of the other wall hidden ways. "There," she opened them again and pointed ahead.

Step by step the witch moved in that direction and the light went with and around her as Loyse had hoped. Steps wide and roughly hewn, rounded by ages of time, loomed to their right. They led Loyse knew to a flat block with certain sinister grooves which lay directly under a break in the roof, so that at intervals light from the sun, or from the moon, bathed it in gold or silver.

Around that platform fashioned of broad steps, they crept on to the far wall. The light of the jewel caught the fall of earth which lay below Loyse's gate. It would be risky to climb that tumble of stone and clay in this gloom, but she was impressed by the urgency of the witch.

The climb was as great a task as Loyse had feared. Though her companion made no complaint, she knew that to use those swollen hands must be torment. When and where she could the girl pushed and pulled the other, tensing together when the rubble shifted under their feet, threatening to plunge them both to the bottom once again. Then they were out, lying on coarse grass with the salt air about them, and a grayish glimmer in the sky telling them that the night was almost gone.

"Sea or land?" asked the witch. "Do you seek a boat along the shore, or do we trust to our two feet and head into the hills?"

Loyse sat up. "Neither," she replied crisply. "This lies at the end of the pastures between the hold and the sea. At this season the extra mounts are turned loose to range here until they are needed. And in a hut near the gate is the horse gear of the rangers. But that may be under guard."

The witch laughed. "One guard? Little enough to stand between two determined women and their desire this night, or rather this morning. Show me this hut with the horse gear and I shall make you free of it with no man the wiser thereafter."

They went across the end of the pasture. The horses, Loyse knew, would be close to the hut where block salt had been set out two days before the storm. The jewel had gone dead when they had emerged from the cavern and they had to pick their way carefully.

A lantern burned over the door of the hut and Loyse saw horses moving back and forth. The heavy war chargers bred to carry an armored man in battle did not interest her. But there were the rough-coated, smaller mounts kept for hunting in the hills, able to withstand hardship and keep going far past the exhaustion point of the costlier animals Fulk fancied for his own riding.

Out into the circle of the lantern light moved two such ponies—almost as if her thought had called them. They seemed uneasy, tossing their heads until their ragged manes flopped on their necks, but they came. Loyse put down the saddlebags, whistling softly. To her delight the small horses came on, snuffling to one another, their forelocks looping over their eyes, with shaggy patches of their winter coats making them look dappled in the dim light.

If they would only prove tractable once she had the gear! She circled about them slowly and approached the hut. There was no sign of the guard. Could he have deserted his post for the feasting? It would be his death if Fulk discovered it.

Loyse pushed inward on the door and it creaked. Then she was peering into a place which smelt of horses and oiled leather, yes, and of the strong drink the village people brewed of honey and herbs, which was enough to make even Fulk blink into sleep at the third tankard. A jug rolled on its side, away from the touch of her boot, and sticky stuff dribbled sluggishly from its mouth. The guardian of the pastures lay on a truss of straw snoring lustily.

Two bridles, two of the riding pads used by hunters and swift riding messengers. They were easy to lift from pegs and ledge. Then she was back in the field and the door pulled to behind her.

The horses remained docile as she bridled them and slapped on the pads, cinching them as tightly as she could. But when both women were mounted and on the upper trail which was the only way out of Verlaine, her companion asked for the second time:

"Where do you ride, blank shield?"

"The mountains." Most of Loyse's concrete plans had dealt only with the mechanics of her escape from Verlaine. Beyond this point where she now rode, equipped, mounted, she had foreseen little. To be free and out of Verlaine had seemed so impossible a happening, so difficult an achievement that she had bent all her wits to the solving of that, with little thought of what would happen after she gained the mountain trails.

"You say Estcarp wars?" She had never really thought of venturing through the wild band of outlaw territory between Verlaine and the southern border of Estcarp, but with one of the witches of that land as a riding companion it might now be the best choice of all.

"Yes, Estcarp wars, blank shield. But have you thought of Kars, lady duchess? Would you look upon your realm in secret and see what manner of a future you have tossed away?"

Loyse, startled, almost kneed her mount into a trot unsafe for the way they threaded.

"Kars?" she repeated blankly.

Something in that worked in her mind. Yes, she had no mind to be Yvian's lady duchess. But on the other hand Kars was the center of the southern lands and she might find a kinsman or two there if she needed help later. In so large a city a blank shield with money in his purse could lose himself. And should Fulk manage to discover something of her trail he would not think to search for her in Kars.

"Estcarp must wait yet awhile," the other was saying. "Trouble stirs through the land. And I would know more of it, and of those who do the stirring. Kars is a starting point."

She had been managed; Loyse knew that, but there was no feeling of outrage in her. It was rather that she had at long last found the end of a tangled cord, one which, if she dared to follow it through all its coils, would bring her where she had always wanted to be.

"We shall ride to Kars," she consented quietly.

3. Venture of Karsten

∞

I
The Hole of Volt

*F*ive men lay on the wave-beaten sand of the tiny cup of bay and one of them was dead, a great gash across his head. It was a hot day and shafts of sun struck full on their half-naked bodies. The smell of the sea and the stink of rotting weeds combined with the heat in a tropic exhalation.

Simon coughed, bracing his battered body up on his elbows. He was one great bruise and he was very nauseated. Slowly he crawled a little apart and was thoroughly sick, though there was little enough to be ejected from his shrunken stomach. The spasm shook him into full consciousness, and, when he could control his heaving, he sat up.

He could remember only parts of the immediate past. Their flight from Sulcarkeep had begun the nightmare. Magnis Osberic's destruction of the power projector, that core of energy supplying light and heat to the port, had not only blown up the small city but must have added to the fury of the storm which followed. And in that storm the small party of surviving Guards, trusting to the escape craft, had been scattered without hope of course keeping.

Three of those vessels had set out from the port, but their period of keeping together had lasted hardly beyond their last sight of the exploding city. And what had ensued had been sheer terror, for the craft had been whirled, pitched, and finally shattered on coastwise rock teeth in a period of time which had ceased to be marked in any orderly procession of hours and minutes.

Simon rushed his hands over his face. His lashes were matted with a glue of salt water and caught together, making it hard to open his eyes. Four men here—Then he sighted that half-crushed head—three men, maybe, and the dead.

On one side was the sea, quiet enough now, washing the tangles of weed ripped loose and deposited on the shore. Fronting the water was a cliff face, broken, with handholds enough, Simon supposed. But he had not the slightest desire to essay that climb, or to move, for that matter. It was good just to sit and let the warmth of the sun drive out the bitter cold of storm and water.

"Saaa . . ."

One of the other figures on the strand stirred. A long arm swept the sand, pushing away a mass of weed. The man coughed, retched, and raised his head, to stare blearily about. Then the Captain of Estcarp caught sight of Simon and regarded him blankly, before his mouth moved in an effort at a grin.

Koris hunched up, his overheavy shoulders and arms taking most of his weight as he crawled on hands and knees to a clear space of water-flattened sand.

"It is said on Gorm," he spoke rustily, his voice hardly more than a croak, "that a man born to feel the weight of the headsman's ax on his neck does not drown. And, since it has ofttimes been made clear to me that the ax is my fate—see how the oldsters are proven right once again!"

Painfully he moved on to the nearest of the still prone men, and rolled the limp body over, exposing a face which was gray-white under its weathering. The Guardsman's chest rose and fell with steady breath and he appeared to have no injuries.

"Jivin," Koris supplied a name, "an excellent riding master." He added the last thoughtfully, and Simon found himself laughing weakly, pressing his fists against his flat middle where strained muscles protested such usage.

"Naturally," he got out between those bursts of half-hysterical mirth, "that is an employment most needed now!"

But Koris had gone on to the next intact body. "Tunston!"

Dimly Simon was glad of that. He had developed, during his short period of life with the Guard in Estcarp, a very hearty respect for that underofficer. Making himself move, he helped Koris draw the two still unconscious men above the noisome welter of tide drift. Then he clawed his way to his feet with the aid of the rock wall.

"Water—" That sense of well-being which had held him for a short space after his own awakening was gone. Simon was thirsty, his whole body now one vast longing for water, inside and out, to drink and to lave the smarting salt from his tender skin.

Koris shuffled over to examine the wall. There were only two ways out of the cup which held them. To return to the sea and strive to swim around the encircling arms of rocks, or to climb the cliff. And every nerve within Simon revolted against any swimming, or return to the water from which he had so miraculously emerged.

"This is not too hard a path," Koris said. He was frowning a little. "Almost could I believe that once there were handholds here and here." He stood on tiptoe, flattened against the rock, his long arms stretched full length over his head, his fingers fitting into small openings in the cliff wall. Muscles roped and knotted on his shoulders; he lifted one foot, inserted the toe of a boot into a crevice and began to climb.

Giving a last glance at the beach and the two men now well above the pull of the water, Simon followed. He discovered that the Captain was right. There were convenient hollows for fingers and toes, whether made by nature or man, and they led him up after Koris to a ledge some ten feet above the level of the beach.

There was no mistaking the artificial nature of that ledge for the marks of the tools which had shaped it were still visible. It slanted as a ramp, though steeply, toward the cliff top. Not an easy path for a man with a whirling head and a pair of weak and shaking legs, but infinitely better than he had dared to hope for.

Koris spoke again. "Can you make it alone? I will see if I can get the others moving."

Simon nodded, and then wished that he had not tried that particular form of agreement. He hugged the wall and waited for the world to stop an unpleasant sidewise spiral. Setting his teeth, he took the upgrade. Most of the journey he made on his hands and knees, until he came out under a curving hollow of roof. Nursing raw hands he peered into what could only be a cave. There was no other way up from here, and they would have to hope that the cave had another opening above.

"Simon!" The shout from below was demanding, anxious.

He made himself crawl to the outer edge of the ledge and look down.

Koris stood there below, his head thrown far back as he tried to see above. Tunston was on his feet, too, supporting Jivin. At Simon's feeble wave they went into action, somehow between them getting Jivin up the first climb to the ledge.

Simon remained where he was. He had no desire to enter the cave alone. And anyway his will appeared to be drained out of him, just as his body was drained of strength. But he had to back into it as Koris gained the level and faced about to draw up Jivin.

"There is some trick to this place," the Captain announced. "I could not see you from below until you waved. Someone has gone to great trouble to hide his doorway."

"Meaning this is highly important?" Simon waved to the cave mouth. "I do not care if it is a treasure-house of kings as long as it gives us a chance of reaching water!"

"Water!" Jivin echoed that feebly. "Water, Captain?" he appealed to Koris trustfully.

"Not yet, comrade. There is still a road to ride."

They discovered that Simon's chosen method of hands and knees was necessary to enter the cave door. And Koris barely scraped through, tearing skin on shoulders and arms.

There was a passage beyond, but so little light reached this point that they crept with their hands on the walls, Simon tapping before him.

"Dead end!" His outstretched hands struck against solid rock facing them. But he had given his verdict too soon, for to his right was a faint glimmer of light and he discovered that the way made a right-angled turn.

Here one could see a measure of footing and they quickened pace. But disappointment waited at the end of the passage. For the light did not increase and when they came out into an open space, it was into twilight and not the bright sun of day.

The source of that light riveted Simon's attention and pulled him out of his preoccupation with his own aches and pains. Marching in a straight line across one wall were a series of perfectly round windows, not unlike ship's portholes. Why they had not sighted them from the strand, for it was apparent that they must be in the outer surface of the cliff, he could not understand. But the substance which made them filtered the light in cloudy beams.

There was light enough, however, to show them only too clearly the single occupant of that stone chamber. He sat at ease in a chair carved of the same stone as that on which it was based, his arms resting upon its broad side supports, his head fallen forward on his breast as if he slept.

It was only when Jivin drew breath in a sound close to a sob, that Simon guessed they stood in a tomb. And the dusty silence of the chamber closed about them, as if they had been shut into a coffer with no escape.

Because he was awed and ill at ease, Simon moved purposefully forward to the two blocks on which the chair rested, staring up in defiance at him who sat there. There was a thick coating of dust on the chair, sifting over the sitter. Yet Tregarth could see that this man—chieftain, priest, or king, or whatever he had been in his day of life—was not allied by race to Estcarp or to Gorm.

His parchment skin was dark, smooth, as if the artistry of an embalmer had turned it to sleek wood. The features of the half-hidden face were marked by great force and vigor, with a sweeping beak of nose dominating all the rest. His chin was small, sharply pointed, and the closed eyes were deep set. It was like seeing a humanoid creature whose far distant ancestors had been not primates but avian.

To add to this illusion his clothing, under its film of dust, was of some material which resembled feathers. A belt bound his slim waist and resting across both arms of his chair was an ax of such length of haft and size that Simon almost doubted the sleeper could ever have lifted it.

His hair had grown to a peak-crest, and binding it into an upright plume was a gem-set circlet. Rings gleamed on those claw fingers resting on ax head and ax haft. And about chair, occupant, and that war ax there was such a suggestion of alien life as stopped Simon short before the first step of the dais.

"Volt!" Jivin's cry was close to a scream. Then his words became unintelligible to Simon as he gabbled something in another tongue which might have been a prayer.

"To think that legend is truth!" Koris had come to stand beside Tregarth.

His eyes were as brilliant as they had been on the night they had fought their way out of Sulcarkeep.

"Volt? Truth?" echoed Simon and the man from Gorm answered impatiently.

"Volt of the Ax, Volt who throws thunders—Volt who is now a boogy to frighten children out of naughtiness! Estcarp is old, her knowledge comes from the days before man wrote his history, or whispered his legends. But Volt is older than Estcarp! He is of those who came before man, as man is today. And his kind died before man armed himself with stick and stone to strike back at the beasts. Only Volt lived on and knew the first men and they knew him—and his ax! For Volt in his loneliness took pity on man and with his ax hewed for them a path to follow to knowledge and lordship before he, too, went from among them.

"In some places they remember Volt with thanksgiving, though they fear him for being what they could not understand. And in other places they hate with a great hate, for the wisdom of Volt warred against their deep desires. So do we remember Volt with prayers and with cursings, and he is both god and demon. Yet now we four can perceive that he *was* a living creature, and so in that akin to ourselves. Though perhaps one with other gifts according to the nature of his race.

"Ha, Volt!" Koris flung his long arm up in a salute. "I, Koris, who am Captain of Estcarp and its Guards, give to you greetings, and the message that the world has not changed greatly since you withdrew from it. Still we war, and peace sits only lightly, save that now our night may have come upon us out of Kolder. And, since I stand weaponless by reason of the sea, I beg of your arms! If by your favor we set our faces once more against Kolder, may it be with your ax swinging in the van!"

He climbed the first step, his hand went out confidently. Simon heard a choked cry from Jivin, a hissed breath from Tunston. But Koris was smiling as his fingers closed about the ax haft, and he drew the weapon carefully toward him. So alive did the seated figure seem that Simon half expected the ring-laden claws to tighten, to snatch the giant's weapon back from the man who begged it from him. But it came easily, quickly into Koris' grasp, as if he who had held it all these generations had not only released it willingly, but had indeed pushed it to the Captain.

Simon expected the haft to crumble into rottenness when Koris drew it free. But the Captain swung it high, bringing it down in a stroke which halted only an inch or so above the stone of the step. In his hands the weapon was a living thing, supple and beautiful as only a fine arm could be.

"My gratitude for life, Volt!" he cried. "With this I shall carve out victories, for never before has such a weapon come into my hands. I am Koris, once of

Gorm, Koris the ugly, the ill-fashioned. Yet, under your good wishing, O Volt, shall I be Koris the conqueror, and your name shall once more be great in this land!"

Perhaps it was the very timbre of his voice which disturbed age-old currents of air; Simon held to that small measure of rational explanation for what followed. For the seated man, or manlike figure, appeared to nod once, twice, as if agreeing to Koris' exultant promises. Then that body, which had seemed so solid only seconds before, changed in front of their eyes, falling in upon itself.

Jivin buried his face in his hands and Simon bit back an exclamation. Volt—if Volt it had really been—was gone. There was dust in the chair and nothing else, save the ax in Koris' grip. Tunston, that unimaginative man, spoke first, addressing his officer:

"His tour of duty was finished, Captain. Yours now begins. It was well done, to claim his weapon. And I think it shall bring us good fortune."

Koris was swinging the ax once more, making the curved blade pass in the air in an expert's drill. Simon turned away from the empty chair. Since his entrance into this world he had witnessed the magic of the witches and accepted it as part of this new life, now he accepted this in turn. But even the acquiring of the fabulous Ax of Volt would not bring them a drink of water nor the food they must have, and he said as much.

"That is also the truth," Tunston agreed. "If there is no other way out of here then we must return to the shore and try elsewhere."

Only there was another way, for the wall behind the great chair showed an archway choked with earth and rubble. And they set to work digging that out with their belt knives and their hands for tools. It was exhausting work, even for men who came to it fresh. And only Simon's new horror of the sea kept him at it. In the end they cleared a short passage, only to front a door.

Once its substance may have been some strong native wood. But no rot had eaten at it, rather it had been altered by the natural chemistry of the soil into a flint-hard surface. Koris waved them back.

"This is my work."

Once more the Ax of Volt went up. Simon almost cried out, fearing to see the fine blade come to grief against that surface. There was a clang, and again the ax was raised, came down with the full force of the Captain's mighty shoulders.

The door split, one part of it leaning outward. Koris stood aside and the three of them worried at that break. Now the brightness of full daylight struck them, and the freshness of a good breeze beat the mustiness of the chamber away.

They manhandled the remnants of the door to allow passage and broke through a screen of dried creepers and brush out onto a hillside where the new grass of spring showed in vivid patches and some small yellow flowers bloomed like scattered gold pieces. They were on the top of the cliff and the slope on this side went down to a stream. Without a word Simon stumbled down to that which promised to lay the dust in his throat, ease the torture of his salted skin.

He raised dripping head and shoulders from the water sometime later to find Koris missing. Though he was sure that the Captain had followed them out of the Hole of Volt.

"Koris?" he asked Tunston. The other was rubbing his face with handfuls of wet grass, sighing in content, while Jivin lay on his back beside the stream, his eyes closed.

"He goes to do what is to be done for his man below," Tunston answered remotely. "No Guardsman must be left to wind and wave while his officer can serve him otherwise."

Simon flushed. He had forgotten that battered body on the beach. Though he was of the Guard of Estcarp by his own will, he did not yet feel at one with them. Estcarp was too old, its men—and its witches—alien. Yet what had Petronius promised when he offered the escape? That the man who used it would be transported to a world which his spirit desired. He was a soldier and he had come into a world at war, yet it was not his way of fighting, and he still felt the homeless stranger.

He was remembering the woman with whom he had fled across the moors, unknowing then that she was a witch of Estcarp and all that implied. There had been times during that flight when they had had an unspoken comradeship. But afterwards that, too, was gone.

She had been on one of those other ships when they had broken out of Sulcarkeep. Had hers fared as badly at the merciless sea? He stirred, pricked by something he did not want to acknowledge, clinging fiercely to his role of onlooker. Rolling over on the grass he pillowed his head on his bent arm, relaxing by will as he had learned long ago, to sleep.

Simon awoke as quickly, senses alert. He could not have slept long for the sun was still fairly high. There was the smell of cooking in the air. In the lee of a rock a small fire burned where Tunston tended some small fish spitted on sharp twigs. Koris, his ax his bedfellow, slept, his boyish face showing more drawn and fined down with fatigue then when he was conscious. Jivin sprawled belly down beside the streamlet, fast proving that he was more than a master of horsemanship, as his hand emerged with another fish he had tickled into capture.

Tunston raised an eyebrow as Simon came up. "Take your pick," he indicated the fish. " 'Tis not mess fare, but it will serve for now."

Simon had reached for the nearest when Tunston's sudden tension brought his gaze to follow the other's. Circling over their heads in wide, gliding sweeps was a bird, black feathered for the most part save for a wide V of white on the breast.

"Falcon!" Tunston breathed that word as if it summed up a danger as great as a Kolder ambush.

II
Falcon's Eyrie

*T*he bird, with that art known to the predatory clans, hung over them on outspread wings. Simon saw enough of those bright red thongs or ribbons fluttering from about its feet to guess that it was not a wild creature.

"Captain!" Tunston edged over to shake Koris awake, and the other sat up, rubbing his fists across his eyes in a small-boy gesture.

"Captain, the Falconers are out!"

Koris jerked his head sharply up and then got to his feet, shading his eyes against the sun, to watch the slow circles of the bird. He whistled a call which arose in clear notes. Those lazy circles ceased and Simon watched that miracle of speed and precision—the strike. For the bird came in to settle upon the haft of Volt's ax where the weapon lay half-hidden in the grass of this tiny meadow. The curved beak opened and it gave a harsh cry.

The Captain knelt by the bird. Very carefully he picked up one of the trailing cords at its feet and a small metal pendant flashed in the sun. This he studied.

"Nalin. He must be one of the sentries. Go, winged warrior," Koris addressed the restless bird. "We be of one breed with your master and there is peace between us."

"A pity, Captain, that your words will not carry to the ears of this Nalin," commented Tunston. "The Falconers are apt to make sure of the borders first and ask questions later, if any invaders are left alive to ask them of."

"Just so, vagabond!"

The words came from immediately behind them. Almost as one, they whirled, to see only rocks and grass. Had it been the bird that spoke? Jivin eyed the hawk doubtfully, but Simon refused to accept that piece of magic or illusion. He fingered his only weapon, the knife which had been in his belt when he had made the shore.

Koris and Tunston showed no surprise. It was apparent they had expected some such challenge. The Captain spoke to the air about them, distinctly and slowly, as if his words must carry conviction to the unseen listener.

"I am Koris, Captain of Estcarp, driven upon this shore by storm. And these are of the Guards of Estcarp: Tunston, who is officer of the Great Keep, Jivin, and Simon Tregarth, an outlander who has taken service under the Guardian.

By the Oath of Sword and Shield, Blood and Bread, I ask of you now the shelter given when two war not upon each other, but live commonly by the raised blade!"

The faint echo of his words rolled about them and was gone. Then once more the bird gave its screeching cry and arose. Tunston grinned wryly.

"Now I take it, we wait for either a guide or a dart in the back!"

"From an invisible enemy?" asked Simon.

Koris shrugged. "To every commander his own mysteries. And the Falconers have theirs in plenty. If they send the guide, we are indeed fortunate." He sniffed. "And there is no need to go hungry while we wait."

Simon gnawed at the fish, but he surveyed the small meadow cut by the stream. His companions appeared to be philosophical about the future, and he had no idea how that trick with the voice had been worked. But he had learned to use Koris as a measuring instrument when in a new situation. If the Guard Captain was willing to wait this out, then they might not have to face a fight after all. But on the other hand he would like to know more about his might-be hosts.

"Who are the Falconers?"

"As Volt," Koris' hand went to the ax, slipping in caress down its handle, "they are legend and history, but not so ancient.

"In the beginning they were mercenaries, come overseas in Sulcar ships from a land where they lost their holdings because of a barbarian invasion. For a space they served with the traders as caravan guards and marines. Sometimes they still hire out when in their first youth. But the majority did not care for the sea; they had a hunger for mountains eating into them, since they were heights born. So they came to the Guardian at Estcarp city and suggested a pact, offering to protect the southern border of the land in return for the right to settle in the mountains."

"There was wisdom in that!" Tunston broke in. "It was a pity the Guardian could not agree."

"Why couldn't she?" Simon wanted to know.

Koris smiled grimly. "Have you not dwelt long enough yet in Estcarp, Simon, not to know that it is a matriarchate? For the Power which has held it safe lies not first in the swords of its men, but in the hands of its women. And the holders of Power are in truth all women.

"On the other hand the Falconers have strange customs of their own, which are as dear to them as the mores of Estcarp are to the witches. They are a fighting order of males alone. Twice a year picked young men are sent to their separate villages of women, there to sire a new generation, as stallions are put out to pasture with the mares. But of affection, or liking, of equality between male and female, there is none recognized among the Falconers. And they do not admit that a woman exists save for the bearing of sons.

"Thus they were to Estcarp savages whose corrupt way of life revolted the civilized, and the Guardian swore that were they to settle within the country with the consent of the witches the Power would be affronted and depart. So were they told that not by the will of Estcarp could they hold her border. However they were granted leave to pass in peace through the country with what supplies they needed, to seek the mountains on their own. If there they wished to carve out a holding beyond the boundaries of Estcarp the witches would wish them well and not raise swords against them. So it has been for a hundred years or more."

"And I take it they were able to carve out their holding?"

"So well," Tunston answered Simon's question, "that three times have they beaten into the earth the hordes the Dukes of Karsten have sent against them. The very land they have chosen fights upon their side."

"You say that Estcarp did not offer them friendship," Simon pointed out. "What did it mean then when you spoke of the Oath of Sword and Shield, Blood and Bread? It sounded as if you *did* have some kind of an understanding."

Koris became very busy picking a small bone from his fish. Then he smiled and Tunston laughed openly. Only Jivin looked a little conscious, as if they spoke of things it was better not to mention.

"The Falconers are men—"

"And the Guards of Estcarp are also men?" Simon ventured.

Koris grin spread, though Jivin was frowning now. "Do not misunderstood us, Simon. We have the greatest reverence for the Women of Power. But it is in the nature of their lives that they are apart from us, and the things which may move us. For, as you know, the Power departs from a witch if she becomes truly a woman. Therefore they are doubly jealous of their strength, having given up a part of their life to hold it. Also they are proud that they are women. To them the customs of the Falconers, which deny that pride as well as the Power, reducing a female to a body without intelligence or personality, are close to demon-inspired.

"We may not agree with the Falconers' customs, but as fighting men we Guards pay them respect, and when we have met with them in the past there was no feud between us. For the Guards of Estcarp and the Falconers have no quarrel. And," he tossed aside the spit from which he had worried the last bite of fish, "the day may be coming soon when the fact shall be an aid to us all."

"That is true!" Tunston spoke eagerly. "Karsten has warred upon them. And whether the Guardian wills it or not, if Karsten marches upon Estcarp the Falconers stand between. But we know that well and this past year the Guardian turned her attention elsewhere when the Big Snow struck and grain and cattle moved southward to Falconer villages."

"There were women and children hungry in those villages," Jivin said.

"Yes. But the supplies were ample and more than villagers ate," countered Tunston.

"The Falcon!" Jivin jerked a thumb skywards, and they saw that black-and-white bird sail through the air over their campsite. It proved this time to be the forescout of a small party of men who rode into view and sat watching the Guards.

The horses they bestrode were akin to ponies, rough-coated beasts that Simon judged were nimble footed enough on the narrow trails of the heights. And their saddles were simple pads. But each possessed a forked horn on which perched at ease one of the falcons, that of the leader offering a resting place to the bird that had guided them.

As did the Guards and the men of Sulcarkeep, they wore mail shirts and carried small, diamond-shaped shields on their shoulders. But their helms were shaped like the heads of the birds they trained. And, though he knew that human eyes surveyed him from behind the holes in those head coverings, Simon found the silent regard of that exotic gear more than a little disquieting.

"I am Koris, serving Estcarp."

Koris, the great ax across his forearm, stood up to face the silent four.

The man whose falcon had just returned to its perch held up his empty sword hand palm out in a gesture as universal and as old as time.

"Nalin of the outer heights," his voice rang hollow in the helm-mask.

"Between us there is peace," Koris made that half-question, half-statement.

"Between us there is peace. The Lord of Wings opens the Eyrie to the Captain of Estcarp."

Simon had doubts about those ponies carrying double. But when he mounted behind one of the Falconers he discovered that the small animal was as sure-footed on the slightest of trails as a burro and the addition of an extra rider appeared to be no inconvenience.

The trails of the Falconer's territory were certainly not laid to either entice or comfort the ordinary traveler. Simon kept his eyes open only by force of will as they footed along ledges and swung boots out over drops he had no desire to measure.

Now and again one of the birds soared aloft and ahead, questing out over the knife-slash valleys which were a feature of the region, returning in time to its master. Simon longed to ask more concerning the curious arrangement between man and bird, for it seemed that the feathered scouts must have a way of reporting.

The party came down from one slope onto a road which was smooth as a highway. But they crossed that and bored up into the wilderness once more. Simon ventured to speak to the man behind whom he rode.

"I am new to this southern country—is that not a way through the mountains?"

"It is one of the traders' roads. We keep it open for them and so we both profit. You are this outlander, then, who has taken service with the Guards?"

"I am."

"The Guards are no blank shields. And their Captain rides to a fight and not from it. But it would seem that the sea has used you ill."

"No man may command storms," Simon returned evasively. "We live—for that we offer thanks."

"To that give thanks in addition that you were not driven farther south. The wreckers of Verlaine haul much from the sea. But they do not care for living men. Someday," his voice sharpened, "Verlaine may discover that none of her cliffs, nor her toothed reefs shall shelter her. When the Duke sets his seal upon that place then it will no longer be a small fire to plague travelers, but rather a raging furnace!"

"Verlaine is of Karsten?" Simon asked. He was a gatherer of facts where and when he could, adding them piece by piece to his jigsaw of this world.

"Verlaine's daughter is to be wed to the Duke after the custom of these foreigners. For they believe that holding of land follows a female! Then by such a crooked right the Duke will claim Verlaine for its rich treasure seized out of storm seas, and perhaps enlarge the trap for the taking of all coastwise ships. Of old we have given our swords to the traders, though the sea is not our chosen battlefield, so shall we perhaps be summoned when Verlaine is cleansed."

"You reckon the men of Sulcarkeep among those you would aid?"

The bird's head on the shoulders before him nodded vigorously. "It was on Sulcar ships that we came out of blood, death and fire overseas, Guardsman! Sulcar has first claim upon us since that day."

"It will no more!" Simon did not know why he said that, and he regretted his loose tongue immediately.

"You bear some news, Guardsman? Our hawks quest far, but not as far as the northern capes. What has chanced to Sulcarkeep?"

Simon's hesitation was prolonged into no reply at all as one of the falcons hung above them, calling loudly.

"Loose me and slide off!" his companion ordered sharply. Simon obeyed, and the four Guardsmen were left on the trail while the ponies forged ahead at a pace reckless for the country. Koris beckoned the others on.

"There is a sortie." He ran after the fast-disappearing ponies, the ax over his shoulder, his slender legs carrying him at a muscle-straining trot which Simon alone found it easy to equal.

There were shouts beyond and the telltale clash of metal meeting metal.

"Karsten forces?" panted Simon as he drew abreast of the Captain.

"I think not. There are outlaws in these wastes, and Nalin says they grow bolder. To my mind it is but a small part of all the rest. Alizon threatens to the north, the Kolder moves in upon the west, the outlaw bands grow restless, and Karsten stirs. Long have the wolves and the night birds longed to pick the bones of Estcarp. Though they would eventually quarrel over those bones among themselves. Some men live in the evening and go down into darkness defending the remnants of that they reverence."

"And this is the evening for Estcarp?" Simon found breath to ask.

"Who can say? Ah—outlaws they are!"

They looked down now upon a trade road. And here swirled a battle. The bird-helmeted horsemen dismounted as the level ground was too limited to give cavalry any advantage, to strike in as a well-trained fighting unit, cutting down those who had been enticed into the open. But there were snipers in hiding and they took toll by dart of the Falconers.

Koris leaped from ledge to trail, coming down in a pocket where two men crouched. Simon worked his way along a thread of path to a point where, with a well-aimed stone, he brought down one who was just shooting into the melee. It took only a moment to strip that body of gun and ammunition and turn the weapon against the comrades of its former owner.

Hawks flew screaming, stabbing at faces and eyes, raking with savage claws. Simon fired, took aim and fired again, marking his successes with dour satisfaction. A fraction of the bitterness of their defeat at Sulcarkeep oozed from him during those few wild moments while there was still active resistance around and below.

A squeal of horn cut the shrieks of the birds. Across the valley a rag of flag was waved vigorously and those of the outlaws who still kept their feet fell back, though they did not break and run until they reached cover where mounted men could not pursue. The day was slipping fast into evening and a host of shadows swallowed them up.

Hide from the men they might, but concealment from the hawks was another matter. The birds swirled over the rising ground, striking down, sometimes finding a quarry as screams of pain testified. Simon saw Koris on the road, ax still in hand, a dark stain on the blade of that weapon. He was talking eagerly with a Falconer, oblivious of those who walked from one body to the next, sometimes making sure of its status with a quick sword stroke. There was the same grim finality to this engagement as there had been after the ambush of those from Gorm. Simon busied himself with the buckling on of his new arms belt, taking care not to watch that particular activity.

The hawks were drifting back down the arch of the evening sky, coming in answer to the whistles of their masters. Two bodies in bird helms were lashed across the pads of nervous ponies, and other men rode bandaged, supported by their fellows. But the toll among the outlaw force had been far the greater.

Simon rode behind a Falconer again, not the same man. And this one was not inclined to talk as he nursed a slashed arm across his breast and swore softly at every jolt.

Night came quickly in the mountains, the higher peaks shutting out the sun, enclosing growing pools of gloom. The track they took was a broader one and smooth as a highway when compared to their earlier trails. It brought them at last, up a stiff climb, to the home the Falconers had made for themselves in their exile. And it was such a keep as drew a whistle of astonishment out of Simon.

He had been truly impressed by the ancient walls of Estcarp with their air of having been wrought from the bones of the earth in the days of its birth. And Sulcarkeep, though it had been cloaked with the spume of that unnatural fog, had been indeed a mighty work. But this was a part of the cliffs, of the mountain. He could only believe that the makers had chanced upon a peak where there were a series of caves which had been enlarged and worked. For the Eyrie was not a castle, but a mountain itself converted into a fort.

They entered over a drawbridge spanning a chasm luckily hidden in the twilight, a drawbridge giving footing to only one horse at a time. Simon released his indrawn breath only when the pony he bestrode in company passed under the wicked points of a portculis into a gaping cave. He aided the wounded Falconer to the pavement and into the hands of one of his fellows, and then looked about for the Guardsmen, sighting Tunston's height and bare dark head before he saw the others.

Koris pushed his way to them, Jivin at his heels. For a space they seemed to be forgotten by their hosts. Horses were led away, and each man took his falcon upon a padded glove before going into another passage. But at last one of the bird heads swiveled in their direction and a Falconer officer approached.

"The Lord of Wings would speak with you, Guardsmen. Blood and Bread, Sword and Shield to our service!"

Koris tossed his ax, caught it, and turned the blade away from the other with ceremony. "Sword and Shield, Blood and Bread, man of the hawks!"

III
A Witch in Kars

Simon sat up on the narrow bunk, knuckles pressed to his aching head. He had been dreaming, a vivid and terrifying dream of which he could recall only the terror. And then he awakened to find himself in the cell-like quarters of a Falconer with this fierce pain in his head. But more urgent than the pain was a sense of the need to obey some order—or was it to answer a plea?

The ache faded, but the urgency did not and he could not remain in bed. He dressed in the leather garments his hosts had provided and went out, guessing that it was close to morning.

They had been five days at the Eyrie and it was Koris' intention to ride north soon, heading to Estcarp through leagues of outlaw-infested territory. Simon knew that it was in the Captain's mind to bind the Falconers to the cause of the northern nation. Once back in the northern capital he would bring his influence to work upon the prejudices of the witches, so that the tough fighting men of the bird helms might be enlisted in Estcarp's struggle.

The fall of Sulcarkeep had aroused the dour men of the mountains, and preparations for war buzzed in their redoubt. In the lower reaches of the strange fortress smiths toiled the night through and armorers wrought cunningly, while a handful of technicians worked on those tiny beads strung on the hawk jesses through which a high circling bird reported and recorded for his master. The secret of those was the most guarded of their nation, and Simon had only a hint that it was based on some mechanical contrivance.

Tregarth had been often brought up short in his estimation of these peoples by just some curious quirk such as this. Men who fought with sword and shield should not also produce intricate communication devices. Such odd leaps and gaps in knowledge and equipment were baffling. He could far more readily accept the "magic" of the witches than the eyes and ears, and when necessary, voices which were falcon borne.

The magic of the witches—Simon climbed stairs cut in one of the mountain burrows, came out upon a lookout post. There was no mist to mask a range of hills visible in the light of early morning. By some feat of engineering he could see straight through a far gap into that open land which he knew to be Karsten.

Karsten! He was so intent upon that keyhole into the duchy that he was not aware of the sentry on post there until the man spoke:

"You have a message, Guardsman?"

A message? Those words triggered something in Simon's mind. He experienced for an instant the return of pain to press above his eyes, that conviction there was something for him to do. This was foreknowledge of a kind, but not such as he had known on the road to Sulcarkeep. Now he was being summoned, not warned. Koris and the Guardsmen would ride north if they willed, but he must head south. Simon put down his last guard against this insidious thing, allowed himself to be swayed by it.

"Has any news come out of the south?" he demanded of the sentry.

"Ask that of the Lord of Wings, Guardsman." The man was suspicious after the training of his kind. Simon headed for the stairs.

"Be sure that I shall!"

Before he went to the Commander of the Falconers, he tracked down the

Captain, finding Koris busied with preparations for taking the trail. He glanced up from his saddlebags to Simon, and then his hands stopped pulling at buckles and straps.

"What's to do?"

"Laugh if you will," Simon replied shortly. "My road lies to the south."

Koris sat down on the edge of a table and swung one booted foot slowly back and forth. "Why does Karsten draw you?"

"That is just it!" Simon struggled to put into words what compelled him against either inclination or sense. He had never been an articulate man and he was discovering it even harder here to explain himself. "I am drawn—"

The swinging foot was still. In that handsome, bitter face there was no readable expression. "Since when—and how has it come upon you?" That demand was quick and harsh, an officer desiring a report.

Simon spoke the truth. "There was a dream and then I awoke. When I looked just now through the gap into Karsten I knew that my road leads there."

"And the dream?"

"It was of danger, more I cannot remember."

Koris drove one fist into the palm of the other. "So be it! I wish you had more power or less. But if you are drawn, we ride south."

"We?"

"Tunston and Jivin shall carry our news to Estcarp. The Kolder cannot cut through the barrier of the Power yet awhile. And Tunston can rally the Guard as well as I. Look you, Simon, I am of Gorm and now it is Gorm which fights against the Guard, though it may be a Gorm which is dead and demon-inspired. I have served Estcarp to the best of my ability since the Guardian gave me refuge, and I shall continue to serve her. But it may be that the time has come that I can serve her best outside the ranks of her liege men instead of within them.

"How do I know . . ." his dark young eyes had shadow smudges under them, tired eyes, worn with a fatigue which was not of body, "how do I know that through me because I am of Gorm danger cannot strike at the very heart of Estcarp? We have seen what the Kolder have done to living men whom I knew well, what else that devil-haunted brood can accomplish what man may tell? They flew through the air to take Sulcarkeep."

"But that may be no fruit of magic," Simon cut in. "In my own world air flight is a common mode of travel. I wish I had had sight of how they came—it could tell us much!"

Koris laughed wryly. "Doubtless we shall be given numerous other occasions in the future to observe their methods. I say this to you, Simon, if you are drawn south, I believe it to be by intelligent purpose. And two swords, or rather," he corrected himself with a little smile, "one ax, and one dart gun, is of greater force than one gun alone. The very fact of this summoning is good hearing, for it must mean that she who went with us to Sulcarkeep still lives and now moves to further our cause."

"But how do you know it is she, or why?" Such a suspicion had been Simon's also, to have it confirmed by Koris carried conviction.

"How? Why? Those who have the Power can send it forth along certain lanes of mind, as these Falconers dispatch their birds through the reaches of the air. And if they meet any of their kind, then they call or warn. As to why—it is in my mind, Simon, that she who sends must be the lady you saved from the pack of Alizon, for she would be well able to communicate with one she knows.

"You are not blood of our blood, bone of our bone, Simon Tregarth, and it would seem in your world the Power lies not only in the hands of women. Did you not smell out that ambush on the shore road as well as any witch might do? Yes, I shall ride into Karsten on no more proof than you have given me at this hour, because I know the Power and because, Simon, I have fought beside you. Let me give Tunston his instructions and a message for the Guardian, and we shall go to cast in troubled waters for important fish."

They rode south well equipped with mail and weapons taken from vanquished enemies, blank shields signifying that they were wandering mercenaries open for hire. The Falconer border guard escorted them to the edge of the mountains and the traders' road to Kars.

With no more than that tenuous feeling as a guide Simon wondered at the wisdom of their venture. Only the pull was still on him night and day, though he had no more nightmares. And each morning found him impatient to take the highway once more.

Karsten had villages in plenty, growing larger and richer as the travelers penetrated into the black-earthed bottomlands along the wide rivers. And there were petty lordlings set up in fiefs who offered employment to the two from the north. Though Koris laughed to scorn the wages they suggested and thus increased the respect with which he and his ax were regarded, Simon said little, but was alert to everything about him, mapping the land in his head, and noting small customs and laws of behavior, while, between times when they journeyed alone, he pumped the Guard Captain for information.

The Duchy had once been a territory sparsely held by a race akin to the ancient blood of Estcarp. And now and then a proud-held dark head, a pale face with cleanly cut features, reminded Simon of the men of the north.

"The curse of the Power finished them here," Koris observed when Simon commented on this.

"The curse?"

The Captain shrugged. "It goes back to the nature of the Power. Those who use it do not breed. And so each year the women who will wed and bear grow fewer. A marriageable maid of Estcarp may choose among ten men, soon among twenty. Also there are childless homes in plenty.

"So it was here. Thus when the sturdier barbarians came overseas and settled along the coast they were not actively opposed. More and more land came to their hands. The old stock withdrew to the backlands. Then warlords arose among the newcomers in the course of time. So we have the Dukes, and this Duke last of all—who was a common man of a hired shield company and climbed by his wits and the strength of his sword arm to complete rule."

"And so will it go with Estcarp also?"

"Perhaps. Only there was a mingling of blood with the Sulcarman, who, alone, it seems, can mate with Estcarp and have fruit of it. Thus in the north there was a stirring of the old blood and a renewing of vigor. However, Gorm may swallow us up before there has been a proving of anything. How is it, Simon; does this town we approach beckon you? It is Garthholm on the river, and beyond it lies only Kars."

"Then we go to Kars," Simon answered wearily after a long moment. "For the burden is still on me."

Under his plain helm Koris' brows rose. "Then it is indeed laid upon us to walk softly and watch over our shoulders the while. Though the blood of the Duke is not high and he is eyed sidewise by the nobles, yet his wits are far from blunt. There will be eyes and ears within Kars to mark the lowliest stranger and questions asked of blank shields. Especially if we do not strive to enlist at once under his banner."

Simon gazed thoughtfully at the river barges swinging at anchor by the town quay.

"But he would not be inclined to enlist a maimed man. Also are there not doctors within Kars who would treat one injured in battle? A man, say, who ailed from a blow on the head so that his eyes no longer served him well?"

"Such a one as would be brought by a comrade to see the wise doctors of Kars?" chuckled Koris. "Yes, that is a fine tale, Simon. And who is this injured warrior?"

"I think that role is mine. It would cover any awkward mistakes which a keen-witted eye-and-ear of the Duke would note."

Koris nodded vigorously. "We sell these ponies here. They label us too much as being from the mountains, and in Karsten mountains are suspect. Passage can be bought on one of the river boats. A good enough plan."

It was the Captain who carried out the bargaining over the ponies, and he was still counting the wedge-shaped bits of metal which served as payment tokens in the duchy as he joined Simon on the barge. Koris grinned as he slapped the handful into his belt purse.

"I have trader blood and today I proved it," he said. "Half again what I was prepared to take, enough to aid in any palm-greasing when we come to Kars, should that be needed. And provisions to keep us until that hour." He dumped the bag he carried on board along with the ax from which he had not been parted since he took it from the hands of Volt.

There were two days of lazy current gliding on the river. As it neared sunset on the second, and the walls and towers of Kars stood out boldly not too far ahead, Simon's hands went to his head. The pain once more shot above his eyes with the intensity of a blow. Then it was gone, leaving behind it a small vivid picture of an ill-paved lane, a wall, and a door deep set therein. That was their goal and it lay in Kars.

"This is it then, Simon?" The Captain's hand fell on his shoulder.

"It is." Simon closed his eyes to the sunset colors bending the river. Somewhere in that city he must find the lane, the wall, the door, and meet with the one who waited.

"A narrow lane, a wall, a door—"

Koris understood. "Little enough," he remarked. His gaze was for the city, as if by the force of his will he could hurl them across the space still separating the barge from the waiting wharf.

Soon enough they came up the quay to the arch in the city wall. Simon moved slowly in his chosen role, trying to walk with the timidity of a man who could not trust his sight. Yet his nerves were prickling, he was certain that once within the city he could find the lane. The thread which had drawn him across the duchy was now a tight cord of direction.

Koris talked for them at the gate and his explanation of Simon's disability, his plausible story—as well as a gift passed under hand to the sergeant of the guard—got them in. The Captain snorted as they passed down the street and turned the corner.

"Were that man in Estcarp I'd have the sign off his shield and his feet pointing on the road away before he had time to name me his name! It has been said that the Duke grows soft since he came into rule, but I would not have believed it so."

"Every man is said to have his price," Simon remarked.

"True enough. But a wise officer knows the price of the men under him and uses them accordingly. These are mercenaries and can be bought in little things. But perhaps if the code still prevails, they will stand firm in battle for him who pays them. What is it?"

He asked that sharply for Simon had stopped, half swung around.

"We head wrong. It is to the east."

Koris studied the street ahead. "There is an alley four doors from here. You are sure?"

"I am sure."

Lest the sergeant of the gate be more astute than they judged him, they went at a slow pace, Simon being guided. The eastward alley led on into more streets. Simon sheltered in a doorway while Koris sniffed their back trail. In spite of his distinctive appearance the Captain knew how to take cover, and he came flitting back soon.

"If they have set any hound on us he is better than Estcarp's best, and that I do not believe. So now let us get to earth before we are remarked to be remembered. East still it is?"

The dull pain in Simon's head ebbed and flowed, he could use it as a "hot" and "cold" guide in a strange fashion. Then a particularly bad blast brought him to the mouth of a curving lane and he stepped within. It was walled with blank backs of buildings and what windows looked out on it were dark and curtained.

They quickened pace and Simon shot a glance at each window as they passed, fearing to see a face there. Then he saw it—the door of his vision. He was breathing a little hard as he paused before it, not from the exertion of pace, but rather from the turmoil inside him. He raised his fist and rapped on the solid portal.

When there was no answer he was absurdly disappointed. Then he pushed, to encounter a barrier which must be backed with bars.

"You are sure this is it?" Koris prodded.

"Yes!" There was no outer latch, nothing he could seize upon to force it open. Yet what he wanted, what had brought him there, was on its other side.

Koris stepped back a pace or two, measuring the height of the wall with his eye.

"Were it closer to dark we could mount this. But such a move now might be noted."

Simon threw away caution and pounded, his assault on the wood that of a drum. Koris caught at his arm.

"Would you rouse out the Duke's companies? Let us lay up in a tavern and come back at nightfall."

"There is no need for that."

Koris' ax lifted from his shoulder. Simon's hand was on his gun. The door showed a wedge of opening and that low, characterless voice had come through it to them.

A young man stood in that crevice between wood and brick. He was much shorter than Simon, less in inches even than Koris, and light of limb. The upper part of his face was overhung with the visor of a battle helm, and he wore mail without the badge of any lord.

From Simon he looked to the Captain, and the sight of Koris appeared oddly to reassure him, for he stepped back and motioned them within. They came into a garden with brittle stalks of winter-killed flowers in precise beds, past a dry fountain rimmed with the mark of ancient scum where a stone bird with only half a beak searched endlessly for a water reflection which no longer existed.

Then another door into a house, and there the stream of light was a banner of welcome. The young man pushed before them, having sped from the barring of the wall door. But another stood to bid them enter.

Simon had seen this woman in rags as she fled from a pack of hunting hounds. And he had seen her in council, wearing the sober robes of her chosen order. He had ridden beside her when she went girt in mail with the Guards. Now she wore scarlet and gold, with gems on her fingers and a jeweled net coifing her short hair.

"Simon!" She did not hold out her hands to him, offered no other greeting save the naming of his name, yet he was warmed and at peace. "And Koris." She voiced a gentle laughter which invited them both to share some private joke, and swept them the grand curtsy of a court lady. "Have you come, lords, to consult the Wise Woman of Kars?"

Koris grounded the haft of his ax on the floor and dropped the saddlebags which had been looped over his wide shoulder.

"We have come at your bidding, or rather your bidding to Simon. And what we do here is for your saying. Though it is good to know that you are safe, lady."

Simon only nodded. Once again he could not find the proper words to express feelings he shrank from defining too closely.

IV
Love Potion

Koris put down his goblet with a sigh. "First a bed such as no barracks ever boasted and then two meals like this. I have not tasted equal wine since I rode out of Estcarp. Nor have I feasted in such good company."

The witch clapped her hands lightly. "Koris the courtier! And Koris and Simon the patient. Neither of you have yet asked what we do in Kars, though you have been a night and part of a day under this roof."

"Under this roof," Simon repeated thoughtfully. "Is this perchance the Estcarp embassy?"

She smiled. "Now, that is clever of you, Simon. But, no, we are not official. There *is* an Estcarp embassy in Kars, housing a lord with impeccable background and not a single smell of witchcraft about him. He dines with the Duke upon formal occasions and provides a splendid representation of respectability. This house is located in quite a different quarter. What we do here—"

When she paused Koris asked lightly:

"I gather our aid is needed or Simon would not have had that aching head of his. Do we kidnap Yvian for your pleasure, or merely split a few skulls here and there?"

The young man who moved quietly, spoke little, but was always there, whom the witch named Briant and yet had not explained to the Guardsmen, reached for a dish of pastry balls. Stripped of the mail and helm he had worn at their first meeting, he was a slender, almost frail youngster, far too young to be well schooled in the use of the weapons he bore. Yet there was a firm set to his mouth and chin, a steady purpose in his eyes which argued that the woman from Estcarp had perhaps chosen wisely in her recruiting after all.

"How, Briant," she said to him now, "shall they bring us Yvian?" There was something approaching mischief in that inquiry.

He shrugged as he bit into the pastry. "If you wish to see him. *I* do not." And that faint emphasis on the "I" was lost on neither of the men.

"No, it is not the Duke we plan to entertain. It is another member of his household, the Lady Aldis."

Koris whistled. "Aldis! I would not think—"

"That we have any business with the Duke's leman? Ah, you make the mistake of your sex there, Koris. There is a reason I wish to know more of Aldis, and an excellent one to urge her to come."

"Those being?" prompted Simon.

"Her power within the duchy is founded upon Yvian's favor alone. While she holds him to her bed she has what she wants most, not gauds and robes, but influence. Men who wish to further some scheme must seek out Aldis as a passage to the Duke's ear, even if they are of the old nobility. As for women of rank—Aldis has repaid heavily many old slights.

"When she first climbed to Yvian's notice the gauds and glitter sufficed, but through the years her power has come to mean more. Without that she is no better than a wench in a dockside tavern, as well she knows."

"Does Yvian grow restive now?" Koris wanted to know.

"Yvian has wed."

Simon watched the hand at the pastry dish. This time it did not complete its mission, but went instead to the goblet before Briant's plate.

"We heard talk in the mountains of the wedding of Verlaine's heiress."

"Ax marriage," the witch explained. "He has not seen his new bride yet."

"And the present lady fears a competition. Is the lady of Verlaine then counted so beautiful?" Simon asked idly but he caught a sudden swift glance from Briant.

And it was the boy who answered. "She is not!" There was a note in that hot denial which baffled Simon with its bitter hurt. Who Briant was or where the witch had found him, they had no idea, but perhaps the boy had nursed a liking for the heiress and was disappointed by his loss.

The witch laughed. "That, too, may be a matter of opinion. But, yes, Simon,

I think that Aldis does not lie easy of nights since she heard the decree read forth in Kars' market place—wondering how long Yvian will continue to reach for her. In this state of mind she is ripe for our purpose."

"I can see why the lady might seek aid," Simon conceded, "but why yours?"

She was reproachful. "Though I do not go under my true colors as a Woman of Power out of Estcarp, I have a small reputation in this city. It is not my first visit here. Men and women, especially women, are ever intrigued to hear of their futures. Two of Aldis' waiting maids have come here in these past three days, armed with false names and falser stories. When I named them for what they are and told them a few facts, they went scuttling back wry-faced to their mistress. She will come soon enough, never fear."

"But why do you want her? If her influence with Yvian is on the wane—" Koris shook his head. "I have never pretended to an understanding of women, but truly am I now in a maze. Gorm is our enemy—not Karsten, at least, not actively."

"Gorm!" There was some emotion stirring behind the smooth facade of her face. "Here also Gorm finds roots."

"What!" Koris' hands slapped down hard on the table between them. "How comes Gorm to the duchy?"

"It is the other way around. Karsten goes to Gorm, or a part of her man-power does." The witch, resting her chin upon her clasped hands, her elbows on the board, spoke earnestly.

"We saw at Sulcarkeep what the Kolder forces did to the men of Gorm, using them for war weapons. But Gorm is only a small island and when she was overrun many of her men must have died in battle before they could be . . . converted."

"That is true!" Koris' voice was savage. "They could not have netted too many captives."

"Just so. And when Sulcarkeep fell Magnis Osberic must have taken with him the major parts of the invading force with the destruction of the hold. In that he served his people. Most of the trading fleet were at sea, and it is the custom of the Sulcarmen to carry their families with them on long voyages. Their haven on this continent is gone, but their nation lives and they can build again. Only, can the Kolder so easily replace the men *they* lost?"

"It must be that they lack manpower," Simon half questioned, his mind busy with the possibilities that suggested.

"Which may be true. Or for some other reason they cannot or will not face us openly themselves. We know so little concerning the Kolder, even when they squat before our door. Now they are buying men."

"But slaves are chancy as fighting men," Simon pointed out. "Put weapons in their hands and you ask for revolt."

"Simon, Simon, have you forgotten what manner of men we flushed from ambush on the sea road? Ask yourself if they were ready for revolt. No, those who march to Kolder war drums have no will left in them. But this much is also true: for the past six months galleys have come to an island lying off the sea-mouth of Kars' river and prisoners from Karsten are transferred to those ships. Some are from the prisons of the Duke, other men are swept up on the streets and docks, friendless men, or ones not to be missed.

"Such dealings cannot be kept secret forever. A whisper here, a sentence there—piece by piece we have gathered it. Men sold to the Kolder for Kolder purposes. And if thus it happens in Karsten, why not in Alizon? Now I can better understand why my mission there failed and how I was so speedily uncovered. If the Kolder have certain powers—as we believe that they do—they could stalk me or any such as me, as the hounds hunted us by scent on the moors.

"It is our belief now that the Kolder on Gorm are gathering a force to the purpose of invading the mainland. Perhaps on that day Karsten and Alizon shall both discover that they provided the weapons for their own defeat. That is why I deal with Aldis, we must know more of this filthy traffic with Gorm and it could not exist without the Duke's knowledge and consent."

Koris stirred restlessly. "Soldiers gossip also, lady. A round of wine shops made by a blank shield with tokens in his purse might bring us tidings in plenty."

She looked dubious. "Yvian is far from stupid. He has his eyes and ears everywhere. Let one such as you appear in the wine shops you mention, Captain, and he shall hear of it."

Koris did not appear worried. "Did not Koris of Gorm, a mercenary, lose his men and his reputation at Sulcarkeep? Doubt not that I shall have a good story to blat out if any should ask it of me. You," he nodded to Simon, "had best lie close lest the tale we told to get through the gates trips us up. But how about the youngling here?" He grinned at Briant.

Somewhat to Simon's surprise the generally sober-faced youth smiled back timidly. Then he looked to the witch as if for permission. And, equally to Simon's astonishment, she gave it, with some of the same mischief she had shown earlier.

"Briant is no ruffler of the barracks, Koris. But he has been prisoned here long enough. And don't underrate his sword arm; I'll warrant he can and will amaze you—in several ways!"

Koris laughed. "That I do not doubt at all, lady, seeing that it is you who say it." He reached for the ax by his chair.

"You'd best leave that pretty toy here," she warned. "It, at least, will be remarked." She laid her hand on the shaft.

It was as if her fingers were frozen there. And for the first time since their arrival Simon saw her shaken out of her calm.

"What do you carry, Koris?" her voice was a little shrill.

"Do you not know, lady? It came to me with the goodwill of one who made it sing. And I guard it with my life."

She snatched back her hand as if that touch had seared flesh and bone.

"Willingly it came?"

Koris fired to that doubt. "About such a matter I would speak only the truth. To me it came and only me will it serve."

"Then more than ever do I say take it not into the streets of Kars." That was half order, half plea.

"Show me then a safe place in which to set it," he countered, with openly displayed unwillingness.

She thought a moment, her finger rubbing at her lower lip. "So be it. But later you must give me the full tale, Captain. Bring it hither and I shall show you the safest place in this house."

Simon and Briant trailed after them into another room where the walls were hung with strips of a tapestry so ancient that only the vaguest hints of the original designs could be surmised. One of these she bypassed to come to a length of carved wall panel on which fabulous beasts leered and snarled in high relief. She pulled at this, to display a cupboard and Koris set the ax far to its back.

Just as Simon had been aware of the past centuries within Estcarp city, solid waves of time beating against a man with all the pressure of ages, as he had also known awe for the nonhuman in the Hole where Volt had held silent court for dust and shadows, so here there was also a kind of radiation from the walls, a tangible something in the air which made his skin creep.

Yet Koris was brisk about the business of storing his treasure and the witch shut the cupboard as might a housewife upon a broom. Briant had lingered in the doorway, his usual impassive self. Why did Simon feel this way? And he was so plagued by that that he stayed when the others left, making himself walk slowly to the center of the chamber.

There were only two pieces of furniture. One a high-backed chair of black wood which might have come from an audience hall. Facing it was a stool of the same somber coloring. And on the floor between the two an odd collection of articles Simon studied as if trying to find in them the solution to his riddle.

First there was a small clay brazier in which might burn a palmload of coals, no more. It stood on a length of board, polished smooth. And with it was an earthen bowl containing some gray-white meal, which was flanked by a squat bottle. Two seats and that strange collection of objects—yet there was something else here also.

He did not hear the witch's return and was startled out of his thoughts when she spoke.

"What are you, Simon?"

His eyes met hers. "You know. I told you the truth at Estcarp. And you must have your own ways of testing for falsehood."

"We have, and you spoke the truth. Yet I must ask you again, Simon—what are you? On the sea road you felt out that ambush before the Power warned me. Yet you are a man!" For the first time her self-possession was shaken. "You know what is done here—you feel it!"

"No. I only know that there is something here that I cannot see—yet it exists." He gave her the truth once again.

"That is it!" She beat her fists together. "You should not feel such things, and yet you do! I play a part here. I do not always use the Power, that is, greater power than my own experience in reading men and women, in guessing shrewdly what lies within their hearts or are their desires. Three quarters of my gift is illusion; you have seen that at work. I summon no demons, toll nothing here from another world by my spells, which are said mainly to work upon the minds of those who watch for wonders. Yet there is the Power and sometimes it comes to my call. Then I can work what are indeed wonders. I can smell out disaster, though I may not always know what form it will take. So much can I do—and that much is real! I swear to it by my life!"

"That I believe," Simon returned. "For in my world, too, there were things which could not be explained with any sober logic."

"And you had your women to do such things?"

"No, it came to either sex there. I have had men under my command who had foreknowledge of disaster, of death, their own or others'. Also I have known houses, old places, in which something lurked which was not good to think about, something which could not be seen or felt any more than we can now see or feel what is with us here."

She watched him now with undisguised wonder. Then her hand moved in the air, sketching between them some sign. And that blazed for an instant in fire hanging in space.

"You saw that?" Was that an accusation or triumphant recognition? He did not have time to discover which, for, sounding through the house was the note of a gong.

"Aldis! And she will have guards with her!" The witch crossed the room to rip open that panel where Koris had stored the ax. "In with you," she ordered. "They will search the house as they always do, and it would be better if they do not know of your presence."

She allowed him no time for protest, and Simon found himself cramped into space much too small. Then the panel was slammed shut. Only it was more spyhole than cupboard, he discovered. There were openings among the carvings, which gave him air to breath and sight of the room.

It had all been done so swiftly that he had been swept along. Now he revolted and his hands went to that panel, determined to be out. Only to discover, too late, that there was no latch on his side and that he had been neatly put into safekeeping, along with Volt's ax, until the witch chose to have him out again.

His irritation rising, Simon pressed his forehead against the carven screen to gain as full sight as he could of the room. And he kept very still as the woman from Estcarp reentered, to be pushed aside by two soldiers who strode briskly about, flipping aside strips of tapestry.

The witch was laughing as she watched them. Then she spoke over her shoulder to one still lingering on the other side of the threshold:

"It seems that one's word is not accepted in Kars. Yet when has this house and those under its roof even been associated with ill dealings? Your hounds may find some dust, a spider web, or two—I confess that I am not a notable housewife, but naught else, lady. And they waste our time with their searching."

There was a faint jeer in that, enough to flick one on the raw. Simon appreciated her skill with words. She spoke as an adult humoring children, a little impatient to be about more important business. And subtly she invited that unseen other to join her in adulthood.

"Halsfric! Donnar!"

The men snapped to attention.

"Prowl through the rest of this burrow if you will, but leave us in private!"

They stood aside nimbly at the door as another woman came in. The witch closed the portal behind them before she turned to the newcomer, who dropped her hooded cloak to let it lie in a saffron pool on the floor.

"Welcome, Lady Aldis."

"Time is wasting, woman, as you pointed out." The words were harsh, but the voice in which they were spoken surrounded that bruskness with layers of velvet. Such a voice could well twist a man to her will through hearing it alone.

And the Duke's mistress had the form, not of the tavern wench to which the witch had compared her, overripe and full-curved, but of a young girl not fully awakened to her own potentialities, with small high breasts modestly covered, yet perfectly revealed by the fabric of her robe. A woman of contradictions—wanton and cool at one and the same time. Simon, studying her, could well understand how she had managed to hold sway over a proved lecher as long and successfully as she had.

"You told Firtha—" again that sharp note swathed in velvet.

"I told your Firtha just what I could do and what was necessary for the doing." The witch was as brisk as her client. "Does the bargain suit you?"

"It will suit me when it is proved successful and not before. Give me that which makes me secure in Kars and then claim your pay."

"You have a strange way of bargaining, lady. The advantages are all yours."

Aldis smiled. "Ah, but if you have the power you claim, Wise Woman, then you can blast as well as aid and I shall be easy meat for you. Tell me what I must do and be quick; I can trust those two outside only because I hold both their lives with my tongue. But there are other eyes and tongues in this city!"

"Give me your hand." The woman from Estcarp picked up the tiny bowl of meal. As Aldis extended her beringed hand, the other stabbed it with a needle drawn from her clothing, letting a drop or two of blood fall into the bowl. She added more moisture from the bottle, mixing it into a batter. And coaxed the charcoal in the tiny stove to a blaze.

"Sit down." She pointed to the stool. When the other was seated, she slapped the board across her knees, putting the stove upon it.

"Think on the one you want, keep him only in your mind, lady."

The batter of that cake was spread out above that handful of fire and the woman from Estcarp began to sing. Strangely enough that something which had so alerted Simon moments earlier, which had thickened and curdled about them in that second when she had traced the fiery sign in the air, was now ebbing from the room.

But in its way her singing wove a spell of its own, changing thought images, evoking another kind of response. Simon, realizing it for what it was, for what it could do, after an incredulous second or two, bit hard upon his lower lip. This—coming from the woman he thought he was beginning to know. Fit magic for Aldis and her like; for the cool cleanliness of Estcarp, no! And it was beginning to work upon him also. Simon screwed his fingers into his ears to close out that sultry heat which seeped from words in the air to the racing blood in his own body.

He took away that defense only when he saw the witch's lips ceased to move. Aldis' face was a delicate pink, her parted lips moist, her eyes fixed before her unseeingly, until the witch lifted from her knees the board and brazier. The woman from Estcarp took up the cake, crumbled it into a square of white cloth and held it out to her client.

"A pinch of this added to his food or drink." The life had gone from the witch's voice; she spoke as one drugged with fatigue.

Aldis whipped the package from her, thrust it into the breast of her gown. "Be sure I shall use it rightly!" She caught up her cloak, already on her way to the door. "I shall let you know how I fare."

"I shall know, lady, I shall know."

Aldis was gone and the witch stood, one hand on the back of the chair as if she needed its support. Her expression was one of weary distaste with a faint trace of shame, as if she had used ill means to gain a good end.

V
Three Times Horned

*K*oris' hands moved in steady rhythm, polishing the ax blade with slow strokes of a silken cloth. He had reclaimed his treasure the minute he returned, and now, perched on a window ledge, with it resting upon his knees, he talked.

"... he burst in as if the Kolder were breathing upon his back and blurted it out to the sergeant who spewed up half the wine I had paid for and was like to choke loose his guts, while this fellow pawed at him and yammered about it. I'd stake a week's looting of Kars that there is a kernel of truth in it somewhere, though the story's a muddle."

Simon was watching the other two in that room. He did not expect the witch to reveal either surprise or the fact that she might already have heard such a tale. However, the youngster she had produced out of nowhere might be less well schooled, and his attitude proved Simon right. Briant was *too* well controlled. One better trained in the game of concealment *would* have displayed surprise.

"I take it," Simon cut through the Captain's report, "that such a story is not a muddle to you, lady." The wariness which had become a part of his relationship with her since that scene with Aldis hours earlier was the shield he raised against her. She might sense its presence, but she made no effort to break through it.

"Hunold is truly dead," her words were flat. "And he died in Verlaine. Also is the Lady Loyse gone from the earth. That much did your man have true, Captain," she spoke to Koris rather than to Simon. "That both these happenings were the result of an Estcarp raid is, of course, nonsense."

"That I knew, lady. It is not our manner of fighting. But is this story a cover for something else? We have asked no questions of you, but did the remainder of the Guards come ashore on the Verlaine reefs?"

She shook her head. "To the extent of my knowledge, Captain, you and those who were saved with you are the only survivors out of Sulcarkeep."

"Yet a report such as this will spread and be an excuse for an attack on Estcarp." Koris was frowning now. "Hunold stood high in Yvian's favor. I do not think the Duke will take his death calmly, especially if some mystery surrounds it."

"Fulk!" The name exploded out of Briant as if it were a dart shot from his side arm. "This is Fulk's way out!" His pale face had expression enough now. "But he would have to deal with Siric and Lord Duarte, too! I think that Fulk has been very busy. That shieldman had so many details of a raid that he must have been acquainted with a direct report."

"A messenger from the sea just landed. I heard him babble that much," Koris supplied.

"From the sea!" The witch was on her feet, her scarlet and gold draperies stirring about her. "Fulk of Verlaine cannot be termed in any way a simpleton, but there is a swiftness of move here, a taking advantage of every chance happening which smacks of something more than just Fulk's desire to protect himself against Yvian's vengeance!"

There was a stormy darkness in her eyes as she regarded all three of them coldly. She might almost have been numbering them among hostile elements. "This I do not like. Oh, some tale from Verlaine might have been expected; Fulk needed a story to throw into Yvian's teeth lest the stones of his towers be rained down about his own ears. And he is perfectly capable of spitting both Siric and Duarte to give added credence and cover his tracks. But the moves come too swiftly, too well fitting into a pattern! I would have sworn—"

She strode up and down the chamber, her scarlet skirts swirling about her. "We are mistresses of illusion, but I will take oath before the Power of Estcarp that that storm was no illusion! Unless the Kolder have mastered the forces of nature—" Now she stood very still, and her hands flew to her mouth as if to trap words already spoken. "If the Kolder have mastered—" her voice came as a whisper. "I cannot believe that we have been moved hither and yon at their bidding! That I dare not believe! Yet—" She whirled about and came directly to Simon.

"Briant I know, and what he does and why, all that I know. And Koris I know, and what drives him and why. But you—man out of the mists of Tor, I do not know. If you are more than you seem, then perhaps we have brought our own doom upon us."

Koris stopped polishing the ax blade. The cloth fell to the floor as his hands closed about the haft. "He was accepted by the Guardian," he said neutrally, but his attention centered upon Simon with the impersonal appraisal of a duelist moving forward to meet a challenge.

"Yes!" The woman from Estcarp agreed to that. "And it is impossible that what Kolder holds to its core cannot be uncovered by our methods. They could cloak it, but the very blankness of that cloak would make it suspect! There is one test yet." She plucked at the throat fastening of her robe and drew forth the dull jewel she had worn out of Estcarp. For a long moment she held it in her hands, gazing down into its heart, and then she slipped the chain from about her neck and held it out to Simon. "Take it!" she ordered.

Koris cried out and scrambled off the ledge. But Simon took it into his hand. At first touch the thing was as smooth and cold as any polished gem, then it began to warm, adding to that heat with every second. Yet the heat did not burn, it had no effect upon his flesh. Only the stone itself came to life; trails of opalescent fire crawled across its surface.

"I knew!" Her husky half-whisper filled the room. "No, not Kolder! Not Kolder; Kolder could not hold without harm, fire the Power and take no hurt! Welcome, brother in power!" Again she sketched a symbol in the air which glowed as brightly as the gem before it faded. Then she took the stone from his hold and restored it to its hiding place beneath her robe.

"He is a *man!* Shape changing could not work so, nor is it possible to befool us in the barracks where he has lived," Koris spoke first. "And how does a *man* hold the Power?"

"He is a man out of our time and space. What chances in other worlds we cannot say. Now I will swear that he is not Kolder. So perhaps he is that which Kolder must face in the final battle. But now we must . . ."

Their preoccupation was sharply broken by the burr of a signal in the wall. Alert, Simon and Koris looked to the witch. Briant drew his gun. "The wall gate," he said.

"Yet it is the right signal, though the wrong time. Answer it, but be prepared."

He was already half out of the room. Koris and Simon sped after him to the garden door. As they reached outside, free from the deadening thickness of the walls of that unusual house, they heard a clamor from the town. Simon was plagued by a wisp of memory. There was a note in that far-off shouting which he had surely heard before. Koris looked startled.

"That is a mob! The snarl of a hunting mob."

And Simon, remembering a red horror out of his own past, nodded briskly. He poised the dart gun to welcome whoever stood without the wall gate.

There was no mistaking the race of the man who stumbled in to them. A bloody gash could not disguise Estcarp features. He fell forward and Koris caught him about the body. Then they were all nearly rocked from their feet as a blast of sound and displaced air beat in on them and the very ground moved under them.

The man in Koris' hold moved, smiled, tried to speak. Deafened momentarily they could not hear. Briant slammed shut the gate and set its locking bars. Together Simon and the Captain half carried, half supported the fugitive into the house.

He recovered enough to sketch a salute to the witch as they brought him to her. She measured some bluish liquid into a cup and held it to his lips as he drank.

"Lord Vortimer?"

He leaned back in the chair into which they had lowered him. "You just heard his passing, lady—in that thunder clap! With him went all of our blood fortunate to reach the embassy in time. For the rest—they are being hunted in the streets. Yvian has ordered the three times horning for all of Estcarp or of the old blood! He is like a man gone mad!"

"This too?" She pressed her hands tight against her temples as if she might so ease some almost intolerable pain. "We have no time, no time at all?"

"Vortimer sent me to warn you. Do you choose to follow him along the same path, lady?"

"Not yet."

"Those who have been horned can be cut down without question wherever they are found. And in Kars today the cutting down does not come swiftly as a clean death," he warned dispassionately. "I do not know what hopes you may have of the Lady Aldis—"

The witch laughed. "Aldis is no hope at all, Vortgin. Five of us . . ." She turned the cup around and around in her fingers and then looked directly to Simon. "More depends upon this than just our lives alone. There are those in the outer parts of Karsten of the old blood, who, warned, might safely get through the mountains to Estcarp, and so swell our ranks. Also what we have learned here, patchy though it is, must be taken back. I could not hope to summon Power enough—you will have to aid me, brother!"

"But I don't know how—I have no use of Power," he protested.

"You can back me. It is our only hope."

Koris came away from the window where he had been peering into the garden.

"Shape changing?"

"It is the only way. And how long will it hold?" she shrugged.

Vortgin ran his tongue across his lips. "Set me outside this cursed city and I'll rouse your countryside for you. I have kin in the backlands who'll move on my word!"

"Come!" She led the way to that tapestried room of magic. But just inside the door Koris halted.

"What I have been given I bear with me. Put on me no shape in which I cannot handle the gift of Volt."

"I would call you lack-witted," she flared back, "if I did not know the worth of that biter of yours. But it is not of human make and so may change shape also in illusion. We can only try. Now let us make ready, quickly!"

She pulled a strip of carpet from the floor as Simon and Koris shoved the chair and stool, bore the other things to the other end of the room. Stooping she traced lines with the jewel of Power and those lines glowed faintly in the form of a five-pointed star. A little defiantly Koris dropped his ax in the center of that.

The witch spoke to Simon. "Shapes are not changed in truth, but an illusion is created to bemuse those who would track us down. Let me draw upon your

Power to swell my own. Now," she glanced around and brought the small clay brazier to sit by the ax, puffing its coals into life, "we can do what is to be done. Make yourselves ready."

Koris caught Simon by the arm. "Strip—to the skin—the Power does not work otherwise!" He was shedding his own jerkin. And Simon obeyed orders, both of them aiding Vortgin.

Smoke curled up from the brazier, filling the room with a reddish mist in which Koris' squat form, the fugitive's muscular body were half-hidden.

"Take your stand upon the star points—one to each point," came the witch's order out of the murk. "But you, Simon—next to me."

He followed that voice, losing Koris and the other man in the fog. A white arm came out to him, a hand reached for and enfolded his. He could see under his feet the lines of a star point.

Someone was singing—at a far distance. Simon was lost in a cloud where he floated without being. Yet at the same time he was warm—not outwardly, but inwardly. And that warmth floated from his body, down his right arm. Simon thought that if he could watch it he would be able to see that flow— blood red, warm—being drained in a steady stream. Yet he saw nothing but the grayish mist, he only knew that his body still existed.

The singing grew louder. Once before he had heard such singing—then it had aroused his lusts, and urged him to satisfy appetites he had beaten under by force of will. Now it worked upon him in another way, and he no longer loathed it fiercely.

He had closed his eyes against the endless swirling of the mist, stood at-tuned to the singing so that each note throbbed within his body to be a part of him, made into flesh and bone from this time forth—yet also did that warm flood trickle out of him.

Then his hand fell limply back against his thigh. The drain had ceased and the singing was fading. Simon opened his eyes. Where the murk had been a solid wall it was now showing holes. And in one of them he caught sight of a brutish face, a beastly caricature of human. But in it sat Koris' sardonic eyes. And a little beyond was another with disease-eaten skin and a flat lid where an eye had once been.

He wearing the Captain's eyes glanced from Simon to his neighbor and grinned widely, displaying decayed and yellowed fangs. "A fair company we shall be!"

"Dress you!" snapped the witch from the disappearing murk. "This day you have come out of the stews of Kars to loot and kill. It is your kind who thrive upon hornings!"

They put on the gear they had brought into Kars, but not enough to go too well clad for the dregs of the city that they seemed. And Koris took up from the floor—not the Ax of Volt—but a rust-encrusted pole set with hooks, the purpose of which Simon would rather not imagine.

There was no mirror to survey his new self, but he gathered that he was as disreputable as his companions. He had been expecting changes in the witch and Briant also—but not what he saw. The woman of Estcarp was a crone with filthy ropes of grayish hair about her hunched shoulders, her features underlined with ancient evil. And the youngster was her opposite. Simon stared in pure amazement, for he fronted a girl being laced into the scarlet-and-gold gown discarded by the witch.

Just as Briant had been pallid and colorless, here was rich beauty, more than properly displayed since her tiring maid did not bother to pull tight breast laces. Instead the crone quirked a finger at Simon.

"This is your loot, bold fellow. Hoist the pretty on your shoulder, and if you grow tired of your burden—well, these other rogues will lend a hand. Play your part well." She gave the seeming girl a shove between her shoulder blades which sent her stumbling into Simon's arms. He caught her up neatly, swinging her across his shoulder, while the witch surveyed them with the eye of a stage manager and then gave a tug to strip the bodice yet farther from those smooth young shoulders.

Inwardly Simon was astonished at the completeness of the illusion. He had thought it would be for the eyes only, but he was very conscious that he held what was also feminine to the touch. And he had to keep reminding himself that it was indeed Briant he so bore out of the house.

They found Kars harbored many such bands as theirs that day. And the sights they had to witness, the aid they could not give, ate into them during that journey to the wharves. There was a watch at the gates right enough, but as Simon approached, with his now moaning victim slung over his shoulder, his raffish fellows slinking behind him, as if to welcome the leavings of his feast, the witch scuttled ahead with a bag. She tripped and fell so that the brilliant contents of her looter's catchall rolled and spilled across the roadway.

Those on guard sprang into action, the officer kicking the crone out of his way. But one man had a slightly higher sense of duty, or perhaps he was more moved by Simon's supposed choice of pillage. For he swung a pike down in front of Tregarth and grinned at him over that barrier.

"You've got you a soft armload there, fishguts. Too good for you. Let a better man sample her first!"

Koris' pole with its rusty hooks snaked out, hooking his feet from under him. As he sprawled they darted through the gate and along the wharf, other guards in pursuit.

"In!" Briant was pulled out of Simon's grasp, thrown out into the flood of the river, the Captain following in a clean-cut dive to come up beside the struggling red-and-gold-clad body. Vortgin took off at a stumbling run. But Simon, seeing that Koris had Briant to hand, looked back for the witch.

There was a flurry down the wharf and a tangle of figures. Gun in hand he ran back, pausing for three snap shots, each taking out a man, dead or wounded. His rush brought him there in time to see that twisted gray-haired body lying still while a sword swung downward aimed at the scrawny throat.

Simon shot twice more. Then his fist struck flesh, crushed it against bone. Someone shrieked and fled as he scooped up the witch, finding her weight more than Briant's. Bearing her over his shoulder he staggered to the nearest barge, his lungs laboring as he dodged among the piled cargo on its deck, heading for the far rail and open water.

The woman in his arms came to life suddenly, pushing against him as if he were indeed a captor she might fight. And that overbalanced Simon so that they went over together, tumbling to strike the river with a force he had not expected. Simon swallowed water, choked, and struck out instinctively, if clumsily.

His head broke the surface and he stared about him for the witch, to see a wrinkled arm, hampered by water-soaked rags cutting in a swimmer's stroke.

"Ho!"

The call came from a barge floating downstream and a rope flicked over its side. Simon and the witch gained the deck, only to have Koris wave them impatiently to the opposite rail into the river again, the craft serving as a screen between them and the city shore.

But here a small boat with Vortgin sitting therein, Briant leaning over the side being actively sick into the water, while he clutched his red robe about him as if indeed he had been the victim of rapine. As they scrambled down to this refuge, Koris pushed them away from the barge, using the point of his hook spear.

"I thought you lost that at the gate!"

Koris' ruffian face mirrored his astonishment at Simon's comment. "This I would never lose! Well, we have us a breathing space. They will believe us hiding on the barge. At least so we can hope. But it would be wise to head to the other shore as soon as this has drifted far enough from the wharves."

They agreed with the Captain's suggestion, but the minutes during which they remained wedded to the barge were very long ones. Briant straightened at last, but he kept his face turned from them as if heartily ashamed of the guise he wore. And the witch sat in the bow surveying the far shore with searching intensity.

They were lucky in that night was closing in. And Vortgin knew the surrounding country well. He would be able to guide them inland across the fields, avoiding houses and farms, until they had put enough distance between them and Kars to feel reasonably safe.

"Thrice horned—yes, that sentence he can enforce in Kars. For the city is his. But the old lords have ties with us, and where they lack such ties or sympathy, they may be moved by jealousy of Yvian. They may not actively aid us, but neither will they help the Duke's men cut us down. It will be largely a matter of their closing their eyes and ears, hearing and seeing naught."

"Yes, Karsten is now closed to us," the witch agreed with Vortgin. "And I would say to all of the old race that they should flee borderward, not leaving escape until too late. Perhaps the Falconers will aid in this matter. Aie . . . aie . . . our night comes!"

But Simon knew that she did not mean the physical night closing about their own small party.

VI
False Hawk

*T*hey lay behind the winter-pressed stack in the field, Simon, Koris, and Vortgin, wisps of the dank straw pulled over their bodies, watching what went on at the crossroads hamlet beyond. There were the brilliant blue-green surcoats of the Duke's men, four of them, well mounted for hard and far riding, and a fringe of the dull-robed villagers. With some ceremony the leader of the small force out of Kars brought his horse beneath the Pole of Proclamation and put a horn to his lips, its silver plating catching fire from the morning sun.

"One . . . two . . . three . . ." Koris counted those blasts aloud. They heard them clearly, all the countryside must have heard them, although what the Duke's men said to the assembly afterwards they caught only as a mumble.

Koris looked to Vortgin. "They spread it fast enough. You'd best be on your way, if any of your kin is to be warned at all."

Vortgin thrust his belt dagger deep into the earth of the field as if he were planting it in one of the blue-coated riders. "I'll need more than my two legs."

"Just so. And there is what we all seek." Koris jerked a thumb at the ducal party.

"Beyond the bridge the road takes a cut through a small woods," Simon thought aloud.

Koris' pseudo-face expressed malicious appreciation of that hint. "They'll soon be through with the chatter. We'd best move."

They crawled away from their vantage point, crossed the river ford, and found the woods track. The roads leading north were not well kept. Yvian's rule in this district had been covertly opposed by noble and commoner alike. Away from the main highways all passages tended to be only rough tracks.

On either side banks rose, brush and grass covered. It was not a safe place for any wayfarer, doubly suspect for anyone in the Duke's livery.

Simon settled into concealment on one side of that cut, Koris chose a stand closer to the river, prepared to head off any retreat. And Vortgin was across from Simon. They had only to wait.

The leader of the messengers was no fool. One of his men rode ahead, studying every bush the wind stirred, every clump of suspiciously tall grass. He passed between the hidden men and trotted on. After him came the one who bore the horn, and a companion, while the fourth man brought up the rear.

Simon shot as the rearguard drew level with his position. But the man who fell from the expertly aimed dart was the lead scout.

The leader swung his mount around with the skill of an expert horseman, only to see the rearguard collapse from his saddle coughing blood.

"Sul . . . Sul . . . Sul!" The battle cry Simon had last heard in the doomed seaport rose shrilly. A dart creased Simon's shoulder, ripping leather and burning skin—the leader must have cat's eyes.

The remaining shieldman tried to back his leader in that attack, until Vortgin arose out of hiding and threw the dagger he had played with. The weapon whirled end over end until its heavy knob struck the back of the other's head at the base of his skull and he went down without a protesting sound.

Hooves pawed the air over Simon's head. Then the horse overbalanced and crashed back, pinning his rider under him. Koris sprang out of hiding and the hooked pole battered down upon the feebly struggling man.

They set to work to strip the riders, secure their mounts. Luckily the horse which had fallen struggled to its feet, frightened and blowing but without any great injury. The bodies were dragged out of sight into the brush and the mail shirts, the helmets and the extra weapons were bound on the saddles before the horses were led to the deserted sheepfold where the fugitives had sheltered.

There the men walked into a hot quarrel. The withered crone, the dark beauty in rent gold and scarlet fronted each other hot-eyed. But their raised voices fell silent as Simon came through a gap in the rotting fence. Neither spoke until they brought up the horses and their burdens. Then the girl in red gave a little cry and pounced upon one of those bundles of leather and mail.

"I want my own shape—and now!" she spat at the witch.

Simon could understand that. At Briant's age a role as he had been forced to assume would be more galling than slavery. And none of them could wish to keep on wearing the decidedly unattractive envelopes the woman from Estcarp had spun for them, even though they had been so delivered out of Kars.

"Fair enough," he endorsed that. "Can we change by our—or rather *your* will, lady? Or is there a time period on this shape business?"

Through her tangle of rough locks the witch frowned. "Why waste the time? And we are not yet out of the reach of Yvian's messengers—though apparently you have dealt with some of them." She picked up one of the surcoats as if to measure it against her own bent person.

Briant glowered, gathering an armload of male clothing to him. The pouting lips of his girl's face set stubbornly. "I go away from here as myself, or I don't go at all!" he announced, and Simon believed him.

The woman from Estcarp gave in. From beneath her ragged bodice she pulled a bag and shook it at Briant. "Off with you to the stream, then. Wash with a handful of this for your soaping. But be careful of it, for this supply must serve us all."

Briant snatched the bag, and, with the clothing, he gathered up his full skirts to scuttle away as if he feared his new possessions might be torn from him.

"What about the rest of us?" Simon demanded indignantly, ready to take off after the runaway.

Koris secured the horses to the moldering fence. His villanious face could not look anything but hideous, but somehow he managed to suggest honest amusement in his laughter. "Let the cub get rid of his trappings in peace, Simon. After all, he hasn't protested before. And those skirts must have irked him."

"Skirts?" echoed Vortgin in some surprise. "But . . ."

"Simon is not of the old race." The witch combed her hair with her long nails. "He is new to our ways and shape changing. You are right, Koris," she glanced oddly at the Captain, "Briant can be left to make his transformation in peace."

The garments looted from the Duke's unfortunate messengers hung loosely on the young warrior who returned at a far bolder gait from the stream. He tossed a ball of red stuff to the back of the shelter and stamped earth over it with an energy which approached attack as Simon and the rest went to the water.

Koris rubbed and laved his rusty hooked pole before he dipped his body, and continued to hold the Ax of Volt as he scrubbed himself. They made a choice from the tumbled clothing, Koris again assuming the mail shirt he had worn out of Kars since no other would fit him. But he shrugged one of the surcoats over it, a precaution followed by both his companions.

Simon handed the bag to the witch when they returned and she nursed it for a moment in one hand, then restored it to its former hiding place. "You are a brave company of warriors. Me, I am your prisoner. With your hoods and your helms Estcarp does not show so strong in you. Vortgin, you alone have the print of the old race. But were I to be seen in my true face I would damn you utterly. I shall wait before I break this shape."

So it was that they rode out of that hiding place, four men in the Duke's colors and the crone perched behind Briant. The horses were fresh, but they held the pace to a comfortable trot as they worked a path across the country, avoiding the open roads until they reached a point where Vortgin must turn east.

"North along the trade roads," the witch leaned from her seat behind Briant to urge. "If we can alert the Falconers they should see fugitives safely through the mountains. Tell your people to leave their gear and bring with them only their weapons and food, what may be carried on pack animals. And may the Power ride with you, Vortgin, for those you can urge into Estcarp will be blood for our veins!"

Koris pulled the horn strap from his shoulder and passed it over. "This may be your passport if you flush any of Yvian's forces before you get into the back country. Luck be yours, brother, and seek out the Guards in the North. There is a shield in their armory to fit your shoulder!"

Vortgin saluted and kicked his horse into a flurry of speed eastward.

"And now?" the witch asked Koris.

"The Falconers."

She cackled. "You forget, Captain, old and shriveled as I seem, with all the juices age-sucked from me, still am I female and the hold of the hawk men is barred to me. Set Briant and me across the border and then seek out your women-hating bird men. Rouse them up as best you may. For a border abristle with sword points will give Yvian something else to think about. And if they can afford our cousins safe passage, they will put us deep in their debt. Only," she plucked at the surcoat on Briant's shoulders, "I would say to you throw these name signs of a lord you do not serve away, or you may find yourself pinned to some mountain tree before you have time to make your true nature known."

Simon was not surprised this time to find they were being observed by a hawk, nor did he think it odd to hear Koris address the bird clearly, giving their true identities and explaining their business in the foothills. He covered the back trail while the Captain took the lead, the witch and Briant riding between them. They had parted with Vortgin in mid-afternoon and it was now close to sunset, their only food during the day the rations found in the saddle-bags of the captured horses.

Now Koris pulled up until the others joined him. While the Captain spoke he still faced into the rising mountains and it seemed to Simon as if he had lost a little of his robust confidence.

"This I do not like. That message must have been relayed by the bird's communicator, and the frontier guards could not have been too far away. They should have met us before now. When we were in the Eyrie they were eager enough to promote a common cause with Estcarp."

Simon eyed the slopes ahead uneasily. "I do not take a trail such as this in the dark without a guide. If you say, Captain, that they are not following custom, then that is all the more reason for staying clear of their territory. I would say camp at the first likely spot."

It was Briant who broke in then, his head up, his attention for the bird wheeling overhead.

"That one does not fly right!" The youngster, dropping the reins of his horse, held his hands together to mimic the wings of a bird. "A true bird goes so—and a falcon so—many times have I watched them. But this one, see— flap, flap, flap—it is not right!"

They were all watching the circling bird now. To Simon's eyes it was the same sort of black-and-white feathered sentry as had found them outside the Hole of Volt, as he had seen on the saddle perches of the Falconers. However he would be the first to admit that he knew nothing of birds.

"Can you whistle it down?" he asked Koris.

The Captain's lips pursed and clear notes rang on the air.

At that same moment Simon's dart gun went up. Koris turned with a cry and struck at Simon's arm, but the shot had already been fired. They saw the dart strike, piercing just the point of the white vee upon the bird's breast. But there was no faltering in its flight, no sign that it had taken any hurt from the bolt.

"I told you it is no bird!" cried Briant. "Magic!"

They all looked to the witch for an explanation, but her attention was riveted on that bird, the dart still protruding from its body, as it made low lazy circles overhead.

"No magic of the Powers." That answer seemed forced out of her against her will. "What this is, I cannot tell you. But it does not live as we know life."

"Kolder!" Koris spat.

She shook her head slowly. "If it is Kolder, it is not nature-tampering as it was with the men of Gorm. What it is I cannot tell."

"We'll have to get it down. It is lower since that dart struck it; perhaps the weight pulls it." Simon said, "Let me have your cloak," he added to the witch, dismounting.

She handed him that ragged garment and looping it over his arm Simon began to climb the wall beside the narrow track they had followed to this place. He hoped that the bird would remain where it was, content to fly above them. And he was sure it drew nearer earth with every circle.

Simon waited, flipping the cloak out a little. He flung it, and the bird flew unwarily into the improvised net. When Simon tried to draw it back the captive fell free, to fly blindly on and smash headfirst against the rock wall.

Tregarth leaped down to scoop up what lay on the ground. Real feathers right enough—but under them! He gave a whistle almost as clear and carrying as Koris' bird summons, for entangled in the folds of torn skin and broken feathers was a mass of delicate metal fittings, tiny wheels and wires, and what could only be a motor of strange design. Holding it in his two hands he went back to the horses.

"Are you sure the Falconers use only real hawks?" he asked of the Captain.

"Those hawks are sacred to them." Koris poked a finger into the mess Simon held, his face blank with amazement. "I do not think that this thing is any of their fashioning, for to them the birds are their power and they would not counterfeit that lest it either turn upon them or depart utterly."

"Yet someone or something has tossed into the air these mountains hawks which are made, not hatched," Simon pointed out.

The witch leaned closer, reaching out a finger to touch as Koris had done. Then her eyes raised to Simon's and there was a question in them, a shadow of concern.

"Outworld—" she spoke hardly above a whisper. "This is not bred of our magic, or of the magic of our time and space. Alien, Simon, alien . . ."

Briant interrupted her with a cry and pointing a finger. A second black-and-white shape was over their heads, swooping lower. Simon's free hand went to the gun, but the boy reached down from his saddle to strike at Tregarth's wrist and spoil his aim.

"That is a real bird!"

Koris whistled and the hawk obeyed that summons in the clean strike of its breed, settling on a rock crown, the tip of the same pinnacle against which the counterfeit had dashed itself to wreckage.

"Koris of Estcarp," the Captain spoke to it, "but let him who flies you come swiftly, winged brother, for there is ill here and perhaps worse to come!" He waved his hand and the falcon took once more to the air, to head straight for the peaks.

Simon put the other thing into one of his saddlebags. In the Eyrie he had been intrigued by the communication devices which the true falcons bore. A machine so delicate and so advanced in technical ability was out of place in the feudal fortress of its users. And what of the artificial lighting and heating systems of Estcarp, or the buildings of the Sulcarkeep, of that energy source Osberic had blown up to finish the port? Were all these vestiges of an earlier civilization which had vanished leaving only traces of its inventions behind? Or—were they grafts upon this world from some other source? Simon's eyes may have been on the trail they rode but his wits were tumbling the problem elsewhere.

Koris had spoken of Volt's nonhuman race preceeding mankind here. Were these remnants of theirs? Or had the Falconers, the mariners of Sulcarkeep, learned what they wished, what served their purposes best from someone, or something else, perhaps overseas? He wanted a chance to examine the wreckage of the false hawk, to try to assess from it if he could the type of mind, or training, which could create such an object.

The Falconers emerged from the mountain slopes as if they had stepped from the folds of the ground. And they waited for the party from Kars to approach, neither denying them passage, nor welcoming them.

"Faltjar of the southern gate," Koris identified their leader. He swept his own helm from his head to display his face plainly in the fading light. "I am Koris of Estcarp, and I ride with Simon of the Guards."

"Also with a female!" The return was cold and the Falcon on Faltjar's saddle perch shook its wings and screamed.

"A lady of Estcarp whom I must put safely beyond the mountains," corrected the Captain in a tone as cold and with the sharpness of a rebuke. "We make no claim upon you for shelter, but there is news which your Lord of Wings should hear."

"A way through the mountains you may have, Guard of Estcarp. And the news you may give to me; it shall be retold to the Lord of Wings before moonrise. But in your hail you spoke of ill here and worse to follow. That I must know, for it is my duty to man the southern slopes. Does Karsten send forth her men?"

"Karsten has thrice horned all of the old race and they flee for their lives. But also there is something else. Simon, show him the false hawk."

Simon was reluctant. He did not want to yield up that machine until he had more time to examine it. The mountaineer looked upon the broken bird he took from the saddlebag, smoothing a wing with one finger, touching an open eye of crystal, pulling aside a shred of feathered skin to see the metal beneath.

"This flew?" he demanded at last, as if he could not believe in what he saw and felt.

"It flew as one of your birds, and kept watch upon us after the fashion of your scouts and messengers."

Faltjar drew his forefinger caressingly down the head of his own bird as if to assure himself that it was a living creature and not such a copy.

"Truly this is a great ill. You must speak yourself with the Lord of Wings!" Clearly he was torn between the age-old customs of his people and the necessity for immediate action. "If you did not have the female—the lady," he corrected with an effort, "but she may not enter the Eyrie."

The witch spoke. "Let me camp with Briant, and you ride to the Eyrie, Captain. Though I say to you, bird man, the day comes soon when we must throw aside many old customs, both we of Estcarp and you of the mountains, for it is better to be alive and able to fight, than to be bound by the chains of prejudice and dead! There is a riving of the border before us such as this land has never seen. And all men of goodwill must stand together."

He did not look at her, nor answer, though he half sketched a salute, giving the impression that that was a vast concession. And then his hawk took to the air with a cry, and Faltjar spoke directly to Koris.

"The camp shall be made in a safe place. Then, let us ride!"

4. VENTURE OF GORM

∞

I
The Riving of the Border

A column of smoke penciled into the air, broken by puffs as more combustible materials caught. Simon reined up on the rise to gaze back at the site of another disaster for the Karsten forces, another victory for his own small, hard-riding, tough-punching troop. How long their luck would hold, none of them could guess. But as long as it did, they would continue to blast into the plains, covering up the escape lines of those set-faced, dark-haired people from the outlands who came in family groups, in well-armed and equipped bodies, or singly at a weaving pace dictated by wounds and exhaustion. Vortgin had done his work well. The old race, or what was left of it, was withdrawing over a border the Falconers kept open, into Estcarp.

Men without responsibilities for families or clans, men who had excellent cause to want to meet Karsten levies with naked blades, stayed in the mountains, providing a growing force to be led by Koris and Simon. Then by Simon alone as the Captain of the Guard was summoned north to Estcarp to recommand there.

This was guerrilla warfare as Simon had learned it in another time and land, doubly effective this time because the men under him knew the country as those sent against them did not. For Tregarth discovered that these silent, somber men who rode at his back had a queer affinity with the land itself and with the beasts and the birds. Perhaps they were not served as the Falconers were by their trained hawks, but he had seen odd things happen, such as a herd of deer move to muddle horse tracks, crows betray a Karsten ambush. Now he listened, believed, and consulted with his sergeants before any strike.

The old race were not bred to war, though they handled sword and gun expertly. But with them it was a disagreeable task to be quickly done and forgotten. They killed cleanly with dispatch and they were incapable of such beastliness as the parties from the mountains had come upon where fugitives had been cut off and captured.

It was once when Simon left such a site, white, controlling his sickness by willpower alone, that he was startled by a comment from the set-faced young man who had been his lieutenant on that foray.

"They do not do this of their own planning."

"I have seen such things before," Simon returned, "and that was also done by human beings to human beings."

The other who had held his own lands in the back country and had escaped with his bare life from that holding some thirty days earlier, shook his head.

"Yvian is a soldier, a mercenary. War is his trade. But to kill in such ways is to sow black hate against a future reaping. And Yvian is lord in this land; he would not willingly rip apart his own holding and bring it to ruin—he is too keen-witted a man. He would not give orders for the doing of such deeds."

"Yet we have seen more than one such sight. They could not all be the work of only one band commanded by a lover of evil, or even two such."

"True. That is why I think we now fight men who are possessed."

Possessed! The old meaning of that term in his own world came to Simon—possession by demons. Well, that a man could believe having seen what they had been forced to look upon. Possessed by demons—or—the memory of the Sulcarkeep road flooded into his mind; possessed by a demon—or emptied of a soul! Kolder again?

From then on, much as it revolted him, Simon kept records of such finds, though never he was able to catch the perpetrators at their grisly work. He longed to consult with the witch, only she had gone north with Briant and the first wave of fugitives.

He launched through the network of guerrilla bands a request for information. And at nights, in one temporary headquarters after another, he pieced together bits and patches. There was very little concrete evidence, but Simon became convinced that certain commanders among the Karsten forces did not operate according to their former ways, and that the Duke's army had been infiltrated by an alien group.

Aliens! As always that puzzle of inequality of skills continued to plague him. Questioning of his refugees told him that the energy machines which they had always known had come from "Overseas" ages past: "Overseas," energy machines brought by the Sulcar traders, adapted by the old race for heat and light, the Falconers also from "Overseas" with their amazing communicators borne by their hawks. And the source of the Kolder was also "Overseas"—a vague term—a common source for all?

What he could learn he dispatched by messenger to Estcarp, asking for anything the witches might have to tell in return. The only thing he was sure of was that as long as his own force was recruited from those of the old race, he had no need to fear infiltration himself. For that quality which gave them kinship with the land and the wild things granted them in addition the ability to smell out the alien.

Three more false hawks had been detected in the mountains. But all had been destroyed in their capture and Simon had only broken bits to examine. Where they came from and for what purpose they had been loosed was a part of all the other mystery.

Ingvald, the Karstenian lieutenant, pushed up beside him now to look down upon the scene of destruction they had left.

"The main party with the booty is well along the hill track, Captain. We have plundered to some purpose this time, and with that fire laid to cross our trail, they will not even know how much has come into our hands! There are four cases of darts as well as the food."

"Too much to supply a flying column." Simon frowned, his mind snapping back to the business at hand. "It would seem that Yvian hopes to make a central post somewhere hereabouts and base his foray parties there. He may be planning to move a large force borderwards."

"I do not understand it," Ingvald said slowly. "Why did this all blow up so suddenly out of nothing? We are not—were not—blood brothers of the coast-wise people. They drove us inland when they came from the sea. But for ten generations we have been at peace with them, each going our way and not troubling the other. We of the old race are not inclined to war and there was no reason for this sudden attack upon us. Yet when it came it moved in such a way as we may only believe that it had long been planned."

"But, not, perhaps, by Yvian." Simon set his horse to a trot matched by Ingvald's mount so they rode knee to knee. "I want a prisoner, Ingvald, a prisoner of such a one as has been amusing himself in those ways we saw in the farm meadow of the fork roads!"

A spark gleamed deep in the dark eyes meeting his. "If such a one is ever taken, Captain, he shall be brought to you."

"Alive and able to talk!" Simon cautioned.

"Alive and able to speak," agreed the other. "For it is in our minds too, that things can be learned from one of that sort. Only never do we find them, only their handiwork. And I think that that is left deliberately as a threat and a warning."

"There is a puzzle in this," Simon was thinking aloud, playing once more with his ever-present problem. "It would seem that someone believes we can be beaten into submission by brutality. And that someone or something does not understand that a man can be fired to just the opposite by those methods. Or," he added after a moment's pause, "could this be done deliberately to goad us into turning our full fury against Yvian and Karsten, to get the border aflame and all Estcarp engaged there, then to strike elsewhere?"

"Perhaps a little of both," Ingvald suggested. "I know, Captain, that you have been seeking for another presence in the Karsten forces, and I have heard of what was found at Sulcarkeep and the rumors of man-selling to Gorm. We are safe in this much: no one who is not truly human can come among us without our knowledge—just as we have always known that you are not of our world."

Simon started, but turned to see the other smiling quietly.

"Yes, Outlander, your tale spread—but after we knew you were not of us—though in some strange way your own akin to our blood. No, the Kolder cannot sneak into our councils so easily. Nor can the enemy venture among the Falconers, for the hawks would betray them."

Simon was caught by that. "How so?"

"A bird or an animal can sense that kind of alien quicker than even one who has the Power. And those like now to the men of Gorm would find both bird and beast against them. So the Hawks of the Eyrie serve their trainers doubly and make safe the mountains."

But before the day was behind them Simon was to learn that that vaunted safety of the mountains was only as strong as those frail bird bodies. They were examining the supplies looted from the train and Simon set aside a portion intended for the Eyrie, when he heard the hail of a camp sentry and the answer of a Falconer. Welcoming the chance to let the latter transport the hawkmen's share and so save his men a trip, Simon came forward eagerly.

The rider had not followed custom. His bird-head helm was closed as if he rode among strangers. It was not that alone which stopped Simon before he gave greeting. The men of his band were alert, drawing in in a circle. Simon felt it, too, that prickle of awaking surmise, just as he had known it before.

Without stopping to reason, he hurled himself at the silent rider and his hands caught at the other's weapon belt. Simon knew fleeting wonder that the hawk perched on the saddle horn did not rouse as he attacked its master. His lunge caught the Falconer by surprise, and the fellow had no time to draw his arms. But he made a quick recovery, slumping his whole weight on Simon, bearing him under him to the ground, where mailed gloved hands tore for Tregarth's throat.

It was like tangling with a steel-muscled, iron-fleshed thing, and within seconds Simon knew that he had attempted the impossible—what was encased in the Falconer's covering could not be subdued with bare hands. Only he was not alone; other hands plucked that fighter off him, held the man pinned to the ground, though the stranger struggled wildly.

Simon, rubbing his scratched throat, got to his knees.

"Unhelm!" He gasped the order, and Ingvald worked at the helm straps, jerking them free at last.

They gathered around the men who held the captive down, for his struggles did not stop. The Falconers were an inbred race with a dominate physical type—reddish hair and brown-yellow eyes like their feathered servants. By his looks this was a true man of the breed. Yet Simon and every man in that clearing knew that what they held was no normal member of the mountain country.

"Rope him tight!" Simon ordered. "I think, Ingvald, we have found what we have been wishing for." He went over to the horse which had carried the pseudo-hawkman into their camp. The animal's hide glistened with sweat, threads of foam spun at the bit hooks; it might have been ridden in a grueling race. And its eyes were wild, showing rims of white. But when Simon reached for the reins it did not try to escape, standing with a drooping head as great shudders moved its sweat-soaked skin.

The hawk had remained quiet, no flap of wings or hissing beak to warn Simon off. He reached up and plucked the bird from its perch, and the minute his fingers closed upon that body he knew he did not hold a living creature.

With it in his hand he turned to his lieutenant. "Ingvald, send Lathor, Karn," he named the two most accomplished scouts in his command. "Let them ride to the Eyrie. We must know how far the rot has spread. If they find no damage done there, let them give warning. For proof of their tale," he stooped to pick up the bird helm of their prisoner, "let them take this. I believe it is of Falconer making, yet," he walked over to the bound man, still silent, still watching them with eyes of mad hate, "I cannot quite believe that this is one of them."

"We do not take him also?" asked Karn, "or the bird?"

"No, we open no doors which are not already breached. We need safe disposal for this one for a space."

"The cave by the waterfall, Captain." Waldis, a boy of Ingvald's homestead who had tracked his master to the mountains, spoke up. "One sentry at the entrance can keep it safe and none know of it save us."

"Good enough. You will see to it, Ingvald."

"And you, Captain?"

"I am going to backtrail this one. It may be that he did ride from the Eyrie. If that is true, the sooner we know the worst the better."

"I do not think so, Captain. At least if he did, it was not by any straight trail. We are well to the westward of the hold. And he entered from the path leading to the sea. Santu," he spoke to one who had helped to rope the prisoner, "do you go and take outpost on this trail and send in Caluf who first challenged him."

Simon threw the saddle on his own horse, and added a bag with rations. On top he thrust in the dummy falcon. Whether this was one of the counterfeit flying things, he could not tell as yet, but it was the first intact one they had. He finished just as Caluf ran in.

"You are sure he came from the west?" Simon pressed the question.

"I will swear it on the Stone of Engis if you wish, Captain. The hawkmen do not care greatly for the sea, though they serve the traders at times as marines. And I did not know they patrolled the shore cliffs. But he rode straight between those notched rocks which give upon the way to the cove we mapped five days ago, and he moved as one who knew the trail well."

Simon was more than a little disturbed. The cove of their recent discovery had been a ray of hope for the establishment of better communication with the north. It was not endangered by reefs and shoals such as fanged too much of the coastline and Simon had planned for the use of small vessels to harbor there, transporting north refugees, and returning with supplies and arms for the border fighters. If that cove was in enemy hands he wanted to know it, and at once.

As he left the clearing, with Caluf and another riding behind him, Simon's mind was again working on two levels. He noted the country about him with an alert survey for landmarks and natural features which might be used in future defensive or offensive action. But beneath that surface activity he was pushing under the constant preoccupation with safety, food, shelter—the job at hand—his own private concerns.

Once, in prison, he had had time to explore the depths within himself. And the paths he had hewn had been bleak, freezing him into a remoteness of spirit which had never thawed since that day. The give and take of barracks life, of companionship in field service he could assume as a cover, but nothing ate below that cover—or he had not allowed it to.

Fear he understood. But that was a transitory emotion which usually spurred him into action of one sort or another. In Kars he had been attracted in another way, and had fought free. Once he had believed that when he took Petronius' gate he would be a complete man again. But so far that was not true. Ingvald had spoken of demon possession, but what if a man did not possess himself?

He was always a man standing apart watching another occupied with the business of living. Alien—these men he led knew it in him. Was he another of the odd mistaken pieces strewn about this world, pieces which did not fit, one with the machines out of their time and the riddle of the Kolder? He sensed that he was on the brink of some discovery, one which would mean much to not only himself but to the cause he had chosen.

Then that second, prying, stand-aside self was banished by the Captain of raiders as Simon caught sight of a branch of a tree, warped by mountain storms, as yet lacking leaves. It was stark against the afternoon sky and the burden it bore, dangling in small, neatly fashioned loops, was starker yet.

He spurred ahead and sat gazing up at the three small bodies swaying in the breeze, the gaping beaks, the glazed eyes, the dangling, crooked claws still bearing their bracelets of scarlet jesses and small, silvery discs. Three of the true falcons, their necks wrung, left to be found by the next traveler along that way.

"Why?" Caluf asked.

"A warning, maybe, or something more." Simon dismounted and tossed his reins to the other. "Wait here. If I am not back within a reasonable time, return to Ingvald and report. Do not follow, we cannot afford to waste men uselessly."

Both men protested, but Simon silenced them with a decisive order before he entered the brush. There was evidence in plenty of those who had been there, broken twigs, scraps of boots on moss, a piece of torn jess strap. He was moving closer to the shore; the sound of the surf could be heard, and what he sought had certainly come from the cove.

Simon had been over that path twice, and he set himself to recall a mental picture of the country. Unfortunately the small valley which gave on the shore was lacking in cover. And the crags on either side were as bald. He would have to try one of those, which meant a roundabout route and some tough climbing. Doggedly he got to it.

As he had crept up to Volt's Hole so did he travel now, crevice, ledge, hand and foothold. Then he crawled on his belly to the edge and looked down into the cove.

Simon had expected many things—a bare strip of sand with no sign of any invasion, a party from Karsten, an anchored ship. But what he saw was very different. At first he thought of the illusions of Estcarp—could what lay below be projected from his own mind, some old memory brought to life for his bafflement? Then a closer inspection of that sharp, clean curve of metal told him that, while it bore some faint resemblance to craft he had known, this was as different from anything in his previous experience as the counterfeit hawk was from the real.

The thing was clearly a seagoing craft, though it had no sign of any superstructure, mast, or method of propulsion. Sharply pointed both fore and aft, it was shaped as might be a cross section, taken lengthwise, of a torpedo. There was an opening on its flat upper surface and men stood by that, three of them. The outline of their heads against the silver sheen of the ship were those of the Falconer bird helms. But Simon was equally sure no true Falconers wore them.

Once again the eternal mystery of this land, for the traders' ships at Sulcarkeep had been masted vessels of a nonmechanical civilization; this ship could be taken out of the future of his own world! How could two so widely differing levels of civilization exist side by side? Were the Kolder responsible here also? Alien, alien—once more he was on the very verge of understanding—of guessing—

And for that instant he relaxed his vigilance. Only a stout helm plundered from Karsten stores saved his life. The blow which struck at him out of nowhere dazed Simon. He smelled wet feathers, something else—half blinded and dizzy he tried to rise—to be struck again. This time he saw the enemy wing out to sea. A falcon, but true or false? That question he carried with him into the black cloud which swallowed him up.

II
Tribute to Gorm

*T*he throbbing beat of a pain drum filled his skull, shaking on through his body. At first, Simon, returning reluctantly to consciousness, could only summon strength enough to endure that punishment. Then he knew that the beat was not only inside him, but without also. That on which he lay shook with a steady rhythmic pound. He was trapped in the black heart of a tom-tom.

When he opened his eyes, there was no light, and when he tried to move Simon speedily discovered that his wrists and ankles were lashed.

The sensation of being enclosed in a coffin became so overpowering that he had to clamp teeth on lips to prevent crying out. And he was so busy fighting his own private war against the unknown, that it was minutes before he realized that wherever he might be, he was not alone in captive misery.

To his right someone moaned faintly now and again. On his left another retched in abject sickness, adding a new stench to the thick atmosphere of their confinement. Simon, oddly reassured by those sounds, unpromising as they were, called out:

"Who lies there? And where are we; does anyone know?"

The moaning ended in a quick catch of breath. But the man who was sick either could not control his pangs, or did not understand.

"Who are you?" That came in a weak trail of whisper from his right.

"One from the mountains. And you? Is this some Karsten prison?"

"Better that it were, mountain man! I have lain in the dungeons of Karsten. Yes, I have been in the question room of such a one. But better there than here."

Simon was busy sorting out recent memories. He had climbed to a cliff top to spy upon a cove. There had been that strange vessel in harbor there, then attack from a bird which might not have been a bird at all! Now it added up to only one answer—he lay in the very ship he had seen!

"Are we in the hands of the man-buyers out of Gorm?" he asked.

"Just so, mountain man. You were not with us when those devils of Yvian's following gave us to the Kolder. Are you one of the Falconers they snared later?"

"Falconers! Ho, men of the Winged Ones!" Simon raised his voice, heard it echo hollowly back from unseen walls.

"How many of you lie here? I, who am of the raiders, ask it!"

"Three of us, raider. Though Faltjar was borne hither limp as a death-stricken man, and we do not know if yet he lives."

"Faltjar! The guard of the southern passes! How was he taken—and you?"

"We heard of a cove where ships dared land and there was a messenger from Estcarp saying that perhaps supplies might be sent to us by sea if such could be found. So the Lord of Wings ordered us to explore. And we were struck down by hawks as we rode. Though they were not our hawks who battled for us. Then we awoke on shore, stripped of our mail and weapons, and they brought us aboard this craft which has no like in the world. I say that, who am Tandis and served five years as a marine to Sulcarmen. Many ports have I seen and more ships than a man can count in a week of steady marking, yet none kin to this one."

"It is born of the witchery of Kolder," whispered the weak voice on Simon's right. "They came, but how can a man reckon time when he is enclosed in the dark without end? Is it night or day, this day or that? I lay in Kars prison because I offered refuge to a woman and child of the old race when the Horning went forth. They took all of us who were young from that prison and brought us to a delta island. There we were examined."

"By whom?" Simon asked eagerly. Here was someone who might have seen the mysterious Kolder, from whom he might be able to get some positive information concerning them.

"That I cannot remember." The voice was the merest thread of sound now and Simon edged himself as far as he could in his bonds to catch it at all. "They work some magic, these men from Gorm, so that one's head spins around, spilling all thoughts out of it. It is said that they are demons of the great cold from the end of the world, and that I can believe!"

"And you, Falconer, did you look upon those who took you?"

"Yes, but you will have little aid from what I saw, raider. For those who brought us here were Karsten men, mere husks without proper wits—hands and strong backs for their owners. And those owners already wore the trappings they had taken from our backs, the better to befool our friends."

"One of them was taken in his turn," Simon told him. "For that be thankful, hawkman, for perhaps a part of the unraveling of this coil may lie with him." Only then did he wonder if there were ears in those walls to listen to the helpless captives. But if there were, perhaps that one scrap of knowledge would serve to spread uneasiness among their captors.

There were ten Karsten men within that prison hold, all taken from jails, all caught up for some offense or other against the Duke. And to them had been added the three Falconers captured in the cove. The majority of the prisoners appeared to be semiconscious or in a dazed condition. If able to recall any of the events leading up to their present captivity, such recollections ended with their arrival at the island beyond Kars, or on the beach of the cove.

As Simon persisted in his questioning however, a certain uniformity, if not of background then of offenses against the Duke, and temperament among these prisoners began to emerge. They were all men of some initiative, who had had a certain amount of military training, ranging from the Falconers who lived in a monastic military barracks for life and whose occupation was frankly fighting, to his first informant from Kars, a small landowner in the outlands who commanded a body of militia. In age they were from their late teens to their early thirties, and, in spite of some rough handling in the Duke's dungeons, they were all able-bodied. Two were of the minor nobility with some schooling. They were the youngest of the lot, brothers picked up by Yvian's forces on the same charge of aiding one of the old race who had been so summarily outlawed.

None of those here were of that race, and everyone declared that in all parts of the duchy men, women and children of that blood had been put to death upon capture.

It was one of the young nobles, drawn by Simon's patient questioning from his absorption with his still unconscious brother, who provided the first bit of fact for the outworld man to chew upon.

"That guard who beat down Garnit, for which may the Rats of Nore forever gnaw him night and day, told them not to bring Renston also. We were blood brothers by the bread from the days we first strapped on swords, and we went to take him food and weapons that he might try for the border. They tracked us down and took us, though we left three of them with holes in their hides and no breath in their bodies! When one of the scum the Duke's men had with him would have bound Renston too, he was told it was no use, for there was no price for those of the old blood and the men-buyers would not take them.

"The fellow whined that Renston was as young and strong as we and that he ought to sell as well. But the Duke's man said the old race broke but they would not bend; then he ran Renston through with his own sword."

"Broke but would not bend," Simon repeated slowly.

"The old race were once one with the witchfolk of Estcarp," the noble added. "Perchance these devils of Gorm cannot eat them up as easily as they can those of another blood."

"There is this," the man beside Simon added in his half-whisper, "why did Yvian turn so quickly on the old race? They have left us alone, unless we sought them out. And those of us who companied with them found them far from evil, for all their old knowledge and strange ways. Is Yvian under orders to do as he did? And who gives such orders, and why? Could it be, my brothers in misfortune, that the presence of those others among us was in some manner a barrier against Gorm and all its evil, so that they had to be routed out that Gorm may spread?"

Shrewd enough, and close to Simon's own path of thought. He would have questioned still further but, through the soft moans and wordless complaints of those still only half-conscious, he heard a steady hissing, a sound he strove hard to identify. The thick odors of the place would make a man gag, and they provided a good cover for a danger he recognized too late—the entrance of vapor into the chamber with a limited air supply.

Men choken and coughed, fought for air with strangling agony and then went inert. Only one thought kept Simon steady: the enemy would not have gone to the trouble of loading fourteen men in their ship merely to gas them to death. So Simon alone of that miserable company did not fight the gas, but breathed slowly, with dim memories of the dentist's chair in his own world.

". . . gabble . . . gabble . . . gabble . . ." Words which were no words, only a confused sound made by a high-pitched voice—carrying with them the snap of an imperative order. Simon did not stir. As awareness of his surroundings returned, an inborn instinct for self-preservation kept him quiet.

". . . gabble . . . gabble . . . gabble . . ."

The pain in his head was only a very dull ache. He was sure he was no longer on the ship; what he lay upon did not throb, nor move. But he had been stripped of his clothing and the place in which he lay was chill.

He who spoke was moving away now; the gabble retreated without an answer. But so clearly had the tone been one of an order that Simon dared not move lest he betray himself to some silent subordinate.

Twice, deliberately, he counted to a hundred, hearing no sound during that exercise. Simon lifted his eyelids and then lowered them again quickly against a stab of blazing light. Little by little his field of vision, limited as it was, cleared. What he saw in that narrow range was almost as confounding as had been his first glimpse of the strange ship.

His acquaintance with laboratories had been small, but certainly the rack of tubes, the bottles and beakers on shelves directly before him could be found only in a place of that nature.

Was he alone? And for what purpose had he been brought here? He studied, inch by inch, all he could see. Clearly he was not lying at floor level. The surface under him was hard—was he on a table?

Slowly he began to turn his head, convinced that caution was very necessary. Now he was able to see an expanse of wall, bare, gray, with a line at the very end of his field of vision which might make a door.

So much for that side of the room. Now the other. Once more he turned his head and discovered new wonders. Five more bodies, bare as his own, were laid out, each on a table. All five were either dead or unconscious, and he was inclined to believe the latter was true.

But there was someone else there. The tall thin figure stood with his back to Simon, working over the first man in line. Since a gray robe, belted in at the waist covered all of his, her, or its body, and a cap of the same stuff hid the head, Simon had no idea of race or type of creature who busied himself with quiet efficiency there.

A rack bearing various bottles with dangling tubes was rolled over the first man. Needles in those tubes were inserted into veins, a circular cap of metal was fitted over the unresisting head. Simon, with a swift jolt of pure fear, guessed that he was watching the death of a man. Not the death of a body, but that death which would reduce the body to such a thing as he had seen slain on the road to Sulcarkeep and had helped to slay himself in defense of that keep!

And he also determined that it was not going to be done to him! He tested hand and arm, foot and leg, moving slowly, his only luck being that he was the last in that line and not the first. He was stiff enough, but he was in full control of his muscles.

That gray attendant had processed his first man. He was moving a second rack forward over the next. Simon sat up. For a second or two his head whirled, and he gripped the table on which he had lain, prayerfully glad it had neither creaked nor squeaked under his change of position.

The business at the other end of the room was a complicated one, and occupied the full attention of the worker. Feeling that the table might tip under him, Simon swung his feet to the floor, breathing strongly again only when they were firmly planted on the smooth cold pavement.

He surveyed his nearest neighbor, hoping for some sign that he, too, was rousing. But the boy, for he was only a youngster, lay limp with closed eyes, his chest rising and falling at unusually slow intervals.

Simon stepped away from the table toward that set of shelves. There alone could he find a weapon. Escape from here, if he could win the door unhindered, was too chancy a risk until he knew more of his surroundings. And neither could he face the fact that in running he would abandon five other men to death—or worse than death alone.

He chose his weapon, a flask half filled with yellow liquid. It seemed glass but was heavy for that substance. The slender neck above the bulbous body gave a good handhold, and Simon moved lightly around the line of tables to the one where the attendant worked.

His bare feet made no sound on the material of the flooring as he came up behind the unsuspecting worker. The bottle arose with the force of Simon's outrage in the swing, crashing upon the back of that gray-capped head.

There was no cry from the figure who crumpled forward, dragging with it the wired metal cap it had been about to fit on the head of the waiting victim. Simon had reached for the fallen man's throat before he saw the flatness on the back of the head through which dark blood welled. He heaved the body over and pulled it free of the aisle between tables to look down upon the face of one he was sure was a Kolder.

What he had been building up in his imagination was far more startling than the truth. This was a man, at least in face, very like a great many other men Simon had known. He had rather flat features with a wide expanse of cheekbone on either side of a nose too close to bridgeless, and his chin was too small and narrow to match the width of the upper half of his face. But he was no alien demon to the eye, whatever he might house within his doomed skull.

Simon located the fastenings of the gray robe and pulled it off. Though he shrank from touching the mess in the cap, he made himself take that also. There was a runnel of water in a sink at the other end of the room and there he dropped the headgear for cleansing. Under the robe the man wore a tight-fitting garment with no fastenings nor openings Simon could discover, so in the end he had to content himself with the robe for his sole clothing.

There was nothing he could do for the two men the attendant had already made fast to the racks, for the complicated nature of the machines was beyond his solving. But he went from one man to the next of the other three and tried to rouse them, finding that, too, impossible. They had the appearance of men deeply drugged, and he understood even less how he had come to escape their common fate, if these *were* his fellow prisoners from the ship.

Disappointed, Simon went to the door. The closed slab had no latch or knob he could see, but experimentation proved that it slid back into the right-hand wall and he looked out upon a corridor walled, ceilinged, and paved in the same monotone of gray which was in use in the laboratory. As far as Simon could see it was deserted, though there were other doors opening off its length. He made for the nearest of these.

Inching it open with the same caution with which he had made his first moves upon regaining his senses, he looked in upon a cache of men the Kolder had brought to Gorm, if this was Gorm. Lying in rows were at least twenty bodies, these still clothed. There were no signs of consciousness in any, though Simon examined them all hurriedly. Perhaps he could still gain a respite for those in the laboratory. Hoping so, he dragged the three back and laid them out with their fellows.

Visiting the laboratory for the last time Simon rumaged for arms, coming up with a kit of surgical knives, the longest of which he took. He cut away the rest of the clothing from the body of the man he had killed and laid him out on one of the tables in such a way that the battered head was concealed from the doorway. Had he known any method of locking that door he would have used it.

With the knife in the belt of his stolen robe, Simon washed out the cap and gingerly pulled it on, wet as it was. Doubtless there were a hundred deadly weapons in the various jars, bottles, and tubes about him, only he could not tell one from the others. For the time being he would have to depend upon his fists and his knife to remain free.

Simon went back to the corridor, closing the door behind him. How long would the worker he had killed be left undisturbed? Was he supervised by someone due to return shortly, or did Simon have a better allowance of time?

Two of the doors in the corridor would not yield to his push. But where the hall came to a dead end he found a third a little way open and slipped into what could only be living quarters.

The furniture was severe, functional, but the two chairs and the box bed were more comfortable than they looked. And another piece which might be either a desk or a table drew him. His puzzlement was a driving force for his mind refused to connect the place in which he stood with the same world which had produced Estcarp, the Eyrie and crooked-laned Kars. One was of the past; this was of the future.

He could not open the compartments of the desk, though there was a sunken pit at the top of each in which a fingertip could be handily inserted. Baffled, he sat back on his heels after trying the last.

There were compartments in the walls also, at least the same type of finger hole could be seen there. But they, too, were locked. His jaw set stubbornly as he thought of trying his knife as a prying lever.

Then he spun around, back against the wall, staring into a room still empty of all but that severely lined furniture. Because out of the very empty air before him came a voice, speaking a language he could not understand, but by the inflection asking a question to which it demanded an immediate answer.

III
Gray Fane

*W*as he under observation? Or merely listening to something akin to a public address system? Once Simon had assured himself that he was alone in the room, he listened closely to words he could not understand and must interpret by inflection alone. The speaker repeated himself—at least Simon was convinced he recognized several sounds. And did that repetition mean that he was seen?

How soon before an investigation would be launched by the unseen speaker? Immediately, when no reply was made? It was clearly a warning to be on his way, but which way? Simon went back into the corridor.

Since this end of the passage was a blank wall he must try the other, repassing the other doors. But there again he met with unbroken gray surface.

With memories of the hallucinations of Estcarp, Simon ran his hands across that blank expanse. But if there was any opening there it was concealed by more than eye-confusing skill. His conviction—that the Kolder, who or whatever they might be, were of a different breed altogether from the witches, achieving their magic according to another pattern—became fixed. They based their action on skills without, rather than a Power within.

To the people of Estcarp much of the technical knowledge of his own world would have ranked as magic. And perhaps alone among the Guards of Estcarp at this moment was Simon fitted to rationalize and partly understand what lay here in Gorm, better prepared to face those who used machines and the science of machines than any witch who could call a fleet up out of wooden ships.

He crept along the hallway, running his hands along first one wall and then the other, seeking any irregularity which might be a clue to an exit. Or did that door lie within one of the rooms? His luck certainly could not hold much longer.

Again from the air overhead came a ringing command in the strange tongue, the vehemence of which could not be denied. Simon, sensing danger, froze where he was, half expecting to be engulfed by a trapdoor or trapped in some suddenly materializing net. In that moment he discovered his exit, but not in the way he had hoped, as on the other side of the corridor a portion of the wall slipped back to show lighted space beyond. Simon pulled the knife from his belt and faced that space, ready for an attack.

The silence was broken again by that bark of disembodied voice; he thought that perhaps his real status had not yet been suspected by the masters of this place. Perhaps, if they did see him, the robe and cap he wore tagged him as one of their own who was acting oddly and had been ordered to report elsewhere.

Deeming it best to act in his chosen role as long as he could, Simon approached that new door with more outward assurance and less commando caution. He nearly panicked, however, when the door closed behind him and he discovered that he was neatly imprisoned in a box. It was not until he brushed against one of the walls and felt through it that faint vibration, that he guessed he was in an elevator, a discovery which for some reason steadied him. More and more he accepted the belief that the Kolder represented a form of civilization close to that he had known in his own world. It was far more steadying to the nerves to be ascending or descending to a showdown with the enemy in an elevator than to stand, for example, in a mist-filled room and watch a friend turn to a hideous stranger in a matter of moments.

Yet, in spite of that feeling of faint familiarity with all this, Simon had no ease, no relaxation of a certain inward chill. He could accept the products of Kolder hands as normal, but he could not accept the atmosphere of this place as anything but alien. And not only alien, for that which is strange need not necessarily be a menace, but in some manner this place was utterly opposed to him and his kind. No, not alien, one part of him decided during that swift journey to wherever the Kolder waited, but unhuman, whereas the witches of Estcarp were human, no matter whatever else they might also be.

The thrumming in the wall ceased. Simon stood away from it, unsure as to where the door would open. His certainty that it would open did not waver and was justified a moment later.

This time there were sounds outside, a muted humming, the snap of distant voices. He emerged warily to stand in a small alcove apart from a room. Partial recognition outweighed strangeness for him once again. A wide expanse of one wall was laid out as a vast map. The trailing, deeply indented shorelines, the molded mountain areas he had seen before. Set here and there upon the chart were tiny pinpoints of light in various colors. Those along the shore about the vanished hold of Sulcar and the bay in which Gorm lay were a dusky violet, while those which pricked on the plains of Estcarp were yellow, the ones in Karsten green, and those of Alizon red.

A table, running the full length of that map, stood below it, bearing at spaced intervals machines which clattered now and then, or flashed small signal lights. And seated between each two of such machines, with their backs toward him, their attention all for the devices they tended, were others wearing the gray robes and caps.

A little apart was a second table, or outsized desk, with three more of the Kolder. The center one of this trio wore a metal cap on his head from which wires and spider-thread cables ran to a board behind him. His face was without expression, his eyes were closed. However, he was not asleep for, from time to time, his fingers moved with swift flicks of the tips across a panel of buttons and levers set in the surface before him. Simon's impression of being in a central control of some concentrated effort grew with the seconds he was left to view the scene undisturbed.

The words which were barked at him this time did not come from the air, but from the man on the left of that capped figure. He gazed at Simon, his flat face with its overspread of upper features, displaying first impatience and then the growing realization that Simon was not one of his own kind.

Simon sprang. He could not hope to reach that last table, but one of those who tended the machines before the map was in his range. And he brought his hand edge down in a blow which might have cracked backbone, but instead rendered the victim unconscious. Holding the limp body as a shield, Simon backed to the wall of the other doorway, hoping to win to that exit.

To his amazement the man who had first marked his arrival there made no move to obstruct him, physically. He merely repeated slowly and deliberately in the language of the continental natives:

"You will return to your unit. You will report to your unit control."

As Simon continued his crabwise advance upon the door, one of the men who had been a neighbor of his captive returned an astounded face from Tregarth to the men at the last table, then back to Simon. The rest of his fellows looked up from their machines with the same surprise as their officer got to his feet. It was clear they had expected only instant and complete obedience from Simon.

"You will return to your unit! At once!"

Simon laughed. And the result of his response was startling indeed. The Kolder, with the exception of the capped man who took no notice of anything, were all on their feet. Those of the center table still looked to their two superiors at the end of the room as if awaiting orders. And Simon thought that if he had shrieked in agony they would not have been so amazed—his reaction to their orders had completely baffled them.

The man who had given that command dropped his hand on the shoulder of his capped companion, giving him a gentle shake, a gesture which even in its restraint expressed utmost alarm. So summoned to attention, the capped man opened his eyes and looked about impatiently, then in obvious amazement. He stared at Simon as if sighting at a mark.

What came was no physical attack, but a blow of force, unseen, not to be defined by the untutored outworlder. But a blow which held Simon pinned breathless to the wall unable to move.

The body he had been using as a shield slid out of his heavy-weighted arms to sprawl on the floor, and even the rise and fall of Simon's chest as he breathed became a labor to which he had to give thought and effort. Let him stay where he was, under the pressure of that invisible crushing hand, and he would not continue to live. His encounters with Power of Estcarp had sharpened his wits. He thought that what trapped him now was not born of the body, but of the mind, and so it could only be countered by the mind in turn.

His only taste of such Power had been through the methods of Estcarp and he had not been trained to use it. But setting up within him what strength of will he could muster, Simon concentrated on raising an arm which moved so sluggishly he was afraid he was doomed to failure.

Now that one palm was resting flat against the wall where the energy held him, he brought up the other. With complaining muscles as well as will of mind, he strove to push himself out and away. Did he detect a shade of surprise on the broad face below the cap?

What Simon did next had the backing of no conscious reasoning. It was certainly not by his will that his right hand moved up level with his heart and his fingers traced a design in the air between him and that capped master of force.

It was the third time he had seen that design. Before, the hand which had drawn it was one of Estcarp, and the lines had burned fire bright for only an instant.

Now it flashed again, but in a sputtering white. And at that moment he could move! The pressure had lessened. Simon ran for the door, making good a momentary escape into the unknown territory beyond.

But it was only momentary. For here he faced armed men. There was no mistaking that rapt concentration in the eyes turned to him as he erupted into the corridor where they were on duty. These were the slaves of the Kolder, and only by killing could he win through.

They drew in with the silent, deadly promise of their kind, their very silence heavy with menace. Simon chose quickly and darted to meet them. He skidded to the right and tackled the man next to the wall about the shins, bringing him down in such a way as to guard his own back.

The smooth flooring of the passage was an unexpected aid. The impact of Simon's tackle carried both past the man's two companions. Simon stabbed up with his knife and felt the sear of a blade across his own ribs under his arms. Coughing, the guard rolled away, and Simon snatched the dart gun from his belt.

He shot the first of the others just in time and the stroke of the sword aimed for his neck sank instead into the wounded man. That brought him a precious second to sight on the third and last of the enemy.

Adding two more dart guns to his weapons he went on. Luckily this hall ended in no concealed doors but a stair, cut of stone and winding up against a wall also of stone, both of them in contrast to the smooth gray surfacing of the passages and rooms through which he had already come.

His bare feet gritted on that stone as they took the steps. At a higher level he came out in a passage akin to those he had seen in the hold of Estcarp. However functional-futuristic the inner core of this place might be, its husk was native to the buildings he knew.

Simon took cover twice, his gun ready, as detachments of the Kolder-changed natives passed him. He could not judge whether a general alarm had been given, or whether they were merely engaged in some routine patrol, for they kept to a steady trot and did not search any side ways.

Time in these corridors where there was no change of light had no meaning. Simon did not know whether it was day or night, or how long he had been within the fortress of the Kolder. But he was keenly conscious of hunger and thirst, of the cold which pierced the single garment he wore, of the discomfort of bare feet when one had always gone shod.

If he only had some idea of the inner plan of the maze through which he was trying to escape. Was he on Gorm? Or in that mysterious city of Yle which the Kolder had founded on the mainland coast? In some more hidden headquarters of the invaders? That it was an important headquarters he was certain.

Both a desire for a temporary hiding place and the need for supplies brought him to explore the rooms on this upper level. Here were none of the furnishings he had seen below. The carved wooden chests, the chairs, the tables were all of native work. And in some of the chambers there were signs of hurried departure or search, now overlaid with dust as if the rooms had been deserted for a long time.

It was in such a one that Simon found clothing which fitted after a fashion. But he still lacked mail or any other weapons than those he had taken from the fighters in the hall. He craved food more than anything else and began to wonder if he must return to the dangerous lower levels to find it.

Though he was considering descent Simon continued to follow up any ramp or set of steps he chanced upon. And he saw that in this sprawling pile all the windows had been battened tight so that only artificial light made visible his surroundings, the light being dimmer in ratio to the distance he put between him and the quarters of the Kolder.

A last and very narrow flight of stairs showed more use and Simon kept one of the guns ready as he climbed to a door above. That swung easily under his hand, and he looked out upon a flat rooftop. Over a portion of this a second sheltering awning had been erected and lined up under which were objects which did not astonish Simon after what he had seen below. Their stubby wings were thrust back sharply from their blunt noses and none could carry more than a pilot and perhaps two passengers, but they were surely aircraft. The mystery of how Sulcarkeep had been taken was solved, providing the enemy had a fleet of those to hand.

Now they presented Simon with a way of escape if he had no other chance. But escape from where? Watching that improvised hangar for any sign of a guard, Simon stole to the nearest edge of the roof, hoping to see something in the way of a landmark to give him a clue to his whereabouts.

For a moment he wondered if he could be back in a restored Sulcarkeep. For what was spread below was a harbor, with anchored ships and rows of buildings set along streets which marched to the wharves and the water. But the plan of this city was different from the town of the traders. It was larger and where the Sulcarmen had had their warehouses with fewer living quarters, these streets reversed that process. Though it was midday by the sun there was no life in those streets, no sign that any of the houses were inhabited. Yet neither did they show those signs of decay and nature's encroachment which would mark complete desertion.

Since the architecture resembled that of Karsten and Estcarp with only minor differences, this could not be that Yle erected by the Kolder. Which meant that he *must* be now on Gorm—maybe in Sippar—that center of the canker which the Estcarp forces had never been able to pierce!

If that city below was as lifeless as it appeared, it should be easy enough for him to get to the harbor and locate some means of boat transportation to the eastern continent. However with the building below him so well sealed to the outer world, perhaps this roof was the only exit, and he had better explore its outlets.

The pile on which he stood was the highest building in the whole small city; perhaps it was the ancient castle where those of Koris' clan had ruled. If the Captain were only with him now the problem might be simplified by half. Simon toured three sides and discovered that there were no other roofs abutting on this one, that a street or streets, fronted each side.

Reluctantly he came to the shelter which housed the planes. To trust to a machine he did not know how to pilot was foolhardy. But that was no reason not to inspect one. Simon had grown bolder since he had gone unchallenged this long. However he took precautions against surprise. Wedged into the latch of the roof door, the knife locked it to all but a battering down.

He returned to the plane nearest him. It moved into the open under his pushing, proving to be a light craft, easily handled. He pulled up a panel in its stub nose and inspected the motor within. It was unlike any he had seen before, and he was neither engineer nor mechanic. But he had confidence enough in the efficiency of those below to believe that it could fly—if he were able to control it.

Before he explored further Simon examined the four other machines, using the butt of one of the dart guns to smash at their motors. If he did have to trust to the air he did not want to be the target for an attack-chase.

It was when he raised his improvised hammer for the last time that the enemy struck. There had been no battering at the wedged door, no thunder of guard feet on the stairs. Again it was the silent push of that invisible force. It did not strive to hold him helpless this time, but to draw him to its source. Simon caught at the disabled plane for an anchor. Instead he drew it after him out into the open—he could not halt his march down the roof.

And it was not taking him back to the door! With a stab of panic Simon realized now that his destination was not the dubious future of the levels below, but the quick death which awaited a plunge from the roof!

With all his will he fought, his reluctant steps taken one at a time, with periods of agonizing struggle between. He tried again the trick of the symbol in the air which had served him before. Perhaps because he was not now fronting the person of his enemy it gave him no relief.

He could slow that advance, put off for seconds, minutes, the inevitable end. A try for the doorway failed; it had been a desperate hope that the other might take his action for a gesture of surrender. But now Simon knew they wanted him safely dead. The decision he would have made had he commanded here.

There was the plane he had meant to use in a last bid. Well, now there was no other escape! And it was between him and the roof edge towards which he was urged.

It was such a little chance, but he had no other. Simon yielded two steps to the pressure, he gave another quickly as if his strength were waning. A third—his hand was on the opening to the pilot's compartment. Making the supreme effort in this weird battle he threw himself within.

The pull brought him against the far wall and the light craft rocked under his scrambling. He stared at what must be the instrument board. There was a lever up at the end of a narrow slot, and it was the only object which seemed to be movable. With a petition to other Powers than those of Estcarp, Simon managed to raise a heavy hand and pull that down its waiting slot.

IV
City of Dead Men

*H*e had perhaps childishly expected to be whisked aloft, but the machine ran straight forward, gathering speed. Its nose plowed across the low parapet with force enough to somersault the whole plane over. Simon knew he was falling, not free as his tormenter had intended, but encased in the cabin.

There was another swift moment of awareness that that fall was not straight down, that he was descending at an angle. Hopelessly, he jerked once more at that lever, pulling it halfway up the slot.

Then there was a crash, followed by nothing but blackness without sight, sound, or feeling.

A spark of red-amber watched him speculatively out of the black. It was matched by a faint repetitive sound—the tick of a watch, the drip of water? And thirdly there was the smell. It was that latter which prodded Simon into action. For it was a sweetish stench, thick and sickening in his nostrils and throat, a stench of old corruption and death.

He was sitting up, he discovered, and there was a faint light to show the wreckage which held him in that position. But the hounding pressure which had battered him on the upper roof was gone; he was free to move if he could, to think.

Save for some painfully bruised areas, he had apparently survived the crash without injury. The machine must have cushioned the shock of landing. And that red eye out of the dark was a light on the control panel. The drip was close by.

So was the smell. Simon shifted in his seat and pushed. There was a rasp of metal scraping metal and a large section of cabin broke away. Simon crawled painfully out of his cage. Overhead was hole framed with jagged ends of timbers. As he watched, another piece of roofing gave way and struck on the already battered machine. The plane must have fallen on the roof of one of the neighboring buildings and broken through that surface. How he had escaped with life and reasonably sound limbs was one of the strange quirks of fate.

He must have been unconscious for some time as the sky was the pallid shade of evening. And his hunger and thirst were steady pains. He must have food and water.

But why had not the enemy located him before this? Certainly anyone on the other roof could have spotted the end of his abortive flight. Unless—suppose they did not know of his try with the plane—suppose they only traced him by some form of mental contact. Then they would only know that he had gone over the parapet, that his fall had ended in a blackout which to them might have registered as his death. If that were true then he was indeed free, if still within the city of Sippar!

First, to find food and drink, and then discover where he was in relation to the rest of the port.

Simon found a doorway, one which gave again on stairs leading downward toward the street level, as he had hoped. The air here was stale, heavily tainted with that odor. He could identify it now and it made him hesitate—disliking what must lie below to raise such a stench.

But down was the only way out, so down he must go. The windows here were unsealed and light made fading patches on each landing. There were doors, too, but Simon opened none of them, because it seemed to him that around them that fearsome, stomach-churning smell was stronger.

Down one more flight, and into a hall which ended in a wide portal he thought must give on the street. Here Simon dared to explore and in a back room he found that leathery journey bread which was the main military ration of Estcarp, together with a pot of preserved fruit still good under its cap. The moldering remains of other provisions were evidence that no one had foraged here for a long time. Water trickled from a pipe to a drain and Simon drank before he wolfed down the food.

It was difficult to eat in spite of his hunger for that smell clung to everything. Although he had been only in this one building outside the citadel Simon suspected that his monstrous suspicion was the truth; save for the central building and its handful of inhabitants, Sippar was a city of the dead. The Kolder must have ruthlessly disposed of those of the conquered of no use to them. Not only slain them, but left them unburied in their own homes. As a warning against rebellion of the few remaining alive? Or merely because they did not care? It would appear that the last was the most likely, and that odd feeling of kinship he had for the flat-faced invaders died then and there.

Simon took with him all the bread he could find and a bottle filled with water. Curiously enough the door leading to the street was barred on the inside. Had those who had once lived here locked themselves in and committed mass suicide? Or had the same pressure methods driven them to their deaths as had been used to send him over the upper roof?

The street was as deserted as he had seen it from that same roof. But Simon kept close to one side, watching every shadowed doorway, the mouth of every cross lane. All doors were shut; nothing moved as he worked his way to the harbor.

He guessed that if he tried any of those doors he would find them barred against him, while within would lie only the dead. Had they perished soon after Gorm had welcomed Kolder to further the ambitions of Orna and her son? Or had that death come sometime later, during the years since Koris had fled to Estcarp and the island had been cut off from humankind? It would not matter to anyone save perhaps a historian. This remained a city of the dead— the dead in body, and in the keep, the dead in spirit—with only the Kolder, who might well be dead in another fashion, keeping a pretense of life.

As he went Simon memorized route of street and house. Gorm could only be freed when the central keep was destroyed, he was certain of that. But it seemed to him that leaving this waste of empty buildings about their lair had been a bad mistake on the part of the Kolder. Unless they had some hidden defenses and alarms rigged in these blank walled houses, it might be no trick at all to bring a landing party ashore and have them under cover.

There were those tales of Koris' concerning the spies Estcarp had sent to this island over the years. And the fact that the Captain himself had been unable to return because of some mysterious barrier. After his own experience with Kolder weapons Simon had an open mind. Only he *had* been able to break free, first in that headquarters room and secondly by the use of one of the planes. The mere fact that the Kolder had not tried to hunt him down was proof of a kind they must believe him finished for good.

But it was hard to think that someone or something did not keep watch in the silent city. So he kept to cover until he reached the wharves. There were ships there, ships battered by storms, some driven half ashore, their rigging a rotting tangle, their sides scored and smashed in, some half-water-logged, with only their upper decks above the surface of the harbor. None of these had sailed for months, or years!

And the width of the bay lay between Simon and the mainland. If this dead port was Sippar, and he had no reason to believe that it was not, then he was now facing that long arm of land on which the invaders had built Yle, ending in the finger of which Sulcarkeep had been the nail. Since the fall of the traders' stronghold it was very probable that the Kolder forces now controlled that whole cape.

If he could find a manageable small craft and take to sea, Simon would have to take the longer route eastward down the bottle-shaped bay to the mouth of the River Es and so to Estcarp. And he was plagued by the idea that time no longer fought upon his side.

He found his boat, a small shell stored in a warehouse. Though Simon was no sailor he took what precautions and made what tests he could to ensure its seaworthiness. And waited until full dark before he took oars, gritting his teeth against the pain of his bruises, as he pulled steadily, setting a crooked course among the rotting hulks of the Gormian fleet.

It was when he was well beyond those and had dared to step his small mast, that he met the Kolder defense head-on. He saw or heard nothing as he fell to the bottom of the boat, his hands over his ears, his eyes closed against that raging tumult of silent sound and invisible light which beat outward from some point within his brain. He had thought his ordeal with the will pressure had made him aware of the Kolder power, but this scrambling of a man's brain was worse.

Was he only minutes within that cloud, or a day, or a year? Dazed and dumb, Simon could not have told. He lay in a boat which swung with the waves but obeyed sluggishly the wind's touch on its sail. And behind him was Gorm, dead and dark in the moonlight.

Before dawn Simon was picked up by a coastal patrol boat from the Es, and by that time he had recovered his wits, though his mind felt as bruised as his boat. Riding relays of swift mounts he went on to Estcarp city.

Within the keep, in that same room where he had first met the Guardian, he joined a council of war, detailing his adventures within Gorm, his contacts with the Kolder to the officers of Estcarp, and those still-faced women who listened impassively. As he spoke he hunted for one among the witches, without finding her in that assembly.

When he had done, and they asked few questions, allowing him to tell it in his own way, Koris tight-lipped and stone-featured as he described the city of the dead, the Guardian beckoned forward one of the other women.

"Now, Simon Tregarth, do you take her hands, and then think upon this capped man, recall in your mind every detail of his dress and face," she ordered.

Though he could see no purpose in this, Simon obeyed. For one generally did obey, he thought wryly, the witches of Estcarp.

So he held those hands which were cool and dry in his, and he mentally pictured the gray robe, the odd face where the lower half did not match the upper, the metal cap, and the expression of power and then of bafflement which had been mirrored on those features when Simon had fought back. The hands slipped out of his and the Guardian spoke again:

"You have seen, sister? You can fashion?"

"I have seen," the woman answered. "And what I have seen I can fashion. Since he used the Power between them in the duel of wills the impression should be strong. Though," she looked down at her hands, moving each finger as if to exercise it in preparation for some task, "whether we can use such a device is another matter. It would have been better had blood flowed."

No one explained and Simon was not given time to ask questions for Koris claimed him as the council broke up, and marched him off to the barracks. Once within that same chamber he had had before they left for Sulcarkeep, Simon demanded of the Captain:

"Where is the lady?" It was irritating not to be able to name her whom he knew; that pecularity of the witches irked him more now than ever. But Koris caught his meaning.

"She is checking the border posts."

"But she is safe?"

Koris shrugged. "Are any of us safe, Simon? But be sure that the women of Power take no unnecessary risks. What they guard within them is not lightly spent." He had gone to the western window, his face turned into the light there, his eyes searching as if he willed to see more than the plain beyond the city. "So Gorm is dead." The words came heavily.

Simon pulled off his boots and stretched out on the bed. He was weary to every aching bone in his body.

"I told you what I saw and only what I saw. There is life walled into the center keep of Sippar. I found it nowhere else, but then I did not search far."

"Life? What sort of life?"

"Ask that of the Kolder, or perhaps the witches," returned Simon drowsily. "Neither are as you and I, and maybe they reckon life differently."

He was only half aware that the Captain had come away from the window, was standing over Simon so that his wide shoulders shut away the daylight.

"I am thinking, Simon Tregarth, that you are different too." Again the words were heavy, without any ring. "And seeing Gorm, how do you reckon its life—or death?"

"As vile," Simon mumbled. "But that shall also be judged in its own time," and wondered at his choice of words even as he fell asleep.

He slept, awoke to eat hugely, and slept again. No one demanded his attention nor did he rouse to what was going on in the keep of Estcarp. He might have been an animal laying up rest beneath his hide as the bear lays up fat against hibernation. When he awoke thoroughly once again it was alertly, eagerly, with a freshness he had not felt for so long, since before Berlin.

Berlin—what—where was Berlin? His memories were curiously overlaid nowadays with new scenes.

And the one which returned to haunt him the most was that of the room of that secluded house in Kars where threadbare tapestries patterned the walls and a woman looked at him with wonder in her eyes as her hand shaped a glowing symbol in the air between them. Then there was that other moment when she stood sick at heart and curiously alone after she had made her sordid magic for Aldis, tarnishing her gift for the good of her cause.

Now as Simon lay tingling with life in every nerve and cell of him, the ache of his bruises, the strain of his hunger and his striving gone out out of him, he moved his right hand up until it lay over his heart. But beneath it now he did not feel the warmth of his own flesh; rather did he cradle in memory something else, as a singing which was no song drew from him, into the other hand he had grasped, a substance he did not know he possessed.

Over all else, the life in the border raiding parties, the experience of Kolder captivity, did those quiet and passive scenes hold him now. Because, empty of physical action though they had been, they possessed for him a hidden excitement he shrank from defining or explaining too closely.

But he was summoned soon enough to attention. During his sleep Estcarp had marshaled all its forces. Beacons on the heights had brought messengers from the mountains, from the Eyrie, from all those willing to stand against Gorm, and the doom Gorm promised. A half dozen Sulcar vessels, homeless, had made port in coves the Falconers charted, the families of their crews landed in safety, the ships armed and ready for the thrust. For all were agreed that the war must be taken to Gorm before Gorm brought it to them.

There was a camp at the mouth of the Es, a tent set up in it on the very verge of the ocean. From its flap of door they could see the shadow of the island appearing as a bank of cloud upon the sea. And, waiting signal beyond that point where the broken ruins of their keep were sea-washed and desolate, hovered the ships, packed with the Sulcar crew, Falconers, and border raiders.

But the barrier about Gorm must be broken first and that was in the hands of those who welded Estcarp's Power. So, not knowing why he was to be one of that company, Simon found himself seated at a table which might have been meant for a gaming board. Yet there was no surface of alternate colored blocks. Instead, before each seat there was a painted symbol. And the company who gathered was mixed, seemingly oddly chosen for the high command.

Simon found that his seat had been placed beside the Guardian's and the symbol there overlapped both places. It was a brown hawk with a gilded oval framing it, a small three-pointed cornet above the oval. On his left was a diamond of blue-green enclosing a fist holding an ax. And beyond that was a square of red encasing a horned fish.

To the right, beyond the Guardian, were two more symbols which he could not read without leaning forward. Two of the witches slipped into the seats before those and sat quietly, their hands palm down upon the painted marks. There was a stir to his left and he glanced up to know an odd lift of spirit as he met a level gaze which was more than mere recognition of his identity. But she did not speak and he copied her silence. The sixth and last of their company was the lad Briant, pale-faced, staring down at the fish creature before him as if it lived and by the very intensity of his gaze he must hold it prisoner in that sea of scarlet.

The woman who had held Simon's hands as he thought of the man on Gorm came into the tent, two others with her, each of whom carried a small clay brazier from which came sweet smoke. These they placed on the edge of the board and the other woman set down her own burden, a wide basket. She threw aside its covering cloth to display a row of small images.

Taking up the first she went to stand before Briant. Twice she passed the figure she held through the smoke and then held it at eye level before the seated lad. It was a finely wrought manikin with red-gold hair and such a life-look that Simon believed it was meant to be the portrait of some living man.

"Fulk." The woman pronounced the name and set the image down in the center of the scarlet square, full upon the painted fish. Briant could not pale, his transparent skin had always lacked color, but Simon saw him swallow convulsively before he answered.

"Fulk of Verlaine."

The woman took a second figure from her basket, and, as she came now to Simon's neighbor, he could better judge the artistic triumph of her work. For she held between her hands, passing it through the smoke, a perfect image of she who had asked for a charm to keep Yvian true.

"Aldis."

"Aldis of Kars," acknowledged the woman beside him as the tiny feet of the figure were planted on the fist with the ax.

"Sandar of Alizon." A third figure for the position farthest to his right.

"Siric." A potbellied image in flowing robes for that other right-hand symbol.

Then she brought out the last of the manikins, studying it for a moment before she gave it to the smoke. When she came to stand before Simon and the Guardian she named no names but held it out for his inspection, for his recognition. And he stared down at the small copy of the capped leader in Gorm. To his recollection the resemblance was perfect.

"Gorm!" He acknowledged it, though he could not give the Kolder a better name. And she placed it carefully on the brown-and-gold hawk.

V
Game of Power

*F*ive images set out upon the symbols of their lands, five perfect representations of living men and a woman. But why and for what purpose?
Simon looked right again. The tiny feet of the Aldis manikin were now encircled by the hands of the witch, those of the Fulk figure by Briant's. Both
were regarding their charges with absorption, on Briant's part uneasy.

Simon's attention swung back to the figure before him. Dim memories of
old tales flickered through his mind. Did they now stick pins in these replicas
and expect their originals to suffer and die?

The Guardian reached for his hand, caught it in the same grip he had known
in Kars during the shape changing. At the same time she fitted her other hand
in a half circle about the base of the capped figure. He put his to match so
that now they touched fingertips and wrists enclosing the Kolder.

"Think now upon this one between whom and you has been the trial of
Power, or the tie of blood. Put from your mind all else but this one whom
you must reach and bend, bend to our use. For we win the Game of Power
upon this board in this hour—or it—and we—fail for this time and place!"

Simon's eyes were on that capped figure. He did not know if he could turn
them away if he wished. He supposed that he had been brought into this
curious procedure because he alone of those of Estcarp had seen this officer
of Gorm.

The tiny face, half shadowed by the metal cap, grew larger, life-size. He
was fronting it across space as he had fronted it across that room in the heart
of Sippar.

Again the eyes were closed, the man was about his mysterious business.
Simon continued to study him, and then he knew that all the antagonism he
had known for the Kolder, all the hate born in him by what he had found in
that city, by their treatment of their captives, was drawing together in his mind,
as a man might shape a weapon of small pieces fitted together into one formidable arm.

Simon was no longer in that tent where sea winds stirred and sand gritted on
a brown painted hawk. Instead he stood before that man of the Kolder in the
heart of Sippar, willing him to open his closed eyes, to look upon him, Simon
Tregarth, to stand to battle in a way not of bodies, but of wills and minds.

Those eyes did open and he stared into their dark pupils, saw lids raise
higher as if in recognition, of knowledge of the menace which was using him
as a gathering point, a caldron in which every terror and threat could be
brought to a culminating boil.

Eyes held eyes. Simon's impressions of the flat features, of the face, of the metal cap above it, of everything *but* those eyes, went, bit by bit. As he had sensed the flow of power out of his hand into the witch's in Kars, so did he know that which boiled within him was being steadily fed by more heat than his own emotions could engender, that he was a gun to propel a fatal dart.

At first the Kolder had stood against him with confidence; now he was seeking his freedom from that eye-to-eye tie, mind-to-mind bond, knowing too late that he was caught in a trap. But the jaws had closed and struggle as he might the man in Gorm could not loosen what he had accepted in an arrogant belief in his own form of magic.

Within Simon there was a sharp release of all the tension. And it shot from him to that other. Eyes were fear-submerged by panic, panic gave way to abject terror, which burned in and in until there was nothing left for it to feed upon. Simon did not have to be told that what he faced now was a husk which would do his bidding as those husks of Gorm did the bidding of their owners.

He gave his orders. The Guardian's Power fed his; she watched and waited, ready to aid, but making no suggestions. Simon was certain of his enemy's obedience as he was of the life burning in him. That which controlled Gorm would be crippled, the barrier would go down, as long as this tool worked unhindered by his fellows. Estcarp now had a robot ally within the fortress.

Simon lifted his head, opened his eyes, and saw the painted board where his fingers still clasped the Guardian's about the feet of the small figure. But that manikin was no longer perfect. Within the hollow of the metal cap the head was a shapeless blob of melted wax.

The Guardian loosened her clasp, drew back her hand to lie limp. Simon turned his head, saw on his left a strained and blanched face, eyes dark smudged, as she who had centered the Power upon. Aldis fell back in her seat. And the lady figure before her was also head ravaged.

That image named for Fulk of Verlaine lay flat and Briant was huddled in upon himself, his face hidden in his hands, his lank, colorless hair sweat-plastered to his skull.

"It is done." The silence was first broken by the Guardian. "What the Power can do, it has done. And this day we have wrought as mightily as ever did the blood of Estcarp! Now it is given to fire and sword, wind and wave, to serve us if they will, and if men will use them!" Her voice was a thin thread of exhaustion.

She was answered by one who moved to the board to stand before her, accompanied by the faint clink of metal against metal which marked a man in full war gear. Koris carried on his hip the hawk-crested helm; now he raised the Ax of Volt.

"Be sure, lady, that there are men to use each and every weapon Fortune grants us. The beacons are lighted, our armies and the ships move."

Simon, though the earth under his feet had a tendency to sway when he planted his feet upon it and levered himself up, arose. She who had sat on his left moved quickly. Her hand went out, but it did not touch his before it fell back upon the board once more. Nor did she put into words that denial he could read in every tense line of her body.

"The war, now completed according to your Power," he spoke to her as if they were alone, "is of the fashion of Estcarp. But I am not of Estcarp, and there remains this other war which is of my own kind of Power. I have played your game to your willing, lady; now I seek to play to mine!"

As he rounded the table to join the Captain, another arose and stood hesitating, one hand on the table to steady him. Briant regarded the image before him and his face was bleak, for the figure, though fallen, was intact.

"I never claimed the Power," he said dully in his soft voice. "And in this warfare it would seem I have been a failure. Perhaps it will not be so with sword and shield!"

Koris stirred as if he would protest. But the witch who had been in Kars spoke swiftly:

"There is a free choice here for all who ride or sail under Estcarp's banner. Let none gainsay that choice."

The Guardian nodded agreement. So the three of them went out from the tent on the seashore: Koris, vibrant, alive, his handsome head erect on his grotesque shoulders, his nostrils swelling as if he scented more than sea salt in the air; Simon, moving more slowly, feeling a fatigue new to his overdriven body, but also buoyed by a determination to see this venture to its end; and Briant, settling his helm over his fair head, coiling the metal ring scarf about his throat, his eyes straight ahead as if he were driven, or pulled, by something far greater than his own will.

The Captain turned to the other two as they reached the boats waiting to pull out to the ships. "You come with me on the flagship, for you, Simon, must serve as a guide, and you—" he looked to Briant and hesitated. But the youngster, with a lift of chin and stare of eye which was a challenge, met that appraisal defiantly. Simon sensed something crosswise between the two which was of their own concern as he waited for Koris to meet that unvoiced defiance.

"You, Briant, will put yourself among my shield men and you will stay with them!"

"And I, Briant," the other answered with something approaching impudence, "shall stay at your back, Captain of Estcarp, when there is good cause to do so. But I fight with my own sword and wield my own shield in this or any other battle!"

For a moment it seemed that Koris might dispute that, but they were hailed from the boats. And when they splashed through the surf to board, Simon noted that the younger man took good care to keep as far from his commander as the small craft allowed.

The ship which was to spearhead the Estcarp attack was a fishing vessel and the Guards were jammed aboard her almost shoulder to shoulder. The other mismatched transports fell in behind her as they took to the bay waters.

They were close enough to see the fleet rotting in Gorm harbor when the hail from the Sulcar vessels crossed the water and the trading ships with their mixed cargo of Falconers, Karsten refugees, and Sulcar survivors rounded a headland to draw in from the seaside.

Simon had no idea of where he had crossed the barrier on his flight from Gorm, and he might be leading this massed invasion straight into disaster. They could only hope that the Game of Power had softened up the defense in their favor.

Tregarth stood at the prow of the fishing smack, watching the harbor of the dead city, waiting for the first hint of the barrier. Or would one of those metal ships, protected past any hope of attack from Estcarp, strike at them now?

Wind filled their sails, and, overladen as the ships were, they cut the waves, keeping station as if drilled. A hulk from the harbor, still carrying enough rags aloft to catch the wind, its anchor ropes broken, drifted across their course, a wide collar of green weed lying under the waterline to slow it.

On its deck there was no sign of life as it bore on its wallowing way. From a Sulcar ship arched a ball, rising lazily into the air, dropping down to smash upon the deck of the derelict. Out of that ragged hole in the planking came red tongues of clean flame, feasting avidly on the tinder-dry fittings, so the ship, burning, drifted on to sea.

Simon grinned at Koris, a brittle excitement eating at him. He could be sure now that they were past the first danger point.

"We have overrun your barrier?"

"Unless they have moved it closer to land, yes!"

Koris rested his chin on the head of Volt's Ax as he surveyed the dark fingers of wharves before what had once been a flourishing city. He was grinning too, as a wolf shows its fangs before the first slash of the fight.

"It would appear that this time the Power worked," he commented. "Now let us be about our part of the business."

Simon knew a twinge of caution. "Do not underestimate them. We have but passed the first of their defenses, perhaps their weakest." His first elation was gone as quickly as it had come. There were swords, axes, dart guns about him. But in the heart of the Kolder keep was a science centuries ahead of such weapons—which might at any moment produce some nasty surprise.

As they came farther into the harbor, faced now by the need for finding passage to the wharves in and among the vessels moldering at anchor, there continued to be no sign of any life in Sippar. Only some of the brooding and forbidding silence of the dead city fell upon the invaders, dampening their ardor, taking a slight edge off their enthusiasm and their feeling of triumph at having passed the barrier.

Koris sensed that. Working his way back through the mass of men waiting to be landed, he found the captain of the ship and urged a quick thrust at the shore. Only to be reminded tartly that while the Captain of Estcarp's Guard might be all-powerful on land, he should leave the sea to those who knew it, and that the master of this particular ship had no intention of fouling his vessel with any of the hulks before them.

Simon continued to eye the shoreline, studying the mouth of each empty street, glancing now and then aloft to that blind hulk which was the heart of Sippar in more ways than one. He could not have said just what he feared—a flight of planes, an army emerging from the streets to the quays. To be met by nothing at all was more disconcerting than to face the high odds of Kolder weapons carried by hordes of their slaves. This was too easy, and he could not find full faith in the Game of Power; some core of him refused to believe that because a small image had ended with a melted head, they had defeated all that lay in Gorm.

They made the shore without incident, those of Sulcar landing farther down the coast to cut off any reinforcements which might be drawn from other points on the island. They scouted up the streets and lanes down which Simon had come days earlier, trying locked doors, investigating dark corners. But as far as they could discover nothing lived nor moved within the husk of Gorm's capital.

And they were well up to the center hold when the first resistance came, not from the air, nor from any invisible wave, but on foot with weapons in hand as the men of this world had fought for generations.

Suddenly the streets were peopled with fighters who moved swiftly, but without sound, who voiced no battle cries, but came forward steadily with deadly purpose. Some wore the battle dress of Sulcarmen, some of Karsten, and Simon saw among them a few of the bird helms of Falconers.

That silent rush was made by men who were not only expendable, but who had no thought of self-protection, just as those in the road ambush had fought. And their first fury carried them into the invasion force with the impact of a tank into a company of infantrymen. Simon went to his old game of sniping, but Koris charged with the Ax of Volt, a whirling, darting engine of death, to clear a path through the enemy lines, and another back again.

The slaves of the Kolder were no mean opponents, but they lacked the spark of intelligence which would have brought them together to re-form, to use to better advantage their numbers. They knew only that they must attack while any strength was left in them, while they still kept on their feet. And so they did, with the insane persistence of the mindless. It was sheer butchery which turned even the veteran Guardsmen sick while they strove to defend themselves and to gain ground.

Volt's Ax no longer shone bright, but, stained as it was, Koris tossed it in the air as a signal for the advance. His men closed ranks leaving behind them a street which was no longer empty, though it was without life.

"That was to delay us." Simon joined the Captain.

"So do I think. What do we expect now? Death from the air such as they used at Sulcarkeep?" Koris looked into the sky, the roofs above them gaining his wary attention.

It was those same roofs which suggested another plan to his companion.

"I do not think you will be able to break in to the hold at ground level," he began, and heard the soft rumble of laughter from within the Captain's helm.

"Not so. I know ways herein which perhaps even the Kolder have not nosed out. This was *my* burrow once."

"But I have also a plan," Simon cut in. "There are ropes in plenty on the ships, and grappling hooks. Let one party take to the roofs, while you search out your burrows, and perhaps we can close jaws upon them from two sides."

"Fair enough!" Koris conceded. "Do you try the sky ways since you have traveled them before. Choose your men, but do not take above twenty."

Twice more they were attacked by those silent parties of living dead, and each time more of their own men were left as toll when the last of the Kolder-owned were cut down. In the end the Estcarp forces parted ways. Simon and some twenty of the Guard broke in a door and climbed through the miasma of old death to a roof. Tregarth's sense of direction had not betrayed him; the neighboring roof showed a ragged hole, the mark of his crash landing in the plane.

He stood aside for the sailors who cast their grapples to the parapet of that other roof above their heads and across an expanse of street. Men tied their swords to them, made sure of the safety of their weapon belts, eyed that double line across nothingness with determination. Simon had recruited none who could not claim a good head for heights. But now when he faced the test he had more doubts than hopes.

He made that first ascent, the tough rope scraping his palms as he climbed, putting a strain on his shoulders he believed from moment to moment he could not endure.

The nightmare ended sometime. He uncoiled a third rope from about his waist, and tossed its weighted end back to the next man in line, taking a turn with the other end around one of the pillars supporting the hangar and so helping to draw him up.

Those planes he had disabled stood where he had left them, but open motor panels and scattered tools testified to work upon them. Why the job had not been finished was another mystery. Simon told off four men to guard the roof and the rope way, and with the rest began the invasion of the regions below.

The same silence which had held elsewhere in the town was thick here. They passed along corridors, down stairs, by shut doors, with only the faint sound of their own quiet tread to be heard. Was the hold deserted?

On they went into the heart of the blind, sealed building, expecting at any moment to encounter one of the bands of the possessed. The degree of light grew stronger; there was an indefinable change in the air which suggested that if these levels were deserted now it had not long been so.

Simon's party came to the last flight of stone steps which he remembered so well. At the bottom that stone would be coated with the gray walling of the Kolders. He leaned out over the well, listening. Far, far below there was a sound at last, as regular in its thump, thump as the beat of his own heart.

VI
The Cleansing of Gorm

*C*aptain," Tunston had moved up to join him, "what do we meet below?"

"Your foreseeing in that is as good as mine," Simon answered half absently, for it was in that moment that he realized he did *not* sense any danger to come at all, even in this strange place of death and half life. Yet there was something below, or they would not hear that.

He led the way, his gun ready, taking those steps cautiously, but at a fast pace. There were closed doors which were locked against their efforts to open them, until they came into the chamber of the wall map.

Here that beat arose from the floor under their feet, was drummed out by the walls, to fill their ears and their bodies with its slow rhythm.

The lights on the map were dead. There remained no line of machines on the table, tended by gray-robed men, though metal fastenings, a trailing wire or two marked where they had rested. But at that upper table there still sat a capped figure, his eyes closed, immobile, just as Simon had seen him on his first visit to this place.

At first Simon believed the man dead. He walked to the table watching the seated Kolder alertly. To his best knowledge this was the same man whom he had tried to visualize for the artist of Estcarp. And he was fleetingly pleased at the accuracy of his memory.

Only—Simon halted. This man was not dead, though those eyes were closed, the body motionless. One hand lay upon the control plate set in the tabletop and Simon had just seen a fingertip press a button there.

Tregarth leaped. He had an instant in which to see those eyes open, the face beneath the metal twist in anger—and perhaps fear. Then his own hands closed upon the wire which led from the cap the other wore to the board in the wall behind. He ripped, bringing loose several of those slender cables. Someone cried out a warning and he saw a barreled weapon swing into line with his body as the Kolder went into action.

Only because that cap and its trailing veil of wire interfered with the free action of him who wore it was Simon to continue to live. He slapped out with his dart gun across the flat face with its snarling mouth which uttered no sound, its stark and hating eyes. The blow broke skin, brought blood welling from cheek and nose. Simon caught the other's wrist, twisting it so that a thin film of vapor spurted up into the vault of the ceiling, and not into his own face.

They crashed back into the chair from which the Kolder had risen. There was a sharp snap, fire flashed across Simon's neck and shoulder. A scream, muted and suppressed, rang in his ears. The face beneath its sweep of blood was contorted with agony, yet still the Kolder fought on with steel-muscled strength.

Those eyes, larger, and larger, filling the hall—Simon was falling forward into those eyes. Then there were no more eyes, just a weird fog-streaked window into another place—perhaps another time. Between pillars burst a company of men, gray robed, riding in machines strange to him. They were firing behind them as they came, unmistakably some remnant of a broken force on the run and hard-pressed.

In a narrow column they struggled on, and with them he endured desperation and such a cold fury as he had not known existed as an emotion to wrack mind and heart. The Gate—once through the Gate—*then* they would have the time: time to rebuild, to take, to be what they had the will and force to be. A broken empire and a ravaged world lay behind them—before them a fresh world for the taking.

The beset fugitives were swept away. He saw only one pallid face flushed red about a wound where his first blow had landed. Clinging about them both was the smell of sorching cloth and flesh. How long had that vision of the valley lasted—it could not have been a full second! He was still fighting, exerting pressure so that he might crack the other's wrist against the chair. Twice he struck it so, and then the fingers relaxed and the vapor gun fell out of their grip.

For the first time since that one scream the Kolder made a sound, a broken whimpering which sickened Simon. A second fading vision of those fleeing men—a moment of passionate regret which was like a blow to the man who involuntarily shared it. They thrashed across the floor to bring the Kolder up against a spitting wire. Simon slammed the other's metal cap hard against the floor. For the last time a fragment of recognition reached from the man to him and in that scrap of time he knew—perhaps not what the Kolder were—but from whence they had come. Then there was nothing at all, and Simon pulled away from the flaccid body to sit up.

Tunston stooped and tried to pull the cap from the head which rolled limply on the gray-robed shoulders. They were all a little daunted when it became apparent that that cap was no cap at all, but seemingly a permanent part of the body it crowned.

Simon got to his feet. "Leave it!" he bade the Guard. "But make sure none touch those wires."

It was then that he was aware that that throb in wall and door, that feeling of life was gone, leaving behind it a curious void. The Kolder of the cap might himself have been the heart, which, ceasing to beat, had killed the citadel as surely as his race had killed Sippar.

Simon made for the alcove where the elevator had been. Had all power ceased so that there was no way to reach the lower levels? But the door of the small cell was open. He gave command here to Tunston, and taking two of the Guardsmen with him, pushed the door shut.

Again luck appeared to be with those out of Estcarp, for the closing of the panel put into action the mechanism of the lift. Simon expected to front the level of the laboratory when that door opened once again. Only, when the cage came to a stop, he faced something so far removed from his expectations that for a moment he stood staring, while both of the men with him exclaimed in surprise.

They were on the shore of an underground harbor, strongly smelling of the sea and of something else. The lighting which had prevailed elsewhere in the pile was centered upon a runway washed by the water on both sides, pointing straight out into a bowl of gloom and dark. And on that quay were the tumbled bodies of men, men such as themselves with no gray robes among them.

Where the living dead who had met them in the street battles had gone armed and fully clad, these were either naked or wore only the tattered rags of old garments about their bodies, as if a need for clothing had no longer concerned them for a long time.

Some had crumpled beside small trucks on which boxes and containers were still heaped. Others lay in line as if they had been marching in ranks when struck down. Simon walked forward and stooped to peer at the nearest. It was clear that the man was truly dead, had been so for a day at least.

Gingerly, avoiding the heaped bodies, the three from Estcarp made their way to the end of the quay, finding nowhere among the dead any armed as fighting men. And none were of Estcarp blood. If these had been the slaves of the Kolder, they were all of other races.

"Here, Captain." One of the Guards lagging behind Simon had halted beside a body and was looking at it in wonder. "Here is such a man as I have never seen before. Look at the color of his skin, his hair; he is not from these lands!"

The unfortunate Kolder slave lay on his back as if in sleep. But his skin, totally exposed save for a draggle of rag about his hips, was a red-brown, and his hair was tightly curled to his scalp. It was plain that the Kolder had cast their man nets in far regions.

Without knowing why, Simon walked clear to the end of that wharf. Either Gorm had originally been erected over a huge underground cavern, or the invaders had blasted this out to serve their own purposes, purposes Simon could only believe were connected with the ship on which he had been a prisoner. Was this the secluded dock of the Kolder fleet?

"Captain!" The other Guard had tramped a little ahead, uninterested in the bodies among which he threaded a fastidious path. Now he stood on the end of that tongue of stone beckoning Simon forward.

There was a stirring of the waters; waves lapped higher on the wharf, forcing all three men to retreat. Even in that limited light they could see something large rising to the surface.

"Down!" Simon snapped the command. They did not have time to return to the lift; their best hope was to play one with the bodies about them.

They lay together, Simon pillowing his head on his arm, his gun ready, watching the turmoil. Water spilled from the bulk of the thing. Now he could make out the sharp bow with its matching needle stern. His guess had been right: this was one of the Kolder ships come to harbor.

He wondered if his own breathing sounded as loud as that of the men beside him did to him. They were more fully clothed than the dead about them; could sharp eyes pick out the gleam of their mail and nail them with some Kolder weapon before they could move in defense?

Only that silver ship, having once surfaced, made no other move at all, rolling in the waves within the cavern as if it were as dead as the bodies. Simon watched it narrowly and then started, as the man beside him whispered and touched his officer's arm.

But Simon did not need that admonition to watch. He, too, had sighted that second boiling upheaval of waves. In those the first ship was pushed toward the quay. It was plain now that she answered no helm. Hardly daring to believe that the vessel was unmanned, they still kept in hiding. It was only when the third ship bobbed into sight and sent the other two whirling with the force of its emergence, that Simon accepted the evidence and got to his feet. Those ships were either unmanned or totally disabled. They drifted without guidance, two coming together with a crash.

No openings showed on their decks, no indications that they carried crews and passengers. The story that the quay told was different, however. It suggested a hasty loading of vessels, intended to attack, or to make a withdrawal from Gorm. And had only an attack been the purpose would the slaves have been killed?

To board one of those floating silver splinters without preparation would be folly. But it would be best to keep an eye upon them. The three went back to the cage which had brought them there. One of the ships struck against the wharf, sheered it off, and wallowed away.

"Will you remain here?" He asked a question of his men rather than gave an order. The Guard of Estcarp should be inured to strange sights, but this was no place to station an unwilling man.

"Those ships—we should learn their secrets," one of the men returned. "But I do not think they will sail out from here again, Captain."

Simon accepted that oblique dissent. Together they left the underground harbor to the derelicts and the dead. Before they took off in the cage, Simon inspected its interior for controls. He wanted to reach some level where he might contact Koris' party, not return to the hall of the map once again.

Unfortunately the walls of that box were bare of any aid to direction. Disappointed they closed the door beind them waiting to be returned aloft. As the vibration in the wall testified to their movement, Simon recalled vividly the corridor of the laboratory and wished he could reach it.

The cage came to a stop, the door slid back, and the three within found themselves looking into the startled faces of other men, armed and alert. Only those few seconds of amazement saved both parties from a fatal mistake, for one of the group without called Simon's name and he saw Briant.

Then a figure not to be mistaken for any but Koris shouldered by the others. "Where do you spring from?" he demanded. "The wall itself?"

Simon knew this corridor where the Estcarp force was gathered: the place he had been thinking of. But why had the cage brought him here as if in answer to his wish alone? His wish!

"You have found the laboratory?"

"We have found many things, few of which make any sense. But not yet have we found any Kolder! And you?"

"One of the Kolder and he is now dead—or perhaps all of them!" Simon thought of the ships below and what they might hold in their interiors. "I do not believe that we have to fear meeting them here now."

Through the hours which followed Simon was proved a true prophet. Save for the one man in the metal cap, there was no other of the unknown race to be discovered within Gorm. And of those who had served the Kolder there were only dead men left. Found, those were in squads, in companies, or by twos and threes in the corridors and rooms of the keep. All lay as they had dropped, as if what had kept them operating as men had suddenly been withdrawn and they had fallen into the nothingness which should have been theirs earlier, the peace which their masters had denied them.

The Guards found other prisoners in the room beyond the laboratory, among them some who had shared captivity with Simon. These awoke sluggishly from their drugged sleep, unable to remember anything after they had been gassed, but thanking such gods as each owned that they had been brought to Gorm too late to follow the sorry path of the others the Kolder had engulfed.

Koris and Simon guided Sulcar seamen to the underground harbor, and in a small boat, explored the cavern. They found only rock wall. The entrance to the pool must lie under surface, and they believed it had been closed to the escape of the derelict ships.

"If he who wore the cap controlled it all," surmised Koris, "then his death must have sealed them in. Also, since he is the one you battled from afar through the Power, he might have already been giving muddled orders to lead to confusion here."

"Perhaps," Simon agreed absently. He was thinking of what he had learned from that other in his last few seconds of life. If the rest of the Kolder force were sealed into those ships, then indeed Estcarp had good reason to rejoice.

They got a line to one of the vessels and brought it alongside the wharf. But the fastenings of the hatch baffled them and Koris and Simon left the Sulcarmen to puzzle it out, returning to the keep.

"This is another of their magics." Koris slid the door of the lift closed behind them. "But seemingly one the capped man did not control, seeing as how we can use it now."

"You can control this as well as he ever did," Simon leaned back against wall, weariness washing over him. Their victory was inconclusive; he had an inkling of the chase yet before him, but would those of Estcarp believe what he had to tell them now? "Think upon the corridor where you met me, picture it in your mind."

"So?" Koris pulled off his helm; now he set his shoulders against the opposite wall and closed his eyes in concentration.

The door opened. They looked out upon the laboratory corridor and Koris laughed with a boy's amusement at an exciting toy.

"This magic I can work also, I, Koris the Ugly. It would seem that among the Kolder the Power was not limited only to women."

Simon closed the door once again, pictured in his mind the upper chamber of the wall map. Only when they reached that did he answer his companion's observation.

"Perhaps that is what we now have to fear from the Kolder, Captain. They had their own form of Power, and you have seen how they used it. This Gorm may now be a treasure-house of their knowledge."

Koris threw his helm on the table below the map, and leaning on his ax regarded Simon levelly.

"It is a treasure-house you warn against looting?" He picked that out quickly.

"I don't know." Simon dropped heavily into one of the chairs, and resting his head on his fists, stared down at the surface on which his elbows were planted. "I am no scientist, no master of this kind of magic. The Sulcarmen will be tempted by those ships, Estcarp by what else lies here."

"Tempted?" Someone had echoed that word and both men looked around. Simon got to his feet as he saw who seated herself quietly a little from them, Briant beside her as if playing her shieldman.

She was helmed and in mail, but Simon knew that she could disguise herself with shape-changing and still he would know her always.

"Tempted," again she repeated. "Well do you choose that word, Simon. Yes, we of Estcarp shall be tempted; that is why I am here. There are two edges to this blade and we may cut ourselves on either if we do not take care. Should we turn aside from this strange knowledge, destroy all we have found, we may be making ourselves safe, or we may be foolishly opening a way for a second Kolder attack, for one cannot build a defense unless he has a clear understanding of the weapons to be used against him."

"Of the Kolder," Simon spoke slowly, heavily, "you will not have to fear too much. There was but a small company of them in the beginning. If any escaped here, then they can be hunted back to their source and that source closed."

"Closed?" Koris made a question of that.

"In the last struggle with their leader he revealed their secret."

"That they are not native to this world?"

Simon's head swung around. Had she picked that out of his mind, or was that some information she had not seen fit to supply before?

"You knew?"

"I am not a reader of minds, Simon. But we have not known it long. Yes, they came to us—as you came—but, I think, from other motives."

"They were fugitives, fleeing disaster, a disaster of their own making, having set their own place aflame behind them. I do not think that they dared to leave their door open behind them, but that we must make sure of. The more pressing problem is what lies here."

"And you think that if we take their knowledge to us the evil which lies in it may corrupt. I wonder. Estcarp has lived long secure in its own Power."

"Lady, no matter what decision is made, I do not think that Estcarp shall remain the same. She must either come fully into the main stream of active life, or she must be content to withdraw wholly from it into stagnation, which is a form of death."

It was as if they two talked alone and neither Briant nor Koris had a part in the future they discussed. She met him mind to mind with an equality he had not sensed in any other woman before.

"You speak the truth, Simon. Perhaps the ancient solidity of my people must break. There shall be those who will wish for life and a new world, and those who shall shrink from any change from the ways which mean security. But that struggle still lies in the future. And it is only a growth of this war. What would you say should be done with Gorm?"

He smiled wearily. "I am a man of action. Out of here I shall go to hunt down that gate which the Kolder used and see that it is rendered harmless. Give me orders, lady, and they shall be carried out. But for the time being I would seal this place until a decision can be made. There may be an attempt on the part of others to take away what lies here."

"Yes. Karsten, Alizon, both would relish the looting of Sippar." She nodded briskly. Her hand was at the breast of her mail shirt and she drew it away with the jewel of power in it.

"This is my authority, Captain," she spoke to Koris. "Let it be as Simon has said. Let this storehouse of strange knowledge be sealed, and let the rest of Gorm be cleansed for a garrison, until such time as we can decide the future of what lies here." She smiled at the young officer. "I leave it in your command, Lord Defender of Gorm."

VII
A Venture of New Beginnings

A dusky red spread slowly up from the collar of Koris' mail shirt, reaching the line of his fair hair. Then he answered and the bitter lines about his well-cut mouth were deep, adding years to his young face.

"Are you forgetting, lady," he brought the blade of Volt's Ax down flatwise on the table with a clang, "that long ago Koris the Misshapen was driven from these shores?"

"And what happened to Gorm thereafter, and to those who did that driving?" she asked quietly. "Have any said 'misshapen Captain of Estcarp'?"

His hand tightened on the haft of his weapon until the knuckles were white and sharp. "Find another Lord Defender for Gorm, lady. I swore by Nornan that I would not return here. To me this is a doubly haunted place. I think that Estcarp has had no reason to complain of her Captain; also I do not believe this war already won."

"He is right, you know," Simon cut in. "The Kolder may be few, most of them may be trapped in those ships below. But we must trace them back to their Gate and make sure that they do not consolidate shattered forces to launch a second bid for rulership. What about Yle? And do they have a garrison in Sulcarkeep? How deeply are they involved in Karsten and Alizon? We may be at the beginning of a long war instead of grasping victory."

"Very well." She stroked the jewel she held. "Since you have such definite ideas, become governor here, Simon."

Koris spoke swiftly before Tregarth could answer. "To me that is a plan to which I agree. Hold Gorm with my blessing, Simon, and do not think that I shall ever rise in the name of my heritage to take it from you."

But Simon was shaking his head. "I am a soldier. And I am from another world. Let dog eat dog as the saying goes—the Kolder trail is mine." He touched his head; if he closed his eyes now he knew he would see not darkness but a narrow valley through which angry men fought a rearguard action.

"Do you venture into Yle and Sulcarkeep and no farther?" Briant broke silence for the first time.

"Where would you have us go?" Koris asked.

"Karsten!" If Simon had ever thought the youth colorless and lacking in personality he was to doubt his appraisal at that moment.

"And what lies in Karsten which is of such moment to us?" Koris' voice held an almost bantering note. Yet there was something else beneath the surface of that tone which Simon heard but could not identify. There was a game here afoot, but he did not know its purpose or rules.

"Yvian!" The name was flung at the Captain like a battle challenge and Briant eyed Koris as if waiting to see him pick it up. Simon glanced from one young man to the other. As it had been earlier when he and the witch had talked across the board, so was it now: these two fenced without thought of their audience.

For the second time red tinged Koris' cheeks, then ebbed, leaving his face white and set, that of a man committed to some struggle he hated but dared not shirk. For the first time he left the Ax of Volt lying forgotten on the table as he came swiftly about the end of the board, moving with that lithe grace which always contrasted with his ill-formed body.

Briant, a queer expression of mingled defiance and hope giving life to his features, waited for his coming, stood still as the Captain's hands fell on his shoulders in a grip which could not have been anything but bruising.

"This is what you want?" the words came from Koris as if jerked one by one by torture.

At the last moment perhaps Briant tried to evade. "I want my freedom," he replied in a low voice.

Those punishing hands fell away. Koris laughed with such raking bitterness that Simon protested inwardly against the hurt that sound betrayed.

"Be sure, in time, it shall be yours!" The Captain would have stepped away if Briant had not seized in turn upon Koris' upper arms with the same urgency of hold the other had shown earlier."

"I want my freedom only that I may make a choice elsewhere. And I have decided upon that choice—do you doubt that? Or is it again that there is an Aldis who has the power I cannot reach for?"

Aldis? A glimmering of what might be the truth struck Simon.

Koris' fingers were under Briant's chin, turning the thin young face up to his. This once was the Captain able to look down and not up at a companion.

"You believe in sword thrust for sword thrust, do you not?" he commented. "So Yvian has his Aldis; let them have the good of each other while they may. But I think that Yvian has made a very ill choice of it. And since one ax made a marriage, another may undo it!"

"Marriage in the gabble gabble of Siric only," flashed Briant, still a little defiant, but not struggling in the Captain's new hold.

"Need you have told *me* that," Koris was smiling, "Lady of Verlaine?"

"Loyse of Verlaine is dead!" Briant repeated. "You get no such heritage with me, Captain."

A tiny frown line appeared between Koris' brows. "That you need not have said either. Rather is it that such as I am must buy a wife with gauds and lands. And never afterwards be sure of the bargain."

Her hand whipped from his arm to his mouth, silencing him. And there was red anger in both her eyes and her voice when she replied:

"Koris, Captain of Estcarp need never speak so of himself, least of all to a woman such as I, without inheritance of lands or beauty!"

Simon moved, knowing that neither were aware of the other two in that room. He touched the witch of Estcarp gently on the shoulder and smiled down at her.

"Let us leave them to fight their own battle," he whispered.

She was laughing silently after her fashion. "This talk of mutual unworthiness will speedily be a step to no talking at all and so to a firm settlement of two futures."

"I take it that she *is* the missing heiress of Verlaine, wedded by proxy to Duke Yvian?"

"She is. By her aid alone I came scatheless out of Verlaine, I being captive there for a space. Fulk is not a pleasant enemy."

Afire to every shade of her voice, Simon's smile became grim.

"I think that Fulk and his wreckers shall be taught a lesson in the near future; it will curb their high spirits," he commented, knowing well her way of understatement. It was enough for him that she admitted she owed her escape from Verlaine to the girl across the room. For a woman of the Power such an admission hinted of danger indeed. He had a sudden overwhelming desire to take one of the Sulcar ships, man it with his mountain fighters, and sail southward.

"Doubtless he shall," she agreed to his statement concerning Fulk with her usual tranquillity. "As you have said, we are still in the midst of a war, and not victors at the end of one. Verlaine and Karsten, too, shall be attended to in their proper seasons. Simon, my name is Jaelithe."

It came so abruptly, that for a full moment he did not understand her meaning. And then, knowing the Estcarpian custom, of the rules which had bound her so long, he drew a deep breath of wonder at that complete surrender: her name, that most personal possession in the realm of the Power, which must never be yielded lest one yield with it one's own identity to another!

As Koris' ax lay on the table, so she had left her jewel behind her when she had moved apart with Simon. For the first time he realized that fact also. She had deliberately disarmed herself, put aside all her weapons and defenses, given into his hands what she believed was the ordering of her life. What such a surrender had meant to her he could guess, but only dimly—and that he knew also, awed. He felt as stripped of all talents and ability, as misshapen, as Koris deemed himself.

Yet he moved forward and his arms went out to draw her to him. As he bent his head to hers, searching for waiting lips, Simon sensed that for the first time the pattern had changed indeed. Now he was a part of a growing design, his life to be woven fast with hers, into the way of this world's. And there would be no breaking it for the remainder of his days. Nor would he ever wish to.

Web
of the
Witch World

Contents

I
Gauntlet Thrown

*J*n the night there had been storm with great gusts of angry wind to batter ancient walls, aim spear-thrusts of rain at the window slits of the chamber. But its violence had been reduced to a sullen mutter outside the South Keep. And Simon Tregarth had found that mutter soothing.

No, this was no troubling of nature—the raw nature man must fight and subdue for his own survival. It was a very different unease he felt as he lay in the early morning, awake and aware as a sentinel listening to sounds beyond his post.

Chill sweat gathered in his armpits, beaded dankly on his slightly hollowed cheeks and square jaw. Gray light overtook the room shadows, there was no sound, but—

His hand went out tentatively before he consciously thought. Nor did he entirely realize that he was yielding to an emotion which he still found new and hard to understand. This was an instinctive appeal for comradeship and support against—what? He could set no name to the uneasiness which held him. Fingers met warm flesh, cupped on soft skin. He turned his head on the pillow. The lamp was unlit, but there was wan light enough to see his bedfellow. Open, watchful eyes met his fearlessly, but their depths were shadowed by a twin to the anxiety growing in Simon.

Then she moved. Jaelithe, she who had been a witch of Estcarp, and was now his wife, sat up abruptly, the black silk of her hair pulling from beneath his cheek to cloak her shoulders, her hands folded over her small high breasts. She no longer gazed at him, but searched the room, open to their sight since the midsummer mildness had led to the bed hangings being looped up for the free passage of night breezes.

The strangeness of that chamber came and went for Simon. Sometimes the present was a dream, ill-rooted and illusory, when he thought of the past. At other times it was the past which had no part of him at all. What was he? Simon Tregarth—disgraced ex-army officer, a criminal who had fled the vengeance of wolves beyond the law, who had taken the final step of the perfect escape known to that evil world—the "gate." Jorge Petronius had opened it for him—an age-old stone seat rumored to take any man daring enough to sit in it to a new world, one where his talents would make him at home. That was one Simon Tregarth.

Another lay here and now in the South Keep of Estcarp, March Warder of the south, sworn to the service of the Women of Power; he had taken to wife one of the feared witches of the age-sombered land of Estcarp. And this was one of the times when the present annulled the past—when he crossed a border he could not describe into a firmer union with the world he had so abruptly entered.

Sharp as any sword thrust into his flesh was that throb, breaking through his momentary wonder concerning himself and what he was doing here. He moved as quickly as Jaelithe had earlier, sitting up so that their shoulders brushed, and in his hand was a dart gun. But even as Simon brought that out from under his pillow he knew the folly of his action. This was not a call to battle, but a clarion summons far more subtle and, in its way, more terrifying.

"Simon—" Jaelithe's voice was shaken, higher than usual and a little unsteady.

"I know!" He was already sliding over the edge of the wide bed, his feet meeting the first step of the dais which supported it above the floor of the chamber, his hands reaching for the garments left on the chair beyond.

Somewhere—either in the pile of the South Keep or near thereto—was trouble! His mind was already busy with the possibilities. A raid by sea from Karsten? He was certain no party from the duchy could have won through the mountains, not when all that country was patrolled by the Falconers of the heights and his own Borderer companies. Or was it some slash-and-go attempt on the part of Alizon, operating by sea? Their sullen unrest had been apparent for months. Or—

Simon's hands did not slack speed in pulling on boots or fastening belt, though his breath came a little faster as he thought on the third and worst possibility—the chance that Kolder was not crushed, that the evil—alien to this world in the same way he was alien—stirred again, moved, lapped closer to them.

In the months since that ruthless enemy had struck and been repulsed, since the Kolder stronghold on the island of Gorm had been taken and cleansed and their supported rising in Karsten failed, they had gone. Nothing stirred from their dark hold of Yle, though none of the Estcarp forces could break through the barrier which locked that cluster of towers from approach by sea or land. Simon, for one, did not believe that the defeat in Gorm had finished the Kolder threat. That would not be done with until the aliens were traced to their overseas stronghold and the nest there destroyed with the vipers in it. Such a move could not be made as yet—not while Karsten smoldered to the south or Alizon remained a battle hound hardly in check in the north.

He was listening now, not only with the sense he could not have named which had warned him out of sleep, but with his ears for the warning tocsin on the tower above. The Borderers who manned this keep were not to be taken unawares. Surely by now the alarm should be booming, vibrating through the stone of the walls!

"Simon!" The summons was so sharp and imperative that he swung around, weapon once again in his hand.

Jaelithe's face was pallid in this half-light, but her lips were unnaturally tight against her teeth. It might have been fear which lighted her eyes so—or was it? A soft crimson robe was clutched about her, held negligently by one hand. She had not put her arms into its wide sleeves and it dragged along the floor as she came around the end of the bed to him, walking stiffly as if in her sleep. But she was awake, very much awake, and that was not fear moving her.

"Simon—I—I am whole!"

It hit him, worse than the summons, with a hurt which registered deep, and which would grow and hurt the more; he sensed this fleetingly. So—it had meant that much to her? That she felt herself maimed, lessened by what had been between them. And another part of Simon, less troubled by emotion, arose to defend her. Witchdom had been her life. As all her sisterhood she had had pride of accomplishment, joy in that usage; yet she had willingly set aside, so she thought, all that when she had come to him, believing that in their uniting of bodies she would lose all which meant so much to her. And his second thought was so much the better one!

Simon held out his hand, though he longed to take her wholly into his arms. And her new joy which blazed from every part of her, as if a fire were lit deep within her skin, bones, and flesh, warmed him also as their clasp went tight, fingers locking about fingers.

"How—?" he began, but she interrupted him.

"It is with me still—it is! Oh, Simon, I am not only woman, but also witch!"

Her other hand dropped its hold on her robe so that the folds collapsed on the floor about her feet. Her fingers went to her breast, seeking what she no longer wore—the witch jewel she had surrendered at her wedding.

A little of that bright look faded as she realized she no longer possessed that tool through which the energy which filled her now could work. Then, with her old-time quick reaction to fact, she broke clasp with Simon and stood, her head slightly atilt, as if she, too, listened.

"The alarm has not sounded." Simon stooped to gather up the robe and wrap her in it.

Jaelithe nodded. "I do not think this is an attack. But there is trouble—evil—on—the move."

"Yes, but where—and what?"

She still stood in the attitude of one listening, but this time Simon knew that she did not hear audibly, but sensed some wave reaching directly to her mind. He felt it, too, that uneasiness which was fast heightening into a push to action. But what kind of action, where, against who, or what?

"Loyse!" A whisper. Jaelithe whirled and made for the coffer which held her clothing. She was dressing with the same haste as Simon had. But not in the robes of her household faring. What she burrowed deep to find was the soft leather which went under chain mail, the clothing of one riding on a foray.

Loyse? Simon could not be so sure, but he accepted her word without question. There were four of them, oddly assorted—four fighters for the freedom of Estcarp, for their own freedom from the evil which Kolder had sown so far in what had once been a fair world. Simon Tregarth, the alien from another world; Jaelithe, the Witch of Estcarp; Koris, exiled from Gorm before its fall into darkness, Captain of the Guard and then Seneschal and Marshal of Estcarp; and Loyse, the Heiress of Verlaine, a castle of wrecker lords on the coast. Fleeing a marriage with Yvian of Karsten, she had brought Jaelithe out of Verlaine, and together they had wrought subtly in Kars for the undoing of Yvian and all that he stood for. Loyse, wearing hauberk, carrying sword and shield, had joined in the attack on Gorm. And in the citadel of Sippar had pledged herself to Koris. Loyse, the pale, small girl who was indeed a warrior strong and brave beyond most counting. And this sending dealt with danger for Loyse!

"But she is at Es Castle—" Simon protested, as he pulled on mail to match that which now clinked softly in Jaelithe's hands. And Es Castle was the heart, if the enemy had dared to strike there—!

"No!" Again Jaelithe was positive. "There is the sea—in this there is the sea."

"Koris?"

"I do not feel him, not in this. If I only had the jewel!" She was tugging on riding boots. "It is as if I tried to track a drifting mist. I can see the drift, but nothing is clear. But Loyse is in danger and the sea is part of it."

"Kolder?" Simon put into words' his deepest fear.

"No. There is not the blankness of the Kolder wall. But the need for help is great! We must ride, Simon—west and south." She had turned a little, her eyes now focused on the wall as if she could really see through it to the point she sought.

"We ride." He agreed.

The living quarters of the keep were yet silent. But as they sped together down the hallway to the stair they heard the sounds of the changing guard. Simon called, "Turn out the Riders!"

His words echoed hollowly, but carried, to be answered by a startled exclamation from below. Before he and Jaelithe were halfway down the stairs, Simon heard the piping of the alert.

This garrison was well prepared for sudden sallies. Through spring and summer the alarm had sounded again and again to set the Borderers loose along the marches. Those who made up the striking force Simon commanded were largely recruited from the fugitive Old Race. Driven out of Karsten when the massacre orders of Kolder were given, they had many causes to hate the despoilers and murderers who now held their lands and who came, in quick stab raids, to try the defenses of Estcarp, the last home of that dark-haired, dark-eyed race who carried ancient wisdom and strange blood, whose women had witch power and whose men were dour, stinging wasps of fighters.

"No beacon, Lord—"

Ingvald, Simon's second in command from the old days when they had fought, ridden and fought again in the high hills, waited him in the courtyard. It was Jaelithe who answered.

"A sending, Captain."

The Karstenian refugee's eyes widened as he looked at her. But he did not protest.

"An attack here?"

"No. Trouble west and south." Simon made answer. "We ride fast—with half a troop. You remain in command here."

Ingvald hesitated as if he wished to argue that, but he did not speak except to say, "Durstan's company has the hill duty for this day and are ready to ride."

"Good enough."

One of the serving women ran from the hall behind them, holding a platter covered with rounds of journey bread, new from the oven and each bearing a smoking slice of meat. Behind her pounded a kitchen lad with filled beakers slopping their contents over his hands as he came. Jaelithe and Simon ate as they stood, watching the troop check mounts and supply bags, ready weapons, for the move out.

"The sender!" Simon heard a small, pleased laugh from Jaelithe.

"She knows! Had I but my jewel in again, we could dismiss her to other duties."

Simon blinked. So Jaelithe, even without her jewel, had communicated with the young witch who was their link with Estcarp command. The warning must even now be on its way to the Guardians' Council. In turn Jaelithe might be able to hold that communication as they rode, stretching it to report.

He began to consider the terrain west and south—mountains, the broken foothill country, and seacoast to the west. There were one or two small villages, market centers, but no other keep or castle. There were also temporary guard points, but all were too small, too far within Estcarp's own territory to house sending witches. So hill beacons passed warning. And there had been no such beacon lighted.

What was Loyse doing there? Why had she come forth from Es Castle and ridden into that wilderness?

"Brought by trick." Jaelithe was reading his surface thoughts again. "Though the manner of the tricking I cannot tell you. The purpose I think I can guess—"

"Yvian's move!" It was the most logical answer to any action against the heiress of Verlaine. By the laws of Karsten she was Yvian's wife, through whom he could claim Verlaine—though he had never set eyes on Loyse, nor she on him. Get her under his hand and the bargain Fulk had made for his daughter would be completed. Karsten was in uproar by all reports. Yvian, the mercenary who had won to power by might of arms, was facing the bared teeth of the old nobility. He would have to answer their hostility firmly or his ducal throne would crumble under him.

And Loyse was of the old blood; she could claim kinsrights with at least three of the most powerful houses. Using her as a tool Yvian's own ability could accomplish much. He had to put Karsten in order in a hurry. Though Simon knew that Estcarp had no intention of carrying war beyond her own borders—save in the direction of the Kolder—Yvian would not believe that.

The Duke of Karsten must rest very uneasy, knowing that his massacre of the Old Race gave more than a little reason to center the vengeance of the witches upon him. And he would not believe that they did not intend to attack him. Yes, Loyse was a weapon and a tool Yvian must be wild to get within his two hands for use.

They rode out of the keep at a purposeful trot, Jaelithe matching Simon's pace in the lead, Durstan's twenty men providing a competent fighting tail. The main road ran to the coast, perhaps four hours' ride away. Before the fall of Sulcarkeep, the traders' city under Kolder attack, this had been one of the trade arteries of Estcarp, linking half a dozen villages and one fair-sized town with that free port of the merchant-rovers. Since Sulcarkeep had been blasted into rubble nearly a year ago the last despairing gesture of its garrison, taking with it most of its enemy, the highway had lost most of its traffic and the signs of its disuse were visible, save where the patrols worked to keep it free of fallen trees and storm wrack.

The troop clattered through Romsgarth, a central gathering point for the farms of the slopes. Since it was not market day their swift passage awoke interest from the early stirring townsfolk and there were calls of inquiry as they passed. Simon saw Durstan wave to the town guard, and knew they would leave a watchful and ready post behind them. The Old Race might be destined to go down to defeat, their neighbors snarling at their borders. But they would take a large number of those enemies with them in the final battle. And that knowledge was one of the things which kept Alizon and Karsten from yet making the fatal move of outright invasion.

Some leagues beyond Romsgarth Jaelithe signaled a halt. She rode bare-head, her helmet swinging at her saddle horn. And now she turned her head slowly from right to left, as if she could scent the path of the quarry. But Simon had already caught the trace.

"There!" The sensation of danger which had been with him since waking focused unerringly. A track split south from the main road. Across it lay a fallen tree and that trunk bore fresh scars on its bark. One of the troop dismounted to inspect.

"Scrapes of hooves—recent—"

"Infiltrate," Simon ordered.

They spread out, not to use the artery of the half-closed path, but working in through brush, among trees. Jaelithe took up her helmet.

"Make haste!"

This ground was right for ambush; to run into attack was the choice of a fool. But Simon nodded. What had brought them here was building to a climax. Jaelithe pressed heels to her mount, jumped the log, headed down the path with Simon spurring to catch up with her again. To any watcher it might seem they were alone, his men remained behind.

The wind in their faces was sea-scented. Somewhere ahead an inlet in the coast waited. Was a ship there—to make a quick pickup and then to sea—to Karsten? What *had* brought Loyse into such danger? He wished for the Falconers and their trained birds to spy on what lay ahead.

Simon could hear the rustling advance of his men—they would certainly not go unheralded in this country. His mount flung up its head and neighed—to be answered from ahead. Then they came out in an open pocket of meadow sloping gently to beach in a cove. Two horses grazed there, saddles empty. And well out stood a ship, its painted sail belly-rounded by the wind, it was far beyond their reaching.

Jaelithe dismounted, ran towards a splotch of color on the beach and Simon followed her. He stood looking down at a woman. Her face was oddly blank and calm, though both her hands were tight upon the blade which had been driven into her. To Simon she was a stranger.

"Who?"

Jaelithe frowned. "I have seen her. She was from across the mountains. Her name—" From storehouse of memory she produced it in triumph. "Her name was Berthora and she once lived in Kars!"

"Lord!"

Simon looked to where one of the troop beckoned. He went to see what was mounted on the very edge of the wave-lapped shore. A spear driven deep into the sand so that it stood uprightly defiant held a mail gauntlet. He did not need any words of explanation. Karsten had been and gone, and wanted that coming and going known. Yvian had declared open battle. Simon's hand closed upon that gauge and pulled it loose.

II
Border Foray

*T*he rays of the lights centered on the glittering thing in the middle of the board, making it seem to ripple with a mindless life of its own. Yet it was but a glove, sweat-stained leather palm down, mailed back up.

"She left two days ago, but the why no one can say—" Bleak voice from which the fellowship had chilled away, leaving only grim purpose. Koris of Gorm stood at the end of the table, leaning forward, his hands so tight about the haft of his war ax that his knuckles were sharp ridges. "Last eve—last *eve* I discovered it! By what devil's string was she tolled here?"

"We can take it," Simon replied, "that this is Karsten's doing and the why we can guess." More "whys" than one, he thought, and meeting Jaelithe's gaze, knew that she shared that guess or guesses. With Koris so emotionally involved this kidnaping would upset the delicate balance of Estcarp defense. Not even witch power was going to keep the young seneschal from Loyse's trail, at least not until he had a chance to cool off and begin to really think again. But had that ship borne away Jaelithe would he, Simon, have been any the different?

"Kars falls." A simple statement, fact when delivered in that tone of voice.

"Just like that?" Simon retorted. For Koris to go whirling over the border now with such a force as he could gather in a hurry was the worst stupidity Simon knew. "Yes, Kars falls—but by planning, not by attack without thought behind it."

"Koris—" Jaelithe's long-fingered hand came out into the light which had gathered about Yvian's battle gage, "do not lessen Loyse!"

She had his attention, had broken through to him when Simon had failed. "Lessen her?"

"Remember Briant. Do not separate those in your mind now, Koris."

Briant and Loyse—again she was right, his witch-wife; Simon gave respect where it was due. Loyse had ridden as the blank-shield mercenary Briant, had lived with Jaelithe in Kars, keeping watch in the very maw of the enemy, just as she had stormed into Sippar. And as Briant she had not only won free of Verlaine, but brought the captive Jaelithe with her at the beginning of her adventure, when all the might of that castle and its lord had been arrayed against her. The Loyse who was also Briant was no helpless maiden, but had a mind, will, and skills of her own.

"She is Yvian's—by their twisted laws!" Koris' ax moved into the light in a sweeping arc which bit deep, severing the stuff of the gauntlet as if it had been fashioned of clay.

"No—she is her own until she wills it otherwise, Koris. What manner of mischief was wrought to get her into their hands, I do not understand. But that it can hold her I doubt. However, think on this, my proud Captain. Go you slashing into Kars as you wish, and she will then be a weapon for Yvian. The Kolder taint still lies there—and would you have her used against you as they can do?"

Koris' head turned to her, he looked up to meet her gaze as he must always do from his dwarfish height. His too-wide shoulders were a little hunched, so that he had almost the stance of an animal poised for a killing leap.

"I do not leave her there." Again a statement of fact.

"Nor do we," Simon agreed. "But look you—they will expect us to be after such bait, and the trap will be waiting."

Koris blinked. "So—and what then do you urge? To leave her wrest herself free? She had great courage—my lady—but she is not a witch. Nor can she, one against many, fight a war on her own!"

Simon was ready. Luckily he had had those few hours, before Koris and his guard had come pelting into the keep, to do some planning. Now he slapped a parchment map down beside the ax head still dividing the severed gauntlet.

"We do not ride directly for Kars. We could not reach that city without a full army and then we needs must fight all the way. Our van will enter the city at Yvian's invitation."

"Behind a war horn?" Koris demanded. "Shape changing—?" He was not so hostile now, beginning to think.

"After a fashion," Simon told him. "We move here . . ."

There was a risk. He had been considering such an operation for weeks, but heretofore he had thought the balance against it too great. Now that they needed a lever against Karsten it was the best he could think of.

Koris studied the map. "Verlaine!" From that dot he glanced at Simon.

"Yvian wants Verlaine, has wanted it from the start. That was partly his reason for wedding Loyse. Not only does the wreckers' treasure stored there beckon him—remember his men are mercenaries and must be paid when there is no loot in prospect—but that castle can also give him a raiders' port from which to operate against us. And now, with the loot from the Old Race exhausted, he will need Verlaine the more. Fulk has been very wise, not venturing to Yvian's territory. But suppose he would—"

"Trade Verlaine for Loyse! You mean that is what we shall do?" Koris' handsome face was frown twisted.

"Allow Yvian to believe he is going to get Verlaine without any trouble." Simon put together the ideas he had been holding in mind. As he spoke Koris' frown faded, he had concentration of a general picking at a piece of strategy seeking weaknesses. But he did not interrupt as Simon continued adding the facts which his scouts had garnered to the reports of the Falconers, lacing the whole together with his knowledge of such warfare from the past.

"A ship on the rocks will bring them out to plunder. Fulk will have a guard still in the castle, yes. But they will not be watching the ways within his own walls which he does not know. Those were Loyse's ways and my lady knows them. A party coming down from the mountains will burrow in thus, and the heart of the keep is ours. We can settle then with those combing the shore for loot."

"It will take time—and a storm—at the proper day and luck—" But Koris' protests were feather-light and Simon knew it. The seneschal would agree to his plan; the danger of a headlong storming into enemy territory was past. At least as long as Koris could be occupied with Verlaine.

"As for time," Simon rolled up the map, "we have been moving to this goal for a day or more. I have sent a message to the Falconers and they have infiltrated the peaks. There are Borderer scouts who know every trail in that cutback, and Sulcarmen will man one of the derelicts from Sippar harbor. With new sails it will ride well enough, the waterlogging setting it deep enough in the waves to seem full cargoed, and it can bear merchant symbols of Alizon. The storm—"

Jaelithe laughed. "Ah, the storm! Do you forget that wind and wave are liegemen to us, Simon? I shall see to wind and wave when the hour ripens."

"But—?" Koris looked up at her again in open question.

"But you deem me now powerless, Koris? It is far otherwise, I assure you!" Her voice rang out joyfully. "Let me but claim back my jewel and you shall have the proof of that. So, Simon, while you ride for the border and your spider's web about Fulk's hold, I will speed to Es Castle and that which I must have again."

He nodded. But deep within him that faint pain pricked once again. She had laid aside the jewel for him—seemingly with joy and content. Only now that she knew she was not bereft of what she thought she had lost, that sacrifice no sacrifice at all, she had put on once again that old cloak to cover the inner places she had revealed to him. And between them was the shadow of division. A chill grew from his fear. Would that division grow stronger—perhaps into a wall? Simon thrust the thoughts away; there was Verlaine to consider now.

Simon sent out the summoning—not by hill beacon which would alert any Karstenian spy in the heights—but by witch sending where it was possible, by rider where it was not. The hill garrisons were thinned—here five men, there ten or a dozen. And those so chosen rode in small parties into the mountains as if on routine patrol, to keep apart until the final word.

Koris dealt with Anner Osberic whose Sulcar merchant-raiders had homed to Es Port now that their coast keep was lost. There was a move to take over Gorm as a base. But as yet men shunned that tragic isle in the bay with its haunted city of Sippar, where the citadel left by the Kolder was sealed under the will of the Guardians of Estcarp, lest the outland knowledge of the enemy be ill-used. Osberic's father had died at Sulcarkeep, his hate for the Kolder and all their ilk ran seadeep and harsh as any storm, and his knowledge of wind and wave, while not that of a witch, was great. If he could not control storms, he could ride them. And he and his men had been demanding action against the enemy. This dangerous game with a wreckers' castle for the bait would please them greatly.

The plan was in motion, all they needed was an agreed striking time. Simon lay flat on a crag ledge. The day was gray, but no fog spoiled his watch of the rounded walls, the two sky-arching towers which were Verlaine. He cupped in his hand one of Estcarp's equivalents of field glasses, a lens of transparent quartz. Down in that gazing oval was tiny, but very distinct and clear, one of the claw-shaped reefs which harvested the sea for the wreckers. Anner would put his pseudo-merchantman on course to crack up on that reef, about midpoint—far enough from the castle to draw the men well away from the walls, but not so far as to suggest danger in garnering the wreckage.

The gray sky, the moist air, warned of a storm. But they needed a controlled fury to work on time schedule. Simon continued to check the terrain before him via glass, but his thoughts strayed. Jaelithe had gone to Es Castle and the Guardians, alive and vibrant in her exultation over her discovery that as a witch she had not been rendered impotent. But since then, no word from out of the north that bore any news of her, none of that mental touch Simon had come to expect as a tie between them. Almost he could believe now that those weeks in South Keep had been a dream, that he had never held the fulfillment of desires he had never realized existed within him, until they had become wrapped in flesh and blood in his arms; he now knew a place which was beyond earth and stars, beyond self, when another shared it.

And that chill fear which had been only a spark in the beginning grew, that wall he sensed took on solid shape. So that he must strive to keep his thoughts away from that path lest he, too, as Koris might, go storming away from duty to seek her.

Time was short, very short. This night, Simon thought, as he slipped the seeing stone back in his belt pocket, this night ought to see their move. Before she had left him Jaelithe had laid the knowledge of the underground ways into his mind. Last night he, Ingvald and Durstan had descended into the cave which was the beginning of those passages, gazed unwillingly at the ancient altar there, raised to gods long since vanished with the dust of those who had worshiped them. They had felt also that throat-choking residue of *something* which still hung there, which fed upon Simon's own gift of extrasense, until he had to impose iron control on his shaking body. More than one sort of power had been in use on this somber continent of an old, old world.

He slipped down from the crag now, made his way to the pocket where three of the Borderer scouts and a Falconer sat cross-legged, as if they would warm themselves at a fire they dared not light.

"No word?"

A foolish question, Simon thought, even as he asked it. He would have known it if she were here. But the boy in the leather and mail of the scout force came lithely to his feet to answer.

"Message from the seneschal, Lord. Captain Osberic has the ship readied. He will loose her on signal, but does not know how long the wind will serve."

Time . . . Simon tried to gauge the wind, though he did not have any sea knowledge. If Jaelithe did not come—then still they must move and risk the greater peril inherent in a true storm, with no aid of witchcraft. It must be tonight, or no later than tomorrow.

A sharp birdcall and the black-and-white falcon that was ears and eyes for Uncar spiraled down to settle on its master's fist.

"The seneschal comes," Uncar reported.

Simon had never understood the tie between man and bird, but he had long ago learned that such reports were accurate and that the hawk range of the Falconers was far more effective than any human scouting in these heights. Koris was on the prowl, and this time Simon would have to agree with the other's urging to move. But where was Jaelithe?

In spite of his ungainly body Koris moved with the economy of action marking an experienced fighting man. The huge ax he had taken from the hand of legendary Volt in the bird-god's hidden tomb was muffled in a riding cloak, but he wore his winged helmet and came armed for battle. That handsome face, so ill supported by his misshapen body, was grimly alight as Simon had seen it before upon occasion.

"This night we move! Anner says that wind and wave favor us. He cannot promise so later." He hesitated and then added in a lower voice, "There is no word from the north."

"So be it! Pass the signal, Waldis. At dusk we move."

The boy disappeared arrow-swift between the rocks. Uncar's lean face showed within the narrow opening of his bird-head helm.

"The rain comes. It will favor us that much more. At dusk, March Warder—" Hawk on wrist he followed Waldis, to bring up his men.

There was no true sunset; the gathering clouds were far too heavy. And the wave action was stronger. Soon Osberic would loose his bait ship. The wreckers had three watch points—two on the reef and one on the center tower of the hold; all would be manned in ill weather. Those on the reef need not be feared, but the sentry post on the tower also overlooked those fields through which the attackers must move. And though they had marked every bit of cover on that approach, Simon was worried. An early rain would give them cover.

But the storm winds came before the rain. And they had only the dusk to cloak them as the line of Borderers and Falconers sifted down to the entrance hole, climbed into the dark beneath. There was a sudden gleam and Simon heard an exclamation from Koris.

The blade of Volt's ax shone with light. And Simon sensed a stir of the force from the crumbling altar, the rising of an energy beyond his ability to describe, but one he feared.

"A battle light!" Koris' humorless laugh followed. "I thank you, Volt, for this added favor!"

"Move!" Simon ordered. "You do not know what may wake here with that blade!"

They found the entrance to the passage quickly. There was a tingling in Simon's skin, his hair lifting despite the weight of his helmet, answering the electricty in this place. Here the walls were slimed with oily streaks of moisture which shone in their journey lights, and a moldering, rotten stench thickened as they went. Underfoot, the flooring vibrated to the pound of rising waves not too far away.

A stair before them, where silvery trails crossed and recrossed the stone, as if giant slugs had made highways there for countless generations. Up and up, all Jaelithe's knowledge of these passages was gained during her flight through them. Loyse had discovered and used them for her purposes, and Simon wished he had her direction now. But he must be certain of his goal and not explore. They would emerge in the tower chamber which had once been Loyse's; from there they could spread to take Fulk's hold—always providing the bulk of his garrison were occupied elsewhere.

The steps rose endlessly, and then Simon's counting ceased. There were still steps ahead, but this landing had counted out correctly for the door. And he could see the simple latch which held on this side. Luckily, the builder who had devised these ways had not concealed such catches. He bore down and a five-foot oval swung away.

Even here they had to use journey lights for the room was dark. A canopied cavern of a bed faced them. There was a chest at its foot, another under the window slits outside of which howled storm wind.

"Signal!" Simon need not have given that order. One of Koris' guard had leaped on the chest, his arm up to thrust open the covering on the slit. Then the beat of the vibration pattern winked through all their journey lights, as it would through Anner Osberic's if he were in position. The ship would be released. Now they had only to wait until the alarm of her coming would awake the castle.

But that waiting was the worst for all of them, keyed to action as they were. Two small parties, one under Ingvald, and one of Falconers under Uncar's command, went back to the wall ways to explore. Uncar reported another door giving upon an empty sleeping chamber, providing a second exit.

Still time dragged and Simon mentally listed the many things which might go wrong. Fulk would be prepared for invasion from without. He had his scouts, as they had discovered in the pass. But this passage had never been discovered as far as Loyse knew.

"Ahhhh—" Someone nearby breathed a sigh of relief, which was swallowed in a blast of brazen clamor from just above their heads, startling them all.

"That is it!" Koris caught at Simon's shoulder and then pushed past him to the door of the chamber. "The wreck tocsin! That will shake these rats out of their holes!"

III
Black Night

*P*atience. Long ago Loyse had learned patience. Now she must use it again as a weapon against fear and the panic which was chill in her, a choking band about her throat, a crushing weight upon her. Patience—and her wits—that was all they had left her.

It was quiet enough in this room where she had been left to herself at long last. There was no need to rise from the chair and try the window shutters or the door. They had even stripped the bed curtains from their supports. Lest she try some mischief against herself, she supposed. But it had not come to that yet; oh, no, not to that. Loyse's lips shaped a shadow smile, but the glint in her eyes was not that of amusement.

She felt very faint, and it was hard to think clearly when the room spun in dizzy side-slips from time to time. Nausea had racked her on board the coasting ship—then she had not eaten for a long time.

How long a time? She began to reckon childishly on her fingers, turning them down in turn, trying to put a memory to each. Three, four, five days?

A face etched on her mind for all time—the dark-haired woman who had come to her in Es Castle in the early morning with a tale. What tale?

Loyse fought for a clear memory of that meeting. And the fear cloud grew thicker as she realized that this was no mental haziness born of nausea and shock, this was a blocking out which had no connection with *her* body or emotions. There had been a woman—Berthora! Loyse had a flash of triumph when she was able to set name to the woman. And Berthora had brought her out of Es Castle with a message.

But what was that message and from whom? Why, oh, why had she been so secretive about riding forth from Es with Berthora? There were fleeting memories of a wooded road, and a storm—with the two of them sheltering among rocks while rain and wind made fury in the night. Then, a meadow sloping to the sea where they waited.

Why? Why had she remained there so calmly with Berthora, feeling no uneasiness, no warning! Ensorceled? Had she been power-moved? But no—that she could not believe. Estcarp was friend, not enemy. And now that Loyse pieced together these ragged tatters of memory, she was very certain that Berthora had moved in haste and as a fugitive in enemy territory. Did Karsten also have its witches?

Loyse pressed her hands against her cheeks, cold flesh meeting cold flesh. To believe that was to negate all she knew of her own land. There were no witches in Karsten since the Old Race had been three times horned, outlawed to be killed on sight. Yet she was certain, just as certain, that she had been spellbound, spell-led, to that meeting with the ship from the south.

There was something more—something about Berthora. She must remember, for it was important! Loyse bit her knuckles and fought her queasiness, the haze in her mind, fought grimly to remember. At last she achieved a bit of a picture . . .

Berthora crying out—first in entreaty, and then in despairing anger—though it was her tone rather than her words that Loyse recalled. And one of those from the ship striking at her with a callous casualness. Berthora stumbling back, her hands on the sword which had given her death, so fast upon that blade that its owner could not pull it free. Then an order, and another man bending over Berthora, fumbling in her riding tunic, bringing forth a hand clenched about something, something Loyse had not seen.

Berthora had delivered her to Karsten, and had been paid with death. But to aid in that delivering Berthora had had some weapon beyond Loyse's knowledge.

How it had been done must not concern her now. That it was done . . . Loyse forced her hand down from her mouth, made it rest on her knee. She was in Kars, in Yvian's hold. If they had sought her in Estcarp, were seeking her now, they could only conjure as to where she had been taken. As for plucking her forth again—It would take an army to break open Karsten, such an army as Estcarp could not put in the field. Loyse had listened enough to the councils of war to know just how precarious was the Old Kingdom. Let them strip the country to invade Karsten and Alizon would snap down from the north.

In Verlaine once she had been one against all the might of Fulk, with no friend within that sea-pounded pile. Here she was one against many again. If she did not feel so sick and dizzy she could think more clearly! But to move made the floor under her dusty riding boots heave and roll as had the deck of the coaster.

The door opened and a flare of a hand lamp struck at her through the dusk, blinding her so that she must squint up at those who stood there. Three of them, two in the livery of ducal servants, one holding the lamp, the other a tray of covered dishes. But the third, that slender figure with a scarf about head and shoulders in masking concealment—

Putting down lamp and tray on the table the serving women left, closing the door behind them. Only when they had gone did that other come into the full light, twitch aside her veiling to view Loyse eye to eye.

She stood taller than the heiress of Verlaine, and her figure had a delicate grace Loyse could not claim. She wore her fair hair looped in intricate plaiting, the whole snooded in a gem-spangled net. And there were more jewels at her throat, her girdle, braceleting her arms above the tight fabric of her sleeves, ringing each finger. As if she had set out the wealth of her gem caskets with purpose to overawe the beholder. Yet, looking beyond all that glitter to her calm eyes, her serene expression, Loyse thought such a gesture could only be a screen. The wearer of that wealth might do it because it was expected of her, not because she needed support of her treasures at this meeting.

Now her hand, with its glinting burden, advanced and she picked up the lamp to hold it higher, facing Loyse with a measuring look which stung, but under which the girl sat unmoving. She could not match the other's beauty. Where this one was golden-haired, Loyse was bleached to fading; where this one was all grace, not studied but instinctive, Loyse was awkward angularity. Nor could she pride herself as to wit, for the Lady Aldis was noted for her astute moves in the murky waters of Yvian's court.

"You must have more to you than appears," Aldis broke the silence first. "But that lies far buried, my lady Duchess." The sober appraisal of that speech became mockery at its close.

Lamp still in hand, Aldis swept a curtsy which made her skirts swing in a graceful swirl not one woman in a hundred could have equaled. "My lady Duchess, you are served—pray partake. Doubtless the fare upon which you were forced to break your fast of late has not been of the best."

She returned the lamp to the table and drew up a stool, her manners a subtly contemptuous counterfeit of a servant's deference. When Loyse neither moved nor answered, Aldis set forefinger to lip as if puzzled, and then smiled.

"Ah—I have not been named to your fair grace, have I? My name is Aldis, and it is my pleasure to welcome you to this, your city of Kars where you have long been awaited. Now, does it please you to dine, my lady Duchess?"

"Is it not rather your city of Kars?" Loyse put no inflection into that question, it was as simply asked as a child might do. She knew not what role might aid her now, but to have Yvian's mistress underrate his unwilling wife seemed a good move.

Aldis' smile grew brighter. "Ill-natured tittle-tattle, gossip, such as should never have reached your ears, my lady Duchess. When the chatelaine is missing, then there needs must be someone to see that all is done mannerly, as our lord Duke would wish. I flatter myself in believing that you shall find little here, your fair grace, that must be changed."

A threat—a warning? Yet if either, most lightly delivered in a tone which gave no emphasis. But Loyse believed that Aldis had no intention of yielding what power she had here to a wife married for reasons of state.

"The report of your death was a sad blow to our lord Duke," Aldis continued. "Where he was prepared to welcome a bride, came instead an account of an open tower window, a piece of torn robe, and the sea beneath—as if those waves were more welcome than his arms! A most upsetting thought to haunt our lord Duke's pillow by night. And how greatly relieved he was when came that other report—that Loyse of Verlaine had been bewitched out of her senses by those hags of the north, taken by them as hostage. But now all is well again, is it not? You are in Kars with a hundred hundred swords to keep a safe wall between you and the enemy. So eat, my lady Duchess, and then rest. The hour is not far off when you must look your best to ravish the eyes of your bridegroom." The mockery was no longer light—cat-claws unsheathed to tear the deeper.

Aldis lifted the covers from the dishes on the tray and the odor of the food turned Loyse's emptiness into a sudden pain. This was no time for pride or defiance.

She smeared her hand across her eyes as might a child who is come to the end of a crying bout, and got to her feet, clutching at the bedpost to steady her steps. A lurch brought her to the table edge and she worked her way along the board to drop onto the stool.

"Poor child! You are indeed foredone—" But Aldis made no move to approach her and for that Loyse was thankful. A small part of her resented fiercely that the other watched while she had to use both hands to bring a goblet to her lips; her weakness was a betrayal.

But Aldis did not matter now. What did was restoring the wavering strength of her body, clearing her head. That Aldis had come here might in turn lead to something. Though Loyse could not yet see the advantage in the visit.

Warmth from the liquid she swallowed spread through her; the surface fear ebbed. Loyse put down the goblet. She did not want a wine-born muzziness clouding her thoughts. Now she pulled a bowl of soup to her and began to spoon it up, the savor of it reaching her. Duke Yvian was well served by his cooks. Against her will Loyse relaxed, relished her supper.

"Boar in red wine," Aldis commented brightly. "A dish you shall find often before you, lady, since our gracious lord relishes it. Jappon, the chief cook, has a master hand for it. My lord Duke expects us to mark his likes and dislikes and be attentive to them."

Loyse took another sip of wine. "Vintage of a good year," she commented, striving to hold her voice to the same even lightness. "It would seem that this lord Duke of yours has also a palate. I would have believed tavern wine more to his taste, since his first man draughts came from such casks—"

Aldis smiled more sweetly. "Our lord Duke does not mind allusions to his somewhat—shall we say—irregular beginnings. That he won Karsten by the might of his sword arm—"

"*And* the backing of his blank shields," Loyse cut in blandly.

"And the loyalty of his followers," Aldis agreed. "He feels pride in that fact and often speaks of it in company."

"One who climbs to heights must beware of the footing." Loyse broke a slice of the nut-flour bread in twain and nibbled its crust.

"One who rises to heights makes very sure that the footing on that height is smoothed," Aldis countered. "He has learned not to leave aught to chance, for Fortune is fickle."

"And wisdom must balance all swords," Loyse replied with a hill proverb. The food had drawn her out of her misery. But—no overconfidence. Yvian was no stupid sword swinger, easily befooled. He *had* won Karsten by wits as well as fighting. And this Aldis—Walk softly, Loyse, walk softly, beware of every leaf rustle.

"Our lord Duke is paramount in all things, with sword, in the council chamber and—in bed. Nor is his body misshapen—"

Loyse hoped her sudden freeze had gone unnoted, but she doubted that. And Aldis' next oblique shaft confirmed that doubt.

"They speak of great deeds done in the north, and that a certain misborn, misshapen churl who swings a stolen ax there led the van—"

"So?" Loyse yawned and then yawned again. Her fatigue was not pretended. "Rumor always wags a wide tongue. I have eaten; is it now permitted that I sleep?"

"But, my lady Duchess, you speak as one who considers herself a prisoner. Whereas you are paramount lady in all Kars and Karsten!"

"A thing I shall keep in mind. But still, that thought, as uplifting as it is, gives me not as much joy as some rest would do. I bid you good eve, my Lady Aldis."

Another smile, a tinkle of laughter, and she did go. But nothing covered the sound Loyse listened for—the scrape of key in lock. Paramount lady she might be in Kars, but this night she was also prisoner within this chamber—and the key lay in other hands. Loyse sucked her lower lip against her teeth as she considered what that might lead to.

She gave the room a measuring survey. The uncurtained bed, as was usual in a room of state, stood on a two-step dais above the flooring. There were windows in two walls. But as she loosed the inner shutters of one after another, she discovered beyond a netting of metal mesh through which she might thrust her fingers to the second joint, but no farther to freedom.

There was a chest against the far wall, wherein lay some garments she did not examine past the first glance. But she was still tired, her whole body ached to stretch out on the bed. There was one more task she set herself to, and it was one which left her weak and trembling. Sleep she must, but no one would come upon her unawares, for the table was now an inner barrier across the door.

Though she was so tired she felt that it would require a vast effort to raise her hand to her head, sleep did not come as Loyse lay there, staring up into the rafter frame which had supported canopy and curtains. She had not turned down the lamp and that made a fine glow by which she could see every part of the chamber.

In the past she had known a similar disquiet—strongest of all in that temple or shrine of the forgotten race where the hidden passages of Verlaine opened to the clean sky. The hidden ways of Verlaine . . . For a moment it was as if their dankness, the acrid odor of them, was about her now. Witchcraft! You could sniff it when you had known it before. Loyse's nostrils pinched as she drew in a deep lungful of air. After all, she did not know all the secrets of Estcarp—and once before she had had a part of one here in Kars, while she and Jaelithe had fished in many pools for such scraps of information as might aid the northern cause. So there could still be agents of the Guardians hereabouts.

The girl's hands balled into the covers on either side of her thin body. If she only had a measure of their Power! If she could loose a sending now— to be picked up by a receptive, friendly mind! She willed that fiercely, crying soundlessly—not really for help, but for a steadying sense of companionship. She had been alone once, but then had come Jaelithe, and Simon, the tall stranger whom she had instinctively trusted and—and Koris. A faint flush warmed her cheeks as she remembered Aldis' sneers. Misborn, misshapen. Not true—never true! Mixed blood, yes—so that he united two strains to his own despite—the squat, powerful body of his Tor mother's kin, the handsome head of his noble Gorm father. But above all men the one her heart fixed upon from the day she had found him with Simon, wearing blank-shield disguises, outside the gate here in Kars, drawn by Jaelithe's sending.

Drawn by a sending . . . But she could not send! Once more Loyse fought her inner barrier, striving to break through. For there *was* the scent of witch-craft or at least of some other thing hereabouts. She was so sure of that! It roughened her skin, made her alert, waiting.

Loyse slipped from the bed, went to set her hands on the table across the doorway. Her arms straightened, she was pushing at that barrier. But something in her still unlulled, still awake, battled against that compulsion to do this.

She backed away to the foot of the bed, facing the door. The key clicked, the latch loosed. The heavy slab swung back. Aldis again! For a moment Loyse relaxed. Then she stared into the other's face. It was the same, exactly the same, feature by lovely feature. Yet—no!

And how it had changed she could not tell. There was even a little mocking smile still playing about those generously curved lips, the same expression on the fair face. Only Loyse knew, with every inch of her, that this was not the Aldis she had seen before.

"You are afraid," Aldis' voice, also. Exact—yet—no! "You have a right to fear, my lady Duchess. Our lord Duke does not like to be crossed. And you have played him several ill turns. He must make you truly his wife, you know that, or his purpose will not be served. And I do not think you will relish the manner of his wooing. No, I do not believe you shall find him a gentle lover willing to sue for your accord in the matter! Because you are in some ways a trouble to me, I shall allow you this much, my lady Duchess."

Flashing through the air to land on the bed by her right hand—a dagger. More a lady's toy than the belt knives she had worn sheathed at her own hip, but still a weapon.

"A sting for you," the Aldis who was not Aldis continued, her voice falling to a soft murmur so that now Loyse could hardly understand her words. "I wonder how you will choose to use it, lady Duchess, Loyse of Verlaine, in one way—or another?"

Then she was gone. Loyse stared at the heavy wood of the now closed door, wondering how she had vanished so swiftly. As if she had been a thing without corporal body—an illusion.

Illusion! The weapon and defense of a witch. Had Aldis indeed ever stood there? Or was this some move on the part of an Estcarpian agent who could only aid Yvian's captive in so much? But she would not nurse that thread of hope unduly.

Loyse turned to look at the bed, more than half expecting to find the blade gone, an illusion. But no. It lay there and under her hand it was solid, the whole slim length of it to needle point. The girl brought it to her breast, fondled it from simple cross hilt to that point. So she was to use it, was she? On whom? Yvian or herself? The choice had not seemed to matter to Aldis, or the semblance of Aldis, who had brought it to her.

IV
Fulk and—Fulk!

Simon stood on the midstep of the stair listening. Below was the din of battle where the forces of Estcarp mopped up the main hall. The loud "Sul! Sul!" of the Sulcarmen echoed faintly to him. But he strained to hear something else, movement above. He had not been mistaken, of that he was sure. Somewhere ahead on this narrow stair was Fulk. And the cornered lord of Verlaine had the advantage of anyone who dare follow him to his last stand.

There! Scrape of metal on stone? What sort of a surprise was Fulk preparing for his pursuers? Yet Fulk, above all, they must take in order to carry out their plan for Karsten. And time worked against them as Fulk's ally.

Simon edged on, his left shoulder pressed to the wall. So far their plan was working. The wrecked ship on the reef had opened Fulk's shore gates, sent out his men, centered the attention of the keep there. So that the invaders had nearly occupied the hold before the castle garrison was aware of their move.

But that had not led to quick surrender; rather the wreckers fought as men must who have no escape behind, and an unforgiving enemy before. Only because Simon had been sent spinning out of one swirling segment of the hall battle had he seen the flight of the tall man, his helm gone so that his red-gold mane identified him. Unlike Fulk of all the legends Simon had heard, this skulker did not seek to rally his men, take the lead in the next furious drive against the Borderers. Instead he had dodged, run, sought this inner stair. And Simon, still with head ringing from the blow which had shaken him out of the press, followed.

Again, metal on stone. He was very sure of it. Some other weapon more forceful than sword or ax being readied? The stair took an abrupt turn to the right just beyond, a yard-square landing was all he could see, the step up the other angle hidden. There was a globe light burning, but pallidly.

The light flickered. Simon drew a quick breath. If the lamp was on the verge of failing . . . But the flickering followed a pulsating pattern, almost as if its power had been sapped at regular intervals. Simon took another step, and another—the third would bring him to the landing and so exposed to what might be waiting on the other flight of stairs.

Flicker, flicker—he found himself counting those blinks. And now he was sure that each drained energy. Simon had never learned the secret of the globe lamps, they could be governed in intensity by tapping on wall plates set below each one. But as far as he knew the globes themselves never had to be re-newed, and no one in Estcarp had been able to explain how they worked. Set in these castle piles ages ago their secret was forgotten.

Flicker again. Now the light was much dimmer. Simon whirled about the angle of the stair, his back to the wall, his dart gun ready. Four, six steps up and then the smooth forward run of a narrow corridor. At the top of those steps a barricade, stuff hastily dragged from rooms above. Was Fulk lying in wait to pick off the first to disturb that erection of stools and a table?

Somehow Simon was worried. Fulk's actions were so contrary to all he had heard of the coast-lord. These were the moves of a man trying to buy time. Time for what? All Fulk's forces were engaged below; he could not be attempting to assemble a relief. No, he was striving to get out himself! Why he was so certain of that Simon did not know, but he was convinced it was so.

Did Fulk know of an inner wall passage, was he hunting the exit now? No more sounds except that the muffled clamor from below lessened, the last of Fulk's men must be cut down.

The blink, blink of the light grew feebler. Then he did hear a faint sound, and fighter's instinct sent him scrambling down the stair angle. The white flash of an explosion! Simon, blinded by that glare, almost lost his footing. He rubbed his eyes.

Light, but no sound at all. Whatever force had been unleashed there was new to him. Now trails of smoke, acrid and throat rasping. Simon coughed, fought to see, but his eyes were still dazzled by the flash.

"Simon! What is here?"

Pound of feet on the stair. Simon caught a hazy glimpse of a winged helm.

"Fulk," he answered. "Up there—but watch—"

"Fulk!" Koris' long arm was out, solidly against the wall, supporting Simon. "But what does he up there?"

"What mischief he can, lord." More steps on the stair and Ingvald's voice to identify them.

"He is late to our meeting," Koris commented.

"Do not rush in—" At last he was able to see again. But the light globe was now far sped. Simon slipped up on the landing, forestalling Koris. The flimsy barrier was gone. Some charred bits of wood, a drift of ash and stains on the wall marked its site.

No sound, no movement from the hall or from the doors opening into that way. Step by step Simon advanced. Then he heard a small scuffling from behind the first door. Before he could move the great Ax of Volt swung down to hit that barrier. The door gave and they looked into a room, the window facing them was open, a trail of rope hung out of it, anchored within by the weight of a chest.

Koris laid the ax on the floor and set his hands to the rope. All the strength of his great shoulders and arms went into an upward pull as Simon and Ingvald moved to the window.

The night was dark, but not too shadowed to hide the scene below. That rope, meant to drop Fulk to a lower roof, was now ascending, even with Fulk's weight upon it, past the point where the wrecker lord would dare leap free. Only—

Simon saw the white oval which was Fulk's face turned up to him. The dangling man, coming up to their waiting grasp through a series of pulls by Koris, deliberately loosened his hold on that line. He screamed aloud, a dreadful cry, as if he were protesting against his own action. Had he, until that last second, really believed he had a chance to land safely? But when he crashed down he lay there. An arm was lifted and fell again.

"He is still alive." Simon reached for the rope. He did not understand the need which moved him now, but he must look upon Fulk's face.

"I must go down," he added as the rope end whipped in the window and he set about making it fast to his own waist.

"There is more in this than seems?" Koris asked.

"I believe so."

"Then down with you. But take care, even a broken-backed serpent wears fangs in its jaws. And Fulk has no reason to let his enemies live after him."

Simon scrambled through the window slit, swung out as they lowered him down. His feet touched the surface of the lower roof. As he threw off the loop, the rope whipped aloft, and he went to that crumpled figure.

His journey light showed the sprawled body clearly. And, as Simon went down on his knee he saw that, in spite of his injuries, Fulk of Verlaine still lived. By some chance the wrecker lord's head turned with infinite and painful effort so that the eyes could meet his gaze.

At that moment of meeting Simon's breath expelled in a hiss. He wanted to cry aloud his repudiation of what he saw there. Pain, yes—and hate. And something which was beyond both pain and hate—an emotion which was not of mankind that Simon knew. He said it aloud: "Kolder!"

This was Kolder, the alien menace in the face of a dying man. Yet Fulk was not one of the "possessed," the walking dead men whom Kolder used to fight its battles, the captives sapped of soul, made to cup within their bodies some enlivening power which clean humanity shrank from. No, Simon had seen the "possessed." This was something else again. Because what had been Fulk was not totally erased; that part which bore pain and hate was growing stronger, and that which was Kolder faded.

"Fulk!" Koris had dropped to the roof, come with a loping stride to join Simon. "I am Koris—"

Fulk's mouth worked, twisted. "I die . . . so will you . . . bog-loper!"

Koris shrugged. "As will all men, Fulk."

Simon leaned closer. "And as will those who are not men also!"

He could not be sure that that remnant of fading Kolder understood. Fulk's mouth worked again, but this time all that burst from his lips was blood. He strove to raise his head higher, but it fell back, and then his eyes were blank of all life.

Simon looked across the body to Koris. "He was Kolder," he said quietly.

"But no—not possessed!"

"No, but still Kolder."

"And of this you are sure?"

"As sure as I am of my own mind and body. Kolder in some manner, but still Fulk also."

"What then have we uncovered here?" Koris was already visualizing horrors beyond. "If they have other servants among us beside the possessed—!"

"Just so," Simon replied grimly. "I would say that the Guardians must know of this, and that speedily!"

"But the Kolder cannot take over any of the Old Race," Koris observed.

"So we shall continue to hope. But Kolder was here, and may be elsewhere. The prisoners—"

Again Koris shrugged. "Of those there are not too many, perhaps a dozen after that last battle in the hall. And they are mainly men-at-arms. Would Kolder pick such for its servants, save as possessed? Fulk, yes—he would be an excellent piece on their playing board. But look you at these and then tell us—if you can."

SUN WAS a thick bar across the table. Simon fought the need for sleep, finding in his smoldering anger a good weapon in his struggle. He knew her, this gray-robed woman with her hair netted severely back from her rather harsh features, the cloudy jewel, which was her badge of office and sword of war, resting on her breast, her hands folded precisely before her. Knew her, though he could not give her a name—for no witch within Estcarp had a name. One's name was one's most private possession. Give that too lightly to the play of many tongues and one had delivered one's innermost citadel into possible enemy hands.

"This then is your only word?" He did not try to modify his hardness of voice as he demanded that.

She did not smile, no expression troubled her calm gaze.

"Not my word, March Warder, nor the word of any one of us, but the *law* by which we live. Jaelithe—" Simon thought he detected a hint of distaste in her voice as she spoke that name—"made her choice. There is no returning."

"And if the power has not departed from her, what then? You cannot say that it is so by merely speaking words!"

She did not shrug, but something in her pose gave him the feeling that she had so dismissed his speech and his anger. "When one has held a thing, used it, then its shadow may linger with one for a while, even though the center core of it be lost. Perhaps she can do things which are small shadows of what once she could work. But she cannot reclaim her jewel and be again one of our company. However, I think, March Warder, you did not summon a witch here merely to protest such a decision—which is none of your concern."

It snapped down, that unbreakable barrier between the witches and those outside that bond. Simon took tight rein on his temper. Because, of course, she was right. This was no time to fight Jaelithe's battle, this was a time when a plan must move ahead.

He spoke crisply, explaining what must be done. The witch nodded.

"Shape-changing—for who among you?"

"Me, Ingvald, Koris and ten men of the Borderers."

"I must see those who you would counterfeit." She arose from her chair. "You have them ready?"

"Their bodies—"

She displayed no change of countenance at that information, only stood waiting for him to lead the way. They had laid them out at the far end of the hall, ten men selected from among the slain, led by the broken-nosed, scarred leader of the last defense who wore the insignia of an officer. And, a little apart, Fulk.

The witch paused by each in that line, staring intently into the pale faces, fitting them into her memory, with every mark of identification. This was her particular skill, and while any of her sisterhood could practice shape-changing upon the need, only one expert in the process could attempt such with the actual features of a man, instead of just a general disguise.

When she came to Fulk her survey was much longer as she stooped low, her eyes searching his face. From that lengthy examination, she turned to Simon.

"Lord, you are very right. There was more in this man than his own mind, soul, thoughts. Kolder—" The last word was a whisper, a husky sound. "And being Kolder, dare you take his place?"

"Our scheme depends upon Fulk entering Kars," Simon returned. "And I am not Kolder—"

"As any other who might be Kolder would detect," she warned.

"That I must risk."

"So be it. Bring your men for the changing. Seven and three. And send all others from the hall, there must be no disturbing this."

He nodded. This was not the first time he had known shape-changing, but then it had been a hurried grasping for quick disguise to get them out of Kars. Now he would be Fulk and that was a different thing altogether.

As Simon summoned his volunteers, the witch was busied with her own preparations, drawing on the stone flooring of the hall two five-pointed stars, one overlapping in part the other. In the center of each she placed a brazier from the small chest her Sulcar escort had carried in for her. And now she was carefully measuring various powders from an array of small tubes and vials, mixing them together in two heaps on squares of fine silk which had lines and patterns woven into their substances.

They could not strip the bodies, lest the stains and rents betray them. But there was plenty more clothing within the castle, and they would use the weapons, belts, and any personal ornaments the dead had worn, to finish off the picture they must present. This was heaped together waiting the end of the ceremony.

The witch cast her squares of silk into the braziers and began a low chant. Smoke arose to hide the men who had stripped and were now standing, one on each star point. The smoke mist was thick, wreathing each man so that he could not believe that there was anything outside the soft envelope about him. And the chanting filled the whole world, as if all time and space trembled and writhed with the rise and fall of words none of them could understand.

As slowly as it had come the smoke mist ebbed, reluctantly withdrawing its folds, returning once again to the braziers from which it had issued. And the aromatic scent which had been a part of it left Simon lightheaded, more than a little divorced from reality. Then he felt the chill air on his skin, looked down at a body strange to him, a heavier body with the slight beginning of a paunch, a feathering of red-gold hair growing on its skin. He was Fulk.

Koris—or at least the man who moved from Koris' starpoint was shorter— they had selected their counterparts from men not too far from their own physical characteristics; but he lacked the seneschal's abnormal breadth of shoulder, his long dangling arms. An old sword slash lifted his upper lip in a wolfish snarl, enough to show a tooth point white and sharp. Ingvald had lost his comparative youth and had fingers of gray in his hair, a seamed face marked by many years of evil and reckless living.

They dressed in clothing from the castle chests, slipped on rings, neck chains, and buckled tight the weapons of dead men.

"Lord!" One of the men hailed Simon. "Behind you—it fell from Fulk's sword belt. There."

His pointing finger indicated the gleam of metal. Simon picked up a boss. The metal was neither gold nor silver, but had a greenish cast and it was formed in the pattern of an interwoven knot of many twists and turns. Simon searched along the belt and found the hooks where it once must have been fastened, snapped it back into place. There must be no change in Fulk's appearance, even by so small an item.

The witch was returning her braziers to the chest. She looked up as he came to her, studying him narrowly, as an artist might critically regard a finished work.

"I wish you well, March Warder," she told him. "The Power be with you in full measure."

"For those good wishings we thank you, lady. It is in my mind that we shall need all such in this venture."

She nodded. Koris called from the door. "The tide changes, Simon, it is time we sail."

V
Red Morning

S ignal flags!" One of the knot of men at the prow of the coaster, now being worked by sweeps up the golden river in the early morning, nodded to the flutter of colored strips from a pole on the bank beside the first wharf of Kars.

He who wore a surcoat gaudily emblazoned with a fish, horns on snout and sloping, scaled head against a crimson square, stirred, his hand going to his belt.

"Expected?" He made an important question of that one word.

His companion smiled. "For what we seem, yes. But that is as it should be. It remains to be seen now whether Yvian is ready to welcome his father-in-law per ax with kindness or the sword. We walk into the serpent's open mouth, and that can snap shut before our reinforcements arrive."

There was a low laugh from the third member of the party. "Any serpent closing his jaws upon us, Ingvald, is like to get several feet of good steel rammed up through its backbone! There is this about blank shields—they are loyal to the man who pays them, but remove that man and they are willing to see reason. Let us deal with Yvian and we shall speedily have Kars thus!" He held out a brown hand, palm up and slowly curled fingers inward to form a fist.

Simon-Fulk was wary of Koris' impetuous estimate of the odds. He did not underrate either the seneschal's fighting ability nor his leadership, but he did question this feverish drive which kept the other at the prow of the coaster all the way up river, staring ahead as if his will could add to their speed. Their crew were Sulcarmen who, as merchants, had made this run before and knew every trick of inducing speed, all of which they had brought into action since they had entered the river's mouth.

In the meantime, the main force of the Estcarpian invaders were coming down through the foothills, ready to dash for Kars when the signal came and that signal . . . Simon-Fulk, for the dozenth time since they had boarded the coaster, glanced at the tall basket cage now draped in a loose cover. In it was the Falconer's addition to their party. Not one of the black-and-white hawks which served the tough mountain fighters as scouting eyes and ears and battle comrades—trained not only to report, but also to fly at the enemy in attack, but a bird which could not be so easily recognized as belonging to Estcarp's allies.

Larger than those hawks which rode at Falconer saddle bows, its plumage was blue-gray, lightening to white on the head and tail. Five such had been discovered overseas by Falconers serving as marines on Sulcar ships. And these had been bred and trained now for three generations. Too heavy to serve as did the regular hawks, they were used as messengers, since they had a homing instinct, and the ability to defend themselves in the air.

For Simon-Fulk's purpose this bird was excellent. He did not dare take one of the regular hawks into Kars, since only Falconers used those birds. But this new breed because of its beauty would catch the attention, and it had been trained to hunt, so that Yvian would welcome it as a gift.

Ten men, a bird, and a whole city against them. This was a wild and foolish expedition on the face of it. Yet once before four of them had invaded this same Kars and had come out with their lives and more. Four of them! Simon's hand slipped back and forth along the ornaments on Fulk's belt. Three of them now—himself, Koris and somewhere, hidden in those buildings, Loyse. But the fourth? Do not think of her now. Wonder why she had not returned, why she had allowed him to hear secondhand from the witch at Verlaine that her mission had failed. Where was she—nursing that hurt? But she had accepted the cost of marriage between them, had come to him first! Why—

"We have welcomers, Lord!" Ingvald drew Simon's attention to the here and now.

A file of men at arms, surcoated alike with the badge of Yvian—a mailed fist holding aloft an ax—were on the wharf. Simon's fingers closed on his dart gun, the edge of his cloak discreetly veiling that movement. But on a barked order from their officer the waiting squad clapped their bared hands together and then raised them for an instant, palm out and shoulder high, the greeting of a friendly salute. Thus they were welcomed to Kars.

There was another turn out of barehanded, saluting troops at the citadel gate. And, as far as they had been able to judge on their march through the city, life in Kars flowed smoothly, no sign of unease.

But when they had been ushered with the formality of court etiquette into the suite of chambers in the mid-bulk of the citadel, Simon beckoned Ingvald and Koris to a bowed window. The seven they had brought with them from Verlaine remained by the door. Simon indicated them.

"Why here?"

Koris was frowning. "Yes, why?"

"Bottle us all up together," Ingvald suggested. "And if such handling gives us warning, they apparently do not care. Also—where is Yvian, or at least his constable? We were escorted by a sergeant-at-arms, no one of higher rank. We may be in guests' quarters, but they skimp badly on the courtesy."

"There is more wrong than insult for Fulk in this." Simon pulled off the dead man's ornate helm and leaned his head against the wall where a breeze ruffled the heavy forelock of red-gold hair which he had borne from the shape-changing. "To pen us together is a security move. And Yvian has no reason to honor Fulk. But here there is more—" He closed his eyes, tried to make that mysterious sixth sense deliver other than just the warning which had been growing stronger every step he took into the enemy's hold.

"A sending—there is a sending?" Koris demanded.

Simon opened his eyes. Once a sending had brought him into Kars, a dull pain in his head which marched him, hot, cold, hot, down streets and alley ways to Jaelithe's lodging. No, what he was feeling now was not the same as that. This—it drew him forward, yes—but that was not all. He tingled with a kind of anticipation, such as one felt on the verge of taking some irrevocable step. But also it was not altogether concerned with him. Rather as if he now moved on the edge of some action; brushed by it, but not the true focus point.

"No sending," he made belated answer. "There is something here on the move . . ."

Koris shifted the ax on which he leaned. Volt's gift was never far from his hand. But for his entrance into Kars it had been disguised with leaf foil and paint into the ornament weapon of a lord's constable.

"The ax grows alive," he commented. "Volt—" His voice sank to a whisper which could not reach beyond the window bay. "Volt guide us!"

"We are in the main block," he added more briskly, and Simon knew that Koris was reviewing mentally the plan of Kars' citadel as they had learned it from reports. "Yvian's private chambers are in the north tower. The upper corridor should have no more than a pair of guards at its far end." He moved towards the door of their own suite.

"How so?" Ingvald looked to Simon. "Do we wait or move now?"

They had planned to wait, but this compulsion Simon could sense . . . Perhaps the bold move was the right one.

"Waldis!" One of the men in Verlaine livery looked up alertly. "We have need for a sack of the bird's grain; it was forgotten in the ship—you seek to send a messenger for it."

Simon pulled aside the covering of the hawk's basket. Those bright eyes, not golden as was usual in that breed, but dark, regarded him intently, having in them a measure of intelligence—not human kind—but yet intelligence. He had never given the bird more than passing heed before, but now he watched it closely as he put hand to the fastening of its prison.

The feathered head turned, away from him, to the door of the room, as if the white one also listened, or strove to hear what could not be picked up by any ear. Then the curved beak opened and the bird uttered a piercing scream at the same moment Simon caught it too—that troubling of the very air about them.

Koris stared at Volt's gift. The shallow disguise of foil could not hide the gleam of the ax head, not brilliant as from sunlight on the burnished metal, but as if the weapon had, for an instant, held fire in its substance. And as suddenly that flash was gone.

The wide, white wings of the hawk fluttered and for the second time the bird screamed. Simon unlatched the cage door, held out his wrist and arm as a bridge. The weight of the bird was a burden, it could never have been carried so, but he held steady as it emerged. Then it fluttered over to perch on the back of a chair.

One of the Borderers held back the door and Waldis came in. He was breathing in great panting gasps and his sword was in his hand, the point of it dripping red.

"They have gone mad!" he burst out. "They are hunting men through the halls, cutting them down—"

It could not be Estcarp forces; they had not yet flown their signal! Nothing to do with them—unless something had gone widely wrong. Ingvald caught the boy's shoulder, drew him closer to Simon.

"Who hunts? Who fights?" he demanded harshly.

"I do not know. All of them by their badges are the duke's men. I heard one shout to get the duke—that he was with his new wife—"

Koris' breath hissed. "I think it is time to move." He was already at the door. Simon looked to the bird mantling on the chair back.

"Open the window casement," he ordered the nearest Borderer. He was being rushed, but that turmoil inside him was a sense of time running out. And if there was already trouble within the citadel they had best make use of that. He motioned and the hawk took off, out through the window, setting a straight course for those waiting. Then Simon turned and ran after Koris.

There was a dead man lying faceup at the end of the hallway—his face gone loose and blank. And he wore no mail, but the tunic of some official by its richness, the small badge of Yvian's service on one shoulder. Ingvald paused by the body long enough to point out a small rod of office, broken in two as if the dead had used it in a futile attempt to ward off the blow which had cut him down.

"Steward," the Borderer officer commented. But Simon had noted something else, the inset belt about the other's loose overrobe. Three rosettes, each set with a small wink of red gem in their heart. But where the fourth should have been to complete a balanced pattern was another ornament, a twined and twisted knot, the same as on the belt taken from Fulk, which he, Simon, now wore. Some new trick of fashion or—?

But Koris was already well up the stairs leading to the next floor, the path which would take them to Yvian's apartments and Loyse—if they were lucky. This was no time to speculate about belt ornaments.

They could hear uproar now, distant shouting, the clash of arms. Clearly an all-out struggle of some kind was in progress.

A shout from above, demanding. Then the thud of hollow-sounding blows. Simon and Koris burst almost together from the stairwell to see men trying to force the door at the far end of the corridor. Two swung a bench as a battering ram, while others of their fellows stood, weapons in hand, waiting for the splintering barrier to give.

"Yaaaah—" No real war cry, but a shattering scream of rage, out of Koris, as if all the impatience and frustration in him was boiling free. With a feline leap he was halfway along the hall. Two of the Karstenians heard him, turned to face this new attack. Simon shot and both went down, one after the other, the darts finding marks. He was never good in cut-and-thrust melee, having come too late to the learning of swordplay, and the niceties of ax attack were not for him. But there were few among either the Guard of Estcarp or the Borderers who could equal his marksmanship with dart gun.

"Yaaaaah!" Koris overleaped the first body, fenced the other toppling man with a shoulder. Now Volt's gift was doing bloody work with those at the battering ram.

Taking no heed for his back, Koris brought the ax down upon the door, and then sprawled forward as whatever bar had held it gave way. The swirl of Borderers had overtaken the remaining Karstenians, passed on after a moment of tight fast work, leaving only dead and dying behind.

Koris was already across the room, now snatching at a hanging to uncover a second and narrower stair. He seemed so sure of his objective that Simon followed without question. Another hall above and, halfway down it, a patch of yellow. Koris grabbed at that, and the folds of a travel cloak billowed out. He tossed it from him as he turned to face the only closed door.

There was no bar here. The first peck of the ax sent it crashing open and they looked into a bedchamber where the bed stood denuded of curtains, its coverings ripped and torn, sliding to the floor in an ominously stained muddle. The man whose fingers were still tightly clawed into those coverlets lay facedown. But his legs moved feebly as they watched, striving perhaps to lift him again. Koris stalked forward and put hand to the hunched shoulder, rolled him over.

Simon had never seen Yvian of Karsten, but now he did not mistake the harsh jet of chin, the sandy brows which were a bushy bar across the nose. The sleekness of soft living had not altogether wiped away the forceful mercenary who had fought battles to become my lord duke.

He wore only a loose overrobe which had fallen apart at Koris' handling so that the powerful body, seamed with old scars, was bare, save for a wide, wet, red band at his middle His breath came in great sobbing gulps, and with every moment of his arching chest, that band grew wider.

Koris kneeled beside the duke, so that he could look into Yvian's face, meet his eyes.

"Where is she?" It was asked with no outer heat, merely a determination to be answered. But Simon doubted if any words could now reach Yvian.

"Where—is—she?" Koris repeated. Under his hand the ax moved, catching light from the window, reflecting it into Yvian's face.

It seemed to Simon that the dying man's attention was not for his questioner, but rather centered on that uncanny weapon, long since fashioned by a nonhuman smith. Yvian's lips moved, shaped a word, and then a second audible enough—

"Volt—" He made an effort which was visible, looking from the ax to him who held it. And there was a kind of puzzlement in his eyes. Koris must have guessed the source of that for he leaned the closer to speak.

"Volt's ax—and I am he who bears it—Koris of Gorm!"

But Yvian's only answer was a ghostly grin, a stretch of lips which matched the slash of his death wound. He struggled to speak a moment later.

"Gorm, is it? Then you will know your masters. I wish them well—hell-cat—"

One hand freed its hold on the covers and he struck up, his closed fist merely touching Koris' jaw before it fell limply back, that last effort having carried him over the final border into the waiting dark.

Save for Yvian they found these chambers bare, nor were the other two entrances unbarred. Koris, who had led that whirlwind search, came back wide-eyed.

"She was here!"

Simon agreed to that, but Yvian's dying words were in his mind. Why had the duke spoke of "your masters" and connected that with Gorm? For Estcarp he would more rightly have said, "your mistresses." All Karsten knew that the council of witches ruled the north. But Gorm had had grim masters—the Kolder! Someone had started the fighting here, and it had not been Estcarp work. Loyse was gone; Yvian given his death wound.

But they had little time to search further. A band of the duke's guards came seeking their commander and the Borderer needs must fight their way to make a stand elsewhere.

It was late night and Estcarp was indeed in Kars, when Simon slumped in a chair and chewed at a strip of meat, trying to listen to reports, to assess what had been done here.

"We cannot continue to hold Kars." Guttorm of the Falconers slopped wine from a bottle into a cup, his hand shaking with fatigue. He had led the vans which had cut their way in from the north gate and he had been ten hours at the business of reaching where he now sat.

"We never intended to do so," Simon swallowed his mouthful to answer. "What we came here to do—"

"Is not done!" The full thud was Koris' ax punctuating his speech, heft butt against the floor. "She is not in the city, unless they have hidden her away so that even the witch cannot sense her, and that I do not believe!"

Ingvald settled a slinged arm with a grimace of pain. "Nor do I. But the witch says there is no trace. It is as if she never was—or now is—"

Simon stirred. "And there is one way of hiding which blanks out the power—"

"Kolder," Koris replied evenly. Simon thought that he already had accepted that dour possibility.

"Kolder," Simon agreed. "What have we learned from our prisoners—that suddenly, shortly after dawn yesterday, within the citadel some of the officers were given messages, all purporting to come from the duke, all definitely ordering them to quietly assemble the men under their command and then move in on each other! Each commander was told that one of his own fellows was the traitor. Could anything cause greater confusion? Then, unable to reach Yvian, even when they were beginning to realize their orders were wrong, the fighting became more intense as the rumor spread that Yvian had been killed by this one or that."

"A cover, and none of our doing," Guttorm stated, "it was only Yvian's own force involved."

"A cover," Simon nodded. "And the only act which might be so covered was Yvian's death. With his forces sadly split, too broken to organize a hunt for any murderer—"

"Maybe not just Yvian," Koris broke in, "maybe also—Loyse!"

"But why?" Frankly that puzzled Simon. Unless—his tired mind moved slowly but it moved—unless Kolder wanted her for bait.

"I do not know, but I shall find out!" Once more the butt of Volt's gift struck the floor with emphatic force.

VI
Duchess of Karsten

*L*oyse sat on the wide bed with her knees drawn up, her arms clasped around them, her eyes for that naked blade resting before her. What was Aldis' purpose? It could not be that the duke's mistress thought she would lose her power over Yvian. His need for Loyse was one of expediency only. And Aldis who had ruled him so long would not be easily unseated.

But—Loyse's tongue tip ran along dry lips as she remembered. When Jae-lithe had been a seeress in Kars months ago, Aldis had come to her secretly, to buy a spell to keep Yvian truly hers. And she must have believed in the necessity and efficiency of that or she would not have come. Then, in that later battle of wills—when the Guardians had used the most potent sendings they could conjure—Aldis (by image) had been the target of Jaelithe's attack. By all the arts of Estcarp certain temporary commands had then been planted in her to use her influence upon Yvian to further the witches' desires.

Now Loyse could not reconcile this present Aldis with the one she had so long thought upon. This Aldis would not have sought out Jaelithe, save for a contest of strengths. Had that been the real purpose of that visit to the witch of Estcarp? No! Jaelithe's own power would have revealed to her any such plan behind Aldis' seeking. She had then come honestly for her love potion.

And it was the truth that Aldis had been put under control for a period at the battle of wills before the taking of Gorm, even though that had been done from a distance and through images only. A failure there, too, Jaelithe would have known immediately.

Loyse gnawed on her lower lip and continued to stare at the dagger. She herself had failed in meeting with the duke's leman—she had been too assured when she should have been simple and bewildered. Somehow she had been turned inside out, assessed, by opposition she must respect—or fear? Aldis was not Aldis as she had expected her to be. And now, Aldis was playing some game of her own, in which she considered Loyse to be a piece to be moved at her pleasure.

Patiently the girl fought down both hot anger and the tinge of fear which followed the facing of that fact. Ostensibly she had been brought out of Estcarp because she was Yvian's wife by ax marriage. What did Yvian gain by her coming? First, what he had wanted from the beginning—Verlaine with its sea-bought treasure, its fortress, its lower harbor which, with the reef knowledge of its men, would give him a fine raiding port from which to prey on Estcarp.

Second, she was of the old nobility, and perhaps that fact might reconcile the aloof houses to Yvian. The tales out of Kars were that he desired to cut old ties with the mercenaries, establish his ducal throne more firmly by uniting with the rulers of the past.

Third—Loyse hugged her knees more tightly—third, her flight from Ver-laine, her joining with his enemies in Estcarp, must have been a goad to personal anger and a wound to his self-esteem. And—those few hints from Aldis—perhaps he chewed now upon the fact that she had sworn betrothal with Koris, that she preferred the outcast of Gorm to the Duke of Karsten. Her lips curled; as if there could be any question between them! Koris was . . . Koris! All she had ever wanted or could want in her life!

Three reasons to bring her here, yet behind them she sensed a shadowy fourth. And, sitting there in the gray of dawn, Loyse tried to summon it into the open. Not Yvian's reason, but Aldis? And why she was sure of that she could not have told either, but that it was true she had no doubt at all.

What could be Aldis' reason? To bring her here, frighten her with those threats of what Yvian had in mind for her—and then deliver into her hand a weapon. So that she might turn that against herself, thus disposing for all time of a rival? A surface reason that, but one which did not quite fit. So that Loyse might turn this length of fine polished metal against the duke when he would have his will of her? But Yvian was Aldis' hold on what she wanted—personal power within the duchy! At any rate Aldis' gift must be considered carefully.

Loyse slid from the bed and went to throw open the window shutters, allowing the wind to sweep across her face, freshen her dully aching head. She thought that it might be mountain wind, though it must have crossed long leagues to be from there. There was a harsh strength to it which she needed to beat against her now.

Somewhere they must be on the move—Koris, Simon, Jaelithe. Loyse did not doubt in the least that they were seeking her. But that they could reach into Kars she did not think possible. No—once more her future depended upon her own resources and wits. She went back to the bed and took up the dagger. Aldis' gift might be in some way a trap, but Loyse knew relief as her fingers closed about the weapon's chill hilt.

Her eyelids were heavy, she dropped back against the bed. Sleep . . . she must have sleep. The table across the door once more? But she could not summon the energy to pull away from the bed and place it so. With the mountain freshening the room she slept.

Perhaps it was those months she had spent campaigning in the border mountains, the need to be alert even in sleep, which had given her that guardian sense. Somewhere in the depths of exhaustion a warning sounded, so that Loyse was out of slumber and awake, though she lay for a long moment with closed eyes—listening, striving with every part of her to learn what chanced.

The faint protest of a hinge—the door! Loyse jerked upright amidst the tumbled covers of the bed. There was morning sun from the window she had left open. The rest of the room was dusky with shadows to which her eyes were more accustomed than were those of the man who entered.

Loyse scrambled to the side of the bed, plunged down, ignoring the dais steps, and put the wide expanse of that massive piece of furniture between her and the invader who had turned his back almost contemptuously as he put the key to lock, this time on the inner side of the door.

He was big—as tall as Simon—and his width of shoulder was not lessened by the folds of his loose bedgown. Big and probably as strong as Koris into the bargain. As he turned to face her with that assured leisureliness, she saw he was smiling a little. And to her mind it was a very cruel and evil smile.

In a way he was like Fulk, but with her father's vivid red-gold coloring blurred into drabber sandiness, the clean-cut features coarsened, a scar seam along his jawline adding an ugly touch. Yvian the mercenary, Yvian the undefeated.

Loyse, her back now against the stone wall, thought that Duke Yvian no longer believed that defeat could ever touch *him*. And that complete self-confidence was in itself a daunting thing to face.

He crossed, with no hurry, to the end of the bed and stood watching her, his smile growing broader. Then he bowed with a mockery bolder than that Aldis had used.

"We meet at last, my lady. A meeting too long delayed—at least I have found it so."

He surveyed her with some of the same contempt Fulk had used to batter her in the past.

"A whey-faced stick indeed." Yvian nodded as if confirming a report. "You have naught to pride yourself upon, my lady."

To answer—would that provoke him into action? Or could silence be a small defense? Loyse wavered between two courses. The longer he talked, the more of a breathing space she had.

"Yes, no man would choose you for your face, Loyse of Verlaine."

Was he trying to goad her into some protest or reply? Loyse watched him narrowly.

"Statecraft," Yvian laughed, "statecraft can drive a man to many things which would otherwise knot his stomach in disgust. So I wed you and now I bed you, lady of Verlaine—"

He did not lunge for her as she feared he might, but advanced deliberately. And Loyse, edging away from him along the wall, read his reason in his eyes. The chase and the capture—that inevitable capture—would provide him with amusement. And, she thought, he would prolong his pursuit of her, savoring her fear, faint hopes born from continued evasion, as long as he wished. Then when he tired, the end would come—at his time and on his terms!

So much would she humor him. With the agility she had learned among the Borderers Loyse leaped, not for the locked door as Yvian might have anticipated, but for the surface of the bed. He had not expected that and his clutch at her fell far short. She sprang again, aided in part by the elasticity of the hide lashings which supported the mattress. Her hands caught the cross ties meant to hold the canopy of state and hangings. Somehow she pulled herself up, perched there, drawing sobbing breaths from the effort which left her momentarily weak, but well above Yvian's reach.

He stared at her. No laughter, no smile now. His eyes narrowed as they must through the visor of his war helm as he looked out upon a battle.

No more talking, he was all purpose. But Loyse doubted if he could climb to rake her down. His weight must be almost double hers and the dusty strips on which she crouched were already creaking when she shifted position. After a long moment Yvian must have agreed on that. His fists closed about a heavy poster of the bed and he began to exert strength against that. Wood creaked, dust sifted into the air. The breath came out of Yvian's chest in heavy grunts. He had been softened by good living, but he still had the frame of a man who had killed more than one in camp wrestling.

The post was yielding and now he pulled at it with short jerks, right and left, loosening it in the bedframe while Loyse's frail perch shook back and forth under her, and only the finger-whitening grip she kept on the timbers held her safe. Then, with a splintering crack, the post broke forward and Yvian stumbled back. Loyse was thrown toward the floor. And the man who had regained his balance with a swordsman's quick double step was waiting for her, the grin back on his sweating face.

She threw herself sidewise as she came and this time she had Aldis' gift ready. Her shoulder met the standing post of the bed painfully, but, even as she cried out, Loyse slashed with the dagger at the hands reaching to crush her. Yvian snarled and dodged that stab. His robe caught in the splintered end of a broken cross piece which sagged across the bed and for a vital second he was a prisoner. He kicked at the girl viciously, but Loyse scrambled to put the bed again between them.

Yvian jerked his arm free. There was a moist white fleck at the corner of his now pinched lips and his eyes . . . Loyse held the dagger breast high and point out, her left arm still numb from the blow against the post. If she had been hampered by skirts she could never have kept out of his hands, but in riding clothes she was limb free and as agile as any boy. Swordplay she knew in part, but knife fighting was an unlearned art. And she was facing a man not only proven in battle, but lessoned in every kind of rough-and-tumble known to blank shields.

He snatched up a draggled sheet from the bed and snapped it at her viciously as a drover would snap a whip. The edge cut her cheek, brought a second cry of pain out of her. But though she gave ground, she did not drop her weapon. Again Yvian lashed at her, and followed that by a lunge, his arms out and ready to engulf her wholly.

It was the table which saved her then. She half fell, half slipped about its end, while Yvian came up against it, taking the full force of that bruising meeting on his thigh, the jar of it slowing him. He found the loose robe hampering and suddenly stopped, fumbling with its belt, striving to throw it off.

His eyes widened, set in a stare aimed across Loyse's hunched shoulder. That device was so old—Loyse's mouth twisted wryly—did he think to catch her in so simple a net? So thinking she was unprepared for the fierce grip

which caught her upper arm, pulling her back. There was a strong musky
scent, a softness of silken robe against her wrist. Then a white hand slipped
down her arm, twisted the knife from Loyse's hand as if she had no strength
at all.

"So you had not the nerve to kill." Aldis' voice. "Well, let one who has
use this!"

Yvian's amazement was now a black scowl. He stood away from the table
to take a quick stride forward. Then he stumbled, gathered balance and came
on, in spite of the steel in his middle, the stain growing on his robe. His hands
clutched for Loyse. She summoned up the last of her strength to thrust him
away. Surprisingly that shove from her made him stagger back and fall against
the bed, where he lay tearing at the covers.

"Why—?" Loyse looked at Aldis where she now stood bending over Yvian,
watching him with a compelling intentness as if willing him to show any
remaining signs of opposition. "Why—?" Loyse could get out no more than
that one word.

Aldis straightened, went to the half-open door. She paid no attention to
Loyse, her attitude was one of listening. Now the girl could hear it, too—a
pounding somewhere below, muffled shouts. Aldis retreated with swift running
steps and her hand was again about Loyse's wrist, but this time not to disarm
but to pull the girl with her.

"Come!"

Loyse tried to free herself. "Why?"

"Fool!" Aldis' face was thrust close to hers. "Those are Yvian's bodyguards
breaking in below. Do you want them to find you here—with him?"

Loyse was dazed. Aldis had thrown the knife which had wounded the Duke,
and his bodyguard were striving to force their way into his chambers. Why
and why and why? Because she could read no meaning into any of this, she
did not resist again as Aldis dragged her to the door. The Karstenian's whole
body expressed the need for haste, the unease. And to know that Aldis shared
fear made it worse for Loyse. To know the enemy was one thing, to be totally
caught up in chaos was infinitely worse.

They were in a small hall and the shouting below was louder. Aldis pulled
her on into the facing chamber. Long windows opened upon a balcony and
Loyse caught glimpses of luxurious furnishings. This must be Aldis' own
room. But the other did not pause. Onto the balcony they went and there faced
a plank set across to a neighboring balcony on the opposite wall. Aldis pushed
Loyse against the railing.

"Up!" she ordered tersely, "and walk!"

"I cannot!" The plank hung over nothingness. Loyse dared not look down,
but she sensed a long drop.

Aldis regarded her for a long moment and then brought her hand up to her breast. She gripped a brooch there as if gaining by that touch additional strength to rule Loyse by her will.

"Walk!" she snapped again.

And Loyse discovered that it was as it had been with Berthora, she was not in command of her body any more. Instead, that which was she appeared to withdraw into some far place from which that identity watched herself climb to the plank and walk across the drop to the other balcony. And there she remained, still in that spell, while Aldis followed. The Karstenian pushed aside their frail bridge so that it fell out and down, closing the passage behind them.

She did not touch Loyse again, there was no need to. For the girl could not throw off the bonds that held her to Aldis' desire. They went together through another room and then into a wider chamber. A wounded man crawled there on his hands and knees. But, his head hanging, he did not see them as Aldis swept her captive on, both of them running now.

Loyse saw other wounded and dead, even the swirl of small fighting groups, but none took any notice of the two women. What had happened? Estcarp? Koris, Simon—had they come for her? But all those they saw locked in combat were Karsten badges, as if the forces of the duke had split in civil war.

They reached the vast kitchens, to find those deserted, though meat crackled on the spits, pots boiled and pans held contents which were burning. And from there they came through a small courtyard into a garden of sorts with straight rows of vegetables and some trees already heavy with fruit.

Aldis pulled the long skirt of her outer robe up over her forearm as she ran. Once she stopped when a tree branch caught in her jeweled hairnet, to break it, but a portion of the twig still stuck out of the net. That she had a definite goal in mind Loyse was sure, but what it might be she did not know until they were splashing among reeds at the borders of a stream. There was a skiff there and Aldis motioned to it.

"Get in, lie down!"

Loyse could only obey, the wash of water wetting through her breeches, over the tops of her boots. Aldis scrambled in and the skiff rocked with her movements as she huddled beside Loyse, pulling over both of them a musty-smelling strip of woven rushes. Moments later Loyse felt the boat move ahead, they were being pulled along by the current, probably toward the river dividing Kars.

The smell of the matting was faintly sickening, and the water washing in the bottom of the boat had a swamp stench to it. Loyse longed to lift her head and breathe clean air again. But there was no disobeying Aldis' orders. Her mind might rage, but her body obeyed.

As the skiff bobbed on Loyse heard sounds which meant they had reached the river. Now where was Aldis going? When she had ridden with Berthora she had accepted all their actions as right and normal, had been so ensorceled that she had not feared or understood what she was doing. But this time she knew that she was under a spell which would make her do just as Aldis wished. But why—why for everything which had happened to her?

"Why?" Aldis' voice soft close to her ear. "You ask why? But now you are duchess, my lady, all this city, all the countryside beyond is yours! Can you understand what that means, my little nothing out of nowhere at all?"

Loyse tried, she tried very hard to understand but she could not.

There came a hail and Aldis sat up, the matting falling away so that the river air was on them. The rounded side of a ship rose not too far away, and Aldis was reaching for a rope tossed to them from that vessel.

VII
The High Walls of Yle

Simon sat in the bowed window, his back to the room and those it held. But he could hear—the panther-pacing of Koris, the men reporting, receiving orders, departing again. This was the nerve center of the Estcarpian invasion force and beyond was the city they had taken in an audacious leap and so precariously held. That they continued to so hold it was rank folly, but whether Koris could be made to accept that truth Simon had some doubts. If the seneschal's present mood continued he might try pulling apart the very stones of the buildings, searching for what he would not admit was gone.

Could he blame Koris for this present single-mindedness which was like to imperil their whole cause? Objectively, yes. A half year ago Simon would have witnessed but not understood the torment which tore the younger man now. But since then he had taken to himself his own demons. Perhaps he did not snarl and pace, pounce upon all comers with a demand for news.

However their cases differed in this much: Koris had been bereft by the enemy of what he had come to treasure most; Jaelithe had gone from Simon by her own will, gone and not returned. And by that he was forced to gauge the depth of the rift which had opened between them. Would she have been content had she not awakened to that shadow of power days ago? Or had that return in part of what she had once had brought home to her the loss as she had not realized it, even when she surrendered her jewel upon their marriage? Simon fought his own thoughts, strove to batter them away and consider the problem at hand—that Kars was theirs for a space, that Yvian lay dead, and that Loyse was gone, and no man they had captured knew the manner of her going.

Estcarp and Kars—the problem to hand—and Koris not able to think straight while in his present mood. Simon came away from the window, to step in the path of Koris' pacing and catch the other's arm.

"She is not here. So we look elsewhere. But we do not lose our heads." Simon put snap in that with a purpose, trying to make his voice serve as might a slap across the face of a man caught in hysterical shock.

Koris blinked, broke Simon's hold with a roll of shoulder. But he had stopped pacing, he was listening.

"If she had run—" he began.

"Then perhaps she would have been seen," Simon agreed. "Think now: why would she have been taken? We come to this place and find that mischief was made among the duke's men. And that purpose could have been the death of Yvian or—"

"Some other reason." The voice made them both turn to face the witch who had ridden in with the Borderers. "For another reason," she continued, almost as if she were clearing her thoughts by putting them into words. "Do you not see, my lord captains, with Duke Yvian dead, his duchess has some claim to Karsten, especially since Loyse is of the old nobility and those clans would rally behind her. They would put her in rule so that they might use her as a shadow screen to cover their own power. This was all done by purpose, but whose purpose? Who is missing—from among the slain, from your prisoners? It would be better not to ask who is dead and why, but who is gone, and the why of that?"

Simon nodded. Good sense—bring Loyse to Kars, confirm her before the duchy as Yvian's consort—with Yvian, perhaps, knowing only a portion of that and believing that portion to be his own plan—and then, dispose of Yvian, use Loyse as a puppet to establish another rule. But which one of the nobles had so devious a mind, such a smoothly running organization as to make it work? As far as Borderer intelligence knew and that was, or Simon had thought it was, very thorough, there was none among the five or six leading families who had either the courage or the ability to set such a complicated plot in action. Yvian would not have trusted any of the once powerful clans to the point that any of their members could have operated so freely within his citadel. And Simon said as much.

"Fulk was not wholly Fulk," the witch replied. "There may be those here who are not wholly what they seem!"

"Kolder!" Koris pounded the fist of one hand into the open palm of the other. "Always Kolder!"

"Yes," Simon replied wearily. "We could not believe that they would give up the struggle with the fall of Sippar, could we? Manpower—or its lack—did we not long ago think that perhaps their greatest weakness? It may be that they can no longer process their possessed armies—at least not here—that what we captured at Gorm has seriously weakened them. If that be so, they may have decided to substitute quality for quantity in their forces, taking over key men—"

"And women!" Koris interrupted him. "There is one whom we should have found here that we have not seen—Aldis!"

The witch was frowning. "Aldis answered to the sending in the Battle of Power before the assault on Gorm. It may be that thereafter she had no place in Kars."

"There's one way to find out!" Simon strode to where Ingvald sat at a table recording data on a small voice machine the Falconers had brought, a refinement of those carried by their hawks on aerial scouts.

"What mention has there been of the Lady Aldis?"

Ingvald half smiled. "More than a little. Three times those messages which set these wolves at each other's throats were delivered by that lady. And she, being who she was in Yvian's confidence, they took her words as sober truth. Whatever coil was woven here that one had a hand deep in its spinning."

The witch had followed Simon across the chamber and now she rubbed her hands together, between their palms the smoky gem of her profession.

"I would see the private chamber of this woman," she said abruptly.

They went in a body—the witch, Simon, Koris, and Ingvald. It was a dainty bower and a rich one, opening from the same upper hall as that room in which they had discovered the dying Yvian. At the room's end long windows opened upon a balcony and the wind stirred the silken curtains of the bed, fluttered a lace scarf drifting from a chest. There was a musky scent which sickened Simon and he went to the open windows.

The witch, her gem still tight between her palms, walked about the room, her hands well out from her at breast level. What she was doing Simon could not guess, but that it had serious meaning he knew. Those hands passed over the bed, down its full length, swept across the two chests, the mirrored toilet table with its assortment of small boxes and vials carved from polished stones. Then, in midpassage over that array, the clasped hands hesitated, poised hawk fashion, and came down in a swoop, though nothing lay below that Simon could see.

She turned to face the men. "There was a talisman here—a thing of Power which had been used many times—but not our Power. Kolder!" She spat that in disgust. "It is a thing of changing—"

"Shape-changing!" Koris cried. "Then she who seemed to be Aldis might not be her at all!"

But the witch shook her head. "Not so, lord captains! This is not the matter of shape-changing which we have long used, this is a changing within, not without. Did you not tell me that Fulk was not Fulk, and still not completely possessed? He was different in that he fled battle where once he would have led his men to the end. But he ran to protect that which was in him, choosing to fall at the last to his death rather than be taken by you while it was a part of him. So will this woman be. For it is firm in my mind that she also carries that inside her which is from Kolder."

"Kolder," Koris repeated between set teeth. Then his eyes went wide and he said that word with a different inflection altogether. "Kolder!"

"What—?" Simon began, but Koris was already continuing.

"Where is the last stronghold of those cursed man stealers? Yle! I tell you— this thing which was once Aldis has taken Loyse and they head for Yle!"

"That's only guessing," countered Simon. Though, he added silently, it was a logical guess. "And even if you are right, Yle's a long way from here, we have good chance to intercept them." And so an excellent reason for prying you out of Kars before disaster is upon us, again he added mentally.

"Yle?" The witch visibly considered that.

Simon waited for an added comment. The witches of Estcarp were no mean strategists, if she had some contribution to make it would be to the point and worth listening to. But, save for that one word, she was silent. Only her gaze went from Koris to Simon and back as if she saw something that neither man could sense. However, she did not speak, and there was no chance of getting it from her by questioning, as Simon knew of old.

That Koris might be right they had proof before moonrise. Not wishing to linger in Kars, the raiders had withdrawn to the ships in the harbor, commandeering transports to take them west to the sea. The sullen crews worked under the guard of Estcarpian forces with a Sulcar commander in each ship.

Ingvald led the rearguard onto the last of the round-bellied merchant vessels and stood with Simon, looking back at the city where the whirlwind, partly of their making, had hit a day earlier.

"We leave a boiling pot behind us," the Borderer commented.

"Since you are of Karsten, would it have been more to your mind to stay to tend this pot?" Simon asked.

Ingvald laughed harshly. "When Yvian's murderers fired my garth and sent their darts into my father and brother, then did I swear that this was no land of mine! We are not of this new breed in Kars and it is better for us that we ride now with Estcarp, since we are of the Old Race. No, let this pot be tended now by who wills. I hold with the Guardians in the thought that Estcarp wants no land or rule beyond her own borders. Look you—do we strive to make Karsten ours now? Then we needs must stamp out a hundred rebel fires down the full length of the duchy. And to do that we should strip the northern keeps. For that Alizon waits—

"We have rid this city of Yvian, the strong man who crested its rule for long. Now will there be five, six of the coastwise lords tearing at each other's flanks to take his place. And, so embroiled, they will have no mind to trouble the north for a space. Anarchy here serves our cause better than any occupation force."

"Lord!" Simon turned as the Sulcar captain of the ship came up. "I have one here with a story. He thinks it worth selling, perhaps he is right."

He shoved forward a man wearing the grimed and stained clothing of a common sailor, who promptly bent knee in the servility of Yvian's enforcement.

"Well?" Simon asked.

"It is thus, lord. There was this ship. She was a coaster, but not of the usual order. Her men, they did not go ashore, though she was dock set for two days, maybe three. And they sent no cargo to the wharves, nor did they ride hold-filled when they came in. So we watched her, m' mate and me. And we saw naught, save that she was so quiet. But when the fighting started in the city, then she came to life. The men, they take out their sculls and cast off. But so did a lot of others, so that was not so different. Only all the others they kept goin' once they started—"

"And this ship did not?" Simon could not see the purpose, but he had confidence enough in the Sulcar captain's recommendation to listen the tale out.

"Just to over stream—" The sailor nodded to the opposite bank of the river, keeping his eyes respectfully on the deck planking. "There they sat on their sculls while the rest of those on the run headed upriver. Then there was this boat, a small skiff just drifting along—like lost from a tow. But they did some fast sculling to get it on the port side where it was hid. And it didn't come out again. Only after that they were on the move, headin' downstream instead of up."

"And you thought that odd?" Simon prompted.

"Well, yes, seein' as how your men were coming from that direction. O' course most of them were ferried across the river by then and hittin' the city. Maybe those others—they thought a try at gettin' back down to the coast was better than headin' inland on the river."

"Picked someone up from the skiff," Ingvald said.

"So it would seem," Simon agreed. "But who? One of their own officers?"

"This skiff, now," the Sulcar captain took a hand in the questioning, "who did you see aboard her?"

"That's what makes it so queer, sir. There weren't nobody. Course we did have no seein' glass on her, but all that showed above the gunnel was a piece of reed mat. There weren't nobody rowing or even sittin' up in her. Was they anybody on board, they was lyin' flat."

"Injured in the fighting?" Ingvald speculated.

"Or simply in hiding. So this ship then headed for the seacoast, downriver?"

"Yes, lord. And that there's queer, too—how she went, I mean. They was men standin' to her sculls right enough—only they was like makin' a play of it, just like the current was runnin' so fast they didn't need to do any more'n maybe just fend her off from some sandbank now and then. There's a current here, sure, but not as strong as that. You need scullin' if you want to make time and the wind's in the wrong quarter—which it was then. But they was makin' time—good time."

The Sulcar captain looked across the bowed head of the seaman to Simon. "I do not know of any way save sculls or wind to move in the river," he reported. "If a ship has such a method of travel, then that kind of ship I have not seen before, nor have any of my brothers. The wind and oars we know, but this is—magic!"

"But not of the Estcarpian kind," Simon replied. "Captain, make signal to the seneschal's ship. Then put me aboard her with this man also."

"Well, Captain Osberic," Koris turned to the Sulcar fleet commander when the story had been repeated to him, "is this a tale poured from some wine bottle, or could it be true?" That he wanted to believe that it was true, had already fitted it into his own quest, was apparent to them all.

"We know of no such vessel—that this man saw what he has told us, yes, that I believe. But there are ships which are not ours."

"This was no submarine," Simon pointed out.

"Perhaps not, but as they seem to copy now our shape-changing, perhaps Kolder might give another covering to a vessel as well. Perhaps in the confusion existing along the river while we were setting our men across, they took a chance on betraying their alienness to gain time they believed they needed."

Koris slipped the haft of Volt's gift up and down in his hand. "Downriver to the sea, then to Yle."

Only perhaps, Simon wanted to remind him. If the ship, small as it must have been to resemble the river craft, was really more than it seemed, it could be heading to Yle—or even overseas to the Kolder nest which lay no man knew where.

But Koris had already made up his mind. "The fastest ship you have, Osberic, our men for the sculls if need be. We're going after."

Only if the ship was ahead of them, it had made good use of its long head start. With night a wind came to fill the sail Osberic had set, and they slipped along at as smart a clip as any river vessel knew, not needing scull labor. Behind them the string of transports was nosing into the northern shore, to disembark the raiders who would ride for the border, leaving chaos behind them. Only Osberic's chosen ship and two others, with Sulcar crews pursued the river chase.

Simon had some hours of sleep, his cloak about him, the discomfort of Fulk's mail still heavy on his limbs. They had rid themselves of their shape-changed disguises, but the borrowed weapons and clothing they still wore. His sleep was uneasy, full of dreams which fell to fragments each time he awoke, though he was plagued with the thought that they were important. And at last he lay watching the stars, listening to the wind, and now and then the murmur of some Sulcar man on duty. Koris lay an arm's length away and Simon thought that perhaps fatigue had struck at last and the seneschal slept.

Yle—and Kolder. There would be no turning Koris aside from Yle—short of putting him in bonds by force. Yet, there was no taking Yle either. Had they not bit again and again on that hard nut these past months? They had won into Gorm because chance had taken Simon as a prisoner into that stronghold and made him aware of certain chinks in Kolder armor. But then Kolder had been confident, almost contemptuous of its opponents with their vulnerability to Kolder might.

The enemies' defeat in Sippar would have taught them a lesson. Had in this much—that there was now an invisible barrier about Yle by both land and sea—a barrier nothing, not even the Power of the witch probe, could pass. For months Yle had been sealed. If the garrison of that stronghold came or went, it was by sea, and not on the surface of that sea. The Kolder ships were submarines, three such had been taken at Gorm. But—

Simon knew again the doubts which had moved him months earlier when he had stood before the Council of Guardians and had given the opinion they had asked for: leave the things found at Gorm alone, be very careful of the alien secrets lest they unleash something they could neither understand nor control. Had he been wrong then? He wavered now. Yet something inside him still argued firmly that he was right, to use Kolder means was to deliver oneself in part to the enemy.

That the witches were exploring the finds on Gorm slowly, carefully, Simon knew. And that did not disturb him, for they would use every possible safeguard, and their own Power was a barrier which Kolder recognized. But to put into the hands of others those machines . . .

Yet they might have a way there of breaching Yle now. Simon had thought of it before, but never, not even to Jaelithe, had he put that thought into words. It might be that he alone could once more crack the shell of a Kolder fortress. Not via submarine—he had not the knowledge for that, and they had not yet discovered what motive force propelled those ships, unless it could be the mental power of the Kolder leader who had died with the metal cap on his head, failing his men at the last. No, not under the sea, but through the air. Those flyers lined up on the rooftop in dead Sippar—they might be the key to Yle. But to mention that to Koris would be the rankest folly.

VIII
Print of Kolder

"It is locked tight—" The curved blade of Volt's gift bit into the thick green turf viciously as Koris would have used it against the enemy. They stood on the heights looking across the seaward valley to Yle.

Gorm had been ravaged from the people of this time and world. But in Yle the Kolder had built on their own. One would, Simon thought, have expected them to raise towers and walls of metal. But they had used the stone common to Estcarpian architecture, the only difference being that buildings throughout the witch land were old, old with the seeming of having been born from the very bones and flesh of the earth which based them, rather than built by men. And this Yle, for all its archaic stone, was new. Not only new, but divorced from the soil and rock about it in a way Simon could feel, but not put into words. He believed that even if he had not known that this was a Kolder hold, he would have realized that it was not of Estcarp or any neighbor nation.

"There was a door there—" Koris pointed with his ax to the face of the now smooth wall below and a little to the right. "Now even that is gone. And no one can get an ell closer than that stream in the valley."

The barrier, much like the one which had kept all intruders out of Gorm, held them now from any closer investigation of the alien pile. Simon stirred uneasily. There was a way. That kept nibbling at his mind through the days since they had left Kars, until he was at war with himself.

"They must enter or leave under the sea, as they did in Gorm."

"So do we turn our backs now and say we are beaten; Kolder has won? That I do not say, not while breath fills my lungs and I have arm strength to swing this!" Once again the ax sliced turf. "There is a way—there must be!"

What pushed Simon then to say what he had sworn to himself that he would not? But the words almost spoke themselves.

"There might be a way—"

Koris whirled, his ungainly body in a half crouch as if he fronted an adversary in a duel.

"By sea? How can we—?"

Simon shook his head slowly. "Remember the fall of Sulcarkeep," he began, but Koris took the words from him.

"By air! Those flying ships at Sippar! But how can we use them, not knowing their magic." His bright eyes demanded things of Simon. "Or do you know that magic, brother? In your tales of your own world you have spoken of such as an aid in your wars. To turn their own weapons against this scum—aha— that would be a good hosting! Aiiiii!" He tossed the great ax into the air and caught it by the haft, his head up so that the sun struck full on his face. "To Gorm then—for these flying ships!"

"Wait!" Simon caught at Koris' arm. "I am not even sure we can fly them."

"If they can be flown to crack this viper den, then we shall do it!" Koris' nostrils were pinched, his mouth a forbidding seam above the grim line of his jaw. "I know that to use alien magic is a chancy thing, but there comes a time when a man grasps all or any weapons to give him aid. I say we go to Sippar and get what we must have."

Simon had not been back to the horror which was Gorm's chief city for months. He had had no desire to be one of those who had combed the buildings which were tombs for the deluded islanders who had welcomed Kolder to aid in a dynastic battle. Simon had had enough of Gorm and Sippar in the fighting which had driven Kolder from that snug nest.

Today he discovered that there was another reason beside those old horrors which moved him to hatred for the halls of Sippar. He stood again in what had been the control chamber of that strange network, where the gray-clad Kolder officers had sat at their tables before their installations, all governed by the capped leader, thinking out—Simon was sure—the orders which had motivated all life within the captured citadel. For moments out of time he himself had shared the thoughts of that leader and so learned the source of Kolder—that these aliens like himself had come through some weird door in space and time to this world, seeking a refuge from disaster at their heels. Yes, he had shared the thoughts of Kolder, and now as he stood there again, once more that scrap of another's memory seemed twice as vivid, as real as if even here and now they were joined mind to mind—though that other mind had been many months dead.

But it was not only with the Kolder that Simon had shared in this hall. It was here that the witch of Estcarp with whom he had shared many ventures had laid aside her jewel, given into his keeping her life, by her standards, when she had spoken her name—that most intimate possession which must not be yielded to another lest Power be passed to that other, Power over one's innermost self. Jaelithe—

Simon waited for the familiar stab of hurt to follow fast on the heels of memory. But this time it was not so sharp, rather as if between them hung a softening shield of indifference. The Kolder memory was far the keener, and Simon knew, with unease, that Jaelithe's defection had not troubled him with the same urgency since he had come out of Kars. Yet—yet they had held a good thing between them, a true thing—or so he had believed. And the loss of that left a wound which might heal in time, yet the scar would not vanish.

Why? The witch had been explicit at Verlaine. For Jaelithe, no return was allowed. Did she hate him now so that she could not bear to see him? No message even. Kolder! Now was the time to think of Kolder and the confounding of that chill evil, and not of things broken past the mending. Simon concentrated on Kolder.

"Simon!" Koris called from the doorway. "The sky ships—they are as we left them."

Ships for the invasion of Yle. Why had he ever thought it wrong to use their own weapons against the enemy? Why did he see danger lurking in the alien machines? Of course Koris was entirely right in this matter. To crack the shell of Yle what better hammer than those its builders had devised?

They climbed to the roof where stood the flyers. Two had been in the process of being repaired, parts and tools still laid out by workmen who had vanished. Simon went straight to the nearest. But this was simple—there was no need to worry about getting it into action again. One did this and this, tightened this . . .

He was working with confidence, some part of his brain directing every movement of his hand, as if conning a detailed chart. Simon slipped the last fitting into place, then climbed into the cockpit, thumbed the starter button, felt the vibration purr. It was all right, he could lift.

A shouting below, loud, and then dying into the distance as the flyer took off. Simon adjusted the controls. Yle, he was bound for Yle—a task of importance waiting him. The barrier could not hold much longer; there had been too many calls upon the central energy. Sooner or later the barbarians would breach it. The pound of the Power of these cursed hags would then shake the walls down.

Cursed hags? Yes, tricky, evil all of them! Wed a man and then walk away from him without a backward look, deeming him too stupid to hold to. Hag— hag!

Simon made a song of that word as he flew over the waters of the bay. Gorm—they had lost Gorm. Perhaps they would lose Yle—for now. But the plan was working. Ah, yes, just let the gate be opened and the great energy tapped, then these stupid savages, those hags would meet with a reckoning! Sippar's fall would be nothing to what would happen in Es. Push here, pull there, move a savage to action, ring in the hags with trouble. Win time—time was what was needed—time for the project at the gate.

So give up Yle now if need be. Let the barbarians believe they had won again, that Kolder was driven away. But Kolder would only withdraw to its source, to wax stronger again—then to move, renewed, straight into the heart of opposition—Es itself!

Simon blinked. Under his confidence, this new and heady knowledge of what was to be done and why, there was a writhing discomfort, as if a fighter held down a still struggling opponent he could not quite master. Ah, there was Yle. And they would be waiting. They had known, they had summoned—and now they waited!

His hands moved on the controls though he was not really conscious of any need for those movements. Flashes inland—the barbarian forces. His mouth shaped a sneer. All right, let them have their worthless triumph here. By the time they broke in with the aid of the hags there would be nothing left worth the gaining. Down now; he must set down on this roof.

The landing gear touched cleanly. For a moment Simon looked about dazedly. This—this was Yle! How had he come here? Koris, the forces . . . His head turned—no, this was true, no dream. He sat alone in a Kolder flyer from Sippar! There was pain in his head, a sickness in his middle. His hand fell from the controls, his fingers without his orders went to Fulk's sword belt, touched a boss there, began to trace its curves and indentations.

Yes, this was Yle and his task was only beginning. They were coming now, those he must take from this place before it fell to the hags and their savages. A square opened in the roof and from that emerged a rising platform bearing two women. That one—she would give the orders—she was the one who had worked so ably to further the plan in Kars. And the one walking under full control by her side—she was the pawn to be played!

Simon pushed open the cabin door and waited, still in the pilot's seat. Loyse—again that stir under the surface within him, but less now, more easily pushed aside. She was staring at him, her eyes wide and wild, but she was under control, they would have no trouble with her. Already she had settled as ordered in the seat behind him. Now that other—Aldis. Aldis?

"To sea."

He did not need that order from her. Simon was pricked by irritation. He knew as well as she where they must fly. They spiraled into the air.

Odd. Mist growing thicker. Aldis leaned forward from beside her charge, eyeing that gathering cloud outside the cabin as if in fear. And she was right— this was some devilment of those hags. But they could not control the flyer, nor turn him from his course, even though they could bewilder his eyes . . . his eyes . . .

Simon stared. Something white moving on the course of the flyer, keeping pace effortlessly, a little above and ahead. Of course, that was his guide—just keep with that and he need not worry about the mist. They flew on but there seemed no end to the fog which enclosed them. The hags fought hard, only they could not control the flyer. Men they might bend to their purposes but not machines, never the machines! With machines one could be sure—be safe!

The mist was more than blinding, it was confusing, too. Perhaps it was not wise to stare into its eddying mass. But if he did not he would lose sight of that white guide. . . . What was it? Simon could not make it out clearly, always some tendril of the mist blurred its outline when he stared intently.

On and on. In the mist time was distorted, too. Some more of their so-called "magic." Ah, they were artful in deceit, all those witches!

"What are you doing?" Aldis leaned forward, her gaze now on one of the dials among the controls. "Where are we going?" Her voice was louder and shriller with that second demand.

"What is ordered." Simon was again irritated by the necessity for answering her. She had done good work, this female, but that was not to say that she had any right to question *him*, his competence, his actions.

"But this is not the course!"

Of course it was! He was obeying orders, following his guide. How dared she say that?

Simon looked down at the dial. Then his hand went to his head. Dizzy—he was dizzy. No need to look at the dials—just follow the white guide, that would make all right. "Be quiet!" he flung at the woman behind him.

But she would not. Now she pulled at his arm. "This is not the way!" She screeched that until her voice hurt his ears. His seat behind the controls was too cramped to let him turn far. But he thrust at her with his right hand pushing her back and away.

She fought back, striving to get at him, her nails raking at the flesh across the back of his hand, and he feared to lose course, have the white guide hidden by the thick enclosure of the mist. A backhand push made her gasp and flinch and Simon's attention was again for that half-seen thing ahead.

Only now he did see it fully—just for an instant. A bird—a great white bird! A white bird! He had known a white bird before—and the mist left his mind. The white hawk, that trained messenger they had carried into Kars—into Kars . . .

Simon twisted, a small choked cry forced out of him. Kolder! Kolder influenced thoughts, leading him—He stared down at his hands on the controls, totally ignorant now of what they must do, of how to keep the flyer aloft. Panic was a sharp, sick taste in his mouth. Somehow he had been used. His left hand groped down hunting—hunting what? Fascinated Simon watched that movement he had not consciously willed. The fingers touched Fulk's belt, slipped swiftly along to that entwined knot of green metal which did not match the other bosses. That!

Now he did use his will to pull his hand away—a struggle which left him sweating. He turned his head. Aldis' hands were tight to her breast, she eyed him with a dark hate, but under that—was it fear?

Simon caught one of her slim wrists, pulled her hand away from what it sought to conceal. Her other hand clung the tighter, but he caught a glimpse of glinting green. Whatever strange talisman had been Fulk's, Aldis wore its match. His own hand jerked, twitched, he could hardly keep it away from the belt ornament.

Under them the flyer lurched, dived through the mist. If he did not replace his hand he would not be able to pilot them safely, that much Simon guessed.

But he would also return to the bondage which had made him serve Kolder. To crash might mean all their deaths. To accept Kolder control at least postponed that for a space, and time might fight on his side. Simon no longer resisted. His fingers flashed to the intricately carved bit of metal, traced its pattern.

He was—where? What had happened? Tricks, the hag tricks—they had befuddled him. No more, no more of those!

A scream—not from any human throat. Coming straight at the cabin window, as if to fly into his face, that bird, its cruel beak open. Simon's hands flew to the controls in reflex action, striving to pull under that determined attack. Out of the curls of mist a shadow—a red shadow which took on too much substance. The flyer sideswiped that, the machine spinning from impact. Aldis' screams were louder and shriller than the hawk's. Simon cursed as he fought for control. They were still airborne but he could not bring them up, gain any altitude. Sooner or later they were going to land and the best he could do was to try to touch down under power.

Simon fought the stubborn machine for that slim chance. They struck, a surface still hidden in a blinding mist—bounced—set down again. Simon's head hit the cabin wall and he was not truly aware when they were still, the flyer tilted at an angle, nose down. Mist pushed exploring fingers through the door, now cracked open. And with it came a rank stench, the smell of swamp, overpowering with stagnant water and rotting vegetation. Aldis pulled herself up, looked about, drew a deep, explorative breath of that exhalation of decay. Her head turned as if impelled by some impulse and her hand stirred on the Kolder token.

She leaned forward, but quickly halted that as the flyer rocked. Her hand caught at Simon, pulled off his helm. With a tight finger hold in his thick hair she dragged his lolling head back.

There was a trickle of blood on his left temple, his eyes were closed. But the fact that he must be unconscious seemed to make no difference to the woman. Her grasp on his hair held his head as close to her lips as she could manage. And now she spoke—no words of Karsten, nor of the older dialect of Estcarp—but a series of clicking sounds, more the beat of metal against metal than any human speech.

Though his eyes did not open, his head moved. He pulled feebly against her hold, but she did not yield to his struggle. For the second time she repeated her message. Then she waited. But he did not rouse. When Aldis released her grip his head fell forward on his chest.

The woman gave an exclamation of irritation. She strove for a view outside and was rewarded by sighting the twisted skeleton of a long dead tree, its broken branches hung with wisps of pallid moss swaying in the wind. The wind was also driving out the mist, clearing a view which did not lead one to optimism.

Green-scummed water in pools, from which a wood of dead trees protruded, as might skeleton hands raised in threat to the sky, bloated growths anchored to the trees. As she watched, one of those came to life, an obscene lizardlike thing of splotched skin and toothed jaws crawling towards the flyer.

Aldis' hand pressed tight against her mouth. She was trying to think. Where could they be? This country was beyond her knowledge and the knowledge of those she served. Yet, her head again turned to the right—*they* were here— or one who served them was. And that meant help. Her hands cupped about the token, she bent all her forces into a summons.

IX
Torman's Land

Simon opened his eyes. The pain in his head seemed one with the greenish light about him. He moved and what supported him responded by rocking in a way which was a warning even his dimmed consciousness could understand. He looked up—to face nightmare!

Only the transparent shell of the cabin window kept that toothed horror from him. Its claws raked the surface of the flyer as it lumbered across the nose of the machine. Unable to move Simon followed that slow progress with his eyes. It had some vague resemblance to a lizard, but its bulk and awkward movements were unlike the eagle litheness of those creatures as he had seen them in his own world. This thing had a leprous, warty skin, as if it had been stricken by some foul disease. Now and then it paused to view him, and there was a malignity in those large whitish eyes which gave terrifying purpose to its deliberate advance.

Simon turned his head with care. The door was open, sprung by the crash. A few more feet, and a little maneuvering by the lizard thing, and it would achieve its goal. He moved his hand by inches, drew the dart gun from his belt holster. Then he remembered the women. With all the care he could muster, Simon changed position, the flyer rocking. The lizard hissed, seemed to spit. A milky liquid hit the cabin window, trickled down its cracked surface.

He could not see Loyse who was immediately behind him. But Aldis sat there, her eyes tightly closed, both hands again over the Kolder talisman, her whole tense position testifying to intense concentration. Simon dare not move far enough to reach the door. The flyer seemed balanced on some point and it dipped nose down at any change of the distribution of weight within.

"Aldis!" Simon spoke loudly, sharply—he must break through the web she had woven about herself. "Aldis!"

If she did hear him the urgency of his voice meant nothing. But there was a breathy sigh from behind him.

"She talks with *them*," Loyse's voice, a shadow of sound, worn and weary. Simon caught at the hope it gave him. "The door—can you reach the door?"

Movement and again the flyer rocked. "Sit still!" he ordered. And then saw that the movement, as dangerous as it had been, had aided them in this much, the lizard thing was slipping, despite all its efforts, down the inclined slope of the flyer's nose. Its claws could not dig into the sleek stuff of the machine's surface.

It opened its mouth and gave voice to a hooting honk as, still scrabbling for a foothold, it went over the edge. On the ground, if the swamp surface could be termed "ground," it might yet find its way to the open door. Simon thought he dared not delay.

"Loyse," he said quickly, "move as far back as you can—"

"Yes!"

The flyer rocked. But the nose was rising, he was sure of that.

"Now!" From the tail of his eye Simon caught a glimpse of hands in action. Loyse was adding to his instructions with an idea of her own as she gripped Aldis by the shoulders and dragged her back in turn. Simon slid along the seat, his hand now on the edge of the open door. But he could not get in the right position to exert much strength and he could not bring it closed.

The flyer rocked violently as Aldis struggled in Loyse's hold, lying back upon the girl who had her in a fierce clutch. Simon struck and the Kolder agent went limp, her hands falling away from the enemy talisman.

"Is she dead?" Loyse asked as she pulled from beneath the limp weight of the other woman.

"No. But she will not trouble us for a space. Here—"

Together they pushed Aldis to the back and that change of weight appeared to establish the flyer so that it no longer swung under them, providing they moved cautiously. For the first time Simon had a chance to survey what lay beyond, though he kept watch on the door, his gun ready.

The half-immersed, dead wood, the scummed pools, and weird vegetation—this was like nothing he had seen before. Where they were he had no idea, nor could he tell clearly how they had come here. The stench of the swamp was in itself a deadening thing which clogged lungs and added to the pain in his head.

"Where is this place?" Loyse broke the silence first.

"I don't know—" Yet far in the back of memory there was something ... A swamp. What did he know of a swamp? Outside the moss on the long dead trees stirred with the dank wind. There was a rustling in a clump of pointed reeds. Reeds ... Simon frowned with pain and the effort at remembering.

Reeds and scummed pools—and a mist—those he remembered from far away and long ago. From his own time and world? No—

Then all at once for a second or two he was an earlier Simon Tregarth, the one who at dawn had come through a gate onto a wild moor under the rain. The Simon Tregarth who had run with a fugitive witch before the hounds of Alizon hunters—and they had skirted just such a bog while the witch had appealed to its indwellers for aid, only to be refused. So they needs must cut across the edge of the swampland and find elsewhere a refuge. The Fens of Tor! Forbidden country which no man save one had been known to enter and return from again. And that man had fathered Koris of Gorm. He had brought his Torwoman out and held her to wife, in spite of his people's hatred and fear of such blood mixing. But the heritage he had so left his son had been sorrow and loss. Tor blood did not mix, the Tor marshes were closed to all outsiders.

"Tor—the Fens of Tor." Simon heard Loyse gasp in answer.

"But—" She put out her hand. "Aldis was calling for aid. And yet Tor does not mix with outworlders."

"What does anyone know of the secrets of Tormarsh?" Simon countered. "Kolder has entered Kars, and I will swear that it walks elsewhere, as in Alizon. Only the Old Race cannot accept the Kolder taint and know it instantly for what it is. That is why Kolder fears and hates them most. Perhaps in Tormarsh there is no such barrier to mingling."

"She called. They will answer—and find us here!" Loyse cried.

"That I know." To go out into that swamp might well mean death, but it held also a thin promise of escape. To remain pent in the crashed flyer would lead but to recapture. Simon wished that his head did not ache, that he knew only a little of where they lay in the swamp. They might be only yards away from the border through which he and Jaelithe had fled. The trees, he decided, provided their best road. For all those which still stood, or leaned, an equal number lay prone, their length in a crazy pattern furnishing at least a footway over the treacherous surface.

"Where will we go?" Loyse asked.

It might be folly, to head into the unknown, but still every nerve in Simon screamed against remaining to be picked up by any force Aldis might have summoned. Slowly he unhooked that belt with its betraying boss. The long dagger and dart gun he would need. He looked at Loyse. She wore riding clothes, but had not even a knife at her belt.

"I do not know," he replied to her question. "Away from this place—and soon."

"Yes, oh, yes!" Carefully she edged about Aldis, balanced to look out the door. "But what of her?" Loyse nodded to the unconscious agent.

"She remains."

Simon looked out below. There were tufts of coarse grass crushed beneath the flyer. The machine had landed on the edge of what might be an islet of solid ground. So far, so good. The grass had been flattened enough so that he thought they need not fear any life lurking in it. Wherever the lizard thing had gone, it had not yet appeared near the door. Simon dropped out, his boots sinking a little into the footing but bringing no ooze of water. Holding out his hands to Loyse, he eased her down and gave a little push towards the rear of the flyer.

"That way—"

Simon pulled at the door, setting the flyer to rocking. But the jammed metal gave as he exerted his full strength. That would shut Aldis in and—well, he could not leave even a Kolder-ruled woman to the things which made this foul country their home and hunting ground.

The ridge of ground on which they had crashed ran back, rising higher. But it was only an island, giving root room to the grass, a bordering of reeds, and some stunted brush. On three sides were murky pools—or perhaps only one pool with varying shallows and deeps. The water was scummed, and where cleared of that filthy covering, an opaque brown beneath which anything might lie in cover. As far as Simon could see the best path out still remained via the sunken tree lengths. How waterlogged and rotted those were was now a question. Would they crumple under the weight of those using them as bridges? There was no way of knowing until one tried.

Simon kept the dart gun, but he handed the knife to Loyse.

"Do not follow on any log until I have already cleared it," he ordered. "We may be only going deeper into this sink, but I do not propose to try the water way."

"No!" Her agreement was quick and sharp. "Take care, Simon."

He summoned up a tired smile which hurt his bruised face. "Be very sure that this is advice I shall hug to me now."

Simon caught a branch of a moss-wreathed tree which stood at the edge of the grass plot. A measure of the ancient bark powdered in his grip, but there remained still a hard core firm to his testing. Holding to that, he swung out, to land on the first of the logs. The wood did not give too much, but bubbles arose in the water, breaking to release so vile a stench that he coughed.

Still coughing he worked his way along to a mass of upended roots where he rested. Not that the mere walking of that way was fatiguing in itself, but the tension in his body had stiffened his joints to make every effort twice as hard. To climb over the roots, find footing again beyond was a task which sapped his strength yet more. He stood there, to watch Loyse come the path he had marked, her pale face set, her body as stiff as his.

How long did it take, that crisscross trailing from log to log? Twice Simon looked back, sure that they must have come some distance, only to see the flyer still far too close to hand. But at last he did leap to another grass-covered ridge, hold out his hands to Loyse. Then they sat together, shivering a little, panting and rubbing the hard muscles of their legs which seemed to have locked during that ordeal.

"Simon—"

He glanced at the girl. Her tongue moved across her lips as she stared at the stagnant water.

"The water—it cannot be drunk—" But that was not a statement, it was a question, a hope that he would say she dared. His tongue moved in his own dry mouth as he wondered how long they would be able to stand up to temptation before they were driven by thirst to scoop up what could be rank poison.

"It is foul," he replied. "Perhaps some berries—or a real spring later on." Very pallid hopes, but they could help to stave off temptation.

"Simon—" Resolutely Loyse had raised her gaze from the slimy pool, was gazing back over the path they had come. "Those trees—"

"What about them?" he asked absently.

"The way that they grew!" Her voice was more animated. "Look, even with those that have fallen, you can see it! That was no grove! They were planted—in lines!"

He followed her pointing finger, studied the logs, the few trunks still standing. Loyse was right, they were not scattered. When they had been rooted firmly they had stood in two parallel lines—marking some long-lost roadway? Simon's interest was more than casual, for that way ended at the islet where they rested.

"A road, Simon? An old road? But a road has to lead somewhere!" Loyse got up, faced away from the trees at the island.

It was little enough to cling to, he knew. But any clue which might be a signpost in this unwholesome bog was worth following. A few moments later in a line from the trees Simon came upon evidence to back their guess. The coarse grass was patchy, rooted only here and there, leaving bare expanses of stone. And that stone was smoothed blocks, laid with a care for the joining of one to the next—a pavement. Loyse stamped upon it with the heel of her boot and laughed.

"The road is here! And it will take us out—you shall see, Simon!"

But a road has two ends, Simon thought, and if we have chosen to go the wrong way this could be only leading us deeper into Tormarsh, to confront what or whom dwells there.

It did not take them long to cross the ridge of higher ground come once more to where water spilled across a dip. But on the other side of that flood stood a tall stone pillar, a little aslant as if the boggy ground had yielded to its weight. On top of that was a ragged tangle of vine, the loops of which drooped in reptilian coils about a carven face.

The beaked nose, the sharply pointed chin, small, overshadowed by that stronger thrust above it, the whole inhuman aspect—

"Volt!" So had that mummy figure they had chanced upon in the sealed cliff cavern appeared in those few minutes before Koris made his plea and took from its dried claws of hands the great ax. What had the seneschal said then? That Volt was a legend—half-god, half-devil—the last of his dead race, living on into the time of human man, giving some of his knowledge to the newcomers because of his loneliness and his compassion. Yet here had once been those who had known Volt well enough to raise a representation of him along some highway of their kind.

Loyse smiled at the pillar. "You have seen Volt. Koris has told me of that meeting when he begged of the Old One his ax and was not denied. There is none of the Old One lingering here, but I take his stone as a good omen, not one of ill. And he shows us that the road runs on."

There was still that stretch of water ahead. Simon searched the bank of the island and found a length of branch. Stripping away its rotten parts for a core tough enough to serve his purpose, he began to sound that waterway. Some inches of ooze and then solid stone, the pavement ran on. But he did not hurry, feeling for each step before he took it, having Loyse follow directly behind him.

Below the pillar bearing Volt's head the pavement emerged on the higher land once more, and as they went, that strip of solid surface grew wider, until Simon suspected that this was no small islet but a sizable stretch of solid ground. Which would provide living space, and so they could not fear dis-covery by the Tormen.

"Others have lived here." None of the vegetation grew tall and Loyse pointed out the blocks of stone which vaguely outlined what had once been walls, stretching away from the road into spike-branched brush. One building? A town or even the remains of a small city? What pleased Simon most was the density of the growth about those blocks. He did not believe that any living thing, save a very small reptile or animal, could force a path through it. And here, on the relative open of the ancient road, he could see any attacker.

The road, which hitherto ran straight, took a curve to the right and Simon caught at Loyse to bring her to an abrupt halt. Those blocks of stone, which had elsewhere tumbled into the negation of any structure, had here been moved, aligned into a low wall. And beyond that wall grew plants in rows, the tending of watchful cultivation plain to read in the weedless soil, the staking of taller stems.

It seemed that here the sunlight, pale and greenish within the swamp world, focused brighter on the plants where buds and blossoms showed as patches of red-purple, while winged insects were busy about that flowering.

"Loquths," Loyse identified the crop, naming a plant which was the mainstay of Estcarp weavers. Those purple flowers would become in due time bolls filled with silken fibers to be picked and spun.

"And look!" She took a step closer to the wall, indicating a small hollow niche constructed of four stones. In that shelter stood a crudely shaped figure, but there was no mistaking the beaked nose. Whoever had planted that field had left Volt to protect it.

But Simon had sighted something more—a well-trod path, which was not a part of the old road, but ran away from it to the right, winding out of sight on the other side of the field wall.

"Come away!" He was sure that they had made the wrong choice, that the road had brought them into Tormarsh and not toward its fringe. But could they retrace their trail? To return to the vicinity of the flyer might be going directly into enemy hands.

Loyse had already caught his meaning. "The road continues—" Her voice was lowered to a half whisper. And the way ahead did look rough and wild enough to promise that it was no main thoroughfare for those of Tor. They could only keep on it.

There were no more fields walled and planted. And even those scattered blocks of ruins disappeared. Only the fact that now and then they spotted a bare bit of pavement told them the road still existed.

But their earlier thirst was now more than discomfort, it was agony in mouth and throat. Simon saw Loyse waver, put his arm about her shoulders to steady her. They were both staggering when they reached the road's end—a stone pier which extended into a hellish nightmare of quaking mud, slime and stench. Loyse gave a cry and turned her head against Simon as he wrenched them both back and away from that waiting gulf.

X
Jaelithe Found

J can go no farther . . ."

Simon kept Loyse on her feet with an effort; her stumbling had become a weaving he could barely support. The sight of the quagmire beyond the road's end had sapped all her strength.

He was hardly in better case himself. The need for water, for food, racked him. And he had kept the girl on her feet only because he was sure that if they gave way now they might never be able to go on again.

Being so lightheaded Simon did not see the first of those balls which had plopped to the ancient roadway and burst to release a cloud of floury particles. But the second fell almost at their feet, and he had caution enough left to stagger back from it, dragging Loyse with him.

But they were ringed in, the dusty puffs rising and melting into a thin wall about them. Simon held Loyse against him, his dart gun ready. Only one could not fight a cloud rising sluggishly. And he had no doubt that this was a deliberate attack.

"What—?" Loyse's voice was a hoarse croak.

"I don't know!" Simon returned, but he knew enough not to try to cross the line of the cloud.

So far these flaky particles had not reached towards the two they confined. And they arose straight from the broken balls from which they had issued as if still attached to those sources. They were not so thick that Simon could not see beyond. Sooner or later someone would come to the sprung trap—then would be *his* turn. There was a full clip of the three-inch needle points in his dart gun.

Now the cloud began to move. Not in at them but around, speeding in that circling until Simon could no longer distinguish particles but saw only an opaque milky band.

"Simon, I think they are coming!" Loyse pulled a little away, her hand was on knife hilt.

"So do I."

But they were to be given no chance at defense. There was another dull popping sound. A ball from which the circle would not let them retreat, fell, to break. From this came nothing they could see. Only they wilted, to lay still, their hands falling away from the weapons they never had a chance to use.

Simon was in a box and the air was driven from his lungs. He could not breathe—breathe! His whole body was one aching, fighting desire for breath again. Simon opened his eyes, choking, gasping in pungent fumes which arose from a saucer being held by his head. He jerked away from that torment and found he *could* breathe now, just as he could see.

A wan and murky light came from irregular clusters on the walls well above where he lay. Stone walls, and the damp and chill of them reached him. He looked to the one who held that saucer. In the pallid light perhaps details of features and clothing were not too clear, but he saw enough to startle him.

Simon lay on a bed for this other sat on a stool and so was at eye level. Small, but still large-boned enough to appear misshapen, too long arms, too short legs. The head, turned so that the eyes met his. Large, the hair a fine dark down, not like hair at all. And the features surprisingly regular, handsome in a forbidding way, as if the emotions behind them were not quite those of Simon's kind.

The Torman arose. He was quite young, Simon thought; there was a lank youthfulness about his gangling body. He wore the breeches-leggings such as were common to Estcarp, but above them a mail jerkin made of palm-sized plates laid scallop fashion one over the other.

With one more measuring stare at Simon the boy crossed the room, moving with that feline grace which Simon had always found at odds with Koris' squat frame. He called, but Simon heard no real words, only a kind of beeping such as some swamp amphibian might voice. Then he completely vanished from Simon's sight.

Although the room had a tendency to swing and sway Simon sat up, steadying himself with his hands. His fingers moved across the bed coverings, a fabric fine and silky to the touch. Save for the bed, the stool on which the young Torman had sat, the room was empty. It was low of ceiling, with the massive beam across its middle forming a deep ridge. The lights were clustered haphazardly about. Then Simon saw one of them move, leave a cluster of three and crawl slowly to join a singleton!

Though the stone walls were damp and chill, yet the swamp stench did not hang there. Simon got warily to his feet. The radiance of the crawling lights was dim, but he could see all four walls. And in none was there any opening. Where and how had the Torman left?

He was still bemused over that when, a second or so later, he heard a sound behind. To turn quickly almost made him lose his balance. Another figure stood on the far side of the bed, slighter, less ill-proportioned than the boy, but unmistakably of the same race.

She wore a robe which gleamed with small fiery glints, not from any embroidery or outer decorations, but from strands woven into the cloth itself. The down which had fitted the boy's head in a close cap reached to her shoulders as a fluffy, springing cloud, caught away from her face and eyes by silver clasps on the temples.

The tray she held she put down on the bed for lack of table. Then only did she look at Simon.

"Eat!" It was an order, not an invitation.

Simon sat down again, pulling the tray to him, but still more interested in the woman than what rested on its surface. The paleness of the light could be deceiving but he thought that she was not young. Though there was no outward signs of age such as might appear among his own kind. It was rather an invisible aura which was hers—maturity, wisdom, and also—authority! Whoever she might be, she was a woman of consequence.

He took both hands to raise the beaker of liquid to his lips. It was without any ornament, that wide-mouthed cup, and he thought it was of wood. But its satiny surface and beautiful polish made it a thing of beauty.

The contents were water, but water in which something had been mixed. This was not ale or wine, but an herb drink. At first the taste was bitter, but then that sharp difference vanished and Simon drank eagerly, relishing it the more with every mouthful he sipped.

On a plate of the same shining, polished wood, were cubes of a solid, cheese-seeming substance. As the drink, they had a wry taste upon the first bite, and grew more savory later. All the time Simon ate the woman stood watching him. Yet there was an aloofness about her; she was doing her duty by feeding one whom she found unacceptable. And Simon began to prickle under that realization.

He finished the last cube and then, his faintness gone, he got to his feet, favored the silent watcher with much the same bow as he would have used to greet one of the Guardians.

"My thanks to you, lady."

She made no move to pick up the tray but came forward, around the end of the bed, so that a large cluster of the crawling lights revealed her more clearly. Then Simon saw that the lights were indeed crawling, breaking up their scattered companies to gather along the beam overhead.

"You are of Estcarp." A statement and yet a question as if, looking upon him, the woman doubted that.

"I serve the Guardians. But I am not of the Old Blood." His appearance, Simon decided, was what puzzled her.

"Of Estcarp." Now it was a statement. "Tell me, witch warrior, who commands in Estcarp—you?"

"No. I am Border Warder of the south. Koris of Gorm is marshal and seneschal."

"Koris of Gorm. And what manner of man is Koris of Gorm?"

"A mighty warrior, a good friend, a keeper of oaths, and one who has been hurt from his birth." From whence had come those words for his use? They were not phrased to match his thinking, yet what he had said was the truth.

"And how came the Lord of Gorm to serve the witches?"

"Because he was never truly lord of Gorm. When his father died his stepmother called in Kolder to establish the rule for her own son. And Koris, escaping Kolder, came to Estcarp. He wishes not Gorm, for Gorm under Kolder died, and he was never happy there."

"Never happy there—But why was he not happy? Hilder was a kindly man and a good one."

"But those of his following would never let Koris forget he was—strange . . ." Simon hesitated, striving to choose the right words. Koris' mother had come from Tormarsh. This woman could even be kin to the seneschal.

"Yes." She did not add to that but asked a very different question. "This maid who was taken with you, what is she to you?"

"A friend—one who has been with me in battle. And she is betrothed to Koris who seeks her now!" If there was any advantage to be gained from the thread of connection between the seneschal and the marsh people, then Loyse must have it.

"Yet they say she is duchess in Karsten. And there is war between the witches and those of Karsten."

It would seem that Tormarsh, for all its taboo-locked borders, still heard the news from outside the swamp.

"The story is long—"

"There is time," she told him flatly, "for the telling of it. And I would hear."

There was a definite order in that. Simon began, cutting the tale to bare outline, but telling of the ax marriage made for Loyse in Verlaine's towers and all that happened thereafter. But when he spoke of the shipwreck on the coast and how he, Koris, and two survivors of the Guard, had climbed to discover themselves in the long-lost tomb of Volt, where Koris had boldly claimed Volt's ax from the hands of the mummified dead, the Torwoman halted him abruptly, made him go into details. She questioned and requestioned him on small points, such as the words, as well as he could remember, that Koris had used when he asked the ax of Volt, and how that ax had been taken easily, with the long-dead body crumbling into dust once the shaft had been withdrawn from the claw hands.

"Volt's ax—he bears Volt's ax!" she said when he was done. "This must be thought upon."

Simon expelled his breath in a gasp. She was gone—as if she had never stood there, solid body on solid pavement. He took two strides to the same spot where she had been standing only an instant earlier, drove his boot down in a stamp which proved the footing as solid as it looked. But—she was gone!

Hallucination? Had she ever been here at all? Or was this one of those mind-twisting tricks such as the witches played? Shape-changing—that was as eerie in it's way as this instant vanishing. So this could be another form of magic, with its own rules, simple enough when one was trained by those rules. And not only the Torwoman practiced it, for the boy had winked out in just the same way. But to those who did not know the trick, this room or others like it would continue to be prison cells.

Simon returned to the bed. The tray with its beaker and plate still rested there. That much was real. And the fact that his hunger and thirst were gone, that he felt strong and able again—that was no hallucination.

He had been captured and imprisoned. But he had also been fed, and so far he had not been threatened. His dart gun was gone, but he had expected to be disarmed. What did these marsh dwellers want? He and Loyse had come into their territory by accident. He knew that they resented all trespassing bitterly, but were they fanatical enough on that subject to hold the innocent equally guilty with any determined invader?

Did they close their borders to everyone? Simon remembered Aldis, her hands tight upon the Kolder talisman, so deeply sunk in her voiceless call for aid that she was unaware of action about her. She must have expected such aid—so Kolder crawled somewhere in Tormarsh as evilly as the lizard thing had crawled upon the flyer.

Kolder. To those of witch blood Kolder was a void, noticeable in its presence because of that void. In the times past he, too, had known Kolder by sensing it—not as a void but as a waiting menace. Could he pick up the canker now the same way?

Simon set the tray on the stool, stretched himself once more on the bed, closed his eyes, and set his will free. He had always had this gift of foreseeing, in part a limping gift, not to be disciplined into any real service. But he was sure that since he had come to Estcarp that gift had grown, strengthened. Jaelithe—the twist of pain which always came now with the thought of Jaelithe. She had used the symbols of Power between them twice and those had glowed in answer. So that she had hailed him as one of her kind, then . . .

Now, though he intended to go hunting for the cancer of Kolder, rather did his mind return again and again to Jaelithe, to pictures of her. First, as he had seen her fleeing in rags with the hounds of Alizon baying on her trail, then as she had ridden in mail and war helm to Sulcarkeep when Kolder had made its first foul move in the present war. Jaelithe, kneeling on the quay of that fortress, breathing witchery into the scraps of sail for the vessels they had hastily whittled from wood, tossing those crude ships into the sea, so that a mighty fleet moved out through the cloaking mist to confound the enemy. Jaelithe acting as a sorceress and reader of fortunes, brewer of love potions in Kars, when her summoning had brought him across many miles to her aid. Jaelithe, shape-changed into a hideous hag and riding in company over the border to rouse Estcarp for war. Jaelithe in Gorm, telling him in her own way that that way was also his from then on. Jaelithe in his arms, being one with him in a way no other woman had ever been before, or would ever be again. Jaelithe excited, bright-eyed, that last morning, in the belief that her witchcraft had not gone from her at all, but that she was all she had been. Jaelithe—gone from him as if she used the traveling magic of these Torfolk.

Jaelithe! Simon did not cry that aloud, but inside of him it was one great shout of longing. Jaelithe!

"Simon!"

His eyes snapped open, he was staring up into the gloom, for the crawling lights had returned to their scattered clusters along the walls.

No, that had not come in any audible voice. Breathing fast, he closed his eyes again. "Jaelithe?"

"Simon." Firm, assured, as she had ever been.

"You are here?" He thought that, trying to shape the words clearly in his mind as a man might fumble about in a foreign tongue of which he knew little.

"No—in body—no."

"You *are* here!" he replied with a conviction he could not explain.

"In a way, Simon—because you are—I am. Tell me, Simon, where *are* you?"

"Somewhere within Tormarsh."

"So much is already known, since we are aware that your flyer dropped there. But, you are no longer Kolder ruled."

"Fulk's belt—one of the bosses on it—their planting."

"Yes, it opened a gate for them. But you were never so much theirs that we could not alter their spell a little. That is why you did not fly seaward at their bidding, but inland. Tormarsh is no ally of ours, but perhaps there is better chance to treat with Tormarsh than Kolder."

"Kolder is here also." Simon told her what he believed to be the truth. "Aldis called their aid, she was calling when we left her."

"Ah!"

"Jaelithe!" That moment of withdrawal frightened him.

"I hear. But if Kolder is with you—"

"I was trying to search for it."

"So? Well, perhaps in that two may be better than one, my dear lord. Think you on Aldis. If she moved to Kolder, perhaps your Power may move with her—to our better knowledge."

Simon tried to picture Aldis as he had seen her last, lying in the flyer as he pushed back the sprung door. But he discovered that he could not visualize that clearly at all. Instead he had momentary flashes of quite another and nonfamiliar scene—of Aldis seated, leaning forward, speaking eagerly to—to a blankness. And upon that the tie, if tie it was, with Aldis snapped.

"Kolder!" Jaelithe's recognition was sharp as any blow. "And they are on the move, I think. Listen well, Simon. The Guardians say that my Power is now only a wisp which will fail with the passing of time, that I have no place now in the Council of Es. But I tell you that between us we have something that I do not understand, for it is different than all else which I have held in my witchhood. Therefore, though it has taken me time to test this thing, to work with it as best I can, I have learned that I am not able to shape or aim it, save with you. Perhaps both of us must be the united vessel for this new strength. Sometimes it rages within me until I fear that I cannot hold it in bonds. But we have so little time to learn it. Kolder is on the move and it may be that we cannot bring you forth from Tormarsh before that move is made—"

"I do not wear their talisman, but it may be that they can control me still," he warned her. "If so, can they reach you through me?"

"I do not know. I have learned so little! It is like trying to shape fire with my two hands! But this we can do—"

Again a snapping—even more sharp than that break which had come between him and the shadow shape of Aldis.

"Jaelithe!" he shouted soundlessly. But this time—no reply.

XI
Kolder Kind

Simon lay very still, sweating now. For this was no half-trance of his own willing. He was motionless in bonds he could not see, his body held by another's will. Then she stood there, clear to the sight, at the foot of the bed, watching him in the level measurement which held no hint of whether she was friend or foe, or merely neutral in this war.

"They have come," she said, "to answer the call of their woman they have come."

"Kolder!" Simon found that he could use his tongue and lips if not the rest of his body.

"The dead ones who serve such," the Torwoman qualified. "Listen, man who obeys Estcarp, we have no quarrel with the witches. Between them and us there is neither friendship nor enmity. We were here when the Old Race came and built Es and their other dark towers. We have been rooted here for long and long, a handful of people who can remember when man was not the ruler of earthside, not even ones who lived widely. We are of those Volt gathered and set apart to learn his wisdom.

"And we want no dealings with those outside Tormarsh. You have come to trouble us with your wars which are no concern of ours. The swifter you are gone from us, the better served we shall be."

"But if you do not favor the witches, then why do you favor Kolder? Kolder hungers for rule over all men—and that includes the race of Tor," Simon retorted.

"We do not favor Kolder, we only ask that we be left to our own mysteries without troubling from beyond the marsh rim. The witches have not threatened us. This you call Kolder has shown us what will happen if we do not yield you to them now. And so it is decided that you go—"

"But Estcarp would defend you against Kolder—" Simon began until she smiled a small, cold smile.

"Will they, with aught save good wishes, Warder of the Border? There is no war between us, but they fear the marsh as a place of ancient mysteries and strange ways. Would they fight to save it? I think not. Also they have no men to throw into such a battle now."

"Why?" She seemed so certain that Simon was startled into a rough demand.

"Alizon has risen. Estcarp needs must throw all her armies northward to hold the marches there. No, we make the best bargain for us."

"And so I am to be delivered to the Kolder." Simon strove to keep his voice even and emotionless. "And what of Loyse? Do you give her also into the hands of the worst enemy this world has ever known?"

"The worst?" The Torwoman echoed. "Ah, we have seen many nations rise and fall, and in each generation there is a powerful enemy to be faced, either with victory or defeat. As for the girl—she is part of the bargain."

"She is also Koris', and I think you will discover that that has a meaning when it comes to extracting a price for such bargaining. I have seen the price he took from Verlaine and from Kars. Volt's gift drank deep in both those holds. Your marshland will not turn him back when it comes to his hunting."

"The bargain is made," her tone was more remote than ever. Then her hands came up in a swift gesture and her fingers moved. Not to shape Jaelithe's symbol of power, but still in an airborne sketch which had meaning.

"So you deem this Koris will come hunting for vengeance here?" she asked. "This pale-faced girl means so much to him?"

"She does, and those who have harmed her have need to fear."

"Ah, but now he must ride to hold back Alizon. It will be many days before he shall have time to think of aught else. Or perhaps he will find an end to all questions and desires among the border hillocks."

"And I say to you, lady, that Volt's gift shall yet swing in Tormarsh if you do as you have said."

"If *I* do, March Lord? I have naught to say in the yea and nay of such bargainings."

"No?" Simon put all the skepticism he could muster into that. "And I say that you are not the least of those among the Tor born."

She did not answer for a long moment, her gaze steady upon him.

"Perhaps once I was not. Now I do not raise my voice in any council. I wish you no ill, Warder of Estcarp. And I think that you mean no ill to me—or any of us. But when need drives, we obey. This much I shall do for you, since the maid is favored by he who was once Lord of Gorm. I shall send a message forth to Es that those there may know where you have gone and why. If then they can move to aid you, perhaps it will not go so ill. More than that I am sworn not to do."

"The Kolder come for us here—how?" Simon demanded.

"They come—or at least their servants come—up the inner river in one of their ships."

"But there *is* no river linking Tormarsh with the sea!"

"No outer one," she agreed. "The marsh drains underground. They have found that way to us, they have already visited us by it before."

By submarine down an underground river, Simon faced that. Even if the promised message reached Es in time to send a small force to the rescue, they could not ferret out the enemies' pathway, or help the prisoners borne so along it. The Guard of Estcarp would not be the answer.

"If you would truly favor us to the point of sending any message," Simon told her, "then send it not to Es but to the Lady Jaelithe."

"If she is your wife, then she is no witch, nor can she do aught to aid you." The Torwoman stared at him again with a curiosity which Simon thought dangerous.

"Nevertheless, if you favor us in so much—then send."

"I have said that I will send, if you wish it. To the Lady Jaelithe it shall be. Now, they come to take you hence, March Lord. If you survive this captivity, remember that Tormarsh is old, there is that within it which has stood long without being stamped into the bog with those who know its ways. Do not think that what is here can be easily swept aside."

"Say that rather to Volt's gift and he who bears it, lady. From Kolder's fingers few escape. But Koris lives, and rides, and hates—"

"Let him ride and hate and show Volt's gift to Alizon. There is the need for action there. Odd, March Warder, there is that in you which does not align itself with your words. You speak as one who resigns himself to fate, yet I do not believe that is so. Now—" Once again she sketched a sign in the air. "The gate is open and it is time you go."

What happened then was beyond any description Simon was ever able to give. He only knew that one moment he was in the doorless cell, and the next, still helpless in whatever hold they had upon him, he was in the open on the bank of a dark lake where the water was thick and murky, with a threatening look to it.

There was the murmur of voices about and behind him, the Torfolk were gathered there, men and women. And a little apart the smaller group of which Simon was an unwilling part.

Aldis, a look of confidence and expectancy on her face, Loyse, standing so stiffly that Simon guessed she was held in the same immobile spell as himself, and two of the Tormen. There was also a fifth from beyond the marsh boundaries.

No Kolder—at least not the Kolder such as he had seen in Gorm. Of middle size, face round and dark of skin, a kind of tan-yellow unlike any Simon had seen in this world, though they had found representatives of unknown races among the dead slaves in Gorm. He wore a tight-fitting one-piece garment of gray, like the Kolder dress, but his head was bare of any cap though he had a silvery disk resting under the fringe of his thin, reddish hair at the temple.

And the stranger was weaponless. However on the breast of his suit there was one of those intertwined knots fashioned of green metal, such as had been on Fulk's sword belt and Aldis carried.

The murmur from the Tormen grew louder, so that individual beepings carried to Simon. For the first time he wondered, with a small surge of hope, if the bargain the woman had told him about had been so widely accepted as she would have him believe. Could an appeal from him now split the ranks, give the prisoners a chance? But, even as Simon thought that, one of the marsh natives, standing with Aldis, raised his arm in a lashing motion. There was a ring of bells, the first really melodious sound Simon had heard in this half-drowned country. As the chain bearing those fell again to the Torman's side there was quiet, instant and absolute.

Quiet enough so that the disturbance in the murky water of the lake broke in an audible bubble on the surface. Then the water poured away as out of the depths arose the mud-streaked surface of a Kolder underwater vessel. There were scars and scrapes along its sides as if it had found whatever passage ran this way a difficult one. It moved without sound closer to shore.

An opening in the rounded upper surface flipped to shore to form a platform bridge uniting land and ship.

Aldis, her eager expression now an open smile, started along that pathway. Then Loyse, as if Aldis pulled her by cords, followed, walking stiffly, her whole body expressing her fear and repulsion. Simon's turn—his muscles, his bones, his flesh, were no longer his own. Only his mind imprisoned in that helpless body struggled for freedom, with defeat for the end.

He walked to that opening in the Kolder ship. Then, still by another's will, his hands and feet found holds on a ladder, and he descended into the space below. But not to freedom. Loyse moved ahead and he after, into a small cabin bare of any furnishings. They stood, he slightly behind the girl, and heard the door clang shut. Then and then only, did the compulsion cease to hold him.

Loyse, with a little moan, slumped and Simon caught her. He lowered her gently to the metal flooring but still held her as their bodies tingled with the vibration reaching them through the structure of the ship. Whatever power moved the submarine was now in force; the voyage had begun.

"Simon," Loyse's head turned so that he felt her breath come in gasps, not far from sobs, against his cheek. "Where are they taking us?"

This was a time when only the truth would serve. "To where we have wished to be—though not under these circumstances—I think, the Kolder base."

"But—" her voice quavered to a pause. When she spoke again it was with a measure of self-control, "That—that lies overseas."

"And we travel underwater." Simon leaned back against the wall. As far as he could see the cabin was bare and they had no weapons. Not only that, but there was that control over them the Kolder appeared able to use at will, leaving all hopes of rebellion doomed. But, perhaps there was one way. . . .

"They will never know where we are. Koris cannot—" Loyse was traveling her own path of thought.

"At present Koris is occupied, they have seen to that also." Simon told her of the invasion from Alizon. "They plan to bay Estcarp around with snarling dogs, letting her wear down her forces with such blows, none of which will yet be fatal, but which will exhaust her manpower and her resources—"

"Letting others do their fighting," Loyse broke in hotly, "ever the Kolder way."

"But one which can win for them as time passes," Simon commented. "They have some plan for us also."

"What?"

"By right of marriage you are now Duchess of Karsten, and so a piece worth controlling in this devious game they play. I am Border Warder. They can use me as hostage or—" He hated to put into words the other reason which might make him valuable to the enemy, the much more logical one.

"Or they can strive to make you one of them and so a traitor to serve their ends among the ranks of Estcarp!" Loyse stated it for him. "But there is one thing we may do so that we cannot be used so. We can die." Her eyes were very somber.

"If the need comes," Simon replied crisply. He was thinking: the site of the Kolder base—that was what they had long wanted to know. Not to snap off the monster's hands and arms, but destroy the head. Only, the world was wide and Estcarp had no clues as to the direction in which such a base lay. The Kolder use of underwater ships meant that they could not successfully be tracked by the Sulcarmen who counted the ocean their true home.

But suppose that Kolder *could* be tracked? The Sulcarmen were not truly land fighters. Certainly their raiders would be now harrying the coast of Alizon with the hit-and-run tactics they had developed to a high art, but that employment would not require the majority of their fleet. And if that fleet were free to track a Kolder ship, find their base—their fighting crews would harass the enemy on their home ground until Estcarp could throw the might of striking power against that hold.

"You have a plan?" The fear which had shadowed Loyse's features was fading as she watched Simon.

"Not quite a plan," he said. "Just a small hope. But—"

It was that "but" which was all-important now. The Kolder ship would have to be traced. *Could* that be done by contact such as he and Jaelithe had had in the Tormarsh village? Would the blight of those barriers the Kolder had always been able to use to cloak themselves against the magic of Estcarp sunder them utterly? So many "ifs" and "buts" and only his scrap of hope to answer all of them.

"Listen—" More to clear his own thinking than because he expected any active assistance from Loyse, Simon outlined what that hope might be. She gripped his arm fiercely.

"Try it! Try to reach Jaelithe now! Before they take us so far away that even thought cannot span that journey. Try it now!"

In that she could be right. Simon closed his eyes, put his head back against the wall and once more bent his whole desire and will-to-touch on Jaelithe. He had no guide in this seeking, no idea of how it might be done, he had only the will which he used with every scrap of energy he could summon.

"I hear—"

Simon's heart beat with a heavier thump at that reply.

"We go . . . on Kolder ship . . . perhaps to their base. Can you follow?"

There was no immediate answer, but neither was that snap of breaking contact which he had known twice before. Then came her reply.

"I do not know, but if it is possible, it shall be done!"

Again silence, but abiding with Simon the sense of union. His concentration was broken, not by his will, nor Jaelithe's, but by a sudden lurch of the ship, sending his body skidding along the cabin wall, Loyse on top of him. The vibration through those walls was stepped up until the vessel quivered.

"What is it?" Loyse's voice was thin and ragged once again.

The flooring was aslant so that the sub could not be on an even keel. And the vibration had become an actual shaking of its fabric and frame as if it were engaged in some struggle. Simon remembered the scars and mud smudges he had seen on its sides. An underground passage by river might not be too accommodating. They could have nosed into a bank, caught there. He said so.

Loyse's hands twisted together. "Can they get us loose?"

Simon saw the wide blankness of her eyes, caught the claustrophobic panic rising in her.

"I would say that whoever captains this vessel would know how to deal with such problems; this is not the first time—by Tormarsh accounts—that they have made the run." But there was always a first time for disaster. Simon had never believed that he would reach the point of joining the Kolder in any wish, but now he did as he tensed at every movement of the ship. They must be backing water to pull loose. The cabin rocked about the two prisoners, spilling them back and forth across its slick floor.

The rocking stopped and then the ship gave a great jerk. Once more the vibration sank to an even purr, they must be free and on course once again.

"I wonder how far we are from the sea?"

Simon had thought about that, too. He did not know where Jaelithe was, how long it would take her to contact any Sulcar ship and send it skulking after them. But Jaelithe would be on that ship—she would have to sail thus in order to hold the tie with him! And they could not assemble a fleet so quickly. Suppose that single Sulcar vessel lurking behind would be sighted, or otherwise detected by the Kolder? An engagement would be no contest at all, the Sulcar ship, and its crew would be helpless before the weapons of the Kolder. It was rank folly for him to encourage Jaelithe to follow. He must not try to reach her again—let her believe that he could not—

Jaelithe—Kolder. They balanced in his mind. How could he have been so insane as to draw her into such a plan?

"Because it is not rank folly, Simon! We do not yet know the limits of this we hold, what we dare summon by it—"

This time he had not tried to reach her, yet she had read all his forebodings as if he had hurled them at her.

"Remember, I follow! Find this noisome nest—and there shall be a clearing of it!"

Confidence. She was riding high on a wave of confidence. But Simon could not match that, he could only see every pointed reef ahead and no discernible course among them.

XII
She Who Will Not Wait

The room was low and long, dark save where the shutters were well open to the call of the sea, the light which came over those restless waves. And the woman who sat by the table was as turbulent within as those waves, though she showed little outward sign of her concern. She wore leather and mail; the chain-mail-scarfed helm, winged like that of any Borderer, sat on the table board to her right hand. And at her left was a tall cage in which perched a white falcon as silent and yet as aware as she. Between her fingers a small roll of bark rolled back and forth.

One of the witches? The captain of the Sulcar cruiser was still trying to assess her as he came from the door to front her. He had been summoned from the dockside to this tavern by one of the Borderers, for what reason he could not guess.

But when the woman looked at him, he thought that this was no witch. He did not see her gem of power. Only, neither was she any common dame. He sketched a half salute as he would have to any of his fellow captains.

"I am Koityi Stymir, at your summoning, Wise One." Deliberately he used the witch address to see her reaction.

"And I am Jaelithe Tregarth," she replied without amplification. "They tell me, Captain, that you are about to put to sea on patrol—"

"Raiding," he corrected her, "up Alizon way."

The falcon shifted on its cage perch, its very bright eyes on the man. He had an odd feeling that it was as intelligently interested in his answer as the woman.

"Raiding," she repeated. "I come to offer you something other than a raid, Captain. Although it may not put loot into your empty hold and it may bring you far greater danger than any Alizon sword or dart you may face in the north."

Jaelithe studied the seafarer. As all his race he was tall, wide of shoulder, fair of hair. Young as he was, there was a self-confidence in his carriage which spoke of past success and a belief in the future. She had not had time to choose widely, but what she had heard of Stymir along the waterfront made her send for him out of all the captains now in port at the mouth of the River Es.

There was this about the Sulcar breed: adventure and daring had a pull on them, sometimes over that of certain gain in trade, loot in war. It was that strain in their character which made them explorers as well as merchant traders in far seas. And she must depend upon that quality now to attract Stymir to her service.

"And what do you have to offer me, lady?"

"A chance to find the Kolder base," she told him boldly. This was no time to fence. Time—that inner turmoil boiled in her until she could hardly control it—time was her slave driver in this venture.

For a long moment he stared at her and then he spoke: "For years have we sought that, lady. How comes it now into your hands that you can speak so, as if you held a map to it?"

"I have no map, but still a method to find it—or believe that this is possible. But time grows short, and this depends upon time." And distance? her mind questioned. Could Simon get beyond the reach of their tie and she lose contact with him?

She twisted the roll of bark which had come out of Tormarsh, which had been an argument with the Guardians.

Her inner conflict might have been communicated to the great falcon, for now it mantled and screamed, even as it might scream in battle.

"You believe in what you say, lady," Stymir conceded. "The Kolder base—" With his finger tip he traced a design on the table board between them. "The Kolder base!"

But when he raised his eyes again to meet hers there was a wariness in them.

"There are tales among us—that the Kolder have a way of distorting minds and so sending those who were once our friends, even our cup-comrades, to lead us into their traps."

Jaelithe nodded. "That is indeed the truth, Captain, and you do well to think about such a risk. But, I am of the Old Race, and I have been a witch. You know that the Kolder taint cannot touch any of my kind."

"Have been a witch—" He caught and held to that.

"And why am I not one now?" She brought herself to answer that, though the need for doing so rasped her raw. "Because I am now wife to him who is March Warder of Estcarp. Have you not heard of the outlander who helped lead the storming of Sippar—Simon Tregarth?"

"Him!" There was wonder in the captain now. "Aye, we have heard of him. Then you, lady, rode to Sulcarkeep for its last battle. Aye, you have met Kolder and you know Kolder! Tell me what you now devise."

Jaelithe began her tale, the one she had set in mind before this meeting. When she had done the captain's amazement was marked.

"And you think this we can do, lady?"

"I go myself to its doing."

"To find the Kolder base—to lead in a fleet upon the finding. Aye, such a feat as that the bards would sing for a hundred hundred years to come! This is a mighty business, lady. But where is the fleet?"

"The fleet follows, but only one ship may lead. We do not know what devices these Kolder have in their below-water ship, how well they may be able to track anything on the surface. One ship above, not too close—that they might not suspect. A fleet could have but one meaning for them, and then, would they knowingly lead us to their den?"

Captain Stymir nodded. "Clearly thought, my lady. So then how do we bring in the fleet?"

Jaelithe lifted her hand to the cage. "Thus. This one has been trained by the Falconers to return whence it came, bearing any message. I have already conferred with those in authority. The fleet will assemble, cruise out to sea. When the message comes, why—then they will move in. But this is a matter of time. If the underseas' ship issues from the marsh river and has too great a lead, then I am not sure we can contact my lord, captive in it."

"This river, draining from Tormarsh . . ." It was plain that the captain was trying to align points along the shore to make a picture he knew. "I would guess it to be the Enkere—to the north. We could pose as a raider on the course to Alizon and so reach that spot without raising any undue interest."

"And may we sail soon?"

"Now if you wish, lady. The supplies are aboard, the crew gathered. We were off to Alizon today."

"This voyage may be longer; your supplies for coast raiding are limited."

"True. But there is the *Sword Bride* in from the south; she carries supplies for the army. We may transship from her if you have the authority. And that will take but a small measure of time."

"I have the authority. Let us be about it!"

The Guardians might not believe that she would retain this power of hers, but they had granted her backing for now. Jaelithe frowned. To have to use one of the Seakeep witches to transmit that request and her message had been galling, but she was willing to face any rebuff to gain her ends. And she had proved, when she had used the falcon and her new perception to confuse Simon in the flyer, that she did have something they could not dismiss as useless. Kolder would only die when its heart was blasted. And if she and Simon, working together, could find that heart, then all witchdom would back them to the limit.

Captain Stymir was as good as his boast. It still lacked several hours of nightfall when his *Wave Cleaver* skimmed out of the harbor, heading towards the black blot of Gorm and so beyond for the open sea. She had chosen better than she knew, Jaelithe decided, when she had picked Stymir from the four captains in the harbor. His ship was small, but she was swift, a cruiser rather than one of the wider-bottomed merchant carriers.

"You have been an opener of ways, Captain?" she asked as they stood together by the great rudder sweep.

"Aye, lady. It was my thought to try for the far north—had this war with Kolder not broken on our heads. There is a village I have visited—odd people, small, dark, with a click-click speech of their own we cannot rightly twist tongue around. But they offer such furs as I have seen nowhere else—only a few of them. Silver those furs, long of hair, but very soft. When we asked whence they came, this click-click speech folk said that they are brought once a year by a caravan of wild men from the north. They have other wares, too. Look you—"

He slipped from his wrist a band of metal and offered it to her. Jaelithe turned the ring about in her fingers. Gold, but a paler gold than she had ever seen before. Old, very old, and there was a design, so worn that it was merely curves and hollows. Yet there was sophistication, a degree of art in that worn design which did not say primitive but hinted of civilization—only what civilization?

"This I traded for two years ago in that village, and all they could tell me was that it came from the north with the wild men. Look you, here and here." He touched with fingertip two points on the band, "That is a star—very much worn away and yet a star. And on the very, very old things of my people there are sometimes such stars—"

"Another trader of your people ages ago who made a voyage there and returned not?"

"Perhaps. But there is also another thought. For we have bard songs, also very old, of whence we first came—and that there was cold, and snow, and much battling with monsters of the dark."

Jaelithe thought of how Simon had come to Estcarp, and of that gate in another place through which the Kolder had issued to trouble them. These Sulcarmen, always restless, ever at sea, taking their families with them on such voyages as if they might not return. Only in the times of outright war were Sulcar ships other than floating villages. Had they, too, come through a gate which kept them searching with some hidden instinct to find again? She gave the band back to Stymir.

"A quest of value, Captain. May there be long years for each of us for the questing we hold in our hearts."

"Well spoken, lady. Now we are approaching the mouth of the Enkere. Do you wish to hunt in your own way for the Kolder water sulker?"

"I do."

She lay on the bunk in the small cabin to which the captain had shown her. It was hot and close and the mail shirt constricted her breathing. But Jaelithe strove to set aside all outward things, to build in her mind the picture of Simon. There were many Simons and all had depth of meaning for her, but it was necessary to forge those into one upon which to center her call.

But—no answer . . . She had been so sure of instant contact that that silence was like an unexpected blow. Jaelithe opened her eyes and gazed up at the roofing of the ship's timbers so close above her head. The *Wave Cleaver* was truly cleaving waves and the motion about her—perhaps that was what broke the contact or kept her from completing it.

"Simon!" Her call searched, demanded. She had had long years of training as a witch, to center and aim her Power through that jewel which was the badge of her office. Was this fumbling now because she must do it all without a tool, with the skepticism of those she had long revered eating at her confidence?

She had been so sure that morning when she had had that sending concerning Loyse and when she had ridden to Es with that flaming desire to be one of the Power again—only to find doors and minds closed against all her knocking. Then, because she had been so sure she was right, she had gone apart, as dictated by her past training, to study this thing, to strive to use it. And when she had had the tidings that Simon had acted against all nature, she had guessed that the Kolder blight had touched him, then she had used that new power, little as she knew about it, in the fight for Simon which dropped him into the forbidden tangle of Tormarsh. After that, she had tried again with purpose. But were the Guardians right, was this new thing she thought she had found merely the dying echo of the old Power, doomed to fail?

Simon. Jaelithe began to consider Simon apart from a goal at which to aim thought. And from the fringe consideration of Simon she looked inward at herself. She had surrendered her witchdom to Simon when she wedded him, thinking this union meant more to her than all else, accepting the penalty for that uniting. But why then had she been so eager to seize upon this hope that her sacrifice had been no sacrifice at all? She had left Simon to ride to Es, to best the Guardians and prove that she was not as others, that she was still witch as well as wife. And when they would not believe, she had not sought out Simon, she had kept to herself, intent upon proving them wrong. As if—as if Simon was no longer of importance at all! Always the Power—the Power!

Was that because she had known no other force in her life? That what Simon had awakened in her was not lasting emotion, but merely a new thing which had been strange and compelling enough to shake her from the calm and ordered ways of her kind, but not deep enough to hold her? Simon—

Fear—fear that such reasoning was forcing her to face something harsh and unbearable. Jaelithe concentrated again on Simon: standing so, with his head held high, his grave face so seldom alight with any smile—and yet in his eyes, always in his eyes when they met hers—

Jaelithe's head turned on the hard pillow of the bunk. Simon—or the need to know that she was still a witch. Which drove her now? As a witch she had never known this kind of fear—not without—but within.

"Simon!" That was not a demanding summons for communication; it was a cry born of pain and self-doubt.

"Jaelithe . . ." Faint, far off, but yet an answer, and in it something which steadied her, though it did not answer her questions.

"We come." She added as tersely as she could what she had done to further his plan for tracking.

"I do not know where we are," he made answer. "And I can hardly reach you."

That was the danger: that their bond might fail. If they only had some way of strengthening that. In shape-changing one employed the common linkage of mutual desire to accomplish that end. Mutual desire—but they were only two. Two—no. Loyse—Loyse's desire would link with theirs in this. But how? The girl from Verlaine had no vestige of witch power. She had been unable to perform the simplest spells in spite of Jaelithe's coaching, having the blindness in that direction which enfeebled all but the Old Race.

But shape-changing worked on those who were not of the Old Race; it had once worked on Loyse in Kars. She might not be able to pull on the Power itself, but it could react upon her. And was this still *the* Power?

Without answering Simon Jaelithe broke the faint link between them, set in her mind instead the image of Loyse as she had last seen the girl weeks ago in Es and using that as anchorage she sought the spirit behind the picture.

Loyse!

Jaelithe had a blurred, momentary glimpse of a wall, a scrap of floor, and another crouching figure that was Simon! Loyse—for that single instant she had looked through Loyse's eyes!

But possession was not what she wanted, contact rather. Again she tried. This time with a message, not so deep an identification. Foggy, as if that wisp of tie between them fluttered anchored for an instant, and then failed. But as Jaelithe struggled to make it firm, it did unite and become less tenuous. Until it held Loyse. Now for Simon—

Groping, anchorage! Simon, Loyse—and it *was* stronger, more consistent. Also—she gained direction from it! What they had wanted from the first— direction!

Jaelithe wriggled from the confines of the bunk, kept her footing with the aid of handgrips as she sought the deck. There was wind billowing the sails, the narrow knife of the bow dipped into rising waves. The sky was sullen where the sun had gone, leaving only a few richly colored banners at the horizon.

That wind whipped Jaelithe's hair about her uncovered head, sent spray into her face until she gasped as she reached the post beside the rudder where two of the crew labored to hold the ship on course, and Captain Stymir watched narrowly sky, wind and wave.

"The course," Jaelithe caught at his shoulder to steady herself at an unexpected incline of the decking. "That way—"

It was so sharp set in her head that she could pivot in a half turn and point, sure that her bearings were correct for their purpose. He studied her for a second as if to gauge her sincerity and then nodded, taking the helm himself.

The bow of the *Wave Cleaver* began to swing to Jaelithe's left, coming about with due caution for wind and wave, away from the dark shadow of the land, out into the sea. Somewhere under the surface of all this turbulence was that other vessel, and Jaelithe had no doubts at all that they were going to follow the track of that, as long as that threefold awareness linked Simon, Loyse and herself.

She stood now wet with spray, her hair lankly plastered to her skull, stringing on her shoulders. The last colors faded from the sky or were blotted out by the cloud masses. Behind them even the shadow of Estcarp's coast had gone. She knew so little of the sea. This fury of wind and wave spelled storm, and could storm so batter them from the course that they would lose the quarry?

Jaelithe shouted that question to the captain.

"A blow—" His words came faintly back. "But we have ridden out far worse and still kept on course. What can be done, will be. For the rest, lady, it lies between the fingers of the Old Woman!" He spat over his shoulder in the ritual luck-evoking gesture of his race.

But still she would not go below, watching in the fast-gathering darkness for something she knew she would not be able to see with the eyes of her body, making as best she could an anchor past breaking for the tie.

XIII
Kolder Nest

*T*ime was hard to measure in this ship's cell. Simon lay relaxed on a narrow shelf bunk, but still he held to that ribbon of communication which included not only Jaelithe, but now Loyse in a lesser degree. Though the girl no longer shared his quarters, she was present in his mind.

Simon had seen none of his captors since, shortly after this voyage had begun, Aldis appeared and took charge of Loyse, leaving him alone. A second inspection of the narrow cabin had provided some amenities: a bunk which could be pulled out and down from the wall, a sliding shelf on which, from time to time, a tray of food appeared—coming from the wall behind.

The food was emergency rations, he thought, thin wafers without much taste, a small can of liquid. Not appetizing but enough to keep hunger and thirst under control. Otherwise there was no break in the long, silent hours. He did sleep a little while Loyse took over, holding the tie. Simon gathered that she now shared Aldis' cabin, but that the Kolder agent was leaving her alone, content that she was passive.

Seven, now eight mealtimes. Simon counted them off. But that gave him no reasonable idea of the number of hours or days he had been here under the unchanging glow of the walls. They could be feeding him twice daily, or even once; he could not be sure. This was a period of waiting, and to any man who had depended most of his life upon the stimulation of action, waiting was a harsh ordeal. Only once before had it been so—during a year in jail. Waiting then, warped by the bitterness of knowing that he had been duped into taking punishment for those he hated, he had spent that time striving to work out schemes for repayment.

Now he was facing a blind future without even a good knowledge of the nature of the enemy. All he had was that mental picture from the past of the Kolder leader dying in Gorm, a narrow valley down which strange vehicles dashed while those in them fired back at pursuers. There had been another world for the Kolders and something had gone wrong there.

Somehow they had discovered a "gate" and come through—into this time and place, where the civilization of the Estcarpian Old Race was on the wane, a slow slip into the age-old dust which already rose about Es and the villages and cities of their kind. Along the coast—in Alizon and Karsten—a more barbaric upswing was rooted, newer nations, elbowing aside the Old Race, yet so much in awe of their legendary witches that they dared not quite challenge them—not until the Kolder began to meddle.

And if Kolder was not uprooted, Alizon and Karsten would go the way of Gorm: ingested into the horror of the possessed. Yet Kolder played upon this older enmity and fear to make their future victims their present allies.

The nature of Kolder. Simon began to concentrate upon that. Their native civilization was a mechanical, science-based one—that fact had been amply proven by what they had found in Gorm. The Estcarpian command had always believed that the Kolder themselves must be few in number, that it was necessary for them to have the possessed captives in order to keep their forces in the field. And now that Gorm was gone and Yle evacuated—

Yle evacuated! Simon's eyes came open, he stared at the ceiling of the cabin. *How* had he known that? Why was he so very sure that the Kolder's only stronghold on the coast was now an empty shell? Yet certain he was.

Were the Kolder now drawing in all their forces to protect their base? Kolder manpower—there had been five left dead in Gorm, the majority in their own apartments—not killed by any sword or dart, but as if they had willed their own dying—or some animating spark, common to all, had failed. But five! Could the death of only five so weaken the Kolder cadre that they would have to pull in all their garrisons?

Hundreds of the possessed had died in Gorm. And then there were their agents in Karsten—Fulk—and the others such as Aldis who were still alive and about their business. Not true Kolder, but natives who had come to serve the enemy—not as mindless possessed, but with wit and awareness. Not one of the Old Race could be so bent to Kolder use; that was why the Old Race must go!

Again Simon wondered at whence that emphatic assertion had come. They had known that the Kolder wanted no Old Race captives for their ranks of possessed. They had suspected that this was the reason, but now it was as clear in his mind as if he had had it from Kolder lips.

Heard it? Did the Kolder have their form of communication such as that he now held with Jaelithe and Loyse? That thought shook him. Quickly Simon sent a warning to she who followed and caught her unease in return.

"We are sure of the course now," she told him. "Break. Do not send again unless there is great need."

"Great need . . ." That echoed in his mind, and then Simon became aware that the vibration which had been so steady in the walls about him was muted, humming down scale as if the speed they had maintained was being cut. Had they reached their port?

Simon sat up on the bunk, faced the door. Would they lock him with the same stiff control which had kept him prisoner before? He had no weapons, though some skill in unarmed combat. But he hardly thought that the Kolder would try a scuffle man-to-man.

He was right, even as the door to the cabin opened, the freeze was on him. He could move—by another's will—and he did, out into the narrow corridor.

Men there, two of them. But looking into their eyes Simon controlled a shudder only because he could not move save an order. These were possessed, the dead alive of the Kolder labor horde. One was Sulcar by his fair head, his height; the other of the same yellow-brown-skinned race as the officer who had brought Simon on board.

They did not touch him, merely waited, their soulless gaze on him. One turned and started along the passage, the other flattened back against the wall to allow Simon by, and then fell in behind him. Thus, between the two, he climbed the ladder, came out on the surface of the submarine.

Above was an arch of rock. The water lapped sullenly against a waiting quay and Simon saw here a likeness to the hidden port beneath Sippar, evidently a familiar pattern for the enemy. Still moved by remote control he walked ashore on the narrow gangway.

There was activity there. Gangs of almost naked possessed shifted boxes, cleared spaces. They worked steadily, as if each man knew just what was to be done, and the quickest way of doing it.

No voices raised, no talk among the work gang. Simon stalked stiffly behind his guide, the Sulcar bringing up the rear, and no one looked at them. The quay was long and two other subs nosed against it. Being unloaded Simon noted. Signs of withdrawal from other posts?

Before them were two exits, a tunnel and a flight of stairs to the left. His guide took that way. Five steps and then a waiting cubby. Once they were inside the door closed and they rose in an elevator such as had been in Sippar.

The ride was not long, the door slid open upon a corridor. Sleek gray walls with a metallic luster to their surfaces, outlines of doors, all closed. They passed six, three to a side, before they came to the end of the hall and a door which was open.

Simon had been in the heart center of Sippar and he half expected to see here again the seated Kolder, the capped master at a cross table, all the controls those men had run to hold their defenses tight.

But this was a much smaller room than that. Light, a harsh burst of it, came from bars set in the ceiling in a complicated geometric pattern Simon had no desire to examine closely. The floor had no discernible carpeting, yet it yielded to cushion their steps. There were three chairs, curved back and seat in one piece. And in the center one a true Kolder.

Simon's guards had not entered with him, but that compulsion which had brought him out of the submarine now marched him forward a step or two to face the Kolder officer. The alien's smocklike overgarment was the same gray as the chair in which he sat, as the walls and the flooring. Only his skin, pallid, bleached to a paper white, broke that general monotone of color. Most of his head was covered by a skullcap, and as far as Simon could see, he had no hair.

"You are here at last." The mumble of an alien tongue and yet Simon somehow understood the words. Their meaning surprised him a little, one could almost believe that they were not captor and prisoner but two who had some bargain in prospect and needed only to come to a final agreement. Caution kept Simon silent—the Kolder must reveal his game first.

"Did Thurhu send you?" The Kolder continued to study Simon and now the other thought that there was a spark of doubt in that question. "But you are not an outer one!" The doubt flared into hostility. "Who are you?"

"Simon Tregarth."

The Kolder continued to hold him with a narrowed stare.

"You are not one of these natives." No question but an assured statement.

"I am not."

"Therefore you have come from beyond. But you are *not* an outer one, and certainly not of the true breed. I ask you now—what are you?"

"A man from another world, or perhaps another time," Simon saw no reason not to tell the truth. Perhaps the fact that he was a puzzle for the Kolder was to his advantage.

"What world? What time?" Those shot at him harshly.

Simon could neither shake his head nor shrug. But he put his own ignorance into words.

"My own world and time. Its relation to this one I do not know. There was a way opened and I came through."

"And why did you journey so?"

"To escape enemies." Even as you and yours did, Simon added in his mind.

"There was a war?"

"There had been a war," Simon corrected. "I was a soldier, but in peace I was not necessary. I had private enemies—"

"A soldier," the Kolder officer repeated, still appraising him with that unchanging stare. "And now you fight for these witches?"

"Fighting is my trade. I took service with them, yes."

"Yet these natives are barbarians, and you are a civilized man. Oh, show no surprise at my guess, does not like always recognize like? We, too, are soldiers and our war brought us defeat. Only it has also brought us victory in the end since we are here and we hold that which shall make this world ours! Think you on that, outsider. A whole world to lie thus—" He stretched forth his hand, palm up, and then closed his fingers slowly as if he balled something tangible within his fist. "To serve as you will it! These natives cannot stand against what we have to back us. And—" he paused and then added with slow and telling emphasis, "we can use such a man as you."

"Is that why I am a prisoner here?" Simon countered.

"Yes. But not to remain a prisoner—unless you will it. Simon Tregarth, March Warder of the south. Ah, we know you all—the mighty of Estcarp." His expression did not change, but there was a sneer in his voice.

"Where is your witch wife now, March Warder—back with those other she-devils? It did not take her long to learn that you had nothing she cared to possess, did it? Oh, all that passes in Estcarp, Karsten and Alizon is known to us, to the minutest detail it is known. We can possess you if we wish. But we shall give you a choice, Simon Tregarth. You owe nothing to those she-devils of Estcarp, to the wandering-witted barbarians they control with their magic. Has not that witch of yours proved to you that there can be no loyalty with them? So we say—come with us, work in our grand plan. Then Estcarp will lie open for *your* plucking, *your* terms—or strike any other bargain you wish. Be March Warder again, do as Estcarp wishes, until the word comes to do otherwise."

"And if I do not accept?"

"It would be a pity to waste one of your potential. But he who is not with us is against us, and we can always use a strong back, legs, arms to labor here. You have already tasted what we can do—your muscles do not obey you now, and you cannot take a step unless we will it so. This can be used otherwise. Would you care to breathe only by our favor?"

There was a sudden constriction about Simon's chest. He gasped under that squeezing pressure and panic awoke in him. Less than a second, but the fear did not leave him when he was released. He did not in the least doubt that the Kolder could do as was threatened—keep the air from his lungs, if they chose.

"Why . . . bargain?" he gasped.

"Because the agents we wish cannot be forced. Under such controls you must be constantly checked and watched, you would not so serve our purpose. Accept freely and you will be free—"

"Within your limits," Simon returned.

"Just so. Within our limits, and that will remain so. Do not believe that you can give assent with your lips and keep to your own purpose thereafter. There will be a change in you, but you will retain your mind, your personality, such of your desires and wishes as fit within the framework of our overall plan. You will not be only flesh to carry out orders as those you term possessed and you will not be dead."

"And I must choose now?"

The Kolder did not answer at once. Again his expression was blank, but

Simon caught a faint tinge of meaning in his voice—threat, uncertainty, maybe one and the same.

"No—not yet."

He made no signal which Simon could distinguish but the control brought him about, set him walking. No guards this time, but they were not needed. There was no possible way for Simon to break free, and the threat of constriction about his chest was with him still, so that every time he thought of that he had the need to breathe deeply.

Down the corridor, into the elevator again. Up, an open door; the order to move, another hall and another door. Simon went into the room beyond and the control was gone. He turned quickly, but the door was closed and he did not need to try it to know that it would not open.

The harsh, artificial light of the lower room was gone. Two slit windows were open to the day and Simon went to the nearest. He was in a position of some height above a rocky coastline with a sheer descent to water. By side glimpses he got an idea of the building; it must resemble Yle. Not only was the window slit too narrow to climb through, but there was no way down, save that drop straight to the sea-washed rocks.

Simon crossed to the other window. Bare rocks again, not the slightest sign of vegetation—rocks in wind-worn pinnacles, in table mesas, slashed into sharp-walled canyons and drops. It was the most forbidding stretch of natural territory he had ever seen.

Movement. Simon pushed forward as far as he could in the window slit to see what moved in that tormented wilderness of broken rock. A land machine of some sort, not unlike a truck of his own world, though it progressed on caterpillar tracks, which crunched and flattened the surface at a pace, Simon judged, hardly faster than a brisk walk. There were marks on that surface which the machine followed. This was not the first truck which had gone that way, or perhaps not the first trip this one had made in the same direction.

It had a full cargo and clinging to that lashed-on gear, were four men, their ragged scraps of clothing labeling them slave laborers. The machine lurched and jerked so that they held with both hands and feet. That slow crawl inland with a cargo on board. Simon continued to watch until the truck disappeared behind a mesa. It was only then that he turned to examine his new prison.

Monotone color and a bed which was merely a shelf opening from the wall and covered by a puffed, foamy substance. Closed doors of cupboards—a whole row of them. One upon his investigating turned down into a table, another gave him sanitary arrangements as there had been on the submarine. The rest remained tightly closed. It was a room to induce boredom, Simon thought. Perhaps its very monotony was a piece of careful contrivance.

But there was one thing he was sure of: this *was* the Kolder base. And there was a good chance that they might have him under some form of ob-servation. The fact that he had been released from control might even be because they wished to see how he would use his freedom. Could they suspect the tie? Was he bait in a trap to bring in Jaelithe?

What would the Kolder give to have one of the witches in their hands? Simon thought that under the circumstances they would give a great deal. Suppose that everything—*everything*—which had happened to him since the awakening in Tormarsh when he had found Jaelithe again had really been of their engineering! He could not be sure it was not.

Yet the Kolder depended upon their machines. They affected to despise the Power. So had they any way of detecting what Simon, Jaelithe and Loyse had woven? To contact Jaelithe now . . . would it be right or wrong? Betrayal or report? He had promised to let her know when he reached the base, give her the news which would eventually summon Estcarp. But how long would it take to bring in that armada? And what could darts and swords or even the Power, do against the weapons the Kolder must mount here—things which had not perhaps been in Gorm or Yle? Should he call or stay silent?

More movement. A truck crawling back. Was it the same vehicle he had watched depart? But that hardly would have time to unload and this was empty.

Call—or be silent? Simon could no longer use this useless survey of the land as an excuse for not making up his mind. He went to the bed, lay down upon it. A chance—but everything was a chance now, and if this was not betrayal, then he dared not delay.

XIV
Witch Weapon

*J*aelithe had journeyed on Sulcarships before, but never into the void of midocean. There was a vast impersonality about the sea which undercut her confidence in herself in a way she had never known before. Only the knowledge that her witchdom had not been swept away was her support. The witches had the reputation of being able to control natural forces. Perhaps on land they could summon up a storm, a mist or weave hallucinations to control the mind. But the sea was a power in itself and the farther the *Wave Cleaver* sailed the less sure Jaelithe was.

Simon's fear that they might have awakened the suspicions of the Kolder, oddly enough, steadied her. Men—even the Kolder, alien as they were—she could face better than this rolling immensity of wind-driven wave.

"There is no land reckoned hereby on any chart." Captain Stymir had out his rolls of sea maps.

"Have none of your exploring ships ever reached in this direction before?" Jaelithe asked, seeing in his very bewilderment something strange.

Stymir continued to study the top chart, tracing markings with hs finger. Then he called over his shoulder, "Pass the word for Jokul!"

The crewman who came in answer to that hail was a small man, bent by the years, his brown face seamed and salt-dried. He walked with a lurch and go and Jaelithe saw his right leg was stiff and a little shorter than the left.

"Jokul," Stymir flattened the chart with a broad hand, "where are we?"

The smaller man's head came up. He pulled off a knitted cap so that the wind lay over his tight braids of faded hair, his somewhat large nose pointed into that breeze.

"On the lost trace, Cap'n."

Stymir's frown grew the deeper. He studied the filled sails above them as if their billowing had taken on a sinister meaning. Jokul still sniffed that wind, advancing a step or two down the deck. Then he pointed to the sea itself.

"The weed—"

A thread of red-brown on the green, whipped up and down with the rise and fall of the swell, trailed on near to another patch. Jaelithe's gaze, following that, saw that closer to the horizon there was an all-red-brown patch. And the change in the captain's expression made her break silence.

"What is it?"

He brought his fist down with a thumping blow. "That must be it!" His frown was gone. "This is why—the weed and the lost trace!" Then he turned to her. "If your course leads there, lady, then—" His hands were up and out in a gesture of bafflement.

"What is it?" she demanded for the second time.

"The weed, it is an ocean thing, living on the surface of the waves in these warmer waters. We have known it long and it is common. One may find bits of it washed ashore after any storm. But there is this about the weed—it has been increasing and now the patches have that on them which kills—"

"Kills how?"

Stymir shook his head. "We do not know, lady. A man touches it and it is as if his hands are burned in a fire. The burns spread upon his skin, his body, and afterwards, he dies. It is some poison in the weed—and wherever it floats we no longer go."

"But if it is in the water and you are onboard ship, do you need to fear the touch?" she countered.

"Let a ship touch it and it clings, clings and grows—aboard!" Jokul broke in. "It has not always been so, lady, only for some years now. So the ocean paths it takes we must now avoid."

"Only lately," Jaelithe repeated. "Since the Kolder have grown so bold?"

"Kolder?" Stymir stared at the floating weed in open bewilderment. "Kolder—weed—why?"

"The Kolder ships go under the surface of the sea," Jaelithe pointed out. "How better could they protect their trail than to sow trouble above where any enemy must follow?"

The captain turned to Jokul. "The lost trace—where did it lead?"

"Nowhere that we wished to go," the crewman answered promptly. "A few barren islands which have nothing. Water, food, people, even the sea birds are scarce there."

"Barren islands? Are they not on your chart, Captain?"

He flattened out the top one again. "Not so, my lady. But if this is the lost trace, then it may be that we cannot follow it farther. For the nature of the weed is such that first it appears in such strings as yonder, then in patches, as you see farther beyond. These patches thicken, not only in number but in depth, so that they make small islets borne on the sea, and then larger islets, and at last, if anyone has the folly to push in, they are a solid mass. This, too, was not always so. The weed made islands, aye, but not so solid—nor was it death to hunt there. I have harvested crabs for the eating. But now no man goes near that ocean stain. Does it not seem as blood washing from a gaping wound? The very sign of the death it is!"

"If one cannot penetrate so far how does one know of these isles?"

"At first we did not know the danger. A floating ship with dying men on her deck drifted out of the weed. And of those who chanced upon that vessel and went to their rescue five more died because the weed had fastened to her hull and they had brushed against it. So did we learn, lady. If the Kolder have indeed set this defense about their hold, it is one we cannot face unless we work out some plan against the weed."

The floating weed—Jaelithe had to accept their word upon its danger. The Sulcar kind knew the sea and all its concerns—that was *their* mystery. The weed . . . But she no longer saw that trail like blood on the sea. Her hands went to her head and she swayed at an imperative summons. Simon!

Simon in the Kolder base—that way—beyond the floating death. They must head into—through—that.

"Simon," her reply sought him urgently, "there is danger between us."

"Stay off! Do not risk it."

Curtain between them now. She could not penetrate that despite frantic efforts. Kolder curtain. Did they *know*, or was that only usual precautions? Simon!

Jaelithe felt as if she had screamed that name, it was a tearing pain in her throat. But when she opened her eyes Stymir showed no alarm.

"What we seek lies beyond there," she said dully, pointing to the horizon where rode the weed. "Perhaps they also know that we come—"

"Captain! The weed!" Not a warning from Jokul, but a cry from the main-mast lookout.

One trail—one patch. No! A dozen trails now, all reaching out deadly tendrils for them. Stymir roared orders to bring the ship about, send it back-tracking. Jaelithe sped for the cage amidships.

The great white falcon welcomed her with a scream as she clicked open the latch of the cage. She stiffened her arm to support its weight as it hooked its heavy claws about her flesh and bone, sidled out to freedom. Fastened to one of those strong legs was what she sought, a tiny mechanism in a rod which the bird could carry with ease. Jaelithe drew a deep breath, to steady her nerves and quiet the racing of her heart. This was a delicate business and she dared make no mistakes. Her fingernail found the tiny indentation in the rod, and she pressed that in code pattern. The bird in flight would automatically register, on this triumph of the Falconers' devices, the course and distance. But the tale of the weed was another matter which she must record for the Falconers to decode.

That done she carried the bird to the afterdeck, speaking to it softly mean-while. Falconers' secrets remained secrets as far as their allies were concerned. How much the bird actually understood Jaelithe could not tell. Whether it was training or bred intelligence which made this falcon superior was a matter for argument. But that it was their only chance to warn the fleet following she knew.

"Fly straight, fly fast, winged one." She drew a finger down the head as those fierce eyes met hers. "This is your time!"

With a scream the falcon tore skyward, circled the ship once, and then shot as a dart back towards the long-vanished land. Jaelithe turned to the sea. The tendrils of weed advanced, a swelling web of them reaching for the ship. Surely, surely their rapid drawing in upon the vessel was not natural. How could floating weed move so swiftly and with a purpose, as she was sure was happening now. Oh, if she only had her jewel! There was more than halluci-nations to be controlled through that. At times of great emergency it could pull upon a central store of energy, common to all the witchdom of Estcarp, and so accomplish tangible results.

But she had no jewel, and what she could use was not the Power she had known before. Jaelithe watched the fingers of the weed and tried to think. It lay upon the surface—and so far there were no thick islands such as Stymir had feared. Under the water was safe, but the *Wave Cleaver* could not go below as did a Kolder ship.

Water gave the stuff support and life. Her fingers moved in a studied pattern on the rail before her. Jaelithe found herself reciting one of the first and earliest of the spells she had ever learned: one to impress upon a child's mind the base for all "changing."

"Air and earth, water and fire—"

Fire—the eternal opposition to water. Fire could dry water, water could quench fire. Fire—the word lingered with a small beat in her mind. And Jaelithe knew that beat of old, the sign every witch waited for, the signpost of a spell ready to work. Fire! But how could fire be the answer on the ocean—a weapon against drifting weed which was poison to what it touched?

"Captain!" She turned to Stymir. He scowled at her as if she was only a distraction in his battle to save his ship.

"Sea oil—you have sea oil?"

His expression changed to one of a man facing a hysterical woman, but she was already continuing.

"The weed, will it burn?"

"Burn—on the water?" His protest was halted as if a thought struck home. "Sea oil—fire!" He connected those with the rapidity of a man who had improvised before in the face of danger. "No, lady, I do not know whether it will burn—but one can try!" He shouted an order.

"Alavin, Jokul, get up three skins of oil!"

The skins of thick oil, skimmed from the boil off langmar stems, kept for use in storms, were brought to the deck and Stymir himself made the small cuts on their upper surfaces before they were lowered on lines to drag behind the *Wave Cleaver*. The oil began to ooze forth some distance from the ship.

It showed as a distinct stain on the waves, spreading as the leaking bags were rolled and mauled by the force of the waves. When that dark shadow made a goodly streak, one of the marines went aloft. His dart gun had been checked by Stymir and a round dozen in the clip load were the burst-fire type, used to set aflame an enemy's rigging and sails.

They watched the patch eagerly. The strings of weed had reached it, had pushed on so that weed was discolored. There was a burst of eye-searing white fire on one of those soggy tendrils. Soaring flames licked along the oil slick—from more than one place now as the marksman placed his darts.

Smoke rose in a haze and the wind drove to them a stench to set them coughing. Flames roared higher and higher. Stymir laughed.

"More than oil feeds that! The weed burns."

But would more than just the oil-soaked tendrils burn? That was the important question now. Unless those branches of weed ignited and the fire spread to the other patches, they had not gained more than a small measure of time, a very small measure.

If she only had the jewel! Jaelithe tensed, strained against the bond of impotence. Her lips moved, her hands cupped as if she did hold that weapon. She began to sing. No one had ever understood why the gems worked to focus the magic wrought by will and mind. If their secret had once been known to her people, it lay so far back in the dim corridor of their too-long history as to be buried in the dust of ages. The making of the jewel itself, the tuning of it to the personality of she who was to wear it, probably for the rest of her life, that they could do. And the training of how to use it properly, that was also a matter of lessoning. But *why* it worked so and who first discovered this means . . .

The archaic words of her chant meant nothing now either. Jaelithe only knew that they had to be used to raise the Power within her, make it flood her body, and then flow outward. And, though she had no jewel, she was doing now what she would have done had it lain on her palm, pulsating with her song.

She was no longer aware of the captain, of the crew, even visual and tactile contact with the ship was gone. Although no mist born of magical herbs and gums wreathed her in as it must for the difficult raisings, Jaelithe was as blind as if she were so enfolded. And all the will which seethed within her body, had been bottled in her since she laid aside the witch gem, was thrust at the fire, as if she held a spear within her two hands and aimed it at the centermost point of the flames.

Those were reaching higher and higher into the sky; then their red tips bent—not towards the ship, but away—back at the center mass of the weed on the borders of which they fed. Away and down. Jaelithe's chant was a murmur of storm afar. They might have loosed a whole shipload of oil rather than three skins. Stymir and his crew stood agape at the holocaust spouting behind them. A forest in full blaze could hardly have produced more cloud-reaching tongues of flame.

There was a clap of noise and a second before they were hardly more than conscious of the first.

Jaelithe stiffened, for a moment her voice wavered. Kolder—Kolder devices within the weed! She aimed her will—the fire against Kolder blankness. Were there underwater ships slinking out to do battle? But the fire continued to bend to her will.

Those sharp explosions were coming faster. Half the horizon was aflame and the heat of it struck at the ship, the stench of the burning made a gas to set them choking. Still Jaelithe sang and willed, fought for the death of the weed. And the weed died, shriveled, cooked, became ash awash on the waves. Jaelithe knew a swell of triumph, a wild joy which, in its way, could be as defeating as the fire. She fought against that sense of triumph, beat it down with all her might.

No more red trails across the water, the flames had eaten those into noth-ingness. Now the fire fed on the larger mass behind them. The *Wave Cleaver*'s crew watched as the day went and night drew in, but still there was a distant glow along the horizon. And then Jaelithe slumped against the rail, her voice naught but a husky croak. Stymir steadied her while one of the men went running for a cup of ship's wine, thin and sour, but wet to ease somewhat the dried agony of her mouth. She drank and drank again, and then smiled at the captain.

"The fire will eat it to the end, I think," she said in the whisper which was the only voice left her.

"This was great magic, lady." And the respect in his voice was that a Sulcarman kept for some great feat of seamanship or notable stroke in battle.

"How great you do not know, Captain. The oil and the fire darts gave it birth, but the shaping by will set it deep. And—" She raised her empty hands and stared at them now with wonder, "And I had no gem! I had no gem!" She strove to stand away from Stymir and staggered, as weak as one risen from a sickbed of long enduring.

The captain half led, half carried her below, helped her to stretch out on the bunk, where she now lay, trembling with a terrible fatigue. She had felt nothing such as this since her earliest days of training. But before she lapsed into the unconsciousness which lapped about her as the sea lapped the ship, Jaelithe caught at Stymir's hand.

"Do you now sail on?"

He studied her. "This may be only the first of their defenses and the least. But after what I have seen—aye—for now we sail on."

"If there is trouble—call—"

Now there was a smile about his lips. "Be very sure of that, lady. A man does not hesitate to use a good weapon when it lies to hand. And we still have several skins of oil below."

He left and she pillowed her head with a sigh of half content, too tired now to examine this new knowledge, to taste it, feel it warm about her like a cloak against the chill of a winter storm. She thought that her tie with Simon had been her new skill, but it would seem there was another—and there could be more to discover. Jaelithe stretched her aching body and fell asleep, smiling.

XV
Magic and—Magic

Simon stood at the seaward window of his prison cell. Along the horizon now there was no night such as hung over the rock perch of the Kolder fortress, but a curtain of living fire reaching from the sea to heaven, as if the very substance of the ocean unnaturally fed that flame. Every nerve and muscle in him wanted action. Behind that wall of fire somewhere—Jaelithe! But there was no tie between them. He had only her last message, which was in part a cry for help. This was some Kolder trick. No wooden-walled Sulcar ship could dare push through that barrier.

Yet, there was a stir along the cliffs below, a buzz of activity at the seashore where those who served Kolder stood to watch the distant flames. And once Simon was sure that he had seen a true Kolder there, gray smock, capped head, as if what was happening out at sea had so much import that one of the masters must see for himself and not depend upon reports from inferiors.

There had been activity on the land side, too. More of the caterpillar vehicles crawled out into the wilderness of the tortured rock, now with broad beams of light fanning out before them to mark the safest path across the rough terrain. And Simon was sure that he could make out a haze of more light beyond, rising from behind the mesa some miles away.

The Kolder were in haste. But there could be no armada of Estcarp yet at sea. At least no fleet near enough to threaten this keep. And the fire would hold any off a while. So, why all this step-up? No one had approached him since he had been sent here. He could only watch and guess. But only one answer fitted for Simon. The Kolder were under pressure—and time supplied that pressure. Whatever they did which was so important lay in the interior. And that could be their gate! Did they contemplate a return to their own world? No—the Kolder wanted power in this one, and they proposed to gain that by the aid of superior arms, though their numbers must be very few. So, did they wish to recruit from beyond that gate—or bring out new weapons?

But they had been driven out of their own world. Would they dare venture back? More likely they strove to bring out more of their own kind.

He bent his head to rest his forehead against the cool wall and tried again, vainly, to reach Jaelithe. The need for knowing how she fared was as great as his desire for action. But—Kolder blankness there . . .

Loyse! Where in this pile was Loyse? As he had not had any touch with the girl since he had been here he did not know. Now Simon fixed his mind on Loyse, called her.

"Here—"

Very faint, wavering, but still an answer. Simon concentrated until that effort became pain. Their contact had never been clear, it was like trying to clasp in his hands an elusive fog which weaved and ebbed, slipped between his fingers.

"What chances with you?"

". . . room . . . rocks . . ." Contact faded, renewed, faded again.

"Jaelithe?" He asked without much hope.

"She comes!" Much stronger, carrying conviction.

Simon was startled. How did Loyse know that? Tentatively he tried again to reach Jaelithe; the barrier held. But Loyse had seemed so sure.

"How do you know?" He made a sharp demand of that.

"Aldis knows—"

Aldis! What part did the Kolder agent play in this? And how? A trap being set? Simon asked that.

"Yes!" Clear again, and forceful.

"The bait?"

"You, me . . ." Again an ebb and when Simon tried to pursue that further, no answer at all.

Simon turned away from the window to look about the room. He had investigated its possibilities when he had been sent here. There was no change. But still he must do something—or go mad! Somewhere there had to be a way out of this room, a way to stop the Kolder trap.

The cupboards which had remained obstinately shut to his earlier search—Simon set himself to the task of remembering all he had learned concerning the Kolder headquarters in the heart of Sippar. He had found living quarters there also, hidden out in them after he had escaped the horrors of that laboratory where the possessed were fashioned from living but unconscious men. And there also had been cupboards and drawers which defied his opening.

But there had been one mechanical device within the fortress which the Estcarpian invaders had learned to use, first in awe, and then as matter of course: the elevator which ran on the power of thought direction. One designated the desired floor mentally and arrived there promptly. An engine may have supplied the power, mind supplied the directive. In fact, had not mental control existed throughout Sippar? That Kolder leader with the metal cap wired to the installations, whose death had meant the death of the hold in turn—he had been thinking life into the other world machines. So mind ran the Kolder installations.

And in Estcarp the witches' Power was really mental; they could control the forces of nature by thought—without the intermediary of the machines the Kolder depended upon. Which meant that witch Power might be the stronger of the two!

Simon's hands balled into fists. He could not face the Kolder with hands, he had no weapons, which left him only his mind. But he had never tried to fight in that fashion. Jaelithe—even the Guardians had conceded—that he had strength in that way which no male of this world had ever displayed. But it was a pallid thing compared to the energy which the witches were able to foster, trim, turn, use—And he had had no training in its use, save that which conditions had forced upon him these past few months.

Simon looked from his useless hands to the cabinets in the wall. He might be battering his mind and will uselessly against an unbreakable barrier, but he had to do *something*!

So—he willed. He willed a door to open. If there was some mechanism within which would answer to thought, then he willed it to yield to him. He visualized a lock such as might exist in his own world, then he went through the steps of unlatching. Perhaps the alien mechanism was so unlike what he thought of that his efforts would have no effect. But Simon fought on, until he swayed dizzily on his feet, stumbled to the bunk and sat there. But never did he take his eyes from that door, from the movements of the lock which must answer his will!

He was trembling with effort when the panel moved and he looked into the interior of the cupboard. For a moment he sat where he was, hardly able to believe in his success. Then he went forward on his knees, ran his hands about the doorframe. This was no self-deceiving hallucination—he had done it!

What lay inside could not provide him with either the means of escape or a weapon. A pile of small boxes, which when opened held narrow metal strips coiled into tight rolls, series of indentations along their surfaces making Simon believe them records of sorts. But it was the method of lock he wanted most to see. Lying on his back, putting his head into that cubby, using fingers to help his eyes, Simon gained some idea of the mechanism.

Now Simon sat up to face the second cupboard. No exhausting struggle this time. When the second door opened he looked in at what might be his passport for exploration outside this room. Kolder clothing was stored in transparent bags.

Unfortunately the owner was smaller than Simon. When he pulled on the gray smock he found that it did not reach far past his knees and was bindingly tight about the shoulders. But still it might serve after a fashion. Now—the room door.

If it just worked on the same principle as the cupboards—With the Kolder smock about him Simon turned to face that last barrier. Outside the night was solidly black, but there was a dim glow coming from the walls. Simon thought of the lock . . .

Open! Slide open!

An answering click. The portal had not rolled away as did the cupboards, but it gave when he pushed. With the ill-fitting clothes on him, Simon looked into the corridor. He remembered how in Sippar a voice had come from the air, as if his movements had been monitored. The same could exist here, but he could not know. He walked out into the hall, listening.

Using the elevator which had brought him here he could return to sea level, but that would also take him into the center of activity. What he wanted was to be out of the hold entirely. Loyse. Frowningly Simon considered the problem of Loyse. Aldis and Loyse—the latter to be used as bait for Jaelithe. But where in this pile could he find the girl? He dared not trust mind contact again.

Four more doors along this hallway—it could be that they put their prisoners close together. What had Loyse said? ". . . room . . . rocks." Which might well mean that her windows gave her sight of the rocky interior. His room had been the sea and interior, but the two rooms now to his left would have outlet only for the rocks.

Simon tried the panel of the first door. It moved under his touch for an inch or so and he stepped quickly to the next. They did not give. He drew one fingertip along its resistance and thought. A locked door did not necessarily mean that Loyse was behind it—a big mistake could be made either way.

He concentrated on the lock. It was far easier now that he had the pattern fixed. And his confidence grew. Within the Kolder keep he was no longer a prisoner. With that freeze they could take over his body; could he defeat that now as he could their simpler safe guards? Simon did not know—nor did he long to put that to the test.

The door moved when he tried it the second time. Slowly he pushed it into the wall at his right. Loyse stood with her back to him, her hands on the sill of the window, staring out into the night. And she looked very small and drawn together, as if hunching her thin shoulders and stooping made her less vulnerable to what she feared.

In Simon's path of vision she was alone, but of that he could not be sure. Now he attempted another use of his newfound strength, willing her to turn and face him. There was a soft cry as she came about, as if she could not stay her movements. Then, sighting him, her hands came up to cover her face and she cowered back, as if she longed to sink into the surface of the wall.

Simon, startled by her reaction, stepped on in and then thought of his smock. She must believe him one of the Kolder.

"Loyse—" He kept that to a whisper, pulling off the tight-fitting skull cap of the Kolder disguise.

Simon could see the shudder which shook her, but she dropped her hands, did look at him. Then fear became astonishment. She did not speak, instead she launched herself from the wall, running to him as she might have run for sanctuary. Her fingers gripped the smock where it strained over his chest, her eyes were wide, her lips thinned against her teeth as if to choke back a cry.

"Come!" Simon's arm tightened about her shoulders as he pulled her into the corridor. A moment to close and relock the door, then to choose their way.

But all he knew of the hold were two hallways—this one and that below leading to the room where the Kolder leader had interviewed him. The lower stories of this rat-held warren must be alert and alive with those dispatching supplies and men to the interior. His Kolder disguise would not pass more than the most casual glance. But, those workers on the dockside—the possessed. They had paid no attention to him and his guards when he had landed from the ship, would they be as unnoticing now if he and Loyse ventured among them? And did that port have any outer door?

"Aldis!" Loyse held to his arm, both of her hands braceleting his wrist in a fierce grip.

"What of her?" They were at the elevator, but he could only send it and them into danger.

"She will know that I am gone!"

"How?"

Loyse shook her head. "The Kolder talisman—it is somehow aware of me. That is how she followed the thought path, learned of Jaelithe. She was with me when we made contact. She has a watch on my thoughts!"

After his own experiences Simon dared not scoff at that idea. But he could not summon the elevator without better idea of where to go. There was one place—again a gamble, perhaps the biggest of all. But if Loyse was right and the hunt might be up almost at once, he knew of no better battlefield.

Simon pushed the girl ahead of him. He pictured the corridor which led to the Kolder officer and the door closed behind him. Then he spoke to Loyse.

"Do you feel her? Can you tell when she is in contact and where she is now?"

She shook her head. "No, she is part of their new plan. They want Jaelithe—a witch. And when they found she followed us they were excited. They knew there was a surface ship out there but of that they were not afraid. But something went wrong with their defense and then they made this plan. Aldis was pleased." Loyse was grim. "She said everything was working for them. But why are they so excited—Jaelithe is no longer a witch."

"Not in the manner as before," Simon told her, "but could she have kept contact with us had she no Power at all? There is magic and magic, Loyse." But could his magic and Jaelithe's stand against the full force of Kolder?

A faint whisper and the door opened. Here was the corridor he sought. He and Loyse had taken only a few steps along it when that invisible lock caught him. But they continued to march along, helplessly, towards the waiting Kolder.

Helpless? Simon's mind asked. Had he not solved the problem of the doors in the room above he might not have had the temerity to challenge this. He was under a compulsion controlled by the Kolder. But why could he not master that, too? Would he have the time?

The door panel was open. With Loyse, Simon came face-to-face with those who waited there. Kolders—two of them—one the officer he had fronted earlier. The other wore a metal cap, his eyes were closed, his head tilted back against his chair, his whole attitude one of deep concentration on something afar from his present company. There were two of the possessed bearing guard weapons, and to one side, Aldis, her attention all for the prisoners, an alert excitement in her slightly parted lips, her shining eyes.

The Kolder officer spoke first. "It seems that you are more then we expected, Warder of the Marches, and that you have certain qualities we did not take into consideration. Perhaps it would have been better for you if you had not. But before all else you are going to help us now. For it also seems true that your witch wife has not left you for good after all, but is coming to your side in trouble, as a proper wife should. And Jaelithe of Estcarp is of importance to us—of such importance that we intend nothing shall go amiss in the plans we have for her. So, let us be about the accomplishing of those plans."

Simon's body obeyed that other will. He turned for the door, the two guards again before and behind him. Then came Aldis, the whisper of her robe was unmistakable. The Kolder, too? Only one, he discovered as they reached the elevator. The man in the metal cap remained behind.

Down again. But within the bonds of the control Simon was flexing his new sense of Power, beginning to test that compulsion as a man might chip away here and there at some confining shell, seeking the weakest point of its surface. By the time they had reached the water level he was ready for his great effort; however, he reserved that until the proper moment.

The quays were now empty, the undersea vessels there—four of them—inert, nosed against the dock as if they were now useless. And all the laborers were gone. But Simon's party heading on around the water came to a slit in the rock in which steps had been chiseled and they climbed until the air of night and the open shore blew in on them.

Still Simon marched, and then Loyse and Aldis, the Kolder officer to the rear. That fire which had made a scarlet line across the horizon was gone. Though drifts of smoke still arose to cloud the low-hanging stars. The ground here was rough, a scrap of beach walled with many rocks. And this was their final goal. Simon and Loyse faced about. He could not see the guards, but they were there.

"Now—" The Kolder officer ordered Aldis. "Use the girl!"

Simon heard Loyse cry out in pain and terror. He felt the brush of the mental command against his own mind. But at that moment he also struck. Not for his body freedom, not against Aldis or her master here, but at the metal-capped man they had left behind. All the will which had freed Simon from the room locked into a single dart, thrust at the alien. If he had drawn the right conclusions that was the proper focal point.

There was resistance—he had not expected it to be otherwise. But perhaps the very unexpectedness of that assault carried him past barriers too late alerted. Confused thoughts, then rage, finally fear—fear and a quick counter-attack. Only that hampered defense had come too late. Simon hammered home his will. And—his bonds were gone.

But still he stood stiffly, waiting. . . .

XVI
Gateway

*I*t edged in through the shadows, another shadow close lying on the sea, its prow pointed for the strand just below their stand. Now Simon could hear the faint hiss of water on oar—no sailing vessel, but a ship's boat making a rash touch on enemy territory. He could make out two—three in the boat and he knew that one was Jaelithe.

Beside him Loyse started forward as if to greet the newcomers, her stride stiff, limited. She was under control. And Simon did not need to see what menace hid in the shadows.

"Sul!" He gave voice to the war cry they had heard so many times in battle and threw himself, not at the girl, but at the watching Kolder.

The alien went down with a startled cry as Simon closed. Then the attacker discovered that if the Kolder used machines and possessed, they could also fight hard to save their own skins. This was no easy knockout but a vicious struggle with a fighter who had combat knowledge of his own. The initial surprise of his spring again gave Simon a small advantage which he used to the uttermost.

How it went on the shore he did not know, all his attention on his fight to take the most dangerous opponent out of the melee. At last that body suddenly went limp under him and he waited, his hands still locked about the Kolder's throat, for any quiver of returning energy.

"Simon!"

Through the blood which pounded against his eardrums he heard that. But he did not loosen his hold on the Kolder, only turned his head a fraction to answer.

"Here!"

She came over rocks and sand, only a dark shape to be seen. Behind her moved others. But she would not have come so unless their struggle, too, was done. Now she was beside him, her hand touching his hunched shoulder. There was no need for more between them—not now, Simon thought with a rich exultation rising within him—or ever.

"He is dead," Jaelithe said and Simon accepted her judgment, rising from the huddled body of the Kolder officer. For a moment he caught at her upper arms, drew her to him in what was not quite an embrace, which he needed to assure himself that this was no dream but truth. And he heard her laugh, that small happy sound he had heard before upon occasion.

"I have me a warlock, a mighty warlock lord!" Her voice was a whisper which could not have carried far beyond the two of them.

"And I have me a witch, lady, with more than a little Power!" Into that he put all the pride he felt.

"So having paid tribute," now her tone was light amusement for his sharing, "we advance to realities. What do we have here, Simon? The nest of the Kolder in truth?"

"How many are with you?" Simon did not answer her question, but went to the main point.

"No army, March Warder—two Sulcarmen to row me ashore—and these I am pledged to return to their ship."

"Two!" Simon was astonished. "But the ship's crew—"

"No. Upon them we cannot depend until the fleet comes. What is to be done here?" She asked that briskly as if indeed she had captained in a troop of his Borderers.

"Very little." His amusement was irony. "Merely a Kolder fortress to face—and their gate—"

"Lady!" A low but imperative call from the shore.

However, before they could answer, light—an eye-dazzling beam of it, striking to the water, lashing a path along the waves from which steam arose.

"Back!" Simon kept his hold on Jaelithe, drawing her with him into rocks which rose more than their height. He pushed her to her knees with an emphatic order, "Stay!" And ran for the beach.

The boat was still drawn up on the shingle, a body lying by it. There were startled cries.

"Get under cover—back here! Loyse—?"

He heard her answer from the left. "Here, Simon—what is that?"

"Some Kolder deviltry—come!"

Somehow he blundered to her, pulled her along, heard a curse in the Sulcar tongue as other figures followed him.

When they reached the rocky space where he had left Jaelithe, Simon found they were a party of six, two Sulcarmen having dragged a silent third form with them. As one they turned to watch the stormy display on the bay. That light, whatever it might be, cut back and forth with the precision of a weapon designed to make sure nothing alive remained afloat on the surface it now lashed. Under its touch the water boiled and frothed into steaming foam.

On the strand was another fire where the skiff had caught and burned as brightly as if it had been soaked in oil. Simon heard Sulcar curses twice as hot from the man crouched on his right.

But Jaelithe was already speaking into his ear, her voice raised above the crackling of the display in the bay.

"They will come, they are coming—"

Simon caught that warning himself, a tingling in his bones. To get away from the bay was necessary. But where to head in this maze of broken rock? The farther from the Kolder keep for now the better. Simon said as much.

"Aye!" That was the Sulcarman beside him. "Which way then, lord?"

Simon stripped off the Kolder smock since he lacked a belt. "Here." He thrust the end of that into the Sulcarman's hold. "Take off your belt, let your mate take the end of that. Through the dark it is best we go linked. What weapons have you?"

"Dart guns, sea swords—we are marines, Lord."

Simon stiffled a sound which dared not be laughter. Side arms—against the Kolder wealth of weapons in their home arsenal! However, night and the rough ground might aid the fugitives.

They moved out, Jaelithe paired with him, Loyse with one of the Sulcar marines, and the silent Aldis with the last. They had tied her hands, but she had not spoken since they had brought her from the shore, only moving at their pushing. Simon argued against the need of taking her with them, fearing betrayal. But Jaelithe had protested, saying she might have some use.

Their pace, of a necessity, could not be fast, but they were well away from the shore and the burning boat by the time they saw lights gather there, scatter out through the rocks marking a search. Simon kept them behind what cover he could and his precautions proved just. For they were in a pocket between two knife-edged, jutting ridges when that searing light burst over their heads.

The fugitives threw themselves facedown, the heat of that ray harsh on their backs, although it whipped well above them. Back and forth across the countryside it played, and they cowered in the cut they had so luckily found. Then it flared on. Simon waited. This shift might be a device to entice them into the open. He sat up to watch the sky, studied the path of the ray as reflected there. At last it vanished. Perhaps the Kolder believed them caught and cooked.

There was one direction in which the enemy would not dare to aim that weapon—towards whatever lay behind the mesa to which he had watched those caterpillar trucks crawl. To head for that would give them some insurance against being wiped out. He told them of that.

"This Gate—their Gate—you think it lies there?" Jaelithe asked.

"Only a guess, but I believe it a good one. They are either reaching through that again, or preparing to. For some reason they must have contact with their home world."

"And that is where we may also find most of their fighters." One of the Sulcarmen observed.

"It is that—or the fortress. And frankly I would rather be in the open than in that Kolder shell again."

The Sulcarman grunted what might be an assent to that. "Open—that is best. Ynglin, this will be a night to notch on the sword hilt before it is done."

"The sword of Sigrod has already been well notched," his fellow replied. "Lord, do we also take this woman with us?"

"Yes!" Jaelithe answered first. "She is needful to us, how I cannot yet see—but yet she will be needful."

Simon was willing to trust to Jaelithe's instinct in this. Aldis had not even gasped when the heat ray skimmed so close to their hiding place. Whether the Kolder agent was in a state of shock, or whether she was familiar with her masters' weapons and merely waited for nemesis to catch up with the fugitives, Simon could not tell. But he felt uneasy over the talisman she carried and what that might do to entangle them again.

"We should take her Kolder symbol—" He spoke that last thought aloud.

But again Jaelithe countered with: "No—in some way that is a key and it may open doors for us. I do not think it will work so, save when Aldis uses it. But no thing of Power is to be lightly discarded. And I shall know if she tries to use it, that I shall surely know!" The confidence in her words was complete, though Simon still had shadowy reservations.

Again linked together they began a slow journey, since none of them denied the wisdom of seeking the bottom of each cut or canyon which led in the general direction of the interior. In the dark Simon was the guide, testing and feeling for each step at times. And their progress was painfully slow.

At intervals they rested and all of them nursed bruises, scrapes, a cut or two, from falls and slips among the rocks. The dawn showed them as grimed and dirty scarecrows. But with the early light also came sound . . .

Flattened on a rock slope they could watch, over the spine of a ridge, a crawling vehicle, its arcs of light cutting ahead to dazzle the fugitives' eyes. Simon sighed with relief. Hs worst fear had been that they were lost in this wilderness of rock. Now he believed they must be close to what they sought.

This crawler was returning to the keep, empty of supplies. Supplies. Simon swallowed. Food, water—both in this barren country would be found only in Kolder hands. Already the need of water pressed him; it probably was as hard for the others. Five of them and a prisoner—and there the might of the Kolder. Perhaps it would have been simpler to invade the keep.

"Simpler—" Jaelithe's answer was almost a part of his own flow of thought. For seconds Simon did not realize that it was not. "Perhaps simpler, but not the right answer."

He glanced at her where she lay, her mail-clad shoulder nearly rubbing against his. With her helm on her head and the loose scarf of metal links depending from it wound about chin and throat, half her face was veiled. But her eyes met his squarely.

"Reading of thoughts?" Again she answered an unvoiced question. "Not quite that, I think, rather that a similar path is followed by us both. You are aware, too, that this is necessary for our venture. And the answer is not safety—not for us—but something far different."

"The Gate!"

"The Gate," she affirmed. "You believe that these Kolder must have something from there to aid in what they would do in our world. That I believe also, therefore they must not succeed."

"Which depends upon the nature of their gate."

The one which had brought Simon into this world had been a very simple affair—a rough stone between pillars of the same crudely hewn substance. A man sat himself there so—hands at his sides fitting into depressions such as also cupped his buttocks. He then waited for dawn and the gate was open. The Guardian of that way had told Simon legends in the hours he had passed of a long night waiting for the dawn. The tales told that this was a stone of great story: the Siege Perilous of Arthur's use, an enchanted stone which somehow read a man's soul and then opened to him the world in which he best fitted.

But whatever gate had let the Kolders through to defile this world had not been that kind. And what five of them could do to close it, Simon had not the least idea. Only Jaelithe was also right—this was the thing which must be done.

They skulked along the heights as the light grew stronger, able to follow the marks of the caterpillar trucks below. One of the marines climbed the mesa wall to scout beyond. The others took turns in sleeping in a hidden crevice. Only Aldis sat, staring before her, her hands, though bound at the wrists, resting tight against the Kolder talisman on her breast, as if such touch brought her strength.

She had been a rarely beautiful woman, but now she aged before their eyes, her flesh thinning until the bones were stark in jaw and cheek, her eyes sunken in ridged sockets. Her tangled golden hair was as incongruous as a girl's wig on an old woman. Since they had begun the march her sight had never focused on any of them; she might have been one of the possessed. Yet Simon thought it was not the quenching of life which made her so, but rather a withdrawal to some hiding place deep within her, from which spirit and life would waken when the need came.

And so, for all her present passivity, she was to be watched—if not feared. Loyse was the watcher and Simon thought she took more than a little pleasure in the knowledge that their roles were now reversed, that it was she who controlled, Aldis who obeyed.

Simon lay with his eyes closed, but he could not sleep. The energy he had expended in the Kolder keep and after, instead of tiring him, seemed to set ferment to working. He had the sensation of one faced with a problem, clues close to hand, and the driving need to solve it. More used to weapons he could hold, touch, this new ability to work mentally kept his mind restless, awoke uneasiness in him. He opened his eyes to find Jaelithe watching him across the narrow cleft in which they sheltered. She smiled.

And for the first time he wondered a little at the form of their meeting. That barrier he had thought so thick, growing thicker, had vanished utterly. Had it ever been there at all? Yes—but now it seemed as if it had existed for two other people, not for them.

She did not touch him by hand, or mind, but suddenly there was a flow of warmth and feeling about him, in him, which he had never experienced before, though he thought he had known the ultimate in union. And under that caressing warmth he at last relaxed, the pitch of awareness no less, but not so taut and binding.

Was this what Jaelithe had known as a witch, what she had missed and then thought she had found again? Simon understood perfectly how great that loss must have seemed.

Scrape of boot on rock—Simon was on his feet, looking to the end of the crevice. Sigrod swung down. He pulled off his tight-fitting, crestless helm, wiped his arm across his sweating face. His cheeks were flushed.

"They are there right enough, a whole camp of them—mostly possessed. They have a thing set up." He was frowning a little as if trying to find the words in his seaman's vocabulary to best describe what he had seen. Then he used his fingers to support description. "There are pillars set so . . ." Forefinger pointed vertically. "And a crosspiece—so." A horizontal line. "It is all made of metal, I think—green in color."

Loyse moved. She jerked aside one of those hands Aldis kept folded over her Kolder talisman, displaying a part of the alien symbol. "Like this?"

Sigrod leaned closer, eyeing the talisman carefully.

"Aye, but it is big. Four—five men can march through at once."

"Or one of those crawling vehicles of theirs?" Simon asked.

"Aye, it will take one of those. But that is all there is to it—an archway out in bare country. Everything else well away from it."

"As if it is to be avoided," Jaelithe commented. "Yes, they must be dealing with strange and powerful forces here. Dangerous forces if they strive to open such a passage."

An archway of green metal, alien technology to be unleashed through it. Simon made his decision.

"You," he nodded to the crewmen, "will remain here with the Lady Loyse. If we do not return within a full day strike for the shore. Perhaps there you can find that which will take you to sea and so escape—"

Their protests were ready, he could read them in their eyes, but they did not attempt to deny his authority. Jaelithe smiled again, serenely. Then she stooped and touched Aldis on the shoulder.

Though she did not exert any other direction, the Kolder agent rose in turn and moved to the end of the crevice, Jaelithe behind her. Simon sketched a half salute, but his words were for Loyse.

"Your part in this is done, Lady. Go with fortune."

She, too, was all protest which she did not utter. Then she nodded.

"To you, also, fortune—"

They did not look back as they began that long tramp, about the base of the mesa so that they might come upon the Kolder camp from the south. The sun was already warm on the twisted rocks about them. It might make this land a furnace before they were out of it. Out of it where? In hiding near the Kolder gate—or—? Somehow Simon was now sure that the gate was not their only goal.

XVII
Blasted World

*T*he sun was high and, as Simon had foreseen, hot, so that the weight of mail shirt on his shoulders was a burden. He had twisted his Kolder smock about his head turban-wise in place of his missing helm, but the heat beat at his brain as he looked to the Kolder gate. As with the Siege Perilous in Petronius' garden so long ago, he could see nothing beyond it but the same desert of rock. Did this one also need a certain time of day to activate it? He judged that the gate was complete, for no one worked there. Though men lay about the campsite as if struck down in exhaustion.

"Simon!"

Jaelithe and Aldis were in the shadow of a rock pinnacle, sheltered in the only way possible from the glare of this grim waste. The Kolder agent was on her feet, looking not to her companions, but straight out through the shimmering heat waves to the gate. Her hands were again over the Kolder talisman. But her face had come alive. There was an avid eagerness in her expression, as if all she had ever wanted lay just before her for the taking. She began to walk forward at a pace which quickened as she went.

Simon would have intercepted her, but Jaelithe raised a warning hand. Aldis was out in the open now, paying no heed to the heat or the sun, her tattered robe streaming behind her as she began to run.

"Now!" Jaelithe was running in turn and Simon joined her.

They were closer to the gate than those in the camp, and for part of that distance they would be screened from sight as the Kolder party sheltered behind two of the crawler trucks and some of the piled boxes.

It was the gate which was drawing Aldis, and, though she had stumbled and drawn back during their journey about the mesa, she showed no signs of fatigue now. In fact her speed of flight was almost superhuman as she pulled ahead of both her pursuers.

There was a shout from the camp. Simon dared not turn his head for they had come upon a smoothed stretch over which Aldis sped like a winged thing. He doubted if he could match her pace, though Jaelithe was not too far behind her. The gate structure loomed taller in the heat waves.

Jaelithe put on a burst of speed which allowed her to grasp Aldis' torn robe. The fabric ripped the more under her clutch and the other's struggles, but she held fast, although Aldis still pulled her towards the gate. Simon pounded up, his heart beating heavily in his chest, unsteady on his feet from the effort.

Something crackled overhead. Only one of Aldis' wild plunges took them out of the path of that. They were under fire from the camp and in the open they were easy targets. Simon could see only one possible escape. With all his strength he threw himself against both of the women as they struggled, and so rushed the three of them under the crossbar of the gate.

It was plunging from midday into night in a single instant. The sensation of venturing where his kind had no right to go lasted for seconds which were eternity. Then Simon fell into gloom with a lash of rain beating across his body. While overhead crackled such a display of lightning that he was dazzled blind when he raised his head. Jaelithe lay within the circle of his arm and she twisted about, her cheek now close to his.

Water washed about them, dashed into their faces as if they lay in the bed of a swiftly rising stream. Simon gasped and pulled himself up, dragging Jaelithe along. Then she cried out something drowned by the drumming of the storm. By a lightning flash Simon could see that other body, the water striking against it as it lay crosswise, damming the stream. He reached for Aldis. Her eyes were closed, her head rolled limply. Simon thought that he might be carrying a corpse, but he brought her up from the bed of the rapidly filling stream.

They were in a valley between high walls and the water was pouring down very fast. Objects bobbed on its surface, arguing of a flash flood. Simon struggled to the wall and eyed it for possible footholds. They were there but to make that ascent with Aldis was a task which exhausted them both. So that once at the top of the rise he lay again with Jaelithe, his back to the rain, his head pillowed on his arm as he breathed in great sobs.

Neither of the women stirred as at last he levered himself up to gaze about. The sky was dark and the rain continued to pour. Not too far away loomed a bulk promising shelter. Simon shook Jaelithe gently until she blinked up at him.

"Come!" Perhaps she did not hear that word in the fury of the storm but she wavered to her hands and knees and then to her feet with his support. He got her under cover and went back for Aldis.

It was only when he returned that Simon was aware of the nature of their quarters. This was no rock nor crevice cave such as they had used for refuge in the Kolder territory, but a building. Lightning flashes revealed only fragmentary glimpses of the remains. Remains because in the far end of the room in which they stood the roof was partly ripped away, the wall had a great gash down it.

That the break was old was apparent by the straggling bunches of grass which had rooted here and there on the broken flooring. And, in spite of the freshness of the rain-filled wind, there was a musty smell to the whole place.

Simon moved cautiously down the length of the room to that break. There was debris on the floor, twice he nearly lost his footing in a stumble. He trod upon something which crackled and broke under his weight, and caught a glint of lightning flash. With his hands he felt about. Fabric—something rotten which went to slimy shreds, making him wipe his hands on a bunch of grass. Then metal—a rod. Simon picked that up and came back to the doorway where the gloom of the storm seemed lessening, or maybe his sun-dazzled eyes were now adapting to it.

What he held could only be a weapon, he decided. And it bore some resemblances to the rifle of his own world. There was a stock and a barrel. But the metal was lighter in weight than that of any firearm he had known.

Jaelithe had her hand on Aldis' forehead.

"Is she dead?" Simon asked.

"No, she must have hit her head when she fell. This is the world from which the Kolders came?" There was no fear in her voice, merely interest.

"It would seem so." One thing he was certain of: they must not get too far from this spot, from where they had come through the gate. To lose their way meant perhaps no return.

"I wonder if there is any sign of the gate on this side." As usual now Jaelithe's thoughts had followed his. "They must have some guide if they come through and wish to return again."

The wild storm was dying. The night-darkness which had enveloped them when they had come through the gate was now modified with a gray approaching dawn light. Simon surveyed the terrain with the intentness of a scout. This was not desert such as lay on the other side of the Gate. There were evidences of onetime occupation of the country all about him, as if this had once been thickly settled land. What he had first believed rocky hills on the other side of the cut turned out to be the shells and ruins of buildings.

There was a familiarity about all this. He had seen such before when armies had fought their ways across France and Germany years ago. War-torn—or at least visited by some great disaster. And sometime in the past, for vegetation grew among the ruins, rank and high, as if the very destruction of those buildings had provided fertilizer for the plants and shrubs.

No sun showing yet, but the light was that of full day. By that he could see the scars cutting deep into the ruins, where the very ground seemed frozen in a curdled slag, and the nightmare of his own world hovered. Atomic war? Radioactive land? Yet on a closer inspection Simon did not believe so. An atomic bomb would not have left buildings still erect on the edges of those congealed puddles, taken half a structure and spared the balance to stand as a ragged monument. Some other weapon—

"Simon!"

He did not need Jaelithe's alerting whisper for he had seen that movement behind a ruined wall. Something alive, large enough to be formidable, perhaps on the stalk, was moving in the general direction of the hideout. Jaelithe's hand went to her belt where sword and knife still hung. Simon looked for the weapon he had found on the floor.

Its similarity to a rifle, in spite of its light weight, made him consider it seriously. But the narrow opening in the barrel puzzled him—too small to emit even the needle darts of the Estcarpian sidearms. What *had* been the purpose of that slender tube? Simon held it in firing position. There was no trigger, merely a flat button. And, without believing there would be any result, Simon pressed that.

The bush on which he had sighted the alien weapon shivered, rainwater shaking from the leaves. The whole plant quivered and it continued to quiver while Simon watched, hardly believing what he saw. Now the limbs bent earthward, the growth was withering, the leaves shriveling up, the stems twisting visibly. He heard a gasp from Jaelithe as the mass was at last still, a seared and wrinkled lump on the ground. There had been no sound, no visible ray— nothing, save that result of his firing the alien gun.

"Simon! Something coming—" Jaelithe looked beyond the withered bush.

He could see nothing; but feeling—that was different. The sense of danger grew acute. Her hand touched the arm which still supported the weapon.

"Be ready." On the words came another sound from her throat, low—no words—just a murmur.

Cover—three good patches of cover out there. Whatever lurked could hide in all or any. Jaelithe's purring call was louder. He had once seen her spill a Kolder ambush out of hiding; was she trying the same tactics now?

The alert in him was reaching a climax. Then—

From all three covers they came, running silently. One from behind a wall, another from a thick brush, the last from behind a half-fallen building. They were men—or, Simon corrected that as they came into plain sight—they had the general appearance of men. Rags of clothing still covered parts of their bodies, but that only added to the horror, rather than made them more human. For those bodies were thin, arms and legs showing as bone covered with skin, no flesh or muscle underneath. The heads they held high on stick necks were skulls. It was as if the ruins had given up the long dead to stalk the living.

Simon swung up the alien rifle, swept it across that trio. For some heart-choking seconds he thought that the first firing had exhausted whatever strange ammunition that weapon held. Then they halted their silent rush, stumbling only a step or two farther. Their bodies jerked as the bush had quivered.

They were no longer silent, instead there came a thin, high, squealing unlike any human speech, as they jerked and danced, until they toppled to lie still. Simon fought down the nausea which was a bitter taste in his mouth. He heard Jaelithe cry out, and he put his arm about her, drawing her close so they clung together.

"So—"

Both of them were startled by the voice from behind. Aldis, on her feet, one hand steadying her against the cracked wall, came to the door of the building. The smile on her face, as she looked out at the row of doubly dead added to Simon's sickness. It accepted that scene and was pleased by it.

"They still live then—the last garrison?" She paid no attention to either Jaelithe or Simon; they might not have existed. "Well, their vigil is about to end."

Jaelithe moved out of Simon's hold. "Who were these?" She asked in a voice which demanded an answer.

Aldis did not turn her head. Still smiling, she continued to study the dead.

"The garrison—those left to hold the last barrier. Of course, they did not know that that was their only duty—just to hold while the Command reached safety. They believed, poor fools, that it was only a withdrawal to re-form, that help would reach them. But the Command had other problems." She laughed. "However, this is a surprise for the Masters, for it seems they have held longer than was expected."

How could she know all this? Aldis was not Kolder born. In fact, as far as any knew, there were no women at all among the Kolder. But somehow Simon did not doubt that it had happened just as she said. Jaelithe made a small gesture with her hand as a scout might wave caution.

"There are more—"

Again he did not need her warning. The sense of danger had not greatly lessened. But he could sight no movement about the stretch of open ground before them. And this time Jaelithe did not strive to bring them out. Instead, she turned to gaze at the cut from which they had climbed.

"They gather—but not against us—"

There was a sound from Aldis—not a laugh, but a titter which scaled past the bounds of sanity.

"Oh, they wait," she agreed. "They have waited, a long time they have waited. And now come those who would hunt for us—only there will be a second hunt." Again that titter which was worse than any cry of pain or terror.

But what she said was not insane; it made sense. The Kolder could be coming through the gate to hunt for the three of them. And these—these things—which lingered here were gathering to meet them. Did the Kolder know what they faced?

Simon gave a hasty glance along the edge of the drop. To go out might make them the quarry for those who were moving in, but only so could they see the gate in action. And the nagging fear which had ridden him since they had crashed through had been that return might be denied.

There was a solid-looking base out there, perhaps it had once supported a superstructure of which only a single rod pointing skyward remained. With their backs to that base they would have a vantage point from which to watch the gate. Cradling the rifle in his arm, Simon caught at Aldis and pulled her along, Jaelithe following fleetly.

What Simon had believed during the storm to be a streambed now showed as the remnants of a paved road, half covered by falls of debris from the heights. A stream still ran down its middle. A little to the right of their present stand, but down on the level of the road, the wall of the cut, on either side, had blocks of green metal set as pillars.

"The gate," Simon said.

"And its defenders," Jaelithe added in a half whisper.

Those were to be seen now, moving along the cut. For all their unearthly, un-human aspect, they were setting up an ambush with the cunning of intelli-gence, or what had been born from intelligence which had once existed. Here and there Simon marked such weapons as the one he held in his own hands.

"They are coming through!"

There was no change in the metal pillars, no sign that the gate was in use, until those men suddenly appeared as if from the air itself. Possessed fighting men, yet they showed caution as they fanned out, moved up the break. There was no hint from those in hiding. And the controlled warriors of the Kolder advanced without facing attack. A full company of them came through, were well along the cut from which every sign of those in ambush had vanished. Now the nose of one of the crawlers appeared, followed by the rest of its ponderously moving bulk. One of the possessed at the controls, but beside him a Kolder agent.

Around, from below, from across the cut, Simon sensed that upsurge—an emotion in the air, dark and heavy.

"They hate—" Jaelithe whispered. "How they hate!"

"They hate," Aldis mimicked her tone. "But still they wait. They have learned to wait, for that is what they have lived to do."

A second truck crawled out of nothingness. Now the invaders' foot force was well down the old road. This second vehicle had a larger cabin on its body, the top of which was a transparent dome. And in that sat true Kolder, two of them—one wearing a metal cap.

The smoldering cloud of emotion was so strong now Simon expected it to rise as a visible fog. But still those in ambush made no move. A smaller party of possessed, marched stolidly along—labor ready for the need.

Then—nothing more.

"Now!"

Sound, lower than thunder but with a bestial hate which made it one with elements, which owed nothing to intelligence or human understanding. The fury which had been building boiled into action as the possessed shivered, jerked, fell.

There was not enough room in the cut for the trucks to turn. But the one bearing the Kolder officers reversed, crawled backward, so that the possessed who followed it were crushed and broken beneath its treads. Then the driver jerked and quivered in turn. He fell out of sight in the cabin, yet still the truck retreated, or strove to withdraw, though its backward run was now far more unsteady. At last it crashed into one of the piles of debris and slowly tilted, as the treads clawed vainly to keep it upright.

The Kolder wearing the cap had not moved, even his eyes remained closed. Perhaps it was his will which had kept the truck going, even protected him and his fellows now as neither seemed affected by the attack which withered and slew those about them.

His companion turned his head from side to side, studying the route. But no expression Simon could read crossed his white face.

"They have what they want now," Aldis again with that tittering laugh. "They have caught a master to give them a key to the gate."

They had come out of hiding, those skeletons—the bait of the Kolder drawing them free of caution. Many of them were bare-handed as they swarmed about the truck, strove to climb to the bubble-topped cabin.

Mewling cries—half that company fell back, their bodies blackened, their limbs moving spasmodically. But still more gathered, not quite as unwary now. Until several came together, bearing with them a loop of metallic chain. Three flings before it fell into position about the bubble. Then fire ran around it in a spitting line. When that was pulled away and they climbed again, there was no trouble. The bubble shattered and they were at their prey.

Jaelithe covered her eyes. She had seen the sacking of cities and the things done in Karsten when the Old Race had been horned into outlawry. But this was something she could not watch.

"Only one—" Aldis babbled, "he must be saved for the key—they must have their key!"

The metal-capped Kolder hung limply in his captors' clutches, his eyes still closed. The skeletons were gathering along the cut, to form up as a grotesque demon army behind that captive and those who held him. There were the alien rifles among them, but others had armed themselves with the weapons of the possessed. And their hate was still high and hot. Then, holding the Kolder to the fore, they marched, as if a forgotten training was revived in their union of purpose—for the gate.

Simon moved as the first of them stepped between the pillars and vanished. The Kolder—now these—what evil would be loosed in the world he had come to consider his own?

"Yes, oh, yes!" Jaelithe cried. "A wind, then a whirlwind—and we must face the storm!"

XVIII
Kolder Besieged

*O*nly the dead lay in the cut, that sense of alien presence had accompanied that sinister army through the gate. How many had been in that force? Fifty. A hundred? Simon had not counted them, but he believed not over a hundred. And what could so few do against the entrenched might beyond? This was not to be a matter of laying an ambush.

But the Kolder should be too occupied now to remember the fugitives, and this was the time to return with the force before them.

"We go back—"

Aldis gave one of those eerie, tittering laughs. She had crept away from them, was moving along the edge of the ravine, looking at them over her shoulder, a sly grin on her lips. Almost she was coming to resemble the skeletal inhabitants of this land. The last vestiges of beauty had been bleached from her.

"How will you go?" she called. "Door without key, door you cannot batter down. How do you go, mighty warrior and lady witch?"

She was running in a zigzag, fleetly, back into the waste.

"After her!" Jaelithe scrambled by him. "Do you not see? That talisman—it is the key—for her—for us!"

If she were right—Simon followed. Light as it was to carry, the alien rifle was an awkward burden as they smashed through brush. But he clung to it. In spite of the veil of vegetation growing over the debris of the buildings, the ruins were impressive. This had been, if not a city, a fort or settlement of some size. And the number of hiding places among the broken walls were beyond counting. As he and Jaelithe burst into an open space, Simon stopped her with an outthrust arm.

"Where?" He made the one word into a demand and saw her gaze about with dawning comprehension. "She might be within arm's distance or well away, but where?" He hammered home the hopelessness of their unthinking pursuit. This warren of ruins was made for endless hide-and-seek.

Jaelithe raised her hands and cupped them over her eyes, standing very still while her breathing quieted. Simon did not quite know what she would do, but in confidence he waited. She pivoted, partway around, and then dropped her hands to point.

"Thus!"

"How do—?"

"How do I know? By what is not there—Kolder barrier—and she wears the Kolder talisman."

A thin clue—there could be other Kolder traces in this land. But it was the only one they had. Simon nodded and accepted her guidance. It was a crooked path Jaelithe set them, and it bored on into the mass of ruins away from the cleft. Simon marked a back trail as they went, blazing growths, or scratching stones. But the time this chase was taking he regretted.

They came out on a large paved space, ringed by buildings in a better state of repair than those nearer the cut. There was a different look to these structures—not quite the sealed appearance of the Kolder holds, yet with some of their stark rigidity of design. Grace and beauty in the sense his world knew them, Jaelithe's people held, were totally foreign to the minds which had conceived and built these. And any one of them might provide Aldis with numerous hiding places.

"Where?" Simon asked.

Jaelithe put her hand on the top of a low wall which ran about that open space. Her breath came fast and the dark finger marks of fatigue under her eyes were plain. They had drunk their fill of rainwater in the storm, but there had been no food for a long time. Simon doubted if they could hold this pace much longer. And now Jaelithe shook her head slowly.

"I do . . . not . . . know. It has gone from me—" Her hurried breaths were close to sobs. Simon caught her, drew her against him, and she came willingly as if very grateful for his strength, his touch which held comfort.

"Listen," he spoke softly, "do you think you could sing her out, as you did in those in ambush?"

"We must. We must!" Her voice was a husky whisper with an element of hysteria in it.

"And we can! Remember once—back in Kars when there was need of shape-changing and you said that you would call upon me for that which you needed to make the ceremony a swift one? Now it will be the same: call upon me for what you need."

She turned in his arms, though she did not step away from him, only faced outward. And her fingers grasped his in a grip which tightened with her need for the effort. Once more she began to sing that song of invocation which started as a hum and rose higher. And Simon felt, as he had on that day in Kars, that flowing from him, down his arms, through his hands, into her, draining him so he used iron will to stand unmoving.

All this world became one with that singsong, so that he did not see the drab stones about him, nor the patches of encroaching vegetation—only a kind of silvery sheen which was within him and without him at one and the same time. But there was no time either; only this—this—this—

Then that chant which beat in his veins died, and he saw again this deserted city. There was movement, something in the shadows. Coming into the open, crawling . . . Aldis crawling. She did not try to get to her feet, instead she collapsed and lay still. Jaelithe released her hold on Simon.

"She is dead—"

Simon hurried to turn over the limp body. Blood, his hands were wet with it, yet there was more flowing, so much more. Her wan face was untouched but below, the wound flowed blood.

And torn flesh was one with torn robe where she had worn the Kolder talisman. Jaelithe cried out. But Simon caught at one of the bruised hands which was a fist tightened in death to still protect. He worked the rigid fingers until he released what they had gripped to the end of reason and life. Whatever had striven to tear from Aldis the Kolder device had not succeeded in winning its desire. She had lost her life in that battle, but not what she had fought to retain. He held the talisman.

"Come." Simon stood up, his eyes searching the windows, the doors, for any sign of the one or ones Aldis had met here.

Jaelithe stooped and pulled a fold of the torn robe across the body, veiling the ravaged face and the wound on the breast. Then she made a sign in the air above its quietness.

They worked their way back to the cut at the best pace they could muster. Simon watched the back trail, unable to believe that they would not be stalked by whatever had killed Aldis. Had the possession of the Kolder talisman brought on that assault? He believed that it had, and that it might draw the same fate after them.

The possessed dead lay in the broken road. There was no sign that anyone had passed this way since they had left hours earlier. Only the shadows were longer, the signs of approaching night clear.

They climbed down into the cut and stood on the cracked surface of the road where the wrecked crawler slewed to close it off. There were the pillars marking the gate, the dusk making the green somber streaks. Simon raised his hand, the palm cupping the Kolder talisman, and Jaelithe set her hands on his shoulders, keeping such contact with them as they approached the gate.

Would the talisman take them past? They had been three together when they had made the other crossing. And the skeleton army had needed the Kolder to see them through. Simon walked on.

He did not know what to expect, but he was not surprised when the object in his hand grew cold and colder—this was akin to the Kolder barrier against mind reaching. But Aldis had not been Kolder by blood and it worked for her.

Another step and they were both between those wall strips. Once more the shaking, wrenching sense of being whirled into a nothingness which was highly inimical to their kind—then through it. Simon staggered forward. He was on his hands and knees on rock still warm from the sun of a baking day, Jaelithe beside him.

Sunset was not complete enough to hide what lay before them. There had been a battle here. And it had not all been the way of the other world force as it had on the other side of the gate. The rock was not only heated by sun; great ribbons of black scorch lay back and forth across the whole plain of the gate and there were things lying there. . . .

Simon wavered to his feet, stooped to bring Jaelithe up in turn. Nothing before them moved, this had been left to the dead. What he was going to do now might be the wrong thing, but it was the only blow he could see to strike for the freedom of this world against the Kolder and what the Kolder had drawn upon this world.

He raised the alien rifle and fired whatever energy it controlled at the base of the nearer of the gate columns. For a moment in the half light he thought that either the charge was exhausted or that it had no effect upon the structure. Then came a shimmering, licking up from his point of target, running along all that side, coming to the bar at the top, across it, down the opposite pillar. Shimmering became sparkling motes drifting apart.

Simon cried out and dropped the weapon. His hand—his hand!

The Kolder talisman which had still been in his grasp when he fired that shot or ray fell from him, leaving his flesh blackened and burning! It rolled out midpoint between the gate posts shimmering into nothing—to explode in a flash of green fire. But the gate was also gone and they looked upon barren space.

Together they staggered on to where the Kolder camp had been, where there was still a huddle of machines and about them things neither wished to see clearer; they were thankful the light was half cut away by the shadow of the mesa. Simon lurched to the ground by one of the crawlers, his hand pressed against him, much as Aldis had always pressed the talisman to her. He was only aware of the pain, pain mixed with a rising weakness so that he could not think clearly, pain beyond enduring save for the space of a breath, and another, and another—

Then the pain was not so great, or else he had become accustomed to it, as a man might come accustomed to any torment which lasted. He tasted water and after that a solid substance was put between his lips and a voice urged him to eat. How long had he been apart in that place of pure pain? Simon did not know. But now his head cleared and he knew that it was dark and nearly as cold as the day had been hot, that his head rested on Jaelithe's knee, and that she was striving to wake him, her voice first only a low murmur and then her words making sense.

". . . coming. We cannot stay here—"

It was so good just to lie so, the fiery torment in his hand reduced to a dull pain. Simon strove to move his fingers and found there was a bandage about them. Luckily, he thought dreamily, it was his left hand.

"Please, Simon!" More than a plea—a half command. Jaelithe's hands on his cheeks, gently moving his head back and forth. Then her arm slipped under his neck, striving to raise him. Simon protested.

"We must go!" She leaned closer over him. "Please, Simon—there is someone coming!"

Memory flooded back, he sat up. The pool of shadow which had been there when he collapsed was now inky, all light cut off by the bulk of the mesa. He did not question her warning as he pulled himself to his feet, leaning on the crawler's track. For a moment he nursed a dim hope of using the machine, then he knew that he would not understand its controls. Once erect Simon found himself steadier than he had first thought. He moved out with Jaelithe, stumbling over the ruts left by the crawlers.

"Who comes? Kolder?"

"I think not—"

"Those others?"

"Perhaps. Do you not feel it too?"

But if there was anything to be sensed in the night it remained a secret to Simon and he said so. For the first time in many hours he remembered those they had left when they began this last weird adventure. "Loyse—the Sulcarmen?"

"I have striven to reach them. But there are new forces loosed here, Simon, things strange to me. I cannot pierce a barrier, then—suddenly it is gone! Only to rise immediately in another place. It is my thought that Kolder fights for its life, that those who share that blood are using all weapons to their hands— some material, some outside our reckoning. That which came out of the wilderness beyond the gate is still alive to hate, to hunt. And if we do not wish to be caught up in this struggle we must keep aloof. For Kolder fights that which is also Kolder, or what gave birth to Kolder, and this is no war such as our world has seen before."

As he moved on, Simon's strength continued to return. Jaelithe had plundered the camp for rations; she told him of that quietly and he felt her horror of what she had seen on that quest. So again he drew her to him, and they went on with his arm about her shoulders, his bandaged hand resting on her lightly, momentarily content that they could go thus, divided in neither mind nor body.

They were rounding the bulk of the mesa to reach the place where they had left Loyse and the Sulcarmen when a stone, rattling down the side of that tableland, made Simon sweep Jaelithe behind him. He had dropped the alien rifle by the gate, but he still had the knife Jaelithe had given him. And now as he listened, that was ready in his good hand.

"Sul—" Not a battle cry but a whisper in the dark.

"Sul!" Simon replied.

More stones fell and then a figure swung down with the agility of a man used to making his way about ship's rigging.

"Sigrod," he identified himself. "We saw you come out of nowhere back there, lord. But there have been demons in these hills and they destroy aught that moves, so we dared not join you. Ynglin has the Lady Loyse in good hiding and I have come to guide you."

"What has happened?"

Sigrod laughed. "What has not, lord! These Kolder pushed through that gate and were gone as if they had used a spell for becoming nothing before a man's eyes! Then—why, it was like all Demon Night opening. Out came those others, marching as an army of dead risen out of their graves to bring swords for a cause as dead as they! They came down upon the Kolder camp and—this is the truth I speak, I swear by the Waves of Asper that it be so!—they looked at a man and he shriveled up and died, as if a frost storm or a fire had shot upon him. Witchcraft, lady, but such as I have never seen in Estcarp.

"They overran the camp as if those within it had not the power to raise hand to sword or shoot a single dart. Then there came the same lightning as strove to seek us out when we left the shore, and that smote and smote again, catching many of the demons and rendering them once more of the earth. But others went on, taking with them a Kolder, and they were traveling toward the sea. Since then there have been strange things in that direction. Only from this height have I seen something to sea. Lady, your sending has been obeyed—for there are sails showing!"

Simon functioned again as a field officer. "And if the fleet runs into that fire—" He put his worry into words. A warning—but how could they deliver that? Would the Kolder, if they were beleaguered in their own hold, weaken their defense to use the lashing fire at a new, sea-borne enemy in a three-cornered fight? And what of the skeletons? Would it make any difference to them whether they hunted Kolder or stood up to a new foe? He must know more of what was going on.

They held council after they joined Ynglin and Loyse in a rock-walled cave.

"There is a way to gain the coast without too much effort," Ynglin reported, "and I, for one, feel the safer with water nearby. This country is too well made for the hunting games which favor the pursuer as well as the pursued. There have been no more fire lashings for some time now. Also we have seen only a few of these wandering bags of bones slinking about. They prowl as if they would sniff up some trail; they do not show the fear of broken men who run from a strong enemy."

"Maybe they have the Kolder besieged in the keep," Simon speculated. "If so—to go seaward might take us into them." He tried to think. The fleet out there—no one ever claimed that Sulcarmen were stupid. They would not run recklessly headlong into a Kolder den, knowing only too well the nature of the enemy and the traps which might lie before them. But this was a good chance, which, if handled right, might stamp out evil once and for all.

He did not believe the Kolder could erect another gate in a hurry, not while harassed by these creatures from their own past. Therefore, that retreat was closed to them. A siege. But guesses were not enough; he had to know more and that meant seeing the site of the present activity—the coast and the Kolder keep.

"A scout," he began, when Jaelithe spoke.

"We must go together, all of us. Also, the sea is our answer."

Was that her thought—or his? The sea could be their answer, giving them a chance not only to communicate with the fleet but to scout the Kolder. Simon agreed.

They set out along the way the Sulcarmen had marked during that time when with Loyse they had remained in hiding. It was rough going and in the dusk perhaps doubly dangerous. But night had not yet deepened into full dark and they made the best time they could. The Sulcarmen had raided the Kolder camp before Simon and Jaelithe had returned and the supplies from there, meager as they were, gave them renewed vigor and energy.

Simon took advantage of several rest halts to climb above and try to sight the fleet. At his second failure he commented on that and Sigrod chuckled.

"Aye, they are doubtless coasting. That is a raiding trick which always serves us well. They have split the fleet in twain, each half turning stern to the other. There will be one scouting north and the other south to find a landing."

Simon brightened. He knew next to nothing of naval tactics, and his acquaintance with Sulcar fighting methods had been limited to their service ashore. But this information was helpful. If even one of those divisions now sailing north and south could be contacted . . . He began to question the two marines. They might not be able to reach those now heading north, but the southern half of the fleet was headed in their own direction, and there was an excellent possibility it could be signaled from shore. Ynglin volunteered to try.

Then Simon went on—with the keep as his goal.

XIX
Drink Sword–Up Shield

*T*o shake them out of that, lord, you will need more than a fleet. Such walls cannot be wished away." Sigrod lay belly down on the rock peak beside Simon regarding the sealed enigma of the Kolder hold.

There was movement below. Apparently those who had come through the gate were gathered before those unscalable, unbreachable walls, willing to wait. Though in a matter of siege Simon thought the Kolder had all the advantage. The force without had no supplies and this was a totally barren land. Perhaps they believed that they would still withdraw through the gate. How long before they discovered that no longer existed?

Wish away walls—that comment remained in Simon's mind. All in all, since he had been here he had seen only four of the true Kolder—the two in the hold and the two who had manned the crawler into ambush. And two of those were dead. Of the others he believed that the one in the cap with whom he had dueled long range from the shore might serve the purpose he was beginning to formulate. *If* that one still lived. But could he be reached and how effective would such a try be? Simon signaled a return to where they had left Loyse and Jaelithe.

They listened to him as he not really outlined any concrete plan, but thought aloud.

"These capped ones—they control the rest?" asked Sigrod.

"At least they give orders and control much of the installation, of that I *am* sure. The aliens brought one with them; they used him to get through the gate."

"But he did not take them into the keep," Jaelithe pointed out, "or they would not be down there now with the walls held against them."

"He might have been killed in the assault on the camp," Loyse suggested.

"And this other one, whom you fought," Jaelithe continued, "you believe that you can reach him by the Power, compel him to do your will?"

"*We* might," Simon corrected.

"So open the doors for those demons?" Sigrod nodded. "But let those get within and the nut is still shelled for our cracking. They were Kolder, too, is that not so, lord? Then what if we have only exchanged one set of Kolder for another?"

"Yes," Simon admitted the justice of that. "Therefore we hope that Ynglin will be able to bring us reinforcements and we wait."

Much of this warfare with the Kolder was based on waiting, Simon decided. And waiting was the most tiring of all a fighting man's duties—war was full of "hurry up and wait." He rolled over on his back and lay looking up into what was now the thick dark of a cloudy night sky.

"I will take the first watch, lord." Sigrod started up slope again. Simon grunted assent, still considering the problem ahead, chafing because—as so much else since he had ridden out of the South Keep weeks ago—this must depend on chance. Could one will good fortune or ill? His thoughts slid in another direction. Were the old witchcraft tales of his own world true so one could aim ill luck to strike an enemy as he might fire a dart?

A hand on his forehead, stroking back the sweat-dampened locks of hair which clung damply to his skin.

"Simon." She could always make of his name a singing, an intimate reaching of one to the other. "Simon—" No more than that, just his name.

He reached up and caught that brushing hand with his unbandaged fingers, brought it down against his cheek and then to his dry lips. There was no need for any more words between them. Theirs had always been an inarticulate love, but perhaps, Simon believed, the deeper for its very wordlessness. And now the last vestige of that barrier between them had vanished. He knew that she had those depths and silences to which she must withdraw upon occasion, that he meant none the less to her because of those withdrawals. They were a part of her and so to be accepted. No one could ever occupy all of another's thoughts and emotions. There were parts of him which would be closed to her also. But to take without question what she did have to give, and offer in return, freely and without jealousy, all he had—that was what their union meant.

"Rest." Her hand went back from his lips to his head, soothingly. Simon knew that she had matched him thought for thought in wordless communication. His eyes closed and he surrendered to sleep.

There was the Kolder keep, sealed as Yle had been sealed, and from this height they could also see the forces from the gate drawn up about it. Nothing had changed during the night.

"They have not used the fire whip again," Sigrod observed.

"Might not dare to so close to their own walls," Simon returned.

"Or else it is exhausted."

"That we cannot count upon."

"They lost a lot of the possessed back there. Too many perhaps to try a sally. How long do you think they will keep sitting here like this?"

Simon shrugged. Could you judge the Kolder by any standard he knew? They might well be able to go without food and water, to squat stubbornly at the enemy gates for days, weeks—

"Simon?"

Jaelithe's face was turned up to his as he looked back and down. Her eyes were alight and there was an eagerness in her expression.

"A sending, Simon! Our people come!"

He glanced at the sea but the bay was free of ships; there were no sails on the horizon. Then he slid down into the hollow behind the scout point. Jaelithe was facing south, her head up. Loyse looked to the older woman as she would to a beacon of hope.

"Sigrod!"

"Aye, lord?"

"Head south. Pick up those who come. Have them circle inland and come up behind us, so—" Simon clarified his order with gestures.

"Aye!" The Sulcarman slipped away into the broken country.

Loyse plucked at Jaelithe's mail sleeve. "Koris?" Her lips shaped that name rather than spoke it aloud.

There was a half smile on Jaelithe's face as she made answer.

"That I cannot say, little sister. That Koris' ax will swing for you—as it has swung—that is truth. But that it will do so here, that I cannot tell you."

Once more a waiting. They sipped from the water container taken from the crawler, shared out mouthfuls of the dry dust which was yet food, also from the Kolder camp. And, as the sun climbed, they continued to wait. But the sun was battling clouds, and its glare did not reach into their hole to scorch them. Before midday it was blotted out entirely. Simon manned the sentry post on the crag, seeing no change below. The Kolder fortress remained sealed, the attackers waited with a super or inhuman patience in their own chosen cover.

Shortly after midday Sigrod came down through the rocks, a tail of fighting men at his back. Mostly they were Sulcarmen, used to shore raiding, but with them also a scattering of hawk-headed helms marking Falconers, and one party of dark-featured men who came quickly to Simon, a hard core of his Borderers.

"Lord!" Ingvald lifted sword hilt in salute. He looked about him at the broken terrain. "This be a land to favor our fighting."

"Let us hope that that is so," rejoined Simon.

They held a council of war—four Sulcar captains with the pick of their fighting crews, the corps from the Borderer Guard, the Falconers, so far from their own mountains but at home in this country like to those peaks. And Simon laid before them the only plan which he thought might open the Kolder keep.

"This can be done?" Captain Stymir asked, but not as if he greatly doubted the doing. Sulcar knew too much of the witches of Estcarp. Only the Falconers held aloof from magic—their avoidance of women and all the Powers of women making them fear more than accept such weapons.

"We can only try," Simon replied. He looked to Jaelithe now and she gave an almost imperceptible nod.

From among the outer ranks of the men came another figure who had just caught up with the main body of the troops. As those about her she was mailed and helmed, but she also wore the gray surcoat of Estcarp and above it rested the dull gem of witchhood.

She pushed to the fore and gazed from Simon to Jaelithe and studied Jaelithe the longer.

"This you believe you can do?" she asked, and Simon heard a note of derision in that inquiry.

"This we can do!" Jaelithe made a ringing promise of her answer. "We have done much else in the past days, sister."

A frown on the witch's face. Plainly she did not relish Jaelithe's title of kinship and equality. But she was willing to wait, to wait for them to fail, Simon believed. And her attitude awoke in him the same defiance, though perhaps not to a like degree, that Jaelithe's tone had made plain. Perhaps it was that defiance which gave added force to his try now.

He built up his mind-picture of the room in the keep—of the two Kolder who had faced him there. Then he narrowed that vision to the one in the cap. His will became a solid, thrusting thing, as tangible and deadly as a dart or sword blade.

That will reached out—sought—and found! His first fear was proven needless, the man of the cap lived. Alive, yes, but that which had been within him was empty—gone. Empty space could be filled for the nonce—with purpose! Simon's will entered in, and behind that flowed a vast building strength which fed and enlarged and worked at one with him—Jaelithe!

Simon was no longer aware of the rocks and the waiting men, of the witch's scornful face, even of Jaelithe, save as that other force which was also a part of him. The will ran into the emptiness of the Kolder, making him wholly theirs—as possessed as had been the slaves he and his kind had taken from Gorm, Karsten, Sulcar, all the other nations of this world they strove to bring under their rule.

Somewhere within the keep the Kolder was on the move now, answering the commands given him. A simple one to begin with: Open the close wards. Let in disaster. And, being no longer Kolder but possessed, he obeyed.

Simon caught hazy glimpses of that obedience—of hallways, rooms—once of a man who strove to stand between and so died. But always the obedience.

Then came a final act, a picture of a board overhung with lights, on it many controls. And the Kolder's hands moved, pressed buttons, touched levers. With his actions the defense of the keep faltered . . . died.

Then there was a sharp darkness and nothing—Simon recoiled from that nothingness, a cold terror gripping him. He was out in the open under gathering clouds, his hands clasped in Jaelithe's and the two of them staring into each other's wide eyes, the horror of that last encounter with nonbeing upon them both.

"He is dead." Not Jaelithe, but the witch saying that. And she was no longer aloof, but something of that terror was in her face. But her hand came up in a small salute for their sharing. "You have done as you said."

Simon moved stiff lips. "Was it enough?"

"Sul!" That cry from the spy perch. "Those demons, they are on the move!"

They were on the move indeed. For there was a gap in the foundation of the keep, a break in the wall. And into that break streamed the skeletons from the gate world. They made no outcry, merely surged forward. Half the party were through when a shield dropped, catching two of the invaders between it and the earth in its crushing descent. These behind aimed their withering rifles at the lower edge, still kept from sealing by the bodies. And the gate shivered at that point, fell apart in jagged pieces as the rest of the skeletons beat upon it.

"Down and in!" One of the captains whirled his sword over his head, answered by the full-throated, "Sul! Sul!" of the raiders he commanded. The wave of the Estcarpian force flowed down the slope.

It was not pretty, that taking of the heart of Kolder. And it was more a hunt than a battle. Strange weapons slew men and skeleton alike in those narrow hallways as they fought from room to room. But then those weapons failed as if the heart of Kolder missed a beat.

And, when Simon and his Borderers, together with a detachment of Falconers, fought their way into the room with the control board that heart ceased altogether. For the capped men there, six of them, died together and the great board went dead with them.

Then the second battle began, for the skeletons from the gate turned upon the Estcarpian men. Warriors withered and died, but darts and swords could slay also.

Outside a storm raged over the barren land and inside, at last, that other and bloodier storm was stilled. Men wearied and sick of killing, men dazed from the deaths of those they held in close comradeship or kinship, men unable to believe that this was the heart of Kolder and they had truly severed it with sword, dart and ax, drifted one by one into the hall where were the controls.

"Kolder is dead!" Stymir tossed his ax into the air and caught its haft, to wave it in an exultant circle. Behind him others fired as they understood what had been done this day—in spite of cruel losses.

"Kolder is dead!" Jaelithe echoed him. With the witch and Loyse she had entered the hold as part of the rear-guard. "But the evil it has sown lives still. And this—perhaps others will rise to use this." She motioned to the controls.

"Not so!" The witch had taken her gem from about her throat and held it out at eye level facing the board, "Not so, sister. Let us make sure of that!"

There was a flush on Jaelithe's usually pale cheeks as she moved to stand shoulder to shoulder with the witch. Together they stared at the gem. The light in the walls had been slowly dimming, so that the chamber was dusky instead of brightly alight as it had been when they first found it.

But now there was suddenly bright sparkling on the board. Sharp explosions broke the silence. The sparks ran along the surface setting off more small explosions. A smell of burnt insulation rose in choking puffs and here and there the casing melted. Whatever energy the united Power of the women released, it was fast stilling forever the controls the Kolder had used, perhaps not only to activate this hold, but to reach overseas in that web they had spun.

Simon said as much later when he waited with the captains and Ingvald for the last reports from those combing the now darkening corridors and rooms of the keep to make sure no enemy still lived.

"The web remains." The witch sat a little apart, her face drawn and haggard from her efforts to blast the controls. "And, while Kolder spun that web, the materials—the hates, the greeds, the envies from which it was fashioned— were there before they gathered them into their hands and wove them into a net to take us. Karsten is in chaos and for a space that chaos has served us, because it keeps the eyes of the great lords there from looking north, but that will not last forever."

Simon nodded. "No, it will not. Into the vacuum of no-rule will arise some leader and to him unity might come from fixing all the attention of those who would challenge him on a war beyond their borders."

Jaelithe and the witch agreed as one; Ingvald also. The Sulcar captains showed interest but not greatly so.

"And Alizon?" Loyse spoke for the first time. "How fares the war with Alizon?"

"The seneschal has raged like a moor fire into their country. He has wrought better than even we thought he might. But we cannot hold Alizon, seething with hatred for us, any more than we can take Karsten under our rule. We of Estcarp want nothing—save to be left alone in our evening. For we know it is our evening, sliding into a night for which comes no morning. But these would make that a night of flame and death and torment. No man or woman dies willingly, it is in us to strive to hold to life. Thus if we have a night of war before us—" She raised her hand and let it fall again. "Then we shall fight to the end."

"It need not be so!" There was that in Simon which refused to accept her reading of the future.

She looked from him to Jaelithe, then to Loyse, Ingvald, the Sulcar captains. Then she smiled. "I see that it is in you to will it otherwise. Well, Estcarp may go as Estcarp, but perhaps it is now a field in which we sow strange and different seed, and out of that seed may rise a new fruit. This is a time of change and the Kolder have only precipitated turmoil. Without the Kolder the elements remaining are those we have long known and so we may steady the balance for a space. At least I give you this, comrades-in-arms; this has been a quest of valor such as shall be sung by bards these thousand years until you would not know yourselves as the godlings you shall become. We shall take our victories one by one and have pride in them. And there will be no looking for the last defeat!"

"But there is an end to Kolder!" Ingvald cried out.

"An end to Kolder," Simon agreed. "There are still battles ahead, as this Wise One has said—victories to be won."

His hand went out and Jaelithe's moved to meet it. In this hour he could not visualize defeat—or night for Estcarp. Or anything—save what was his.

Year
of the
Unicorn

Contents

I
News of Far Faring at Norstead

*H*ow does one know coming good from coming ill? There are those times in life when one welcomes any change, believing that nothing can be such ashes in the mouth, such dryness of days as the never-altering flood of time in a small community where the outside world lies ever beyond gates locked and barred against all change. From the bell tower of Abbey Norstead—and how many years had sped since a bell had pealed from there?—one could see the unending rippling of the Dales, on and on to the blue-gray of Fast Ridge. On bright days, when the sun drove away the mist curtain, the darkened fringe of the forest cloaking Falthingdale broke the moss-carpet to the west, and the harsh, sky-clutching claws of Falcon-Fist made a sharp point to draw the eyes eastward. But otherwise there were just the Dales with their age-old shutting out of man and his affairs. They had lain so before his coming; they would remain so at his going. But as yet he had his part in them, and here in Norsdale it would seem that quiet land had conquered the natural restlessness of the breed of mankind, slowing all life force to the pace of those everlasting hills.

Yet this was a land lately embattled, wherein war flashed like a drawn sword, thrust as a cruel spear, sung in the flight of arrows, or lay panting of breath behind a half-riven shield. War . . . uneasy peace for a hand-finger count of years . . . then war again. In the first days open field battle, with one army at the throat of another. And then, as men fell, as time gnawed, small raiding bands flashing out of a wilderness to use wolf-fangs. Then—with the invaders from overseas driven back to their first handhold on the coast—a final destruction and peace which those, who had been nurtured from their cradles under the flapping hawk banners, who had heard naught but sword talk for the span of their lives, met awkwardly and ill at ease.

This we of Norsdale knew, yet the war tongues had never licked inland so far as to sear our valley. And only those who had survived terror and worse and fled to us for refuge bore battle tidings within the gates of the Abbey. We had never seen the Hounds of Alizon at their harrying, and for that, the Dames of Norstead gave thanks on their knees night and morning in the Chapel.

Abbey Norstead held me because of that war tide, and there were times when I thought that its stifling peace would choke me. For it is very hard to live among those who are no kin to you, not only in blood but in spirit and desire and mind. Who was I? Anyone walking those precise paths in the garden below could have given me name and past, and would have told you at the asking:

"That one? Ah, that is Gillan, who works with Dame Alousan in the herbarium. She came here eight years ago with the Lady Freeza, being a handmaiden of her household. She has some small knowledge of herbs, a liking for her own company, no beauty, no great kindred—comes to the Chapel services morn and night, she bows her head, but she takes no vows. She sits with the maids at times and plies her needle as is fit, but she has not asked to serve the Abbey. She speaks little—"

Aye, she speaks little, my Dames, and maids, and those ladies who have taken refuge here. But she thinks much, and she tries to remember. Though that is another thing which time denies, or perhaps the unchanging pattern of this land and life denies.

For Gillan is not of the blood of High Hallack. There was a ship. Always can I remember so much, of the tossing of a ship on a sea where waves ran high, avid to feed upon the work of men's hands. A ship of Alizon, that much also I remember. But that I am of Alizon—no. There was a purpose in my being on that ship, and, small and young a girl child as I then was, I feared that purpose. But he who brought me there was under a mast which the wind and wave brought down upon the deck. And then no other of his company knew why I was among them.

That was during the time of raids when the lords of High Hallack, fighting to free their homeland from the Hounds of Alizon, swept down and struck a lightning blow at the port through which came the invaders' lifeblood of supplies and men. And so was I also swept up with those supplies and taken to one of the mountain holds.

The Lord Furlo, I believe, had some private knowledge or suspicion of my past. For he sent me under guard to his lady wife, with safety in that household for a space. But that also did not last, for Alizon arose in might and the Lords were driven back and back. In the depths of harsh and heavy winter we fled across the barren land and into the upper dales. At last we came to Norstead, but the Lady Freeza came only to die. And her lord lay with an arrow in his throat back in the passes—whatever he had suspected concerning me unsaid. So that I was again adrift in strange, if placid, waters.

I need only to look into any mirror within these walls to know that I was not of the breed of Hallack. Whereas their womenkind were fair of skin, but with a fine color to their faces, their hair as yellow as the small flowers bordering the garden walks in the spring, or brown as the wings of the sweet singing birds in the stream gullies, I was of a flesh which browned under the sun, but held no color in cheek. And the hair I learned to plait tightly about my head, was of a black as deep as a starless night. Also . . . I thought odd thoughts. But even before I came to Norstead, while still I played the part of fosterling, I had learned to keep such thoughts to myself, for they alarmed and dismayed those about me.

There is a loneliness of spirit which is worse than loneliness of body. And in all Norstead during those years, I had found only two to whom I might turn for company of a kind. The Dame Alousan was past the span of middle life when I came. She, too, was apart from her companions of the Order. Her life was in the gardens, and in the rooms wherein she worked with herbs, distilling, combining, making those powders and salves, those flasks of liquids, which soothed, healed, pleasured mankind. Noted she was, so that fighting bands in the high hills would send men trained for swift traveling to beg her for those products of her knowledge and hands which would aid in the healing of sore wounds, or the fevers and rheums which came of living in the open no matter what the season or weather.

And when I was set adrift in Abbey Norstead, she looked upon me, keenly, as usually she looked only on some herb new come to her (for she was sent packets of strange things from time to time, by her ordering of gifts). Then she took me into her service and I found that at first all I needed, for it was learning of a demanding kind, and my mind was thirsty for occupation. For some years thereafter I was content.

I was working in the garden, weeding beds, when I first knew that other one who was to trouble my balance of learning and labor. There was always a humming of bees, since bees and gardens needs must lie close together, each serving the other. But now there came another thread of sound, entering my ears, and then my mind. And I sat back on my heels to listen, because my memory stirred, yet I could not summon aught clearly to the surface of my mind.

As if that humming were a cord to draw me. I arose and went through an arch into the inner garden which was for pleasure only, a place with a fountain and a pool, and flowers according to the season. A chair had been placed there, half in sun, half in shade. And in it, well cushioned, draped about with shawls though the day was warm, was one of the very ancient Dames, those who seldom ventured from their cells, who were almost legend among the younger members of the community.

Beneath her hood and coif, her face was very small and white, yet the wrinkles of age were tight only in the corners of her eyes and about her lips. They were wrinkles, too, such as come from smiling, and looking upon the world with a blithe spirit. Her hands were much crooked with the painful twisting of one of the blights of aging, and they lay in her lap unmoving. But on one of her fingers perched a jeweled lizard, its small head raised, its sparks of eyes fixed upon her as if they two communed happily together.

She looked still at the lizard, but the humming stopped and she said quietly, "Welcome, my daughter. This is a fair day."

So short a speech, and words such as you might hear from any lips, yet they drew me into a warmth of spirit, and I came and knelt by her chair eagerly. Thus did I meet with Past-Abbess Malwinna and from her, too, I learned. But hers was not the lore of plants and growing things, but of those winged, and fourfooted, and wriggling lives which share our world, and yet so often are made servants or foes of man.

But the Abbess was in the far twilight of her life, and she was to be my friend for only a short, so short, a time. In all of Norstead she knew my secret. I do not know just how I betrayed myself to her, but she showed no uneasiness when she learned that sometimes I could see the thing behind the thing that was. On the last meeting between us—she was abed then and could not move the body which imprisoned her free-ranging spirit—she asked me questions, as she never had done before. How much could I remember . . . aught at all behind the ship from Alizon? And when had I learned that I was not like those about me? And to those questions I made the fullest answers.

"You are wise for one so young, my daughter," she said then, her voice the thinnest thread of speech. "It is our nature to mistrust that which we do not understand. I have heard tales of a country overseas where some women have powers beyond the common. And also that Alizon stands enemy to those people, just as her hounds now tear at us. It may well be that you are of that other race, prisoner for some reason."

"Please, Mother Abbess"—I took fire from her words—"where lies this country? How might I—"

"Find your way thither, my daughter? There is no hope of that. Accept that fact. And if you venture to where Alizon may again lay hands upon you—that may be courting greater pain than any sword thrust which ends life cleanly. Do not shadow your years with vain longings. Naught moves save by some purpose of Those Who Have Set the Flames. You will find that which is meant for you to do in the proper time." Then her eyes smiled, though her lips could not. "Ill hearing for the young this promise of a better future. But accept it as the last gift I have to give you, my daughter. I say it by the Flames, there will come that which will fill your emptiness."

But that had been said three winter seasons past. Now there was a stirring within Norstead with the war's end. Lords would come riding to claim wives, sisters, daughters. There would be a marrying season and there was a fluttering in the narrow rooms below my tower perch.

A marrying—which made me think of that other tale which had come to us through many lips—the Great Bargain. Now would come the settling of the Great Bargain.

It was during the days of the first spring flood in the Year of the Gryphon that the Lords of High Hallack had made their covenant with the Were Riders of the waste. They had been sore driven by Alizon, knowing the fading hope of very desperate men, and the fear that they faced the final shadow of all. Thus hate and fear drove them to set up a call banner in the salt dunes and treat with the Riders.

Those who came to speak with the harried lords wore the bodies of men, but they were not humankind. They were dour fighters . . . men—or creatures—of Power who ranged the northeastern wilderness and who were greatly feared, though they did not trouble any who touched not upon the territory of their holding. How many of them there were no man knew, but that they had a force beyond human knowledge was certain.

Shape-changers, warlocks, sorcerers . . . rumor had it they were all that and more. But also when they spoke upon oath they held to that oath-taking and were loyal. Thus they would fight, under their own leaders and by their own strange ways, yet for the right of High Hallack.

The war continued through the Year of the Firedrake, and that of the Hornet, until Alizon was utterly broken and downcast. From overseas came no more ships to supply her men. And now that last port was taken. Her forts on the high places were stinking rubble, and she was erased from the coast she had invaded.

Now approached the new Year of the Unicorn, and the Great Bargain must be kept with the Riders as they had kept theirs with High Hallack. The promises of the Riders had been two: that they would come to the support of the lords; and then, they would ride out of the wastelands, withdrawing from the land they had helped to cleanse, leaving it to the humankind alone.

And the other side of that bargain—the payment the Lords of High Hallack had sworn dire and binding oaths to render? That was to be in their own blood, for the Riders demanded wives to carry with them into the unknown.

As far as the Dales knew, the Riders had always been. Yet among them no female had ever been sighted, or talked of. Whether they were the same, with a life span far beyond that of humankind, was not known. But it was true that no child had ever been sighted among them—though lords from time to time had sent envoys into their camps, even before the Bargain.

Twelve and one maids they asked for—maids, not widows, or those who had chosen to live beyond custom's bonds. And they must not be younger than eighteen years of age, nor beyond twenty. They were also to be of gentle blood, and well of body. Twelve and one to be found and delivered on the first day of the Year of the Unicorn at the borders of the waste, thereafter to ride with their strange lords into a future from which there would be no return.

How would they feel, these twelve and one? Fearful? Yes, fear would be a part of it. For, as Abbess Malwinna had said, fear is our first reaction to that which is alien to us. Yet to some of them it would be an escape. For the girl who had no dowry, nor face bright enough to excuse that lack, no kinfolk who would shield and care for her, or who might perhaps have kin who wished her ill—for such this choice might be the better of two evils.

Norstead now sheltered five maids who answered all the requirements. Two of those, however, were already betrothed, waiting impatiently for marriage in the spring. The Lady Tolfana was the daughter of a lord so highly born that surely a great alliance would be arranged for her, in spite of her plain face and sharp tongue. And Marimme, with her flower face, her winning softness—no, her uncle would have her out of this Abbey and off to the first Fold Gather where he could pick and choose wisely among her suitors for good addition to his standing. Sussia—

Sussia—what did anyone know about Sussia? She was older, she kept her own council, though she talked readily about the small concerns of Norstead in company. Perhaps few realized how little she ever spoke of herself. She was of gentle blood, yes, and had, I thought, a good and even quick mind. Her home was in the lowlands of the seacoast, and so she had been exiled from her birth. She had kin with the host, but how close they were . . . Yes, Sussia was a possibility. And how would she welcome news that such a choice had fallen upon her? Would that outward amicability crack and let us see what lay beneath it?

"Gillan!"

I looked down over the parapet of the tower. There was the sheen of rime, the covering of snow across the gardens. I had a doubled shawl about me against the bite of the wind, yet the sun made a diamond glitter on the cloak of winter and a small, sharp wind tugged at Dame Alousan's coif veil.

To be summoned by my mistress in this fashion was a thing out of daily pattern. And in me stirred a feeling which I had half forgotten since I had so well schooled myself against that which was trouble. The dust of time was being blown upon—Dared I hope for a wind of change?

Though I had learned to walk calmly, with unhurried step according to Abbey custom, yet now I ran down the stairs, round and round the wall of the bell tower, setting a curb on my haste only when I came into the open.

"Dame?" I sketched the curtsy of greeting and she gestured in return.

"There has been a message, and a full convocation is ordered." She was frowning. "Go you and tend the small still. This is not a time when my work should be so interrupted."

She pulled at the flapping ends of her veil and went past me with a firm step as one who would speedily answer some hail that she might the more quickly return to her task.

A message? But no one had ridden through the Dale, past the village. The flapping of wings past the tower when I had first ascended? A bird? Perhaps one of the trained, winged messengers used by the host. Abbess Malwinna had lessoned many of them in her active days. The war—had our belief in peace been only rumor? Did the Hounds now bay on the borders of Norstead?

But these were only thoughts, and come war or lasting peace, if I did not give thought to Dame Alousan's distilling there would be real trouble for me in due time.

The stillroom was odorous as always, though most of those smells were sweet and clean. And now there was a fragrance, arising from the vessel by the still which was so entrancing that I feasted my nostrils as I obeyed the orders laid upon me. That task was done, the liquid safely bottled, the apparatus washed thrice as was the custom, and yet Dame Alousan returned not. Outside afternoon became early winter evening. I blew out the lamps, latched the door, and crossed to the main hall of the Abbey.

There was the twittering of voices, growing the shriller by the moment as women's voices do when there are no lower masculine notes to hold them in scale. Two lay sisters were setting out the meal for guests on the table, but none of the Dames were present. By the fireplace gathered all those who had taken refuge, some for years, within these walls.

I hung my shawl on the proper hook by the door and went to the fire. In that gathering I was neither bird nor cat. I do not think that some ever knew just how to accept me: whether as a fosterling of a noble house once on a time and of the rank, say, of a Captain of company's daughter; or whether I was to be counted one of the community though I did not wear the veil and coif. Now, as I joined them they took no note of me at all, and the chitter-chatter was deafening. I saw that some, usually sparing of word, were now striving to outtalk their companions. Truly a stoat had been introduced into our house of hens!

"Gillan, what think you!" The Lady Marimme was all rounded lips and wide, astonished eyes. "They are coming here—they may reach here by the Hour of the Fifth Flame?"

Kinsmen home from the wars, I thought. Truly something to set the Abbey aflutter. But—why the convocation lasting to this hour? The Dames would not be moved by any such guesting, not even that of a full company of horse. They would merely draw into their apportioned section of the Abbey until the men of the world had departed beyond their gates once again.

"Who comes?" I then named her nearest kin. "Lord Imgry?"

"He and others—the brides, Gillan, the promised brides! They march to the waste border by the north road and they will guest here this night! Gillan, it is a fearsome thing they do—Poor, poor ones! We should offer prayers in their names—"

"Whyfor?" The Lady Sussia came up in her usual unhurried way. She had not the soft beauty of Marimme. But, I thought, she will be regal all her life, and eyes will follow her after other beauty fades with the years.

"Whyfor?" repeated Marimme, "Whyfor? Because they ride into black evil, Sussia, and they will not come forth again!" She was indignant.

It was then Sussia repeated aloud what had been something of my own thinking on the subject. "Also they may ride from evil, birdling. All of us have not soft nests nor sheltering wings about us." She must be speaking for herself. Did she indeed have some foreknowledge that the train which would guest with us this night would take her with it in the morning?

"I would rather wed steel, in truth," cried Marimme, "than ride on such a marriage journey!"

"*You* need not fear," I said then, for I guessed she spoke the truth, if somewhat wildly. Her fear was like a sickness, stretching out its shadow from her mind and heart.

But over Marimme's shoulder I saw Sussia look at me oddly. Again it was as if she had foreknowledge. And in me a second time that warning of my own stirred. I could breathe in trouble as I could the aromatic smell of the leaves burned with the firelogs to freshen the hall.

"Marimme, Marimme—"

I think she was glad to turn from us to answer that call, to join the maids who were betrothed and so safe from alarms, as if their safety could cloak her also. But Sussia still faced me, her face locked as ever against any revealing of herself.

"Watch her, as shall I this night," she said under cover of their chatter.

"Why?"

"Because—she goes!"

I stared at her, for the moment struck dumb with amazement. Still I knew she spoke the truth.

"How—why—?" I did not finish either question for she was speaking swiftly, her hand on my arm drawing me a little away, her voice low and for my ear alone.

"How do I know? I had a private message this seven night. Oh, yes, I thought that I might be chosen, there was much to warrant it. But my kinsmen have had other plans for a year, and when the suggestion was made that I might be included in the Bargain, they made sword troth for me at once. While war raged I was landless. Now that the Hounds are hurled back into the sea from whence they came, I am mistress of more than one manor, being the last of my immediate line." She smiled thinly. "Thus am I a treasure for my kin. I go to a wedding indeed this spring, but one in the Dales. As to why Marimme—beauty draws men, even when there is no dowry to fill the purse or line manor with manor. But a man who wants power can try for it in different ways. Lord Imgry has the granting of her hand. He is a man who hoards power as a captain hoards his men—until the attack trumpet. Then he will risk much to get what he wants. He has offered Marimme in return for certain favors.

And the others believe that such a flower offered the Riders will sweeten the dish, since all the brides are not so choice."

"She will not go—"

"She will go—they shall see to that. But she will die—such a draught is not for her drinking."

I glanced across to Marimme. Her face was flushed, she made quick grace-ful gestures with her hands. There was a feverish gaity about her I did not like. Though what was all this to me, who was an outsider and none of their blood or company?

"She will die," again that statement delivered with emphasis.

I turned to Sussia. "If the Lord Imgry is set on this and the others agree, then she cannot escape—"

"No? Oftentimes have men agreed upon a thing and women changed their thinking."

"But even if another were offered in her place, would they agree to the choice, seeing as how it is her beauty which made her it in the first place?"

"Just so." Sussia continued to watch me with that strange, knowing look, almost as if she sensed in me something so closely kindred that we thought with one thought and had no need for words between us. And I was thinking of Norstead, of the dust of changeless years, of my own place and part in this my world. And as many thoughts, some less than half-formed, sped thus through my mind, the Lady Sussia retired a little, dropped her hand from my arm. Once again there was a curtain between us and matters were as they had always been.

I knew a spark of anger then, thinking—"She has used me!" But that lasted only for the space of an eye-wink. For it did not matter what tool of That Which Abides is used to open the future. To let some small resentment cloud one's mind is the action of a fool. Twelve brides would guest here tonight, twelve and one would ride out in the morning. Twelve and—one!

As to planning, I knew much about the Abbey and its inhabitants. Much I could learn through eyes and ears in the hours to come. And proudly I set my wit and will against any of High Hallack, be they Dame, lady, or lords of the host!

II
Brides–Twelve and One

*T*he halls of the Abbey were dim with the winter twilight. Here and there a wall lamp gave off faint light, which did not draw back the arras of shadows. To leave the fireside and the company in the great hall was to step into another world, but it was one I knew well. I passed the chamber of convocation. No light showed beneath its ponderous but time-warped door. The Dames must all have returned to their cells in the wing forbidden to their guests.

Their guests—as I sped along that dark and chilly corridor I thought of those guests. Not those who had been so long housed at Norstead that they had become a part of its life, but rather the party which had ridden in before the last close down of night, who had shared our board and fare about the long table.

Lord Imgry, very much in charge of that company—his brown beard cut short to the jawline for the better wearing of battle helm, its wiry strength shot here and there with silver, which showed again above his ears. His was a strong face, but with determination and will in every line of it, deep graven. This was man to yield not to any plaint, save when it pleased his own plan to do so, when that yielding meant advantage.

With him two others, lesser men, and ones who had little liking for their present task. Soldiers used to the ordering of their coming and going, never looking beyond those orders to what prompted their giving—now ill at ease and more centered upon that unease than upon the surroundings which gave it cause. As for the troop of men-at-arms—they had retired to quarters in the village.

Last of all—the brides. Yes—the brides! My acquaintance with weddings had been limited to those of village maids, when I had accompanied the Dame delegated to represent the Abbey at such festivities. Then there had been smiles, and if tears, happy ones, and singing—a festival, in truth.

Tonight I had faced across the board a new kind of bride. They wore the formal travel garb, robes well padded against winter blasts, skirts divided for the saddle, and, under their cloaks the short tabards, each embroidered with the arms of their houses, that they might proclaim their high birth to the world. But there were no loose locks and flower crowns.

There is a saying that all brides are fair of face on their wedding days. Two or three of these, now glittering of eyes, feverishly flushed, too talkative, were notably pretty. But there were heavy, reddened eyelids, too-pallid cheeks, and other signs of misery among them.

And in my ear had sounded the too-carrying whisper of the Lady Tolfana sharing her knowledge of the gathering with her seat mate.

"Fair? Ah, yes, too fair as her sister-by-blood, the Lady Gralya would tell you. Lord Jerret, her bedmate, is a notable lifter of skirts. It seems that lately he fingers, or would finger, robes closer to home. Thus you see Kildas in this party. Once wedded to a Rider she will not trouble that household again."

Kildas? She was one of the feverishly alive brides. Her brown hair was touched with red-gold in the lamplight, and she had the round chin, the full lower lip of one fashioned for the eyes of men. Even behind the stiff tabard there were hints of a well-rounded body, enough to inflame the lecher her sister's lord was reputed to be. A reason good enough to include Kildas in this company.

Her seat mate was a thin shadow to her ruddy substance. The 'broidery of her tabard was carefully and intricately wrought. Much care and choice had gone into that stitchery, as if it were indeed a labor of love. Yet the robe beneath it was well worn and showed traces of being cut from another garment. The girl sat with her lids tear puffed, downcast and scarce ate, though she drank thirstily from her goblet.

I searched memory for her name—Alianna? No, that was the small girl at the far end. Solfinna—that was it. While Kildas had been sent forth in fine trappings, mayhap salving in some small way the consciences of those who had so dispatched her, Solfinna wore the thread-bareness of poverty long borne. Daughter of an old but impoverished house no doubt, with no dowry, and perhaps with younger sisters to be provided for. By becoming a bride she put the lords under obligation to serve her family.

In spite of Sussia's suggestion, none of the girls were ugly. By the covenant they could not be diseased nor ill formed. And several, such as Kildas, were fair enough to marry well. For the rest, youth granted them some pleasantness or prettiness—thought their unhappiness might cloud that now. I began to consider that the Lords of High Hallack were fullfilling their part of the bargain with honor—save that the brides were unwilling. But then, in High Hallack, weddings did not come of mutual liking and regard, not among the old houses, but rather were arranged alliances. And perhaps these girls were not facing anything worse than they would have faced in the natural course of events.

It was easy to believe that until I looked upon Marimme. She did not display the strained vivacity she had shown in the hall, but now sat still, as a bird when a serpent eyes it coldly. And she ever watched Lord Imgry's face, though she made no attempt to attract his eye, rather turned her gaze from him quickly when it would seem he was about to return it. Had he broken the news to her yet? I thought not. Marimme, who had never been able to retain her composure when faced by small difficulties of the day, would have been in hysterics long since. But it was also plain she suspected something.

And when it did come . . . Plans made on the spur of the moment may go awry, but also may those which have been most carefully wrought over days and years. I was shield-backed now by my own sense that this was one of those times when Fortune not only smiled but put out her hand to aid, and that I needed only keep my wits about me to have matters go as I willed.

So now that the feast was past—mock feast and shadowed as it had been—I sought my own answer for what must happen soon. The shawl over my arm

I whipped about my shoulders. To have sought my own would have perhaps marked my going, so I had one found on the back of a chair—dull green instead of gray, but no color in the night.

The way I took was a private one long known to me by my labors in the stillroom, and it was to that chamber I went, crossing the winter-blasted garden at a run. There were snowflakes, large and feathery, falling. A storm such as this was another stroke of good luck. Within the stillroom the chill was not yet complete, and the good scents hung in the air. What I had come to do must be done swiftly and yet with care.

There were bags on a side shelf, each quilted into pockets of different sizes and shapes. One of these in my hands—and then, moving with care, for I dared not show a light, I made my way about the cupboards and tables, from shelves to chests, thankful that long familiarity made my fingers grow eyes for this task. Phials, boxes, small flasks, each to its proper pocket in the bag, until at last I slung over my shoulder such a bag of simples and healing aids as Dame Alousan had supplied to the war bands. Last, not least but foremost, I groped my way to a far cupboard. It was locked by a dial lock, but that was no bar to me who had been entrusted with its secret years ago. I counted along a row of bottles within, making that numbering twice, then working loose a stopper to sniff.

Faint indeed was the odor—sharp, rather like the vinegar from the orchard apples. But it told me I was right. The bottle was large and difficult to carry. However, to try to decant what I needed for my purpose was impossible here and now. I gripped it tight between crooked arm and breast as I relocked the cupboard.

There was always the chance that Dame Alousan might find it in mind to check her storehouse, even at this hour and season. Until I reached my own room I was in danger of discovery. Yet in me the exultation grew with the belief that all was moving as I wished.

My small chamber was in a turn of the hall, a meeting place between the corridor of the Dames' cells and the portion given to visitors and boarders. Lights shone dully about the frames of some of the latter doors, but only the night lamp was alive at the far end of the cell hallway. My quick breath slowed as I closed my door behind me, though I had as yet taken only the first and far lesser steps on the path I had chosen to walk this night.

I set spark to my own lamp on the small table and set down thereon the flask I had brought out of the stillroom. A tray—so—then the small horn cup always used for medicinal doses, a spoon—all laid out. Last of all—the dose! I poured with care—filling the smaller bottle from my cupboard with the colorless liquid out of the flask. This much, no more—then—into it drops— five, six—from another phial. I counted under my breath, watching the mixture and its changing color, until it was a clear and refreshing green.

Now—to wait—And deep inside me grew a wonder as to how I could be so sure that this would be the way of it. My long suppression of my "power," if that was the word one might apply to my strange bits of knowledge and feeling which warred against controls I kept on them, might that not now have led to deception, a self-confidence which could defeat me? I could not sit still, but stood by the narrow window looking out into the night and the snow. There were lights in the village, marking the inn where Lord Imgry's escort now took their ease. Beyond that only the dull dark of the dale. North—the brides were riding north to the waste border—down Norsdale, and on past the Arm of Sparn, into Dimdale, and Casterbrook, and the Gorge of Ravenswell, off the map of our knowing—

Yet all the time my eyes watched the outer world my ears listened for sounds of the inner one, for I had carefully left my door ajar to better that hearing. And in me excitement bubbled and boiled.

The swish of a robe, the quick beat of slipper heels on uncarpeted stone— All that was in me wanted to rush to the door, throw it open to greet who came. But I kept control and at the scratch of nails on the wood, I moved with deliberation.

It was no surprise to front the Lady Sussia. Nor was she in turn amazed, I was sure, to find me still dressed as if I awaited a summons.

"Marimme—you are needed to tend her with your healcraft, Gillan." Her eyes swept past me to the table where waited the tray and its burden, and there was the faintest curve of smile to her lips as she then glanced back to me. Again there were no words between us, but understanding. She nodded as if agreeing to some comment unheard by me.

"I wish you good fortune for what you do," she said softly. But it was not of heal-craft that she spoke, and we both knew it.

I went down the hall, bearing the tray. As I came to the door of Marimme's room I saw that it also stood ajar and there were voices to be heard. One was low, a murmur which seldom arose to intelligible speech. The sound of it stopped me, struck against the confidence which had been heady wine for my drinking all evening.

Abbess Yulianna! To govern any Abbey-stead was a task demanding wit and force of character which made any Abbess a formidable adversary. And Yulianna was not the least of those who had ruled here. To play my game before her required far more skill than any I thought would be demanded of me. Still I had long passed the point where withdrawal from battle-to-be was allowed.

"—maidish vaporings! Yes, Lady Abbess, this I will make allowance for. But time marches along the hills. We ride with the morn to keep our covenant. And she goes to the marriage made for her! Also she goes without wailing. I have heard you are skilled in heal-craft. Put down her some potion to end these mad humors she has treated us to this past hour. I would not take her gagged or tied in the saddle—but if that must be—so it will! We keep our bargain with those we have hand-sealed to the treaty."

Not choleric was Lord Imgry—no—cold and as one stating facts which not even the winds and tempests of the heavens could nay-say. He was one who would be as unyielding as the earth and the stone bones of the Dales.

"Those who use heal-craft for ill are not among us, my lord." As unyielding in turn was the Abbess. "It remains, do you wish to reach your trysting place with a girl out of her wits with fear? For this is what well may happen should you force this matter—"

"You enlarge upon this past all reason, Lady Abbess! She is startled, yes, and she had heard too many wild tales. Makes she any marriage she will do it to order and not to silly liking. We tryst within three days, so we ride in the dawn. By honor are we bound to give twelve and one brides into their lords' care. Twelve and one we have under this roof tonight. We do not take fewer with us—"

I steadied the tray upon my right hand and scratched upon the door with my left during the small interval of silence which followed his cool statement, one which he certainly did not intend to be challenged.

There was an exclamation and the door was opened. Lord Imgry looked out and I dipped knee in curtsy, but as would an equal in blood.

"What's to do?"

"The Lady Sussia says that heal-craft is needed," I schooled my voice. I waited an answer, not from him, but from her who stood by the bed on which lay Marimme. Her veil was pushed a little back so that her face was in the light. On it, however, I could read no expression as Lord Imgry stepped back to allow me entrance.

"Come in, then. Come in and be about your work—"

I think he paused then because he did not know just how to name me. Though my underrobe was drab of color, I wore neither coif nor veil. Instead I had on a feasting tabard bright with stitchery. No crest for a nameless, landless one, of course, yet the fabric was richly stiff with an intricate design of my own wandering fancy.

But for now the Lord Imgry was not my concern. I continued to watch her who looked over his shoulder. And toward the Abbess Yulianna I launched the full force of what power of will I could summon, even as an archer on a field of grave doubt would loose the last of his shafts at the captain of the enemy. Though in this time and wise I did not wish to compel foe but one who might stand my friend.

"This is not your healer," Imgry said sharply.

I waited then for the Abbess to nay-say me in agreement. But rather did she move a step or two aside and wave me to the bed.

"This is Gillan who is help-hand to our healer and lessoned in all such matters. You forget, my lord, it is past the Hour of Last Light. Those of the community must soon be in the Chapel for night prayer. Unless the need approaches great danger, the healer cannot be summoned from such a service."

He gave a bitten-off exclamation, but even his confidence could not prevail against the custom and usage under this roof. Now the Abbess spoke again:

"You had best withdraw now, my lord. Should Marimme awake from her swoon to find you here—then perhaps needs must we again have the wailing and crying which you so dislike—"

But he did not move. There was no scowl on his face . . . only the lines of determination which I had marked at the table grew a fraction deeper. For a moment there was silence and then the Abbess spoke, and now her tone was that which I had heard now and again, infinitely remote and daunting.

"You are her guardian-by-rule-and-blood, my lord. We know well the law and will not move against your will, no matter how ill we think your decision. She shall not be spirited away in the night—how could she be? Nor is it necessary for us to give oath on such a point under this roof!"

He did then look a little ashamed, for it was plain she had read aright his thoughts. Yet at the same time her voice carried the conviction of one taking that oath she had denied the need for.

"My daughter," again her eyes sought mine and held them. *I* could not read her thoughts. If she read mine, or guessed my intention, she did not reveal the fact. "You will heal as you can, and watch through the night, should that be needful."

I made no direct answer, only bent knee in curtsy, and that more deeply than I had to my lord. He was at the door, still hesitating there. But as the Abbess advanced upon that portal he went, and she, following, closed it with a click of falling latch.

Marimme stirred and moaned. Her face was flushed as one in a fever, and she breathed in uneven gasps. I set the tray on the table and measured by spoon a portion of the liquid into the horn cup. I held it for a moment in my hand. This was the last parting between present and future. From this point there was no back-turning—only complete success, or discovery and ill will of the kind I could never hope to escape. But I did not hesitate long. My arm behind her shoulder raised Marimme. Her eyes were half-open, she muttered incoherently. The horn cup to her lips . . . then she swallowed with soft urging from me.

"Well done."

I looked around. Sussia stood by the door, but it was safely closed behind her. Now she came forward a step or two.

"You will need an ally—"

That was true. But why—?

Again it was as if we were mind to mind, one thought shared.

"Why, Lady Gillan? Because of many things. First, I have more than a little liking for this soft creature." She came to the end of the bed and stood looking down at Marimme. "She is a harmless, clinging one of the kind who find the world harsh enough without bending and breaking under blows never meant for their shoulders. No—you—and I—we are of a different breed—"

I settled Marimme back on her pillows and stood up, putting down the horn cup with a hand I was pleased to see was steady.

"And second, I know you, perhaps better than you think, Gillan. This Norstead has become a prison to you. And what other future could you look to but endless years of like living—"

"The dusty years—" I had not realized I spoke aloud until I heard her small chuckle of amusement.

"I could not have said it better!"

"But why should my fate be a matter of concern to you, my lady?"

She was frowning a little. "To me that is also a puzzle, Gillan. We are not cup-fellows, nor sister-friends. I cannot tell why I wish to see you forth from here—only that I am moved to aid you so. And I think this is truly a venture for you. It is one which I would have chosen, had I been allowed a choice."

"Willingly?"

She smiled. "Does that surprise you?"

Oddly it did not. I believe that Sussia would have ridden on such a bride trek with tearless eyes, looking forward with curiosity and desire for adventure.

"I say it now again, we are of one breed, Gillan. Therefore this Abbey is not for you, and since there is naught else within High Hallack for you—"

"I should go forth with a high heart to wed with a shape-changer and sorcerer?"

"Just so." Still she smiled. "Think what a challenge and adventure that presents, my Gillan. Greatly do I envy you."

She was right, very right!

"Now," she spoke more briskly. "What dose have you given her? And what do you plan?"

"I have given her sleep, and shall give it again. She will wake refreshed a day, perhaps more, from now. And also she will awake with soothed mind and nerves."

"If she sleeps here—" Sussia put fingertip to lips and chewed upon it.

"I do not intend that she shall. In her sleep she will be open to suggestion. As soon as the Hour of Great Silence begins I shall take her to my chamber."

Sussia nodded. "Well planned. You are taller than she, but in the morning dark that will not be marked. I will bring you riding robe—and with her tabard, and the cloaks—You can be allowed some weeping behind a wind veil. I do not think Lord Imgry will question if you walk with face hidden to your horse.

But there is the leave-taking with the Abbess, she is to bless the brides at the Chapel door—"

"It will be very early, and if it snows—Well, there are some things one can only leave to chance."

"A great deal in this ploy must be left to chance," she countered. "But what I can do, that I will!"

Thus together we pushed onward my plan. Marimme lay at last in my bed and beside it I did don the underclothing for a long winter ride, setting over it the divided robe Sussia brought me. It was a finer stuff than I had worn for years, though plain of color, being a silver gray to match the cloak she also gave me. Over it the tabard was a bright splash of color, the striking hippogriff of Marimme's crest picked out in bright scarlet with touches of gold, prancing over a curve of blue-green representing the sea.

I braided and pinned very tight my dark hair and then coiled a travel veil and hood over that, leaving veil ends loose to be drawn mask-fashion over my face. When I was done, Sussia surveyed me critically.

"To one who knows Marimme well, this would be no true counterfeit, I fear me. But the Lord Imgry has seen her little, and those you will ride with on the morn do not know her at all. You must use all wits to keep the play going until they are past the place from which they might return. The time for the meeting with the Riders comes very close, ill weather in the highlands could mean more delay, so Lord Imgry would not dare return. After all, he needs but twelve and one brides, and those he shall have. That will be your safeguard against his wrath when discovery is made."

And that was the only safeguard I would have. A little shiver ran through me, but that I would not let Sussia guess. My confidence must be my armor.

"Good fortune to you, Gillan."

"I shall doubtless need all such wishes and more, too," I replied shortly as I picked up the bag of herbs and simples I had earlier packed. Yet at that moment had I been given a chance to retrace all I had done that night and be free of the action I had embarked upon, I would have scornfully refused it.

Back in Marimme's chamber I rested for the rest of the night, having fortified myself with another cordial from my store, so that while I did not sleep much, I was vigorous and eager when there was a morning scratching at my door.

I had my veil about my head, my cloak over my arm. For a moment I did not move to open and then I heard a whisper:

"Ready?"

Sussia again. When I came forth she put her arm quickly about my shoulders as one who supported a friend in distress. Thus I adapted my action to her suggestion, and walked in a feeble, wavering fashion down to the hall. There was food waiting: cakes of journey bread and hot drink. And of this I managed to eat more than appeared with Sussia sitting as a cup-companion, urging me on in a solicitous fashion. She told me in whispers that she had warned off Marimme's other friends, saying that I was so distraught that their sympathy might prove disastrous. And after Marimme's hysterical fit of the night before when the news was broken to her, they believed this readily.

Thus it went as we had hoped. When Lord Imgry, who had avoided me heretofore, came to lead me forth, I went bent and weeping, so I hoped, in a piteous fashion. The last test came as we knelt for the Abbess's blessing. She gave each the kiss of peace and for that I needs must throw back my veil for a moment. I waited tensely to be denounced. But there was not a flicker of change on the Abbess's face as she leaned forward to press her lips to my forehead.

"Go in peace, my daughter—" She spoke the ritual words, but I knew they were truly meant for me and not Marimme. Thus heartened, I was aided by Lord Imgry into the saddle and so rode out of Norstead forever, after some ten years of life within its never-changing walls.

III
The Throat of the Hawk

*I*t was cold, and the falling snow thickened as the road wound out of Norsdale, across the uplands, where the fringe forests made black scars against the white. In the spring, in the summer, in autumn, the dale lands were green with richly rooted grass and tree, bush and briar, but in winter they held aloof, alien to those who dwelt in village or upland farm.

Into Harrowdale the road narrowed. Before the long war of the invasion, men had spread out and out to north and west, putting under tillage land uncut by plow before. And then there had been travel on these roads, pack merchants, hill lords and their men, families with their worldly possessions on carts, driving their stock, moving out to fresh new lands. But since the war years communication across the Dales had dwindled, and what had been roads became mountain tracks—narrowed and blurred by the growth of vegetation.

There was little or no talk among our party as we rode, not mounted on such horses as the host kept for raiding and battle, but rather on shaggy-coated, short-legged beasts, ambling of pace, yet with vast powers of endurance and deep lungs to take the rough up-and-down going of the back country with uncomplaining and steady gait.

At first we rode three and four abreast, one or two of the escort with each pair of women. Then we strung out farther as the brush encroached and the road became a lane. I was content to keep silence behind veil and hood. For a space I had ridden stiff of back, tense, lest some call from the Abbey . . . a rider sent after . . . would reveal me for what I was. Still did it puzzle me that the Abbess Yulianna had not unmasked me in that farewell moment. Did she have such tenderness for Marimme that she was willing to let the deception stand to save a favorite? Or did she consider me a disturbing factor in her placid community, of whom she would be well rid?

Every hour we traveled lessened the chance of any return. And Imgry forced the pace where he could, conferring with the taciturn guide who led our party at least twice during the morning. How far away was our rendezvous? I only knew that it lay upon the edge of the waste at some point of landscape which was so noteworthy as not to be mistaken.

Harrowdale with its isolated farms was gone, and yet the road climbed with us. Save for our own party we might have passed through a deserted countryside. No animal, no bird—and certainly no man—came into sight. When winter wrapped the farms their people kept much indoors, the women busy at their looms, the men at such tasks as they wished.

Now followed the sharper descent into Hockerdale and the murmur of water, for the swift-flowing stream there was not yet completely ice roofed. We passed a guard post at the head of that dale, and men turned out to salute our leader and exchange words with him and the guide. It was at that pause another pony edged close to mine and she who rode it leaned a little forward in her saddle.

"Do they mean to never give us any ease?" she asked, perhaps of me, perhaps only of the air, that her words might carry to Lord Imgry.

"It would seem not so," I made my answer low-voiced, for I did not want to be heard abroad.

She pulled impatiently at her veil and her hood fell back a little. This was that Kildas whom Tolfana had pricked with her spite at the table. There were dark shadows under her green-blue eyes in this wan light, a pinching about her full-lipped mouth, as if both harsh dayshine and the cold had aged and withered her for the nonce.

"You are his choice," she nodded to Lord Imgry. "But you ride mum this morning. What whip of fear did he use to bind you to his purpose? Last eve you swore you would not come—" There was not any sympathy in her, just curiosity, as if her own discomfort might be eased a little by seeing the sores of another sufferer exposed.

"I had the night for reflection," I made the best reply I could.

She laughed shortly. "Mighty must have been those reflections to produce so collected a mind this day! Your screams had the halls ringing bravely when they took you forth. Do you now fancy a sorcerer bridegroom?"

"Do you?" I countered. The thought that Marimme had made such a show of her fear and revulsion was a small worry now. I was not Marimme and I could not counterfeit her well. Lord Imgry had been engrossed all morning in his urge for speed. But what would happen when he found he had been be-fooled? He needed me to make up the tale of the Bargain, and that should protect me from the full force of any wrath that he would feel upon learning of the substitution.

"Do I?" Kildas drew me out of my thoughts. "As all of us, I have no choice. But—should these Weremen share much with those of our own kind, then I do not fear." She tossed her head, strengthened by her confidence in herself and those weapons chance and nature had given her. "No, I do not fear that I shall be ill received by him who waits my coming!"

"What are they like? Have you ever seen a Rider?" I set myself to explore what she might know. Until this time I had been far more intent upon escape and what lay behind me, than what waited at this ride's end.

"Seen them?" she answered my last question first. "No. They have not come into the Dales, save on raids against Alizon. And they are said then to travel by night, not day. As to what they are like—they wore man forms when they treated with us, and they have strange powers—" Kildas' confidence ebbed and again her fingers pulled at the veil about her throat as if she found it hard to breathe and some cord pressed there against her flesh. "If more is known—that has not been told us."

I heard a catch of breath, not far removed from sob, to my left. Another had come level with us. Her travel-worn robe—she was Solfinna who had shared Kildas' plate the night before—her poverty put further to shame by the other's display.

"Weep out your eyes if you wish, Solfinna," snapped Kildas. "A pool of tears as deep as the sea will not change the future."

Solfinna started, as if that voice, whip-sharp, was indeed a thong laid about her hunched shoulders. And I think that Kildas then took shame, for she said in a softer voice:

"Think you—this was a free choice for you. Thus are you the greater than the rest of us. And since you believe in prayer, do you not also believe that right and good come to just rewards, even if there must be a time of waiting?"

"You chose to come?" I asked.

"It—it was a way to help." Solfinna paused and then spoke more firmly, "You are right, Kildas. To do a thing because it is right, and then to bewail the doing because one fears, throws away all that one must believe in. Yet I would give much to see my lady mother, and my sisters and Wasscot Keep once again. And never shall I."

"Would that not also be so in regular marriage?" Kildas asked with a gen-tleness she had not shown before. "If you had been betrothed to lord or Captain of the south Dales, there would have been no returning."

"So do I remember. To that thought I hold," Solfinna said quickly. "We

are betrothed, in truth. We go to our weddings. It is as it has been for womenkind for untold years. And for my going so, those left behind gain much.
Yet the Riders—"

"Look upon this thought, also. Test it in your mind," I said. "These Riders
so wanted wives that they set up a war bargain to gain them. And when a
man so much wants a thing that he will gamble his life to its gaining, then I
think once it is in his hands he will cherish and hold it in no little esteem."

Solfinna turned to look at me more closely. Her red-rimmed eyes blinked
as if she would focus them upon me for keener sight. And I heard a little
exclamation from Kildas, who urged her mount even closer.

"Who are you?" she demanded with a force which disputed any denial.
"You are not that wailing maid they carried from the hall last night!"

Need I try to play the counterfeit with my fellows in the train? There was
no great reason for that. Perhaps we were already past the point where Lord
Imgry could make adequate protest.

"You are right. I am not Marimme—"

"Then who?" Kildas continued to press, while Solfinna watched me now
with eyes rounded by astonishment.

"I am Gillan, one who dwelt at the Abbey for some years. I have no kin
and this is my free choice."

"If you have no kin to compell you, nor to profit from your free choice,"
that was Solfinna her amazement now in her voice, "why do you come?"

"Because, perhaps there are worse things then riding into an unknown future."

"Worse things?" prompted Kildas.

"Facing a future too well known."

Solfinna drew back a little. "You have done that which—"

"Which makes this the lesser choice of ill fate?" I laughed. "No, I leave
no crimes behind me. But neither do I have any chance of life outside the
Abbey-stead, and I am not of a nature to take veil and coif and be content
with such a round, one day so like unto another, so that during the years they
become just one endless series of hours none differing from its fore or following companion."

Kildas nodded. "Yes, I think that could be so. But what will chance when
he," she nodded towards Lord Imgry, "discovers the truth? He was set upon
Marimme because of some project of his own. And he is not a man to be
lightly balked."

"That I know. But there is this drive he has shown, a fear of passing time.
He will not be able to return to Norstead and he is honor bound to furnish
the full toll of brides."

Again Kildas laughed. "You have a good way of thinking to a purpose,
Gillan. I believe that both your weapons against him will serve."

"You—you do not fear the—the wild men? You chose for yourself alone?" Solfinna asked.

"I do not know about future fears. It is best not to see shadows on mountain crests while you still ride the valleys at their feet," I replied. Yet I thought that I could not claim unusual courage in this. Perhaps I had turned my back on a lesser trouble to embrace a greater. Still I would not admit that now, even to myself.

"A good philosophy," Kildas commented, but there was more a note of raillery than approval in that. "May it continue to guide and preserve you, sister-bride. Ah, it appears that we shall be granted a rest within after all—"

For at word from Lord Imgry the men of the escort came forward to help us dismount and lead us into the post. In the guardroom we crowded to the fire, holding out our hands, moving about to drive the stiffness from our legs and backs. As always I kept as far from our leader as I might. Perhaps he would believe that my avoidance of him was only natural, that Marimme's fear and hatred would keep her from the man solely responsible for her being here. If he believed so, he meant to leave well enough alone, for he did not approach me where I stood with Kildas and Solfinna, sipping now at the mugs of hot stew-soup dipped out of a common kettle.

We were not yet finished with this meal, if meal it might be named, when Lord Imgry spoke out, addressing us as a company.

"The snow has stopped in the heights. Though it is uncomfortable, yet we must press on to the Croffkeep before night. Time grows short and we must be at the Throat of the Hawk in another day's time."

There was some under-the-breath complaining at his words, but none of them spoke out loud. He was not a man to be fronted on a matter of comfort alone. Throat of the Hawk—the name meant nothing to me. Perhaps it was our ordained meeting place.

My luck still held. When we reached the Croffkeep, a mountain fort now only a quarter manned, we were given a long room to ourselves, with pallets laid on its floor, reducing us to the "comforts" of those who had fought from this rocky perch in years past.

Fatigue pushed me into sleep, deep and dreamless. But I awoke from that suddenly, alert of mind, as if I had been summoned. Almost I could hear the echo of some well known voice—Dame Alousan's?—calling me to a necessary task. And so strong was that feeling that I blinked at the dim lamp at the far end of the room, found it hard for the moment to recognize the sounds of heavy breathing from the pallets around mine and realize where I lay and for what purpose.

My weariness was gone. Instead I was filled with a restlessness, the kind of anticipatory unease which haunts one before some momentous and life-changing event. And also my old talent, which had been stirring in me since I first thought of this, was as awake as I.

There was that reaching out in me which I did not exactly fear, which some inner part below the level of my daymind knew and welcomed, as one drinking a cordial for the first time might know the refreshment of an herb the body craved but which hitherto had been denied it. It was a brave excitement and it worked in me so that I found it impossible to lie still.

With what stealth I could summon, I put on my outer clothing. The divided skirt of my riding robe was still damp and the chill unpleasant but that did not matter to the thing forcing me into the night and the open, as if I must have freedom in which to breathe.

Kildas stirred in her sleep as I rounded the end of her pallet, next to mine, and murmured—a name perhaps. But she did not wake, and then I laid hand on the door latch. I could hear the tread of a sentry in the corridor. Yet my need for the open drove me on.

When I edged open the door he was back towards me at the end of his beat. I had taken but a step or two without when he began to turn. And in that moment I was possessed by that which I had known only dimly—a will which was as much of the body as it was of the mind. I looked upon that man who in a moment would see me, and I willed, fiercely and with all the force in me, that he would not do so—not for the seconds which would see me gone.

And he did not! Though, as I reached the side corridor, I leaned limply against the cold stone of the wall, spent with the effort of that willing. And the excitement in me was augmented by another emotion—that of wonder and triumph mixed. For a period out of real time I stood so, savoring what I believed I had done—but one cool portion of me doubted, acted as a brake. Then I went up the stairs facing me and out onto a terrace or lookout walk. The snow gave a certain lightness, but the bulk of the dark heights were only slightly silvered by the moon veiled by drifting clouds.

There was a wind, fresh, as it blew from yet higher peaks—free lands where the dust of the Dales could never linger. Only, now that I had reached this place, that urge which had brought me here was fast dying, and I could find no reason for it. In spite of my cloak I shivered in the wind, drew back to the doorway for protection.

"What do you here?"

There was no mistaking that voice. Why or how Lord Imgry shared my need for deep night wandering, I did not know. But our meeting I could not escape.

"I wished the fresh air—" My reply was stupid, meaningless. But to seek delays was useless.

As I turned I held my hand to my eyes for he swept me with the dazzling light of a hand lamp. He must first have read the device on Marimme's borrowed tabard, for his hand flashed out and gripped my shoulder with punishing force, dragging me closer to him.

"Fool! Little fool!" Passion stirred under that adamant tone, not one soft-turned to Marimme, but rather one concerned with his good or ill. And somehow that thought armored me and I dropped my masking hand to meet him eye to eye.

"You are not Marimme." He kept grip on my shoulder, swung the lamp still closer to me. "Nor are you any other rightfully of this company. Who are you?" And his fingers were five sword points in my flesh, so that I could have cried out under their torment but did not.

"I am of this company, my lord. I am Gillan, out of Norstead—"

"So! They would dare, those mouse-squeak women, to do this—"

"Not so." I did not strive to throw off his hold, since I knew that I could not, but I stood straight-shouldered under it. And I think my denial of his accusation broke the surface of his anger and made him listen. "This was of my own planning—"

"You? And what have you to do with decisions beyond your making? You shall rue this—"

Passion curbed, but perhaps all the more deadly for that curbing. But to meet his anger I summoned will. Somehow I knew that I could not impress upon this man my desire as I had upon the sentry—if I had—still will gave me a shield to arm-sling for my own protection.

"The time for rue is past—or has not yet come," I tried to choose my words with care, those best to hold attention and make him think. "Time is not one of your menie this night, my lord. Return me to Norstead and you have lost. Send me back with one of your men, and again you have lost—for at the Throat of the Hawk there must be twelve and one, or honor shall be broke."

His arm moved and he shook me to and fro, his strength so that in his grasp I was a straw thing. But my will held and I faced him. Then he flung me away so I slipped in the snow and went to my knees, jarring against the parapet of that walk. And I do not believe in that instant he would have cared had I been hurled over it and down.

I pulled to my feet and I was shaking, my bruised shoulder all pain, the fear of what might have been brushing me still. But I could face him head up and still clear of thought, knowing what I must say.

"You were to provide one of the brides, my lord. I am here, nor will I nay-say that I am here through your will, should witness be needed. And still you have Marimme who is of such beauty as to make a fine match. Have you truly lost aught by this?"

I could hear his breathing, heavy as that of a man who had tried to outrace

enemy horse and then been cornered in some rock hole. But, though his pas-
sions were hot, I had read him aright as one of those men who had full control
when that was needed to further his plans. Now he came to me, moving with
deliberation, holding up the lamp. However I knew that the moment of greatest
danger was past. Imgry might hate me for my deception, but he was greater
than some men, able to swallow that which might have been humiliation at
being befooled, because it best suited. His mind was already working ahead,
chewing upon what I said.

"Gillan." My name was flat from his lips, sounding harsh and dull. "And
you fulfill the condition?"

"I am maid, and I think I am some twenty years of age. I was fostering to
Lord Furlo of Thantop and his wife, having been found as a small child a
prisoner of Alizon. Since the Hounds had preserved my life Lord Furlo believed me of some consequence—thus you might deem my birth worthy."

He was surveying me insolently from head to foot and back again. It was
shameful, that raking stare, and he knew it, making it so deliberately. I knew
anger and kept it leashed, and I think he understood that also. Though what
my inner defiance meant to him I could not tell.

"You are right—time presses. Twelve and one brides they shall have. You
may not find this will be as you hope, girl."

"She who expects neither good nor ill has an equal chance of either," I
replied as sharply as I could.

A faint shadow of expression crossed his face, one I could not read.

"From whence did the Hounds have you?" There was interest in that, in
me as a person, not just one of the playpieces he pushed about his private
board.

"I know not. I remember only a ship in a storm, and after that the port
where Lord Furlo's raiders found me." I gave him the truth.

"The Hounds war also overseas. Estcarp!" He flung that last word at me as
if to provoke response, perhaps betrayal.

"Estcarp?" I repeated, for the word meant nothing, though I added a guess
as a question.

"That is enemy to Alizon?"

Lord Imgry shrugged. "So they say. But it is of no moment to you now.
You have made your choice. You shall abide by it."

"I ask no more than that, my lord."

He smiled and it was not a good smile. "To make sure—just to make
sure—"

Thus he brought me back to the sleeping chamber, pushed me inside. I
heard him summon the guard to stand outside that door. Then I came back to
my pallet and lay down. That which I dreaded since I had left the Abbey was
now behind me. I had overleaped the second of the walls between me and

what I sought. And the third—now my mind turned to the third—he who might wait for me at the Throat of the Hawk.

Mankind was known only at the Abbey-stead through speech, and now and then, at long intervals, by the kin of those refugee ladies who made visits. At such times I had been classed among the Dames and had seen such visitors only at a distance. I knew of men, but I did not know man. Though, this too was a custom among those of gentle blood.

Marriage is a far-off thing which lies in a maid's mind but is not early brought to the surface, unless she is among those to whom it is of importance. Perhaps in this way I was far younger than those, or most of those, I rode among. For the Dames marriage had no existence, and they did not discuss it. Now, when I tried to think of what my choice might lead me to, I had little to build upon. Even the fears of my companions were not real to me, since an ordinary man seemed as equally strange as one of the Were Riders with his dark reputation. And I needs must apply my own advice—that which I had so easily given to Solfinna—not to seek trouble until its shadow could not be denied.

There was no mention in the morning between Lord Imgry and me of our night meeting. I used my masking veil prudently, lest others in the company remark that I was not Marimme. But I believe that the closer we drew to the end of our journey, the more each turned inwards, dealing with her own hopes and fears to the best of her ability, and the less attention they spared for those about them. We were very quiet during that day's riding.

As far as I knew the world about us we had ridden off the map of the Dales. The road was a track along which two might file, ponies shoulder to shoulder, and it brought us down again from the heights to a plain, brown with winter. Dark copses of trees looked smaller than those of the Dales, as if they were stunted in growth. There was little underbrush. Sere grass showed in ragged tuffs through snow which lay thinly here.

We crossed a river on a bridge, man-built of timbers rudely cut and set in hardened earth. But there had been no recent travelers on this way, no tracks broke the snow. Again we moved through a deserted world which would lead one to believe that mankind had long passed away.

Once more we began to climb a slope, a little steeper than before. And our way led now to a notch between two tall cliffs. We came out on a level space where stones had been built into a rude half shelter and a pit, lined with rocks, was marked with the black of past fires. There we came to a halt. Lord Imgry joined with one of our guards and the guide before he faced us to say:

"You will rest here."

No more. He was already riding off with those two. Stiff and tired, we dismounted. Two of the escort built a fire in the hold and then shared out trail provisions, but I do not think that any of us ate much. Kildas touched my arm.

"The Throat of the Hawk—" she motioned toward the cut. "It would seem that the brides are more willing than their grooms. There is no sign of any welcome."

As she spoke the gathering dusk was broken, deep inside that cut, by light. Nor the yellow of lamp shine, nor the richer red of fire, but with a greenish glow strange to me. Outlined blackly against it were the three who had left us—just them—no one else appeared in the pass.

"No," Kildas repeated, "one cannot name them eager."

"Maybe," there was hope in Solfinna's voice, "maybe they have decided—"

"That they do not want us after all, child? Never think it! In a songsmith's tales such an ending might be granted us—in real life I have found it always goes differently." As on the day previous her face of a sudden had an aged, pinched look. "Do not hope. You will only be dashed the deeper when you know the truth."

We stood within the range of the fire where there was warmth, but perhaps all of us shivered within as we looked upon the Throat of the Hawk and that ever-steady green fire well within it.

IV
Unicorn Morn

"*K*now you what night this is?" She who tossed back her veil and loosed her hood so that fair hair strayed limply from beneath its edge was Aldeeth who had lain to my left the night before. From the southlands she had come, and her blazon of salamander curled among leaping flames was one I did not know.

Kildas made answer. "If you mean we stand at year's end, to greet a new one with the dawn—"

"Just so. We pass now into the Year of the Unicorn."

"Which some might take as a good omen," Kildas responded, "since the unicorn is the guardian of maidens and the banner of the innocent."

"Tonight—" Solfinna's voice was very low, "we would gather in the great hall, with ivy and holly on the board so each might have a sprig for wearing— holly for the men, green ivy for us. And we would drink the year's cup together and feed the Strawman and the Flaxwoman to the flames, burning them with scented grasses, so that the crops would be fair and plentiful and luck would take its abode under our high roof tree—"

I had memories of the household meeting she put tongue to—a simple one, but carrying meaning for those who lived upon the fruits of the soil. Each silent and dark farmstead we had passed would be doing likewise this night, as would they with more revelry in a great hall. Only at the Abbey there would be no feasting nor burning of symbols, as the Dames allowed no such pagan ceremonies within their austere walls.

"I wonder whether our lords-and-masters-to-be welcome in the year's beginning in some such manner," Kildas broke the silence of our memories. "They worship not the Flames, since Those by their very nature are alien to the Riders' world. To what gods do they bow? Or have they any gods at all?"

Solfinna gave a little gasp. "No gods! How may a man live without gods, a power greater than himself to trust upon?"

Aldeeth laughed scornfully. "Who says that they are men? They are not to be judged as we judge. Have you not yet bit full upon that truth, girl? It is time to throw away your cup of memory, since you and we were born under ill-fated stars which have determined we pass so out of one world into another, even as we pass from the old year into the new."

"Why do you deem that that which is unknown must likewise be ill?" I asked. "To look diligently for shadows is to find them. Throwing aside all rumor and story, what evil do we know of the Riders?"

They spoke then, several together, and Kildas, listening to that jumble of speech, laughed.

" 'They say'—'they say'—this and that *they* say! Now give full name and rank to *they* I'll warrant that this, our sister-comrade has the right of it. What *do* we know save rumor and ill-wishing? Never have the Were Riders lifted sword or let fly arrow against us—only have they ravaged the enemy in our behalf, after making covenant and bargain with our kin. Because a man grows black hair upon his head, wears a gray cloak, likes to live in a land of his own choosing, is he any different in blood, bone and spirit from he who had fair locks beneath his helm, goes with scarlet about his shoulders, and would ride in company along a port town street? Both have their part to play in the land. What evil of your own knowing has ever been from Rider hand?"

"But they are not *men!*" Aldeeth wished to make the worst of it.

"How know we that, either? They have powers which are not ours, but do all of us have talents alike? One may set 'broidery on silk so as to make one wish to pluck the stitched flowers and listen to the singing of the birds she has wrought. Another may draw her fingers across lute strings and voice such a song as to set us all a-dreaming. Do we each and every one of us do these things in a like measure? Therefore men may have gifts beyond our knowing and yet be men, apart from those talents."

Whether she believed what she spoke or not, yet she was doing valiant service here against the fear which sucked at us all.

"Lady Aldeeth," I broke in, "you wear upon your tabard a salamander easy among flames. Have you seen such a creature? Or does it not have a different meaning for you and your house—and its friends and enemies—than a lizard encouched on a fiery bed?"

"It means we may be menaced but not consumed," she replied as if by rote.

"And I see a basilisk here, a phoenix, a wyvern—do these exist in truth, or do they stand for ideas which each of your houses have made their guiding spirits? If this is true, then perhaps those we go to have also symbols which may be misunderstood by those who are not lettered in their form of heraldry." So did I play Kildas' game, if game it was.

But still the green light glowed unchanged in the pass and Lord Imgry and his companions did not return. While waiting always frays the nerves of those who have only time to think.

We were sitting on stones, still huddled around the fire, when he who was Imgry's lieutenant returned with the message that we were to move on, into the Throat. And while I cannot answer for the others, I believe that each of them shared what I was feeling, an excitement which was more than half fear.

But we rode not into any camp of men prepared to do us welcome. Rather did we find at the end of the pass a wide ledge and on that set shelter-tents of hide. Within were couches covered with the skins of beasts, and some of them of beasts we had never seen, and the floors were so carpeted also. There was a long, low table in the largest tent and it was spread with food.

I stroked a fine, silver-white fur, beautiful enough to form a mantle for the lady of a great lord. It was dappled with a deeper gray and so well cured that it was as soft in my hands as a silken shift. Though all about us was leather or fur, still there was a magnificence which spoke of honor offered and comfort promised.

Lord Imgry stood at the foot of the table as we finished those viands left for us, a bread with dried fruit baked therein, smoked meat of rich flavor, sweets which had the taste of wild honey and nutmeats. He had a shadow about him, I suddenly thought, as if between him and our company was forming a barrier—that indeed we were already forsaking our kind. But there was this time no fear in that thought, only again did I feel that prick of eagerness to be away—to be doing—where and what? I could not name either.

"Listen well," his voice was unduly harsh, sending us all into silence. "In the morn you shall hear a signal—the calling of a horn. Then will you take the marked path leading from this tent, and you will go down to where your lords await you—"

"But—" Solfinna protested, "there will have been no marriage, no giving by cup and flame."

He smiled at her as if that shaping of the lips came, for him, with vast effort.

"You pass from those who deal by Cup and Flame, my lady. Marriage awaits you true enough, but by other rites. However, they will be as binding. I bid you," he paused and looked at each in turn, coming at last to me, though his gaze did not linger, "good fortune." His hand moved in the green light of the table lamps. He was holding a cup. "As he who stands for all of you as father-kin, do I drink long years, fair life, and easy passing, kin-favor, roof-fortune, child-holding. Thus be it ever!"

So did the Lord Imgry perform for the twelve and one he had brought hither the father-kin farewell. And then he was swiftly gone before any found tongue.

"So be it." I stood up and in that moment of bewilderment their eyes all swung to me. "I do not think we shall see my lord again."

"But to go alone—down to strangers—" one of them made protest.

"Alone?" I asked. Swiftly Kildas came in, as might a shield companion in a sharp skirmish.

"We are twelve and one, not one alone. Look you, girl—this may not be a festive hall, yet I think we have been made good welcome here." She drew to her a lustrous length of black fur, with small diamond sparkles touching the hair tips in the light.

I had half expected trouble after the going of Imgry. But, while there was little talk among them as they prepared for the waiting couches, also there was more a sense of expectancy and content. Almost as if each in truth did wait for a wedding she might have hoped for in the usual passing of time. They were quiet as if their thoughts were turned inward, and, now and again, one had a shadow of smile about her lips. As I drew the silver fur about my shoulders I wondered a little.

But I slept that night deeply dreamless, and knew no waking until the morning sun lay from the tent's entrance as a thin spear.

"Gillan!"

Kildas stood there. She had looped aside the flap to look out, and now she glanced at me, plainly disturbed.

"What make you of this?"

I crawled from my warm nest of furs and joined her. The horses we had ridden the night before were gone from the picket line our escort had set up. The other tent still stood, its flap looped up to show it empty. To all appearances the camp was deserted, save for the brides.

"It would seem they feared some last-minute changes of mind," I commented.

She smiled "I think they need not have harbored such doubts. Is that not true, Gillan?"

With her asking I knew it was true. On this morn, had all the powers that ruled High Hallack stood ranged before me and offered me the greatest desire of my heart's wishing—still would I have chosen to go down the Throat to the north, rather than return to the world I knew.

"At least they were thoughtful enough to leave our bridal fairings, and did not condemn us to make a poor showing over-mountain." She pointed to packs set out in an orderly fashion. "I do not know how long we have before our lords summon us to a bridal, but I think it might be well for us to waste no time. Rouse you!" She raised her voice to summon the others already beginning to stir and murmur on their beds. "Greet the Unicorn and what it has to offer us."

In the deserted tent we found bowls of a substance like unto polished horn and with them ewers of water, still warm and scented with herbs. We washed and then shared out equally the contents of the packs, so that shabbiness was forgotten and each adorned as fairly as might be. Nor did this oneness on property seem strange, though some had come poorly provided for and others, such as Kildas, with the robes due a bride of a noble house.

We ate, too, with good appetite, of what was left from the night before. And it seemed we had timed matters very well. For, as we put down our cups from a toast Kildas had proposed to fortune, there was a sound from beyond our small world in the pass. A horn—such as a hunter might wind—no, rather as the fanfare of one greeting a friendly keep.

I arose and turned to Kildas and to Solfinna.

"Shall we go?"

"There is no need to linger." Kildas put aside her cup. "Let us see what the fortune we have drunk to has in store for us."

We went out into a curling mist, which cloaked that lying below, but not the path ahead as we walked. And the road was neither steep nor difficult. Behind us followed the rest, holding their skirts from sweeping the earth, their bride veils modestly caught across their faces. None faltered, nor hung back, and there was no trace of hesitation or fear as we went silently.

The horn sounded thrice, when we first obeyed its summons, again when we left the pass behind hidden in the mist, and then a third time. On that the mist before us cleared as if drawn aside by a giant hand. We came into a place which was not winter but spring. The soft turf was short and smooth and of a bright and even green color. A wall of bushes made an arc beyond, and on these small flowers hung as white and golden bells, while from them came the scent of bridal wreaths.

Yet no men stood in our sight, but rather was there a strange display. Lying hither and thither, as if tossed aside in sport, were cloaks. And these were wrought of such fine stuff, so bedecked with beautiful embroidery, with glints of small gems in their designs, that they were richer than any I believe any of us had seen in our lifetimes. Also, each varied from his fellow—until one could not believe so many patterns could exist.

We stood and stared. But, as I looked longer at what lay before me there I was twice mazed, for it seemed that I saw two pictures, one fitted above the other. If I fastened my will on any part of that green cup, the flowering bushes, or even the cloaks, then did one of those pictures fade, and I saw something else, very different, which lay below.

No green turf, but winter-brown earth and ash-hued grass such as had covered the plain across which we had ridden yesterday; and no sweetly flowering bushes, but bare and spiky limbs of brush, lacking either leaf or blossom. While the cloaks—the beauty of the stitchery and gem was a shimmer above darker color, where there were still designs, but these oddly like lines of runes for which I could summon no meaning, and all were alike in that they had the ashen hue of the earth on which they lay.

The longer I looked and willed, so more did the enchantment fade and dim. Glancing to left and right at the rest of my companions I saw that with them this was not so, that they saw only the surface and not that which lay beneath it. And their faces were rapt, bemused, those of mortals caught in a web of glamourie. They looked so happy that I knew no warning of mine could break that spell, nor did I wish to.

They left me, first Kildas and Solfinna, and then all the rest, passing by me swiftly into that enchanted dell. And each was drawn by herself alone, to one of the cloaks which lay beckoning with that semblance of what it was not.

Kildas stooped and gathered up to her breast one of blue, brilliantly rich, with a fabulous beast wrought upon it in small gems—for the double sight came and went for me and it seemed as if I could see now and then through those ensorceled eyes as well. Holding it to her as a treasure beyond all reckoning, she moved forward as one who saw perfectly her goal and longed only to reach it. She came to the bushes, passed through a space there and was gone, for beyond still held the mist curtain.

Solfinna made her choice and was gone. Aldeeth and all the rest followed. Then with a start I realized I alone remained. My double sight was a thing to fear, and to hesitate now might be a risk of peril. But when I looked at the remaining cloaks, for there was more than one, their beauty was vanished and they were all alike. Still not entirely so, I decided when I studied them more closely—for their bands of rune writing differed in number and width.

There was one cloak lying well away from the rest, almost to the hedge which set the boundary of the dell. The runes did not run on it as an uninterrupted edging, but rather were broken apart. For a moment I strove to see it enchanted—green—or blue—or something of them both—and on it a winged form wrought in crystals. But that glimpse was gone so quickly that I could not have sworn to it a moment later. I was drawn to it—at least it drew my eyes more than did the others. And I must make a choice at once, lest I be suspect—though why I thought that I could not tell.

So I crossed dead and frozen ground, and I picked up the cloak, holding it before me as I went on, through bare bushes and the chill of the mist, leaving yet perhaps a half score cloaks still lying there, their spells fled, their color vanished.

I heard voices in the mist, carefree laughter, joyful sounds. But I saw no one and when I tried to follow any of the sounds, I could not be sure of my direction. In the filmy entrapment my uneasiness grew and all the dark of dread rumor whispered in memory. The cloak between my hands was heavy, lined with the white-gray fur which was harsh to my skin. Also I was chilled, and my borrowed finery dew-wet, little protection against the mist.

A darkness within that cloud, a figure coming towards me. In that moment it was as if I were being stalked, cunningly and with no hope of escape.

Shape-changers, that was the cry in one's ears when the Were Riders were named. Man—or beast—or both? What did I face now—a darkish shadow—but it walked on two feet as a man. Did a beast's head rest upon its shoulders? Whatever my companions had met with in that disguising fog, they had not feared, or voices would not continue to rise with so happy a ring, even though the words they spoke I could not distinguish.

I halted, holding still the cloak which grew ever heavier in my hands, dragging them down with its weight. Man, yes, the outline of the head was human, not that of a shaggy beast. And still I had clear sight, for the gray-brown cloak I held proved that.

A last whisp of the fog between us was sundered and I looked upon this stranger from another breed who had come a-hunting me. He was tall, though not of the inches of a hill warrior, and slim as any untried boy on his first foraging would be slim. Smooth of face as a boy, also. Yet the green eyes beneath slanting brows were not a boy's eyes, but weary and old, still ageless also.

Those brows slanting upward, made the eyes in turn appear angle-set in a face with a sharply pointed chin, and were matched in outline by his thick black hair which peaked on his forehead. He was neither handsome nor unhandsome by human standard, merely very different.

Though his head was bare of war-helm he wore a byrnie of chain-link, supple by his easy movements within its casing. This reached to midthigh and beneath it breeches, close fitting, of furred hide, a silvery fur shorter in the hair than the pelt which had taken my fancy at the tent though still of the same nature. His feet were booted, but also in furred leather, their color being a shade or two the darker than his breeks. About his slender waist was a belt of some soft material, fastened by a large clasp in which were set odd milky gems.

Thus did I face for the first time Herrel of the Were Riders, whose cast cloak I had gathered to me, though not through the same weave spell as intended.

"My—my lord?" I used the address courteous, since he did not seem disposed to break the silence between us.

He smiled, almost wryly.

"My lady," he returned and there was a kind of mockery in his voice, but I did not feel it was turned upon me. "It would seem that I have woven better than was deemed possible, since that is my cloak you bring."

He reached out and took it from me. "I am Herrel," he named himself as he shook out the folds of cloth and fur.

"I am Gillan," I made answer, and then was at a loss as to what was expected of me. For my planning had not reached, even in fancy, beyond this point.

"Welcome, Gillan—"

Herrel swung out the cloak and brought it smoothly about my shoulders so that it covered me, from throat almost to the ground now lost in the mist.

"Thus do I claim you, Gillan—it being your wish?"

There was no mistaking the question in those last words. If this be some form of ceremony, then he was leaving me a chance of withdrawal. But I was committed now to this course.

"It is my wish, Herrel."

He stood very still as if awaiting something more, I knew not what. And then he leaned a little toward me and asked, more sharply than he had yet spoken:

"What lies about your shoulders, Gillan?"

"A cloak of gray and brown and fur—"

It was as if he caught his breath in a swift gasp.

"And in me what do you see, Gillan?"

"A man young and still not young, wearing chain mail and furred clothing, with a belt about him buckled with silver and milk white stones, with black hair on his head—"

My words dropped one by one into a pool of quiet which was ominous. His hand came out and took from my head the bride's veil, so swiftly and with such a jerk that it dislodged the pinning of my braids, so they loosened and fell upon my back and shoulders over the cloak he had set about me as a seal.

"Who are you?" His demand came with some of the same heat as Lord Imgry had shown at our night meeting.

"I am Gillan, beyond that I do not know." The truth I gave him because even then I knew that the truth was his right. "A war captive from overseas, fostered among the Dales of High Hallack, and come here by my own will."

He had dropped the veil into the mist, now his fingers moved in the air between us, sketching, I believe, some sign. There was a faint trail of light left by their moving so. But the smile was gone from his mouth and now he wore a battle-ready face.

"Cloak-bound we are—and there is no chance in that, only destiny. But this I ask of you, Gillan, if the double sight is yours—see with the outer eyes only for this while—there is danger in any other path."

I did not know how to regain the less from the greater, but I tried fumblingly to see green grass under my feet, color about me. And there was a period of one wavering upon the other, then I stood with rippling splendor about me, green-blue hung with crystal droplets. And Herrel wore a different face more akin to that of humankind and strongly handsome—yet I found it in me to like his other guise the better.

He took my hand without more words and we walked from the never-never land of the mist into more green and flowering trees. There I found my companions, each companied with a man like unto Herrel, and they were seated on the grass, drinking and eating, each couple from a common plate, even as was the custom at bride feasts in the Dales.

To one side there were more men, and these were without companions, nor did the feasters appear to note them. As Herrel drew me onward we passed close to these apart and almost as one they turned to stare at us. One started forward with a muffled exclamation, and it was not a pleasantry I knew. Two of the others shouldered him back into their midst. Nor did they do aught more as we passed and Herrel brought me to a small nook between two sweet flowered bushes and then vanished, to speedily return with food and drink, set out in crystal and gold, or that which had such seeming.

"Laugh," he told me in a low voice, "put on the happiness of a bride, there are those who watch, and there is that which must be said between us which other ears—or minds—or thoughts—must not share."

I broke a cake and held a portion to my lips. From somewhere I summoned a smile and then laughter. But in me there was a sentry now alert.

V
Trial by Spell

I give you good fortune," Herrel was smiling too as he raised cup in formal courtesy and sipped of the sparkling amber fluid it held.

"But," I returned, low voice, "that may not be . . . is that what you must say? If so—why?"

He held out the cup to complete the fair-wishing, and I drank in turn, but over its rim my eyes held his.

"For several reasons, my lady. First, this was not meant to be worn, by any of you—" Herrel put his hand to the cloak which still spread a shimmer of glory about my shoulders. "By Pack Right they could not deny any the weave-spell. But neither did Halse, or Hyron, believe that mine would draw a bride. You have chosen ill, Gillan, for in this company I am the least—"

He said that easily, as if no shame or hurt lay behind his words, but as if some sentence had been passed upon him and accepted.

"That I do not believe—"

"Smile!" He broke a bit from a cake. "You speak from courtesy, my lady wife."

"I speak what is mine to say."

And now it was his turn to fall serious, and his eyes searched my face, looked into mine as if he would indeed enter into my mind and shift the thoughts there, both those I knew and what other lay beneath them. He drew a sudden deep breath.

"You are mistaken. I have been wrought in such a way that I fumble where others move easily to their goals. I am of their blood, yet within me something has gone awry so that the powers I use may sometimes be as I wish, and other times fail me. Thus, you have come to a man who is held by his fellows to be less than they."

I smoothed the cloak about my shoulders. "It was this which drew me, thus it would seem that this time your power did not fail."

Herrel nodded. "So have I stepped where I should not tread—"

"And this is a reason to fear disaster?" But I did not think he feared, this was no rear-line warrior, whatever else he might deem himself.

"You know not." He did not say that sharply. "But I would have you learn at this first hour that there may not be a clear road for our riding. Twelve and one brides did we bargain for, but near twice that number are in this war band. We left it to the spell that our destiny be read, but there are those who will not accept what does not match with their desire. Also—war captive from overseas you have named yourself, and then fosterling in the Dales. But you are not of High Hallack blood, none of them have the true sights. Therefore you may be far kin to us—"

And not of humankind therefore? questioned that within me which had awakened and thirsted to grow.

"I know not who I am, Herrel, save that my memory is of being captive on a vessel of Alizon, thereafter being taken by raiders from the port. I came here of my own choice, replacing one who dreaded it—"

"Let no one else suspect that you possess the true sight. In these late years that which is not of us is mistrusted—perhaps doubly so for one who took up *my* cloak." He looked down into the wine in the cup as if some picture of the future might be mirrored there. "Walk softly in the night when the enemy sleeps nearby. Do I fright you with raider talk, Gillan?"

"Not greatly. I do not think I need hold a mirror before you for my protection."

"A mirror?"

"A mirror to kill demons. Seeing themselves their fright kills or repels them. See, I am learned in the ancient lore."

And this time his laugh was no matter of study and need, but came lightly.

"Perhaps *I* should have the mirror, my lady. But I think not, for one so fair need only look in such to learn how much she pleases."

"Is this—" I was warm of cheek from such a speech as had not ever been made me before, "your camp?"

"For an hour or two." Still he smiled and I knew he read my discomfiture—which added to it. But courteously he spoke now of other things.

"If you look for a snug keep to sit between you and the air, or the walls of a great hall, then you will search in vain, my lady—for the while. We have now no home save the waste—"

"But you go from here—that was part of the Bargain! Where then do we ride?"

"North—yet farther north—and east." His hand was on his belt, fingers upon the milky gems of its buckle. "We are exiles, now we are minded to turn homeward once again."

"Exiles? From what land? Overseas?" It might be true then that we were distantly of one blood.

"No. Afar perhaps in space and time, but not sundered from this land. We come from a very old people, and those of High Hallack from a new. Once we had no boundaries on our far-faring. All men and women held a sway over Powers which could build, or serve according to their wishes. If one wished to savor the freedom of a horse running before the wind, then one could be that horse. Or a hawk or eagle in the heavens. If one wished raiment soft and silken for one's wearing, jewels for the bedecking, under will they were his, to vanish when he tired of such. Only, to have such Power and use it ever brings with it a great weariness, so that in time there is naught left to wish for, no new delight for one's eyes and heart and mind.

"This then is a time of danger, when those who grow restless turn from the known to the unknown. Then may doors be opened on forbidden things and that loosed which cannot be controlled. We grew older, and more weary of mind. And some of the restless and yet curious tried other ways of amusement. Indeed did they loose what they could not rule, and death, and worse than clean death, stalked the land. Men who have been brethren now looked upon their fellows with suspicion, or hate. There was killing, sword-blooding and with it another kind of killing which was worse.

"Until, after one great battle there was set upon us all a bond. Those who were born among us from that time forward with a restless spirit they must issue out of the land to which our kin withdrew and become wanderers. Not by choice though some did choose so—but because they were deemed to be disturbing to a peace which must be kept or our breed would perish. And they must wander for a set number of years, until the stars moved into new patterns. When that was accomplished, then once more they might seek out the gate and ask for admittance. And if they could pass the testing there—then they would know again the homeland of their kind."

"But the men of High Hallack say that always since they have pushed into this country have they known the Riders—"

"The years of man and our years are not one and the same. But now the day comes when we may essay the gate. And whether we win or fail, we shall not let our breed die. Thus we take brides from among men, that there will be those after us."

"Half blood is not always as great as full blood."

"True. But, my lady, you forget that we do have Powers and arts. Not all the changes we can make are to confuse the eye only."

"But will their eyes continue to be confused?" I glanced about me. Those who had preceded me were rapt, ensorceled, so that they looked only upon those with whom they shared cup and plate. Whether this was for good or ill, I could not tell.

"For now," he said, "they see what they are designed to see, according to the desires of those whose cloaks they wear."

"And I?"

"And you? Perhaps, if more than one will was bent to the task, you might see at another's bidding—but that I do not know. I only say, with all my cunning as a warrior, it is best that you pretend to see. There are those within this company who would not welcome a will they believed they could not dominate. Fortune, my lady—"

His change of tone and word were so abrupt that I was startled and then alerted. Someone approached us from behind. But taking my cue from those about me, I showed no sign of knowing this, and I looked only to Herrel as if he alone meant anything in a narrow world.

He who had come up behind me stood silently, but from his very presence there flowed a vast, disquieting cloud of—hate? No, this emotion was too contemptuous, too self-confident for hate. That we save for those who are our equals or superiors. This was the kind of anger one directs at lesser things which have crossed a will which believes it should have no limits. And how I knew this I could not have said, save that within this enchanted place perhaps emotions were made keener by design, and mine, not having been snared in the set trap, thus scented out the stranger's.

"Ah, Halse, come to drink bride cup?" Herrel looked up to the one who stood behind me. There was no unease open in him. But once in Norstead village at a feasting I had watched a wrestling match. And it was said that those who pitted their strength against one another so bore ill will, so the battle was not in sport or play. Then I had witnessed that small narrowing of the eyes, that stiffness of shoulder for the instant before they sprang at one another. And so was I sure that this Halse was no good friend to Herrel, but one of those whom he expected might show anger that his cloak-spell had succeeded. But still I schooled myself to watch only Herrel, with the bemusement of the other girls.

"Bride cup?" Derision on that, laid over anger. "For once it would seem, Herrel the Wrong-handed, you set a spell aright. Let us see how well you set it—what kind of a bride came to your cloak!"

In one fluid motion Herrel was on his feet. He was weaponless yet it was as if he stood with bared steel to take up the challenge the other had so plainly flung at him.

"My lord?" Had I put into that the proper amount of wonder? It would appear that I must continue to play the part of one I was not. Putting forth my hand I caught at Herrel's where it hung by his side. Under my touch his flesh was cool and smooth. "My lord, what's to do?"

Exerting unusual strength he drew me up and then I was at last able to turn and face the other. He was perhaps a finger taller than Herrel, and, of the same slim and wiry breed. Yet his shoulders were the wider. In general appearance though he differed only from his troop-mate in that his breeches and boots had been fashioned from a rusty brown fur and the belt around him had small red stones to its clasp. But beneath the general resemblance of one to the other—for they might have been brothers, or at least close kinsmen—there was a parting of spirit. Here indeed, I thought for a moment almost wildly, I might well raise my demon-repelling mirror. Anger, arrogance, a self-belief so great that he deemed naught in the wide world could withstand his will were Halse's. And to me he was one whom I would have fled as a small frightened mousething would flee the strike of a hunting owl. But that very fear worked within me to build ramparts for defense.

"My lady," Herrel's hand still held mine in a warm, sustaining grip. "I would make known to you this my fellow Rider. He is Halse the Strong-armed."

"My lord," I strove valiantly to play well my role, "friends and comrades of yours are high in my sight and regard—" The words were formal but perhaps that was not wrong.

Halse's eyes glowed not green but red. And his smile was like a whip laid upon bare skin for those who could see.

"A fair lady indeed, Herrel. Luck has played you good wisher this time. And what think you, my lady, of luck's efforts?"

"Luck, my lord? I do not know what you mean. But by the Flame," thus did I retreat upon the language of the Dales, "I have grasped great happiness this hour!"

Now *I* had aimed whiplash, though I had not intended so. He continued to smile, but under that stretching of skin and lip boiled emotion he kept in check—so much emotion that I began to wonder if more lay behind his exchange with Herrel than that explanation given me.

"May it continue, my lady." He bowed and stepped aside, going with no more farewell.

"So be it," commented Herrel. "Now, I think, we face war. And for your own sake, Gillan, guard your tongue, your smiles, your frowns, your very thoughts! Never did Halse believe that he would be one to ride hence unaccompanied by a cloak-mate, and to have me succeed where he failed sets him doubly afire."

He held out his hand again and I noted that those about us were also rising, their feasting done.

"It is time to go?"

"Yes. Come—" He set his arm about my waist and drew me with him, walking as all those other couples under the flowering trees and out of the bower, to a place where horses stood.

A shaggy pony of the hills, surefooted and yet slow of pace, had carried me here. But these mounts were far different. They were strangely dappled of coat, gray and black so intermingled that unless they made some movement they were hidden in plain sight because of their melting into the winter landscape, for we had passed once more from spring to winter.

Tall were these horses of the Riders, thinner of body, longer of leg than any I had seen in the Dales. Their saddle cloths were furred and the saddles smaller, less cumbersome. All suggested a need for speed. Some wore packs, though I noted that, just as we had left behind all that had been in the tents, so also we appeared to abandon that which had refreshed us in the bridal valley.

Herrel brought me to one of the mounts and it swung its head about, surveying me as if it were no mere beast, but carried intelligence akin to mine in its narrow head.

"This is Rathkas, and she will serve you well," Herrel told me.

Still the mare looked upon me in that measuring fashion. I stepped forward and laid hand upon her shoulder. She shivered throughout her body, then throwing up her head she whinnied. Around the other horses looked at me.

Herrel moved quickly, laying his hand above mine on the mare's neck. She dropped her head and looked no more at me, while the others also lost interest. But I saw Herrel's lips were tight set, and once again his eyes held the wrestler's watchfulness.

"Guard," he made a whisper of that word as he aided me to the saddle. And he glanced over his shoulder, but it would seem that none of those near us had marked that small happening.

Thus we rode from our wedding. Though I did not feel that I was truly bride, nor Herrel groom. It was plain that such doubts were not shared elsewhere in that company. So once again I was set apart from those whose life I was destined to share.

This was no amble of a pony in the hills, this was a swift, tireless covering of ground at a pace I had not thought possible for any four-footed creature. Though none of the mounts showed any signs of distress at holding to it as time passed. Time, also, took on a different rhythm—hours—what hour held us now? I could not truly answer that. It had been morning when we had come to the place of the cloaks—was it even the same day? For I had the feeling that the Riders might, with their bedazzlement, also alter time at their pleasure.

Perhaps there was that in the food and drink which we had shared that banished both fatigue and hunger for a space as we did not rest nor eat. We rode—through the night, and into the day, and again into night. Horses did not tire and the hours were part of a dream, flowing together. I do not believe that any of the others marked any passing of time, for they rode with tranced faces in which a kind of delight had frozen. And this also I tried to maintain, though it was hard, for I could not hold long to the surface sight, my will not being equal to my desire.

Those such as Halse, who had gone unpartnered from the wedding, mustered at the head and rear of our party, as if set on guard against danger. But though the land was wild and barren, we saw no life through the miles.

Bleak though that country was, I saw so little difference between it and the lesser dales, that I wondered why it was spoken of always as "the waste," a word which brought to mind desert unfriendly and sealed to man. Here were open plains with the brittle brown grass of yesteryear covering them, showing in hillocks through light snow. And there were tree copses and brush.

No, it was not the land itself which did not welcome man, it was rather what brooded over that territory. For as we rode I knew a heaviness of spirit, a fear, of what I did not know. This grew the more with every mile, until I had to summon power of will against crying out, that my voice might break that shadow spell.

We came at last to higher ground and here I saw first the handiwork of man, for a wall of boulders had been set up, standing perhaps the height of two men or a little more, roofed above with an untidy thatching of tree limbs and brush. Or so *I* saw it. For I heard Kildas say:

"My lord, fair indeed in this hall!"

Then once more I put will to the task of seeing as the Riders would have me see. Thus I, too, rode into a courtyard where stone was cunningly wrought and finely carved wood roofed the buildings set around. Herrel turned to me, saying:

"This is our biding place until we go hence, my lady."

As I dismounted all the fatigue which should have been mine from the hours behind me, struck, and I think I would have fallen had Herrel's arm not been there to steady me. Of the rest, it was a dream of which I could not·sort out true or false, a dream which became sleep indeed. . . .

Until I awoke in the dark! And beside me there was quiet breathing so that I knew I had a bedfellow. I lay taut and tense to listen. Save for that come and go of breath there was no sound. Only I had come from sleep at some summons, the call was still clear.

It was very dark, I could see only denser shadows against the lighter. Moving with caution I sat up in bed, harking ever for any change in that small sound to my left. The room was warm as if a fire blazed on a hearth where there was neither flame nor fireplace. I wore my shift only yet I was not chilled—not outwardly. But in my body there was a spreading cold. All of a sudden it was very necessary to see—to see not only the room, the bed, but most of all what lay upon that bed and slept so soundly.

My bare feet were on deep fur, skins must make a carpet. I moved on one step at a time, sweeping my hands before me lest I stumble against some piece of furniture. How did I know that somewhere before me lay a source of light and that would satisfy my desperate need?

A wall—across its surface my hands moved with haste which was not of my conscious willing. A window—surely this was a window—shuttered and with a bar across. My fingers tugged at the bar. I thrust at the shutters, sending them flying open. Moonlight—it was very clear and brighter than I had ever seen it before, so bright as to dazzle my eyes for a moment.

"Ahh—" Voice—or snarl?

I turned to look to the bed I had left. What lifted heavy head and looked at me green-eyed? Fur, sleek and shining fur, the fanged mask of awakening fury—A mountain cat, yet not a cat—but also death. The lips wrinkled, showing even more the fangs meant to tear, to devour—It was horror beyond any horror I had ever dreamed upon.

This—this you have chosen!—

In that moment by the words which rang in my head, did evil defeat itself. Mayhap with another it would have succeeded—but for me that broke the spell. And what I looked upon now was two, one overlying the other, furred hide above smooth skin, a beast mask over a face—only the green eyes were not two but one. And if they had flashed battle on their opening, now did they show intelligence and knowledge.

I went towards that thing which was now beast, now man. But because I could see the man I was no longer afraid of what shared my chamber. Though of that which had awakened me, sent me to the window—of that I was frightened.

"You are Herrel—" I said to the beast-man. And with my speech he became wholly man, the beast vanishing as if it had never been.

"But you saw me—otherwise—" He made a statement, he did not question.

"In the moonlight—I did."

He moved, out of the bed until he stood at its foot. Faced towards the door I could now see, he moved his hands in the air, at the same time uttering words in a tongue I did not understand.

There was a glow by the door which was not silver clear as the moon, but carried the green tinge of the Rider lamps, and from that glow were two small runnels of light, one to the bed where he had lain, the other to my feet.

Once again I witnessed the mergence of man and beast, this time because of anger burning in him. But control won and he was man again. Herrel caught up a cloak and threw it about his shoulders, went to the door. Then, his hand already set to the latch, he looked back at me.

"Perhaps it is just as well—" he could have been arguing with himself. "Yes, it is better—Only," now he did speak to me, "let them see that you have had a fright. Can you scream?"

What play he intended I could not guess, but I had faith in his wisdom for us both. Summoning up what art I could, I screamed, and surprised myself with the shrill note of terror I put into that cry.

No longer was the building silent. Herrel threw open the door and then ran back to me. His arms drew me close as one who would comfort and his whisper in my ear suggested further display of terror on my part.

There were more outcries, running feet, and then lamplight. Hyron was there, looking at us. Captain of the Riders, I had seen him only at a distance, now he wore the face of a man wanting a satisfactory explanation.

"What chances here?"

Herrel's moment of counciling aided me. "I awoke and was warm—too warm. I thought I must open wide the window—" Now I raised my hand uncertainly to my head as if I felt faint. "Then I turned and saw a great beast—"

There was a moment of silence and Herrel had the breaking of it.

"Look you—" that was more order than request. He pointed before me to where that green line crawled across the floor. Faded now from our first sighting though it was, it was still visible.

Hyron looked, and then, grim faced, he raised his eyes again to Herrel.

"You want sword right?"

"Against whom, Captain? I have no proof."

"True enough. And it would be well not to seek it—in these hours."

"Do you lay that upon me?" Herrel's voice was very cool and remote.

"You know where we must ride and why. Is this the time for private quarrels?"

"The quarrel is none of my provoking."

Hyron nodded, but I felt that his assent was given reluctantly, that he had taken the matter ill, as though this was some trouble pushed upon him which only duty made him consider seriously.

"This game or others like it must not be played again," Herrel continued. "There is no nay-saying cloak-spell. Did we not all swear to that, weapon-oath?"

Again Hyron nodded. "There will be no trouble." And that also rang like an oath.

When we were again alone I faced Herrel in the moonlight.

"What arrow was aimed at us this night?"

But he did not answer that, rather did he look at me very searchingly and ask:

"You saw a beast, yet you did not flee?"

"I saw a beast and a man, and of the man I had no fear. But tell me, for this was clearly sent by malice, what chanced?"

"A spell was set, to disgust you with me, perhaps to send you running to another who waited. Tell me. Why did you seek the window?"

"Because I was—ordered—" That was it! I had been ordered from my sleep to do just that. "Is it false?"

"It might well be. Or there are others—I told you, none believed that you or any woman would choose my cloak. Having accomplished this, I have questioned their Power in their own eyes. Thus, they would like to see me fail now. By frightening you with shape-change they would drive you away."

"Shape-change—Then you *do* wear this guise when it is needed?"

But to that he did not answer at once. He went to the window and looked out into the silence of the night.

"Does it give you fear of me to know this?"

"I do not know. I feared, yes, when I first saw—But with the undersight perhaps you will always be a man to me."

He turned back to me, but his face was now in shadow. "I promise you this weapon-oath, Gillan, willingly never will I fright you!"

For an instant only did I see fur on his shoulders, a mountain cat's muzzle in place of his face? But I willed to see a man, and I thereafter did.

VI
Trial by Sword

*A*re there no mirrors in your household? Does demon lore speak true thereof?" I strove to rebraid my hair. By touch alone that was an unhandy business.

A laugh behind me, and then, swept over my head and down, held for my convenience, a mirror indeed. But this of shining metal, meant rather to ward battle stroke than to provide an aid for adornment. Wan and strange did my reflection look back at me from that shield surface; still it did guide my hands in the ordering of my hair. My pins were half missing and the final coiling looser than I wished.

"You have taken up rough housing, Gillan—unless you wish to see it as the others do—" There was question in that.

"Matters as they are suit me very well indeed," I made quick reply. "I have a liking for facing what I must with a clear head. Herrel, what *do* we have to fear?"

"Most of all discovery." He had slung sword on a shoulder baldric which was set with the same milky gems as those of his belt buckle. And now he held in his two hands a helm, wrought of silver, or so it looked. For a crest it had no plume such as those worn by the fighting lords of High Hallack, but a small figure, marvelously made, a thing of rare beauty, in the form of a crouching, snarling mountain cat, preparing to launch in attack-spring.

Discovery, he said. And the burden of escaping such discovery fell largely on me. Herrel must have read my dawning knowledge in my face for he came to me swiftly.

"I do not think we have aught to fear this day, for the trickery in the night will make them wary. But if you again sense anything strange, tell me. There is this," beneath his helm his eyes had the same cold glitter of the jewels in the eye sockets of the silver cat, "perhaps you have chosen ill after all, Gillan. I cannot stand against Halse, or the others in spell weaving. But should I learn which one would attack so, then I may challenge sword battle, and they cannot nay-say me. Only, to so speak I must have proof that he who I would meet is indeed guilty. I can lay no wall about you—"

"Perhaps I have another safeguard—I had forgotten it."

It was so slender a thread, but one about to fall will clutch any rope. I pulled aside the cloak on the bed, the one which had plunged me into this. Under that lay the one thing I had brought out of Norstead for my own, the bag of simples. Why I had clung to it, I could not tell, but now perhaps I could be glad.

Healing salves and balms, most of them. But in the last pocket a small amulet which I had made for an experiment and which I had never shown to Dame Alousan, lest she turn on me for following the country beliefs in a fashion unbefitting one who dwelt in a holy place.

Wild angelica, and the dried flowers of purple mallow, with a pressed ivy leaf or two, and also the berries of rowan, sewn into a tiny packet, with certain runes stitched on it. All lore coming from records, yet never so combined before. There was a cord to it, and I looped that about my throat where it could not be seen under the high collar of the tabard. Dame Alousan herself had admitted that some old lore had a foundation of truth, the which she had proved by her own experiments. But this was from tradition older than her religion and alien to it.

Against my skin it felt warm, almost as if some heat generated within it. I turned to face Herrel. His hand went up as if he could ward me off.

"What is it?" he demanded.

"Herbs, leaves, berries from the field."

His hands moved in gestures and then he gave a sharp exclamation and the fingers of one went to his lips, his tongue licking as if he would so cool them against some heat.

" 'Tis a bane, right enough." He smiled. "And perhaps not a thing they will be expecting. Or, if they find it, they will deem it a safeguard natural. I do not know how that will hold against any determined sorcery. Let us hope it will not be put to any such test."

Our company rode forth from the hold of the Riders, and this time there were more horses with packs, for there would be no returning. We were bound for the gate of their vanished homeland. Our pace was less demanding on our mounts, but the land through which we traveled repudiated us as it had the day before, inimical to man, and perhaps to the Riders also. Or was that aura some defense they had set against those not of their blood and kin?

The heights on which the hold had been set was only the beginning of land which climbed. It did not snow, but the wind cut coldly. And we were glad when the unmarked trail we followed wound through woods shelter which kept off the worst of the blasts.

Herrel rode at my left hand, but he spoke little. Now and then he held high his head, his nostrils expanding as if he would scent something in the air which might be the odor of danger. As I looked cautiously about me, I saw that others of his company did likewise, though the girls were still deep in their contented bemusement. Herrel's crest was that of the mountain cat, but that of the man who rode with Kildas was a bird—an eagle perhaps—its wings outstretched a little as if it were about to launch into the air. And beyond him was one who wore the semblance of a bear, the viciously tempered, red-brown-coated dweller in the mountain forests, wily and cunning so that hunters dreaded it almost beyond any other beast.

Bear-helm turned his head, and I recognized him for Halse. Bear, cat, eagle, I strove to identify the others—finding, without making too obviously my eye-search, a boar, tusked and head lowered for the charge—a wolf—Shape-changers, sorcerers, were they also beast and bird at will? Or was what I had seen last night merely part of a spell sent to disgust me with Herrel?

I felt no disgust, however fear, a little, as the unknown always awakens first the emotion of fear. How *had* the Were Riders proved so formidable in war? As men bearing swords and bows, fighting as the men of High Hallack fought, or as beasts with the brains of men, tearing, stalking, leaping as the furred and the feathered? Before the day was out I was to have my answer.

Our ride was not steady, though it was undoubtedly ground covering. We paused in a small clearing to break our fast when a pale sun marked a nooning. And I thought we were swinging farther to the east than our track had been heretofore. Herrel was uneasy, that I noted first. His testing of the wind increased. And I saw that others of the Riders moved restlessly about, their pacing almost being that of animals scenting a danger yet afar.

Those without brides gathered to Hyron by the picket line and three of them rode out. None of the girls appeared to note any of this so was I restrained to be likewise unheeding. But when Herrel brought me a cup of the amber-hued wine, I dared to whisper:

"What has gone amiss?"

He did not fence with me. "There is danger—to the east. Men—"

"High Hallack?" But I could not believe they were so honor-broke, for the code binding the High Lords to certain customs was not easily shattered.

"We do not know. It may be Alizon—"

"But Alizon is finished on these shores! There are no more—" I could not at once tame my surprise.

"Alizon was broke. But there might be those who fled. Desperate would they be with their ships gone and no path left for their returning home. Such a band under an able leader would try to turn Hallack's tricks upon her lords and live in the wilderness to raid. They are not soft men, the Hounds, nor ones to throw down swords and call for peace because the tide turns against them."

"But this far north—"

"One of their long boats could slip along the coast, that would take them away from the ports fallen to their enemies. And they would come north because they know that High Hallack does not patrol in this direction—leaving the waste to us—"

"But surely they also know—"

"That the Riders bide here?" His lips drew back, and for a second did I see a faint shadow form across his face? "Do not misjudge the Hounds, Gillan. Long did the Lords of High Hallack fight them. But all men are not formed the same. Oh, they have two arms, two legs, a head, a body, a heart, a mind—But what lies within to animate all that—that may differ much. There were those of the coast lands, of Dales' blood, who did lay down sword and accept Alizon's overyoke years ago. Many were hunted down and put to the sword when we finished off the invaders. Still perhaps not all turncoats were so finished. And do you not think that there has not been much talk through these years just past the Great Bargain? What better stroke might a band of desperate men deliver than to cut us off now, leaving dead whom they could, perhaps making us believe that Hallack broke faith, so in turn we would return to rend the Dales?"

"You believe this?"

"It is a suggestion we do not throw away without question."

"But to attack the Riders—" So deeply had I been schooled in the beliefs of the Dales that I had come to accept the common opinion that those I now rode among were invincible, and no man, lest he be bereft of his sense, would go up against them willingly.

"Gillan," Herrel was smiling a little, "you do us too much honor! Powers we have which those of other races do not use. But we bleed when a sword pierces, we die when it cuts deeply enough. And we are now only as many as you see. Also, we cannot detour too far from our chosen trail lest we do not reach the gate we seek in the appointed time, and so must rove on unsatisfied."

Thus once more was I caught in another race against time. Only I could not credit that the Were Riders were not as all-powerful as their reputations made them. Perhaps my face mirrored my doubt for Herrel then fitted another portion of the puzzle into place for me.

"Do you not understand that to maintain an illusion or bind a spell on another's mind wears upon a man? Twelve in this company ride in spell. More than just the will of he who companies with each holds steady that illusion. You asked me last night—was I as you saw? Yes. I am that, at times—in battle. For our own sakes in fighting we are all shape-changers. But to put on one shape or another is an effort of mind and will. These maids from High Hallack see as it is laid upon them to see. Should we be attacked then they would see what you have witnessed. From that true seeing could come an end to all we sought in the Bargain. Speak now the full truth, Gillan—which of those who rode hither with you would accept such a full sight and have it make no difference?"

"I do not know them well, I cannot say—"

"But you can venture a guess, and what is that?"

"Very few." Perhaps I was misspeaking the maids of Hallack, but remembering their murmuring on the ride to the Throat, and the stark fear which some showed then, I did not think I was so far in error.

"So. Thus are we now crippled. And those who might attack us have the courage of men who have been stripped of all—who have nothing left to lose. So would they come into battle with the advantage."

"What will you do?"

He shrugged. Just such a gesture as I would have expected from Lord Imgry in such a strait. "What do we do? We send out scouts to spy us a trail, we strive to find a swift passage, we hope that we do not have to fight for it."

But his hopes were in vain. We struck a fast pace leaving that halting place. Within the hour we split into two parties. Those who were unpaired, save for three of their number, took a branching way yet farther east and rode from us at a gallop. While for the remainder we had a trail straight ahead. One of our three guards, who ranged up and down the line, as I had seen men of the Dales ride herd while moving cattle, was Halse. Each time he swung past it seemed to me that he turned his head, so that the baleful gems in that bear-topped helm flickered, the ornament almost appearing a small living creature fully aware of all it saw.

In winter, twilight comes early. Shadows crept across our way which was now clear of forest or many trees, but which wound about to avoid outcrops of snow-crowned rock. Herrel's mount was dropping behind and I reined back. The last of the party were now out of sight and we were alone.

"What is the matter?"

He shook his head. "I do not know. There is no reason—" He had stopped, now his head went up, his nostrils expanded, as he half turned in the saddle to look back along our trail. His hand moved in an imperative gesture for quiet.

I could hear the clop-clop of hooves ahead, the creak of saddles, growing fainter by the moment. Surely Halse or one of the others would come pounding back to see what delayed us.

Herrel dismounted. He looked up at me, his face a blur not easily read beneath the shadow of his helm.

"Ride!"

He went down on one knee to examine the forefeet of his mount, not looking at the hooves but rather in the longish hair above them. His fingers stilled and his whole body tensed.

"What is it?" I asked for the second time.

But there was no answer—only singing in the air, shrill, ear-piercing in high notes. Herrel's mount reared, screamed, striking out, and sending the man at its feet rolling.

There was no controlling my mare either. She dashed ahead so wildly that she might have been blind. I fought against her terror with hands on reins and my will—that same will which leapt ever to my defense when there was need. Then, when it seemed she was truly mad, I leaned forward in the saddle, grasping her mane. Against my breast I felt a burning coal, eating into my flesh. The amulet—but why? I dared loose hold with one hand, clutched for that packet. Why I did then what I did I had no knowing, any more than why I had performed many actions these past days.

Jerking the cord until it broke, I pressed the amulet between my palm and the mare's foam-spattered neck. She ceased the terrible neighing which had been bursting from her as a woman might scream; her wild run slackened. My will caught her—we turned back. I was sure that what had moved her and Herrel's horse had been no freak of nature but a deliberately planned blow.

Almost I feared I could not find my way back. The rocky outcrops all looked the same. But I urged the mare on, my amulet still pressed on her sweating hide. And I could feel the shivering which racked her. Fear was a stench in the air, and mine a part of it.

Behind me the pounding of hooves. Halse drew even, his cloak swept back on his shoulders. I could see sparks of fire . . . man's eyes . . . bear's eyes. He leaned forward as if to grasp at my rein, bring me to a halt. And I flung out my hand to ward off his. The amulet swung forward on its broken cord, struck across his bare wrist.

"Ahhh—" A cry of pain, as if I had laid a whip there in earnest. He jerked back and his horse reared with a startled neigh. Then I was out of his reach, riding on to where I had seen Herrel roll away from his mount's striking feet.

His horse stood there, spraddled of leg, muzzle close to the ground. It shivered, plunged once as I moved up, yet did not run. While on a rock ledge of the outcrop crouched that which I had last seen by moonlight on a bed.

"Man—man!" My mind fought fear. But this time my will did not dislodge a phantom. The great cat was silent, it did not even look at me. Those green, glowing eyes were turned elsewhere, down slope, and above its head was a flicker of slender green flame.

"Herrel?" So intent was I on winning man back from cat that I forgot all caution. I slid from the saddle, ran to the rock. As I called the cat's stare broke, it arose in a great bound to clear the fear-stricken horse and reach the ground beyond.

The hair along its spine rose, its ear flattened against the skull, and the long tail quivered at tip. Still it looked back down our trail. Then for the first time it yowled.

Herrel's horse plunged and screamed. My mare bolted. Now the cat growled, slinking into a crevice between two rocks, belly to the ground. Seeing that hunter's creep I shrank back against the outcrop, losing touch with the reality of the world I had always known.

I still held the amulet, though I did not remember that until once more in my hand it was burning hot. When I snatched away my fingers I saw, standing out from a crack in the stone, a strange thing. It was perhaps as long as my forearm, and it glowed when the amulet approached it. There was such an effluvium of evil exuding from it that before I thought clearly I pulled it free and flung it to the ground, setting my bootheel upon it as I might upon some noxious insect, grinding against the stone until it splintered.

"Harroooo!" Echoed, changed by the rock walls and the wind, but still that was no animal cry. It had come from a human throat, and with it other shouts and a beast's growling.

By me, with more speed than I could have thought possible for such a clumsy seeming body, raced a bear, on its way down trail. A whistle of wings in the sky and a bird, beyond my reckoning large, followed after. A great gray wolf, another cat—this one with fur spotted black on tawny-red, a second wolf, black—the company of the Riders on their way to battle. But that struggle I did not see. Perhaps that was well, for there came a cry so horrible that my hands went to my ears and I crouched against the outcrop with no courage left, only filled with a desire not to see, hear, or think, of what passed where men met beasts in the twilight.

I found myself then, one who had never believed in the service of the Abbey, muttering prayers I had heard there years on end, as if those words could build a wall between me and terror unleashed to walk the earth. And I strove to concentrate upon the words and their meanings, using them as a shield.

Hands upon my shoulders—I tried to free myself as if they had been claw-set paws. Still I would not open my eyes. For how could I bear now to look upon a man who was also a beast?

"Gillan!" The grasp which held me tightened. I was shaken to and fro, not in punishing anger as my Lord Imgry had used me, but as one would awaken another caught in a nightmare.

I looked—into green eyes, but they were not set in a beast head. Only, still could I see them so. And above them was that helm on which crouched a cat—a stark reminder. I was too weak to pull away from Herrel's hold, yet my flesh shrank from it.

"She saw us—she knows—" Words from beyond the narrow world which was mine, in which only the twain of us stood.

"She knows more than you think, pack brothers. Look upon what she has in her hand!"

Anger rising about me. Almost I could see that with my eyes as a dull red mist. I stood on a high and open place and they would stone me with rocks of their hate.

"Doubtless sent to lead us into some trap—"

There was an arm about me, holding me close, promising security. Once I thought I could accept that with open eyes. Now there was such a revulsion working in me that I had to force my will to stand fast, lest I run screaming into the wilderness. And the anger continued to thrust spears of rage at me.

"Cease! Look you well, this is what she holds within her hands. Take it— you, Harl, Hisin, Hulor—Magic, yes, but where is there any evil in it, unless evil was intended in return? Harl, say the Seven words while it rests in your fingers."

Words—or sounds—so sharp they hurt ears, rang into one's skull—words of alien Power.

"Well?"

"It is a charm, but only against the Powers of darkness."

"Now—look yonder!"

The red wall of anger was gone. I saw again with my eyes and not my emotions. From where I had trampled and broken that shaft I had found in the rock arose a line of oily black smoke, as if from a fire feeding on rotten-ness. And there was a sickly smell from it. The smoke swirled, formed into a rod which had the likeness of the unbroken shaft.

"A screamer, and one under a dark Power!"

Again they spoke words, this time several voices together. The rod swayed back and forth, was gone in a puff.

"You have seen," Herrel said, "you know what kind of a spell that bore. One who wears such an amulet as Gillan cannot dabble in dark learning. And there was another charm here also. Harl, I ask of you, look to the fetlock of Roshan's left forefoot."

I saw him who wore the eagle go to Herrel's mount, kneel to feel about the hoof. Then he arose with a thread between his fingers.

"A hinder-cord!"

"Just so. And this also do you say is of the enemy, or of my lady's doing? Perhaps," Herrel looked at each of them for a long instant, "it was a trick for amusement. But almost it worked to my bane, and likewise to those of you who came hither. Or was it more than a trick, a hope that I fall behind to some undoing by fate or enemy?"

"You have the right to ask sword-battle then!" flashed Halse.

"So I do, as I shall call upon you all to witness—when I find the one who tried to serve me so."

"This is one thing," boar-crest broke in, "but she—" he pointed to me. "is yet another. She who deals in outland charms, who and what is she?"

"All peoples have their wise women and healers. We know well the skill of those of High Hallack. Gillan had for mistress one who was well learned in such arts. To each race its own Powers—"

"But such a one has no place in our company!"

"Do you speak for all the pack, Hulor? Gillan," Herrel spoke to me, far more softly, as one who would win words from a sorely frightened child, "what know you of this other thing—this shaft?"

And as simple as a child I made answer. "The Amulet burned my hand when I rested it on the rock. There was a break in the stone and that stood within it. I—I pulled it loose and broke it with my foot."

"Thus," he swung back to the others, "it would seem, pack brothers, that we owe herewise a debt. With that still potent what might have happened had we gone into battle shape-changed and then returned, unable to be men, to face so these we would shield from the truth?"

I heard murmurs among them.

"Upon this matter the whole company must have their say," Halse spoke first.

"So be it—with you witnessing as to what happened here," Herrel replied evenly. His arm tightened around me. I fought against the shudders with which my body would have resisted that hold. "Now, we have no threat left behind, but that does not mean it has vanished from the land. Only, hold in mind, pack brothers, that you return now to those whom you cherish as men this night because of the courage and wit of this my lady."

If he expected any outward assent from the others he did not get it. They drew away. Herrel lifted me into the saddle and climbed up behind, the circle of his arms holding me. Yet I was alone, alone in a company who had let me feel the fire and storm of their hate, and in arms which now I thought of as wholly alien.

VII
Night Terrors and Day Dreams

*O*f that night I remember very little, waking, but of sleeping—Even now my mind shrinks from that memory. Dreams seldom linger in the mind far past the waking hour, but such dreams as haunted me that night were not the normal ones.

I ran through a forest, leaved and yet not green—but a sere and faded gray, as if the trees had died in an instant and had not thereafter lost their leaves, but only become rigid ghosts of themselves. And from behind their charred black trunks things spied upon and hunted me—never visible, yet ever there, malignant and dreadful beyond the power of words to make plain.

There was no end to that forest, nor the hunters, nor to my anguish. And there grew in me the knowledge that they were driving me to some trap or selected spot of their own wherein I would be utterly lost. I can yet feel beneath fingertips the rough bark of trees against which I leaned panting, pain a sword in my side, listening—oh, how I listened!—for any noise from those who followed. But there was no sound, just ever the knowledge they existed.

A wild hunt—though the hounds, the hunters I never saw—only the fear which preceded them drove me.

Time and time again I strove to hold to courage, to turn and face them, telling myself that fear faced is sometimes less than fear fled, but never was my courage great enough to suffer me to hold, past a quivering moment or two. And always the dead-alive trees closed about me.

Growing in me was the knowledge that the end would be horrible past all bearing—

And when I broke then and screamed madly, beating upon the trunk of the tree where I had paused, there was a murmur in my head, a murmur which was first sound and then words, and finally a message I could understand:

"Throw it away—throw it away—all will be well—"

It? What was it? Sobbing with breaths which hurt, I looked first to my hands. They were scratched, bleeding, the nails torn—but they were empty.

It? What was it?

Then I looked down at my body. It was bare, no clothing left me. And it was so wasted that the bones showed clearly beneath scarred and scratched skin. But on my breast rested a small bag patterned with runes stitched on in black. Memory stirred faintly, fading before it really told me aught. I caught at the bag. That which stuffed it crunched, and from it rose a faint odor to sting my nose.

"Throw it away!" A command.

There was sound now and not only in my head. With the bag between my fingers I turned to look upon the masks of beasts—standing manlike on their hind legs. Bear, boar, cat, wolf—beasts—and yet more, far more—far worse!

I ran, witlessly, with a pain in me which seemed to burst the ribs about my heart. From the beasts I ran, back towards that which had hunted me. And behind I heard a cat's yowl.

Perhaps I might have died, caught in the horror of that dream. But the pressure of the bag in my clenched hand, from that spread—what? Courage? No, I was too far past the point where courage could return. I was only an animal—or less—filled with fear and a terror beyond what we call fear. But there came a kind of new energy and then an awareness that I had outrun the beasts. And after that, a small ray of hope that there would come an end to all this and perhaps it was better to face that end than go mad with terror.

I did not run any longer. I dropped, my breast heaving, under one of the dead trees, and I pressed both hands with the bag to me.

So—thus was it? Knowledge and then anger, then purpose which in turn drew upon the depths of will. My enemies were blind masks behind which men hid. Masks could be torn away.

They had overreached themselves this time, not knowing the temper of the metal they had striven to destroy. In me that metal hardened. They had not yet the breaking of *me*. Will—I must will myself out of here—

But so little was I used to that weapon that I fumbled. The trees—they were evil—they should be cut away—An ax lay gleaming at my feet.

No wish-ax was the answer. No—that lay elsewhere. Will—I was me—Gillan! At that naming the trees wavered. Gillan—me—I flung that thought at them. I have a will, a power—if the bag I held was in some way a key—then I would turn it. Light routs dark, I held the bag to my dry, cracked lips. Light—I will light!

The gloom beneath the shadow trees thinned. I am Gillan and elsewhere do I have a place which is mine—mine! I will it!

Green of a lamp. In my nostrils the smell of aromatic wood burning, the odor of food. Sounds—of voices, of people moving not too far away. This was the sane world, the world of which I, Gillan, was a part. I was back!

Yet I was so weary that I found it hard to raise my hand, run it along my body, which was clothed as always, under the cover of a fur-lined cloak. There was the light of a cloudy winter morning about us. Outside a shelter of skins, not as formal as a tent, I saw Riders moving. Men—or beasts such as I had seen in the dead forest?

I struggled to lever myself up on my hands, straining to see those men. But between me and them came Kildas. Kildas—how long ago had it been since we had eaten together on another morning and wished each other fortune with a formal toast before answering the summons which had brought us here? I found I could not name the days, they mingled one with the other.

"Gillan." She did not look as bemused as she had since her bridal in the field of cloaks, "How do you feel? You are fortunate that you came from such a fall with no broken bones—"

"Fall?" I repeated, and stared, stupidly I am sure, into her face.

She steadied my swimming head against her shoulder, raised a brimming drinking horn to my lips, and perforce I swallowed a mouthful of its contents. Hot and spicy, yet the heat did not warm me and I shivered as if never again would my body be shielded from any icy wind.

"Do you not remember? Your mount took fright upon the slope and threw you. Since you have lain unheeding through the night."

But what she said was so at variance with the memories now crowding in upon me, that I shook my head from side to side, awaking in it an aching. Were—were those memories born of some hurt I had taken? Evil dreams could come from fever, as well I knew—though my body was cold, not hot. A blow on the head—from that came my beast-men? No, I had seen the cat before—before we had ridden into these wastes. And I could look now and see—I raised my shaking hand to cover my eyes.

Perhaps the Riders had their own heal-craft; they must have had since Herrel had said they, too, knew wounds and hurt. As Kildas urged upon me again the contents of the horn, I grew stronger. My shaking was stilled. But I was cold—so cold—and that cold was fear—

"My lord," Kildas looked beyond my shoulder to one who had come to us. "She has wakened and, I believe, mends—"

"My gratitude to you, Lady Kildas. Ah, Gillan, how is it now with you, dear heart?"

Hands again on my shoulders. I stiffened . . . afraid to turn . . . to look. His words meant nothing. What had happened to me? cried one inner voice. I had not feared before, I had not shrunk from his touch, I had—

I had stood apart, answered something within my mind. All this had been action I watched, which had not engulfed me in its pattern. I had now stepped from one path where I knew, or thought I knew, the trail, into another running on into darkness and fear.

"I mend—from my fall, I mend," I answered dully.

"It was a sorry one."

Not yet did I look to him; it was all I could do to not flinch from his hands upon me. "Do you think you can ride?" he continued, and now there was a difference, a more formal note, in his voice.

"Kildas—" That voice also I knew. He who called wore an eagle-crested helm. Or did he sprout a bird's cruel beak, feathers and claws?

"I am called," she laughed joyfully. "Take good care, Gillan. I hope you will meet no more ill fortune." She left us and when she was gone I summoned will and stood away from Herrel, daring to face him.

"So I fell, and struck my head upon a stone," I said swiftly, making myself look. But he was a man, and I was safe. Safe? Would I ever be safe again?

Herrel did not answer me with words. He lifted his hand to my cheek. And this time I could not control my aversion. I dodged his touch as I might have eluded a blow. His eyes narrowed as a cat's might. I waited for furred mask to appear. But it did not and when he spoke again his voice was very remote.

"So you are now using another sight, my lady. What illusion—"

"Illusion?" I cried. "I am seeing with eyes which are freed, shape-changer! Tell what tale you need. I shall not nay-say it. Perhaps I could not. You and your pack brothers have woven too well your spells. Only they do not blind me—any more than you can conquer me with night fears—"

"Night fears—?"

"Hunting me through the forest of ashes—but you did not have your will there."

"Forest of ashes?"

"Can you do naught but repeat my words, shape-changer? I have run before fear. But be warned, dreaming or waking, Lord Herrel, there comes a time when the whip of fear breaks. One can learn to live under it, which is the first step towards making it servant, not master. Haunt my sleep as you will—"

Now he caught me again in his grip, holding me so I must meet his eye stare directly and in the full. Green—vast green—pool—sea into which I was falling—falling—falling—

"Gillan!"

Eyes only, but not human eyes. Below them a mouth straight set, a face hard as if carved from some white gem stone.

"Not of my doing. Do you understand, Gillan? Not of my doing!"

Not quite coherent those words, yet their meaning reached me. He was denying what I had thrown at him in accusation, not quite believing it all myself. And his denial had an effect. That had been no vivid nightmare; it had been an attack, delivered in a different time and space, but aimed at me.

"Then whose?" I demanded of him.

"Could I point the sword, then I would in this instant! Until I can—"

"I must run haunted and—What was that they spoke of last night—the hinder-cord?" For now memory supplied another bit.

"Something which could have been named a trick if discovered or be my undoing if it had been aided by fate. A spell laid to slow and perhaps lame a horse. But night terrors are not one man's trick, they are a flight of arrows from more than one bow."

"They would be rid of me, wouldn't they? The bear, the eagle, the boar—"

"They must abide by the covenant—or be shape spelled! And I do not think they will try to strike again—"

"Because, warned, you may strike back?"

"I? The least of them? I think they do not deem that possible." He had no shame in that saying. "They may not know me yet, however. Now—can you ride?"

"I think that I had better—"

He nodded. "It will not be for more than a day. We draw near to gate. But, I ask of you, keep in mind that still we deal in illusions and it is best not to fight before we must—"

Herrel spoke as if together we faced danger. Yet in me I was alone, all alone. There was no Herrel I could depend upon, there was a man and a beast, and neither dared I cling to. But that I would not dispute upon now, not when I was so tired in mind and body.

"I fell and hit my head on a stone," I said as one repeating a well learned lesson. "There was no battle?"

"No battle," he agreed.

"In my dream battle then," I pursued the question, "what force trailed us and what weapon did they use which might have destroyed your illusions?"

"You remember it all?"

"I remember—"

"They were Hounds of Alizon. But some one of them must have been schooled in the knowledge they make such a parade of abhorring. What they sent to confuse us was a power of the dark to shape-change and then enforce that change to continue. In this they heaped their own grave mounds—better would they have wrought to keep us men."

"How many of them were there? And why did they attack?"

"Twenty—that we found. It was cleverly planned for they split our party with a false trail and then struck at what they deemed the weaker portion. As for why? They carried Hallack shields and blazons—thus they wished to embroil us with the Dales. It is only the dark arrow we do not understand, that has no place in their armament."

"Herrel—" Hyron, his crest of a rearing stallion plain in the growing daylight, stood at the open end of the lean-to. "Lady—" he sketched a hand salute to me, but I noted that he did not really look in my direction. "It is time we ride. You are able to, lady?"

I wanted to say no, that I could not cling to a saddle, that I had no desire, nor strength to face a day's ride across this land which was enemy to my kind. But I could not say those words; instead I found myself nodding as if what he willed could only be my heart's desire also.

We rode, but in a different pattern from that which we had followed before. Now woman companied woman; the men threw out advance scouts and set a rearguard. I looked to Kildas at my left, Solfinna at my right. Neither seemed apprehensive, nor did they remark upon this division.

"Hisin says that this night shall we bide in the outer way," Solfinna's words broke my absorption. "Soon there will be an end to this journeying, though we are still two days from the appointed hour. Very fair must be the land beyond the Safekeep—" She smiled happily.

"Gillan, you have said so little. Does your head still ache?" Kildas shifted a little in the saddle to look at me more closely.

"It aches, yes, and I dreamed ill in the night."

To my surprise she nodded. "Yes, Herrel was in great concern when you cried out. He strove to wake you, but when he touched you, Hyron bade him cease for you seemed in even greater distress. Then he put something into your hand, and thereafter you quieted."

"Why did that so anger Hyron?" Solfinna broke in. "I could not see that it did harm, rather good."

"Hyron was angered?"

"Yes—" Solfinna began but Kildas broke in:

"I do not think angered, rather concerned. We all were, Gillan, for you cried out strange things we could not understand, which frightened, as if you were caught in a very evil dream."

"I do not remember," I lied. "One may do such after a head blow, that much I know from heal-craft. And this land is so dreary it puts phantoms into one's mind—"

My first real error. Kildas looked at me oddly.

"The land lies under winter, but it is like unto the Dales. Why men speak of it as a waste I do not understand. Look you how the sun touches all to diamond snow and crystal ice?"

Sun? Where shown any sun? We moved under a leaded sky. And the diamond snow was rimed drifts. Icy coated branches spoke only of frozen death. Illusion—Now I wanted to share that illusion for my own comfort. But this time, for all my willing, I could not see the land under the beneficent haze through which my companions moved. All was gray, grim, stark, with branches reaching for us like the misshapen hands of monsters, while every shadow could be granted evil and alien life of its own, lying in wait for the unwary.

I closed my eyes against what was real to me, summoned my will, desired to see . . . only to open sight once more on the same forbidding countryside. Also—the rush of power I had come to associate with my will-summons did not answer—save as a weak and quickly ebbing ripple. And with that discovery self-distrust awoke in me, weakening me yet further. But I needs must guard my tongue and strive to fight my fears.

Now and again one of the Riders came to bear us company for a short while—always the mate of one of the brides. Then I noted that Herrel did not come so, nor had I seen him since we rode out of camp, though Halse passed twice down the line. Once when the bear-man slacked pace and Solfinna jogged ahead, I spoke, perhaps recklessly, but as I thought was only natural.

"My lord, where rides Herrel?"

There was that derisive smile on his face as he made answer courteously enough, but with such under mockery as to be an unseen blow.

"He rides rearguard, my lady. Shall I tell him you wish words with him? Doubtless some message of importance?"

"No. Just tell him all is well—"

Those red eyes searching me, trying to read my thoughts. Could these sorcerers in truth read thoughts? I did not believe so.

"You are wise not to draw him from his duty. Hyron believes him now best employed for the service of the company. And we must rest upon the best defenses we can muster—"

Words innocent enough, but so delivered that a threat ran beneath their smooth surface. And now Halse, in a low voice, added more:

"I would have nay-said Herrel could gain a bride. Has he told you that in this company he is the wrong-handed, the limper? But destiny is right after all, now we consider him well matched—" Still he smiled, and it was enough to make one dread all smiles.

"I thank you, my lord." From some last bulwark of pride and defiance I summoned those words. "Can anyone truly say what a man is, or may come to be? If cloak-spell united us, then you will not miscall your own Power. I am content, if my lord is also." A lie, and a lie he knew, yet one I would continue to cling to.

The method of our pairing from the bridal dale had been such that we knew only he whose cloak we had chosen—knew him? That was not my case certainly. But as to his fellow Riders, what did any of us know? My companions were so bound in illusion woven to hold them apart from the truth, that they would accept any seeing. Me—I was so torn with fear and suspicion that perhaps I saw awry also. Yet Halse I did not like, nor did I take kindly to the gaze Hyron turned upon me. And I had felt the animosity of those others last night.

What of Herrel? Yes, what of Herrel? Our first meeting when he had taken me to wife, in name, by the cloak about my shoulders . . . the night when I had been willed by another's ill wishing to wake and see him as he could be and was, upon occasion. Last night when I had watched him go into battle and heard the horror of that fight—

I had come to our first meeting prepared to accept an alien—or had I really? Can anyone accept what they do not know? Now after testing I was as faint-hearted as Marimme, if able to conceal it better. Was Herrel a beast who could put on the semblance of a man for his purposes, or a man putting on the beast? It was this question ever seesawing at the back of my mind which made my flesh shiver and cringe from his touch, made me rejoice he was not my mate in truth. Kildas, Solfinna, the rest, they harbored no doubts. I believed they were all wives as I was not. But which husbanded them—beast and bird—or human body?

"To have the true sight, my lady," Halse's mount crowded closer to my mare; his voice dropped lower still, "can be a grievous thing. You do not belong here."

"If I do not, my lord, this is a very late hour to make such a discovery. And I think you do not give me much credit—"

He shrugged. "It may be, my lady, that we do you wrong. At least you have not spilled your doubts to these, your sisters. For that we give you due credit. And I shall give your message to Herrel." He wheeled his horse and was gone, leaving me with the feeling that I had done very ill to give him any reason to seek out Herrel.

I urged my mare on and caught up with Kildas, suddenly having a dislike for riding alone.

"Harl says that Halse is sharp-tongued," she commented. "Though he does not seem to lack in proper courtesy. He resents it that he did not win a bride."

"Perhaps his cloak was not eye-catching enough."

She laughed. "Do not tell him that! He is one who fancies that in most companies he is the first to be noted. It is true he is very handsome—"

Handsome? To me he was the bear, danger covered with a deceptively clumsy skin.

"A fine face is not everything."

"Yes. And I do not care much for Halse. He ever smiles and looks content, but I do not think he is. Gillan, I know not what Herrel has told you, but do not speak freely—too freely—with Halse. Harl has said that there is old trouble between him and Herrel, and since the bridals it has grown worse. For Herrel obtained what he would have—"

"Me?" I laughed, startled by her speech which was so far from the truth I knew.

"Perhaps not you, but a bride. He spoke much before our coming as to what his luck would be, and then to have it dashed so, it has been as a burr within his tunic. The other Riders, they have not forgotten his boasts, and they lead him to remember them from time to time. It is odd," she glanced at me, "before we came I thought of the Riders as all alike, gathered into a pack which thought and acted as one. Instead they are as all men, each having thoughts, faults, dreams and fears of his own."

"Harl taught you thus?"

She smiled, a very different smile from that which curved Halse's lips, deeply happy. "Harl has taught me many things—" She was lost in a dream again, a dream which I could not enter.

And so the long day passed and I saw naught of Herrel—though whether that was by his own design or the will of others, I did not know. We came at last to a long and narrow valley. Its entrance was masked with trees and brush, so thick that I would have believed there was no opening, yet he who was our guide wound a serpent's route through which we filed in a long line. The wall of vegetation gave way to an open space walled with steep rock cliffs. Down one was a lace of ice marking the passage of water flowing away in an ice-encased brook. Before us the defile was a slit which was half-choked by rock falls from above.

There were journey tents standing—those before us in the advance guard had made good use of time. Twilight was fast falling, but green lamps winked at us and there was a fire. At that moment it all looked as welcoming to me as the safe interior of any great hall—rough though that might be.

But when we would dismount the man who came to aid me wore a wolf helm.

"Herrel?"

"The rearguard has not yet come in, my lady." A smooth answer, aptly given.

And the truth was that I could not have honestly said that it would have lightened the burden of my fear had the cunningly wrought body of a cat overtopped the face looking up to mine.

That weariness which appeared always to hold off while one was in a Rider's saddle, fell upon me as I made my way, stiff limbed, to the warmth of the fire. Loneliness closed me off from the others, the loneliness of knowledge. I could no longer hold off the thought that I had been left no return. A choice, made too lightly and in overconfidence had long since wiped away a bridge between present and past—the future my mind flinched from considering.

Night—sleep—but I dared not sleep! Sleep held dreams—not as Kildas and the others dreamed by day, but the other, the dark side of that shield.

"Gillan?"

I turned my head stiffly. Herrel was coming from the picket line. And in my loneliness I saw a man, a man to whom I might have some small meaning. My hands went out as I answered:

"Herrel!"

VIII
Power of the Pack

*I*t is well with you?"

"A day in the saddle is not like unto one spent in a bower," I fenced. The impulse of welcome which had made me move a step forward was a break in the wall of my fortress, imperiling me.

"We shall not drive you further, Gillan. And do not build up your defenses; to yield will be more to your profit, I promise you." His hand enfolded mine past my strength to free my fingers unless we struggled in good earnest.

And his touch built illusion. We stood not in a steep-walled, dark cut, but in a place of springtime. Night was about us, yes, but a spring night. Small pale flowers gave sweet perfume to the night, blooming in a turf carpet, a thick cushion for our feet. Ripples of green and gold ran free from lamps along the edges of the tents, outlining them. There was a low table set with a multitude of plates and goblets, with mats for the diners. Those who were not partnered were gone. Only the twelve and one of us who had come out of the Dales and those of our choice remained.

Herrel drew me to the feasting table, and I went without question, as much bemused in that moment as any of the others. It was a relief to push aside reality, to plunge into the illusion, as one might dive into a pool of cooling water when one's body was fevered with summer heat.

I ate from the plate we shared in the courtly fashion. I could not have named the food, only knew that never before in my life had I tasted such viands, so subtle of flavor, so beguiling to the senses, so satisfying of hunger. There was drink in the goblet before me. Not the amber liquid Herrel had brought me in the marriage dell, but darkly red. And from it arose an aroma like the first fruits of bounteous autumn, rich, freighted with the sunlight of summer past.

"To you, my lady," Herrel raised that cup.

That which lay within me stirred, the lull of illusion was troubled, a ripple across the surface of a pool. Did he drink, or did it only appear so? He held out the cup to me. And I no more than wet my lips as I bowed my head in return.

"Can this then be journey's end, my lord?" I asked as I put away the scarce-tasted wine.

"In one fashion. But it is also a beginning. Tonight we feast to that. Yes, a beginning—" He looked down at the table rather than to me.

Alone were we sober in that company. Around us there was soft, fond laughter, the murmur of voices, a kind of beatitude. But that part of the illusion was not ours.

"Ahead lies the gate you must storm?"

"Storm? No, we cannot force a way here. Either the path is freely open, or it remains closed. And if it is closed—" He paused so long I dared to question:

"What then?"

"Why, once more we go a-wandering—"

"By the Bargain you cannot return to the waste—"

"This land is very wide, larger than you of the Dales know. There are other portions in which we may live."

"But you hope not—"

Now he did turn to me, and what I read in his face struck all other questions from my lips. Yet when he answered, the words came evenly, as if he read them from some often-conned book.

"We hope wandering is past."

"When and how will you know?"

"When?—tomorrow. How?—that I cannot tell you."

But his "cannot" was plainly "will not."

"And if we pass this gate, what then shall we find waiting us beyond?"

Herrel drew a deep breath. Always his man face had been that of a youth with the eyes of age, but now when he looked upon me the eyes were young also. And of the beast—had I ever seen the beast?

"How can I tell you? It is far beyond the words we share. Truly life there is different; it is another world!"

"And you came from there—how long ago?"

Once more his eyes were weary with years of looking at what he must see. "I came from there—how long? I—we—do not reckon times save when we must deal with those of this world. I do not know. We were granted one favor when we came forth, that our memories would be dimmed and dulled, that we would only dream, and that infrequently—"

Dreams! I shivered. The table before me, the feast, the lights, shimmered, lost substance. I wanted no dream memories. I reached forward, lifted the goblet to my lips. I was cold—cold—Perhaps the wine would warm me. Yet when it was on my tongue I paused, again within me that warning.

About us one by one the couples arose, arms entwined, going to the tents. What I had unconsciously feared was now before me.

"Dear heart, shall we go?" His voice had changed, he was soft-spoken, not as he had been when telling of the gate.

No! shrilled my mind. But my body did not elude the pressure of his arm about my waist. To any onlooker we would have been another langorously amorous couple.

"A Toast," he glanced at the cup I still held, "to our happiness, Gillan—drink to our happiness!"

No lover's request—an order. And his eyes compelled me to it. I drank. My vision wavered, the illusion mended—could it indeed be illusion? I went with him, for a moment unheeding save that this was ordained.

Lips—gentle, seeking, then demanding, to which demand I responded. And then hands—

Sharp as a sword thrust the awakening in me of denial. No—no—this was not for me! This was an end to the Gillan that was, a small death. And against that death all the will and what I termed "power" arose in savage defense. I crouched on the far side of the pallet, my hands crooked to claw. Herrel's white face I saw and across it a band of bleeding scratches.

Herrel's smooth skin—or was it furred, blurred with fur—and his mouth fanged? Man or beast? I think I cried out and flung up my hand before my eyes.

"Witch—"

I heard him move away. That word he had flung at me—

"So—that is it—witch," he added. "Gillan!"

I dropped my hand shield to look at him. He made no move. Only his face, truly a man's face, was set as it had been when he had fronted his pack brothers after the battle.

"I did not know—" he spoke, not to me, but as one seeking support or assurance from a source greater than he, "I did not know."

He moved and I shrank instinctively.

"Be not afraid. I lay no hand on you this night, nor like to any other night either!" There was bitterness in that. "Indeed Fortune is crossgrained to me. Another—Halse—would force you—to your good and the company's. But that is not in my birthright. Very well, Gillan, you have chosen—upon you be the consequences—"

He seemed to think I understood, yet his words were riddles past my reading. Now he drew the sword from the sheath he had thrown aside, laying the naked blade in the center of the pallet. So doing he laughed without mirth.

"A convention of the Dales, my lady. I shall honor it this night, you may rest without fear—that fear. But perhaps later you will discover that your choice was not altogether a wise one."

He stretched himself beside the sword and closed his eyes. Why? Why? I had so many whys swelling in my mind, but his face was closed. It was as if, though he lay only a hand's distance from me, we were separated by miles of a haunted waste. And I dared not break the silence.

I thought to lie sleepless. But when I came to the other side of that sword barrier I was straightway plunged into dark where there was not thought nor feeling. Nor did I dream.

From sleep to wakefulness I passed in an instant. I have heard that soldiers in the field sleep so, with an inner alert which walks sentry go for their protection. Around me—what could I name it—a quickening?

Though I listened there was naught but silence. Yet it was a silence which was alive. Herrel? My hand went out—there was no cold steel—

"Herrel?" Did I whisper that or only think it?

I opened my eyes. There was a faint gray light—perhaps that of very early morning. And I was alone in the tent. But in me that surging need to be out—about—I had known it back in the hillkeep when it had brought me to the discovery of Lord Imgry, but not as greatly as I did now. I was summoned—summoned! By whom and to what?

Swiftly I ordered my clothes and then pushed out into the morning. The enchantment was gone—cold stone cliffs, a dying fire—No movement, save now and then at the picket line a mount pawed the ground. I felt as if I alone were awake when all else slept. And the need for knowing I was *not* alone swept me.

I came to the next tent, moved by that need. Kildas lay there, covered by a cloak, sleeping. I looked farther, the Riders were gone! Returning to Kildas I strove to rouse her, but I could not. Perhaps she dreamed happily for there was a smile on her lips. Nor were my efforts more fruitful with the rest.

The restlessness possessing me until to sit still was beyond my power, I fed the dying fire. My flesh tingled; I was eaten by a rising excitement I did not, could not understand. Somewhere action was in progress and it drew me—

Drew me! That was the answer. Not my mind—I must blank out my mind and the here and now as I had sought to do to preserve the illusion—the other sight. Let that drawing force take over, it must if I would ease this torment within.

Clumsily I strove to do that. Closing my eyes against the reality of the camp, trying to shut out what I knew and yield to that tugging I felt. I swayed, as one in a wind too great to breast, and then turned to the rubble-filled end of the valley. There—somewhere there—!

Danger—I forgot danger—I was aware of nothing save the drawing. I scrambled through the rubble of the fallen rocks, impatient at the hindrance of my skirts. On and up—on and up!

It was like blood beating in the regular pound of my heart, yet also was it a throb in the air which was not as loud as the pound of a drum—waves beating, becoming a part of my body as I labored up the path to the Safekeep gate.

Sound now, and the tingling in me responded to that sound. But within a growing frustration. I should know—I should! And yet I did not. I was shut outside some door on which I could beat with my fists until they ran blood, yet I could not enter for the knowledge which controlled the door was not mine.

I reached the top of one of the mounds and looked down. I had found the Riders.

They stood in a triple line, facing the end of the valley, and it was indeed an end—a wall of solid rock without break, smooth past any climbing. They were bare of head, their helms and their arms all laid behind immediately below my perch. They faced that wall with empty hands.

And they were calling, not with voices, but from their hearts. It tore at me, that calling. I put my hands to my ears to shut it out. But that gesture was nothing against the evocation rising from below. Hunger, sorrow, loneliness—and a small spark of hope. They hurled emotions against the stone as besiegers would swing rams to batter down a keep gate.

One of them came forth from the line—Hyron, I believed, though I could not see his face. He went forward to the wall, laid the palms of his hands against its surface and stood so, while still they cried silently their desire for admittance. He stepped aside and another took his place, and another, each in turn. Time passed and I was no more aware of that than the Riders. The first line were done with that touching, the second, one by one, and now the third and last. Halse led them. He came to the barrier with an air of confidence, as if it must open for him.

On and on—and now the last—Herrel—wall. I remembered his face as I had seen it the night before, naked, scored by loss and longing. They were not willing down there, they were pleading, humbling themselves, against the nature of their kind.

Answer—Did they expect an answer now? Herrel came away from the wall to his place in the last line. And the beat, beat of their plea was unchecked. Almost I could believe that they had mistaken their gate. That stone must have stood unriven from the beginnings of time. Or had madness, born out of their wanderings in the waste, tainted their minds so they expected the very mountains to break—*Was* there any lost land?

I was accustomed now to the beat in my own body. Now that I knew what they strove to do here perhaps prudence would argue that I make my way back to camp. But when I tried to move from my vantage point I could not. I was one bound to the rock on which I half lay. And the fright that realization gave me brought a cry from my throat.

They would know—would find me here! Only not a head turned, no eyes moved from their steady fix upon the wall. I struggled the more, summoned all my will—and could not break those invisible bonds. On and on the Were Riders called upon whatever Power they sought to reason with, and I lay there helplessly.

Now it seemed endless and I found my fear of the trap which held me broke through my preoccupation with what passed. Will—I would *not* lie here helpless! I *could* move—My fingers stretched across a stone before my eyes. Those I would move—narrow my world and my will to my fingers—

Move, fingers! Flesh and bone arched up in answer, free of the flesh held in prison. My hand curved into a fist, thrust against the rock to push away. Arm—next—arm!

Beat—beat—open gate—*No!* Doggedly I pulled will and mind back to me—me! Arm—raise—

I tasted the salt of my sweat running across my lips, into the corners of my lips. Arm—raise!

Slowly—with such painful slowness—obedience. I could set hand on rock, arm as a brace, lever myself up a little. But the rest of me was unstirring weight. Foot—knee—

Beat—beat—the gate—that was important—the gate—

"No!" Perhaps I flung that denial down upon the heads of those below in an outburst of fury and frustration. Their gate meant nothing to me. They had receded from my life. What was needful was to move a foot, bend a knee, break out of a web I could not see.

I lay back, my shoulders supported by the cliff wall, panting as I drew great gasps of air into my laboring lungs. So far—in this small way I had broken free. Now—on my feet—I must get to my feet! From this new position I could no longer see the Riders, though their wall, still unbreached, was in my line of vision. As it would doubtless continue. They had failed. Why would they not accept that fact?

No—do not think of them! To do so was to lose the small ground I had gained, again it was hard to turn my head. There was nothing, nothing beyond this pocket of stone and earth which held my disobedient body, feet, legs, arms, hands—Will their coming alive!

Now I stood, stiffly, unsteadily, afraid that any attempt at a step would plunge me from my perch. Once more I could look down upon the Riders. And from them now arose no disturbing beat of supplication. But still they stood facing the wall. And it came to me that they awaited their answer.

I edged around. It no longer mattered to me what that answer would be. My world now held only Gillan and her concerns. I was encased in a hardening shell in which I could depend upon myself alone. And, when I thought that, there flashed a vivid picture out of memory, of Herrel setting between us a drawn sword—not of custom, but of severence.

As I managed to drag myself away from the rock where I had lain to watch the Riders my movements became freer. I had to expend less effort of will on making each limb do as I wished it to.

And sunlight found its way down into the valley. It was warm on my face, my hands, scraped raw and bruised. By the time I had turned my back fully on the slide of rock which walled the Riders from me I was moving normally, but with the fatigue which had punished me after my flight through the dream forest. There was on me now another kind of need, to reach the camp—to find there anchorage.

But I was only a few steps upon my way when my isolation was broken. I had heard the mellow gong notes they sound in the Abbey Chapel to tell the hours prescribed for prayer. More rounded than the voice of any bell, richer, deeper. But this note came as if from the rock about me, the sky overhead, the rough ground underfoot. And with it all that was stable moved, shook, was stirred. Stones toppled and fell. I threw myself back against the cliff side. My arm was numb as one struck against flesh and bone.

The echo of that note rolled, now growing fainter and fainter down the chain of the hills, seemed louder, more imperative, than the sound from which it was born. No war trumpet's ring, no temple gong, no sound I had ever heard could compare with it.

So—they had succeeded in opening their long-closed door. Their homeland was before them. Theirs—theirs! Not mine—

A further rattling of rocks—I looked around. Slavering boar eyeing me, and behind its shoulder the narrow muzzle of a wolf, and the beat of eagle's wings. The Weremen—or beasts—coming to me. It was my vision from the dead forest brought into the sunlight of open day. And this time I could not flee.

"Gillan!"

A weaving, watering of the pattern. Men now and not beasts. Herrel had pushed to the front of the pack.

"Kill!"

Did that come from the wolf's jaws, or in the scream of the eagle, or the wild neighing of a stallion? Did I hear it at all, or only read it in their eyes?

"You cannot kill—" that was Herrel, "she is sister stock—"

Their heads swung so they looked upon me, and then to him, and again to me.

"Do you not understand what we have netted by chance? She is wise-stock—witch by blood!"

Hyron had come to the fore, was looking upon me with narrowed eyes, noting my disheveled clothing, the wounds on my hands.

"Why came you here?" His voice was quiet, too quiet.

"I woke—I was—called—" Out of somewhere I chose that word to describe the uneasiness which had impelled me here.

"Did I not tell you?" broke in Herrel. "All of the true blood would answer when we—"

"Silence!" That carried the force of a blow in the face. I saw Herrel's body tense, his eyes glitter. He obeyed, but only just.

"And you came where?" Hyron continued.

"Up there." At that moment I could not have raised hand to point. I used my eyes to indicate the rise from which I had viewed their calling.

"Yet—" Hyron said slowly, "you did not fall, you climbed down in return—"

"Kill!"

Halse? Or another? But Hyron was shaking his head. "She is no meat for our rending, pack brothers. Like draws like." He raised his hand and lined a symbol in the air between us. Green it was as if traced in the faintest curl of mist, and then that green became blue which was gray at its dying.

"So be it." Hyron spoke those three words as if he pronounced some sentence. "Now we know—"

He did not move towards me, but Herrel did. And I yielded to his hand. Together we walked slowly, none of the Riders following closely behind, letting the distance grow between us.

"Your gate is open?"

"It is open."

"But—"

"Now is not the time for talking. We shall have many hours for that ahead of us—"

Then he broke the moment of new silence. "I wish—" he began but did not continue, looking never at me but at the way ahead, picking out ever the easiest footing for me.

"What do you wish?" I did not really care much. I was so tired I wanted nothing but to slip into some dark place and there rest content.

"That there was more—or less—"

More or less what? I wondered mistily, not that it mattered. But to that he made no reply.

We came to the tents. The fire was dead, and there were no signs of life— the others must still sleep. Why had I not been able to share that? Since we had passed through the Throat of the Hawk I had shared nothing—nothing—

Herrel brought me back to the bed where the sword had lain between us. Weary I lay down upon it and closed my eyes. I think that I slept—or swooned—because of my great weariness of body and mind.

Had I been adept in the Power born in me, but which I used only as a clumsy child would play with a weapon which could either save or harm, then I would have been armed, warned, perhaps able to defend myself against what the new night brought. But Hyron, in that testing, knew me for what I was, witch blood right enough, but unskilled, so no foe to stand against what he could summon and aim.

I had thrown away the one defense Herrel might have set between me and what they intended. Though I was not to know that for long to come.

Hyron moved quickly, and he had the backing of all the pack but one in that moving. Illusions they dealt in—but illusions may be common, or very complex. And the opening of the gate allowed them to draw upon sources of energy which had been dammed from their use for a long time.

I roused as Herrel knelt beside me, cup in his hand, concern in his face, his touch tender. He would have me drink—it was the reviving fluid which had restored me before. I could recall its taste, its spicy scent. Herrel—I put out my hand—it was so heavy—so hard to lift. Herrel's cheek bearing my nail brand—Why had I so misused one who—one who—?

But that cheek wore no brand! Herrel—cat—Or *was* it a cat's green eyes watching me? Cat—bear—? My eyelids were so heavy I could not hold them open.

But though I could not see, yet still it would seem that hearing had not foresaken me, the dregs of my Power leaving open that small channel to the outer world. I could hear movement in the tent about me. Then I was lifted, carried—

I was aloof, apart from what my ears reported.

"—fear him—"

"Him?" Laughter. "Look upon him, brothers! Can he move to raise his hand, does he even know what we now would do?"

"Yes, he will be content enough to ride with us in the morning."

It was like that beat of their desire in the valley, but now it formed a huge, stifling cloud of will—their will—pushing me down into darkness—with no hope of struggling against it.

IX
The Hounds of Death

*T*he ashen forest about me again—and the hunt! But this was, in its way, worse than it had been before. I looked down upon my breast for that amulet which had been my safety in a sea of terror. This time it did not warm my flesh. I was bare of any defense. Yet I did not run. As once I had said, when fear comes too often, then it loses its sharp edge. I braced my back against one of the dead trees and waited.

Wind—no, not wind, but a purpose so great it sent its force before it as a wind—stirred the leaves which were pallid skeletons of their living brothers. Still did I make myself stand and wait.

There were shadows—but not dark—these were pale and gray and they flitted about, their misshapen outlines hinting of monstrous things. But, as I continued to stand my ground, they only gathered behind the trees, menacing, not attacking.

A wail to follow on that wind of purpose, so high and shrill as to hurt the ears. The shadows swayed and fluttered. Now down the forest aisles moved those who had substance. Bear, wolves, birds of prey, boar, and others I could not name. They walked erect which somehow made them more formidable to my eyes than if they hunted four-footedly.

The need for speech struggled in my throat. Let me but call aloud their names! Only that relief was denied me, and it was as if I suffocated in the need to scream.

Behind the beasts the shadows gathered thickly, their outlines melting, re-forming, melting again, so all that I knew was they were things of terror, utterly inimical to my form of life. Now the pack of beasts split apart and gave wide room to the leader of their company. A long horse head, the wild-ness of an untamed stallion gleaming in the eyes. And in its human-hands a weapon—a bow of gray-white tipped with silver, a cord which gave off a green gleam.

He who wore the bear's mask held out an arrow. It, too, was green. A spear of light might have been forged into that splinter shaft.

"By the bone of death, the power of silver, the force of our desire—" No spoken words, the invocation rang in my head as a pain thrust, "Thus do we loose one of three, never to be knotted together again!"

The shaft of light set to the cord of light. Now had I desired in that last moment to seek a small and doomed moment of safety in flight, yet I would not have succeeded, for their united wills held me as fast as if I were bound to the tree. And the cord twanged, or else that small sound was sensed rather than heard.

Cold—a bite of frost so bitter and so deep that it was worse than any pain I had ever known. I stood still again the tree—or did I? For in strange double vision now I looked upon the scene as one who had no part in it. There was she who stood, and another she who lay upon the ground. Then she who stood moved forward to that company of beasts, and they ringed her around and vanished among the trees. But she who lay did not move. And now I was she who lay—and the shadows were drawing in to—

I had said fear could become so familiar it no longer was a goad. But there was that in those shadows which caused such a revulsion and terror in me that I answered with a frantic denial of them, of what I saw—And was answered by dark and no knowledge at all—

Cold—piercing cold—I had never known such cold. But cold was my portion now—cold, cold, cold—

I opened my eyes. Over me a leaden sky and from it the falling of snow. Tent—surely there was a tent—?

Slowly I moved, struggled to sit up. Memory also awoke. Those cliffs I had seen before—this was the valley which led to the gate of the Riders' lost land. But it was empty. No tents stood, no mounts in a picket line. Snow drifted a little, but it had not quite yet hidden a ring of fire-blackened stones. Fire—heat to banish this body-aching cold! Fire!

I crept to those stones on hands and knees, thrust my fingers into the ashes. But they were long dead, as cold as the flesh and bone which probed them.

"Herrel—Kildas—Herrel!" I cried those names and had them echoed ghost-fashion back to me. There came no other answer. The camp, all those who had been within it—gone—utterly gone!

That this was another dream I never believed. This was the truth, and one my mind flinched from accepting. It seemed that the Riders had indeed rid themselves of one they did not want, and by the simplest of methods—leaving me behind in the wilderness.

I had two feet—I could walk—I could follow—

Swaying I got to those feet, staggered along. Only to return again to hands and knees, to crawling. And then—there it was—that unbroken cliff wall. Had there ever been a gate? After all I had not seen it. If there had it was firmly closed once more.

Cold—it was so cold—I would lie in the snow and sleep again and from that sleep there would come no waking. But sleep—sleep perhaps meant an ashen forest and the shadow that crept in to—feed! Painfully I made my way back down over the rubble. There, already powdered with snow was the furred rug on which I had lain. I shuffled to it, to find something else—my bag of simples.

My hands were so cold I could hardly feel anything my fingers handled, but somehow I brought out one of the vials, got it to my lips, sipped, waited for inner warmth to follow.

No warmth—cold—cold—As if some part of me had been frozen for all time, or else drawn out to leave an empty void into which ice had molded. But my head cleared, my hands answered the commands of my brain with more skill.

I had the rug on which I had lain, and my bag, the travel-stained clothing I wore. There was naught else—no weapon, no food. I might have been left for dead on some battlefield where the victor cared not to honor the remains of the vanquished.

Cold—so cold—

Wood, some wood left. And they had not been wise to discard my simple bag—no, that had been a grievous mistake on their part. I was better learned in the worth of what I carried so far than they might guess.

I dragged the wood to the fire stones, laid it as best I could, and then smeared on some twigs a fingertip of salve, to which I added drops from another vial. My hands were steady. They moved easily now. Flame answered, caught easily at the branches around. I drew as close as I might to its warmth.

Warm—on my hands, my face, my body, yes, there was warmth. But inside me, cold, cold, cold emptiness! At last I found the right word for that sense of loss. I was empty—or had been emptied! Of what? Not life, for I moved, breathed, knew not hunger and thirst, which I assuaged with handsful of snow. The cordial from my bag had quieted the pangs of physical hunger. Still I was empty—and never would I be whole again until I was filled.

That me which the beasts had taken with them—that was what I must find again. But a dream—? No, not wholly dream, they had wrought some sorcery of their own over me when—last night—many nights ago? By all accounts sorcery could alter the wave of time itself. They had left me to the shadows in the dream world—perchance thus, they believed, to one form of death. And if that failed, as it had, then to this other death in the wilderness. Why had they so feared—or hated—me? Because I could not be ensorceled or shaped, controlled as those others from the Dales?

"Witch," Herrel had named me. And he had spoken as one who knew well of what he spoke.

Dame Alousan was a Wise Woman. She had known more of things outside the beliefs of the Abbey than she had ever said. In her library of old knowledge there were books, books I had understood only in part. Sorcery existed. All men knew that. It was remnants of a kind of learning from a very old day and from other peoples who lived in the Dales before the men of High Hallack came from the south to spread out among the hills. And the Were Riders—all men knew that they controlled Powers and forces beyond human ken.

Some such powers were for the good of those who sought them, or they could be shaped for good or ill. And a third sort were neither good nor evil. But beyond the bonds laid by men, yea or nay. There was a flaw in the use even of good Powers. That had been early impressed on me until I learned it as an undeniable lesson. For the sense of mastery such use gave the one who practiced it led to a desire for more and more. And finally, unless one was strong-willed enough to put aside temptation, one ventured from light into shadow, and into the dark from which there was no return.

No return—there might have been no return from that ashen wood for me. And—also there had been something rift from me there. Cold—cold—I pressed my hands tight to my breasts—so cold! Never would I be warm again, filled again—until I won back from those who had taken it that other self of mine. Won back? What chance had I of that? I would die here in the wilderness, or this part of me would die—Oh, I could keep life in me for a short period using those simples and my knowledge—but it would only stave off an inevitable end.

Cold—would I never be warm again? Never?

If only I knew a little more! If I had not been denied my birthright—birthright? Who was Gillan? Witch, Herrel had laid name to me—witch? But one who could not perform her witchery, who had Power of a sort but could not use it to any great purpose—a witch who was maimed, even as Herrel had claimed to be maimed, unable to be whole. Whole?

I found myself laughing then, and that laughter was so ill a thing to hear that I covered my mouth with both hands, though my shoulders still shook with the force of those convulsions which were not mirth, were very far from human mirth.

Whole? The laughter which had torn me subsided. I must—I would be whole. Slowly I turned my body until I faced the gate which was no longer a gate. What would make me whole had vanished—behind that. But—it pulled me—it did, it did! As my body grew stronger, my mind more alert, so did I feel that pull, as well as if I could actually see a cord trailing away, leading into the stone.

The snow had stopped and the firewood was almost consumed. I could not take the back trail; that which dragged at me would not allow it. Thus I must find some way through the barrier—or over it—

"Stand!"

My head jerked on my shoulders.

Men coming up the valley. As the Riders, these were helmed. But their head covering bore ragged crests and were equipped with eye pieces which fitted down over their eyes mask fashion. They had short coats of furred hide and their boots arose on the outer side of the leg in a sharp point.

Hounds of Alizon!

When they had first come to this continent as invaders they had been armed with weapons strange to the Dales, one of which had shot a searing beam of fire. But when their supply ships had ceased to arrive, some two years ago, these had grown fewer and fewer among them. Now they rode as did the other fighting men of this land with bow, sword, spear, and I saw arrows on cord—

I did not move. It would seem prospective danger was now real. For the fate of any woman in the hands of the Hounds was not good to think upon. I had that in my bag which would give me a last freedom, had I chance to use it.

"A woman!" One of them rode past the archers, slid from his saddle and ran towards the fire. Wearing his mask helm he was more alien even than the beasts.

I had no road of escape. Should I try to scramble over the rocks I could be pulled down with ease, or caught when I came up against the barrier of the gate.

Because I did not flee I surprised him. He slackened pace, looked from the fire to me, glanced about—

"So your friends have left you, wench?"

" 'Ware, Smarkle," an order snapped from the others, "have you never heard of baited traps?"

He halted almost in midstride, and dodged behind a rock. There was a long period of silence wherein the archers sat their saddles, their arrows centered on me.

"You there," a man stepped out from between the horsemen, his shield well up to cover his body, a captured shield since its surface bore a much-defaced bearing of the Dales. "Come out—to us! Come or be shot where you stand!"

Perhaps the best choice would be to disobey, to go down now in clean death with the arrows reaching into that emptiness. But there was a need in me greater than any other, to regain that which I had lost, and it would not let me turn away from life so easily. I walked past the fire, to the rock behind which Smarkle crouched.

"She is one of the Dale wenches right enough, Captain!" His voice rang out.

Still with his shield before him the Captain dodged from one bit of cover to the next in a zigzag course.

"Come, you, on!"

Slowly I went. There were four archers, the two men behind the rocks— how many more might be in the valley I could not guess. Plainly they had trailed our party here, which showed strong determination on the part of these hunted men, since the course brought them deep into the waste and away from the sea which was their path homeward, could they ever find a ship. As Herrel had said, these were desperate, with naught to lose which counted longer, even their lives. And so they were also beasts, perhaps much worse than the Riders.

"Who are you?" The Captain fired a second demand at me.

"One of the Dale brides," I made answer with the truth, knowing now that these men were not as they had been weeks, or even days ago. Even as I they had lost some part of them, worn away by hardship and the abiding loneliness and despair which dwelt in the waste.

"Where are the rest, then?" That was Smarkle.

"Gone on—"

"Gone on? Leaving you behind? We are not fools—"

Small inspiration came to me. "Neither are they, men of Alizon. I fell ill of hill fever—to them it is doubly dangerous. Do you not know that the Were Riders are not as we? What ails us is sometimes doubly fatal to them—"

"What do you think, Captain?" Smarkle asked. "If this be a trap, they would have cut us down by now—"

"Not and risk her. You—go back, beyond that fire, against the rocks! Keep your arrows on her as she goes."

I returned, passing the dying fire, setting at last my shoulders against the stone.

"You—back there—" Now the Captain did not address me, now his own men, but the debris in the valley which masked the gate wall. "Move, and we arrow slit this dainty piece of yours!"

His words echoed about the walls as they waited tensely. And when the last sound died away, he spoke to Smarkle.

"Take her!"

He came at me in a run, dodging about the smoldering fire, slamming his body against mine, pinning me to the rock by his weight. His breath was hot and foul in my face, and through the eye slits of his helm I could see his eyes, aglitter with a vicious hunger.

"Got her!"

They moved, still cautiously, towards us. Smarkle contented himself for the present with whispers, the obscenity of which I could guess, though most of the words he used I had never heard. Then he pulled me away from the rock and held me with my arms clamped to my sides, though I had made no struggle.

"She's no Dale wench." One of the archers leaned forward in the saddle to stare at me. "Did you ever see such hair on one of them, now did you?"

My braids had loosened and fallen, and against the snow their black hue was startlingly dark. The Hounds looked me up and down as Smarkle held me for their inspection, and now I thought I saw a wariness in their eyes. Not as if they feared me to be bait in some baffling trap they had not yet uncovered, but that something in my appearance alone made them uneasy.

"By the Horns of Khather!" swore the archer. "Look upon her, Captain—have you not heard of her like?"

Beneath the half mask of his helm the Captain's lips curled in an evil leer. "Yes, Thacomer, I have heard of her like. Though in this land—no. But have you not heard there is a way to disarm such sorceresses, a very pleasant way—"

Smarkle laughed, his grip tightening painfully on my arms.

"Let us not look into her eyes, Captain. It is so a man is held in spell. Those hags of Estcarp know how to bewitch mortal men."

"So they may. Yet they are also mortal. We have caught us some fine sport."

The sun had come from behind clouds, its westerning rays struck full in my face. Of what they spoke I had no clue. Though that they believed me of a race of old enemies of theirs I could guess.

"Build up the fire," the Captain flung the order to the archers. "It is cold here—these walls hold out the sun."

"Captain," Thacmor asked. "Why would she stay here—unless she means us harm—"

"Harm to us? Perhaps. But rather do I think she was found out for what she is, and so left—"

"But those devils also deal in magic—"

"True. But wolves of a pack turn upon one another when hunger bites deep. There may be some quarrel we do not know. Perhaps even these Dale sheep laid plans and planted her among the rest to bring their 'Bargain' to naught. If so, she has failed or been found out. At any rate they have left her to us. And we shall not nay-say them!"

As yet Smarkle held me, and his touch was an offense it would shame me to put into words. Feeling was left me, like a dim memory of something which had once been alive—and good.

They gathered more wood. At one time this valley must have been a channel for a stream of size and storm drift was still caught among the boulders. They stirred the fire I had kindled into higher blaze. Smarkle threw a loop of hide thong about my shoulders and arms, another about my ankles, making me prisoner.

But with them one kind of hunger seemed greater than the other, for one brought a brace of birds, a large rabbit to the fireside, and these they cleaned and spitted for broiling. One of the archers had a leathern flask. He unstoppered it, strove to drink, and then hurled it from him with a curse.

"Witch," the Captain stood straddle-legged before me. "Where did they go—the Were Riders?"

"On."

"And they left you because they found you out for what you are?"

"Yes." That might or might not be true, but I thought he guessed rightly.

"Therefore their magic was greater than yours—"

"I cannot judge their Power."

He thought on that, and I do not think he relished his thoughts.

"What awaits ahead?"

Again I gave him the truth. "Now—nothing."

"Did they become thin air and float away?" Smarkle twitched the cord about my ankles in a cruel pull. "The same you will not, witch wench!"

"They passed a barrier, it closed behind them."

The Captain glanced up at the sun, now almost gone from this shadowed valley, and then at the choked passage ahead. He did not appear to like its looks, but he was a seasoned warrior and prepared to make sure of his ground. At a gesture from him two of the archers laid aside their bows, drew swords, and worked their way up the piles of slide debris.

To one side lay the fur rug which had been left with me. Smarkle advanced a hand to it, and then lifted it higher with the toe of his boot, scudding across the frozen ground.

"Stupid fool!" The Captain turned on him. "That is a shape-changer's hide. Would you touch it?"

Smarkle shivered, his leering grin gone. He grabbed a branch from those laid ready for the fire and lifted the finely dressed hide, thrusting it yet farther away. A rug—they so feared a fur rug? But these men must have faced the fur of the Riders in their battle guise, to them it was indeed an animal's pelt.

My bag of simples—I could see the end of its carrying strap lying in the shadow of a rock. Doubtless they would deal the same with that should they find it, mistrusting the "magic" it might contain. Were I free and had it in my hands, then I might indeed work "magic"—

But they did not sight it, not yet. And now the Captain came back to his interrogation of me.

"Where did they go? What lies behind this barrier?"

"I do not know—save that they sought another land—"

The Captain snapped up the eyepiece of his helm, took off the head covering. His hair was very fair—not the warm yellow, or light red-brown of a Dalesman—but rather almost white, as if he were an old man—yet that he was not. He had a sharp and jutting nose, not unlike an eagle's beak (an eagle's beak . . . would I ever now look for such signs on a man's face?) and high cheekbones set wide apart—though his eyes were small and narrow lidded so that he appeared to ever squint.

He ran his hand from one temple back up his head. There were marks of fatigue on his face, and that kind of tautness shown by a man driven to the edge of endurance, perhaps beyond. He sat down on a stone, no longer looking at me, but staring into the fire.

Moments later the scouts returned.

"Well?"

"Much fallen rock and then just cliff—they could not have gone that way."

"They came in here," the other scout said, a thin, unsteadiness in his voice. "They could not have doubled back past us. They came in here—but now they are gone!"

The Captain's gaze swung once more to me. "How?" his voice rasped that one word demand.

"To each his own sorcery. They asked a gate to open—it did."

It had opened for them—not me. But that would not stop me, any more than this remnant of broken, fleeing men would stop me. Somewhere beyond that wall was a part of me. It would draw me on, guide me, and I would be whole once again!

"She—she can get us by—" Thacmor nodded at me. "The witches—they say wind and wave, earth and sky, obey them."

"One witch alone, who could not use her Power before?" The Captain shook his head. "Do you think she would have been here, waiting for us, had she been able to break their spells? No, the hunt's lost now—"

Smarkle licked his lips, the others shifted uneasily.

"What do we do now, Captain?"

He shrugged. "We eat, we—" He paused to grin at me, "amuse ourselves. On the morrow we lay plans again."

Some one of them laughed. Another slapped his near companion on the shoulder. They were pushing aside tomorrow, living for the hour as was customary with fighting men whose lives were long forfeit. I glanced at the meat by the fire. It would soon be done, then they would eat and then—after—

So far my passiveness had appeared to serve me. I was bound but they had not otherwise misused me. However my respite was very close to an end. They would eat and then—

If I only had the knowledge. There was that in me, I was sure, which might act as shield and sword at this hour could I release it. Will—I had always thought of it as power of will. Will—power—Could I channel will to make of it a weapon?

X
No Shadow!

*T*he simple bag, my desperate thoughts kept coming back to that. They had scooped up snow, dumped it by the fistful into a small pot now shoved close to the flames. A few drops from a certain small bottle into that and—

But I was as far from achieving that as I was from finding the vanished gate. What I did *not* know was so much more than what I did.

They ate and the smell of the roasting meat, as they tore it with teeth or sawed chunks off with the belt knives, aroused the hunger the cordial had allayed. They offered me none and I knew their purpose. Whatever use they planned to make of me this night, I would not go hence with them in the morning. Why should they wish to burden their troop with a woman who was also a feared witch?

The simple bag. I tried to keep my eyes from it, lest one of them follow my gaze and find it. But when I stole another look I saw, doubtless by some trick of firelight, it was now in the open, could be sighted by any who turned his head. In the open—but how? It had been between two rocks—those two—and now it was inches away!

That shook me—so simple a thing among all the greater. However it is such that tugs at reason when greater shocks will not. The bag had lain there, now it was by so much the nearer to me. As if my desire and will had lent it legs on which to answer my unvoiced summoning. Legs—will? Almost I dared not believe—but I had to.

The flap-cover of the bag—it was fastened so and so. Not daring to look I stared into the flames of my captors' fire and concentrated on building a picture in my mind of that latching. So easy to finger, but for the mind—ah, that was different. How many times can one accurately and minutely describe some well-known possession we handle a hundred times a day? It is so familiar to us that the eye takes no record of its details. To try to recall without looking at it now becomes strange and alien.

Thus and thus—rod into metal loop, turned down—so! I had it correctly pictured, or hoped that I had. Now—to reverse that locking—turn up—slide out—Dared I look to the bag once more to see if it had obeyed my will? Better not—though not to know—

Now—within—how were ranked those contents? I put myself back in the night-filled room of Dame Alousan, the cupboards I had opened, drawers which had yielded to my pull. In what order had I filled those pockets and loops? So deeply did I search memory that the fire and the scene before me blurred. I dared not think on how much time I might have left, as one by one I used memory as a pointer as to what lay now in the shadows. The fifth pocket—it was the fifth pocket! If memory had not foresaken me utterly when I needed it most.

Slender tube, not of glass, but of bone, hollowed and then capped with a stopper of black stone. Out—tube! Greatly daring, I dropped my head forward on my knee, face turned to the darkness. They might well believe me sunk in despair, but now I could see what I wrought, or tried to do—

The tube—out! Movement under the flap of the bag. I do not think it was until that moment, in spite of hope, I dared to believe that I was accomplishing anything. And the sight of my small success almost defeated my efforts by surprise. Again my will steadied, I saw the bone tube work from beneath the leather cover, lie open to sight on the ground.

Tube—pot—one into the other. The meat they were eating was hot and greasy; they would thirst. Tube—into pot. The small bone stirred, arose, pointed for the direction in which I would aim it. I put into that all the force I could muster.

It had no arrow swiftness. Now and then it swayed groundward and my will failed, my concentration broke. But I did it, toppled it into the melting snow water and none of the Hounds had noticed it.

Last of all—the stopper—that black stone. Out—out—! Trickles of moisture from my temples, runnels of it from my armpits. Stopper—out! I kept on the battle, having no way of knowing of my success or failure.

A hand reached for the pot. I held my breath to see a small drinking horn dipped into the contents. Would that archer see what lay within—had it done its purpose? He drank thirstily from the horn, and so did the one next to him. Three—four—now Smarkle. The Captain? So far he had not.

Time—would time serve me now? I knew what the effect of that liquid was under certain controlled conditions. How it might answer this night was something else.

They had finished eating; clean picked bones cast out among the rocks. I had had my respite. Now it was coming to an end. The Captain—one other— had not drunk. And of those who had—I could see no signs they were affected. Perhaps the stopper—but it was too late to regret now—

Smarkle stood up, wiping his hands down his thighs, grinning.

"Do we go to the sport, Captain?"

Now—he was turning to the water pot! Just as I had used my will on the bone vial, so did I now fasten it upon him, urging the need for drink. And he did, deeply, before he made answer to Smarkle's question. Beyond—the other holdout did also.

"If you wish—"

Smarkle gave an obscene crow and strode towards me while laughter and calls of encouragement came from his fellows. He reached down to drag me up against him, thrusting his face into mine, pulling at my clothing—though I struggled as best I could.

"Smarkle—!" A loud cry, but he laughed, blowing foulness into my face. "You will have your turn, Macik. We will do it fair, turn and turn about."

"Captain—Smarkle—" One of the archers came in a leap to tug at his fellow. "Look you—fool!"

His grasp had loosened Smarkle's hold on me, pulled the other a little away from where I fell against a rock. Smarkle mouthed an oath and turned, but something in the other's excitement stopped the blow he had raised his hand to strike.

"Look you!" The archer pointed to the ground. "She—she throws no shadow!"

As the rest I stared down. The fire was bright and the shadows seemed clear and dark, thrown as they were by the men. But—there was none for me. I moved, and no answering black appeared on rock or ground.

Smarkle shook off the other's hold. "She is real enough, I had hands on her—she is real, I tell you! Try her for yourself if you do not believe that!"

But the archer he ordered to that action stepped back and shook his head.

"Captain, you know about the hags," Smarkle appealed. "They can make a man see what is not. She is real, we can break all her magic easy enough—and have a good time doing it."

"They can make you feel as well as see, do they wish it," the archer replied. "Perhaps she is no woman at all, but a shape-changer set here to hold us until his devil pack can come to our blooding. Shoot—prove her real or shadow. Use one of the cursed shafts—"

"If we had one left, Yacmik, do not doubt I would use it," the Captain cut into the argument. "But we do not. Hag or shape-changer, she has Powers. Now we shall see if they can stand against cold steel." He drew his sword and the others fell back as he came to me.

"Ahhhhh—" That sound began as a startled cry and ended as a sigh. He who had first drunk from the pail of snow water lurched back, clutching for support of the man beside him. Then he went down, dragging the other with him. A second man wavered, fell.

"Witch!" The Captain thrust with his sword. But the blade went between my arm and my side, scoring the flesh along my ribs, but not the fatal wound he intended, jarring its tip against the rock which backed me. He blinked at me, his face creasing in a grimace of hatred and fear, and made ready to strike again.

But smothered cries from those about the fire made him turn his head. Some of his men lay prone and still, and others strove to keep on their feet but wavered drunkenly, with manifestly little control over their bodies. The Captain put his hand to his head, brushed across his eyes as if to clear them from some vision. Then he thrust at me a second time, his blade tearing a long rip in my robe, and he went to his knees, to crash forward on his face.

I pressed my hand to my side, feeling the damp of my blood, not yet daring to move for there were some still stumbling about. Two tried to reach me with drawn weapons, but in the end I alone stood among the fallen.

They were not dead, and how long the drug would hold, so diluted and used, I did not know. Before they woke I must be gone. And where was I to go? When I was sure they were all unconscious I went to the bag my will had opened and searched for that which would aid my hurt. That salved and bound, I passed among my sleeping enemies, looking for aught which might aid me in the struggle to keep life in my body.

A long hunting knife was in my belt, and I found some food—the compact rations known to the forces of Alizon, which they must have been saving, trying to live off the country when they could. Swords, bows, arrow-full quivers I gathered and threw upon the fire—which might not harm the blades but would finish the rest. Their horses I freed from the picket line and sent down the valley, flapping a blanket to frighten them.

With the knife I cut away the long skirt of my divided robe, binding what was left to my legs so that I would not be burdened in my climb. For only climbing would take me where I must go. And, even though it was now night, I must be on my way, lest the sleepers rouse to find me still within their reach.

There was no use in attempting the barrier which masked the Riders' "gate"; not so much as a finger- or toehold could be found on its surface. So—there remained the valley walls. And the danger of such a road was marked by the debris of past slides.

Only in me one purpose had grown so great that it filled even the emptiness. The pull which drew me north had strengthened during the passing of hours, not become lesser. I was no longer a creature of flesh and blood alone. That flesh and blood was rather an envelope for something now more acute and desirous than any ordinary human might know. It was as if my ordeal in escaping from the Hounds had awakened, or shaped, yet further that unknown which I had always possessed but been unable to bind to my service.

I began to climb. This much favored me, I had never found it hard to walk high places. And I had heard it said many times by the hunters from the mountains who came to trade their fur take in the Dale towns, that one must never look down or back. Though it seemed to me now that my advance was the journey of an ant compared to the stride of a tall man, as I looked ahead to what still lay before me. Also, I had no lessoning in this, and was ever fearful of a wrong move plunging me down, while I never knew at what moment those I had left might rouse and take to the hunt.

Up and up, moments lengthened until they weighed upon me as full hours.

Twice I clung in stark terror as rocks *did* crash, missing me by very little. At last I came upon a fault in the rock which had better holds within it. So, venturing inside that break, I went on and on until, at last, I pulled out upon a bare and open space which must mark the top of the cliff. There I tumbled forward into a pocket of snow, my body weak and trembling, no longer able to obey my will.

At length I recovered enough to crawl between two pinnacles of rock, and from my back I loosed the fur rug which I had knotted to me with strips of my robe. This I wrapped about me and so huddled in the poor shelter I had found.

There was a moon that night. It had ridden high in the sky as I climbed but now it paled, and so did the glittering stars. I had reached the crest of the guardian cliff, so I must now be on a level with the top of the gate barrier. What I had to face I did not try to guess. I was so tired my mind seemed to float away, out from my aching body.

I did not sleep, I drifted in an odd state of double awareness which was puzzling. At times I could see me huddled between my rocks, a bundle of furred robe, as if another Gillan crouched on one of the pinnacles, detached, uncaring. And at other times I was in another place where there was warmth, light, and people whom I tried to see more clearly but could not.

The scratch on my side had stopped bleeding, the salve had done its duty, and the rug kept out the major part of the cold. But finally I stirred uneasily, the pull on me urging me on. It was past dawn and the rising sun streaked the sky with red. We would have a fair day—we? I—I—I—Gillan who was alone—unless Fortune turned her face utterly from me and the Hounds came baying up my scent.

Beyond the pinnacles which had protected me during the last hours of the dark was a broken country, such a maze of wind-worn rock in toothy outcrops as could utterly bemuse and confuse the would-be traveler. The cliff must be my guide and I should keep to its lip in order not to become lost.

The wall which was a barrier was perhaps twelve feet or more thick—beyond it the same narrow valley continued—no different from the one out of which I had climbed—save that here the walls were sheer past any hope of descent. I must move along the edge hoping to find more favorable territory beyond.

Here in the heights the sun was not veiled and struck fair across the stone, bringing with it warmth, fleeting though that might be. And now I noticed a difference in the rocks about me. Whereas they had been gray, brown or buff-tan, here they were a slatey blue-green. But as I paused by one and let my eyes move to the next outcrop and the next, I perceived that these colorful pieces, many of them taller than my head, were not natural to the terrain they rested on. And also that, tumbled as they were, they yet followed a given course, as if some titanic wall had long since tumbled into rubble. They grew to be taller and taller and more thickly set together, so that many times I had to detour and backtrail to find a path among them. Which course in time drew me farther from the edge of the cliff which was my guide.

I rested and ate of the rations I had plundered from the Hounds. The stuff was dry and tasteless, and it did not give the satisfaction of food, but I thought it would renew the energy I had lost. As I sat there I studied those blue-green rocks and their piling. They were not finished, bore no signs of ever having been dressed or worked; yet they did not arrive here by natural chance, of that I was sure.

Now that I stared at them, I shook my head, closed and opened my eyes. As in the wedding dell of the Riders, I again faced two kinds of sight, melting and running together until I was utterly confused, made dizzy by that flowing and ebbing before me. One moment there was an open pathway a little to my right. But as I watched that closed, rocks rising to bar it. I was sure this was not born from my fatigue, but rather of a shadowing and clouding of mind. If it continued to last I would hardly dare move, lest my eyes betray me into dangerous misstep.

This time my will could not control it, except for very short snatches of time. And each attempt to do so wore on me heavily. Also any prolonged survey of that changing landscape made me giddy and ill. In me the tie urged forward—now—with no delay. But to obey—I could not.

I was on my feet again but the shifting before my eyes made me cling to the rocks. For it seemed that the ground under my feet was no longer stable. I was trapped in this place and there was no escape.

Then I closed my eyes and stood very still. Gradually the dizziness subsided. When I pushed one foot cautiously forward it slid over solid, unchanging ground. I felt before me, grasped rock and drew myself to its reassuring solidity.

Perhaps the trouble was now past. I opened my eyes and cried out—for the whirl about me was worse than it had been, giving no promise of any end. With my eyes closed the world was solid, when I looked upon it there was only chaos. And I must go on.

Shouldering the bag of simples and the rug, I stood for a moment trying to summon logic and reason. I did not believe that my eyes were to blame for this confusion, but that some spell or hallucination was in force. It did not confuse touch, but only sight. Therefore I ought to be able to advance by feeling my way, but to do so would lose me my guide—of the rim of the cliff, the landmarks I had set upon. I could wander about in circles until either I fell or wasted away.

Lacking a guide—but did I lack a guide? It was so thin a cord to which to trust one's life—that which drew me ever onward after the Riders. Could that bring me, blind, through this maze? I did not see that I had aught else to try.

Resolutely I closed my eyes, put out my hands, started in the direction which beckoned me. It was not easy and my progress was very slow. In spite of my hands before me I crashed against rocks, to stagger on, bruised and shaken. Many times I paused to try sight, only to sicken from the vision which was not only double now, but triple, quadruple, and maddening.

I could not be sure if I were making any progress; my fears might be very well founded and I might be wandering in a circle, utterly lost. Only the tugging at me continued, and I believe, as time passed, I was growing more alert to its direction, found it easier to answer. My hands grazed rocks on either side. But then my outstretched palms flattened against a hard surface. Not harsh contact with rough stone—I slid them back and forth across smoothness. And that was so foreign I dared to open my eyes.

Light, dazzling, threatening to engulf me, to burn me to ashes. Yet no heat against my hands. It was blinding and I dared not look upon it.

Back and forth I examined it by touch, up and down. It filled a gap between two walls through which I had come, stretching from beyond a point above as high as I could reach, down to the ground. There was no break, or even rough spot on the whole invisible surface.

I edged back, tried to find some other way past. But there was none, and my guide pulled me ever into the defile which was so stoppered. At last I dropped to the ground. This, then, must be the end. No way forward except one barred, and no guide back if I strove to retrace my steps. I dropped my head to rest on my hunched knees—

But—I sat not on stone—I rode a horse. Daring to open my eyes because this I could not believe—I saw Rathkas' tossing mane, her small ear. We were in a green and golden land, fair to look upon. Kildas—there was Kildas—and Solfinna. They wore flower wreaths on their heads and white blossoms were twisted into their reins. Also they were singing, the whole company sang—as did I.

And I also knew that this was one side of the coin of truth, just as the twisted rock maze and the barrier of light was the other. I wanted to shout aloud—but my lips shaped only the words of the song.

"Herrel!" In me rose the cry I could not voice—"Herrel!" If he knew, he could unite the whole—I would not be Gillan ahorse with the brides of the Dales, nor Gillan lost among the rocks—but whole again!

I looked about me and saw the company strung out along a green banked lane. And the Riders, too, wore flowers upon their helms. They had the seeming of handsome men, not unlike those of the Dales, with the beast quite hidden and gone. And very joyful was that company—yet he I sought was not among them.

"Ah, Gillan," Kildas spoke to me, "have you ever seen so fair a day? It would seem that spring and summer have wedded and that we have the best of both to welcome us to this land."

"It is so," my lips answered for the one who was not wholly Gillan.

"It is odd," Kildas laughed, "but I have been trying to remember what it was like, back in the Dales. And it is like a dream which fades from one's waking hour. Nor is there any reason for us to remember—"

But there is! cried my inner self. For I am of the Dales yet and must be united—

There came a rider up beside me, holding out a branch which flowered with waxy white blooms, giving off such perfume as to make the senses swim.

"Sweet, my lady," he said. "Yet not as sweet as she who would accept my gift—"

My hand went to the branch—"Herrel—"

But as I raised my eyes from the flowers to he who offered them I saw a bear's red eyes on his helm. And beneath that his own narrowed, holding mine in a tight gaze. Then his hand flashed up between us, and in its palm was a small, glittering thing which pulled my attention so that I could not look away.

I raised my head from my knees. Shadows, darkness about me in a pool which denied that green and gold had ever been. I rode not with flowers and spring about me, I crouched along among enchanted stones in the cold of winter. But this I brought with me—the knowledge that there were indeed two Gillans—one who strove to reach the other side of these heights in painful weariness, and one who still companied with those from the Dales. And until those two were one again there was no true life for me.

It had been Halse beside me on that ride, and he had recognized my return to the other Gillan, had driven me back here. But Herrel—where had he been, what had he to do with that other Gillan?

Now I was also aware that in the dark the dizzy many-sight had ceased, that I could look about me without meeting that giddy whirl of landscape. Had the barrier also vanished?

I crept back between the rocks to face—not the blinding light which had been there earlier, but a glow—a wall of green light. I approached it, put my hands to its surface. Yes, it was as firm as ever. And it was sorcery, of that I was certain. Whether of Rider brewing, or merely some long-set safeguard, I did not know. But I must find a way through it, or past it.

Here I could not climb the walls as I had in the valley. And surely I had nothing to dig underneath, I thought a little wildly. With the fading of its day-glare I could see through it.

Beyond lay an open space, an end to the tumble of rocks which had choked my back trail. Perhaps with those behind I need not fear any longer the bewildering of my sight. But how to pass the barrier—

I leaned back against the rock and stared at it hopelessly. It could not be too thick; I could see through it so easily. If I might shape change as easily as those I trailed—wear an eagle's body for a space, this would be no more than a stride. But that was not my magic.

What was my magic—the will which had served me. How could I apply that one poor weapon here? I could see no way—yet find one I must!

XI
That Which Runs the Ridges

$\mathcal{I}$ was cold, I hungered, both for that which I might take into my mouth and swallow, and that which had been rift from me. And I was caged, for there was no return, nor, it would seem, any going forward from this place.

Down in the Dales I had gone afield with Dame Alousan and some of the village women upon occasion, seeking out herbs, and their roots. And in the summer I had seen webs of field spiders spun between two small bushes or tussocks of grass to form a barrier—

Why did I now have such a memory picture? A web set up between two more solid anchors—? As this wall of light confronting me between stones—

I raised my head, looked more closely at those stones. There was no climbing them—twice my height and a little more, they were sleek and had no handholds. For they were a part of this ancient wall or fortification. Yet those portions between which hung the curtain of light were not a part of the bulk, rather posts of a sort, separate from the rest as the supports of a doorway. Creeping forward I discovered I was able to push fingers knuckle deep between them and the other rocks.

A spider's web—Eluding the danger of the sticky cords it could be brought to naught by the breaking of its supports. So wild a thought yet my mind fastened on it, perhaps because I could see no other way. I had brought the bone vial out of the bag by will. But these were no light bottle, these were weighty stones, such as many men might labor to dislodge. And how could I be sure that moving one would break the curtain?

I covered my eyes, leaned back against the stone of the wall. Though the fur rug was about me, still I could feel its chill, its denial of what that wild thought urged me to try. And always on me that pull from beyond—

Now I looked again to the curtain pillars. To my sight they seemed equally deep set, not to be tumbled from that planting. So I turned my eyes upon that one which stood to the left, and I called upon my power of will.

Fall! Fall! I beat my desire upon it as I would have beat body, hands, all my physical strength had such been able to serve me. Fall! Tremble and fall! I did not have to think of time as I had in the camp of the Hounds. Time here was meaningless—there was only the pillar—and the curtain—and the need for passing it. Fall—tremble and fall!

World without vanished, fading from me. I saw now only a tall, dark shadow, and against it thrust small spurts of blue. First at its crown, and then, with better-aimed determination, at its ground rooting. Soil—loosen, roots tremble—I was wholly the will I used—

Tremble—fall!

The dark pillar wavered. That was it! The foot—work upon its foot. Blue shafts in the murk which was none of my world, yet one I should know. Tremble—fall—

Slowly the stone was nodding—away from me—outward—

There was a sound—sound which shook through my body—was pain so intense it conquered mind and will—drove me into nothingness.

I turned my head which lay on a hard and punishing surface. On my face was the spatter of cold rain or sleet, I opened my eyes. In my nostrils was a strong smell, one which I did not remember ever having met before. Weakly I raised myself.

Black scars on the stone. One of those pillars askew, leaning well away as if pointing my way on. And between it and its fellow—nothing. I crawled on. My hand touched the blackened portion of the stone. I snatched it back, fingers burned by heat. Waveringly I got to my feet, lurched through the charred space, came into the open.

It was day—but thick clouds made that twilight. And from the overcast poured moisture which was a mixture of rain and snow, the frigid touch of which pierced to the bones. But I could see clearly, there were no more shifting rocks ahead—only the natural stones of the mountains, familiar to me all my life. And also there was something else—a way cut into the rock.

But weariness dragged at me as I staggered on to that road. I had only taken a few steps along it when I needs must sit down again. And this time I allayed my hunger with some of the rations from the Hounds' supplies.

There were lichens upon the stones about me, whereas among the blue-green walls there had been no growing things. Also, as I breathed deeply I found a taste in the air, a freshness unknown before.

Since I had come from the place of the curtain of light the bond which drew me was stronger, and in a way more urgent. As if the need for uniting was far more important and necessary.

Having swallowed my dry mouthfuls, I arose once more. It was lucky that the forgotten road I followed was a smoother path, for in my present unsteadiness I could not have managed as I had the day before. It was not a wide road, that very ancient cut now paved with splotches of red and pale green lichens. And through some oddity of this country, my sight was limited by a mist, which did not naturally accompany rain in the Dales, but did hang here.

I descended gradually, and now the road was banked with walls of rock. Too narrow for a troop of horse that way. If it had served a vanished fortress, then those who had manned the rubbled walls were all footmen. Stunted trees, wind crippled, grew here and there, with tangles of brush and dried grass in pockets. I turned a curve and came down a last rise into a great open space, how large I could not tell, for about it hung the veils of mist.

The road led under an arch into an area which was walled, but not roofed—nor had it ever been roofed, I believed. And I stood in an oval enclosure. At regular intervals along those walls were niches which had been closed up for three quarters or more of their height, leaving only a small portion at the top still open. On each of those was deep set a symbol carved in the walling stone. Worn they were, and most past any tracing—those at the other end so smooth that only a thin shadow of a design was hinted at, though some, to my right, were more deeply defined. None had any meaning for me.

It was dark within the open portion of those niches. As I paused before the first I staggered. From that space came against me—what? A blow of some unseen force? No—as I swung to face that small opening the sensation was clearer. This was an inquiry, a demanding of who? and what? and why? There was an intelligent presence there.

And I did not find it odd to speak aloud my answer into the silence which held that questioning beneath its surface:

"I am Gillan, out of the Dales of High Hallack, and I come to claim that which is the other part of me. No more—no less, do I seek."

Outwardly, to my eyes, my ears, there was no change. But I felt a waking of some thing—or things—which had stood guardian here for years past human telling, all of whom now stirred, centered their regard upon me. Perhaps my words meant nothing, perhaps they were not of those who deal in words. But that I was sifted, examined, pondered upon, *that* I knew. And I moved along the center way of that place, turning from one niche to its fellow across the way, each in order, facing that which weighed me.

From those niches with the clearer symbols it came no stronger than from those so age worn. These were Guardians, and I was perhaps a threat to that which they had been set to guard. How long had it been since they had last been summoned to this duty?

I reached the end of that oval, stood before the arched way which carried on the road. Now I turned to face back along the path I had come. I waited, for what I did not know—Was it recognition of some kind, a permission to go as I would, goodwill towards the fulfilling of my quest? If I expected aught, I was disappointed. I was free of that questioning, that was all. And perhaps that was all that was necessary. Still I felt a kind of loneliness, wished for more.

Once again the rock-chiseled road ran on, to descend another long slope. More trees showed and brown grass. The rain held, but now it was not so cold. I found a pool hollowed in a block beside the road and drank from my cupped hands. The water was very chill, but it held a trace of sweet taste. As the air—it refreshed.

Now my trail led along the side of a rise, with a drop to my right, the depths of which were hidden by the mist, for that I had not left behind. And in all this time the only sounds I heard were born from the activity of the rain. If any animal or bird made home in this land, then it was snug in den or nest against the fall of water.

My limbs seemed weighted; I was afraid that I could not go much farther, yet the sharp pull was now a pain inside me. I came to the end of that cliff-side walk and found a grove of trees. Though they were winter stripped, yet their tangled branches gave some shelter. I settled myself at the foot of one, pulling the rug closely about me. Though the fur was matted with moisture, yet the hide was waterproof and kept out the rain. From the place I had chosen I could still look upon the road, coming out of the mist above where lay the plateau of the Guardians, continuing on into more mist and a future I could not hope to read. I curled up, pulled a flap of the rug closer so I was completely covered.

This extreme weariness worried me. I had that cordial in my bag; sips of it could strengthen me for a space. Still if I wasted it at the beginning of what might be a long journey, then later I might discover myself helpless in a time of greater need. If I were no stronger in the morning, then I must risk it. Cold—would I always be so cold?

No—not cold—warm—Sun and warmth, and the scent of flowers. Not a horse this time—I opened my eyes and looked out of a tent. The light was that of late afternoon—outside a brook made music. This was the green-gold land of that other Gillan. I saw a man come, his face half-averted from me. But no one could hide him—not by any shaping!

"Herrel!"

His head snapped around, he was staring at me with those green eyes. There was that in his face which was steel-hard, closed—and so it was with his eyes at first. Then they changed as they entered deeply into me.

"Herrel!" I did what I had never done before in my life, I asked aid of another, reached out in need—

He came to me, almost with the leap of a hunting cat, was on his knees before me; our eyes locked.

All that I wanted to say was imprisoned in my throat. Only could I utter his name. His hands were on me; he was demanding in a rush of speech answers—yet I could not hear nor speak. Only my need was so great it was an unvoiced screaming in my head.

There was shouting. Men burst in upon us, fell upon Herrel and dragged him away despite his struggles. Again I looked at Halse. His mouth was ugly with hate, his eyes fire—fire burning me. Once more he held between us that which drove me away—back to the woods and the rain—and the knowledge that I was again in exile.

"Herrel!" I whispered slowly, softly. Somehow I had nursed in me—to learn now it was truth—the thought—the hope—that Herrel had not been one with those who had left me alone in the wilderness. Could he, too, have been deceived by that part of Gillan now riding with the company? Halse had brought that Gillan flowers, as if in wooing. Had that Gillan been turned by their sorcery to favor Halse? How—how far could she have turned?

The chill which was never gone from me was an icy sword in my breast. Halse had the power to exile me from that other Gillan, he used it at once when he knew that we were one—to drive me forth again. Halse—or some-one—but I thought it Halse—had striven to part me from Herrel by showing me him as his shape-change made him. And then he had turned on me readily when the Riders had discovered that I had some power of my own. This being so—why would he now woo me? Fragments of what Herrel had told me made a pattern of sorts.

Herrel had named himself the least of the Riders, one who lacked the full-ness of the talents the others shared, and thus was not reckoned of much account in their company. Because of custom he had set his cloak enchantment that it would draw no bride. But it had me—why?

For the first time I thought back to that moment when I had stood at the edge of the wedding dell, looking upon those cloaks, seeing them with the double vision. Why had I taken up Herrel's? I had not been caught by any enchantment through its beauty. But I had gone to it, passing other cloaks spread there—taken it up in my hands with the same single-minded action as displayed by all the other maids of High Hallack.

Thus—Herrel had succeeded where they wished him failure. And I did not know to this moment why I had chosen his cloak—and so him. But Halse had been passed by, came forth from that bridal morn riding alone, and that had bitten into him. It would seem that he alone of those unmated had deemed Herrel fair game, planning to take what was his. Perhaps any more save to-wards Herrel would have brought retaliation from the pack, and Halse's de-termination was greater than the rest.

If—when they had rift that other Gillan from me—Halse had fastened on that other self, dividing her from Herrel—How much life did that other Gillan have? There were old tales in the Dales—good telling for the winter nights, when a small shiver up the back added to one's feeling of comfort, the hearth fire blazing before, snug company around. I had heard snatches of stories concerning "fetches"—the simulacrum of the living appearing to those away, generally foretelling death. Did a fetch now ride at Halse's side?

No, that Gillan had more substance, or else the appearance of it. Appearance—hallucination—did Halse actually create—with aid—a bride for himself, or merely the appearance of one to assuage his esteem and deceive those who might be led to question my disappearance—say—Kildas? Or had that other Gillan been used to punish Herrel in some manner, he not knowing her real nature? If so, that short meeting in the tent must have awakened him to the true facts. I did not doubt that Herrel had been made aware in those short moments before the others had come upon us, that there was a difference in Gillans.

Now, with that same urge which I had summoned to topple the pillar, I tried to reach that other Gillan—to be reunited. The cord between us still held, but draw along it to her in this fashion I could not. Warned, they must have set up a barrier to that.

The rain had stopped. But there was no lightening of the clouds, and around me the woods were very quiet, save for the drip of water from the branches. But with the coming of night, there were breaks in the silence which had held by day. I heard a cry which might have been the scream of some winged hunter, and farther away, faintly, a baying—

In my belt was the knife I had brought from the Hound camp. Save for that I was weaponless. And even in the Dales there were four-footed hunters not to be faced unshielded and alone. For me fear suddenly peopled this wood, this country, with a multitude of moving shadows, owing no allegiance to any stable thing. Almost I might have been plunged back into the nightmare wood of my dreams.

Move on, run—down the road—in the open—cried one part of my mind. Stay hid in the dark, under the rug I was but one more shadow. Stay—Go—they buffeted me. Back to the oval of the Guardians—the mere thought of walls was steadying. But that which held me to the forward trail would not allow retreat. And if I broke that tie—and could not find it again—I would have no guide—

Stay—Go—

Weariness made my eyelids heavy, pushed my head down upon my knees. That argument which had no end was lost in sleep.

The scent reached me first, for I came to my senses gasping, choking at the foulness of a fog which came in gathering intensity from the road. The stench was throat-clogging, lung-searing—

This was not the mist which still cloaked the distances from my eyes, but a yellowish cloud of corruption which held a faint phosphorescence in its swirls. I retched, coughed. Nothing so foul had ever polluted any world I knew.

Under my body was the ground, and through that came a vibration. Something moved out there, along that road, with force enough to send those waves through the earth. The time for retreat was gone. I could only hope that stillness, the robe shadow—something—would keep me from discovery. I put my palm flat on the wet and muddy ground, since I dared not so bend my head, hoping that thus I might better read the vibrations. And it seemed to me that it was not the ponderous slow step such as one might assign to some great bulk, but rather a rapid beat as from a company running—

The muddy fog was thick. If it hid the road from me, then certainly it should in turn hide me from what passed that way! But that was only a small hope, such as we are wont to cling to in times of great peril.

That this was such a time, I doubted not. I shrank inside and out from the fog and what it held—so alien to my flesh and spirit that to come even this close to it was befoulment beyond the finding of words.

Now the passage of what the fog hid was not only vibration through the ground to my touch; it was sound for my ears. The beat of steps, and of more than one pair of feet—but whether of beast or things two footed and running in company I could not tell.

The phosphorescent quality of that evil cloud grew stronger, its yellow taking on a sickly red tinge, as of watered blood. And with that a low droning noise, which one's ears strained to break down into the tones of many voices chanting together, but which ever eluded that struggle for clarity. It was coming up the road, not down from the place of the Guardians.

I bit hard upon my knuckles, scoring them with my teeth until I tasted blood, so keeping from the outcry my panic held ready in my throat to voice. Was it better to see—or far, far better to be blinded against this runner, or runners in the night? Flecks of darker red in the fog. And the drone so loud it filled my head, shook my body. I think my very terror worked on my behalf to save me that night, for it held me in a mindless, motionless state very close to the end of life itself. Fear can kill, and I had never met such fear as this before. For this did not lurk in any dream, but in the world I had always believed to be sane and understandable.

Blood on my hands and in my mouth, and that stench about me so that I would never feel clean again unless I could flee it. But I no longer saw those red flecks, and the drone was easing—it was past me.

Still I could not move. All strength had seeped out of my body as it might have drained from an open and deadly wound. I sat there, terror bound, under the leafless tree.

Vibration now, rather than sound, told me it was still on its mysterious way. Where? Up to the place of the Guardians, then on to the shifting stones—

With the greatest effort I had forced upon my body since I had ridden out of Norstead, I dragged myself to my feet. To leave the shadow of the trees, go out to the edge of the road, was torture. But neither dared I remain here, to perhaps face the return of that which ran the ridges in the night. I had nigh reached the end of all my strength and beyond that lay death—of that I was sure.

To go out on the road itself I did not dare. I stumbled along under the edge of the trees, heading away from what had passed me. The mist seemed thicker, closing about me at times so I could see only a few steps ahead; there lingered, too, the noisome smell of the fog.

For a while I had the wood on my right hand and that small promise of shelter. Then once again I had to take to the road for the ground fell on one side and climbed on the other. Always must I listen for what might come behind—

The slope of the road grew steeper. I slowed my pace even more. And I was panting heavily as I paused to rest for a few moments. Then—away and afar—behind—came a cry—a screech which, faint as it was, made me gasp and cry out. For the alien malignancy which frightened it was that of some utterly unbelievable nightmare. Faint and far, yes, but that did not mean it was not returning this way—

I began to run downhill, weaving from side to side, blindly, without caution, only knowing that I *must* as long as I could stand on my feet. Then I must crawl, or roll, or claw my way as long as I continued to live.

This was dream panic relived in reality. I caught at stones, at the cliff side, to steady myself. A mud patch on the road—I slipped, went to my knees. Gasping, I was up again, staggering on. Always did I fear to hear that cry repeated—closer—

I had not realized that the mist was thinning until I saw farther ahead. And there was light—light? I pressed my hands to my aching side and stared stupidly as I reeled back against the cliff wall. Light—but no lamp—no star—no fire—nothing I could relate it to. Yellow-white, streaking here and there as if it flashed at random from widely separated sources. Not beams of light, but small sparks, winging here and there—

Winging! Lights which flew, detached from any source of burning, dancing sometimes together, sometimes racing far apart or circling one after the other—in no set pattern which would suggest any purpose. One settled for a moment on a tree below, gleamed brightly, vanished—In and out, up and down, to watch them made me almost as dizzy as it had to watch the shifting stones.

They did not warn me of danger, and after a moment or two of watching them I went on. One sped apart from its fellows towards me. I flinched and then saw it was well over my head. There was a buzzing and I made out beating wings, many faceted eyes which were also sparks of fire. An insect or flying thing—I did not believe it a bird—perhaps as large as my hand and equipped with a rounded body which glowed brightly—

It continued to fly well above my head, but made no move to draw closer, and I gathered the remnants of my tattered courage to go on. Two more of the lightbearers joined the one who escorted me, and with their combined light I no longer had to pick my way with care. The road became level once again. Here were trees, I could see leaves and smell the scent of growing things. I had come from winter into spring or summer. Was this the green-gold land of the other Gillan?

At least our bond led me forward. And my lightbearing companions continued with me. Here the trees grew back from the road, leaving a grassy verge on either side of its surface and there was a welcome which was as soothing as an ointment laid upon a deep burn. I could not conceive that that from which I fled could walk through such a land as this. But it had come from this direction and I dared not allow myself to be so lulled.

The road no longer ran so straight, it curved and dipped and came out at last by a river. There was a bridge, or had been a bridge, for the center span was gone. Under that water rushed with some force. To cross here, unless driven, in the night was madness. I dropped down on the entrance to the bridge and half lay, half sat, content for the moment just to have come so far unharmed.

Scent turned my head to the left. One of the light creatures settled on a beflowered branch which swung under its weight. The waxen flowers—those were the kind Halse had offered Gillan on the road. In this much had I come on my journey; I had reached the land behind the gate—that which the Riders had so longed for during their years of exile. Fair it was—but what of that which ran the ridges in the night? Could this land be also greatly foul? I was not spell-entranced, one ensorceled as that other Gillan and her companions. Would my clear sight here serve to warn and protect—or hinder?

XII
Land of Wraiths

*D*awn came gently, and with color; not in the grayness of the waste and the peaks. The light-bearers flitted away before the first lighting of the world about me, and now birds began to sing. I no longer was lonely in a country which rejected my kind. Or so I thought on that first morn in the forbidden land.

In me blood ran more swiftly. I had drawn back my fled courage, my waning strength. That which ran the ridges haunted a former life far behind.

Though the river ran swiftly enough to delay my passage yet there was a small backwater below where I rested, having the calm of a pool. Over this leaned trees with withy branches which bent to the water's surface and those were laced with pink flowers from which each small breeze brought a shower of golden pollen sifting down, to lie like yellow snow upon the water. Slender reeds of brilliant green grew along the bank, save for where a broad stone was deep set, projecting a little into the water, as if meant as a wharf for some miniature fleet.

Stiffly I found my feet and climbed down to that stone, skimming some of the pollen from the water with my hand, letting the clear drops run down my skin. Cool and yet not too cool. My fingers went to buckles, clasps and ties and I dropped from me the travel-stained clothing, with all its tears and the mustiness of too long wearing, to wade out into that back eddy of the stream, washing my body. The wound on my side was a pink weal—already more than half-healed. Some of the blossomed withes rubbed my head and shoulders, and the perfume of the flowers lingered on my skin and hair. I luxuriated in that freedom, not wanting to return to my clothing, to that urge which sent me on. If I moved in illusion, then it was so strong as to entrap me utterly—nor did I want to break the spell.

But at length I returned to the bank and pulled on garments the more distasteful for my own cleanliness. Having eaten I again studied the bridge. It looked as old as time, its gray stones patterned with moss and lichen. The center span must have vanished years ago. No, the only way to cross the river must be to—

I stared at the gap in the bridge. Then, tenuous as a spider's transport thread—there was something there. Illusion? I willed for true sight. There was the dizziness of one picture fitted over another. But I could see it. The old, old bridge, half-gone and another intact, with no break! And—the intact bridge was the true one. But it still remained, for all my concentration, a shadowy, ghostly thing. I glanced away to the pool where I had bathed, to the flowering shrubs and trees, the green generosity of this smiling country. But that showed no ghosts of overfitted illusion—only the bridge did so. Another safeguard of this land, set up to delay, to warn off those who had not its secret?

Slowly I stepped upon the stone I could see well, heading towards that ghost. Or was it another and more subtle illusion, beckoning the wayfarer on for a disastrous fall into the flood below? As I closed upon the broken gap mended by that dim rise, I went down on hands and knees, creeping forward, warily testing each stone before me, lest a dislodged block turn and precipitate me down. It was very hard to believe in—that shadow portion.

I reached the end of the solid stone, or what one sight reported solid stone. My hand moved out, expecting to thrust into nothingness, but the shadow was firm substance. I crept on, hardly daring to look about me. For my eyes said that I was coming onto a span of mist, too ephemeral a thing to support my weight. And below the water boiled and frothed about the support pillars. My touch told me that the mist was real, the break was not. Almost it was as confusing as the shifting stones on the heights.

Across what I could see only as a shadow I went, still on hands and knees until I came to the solid stone. As I stood upright, supported by one hand on the parapet, breathing hard, I knew that once again I must ever be on guard, not disarmed by the smiling peace of this land, so that my double sight could aid and warn.

The road wound on, now through fields. No cattle nor sheep grazed there, nor were any crops sown. At intervals I called upon my double sight, but no hazy outlines formed. There were birds in plenty, and they showed no wariness of me, scratching in the dust near my feet, soaring within a hand's distance, or swinging on some bush limb eyeing me curiously. They were brighter plumaged than the ones I knew from the Dales, and of different species. There was one with stiffly curled tail feathers of red and gold, wings of rust red, that did not fly at all, but ran beside me for a space in company, calling out at intervals a small questing note as if it expected some coherent answer. It was larger than a barnyard fowl and more assured.

Twice I saw furred things watching me as unafraid. A fox surveyed my passing, sitting up as might a hound. Almost I expected it to bark a greeting. And two squirrels, these a red-gold, rather than the gray that lived in Norstead gardens, chattered together, manifestly exchanging opinions concerning me. Were it not for that cord ever drawing me onward, that sense of necessity and need, I would have traveled with a light and joyous heart.

Still caution walked with me and I did not forget to use the sight as a check upon the countryside. The sun arose, was warm, so that the fur rug which had been such a boone in the hills was now a sorry drag upon my arm. I was folding it for the fourth time when I chanced to look upon the ground and a small chill froze me in mid-gesture.

I threw no shadow—that dark mark of any standing or moving thing in a lighted world was no longer mine! Smarkle had accused me of that in the Hound camp, but I had been too intent upon escape for it to make much impression on my mind. But I *was* real—solid—flesh and bone! Around me trees, bushes, tall clumps of grass all had their proper patch of corresponding shade to mark their presence. But it was as if I were as unsubstantial as that piece of bridge had been in my sight.

Was I only real to myself? But the Hounds had seen me, laid hands upon me, had thought to do even more. To them I had been solid, had had life. That I hugged to me, though I had never thought to be thankful for my meeting with those ravagers and outlaws.

Now I moved my hands, striving to win an answer to that movement on the ground. And the confidence built up during my morning's wanderings ebbed somewhat. So small a shadow, something we seldom think on. But to lack it—ah, that was another matter. Suddenly it became one of the most important possessions, as needful as a hand, a limb—as needful to one's sense of sanity.

Even the double sight gave me no shadow. But I used it on the surrounding country and saw—

I was no longer in a world empty of inhabitants. Mist formed, grew more visible as I concentrated, stiffened, became opaque and solid seeming. To my left there was a lane turning from the road, and at the end of that lane a farm garth. An old house with a sharply gabled roof, outbuildings, a walled enclosure which might mark a special garden. It was unlike the holdings of the Dales with that steeply pitched roof, with the carvings scalloped around the eaves and dormer window. The front faced a paved yard in which I saw figures passing. And the more I studied it, the clearer my sight came to be. This was the true sight, the empty fields the illusion.

Without making any real decision I turned into that lane, hurried my steps to the paved yard. And the closer I came the more imposing the house. The roof was covered with slates, the house itself was of stone—that same blue-green stone I had found on the heights. But the carvings were touched with gold and a richer green. Over the main door was set a panel bearing a device like unto the arms of the Dales, yet different, since it made use of intertwined symbols and not the signs of heraldry. And about it was the feeling of age, not an age which drains and exhausts by the passing of years, but an age which adds and enriches.

Those who went about their business outside were two, a man who led horses from the stable to drink at a trough, and a capped maid shooing fowls before her—fowls of brilliant feathers and long slender legs.

I could not see their faces clearly, but plainly they were made like unto me and human seeming. The man wore silver-gray hosen, and an overjerkin of gray leather, clipped in at the waist with a belt on which gleamed metal. And the maid had a gown of russet, warm as a hearth fire and over it a long apron-shift of yellow, the same color as her cap.

The pavement of the yard was solid under my boots. And the maid approached me, sowing grain for the birds from a shallow basket on her arm.

"Please—" Suddenly I needed contact, for her to see me, answer—I had spoke aloud but she did not glance at me, even turn her head in my direction.

"Please—" My voice was thin but loud. In my own ears it rang above the sounds made by the fowls. Still she did not look to me. And the man, having watered the horses, returned with them to the stables, passing close by. He looked, yes, but manifestly he did not see. There was no change of expression on his thin face with its slanted brows and pointed chin—like in that much to the Riders' features.

I could stand their indifference no longer. Reaching out I caught the maid's sleeve. She gave a little cry, jerked back and stared about her as one bewildered and a little afraid. At her ejaculation the man turned and called query in a tongue I did not know. Though both of them looked to where I stood, yet they did not show that they saw me.

My concentration broke. They began to fade, that age-old house, man and maid, buildings, fowls, horses—thinner and thinner—until they were gone and I stood in the middle of one of the fields utterly alone again. Still in me I knew that my sight was reversed—where once I had seen good slicked over ill, now I saw ill slicked over good. To me this was a land of wraiths—and to them *I* was the wraith!

I stumbled back to the road and sat down on its verge, my spinning head in my hands. Would I ever be real in this land? Or not so until I found the other Gillan? Was she real here?

The Hound rations were only a few crumbs now. Where would I find sustenance, this wraith who was me? Perhaps I could break the illusion long enough at some garth or manor to find food, though I might have to take it without asking, if those who dwelt there could not see me. Let me only reach that other Gillan, I prayed—to what Power might rule in this land—let me be one again—and real—complete!

For a while I no longer tried to see what lay beneath the overriding cover to emptiness. How well these people had chosen their various skins of protection—the Guardians—that horror on the mountain road, and this new blanket to meet the eyes of any invader. A company of Hounds might ride here, mile after mile, and see naught to raid. How much had I passed by chance without knowing that it was there? Keeps, manors, towns?

More food I must have, and if I must raid for it, then it would be necessary to see. Two manors I sighted dimly as I went on were too far from the road, and I clung to that because it was real. And it led, my invisible guide told me, in the right direction.

It was midafternoon when I saw the village. Again it lay on a side way. And I speculated as to why all the dwellings I had seen did not abut on this highway but stood always some distance from it. Was the road itself a trap of sorts, to lead an invader across open country well apart from any inhabited place where blundering chance might inform him that all fields were not as they appeared?

A small village, perhaps a score of houses, with a towered structure in their midst. The people in its two streets were shadows to me. I did not try to see them better. It was enough that I could distinguish them and avoid their movements. But the houses I concentrated upon.

The nearest I dared not approach, for a woman sat on the stoop spinning. The next, children ran about the yard engaged in a vigorous game. And the third showed a closed door which might be latched against all comers. But the fourth was a larger building and a signboard with a painted symbol swung out over its main door—it could well be an inn.

I strained my Power to keep it real and visible as I went in the half-open door beneath that board. There was a short passage, a door in it to my left, giving upon a long room in which were trestle tables and benches. Set out on one of those tables a plate with a brown loaf, next to it a round of deep yellow cheese from which had been cut a wedge. Almost I thought they might fade into nothingness as my fingers closed about them. But they did not. I bundled both into a fold of the rug and turned to go, well content.

A figure flickered in the doorway—one of the misty people of the village. I backed to the wall. But the newcomer came no farther in. A little alarmed, I strove to build that wavering outline into a solid person. A man—he wore leather breeks, boots, chainmail under a short surcoat of silky fabric, like in fashion to that of the Riders, save his were not furred. Instead of a helm a cap covered his head, its front turned up and fastened with a gemmed brooch.

He was looking intently into the room, searching, once his eyes swept across me without pausing. Still I read suspicion in his manner. Though he had not drawn it, there was a sword in his baldric, and, being of this land, perhaps he had also other guards and weapons which did not show as openly.

There was another door to the chamber, but it was closed, and to open it might instantly betray me. If he would only come farther into the room, I could slip along the wall and be out—But that helpful move he did not seem inclined to make.

It was a struggle to keep him so sharply in my sight. I was fast discovering that it was easier to "see" the buildings than the people who inhabited them.

I saw his nostrils expand, as if he would sniff me out. Always his eyes searched the room, his head turned from side to side. Then he spoke, in the language I did not understand.

His words had the rising inflection of a question. I tried to hold my breath, lest the sound of the quickened breathing I could not control would reach his ears.

Again he asked his question, if question it was. Then at last, to my great relief, he took several steps into the room. I began my sidewise creep to reach the door, afraid my bootheels would scrape. But the floor was carpeted with a woven stuff which had been, in turn, needleworked in a sprawling design and that deadened any sound. I was within a foot of escape when the stranger, who by now reached the table from which I had taken the bread and cheese, tensed, swung around. At first I thought that by some ill hap he had seen me. But, though he was now staring straight into my face, there was no change in his listening, wary expression. Only—he was coming for the door.

With a last effort I was at it, through, intent on leaving the hall behind me. He shouted. There was an answer from the road. I saw another figure before me. Desperately I threw myself forward, one arm held out stiffly. That met solid flesh and bone, though what I saw was a faded blur. There was a cry of surprise as the newcomer reeled back. Then I was out, running in the street, away from the village, back to the road which I was beginning to consider a haven of safety.

Sounds of cries, of pounding feet behind me. Did they see me, or was I safe by that much? I dared not look back. And I let my defense against illusion drop, saving all my energy for that dash across field.

On the verge I stumbled, sprawled forward, to lie for a few seconds to quiet my racing heart and laboring lungs. When I at last sat up and turned my head it was to face nothing but meadow and sky. But I could hear. There was still shouting back there, and now the sound of a horse galloping, nearer and nearer. I caught up my booty bundled in the rug and began to run, along the road, away from the vanished lane. When at last I paused, breathless, there was nothing to be heard, save the twittering of a bird. I had aroused suspicion but they had not really seen me. I had nothing to fear, at least for now.

But still I put more distance behind me before I sat down on a grassy hillock beside the road and tasted my spoils. Better than any feast the Riders had spread for their brides it was on the tongue—that bread pulled apart in ragged chunks, the cheese I crumbled in my fingers. The Hound rations had given me energy, but this food was more than that—it was life itself. After my first ravenous attack I curbed my appetite. Perhaps a second such raid could not be carried out and I must hoard my supplies.

A bird hopped out of the bushes to pick up crumbs, chirped at me as if asking for more. I dropped some bits to watch their reception. There was no doubt that the bird saw me, as had the fox, the squirrels, the other birds during my day's travel. Why then was I a wraith to those made in the form of humankind? Was it the other side of their defense? For now I was convinced that this coating of illusion was their defense.

Already the sun was well west. Night was coming and I must find some kind of shelter. Ahead I could see a darker patch which might mark a wood. Perhaps I should try to reach that.

I was so intent upon my goal that only gradually did I become aware of a change in the atmosphere about me. Whereas I had felt at ease and light of spirit all day, so now there was a kind of darkening which did not come from the fading of the day, but within me. I began to remember, in spite of my struggle to shut such mind pictures away, the terror of the night before, and all the other shocks of mind and body which had come upon me since I left the Dales. The openness of the land beyond the borders of the road no longer meant light and freedom, but plagued me with what might lie hidden in illusion.

Also—the sensation of being followed became so acute that I turned time and time again, sometimes pausing for minutes altogether, to survey what lay behind me. There were more birds fluttering and calling, doing so in increasing numbers along the verges of the road, or flying low about me. And I had an idea that things peered and spied from farther back.

So far this was no more than a kind of haunting uneasiness. But now I did not like the idea of night in this land. And the trees ahead which had promised shelter at my first thinking threatened now.

It was a wood of considerable size, spreading from north to south across the horizon. Almost did I decide to halt where I was, lie to rest on the verge of the road apart from fields which could hold so much more than I saw. But I did not—I walked on.

These trees were leafed, though the green of those leaves had a golden cast, particularly to be marked along their rib divisions and their serrated edges so that the effect of the woods was not one of dark, but of light. The road continued to run, though the verge vanished and boughs hung across as if the trees strove to catch hands above. It was narrower here, more like the track in the heights. I dared not allow my thoughts to stray in that direction.

There was a lot of rustling among those leaved branches and around the roots of the trees. Though I sighted squirrels, birds, another fox, yet I was not satisfied as to an innocent cause for all that activity. To me it was rather that I was being carefully escorted by a woodland guard of bird and beast—and not for my protection!

Though I kept watch for anything which might promise shelter for the coming night, I saw no place which tempted me to turn aside from the road. And I had come to think it might be well to settle in its center, hard though the pavement promised to be, rather than trust to the unknown under the trees.

It was then that the road split into two ways, each as narrow as a footpath. In the center between those was a diamond-shaped island of earth on which was based a mound, following the same outline as the portion of ground and leveled on its top. Set equidistant down there were three pillars of stone, that in the middle being several hands' taller than the two flanking it.

They bore no carving, no indication that they were aught but rocks, save that their setting was so plainly the work of man, or some intelligence, and not natural chance. Oddly, once I had sighted them much of my uneasiness fled. And, though the position was exposed, I was drawn to that earthy platform beneath the central pillar's long shadow.

Slowly I climbed and unrolled the rug, sitting on it so that I could pull the flaps up about me when I wished. The pillar was at my back and I leaned against its support, while before me stretched the road, uniting beyond the point of the islet, to run on and on, though it was hidden by the trees not too far away.

Once more I ate from the bounty the inn had supplied, far less than I wanted. I was thirsty and it was hard to chew the bread, but the cheese had a measure of moisture and went down more easily.

It was past sunset now. I pulled the rug about my shoulders. The voices of the wood were many, a kind of murmur which kept me straining to identify just one sound and so bring a measure of the familiar past to comfort me in this strange present. But sleep was heavy on me, a burden weighting my tired body.

I awoke in the dark, my heart pounding, my breath fast and gasping. Yet it was no dream terror that shook me into wakefulness. My head lay against the pillar's foot. There were streaks of moon on the road. But around me the light was very full and bright. Under its touch the pillars glowed silver.

Again I was as one blindfolded, stumbling about a room which held a treasure of great importance. Only I could not guess what that was. That I had unwittingly been drawn to a place of real power, I was sure. But the nature of that Power—for good or ill—was past my reading.

There was no fear in me, just a kind of awe, a despair because I could not receive the messages which flowed about me, which might mean so much—

How long did I sit there, entranced, striving to break the bonds of my ignorance and reach out for riches, the nature of which I could not name?

Then it broke, failed. And another emotion swept in, a need for awareness, for being prepared—a warning which again I could not read past its general alerting.

Sound—the pound of hooves on the road. That did not come from behind, but from ahead. Someone rode toward me at reckless speed. Around my island the forest stirred. A multitude of small, unseen things fled away from the road and from me who they had been watching with set purpose.

Yet under my silver pillar no fear touched me . . . only the need to be ready, an expectancy. The rider must be very close—

Out into the moon came a horse, flecks of white foam on its chest and shoulders. The rider reined in so suddenly the animal reared, beat the air with forefeet.

A Were Rider!

The horse neighed and again beat with forefeet. But the rider had full mastery. Then I saw clearly the crest of his helm and I was on my feet, the rug falling from about me. It tripped my feet as I would have run to the end

of the mound, and I kicked at its folds. I shook free. My hands were out as I
called—called?—rather shouted:

"Herrel!"

He swung from the saddle, started to me, his cloak flung back, his head
lifted so that his eyes might seek mine, or so I believed. But his face was still
overshadowed by the helm.

XIII
Beast into Man

*T*his was like journeying down a dark way in the cold of a winter's night,
making a turn, and seeing before one the open door of an inn from
which streamed warmth and light, the promise of companionship with one's
kind. So did I scramble down from the safety of my moonlit mound-island
and run to meet him who had ridden in such haste.

"Herrel!" Even as I had called to him from the tent when I was for a short
space that other Gillan, so did I now reach out to him, voice and hand—

But a swirl of that green light which was the Riders' mark coiled between
us serpent-wise, threatening—and when it vanished—

I had seen the beast which had crouched on the ledge before it leaped to
go hunting the Hounds of Alizon. But then I had not fronted it—only watched
it in lithe action. Now beast eyes were on me, lips raised in a snarl over cruel
fangs—and there was nothing left I could reach.

"Herrel!" I do not know why I named that name—the man had gone.

Stumbling I tried to back away as that long, silver-furred shape stooped
low to the ground in a threatening crouch and I knew that I looked upon death.
The firm earth of the mound was hard behind my shoulders, but I dared not
turn my back upon that death to climb to what small safety its summit might
offer.

There was a knife at my belt, but my hand did not go to it. This I could
not meet with steel. Nor perhaps would my other weapon be any more than
a reed countering a sword stroke. Still it was all I had left me.

Deep did I stare into those green eyes which now held nothing of man in
them, were only alien pools of threat. Within the beast was still Herrel—
hiding, submerged, yet there. Or else man could not rise again from cat. And
if my will—my Power—could find the hidden man, then perhaps I could draw
him once more to the surface. For to front an angry man was far, far better
than to be hunted by a beast.

—Herrel—Herrel—I besought him by mind rather than voice. Herrel!

But there was no change, only a small, muted sound from that furred throat, of anticipation—hunger—And from that thought my mind recoiled sickened, and my will nearly broke. But I fought our battle as best I could.

Suddenly that round head with the ears flattened back against the skull arose a little and from the beast bubbled a yowl such as it had voiced before the Hound attack.

—Herrel!—

Its head waved from side to side. Then it shook it vigorously, as if to throw off some irritating touch. One paw, claws unsheathed, was outstretched in the first step of a stealthy advance which could only end in a hunting spring.

—Man, not beast—you are a man!—

I hurled that at him—or it. For now was leaving me the conviction that man did lie within the cat. This was its own land. What new Power or source of power lay open to it here?

—Herrel!—

Long ago I had lost the talisman I had brought out of the Dales. I knew no power which might lie over this land to which I could raise voice in appeal—in protest—against this ghastly thing which was to pull me down. It is very daunting to stand alone with riven shield and broken sword as I did then.

I cried out—no longer his name—for what or who I had known as Herrel was gone as surely as if death had severed our worlds one from the other. I closed my eyes as my small Power was swept away in a rush of hate. The beast sprang.

Pain raking along the arm which I had flung across my face in that last instant. A weight pinning me against the mound so that I might not move. I would not look upon what held me, I could not.

"Gillan! Gillan!"

A man's arms about me, surely—not the claws of a beast rending my flesh. A voice strained and hoarse with fear and pain, not the snarling of a cat.

"Gillan!"

I opened my eyes. His head was bent above me, and such was the agony in his face that I knew first a kind of wonder. Held me in a grip to leave bruises on my arms and back, and his breath came in small gasps.

"Gillan, what have I done?"

Then he swung me up as if my weight was nothing, and we were on the platform on the mound where the moon was very bright. I lying on my robe while, with a gentleness I had not thought in him, Herrel stretched out my arm. The torn cloth fell away in two great rents and revealed dripping furrows.

He gave a sharp cry when he saw them clearly, and then looked about him wildly, as if in search of something his will could summon to him.

"Herrel?"

Now his eyes met mine again and he nodded. "Yes, Herrel—now! May yellow rot eat their bones, and That Which Runs the Ridges feed upon their spirits! To have done this to you—to *you*! There are herbs in the forest—I will fetch—"

"In my bag there are also cures—" The pain was molten metal running up my arm, into my shoulder, heavy so that I could not breathe easily, and around me the moonlight swirled, the pillars nodded to and fro—I closed my eyes. I felt him pull the bag from beneath the rug and I tried to control my wits so that I might tell him how to use the balms within it. But then he laid hands upon my arm again and I cried out, to be utterly lost in depths where there was neither pain nor thought.

"Gillan! Gillan!"

I stirred, reluctant to leave the healing dark—yet that voice pulled at me.

"Gillan! By the Ash, the Maul, the Blade that rusteth never, by the Clear Moon, the Light of Neave, the blood I have shed to Him Whose semblance I wear—" the murmur flowed over and around me, wove a net to draw me on out of the quiet in which I lay.

"Gillan, short grows the time—By the virtue of the Banebloom, and the Lash of Gorth, the Candles of the Weres—come you back!"

Loud were the words now, an imperative call I could not nay-say. I opened my eyes. Light about me, not that of day, but of green flames. A sweet scent filled my nostrils and the petals of flowers brushed my cheeks as I turned my head to see him who spoke. Herrel stood against a silver pillar, his body to the waist pale silver too, for he had stripped off mail and leather and was bare of skin to his belt—save that across his upper arms and shoulders were welts, angry, red, and on some of them stood beads of blood. Between his hands was a whip of branch broken in the middle.

"Herrel?"

He came quickly, fell to his knees beside me. His face was that of a man who has come from a battlefield, gaunted by exhaustion, too worn to care whether he held victory in his hand, or must taste the sour of defeat. Yet when he looked down at me he came alive again. His hand came out as if to touch my cheek, then dropped upon his thigh.

"Gillan, how is it with you?"

I wet my lips. Far within me something was troubled, as if it had reached and been denied. I moved my arm; faint pain, the lingering memory of that agony which had rent me earlier. I sat up slowly. He made no move to aid me. There was a bandage about my arm and I smelled the sharp odor of a salve I knew well; so he had plundered my bag. But as I so moved a covering of flowers cascaded down my body, and with them leaves hastily torn into bits, from which came the scent of herbs. I had lain under a thick blanket of them.

Herrel made a gesture with his hand. The green lights snuffed out. Nor could I see from what they had sprung, for they left no sign of their source behind them.

"How is it with you?" he repeated.

"Well, I believe well—"

"Not wholly so. And the time—the time grows short!"

"What do you mean?" I gathered up a handful of that flowery covering, raised the bruised blossoms, the aromatic leaves to sniff them.

"You are two—"

"That I know," I broke in.

"But perhaps this you do not know. For a space one may be made two—though it is a mad and wicked thing. Then, if the two do not meet once again—one fades—"

"That other Gillan—will go?" The flower petals dropped from my hand, once more I felt that cold within me, that hunger which could not be appeased by any food taken into the mouth, swallowed by the throat.

"Or you!" His words were simple, yet for a moment the understanding of them was not mine. And he must have read that in my face, for now he got once more to his feet, brought down his bare fists against the side of the pillar as if he smashed into the face of an enemy.

"They—wrought this—thinking that you—this you—would die in the waste—or in the mountains. This land has mighty safeguards."

"That I know."

"They did not believe that you would live. And if you died, then would that Gillan they had summoned be whole—though not as you, save in a small part. But when you came into Arvon—they knew. They learned that a stranger troubled the land, and guessed that it was you. So they turned again to the Power and—"

"Sent you—" I said softly when he did not continue.

He turned his head so that once more I could read his face, and what lay there was not good to behold. There were no words in me which I could summon to assuage that wound as my balms and salves could have healed torn flesh for him.

"I told you—at our first meeting—I am not as they are. They can, if they wish, compel me, or blind my eyes, as they did when they brought forth that other Gillan who turned aside from me to welcome Halse—as he wished from the beginning!"

I shivered. Halse! Had that other me lain happily in Halse's arms, welcomed him? I put hands to my face, knowing shame like a devouring fire. No—no—

"But I am me—" I could not set my bewilderment into words clear enough even for my own understanding. "I have a body—am real—"

But was I? For in this land I was a wraith, as its people were wraiths to me. I ran my hand along that bandaged arm, welcoming the pain which followed touch, for it spelled the reality of the flesh which winced from finger pressure.

"You are you, she is also you—in part. As yet a far lighter and less powerful part. But, should you cease to exist, then she is whole, whole enough for Halse's purpose. They fear you, the Pack, because they cannot control you as the others. Therefore they would make one by sorcery that they can."

"And if—if—"

Again he picked the thought from my mind. "If I had done as they intended and slain you? Then they would not have cared had I learned the full truth, once I had accomplished their purpose. They do not fear me in the least, and if I had done myself harm on discovery of the murder they set me to, well, that would have merely removed another trouble from their path. To their thinking this was a fine plan."

"But you did not kill."

There was no lighting of his face. Still he was as one who had fallen into Hounds hands and been subjected to their cruel usage.

"Look upon your arm, Gillan. No, I did not kill, but in this much did I serve their purpose. And should this hurt keep us from the road we must take, then I have done as commanded—"

"Why?"

"Time is our enemy, Gillan. The longer the twain of you are apart, so will you fail in strength—so finally you may not reach uniting in time. I speak thus that you may know what truly lies before us, for I do not believe that you are one to be soothed with fair words and kept in ignorance."

Perhaps he paid me a compliment in that judging. I do not know. Only then I wished that he had not thought so highly of my courage, for I was shaken, though I tried not to let him know it.

"I think," I tried to push aside fear for a space and think on other things, "that you are more than you believe—or they give you credit for being. Why did you not carry through this geas they set upon you? I have heard, by legend, that a geas is a thing of great Power, not lightly broken."

Herrel came away from the pillar, stooped and took up from the ground a shirt which he drew on over his welted shoulders.

"Do not credit me with any great thing, Gillan. I give thanks to the forces above us, that I awakened from their spell in time. Or that you awoke me— since your voice came to me in that darkness where they had me bound. If you believe you can ride, then we must be gone. To catch up with the pack is what we need to do—"

He donned leather underjerkin and then his mail, belting it about him. But when he picked up his helm he stood for a long moment, staring down upon the snarling cat crest and his eyes were hooded as if he looked upon that which he would like to thrust from him. However, after that short pause he put it on his head.

Then he turned to me, aiding me to my feet, putting about my shoulders not the heavy rug, but his own cloak. Then he half led, half carried me from the mound.

The moonlight was waning; it must not be far from dawn. Herrel whistled and his horse came to us, snorting a little, glancing from side to side, as if it perceived more lurking in the forest shadows than we could see. Yet Herrel displayed no interest in the woodland. He lifted me to the saddle and then mounted behind me. The stallion showed no distaste for a double burden but set off at a steady, ground covering pace.

"I do not understand," I began. Herrel's arms were about me warm and safe, the mail of his sleeves not harsh to the touch but rather reassuring in its rigidity. "I do not understand why Halse wanted me. Was it because his pride suffered when you fared well and he went brideless?"

"It may have begun so," he answered me. "But there was another reason, which came because you are you, and no maid of the Dales. From the first, the rest were one with those whose cloaks they wore in spell. You were not held so. They feared that. There was a chance, a last chance to bind you to us. When that failed, then you were open to what they would do."

"A chance—?"

His voice was low, and I was glad he was behind me, that he did not see my confusion when he made answer.

"That night in the Safekeep, you refused me. Had it been otherwise, then all their spells could not have prevailed."

I broke the silence which followed. "Then you named me witch, Herrel. Was that out of anger—or out of knowledge?"

"Anger? What right had I to anger? I do not take by force that which one chooses to withhold from me—for such must be freely given and in liking, or it has no meaning, not in my sight, nor that of Neave. I named you as what I think you are. Being so—you could do no else than say me nay—"

"Witch," I repeated thoughtfully. "But I am not learned in aught but healing lore, Herrel. That is a craft, yes, but owes nothing to sorcery. Had I been what you named me, then never could I have dwelt at the Abbey-stead. They would have expelled me within an hour of my coming. The Flames and sorcery had naught to do with one another, and the Dames of the Abbey-stead would have thought themselves defiled by my presence."

"Witchery is not the evil the Dalesmen think. There are those of another blood who are born to it. Lessoned in its use they must be, but the Power over wind and water, earth and fire, is theirs by natural gift and not just from study. In the old days Arvon was not walled against the rest of the world. For all men then had touch with Powers which lay not in their strength of arm, nor their minds, save as their minds could control such forces. We knew of other nations over seas which also used sorcery as a way of life. There was one wherein witches walked. And when we rode the waste, still we heard of that land, or what had come from its dwindling, for as Arvon, it had aged. There are witches still in Estcarp and with them Alizon wars."

"You think then I am of this witchblood?"

"True. You have not the lessoning, but within you lies the force. And there is this. They believe that a witch who gives her body to a man must put aside her witchhood."

"If they never do, then how does their nation survive?"

"It dwindles amain by report. Also, this was not always true. It followed when some blight fell upon them long ago. Not all women of that land are witches, though they may mother daughters with the Power. But she who has it is not wont to put it aside."

"But I have had no lessoning. I am not truly witch."

"If the Power is in you, then it will strive to make you a proper vessel for its encompassing."

"And the other Gillan?"

"The Gillan they try to fashion is not witch. They would not take such a threat among them."

With each measured word Herrel sent me further and further into my own waste of exile. Would there ever be any rate for my return?

"Herrel—when I was with that other Gillan for a space—in the tent—and called to you—you knew me?"

"I knew—and learned then what had happened."

"They dragged you away—then Halse sent me out of her."

"Yes."

"Would you have come searching for me, even if they had not sent you under geas?"

"I am not greater than the pack." It seemed to me that he wished to evade my question. "I came—to their bidding."

I had never been good at the understanding of people, the weighing of any emotions other than my own. Still, at this moment, was granted me a small flash of insight as profound, perhaps, as that any witch in the glory of full Power could gain.

"You came because they could use your wish to lay the geas. Had there been no—no tie between us, then perhaps their bidding would not have sent you—"

I heard a sharp sound, or else a breath drawn in pain.

"Also, it was because of your thought of me that you broke that geas, Herrel! Remember that. For never have I heard of a man breaking a geas set in earnest spell—"

"What have you heard," he demanded harshly, "save what lies in song and legend? The Dalesmen spin tales, and in them the kernel of truth is very small and hid. Do not find in me any virtue that I did not kill you to their bidding. I know well my shame—"

"Too long—" I put out my hands, resting them on his where he held the reins before my waist, "too long have you accepted a lesser naming, Herrel. Remember, I came to your cloak, when those others laughed to see you leave it. Through their clouds of sorcery, ill meant, have we broken thus far. You have not failed in battle, or you would not have continued to ride with the Pack." I paused, but he said nothing, so I continued:

"An arrow shaft alone can be broken between a man's two hands by small effort. Set two arrows together and the task is less easy. All my life I have walked alone, an onlooker of the lives of others. So perhaps have you. But do not tell me that you are less than Halse, or Harl, or Hyron. That I do not believe!"

"Why did you pick up my cloak?" he asked abruptly.

"Not because it lay the nearest, or because I saw it of great beauty. For, remember, I saw it as it was. But because when my eyes fell upon it, I could not turn aside, or do aught else than gather it up." The mailed arms about me tightened, and relaxed.

"This then—this much I did!"

"And the spell you laid, Herrel, must have been greater than the others, for I saw beneath the illusion. And you as you are—"

"Did you?" The momentary elation was gone from his voice. "Are you sure that you did not rather see the truth this night? Halse showed it you once in your very bed—"

"Truth may be not a sword with only two sides to the blade, so you look upon one and then the other. Rather it is like a faceted jewel with many faces. You may think you know one well, and another; then you discover a third, a fourth. Still they are all truth, or truths. I have seen you as illusion would make you for a bride's beglamoured eyes, as a Were Rider from the waste, as the beast—And I think perhaps there are still more Herrels I have not met. But it was Herrel's cloak which brought me here and I have no regrets of that choice."

Again he made no answer for what seemed a long time. Around us the gray light grew stronger; we were coming into the new day, although in the wood the transition from dark to light might be delayed. The stallion held to his steady trot, now looking forward as if he, too, sensed the need for reaching some goal with as little delay as possible.

"You build too high on a hope—" Herrel might have been speaking to himself rather than to me. "However we only live by hope and mine hitherto has been a poor, weak thing. But, Gillan, listen to me—the worst is not now behind us—rather does it lie ahead. Their geas is broken, but they have that Gillan of their fashioning. And we must get her forth from them. To do that the Riders have to be faced—in one guise or another."

"Will they meet us as beasts?"

"You they can face so. With me, no—to me they must give Pack right—if I have my chance to demand it."

"Pack right?"

"I may demand to meet Halse sword point to sword point in Right and Judgment—since he has taken the other Gillan. And with you at hand I have proof of that."

"And if you win?"

"If I win, then I can demand repartment from Halse—perhaps of the rest. But they will do all they can to keep me from such a challenge. And here in Arvon they can bend much to their will. From this hour on we ride in danger. I know not what they may send against us. Were it otherwise we would ride for the border, but without that other Gillan that would bring you naught but ill."

We came out of the woods at last, but the level meadowlands through which the road had led me before now gave way to rolling country, not too unlike the Dales, though perhaps their rises and valleys were not as steep. A bird flew from nowhere to hang above us.

I heard Herrel laugh shortly. "They are well served—"

"It means us some harm?" I questioned. The bird was small, rusty brown, unlike any hawk or winged instrument of war.

"In this much, it watches our path. But they need not keep such a check upon us. There is only this road for us."

He called aloud in another tongue, that, I believe, of the wraith people. The bird swooped as if to fly at our heads, veered, and shot away into the morning sky.

XIV
The Shadowed Road

*H*as this land of yours no water?" I ran tongue over dry lips. "Also, one of humankind cannot live on hope and words alone—there needs must be bread and meat—"

"Ahead—" his answer was one curt word where I had attempted to make my complaint light. Broken as the land about us was, yet did it seem empty of all but us and the birds. But the meadows had not been empty yesterday, save to the outer sight. And mayhap Herrel saw more here than I did. That I must know.

"Herrel—is this land empty as I see it under the illusion, or is it inhabited?"

"Under the illusion—how so?" He sounded genuinely perplexed, so I told him of the manor and the village, and how I had run from there because I believed I had been detected, if not really seen.

"This man in the inn room, of what manner was he?" Out of all my story Herrel caught upon that first.

From memory I tried to build a picture of him. When I had done I ended with a question: "Who was—is—he? And how could he have known I was there?"

"He was of the Border Guard by your description. As such he is sensitive, one trained to the ferreting out of any invader. Hard though the way into Arvon may be, still through time men have come into these lands unknowing. For the most part the illusion holds, they see naught but the road, or some ruins. And they are worked upon by threats to the spirit which gives them a dislike of the place, so they pass through. But when you sought the inn, the guard would know an alien presence was there, and that it was aware of more than an empty land. That was why the alarm went forth. You after kept to the road, which was your safety—had you known it—"

"Why can I see only the illusion, save when I call upon my Power?"

"You entered not by the Gate, but by the mountain." Again his arm tightened about me. "And those are filled with many entrapments. How you came safely by all those snares, that is also magic—yours. Tell me, what of that road, and how did you find it?"

So I went back to my awaking in the deserted camp and when I spoke of the coming of the Hounds, then did I hear his breath quicken with a sound like unto a cat's hiss of anger. I told of the vial and the way I freed it from my bag and there he interrupted:

"True witchery! There is no denying your gift. Had you the proper lessoning in it then—"

"Then what?"

"I do not know, it is not our sorcery. But I think in some ways you might challenge the whole Pack and come off unscathed. So you left those dogs of Alizon asleep in the snow. Let us hope that winter cold made that sleep death! But the Gate was closed—spell laid and bound again—so how found you another way?"

"Up and over the heights—" I told him of that climb, of my blind struggle with the shifting stones.

"Those were the ruins of Car Re Dogan—reared by wizardy to be a fortress against the evil which once roamed the waste and which is long since gone. You found a very ancient way, one our race has not trod for half a thousand of Dale years."

I spoke of the barrier of light and its overthrow, and then of my coming into the places of the Guardians.

"The Setting Up of the Kings," Herrel identified for me. "They were the rulers of an elder age. When we first came to Arvon those of that blood were very few, but we mingled with them and took from them some customs which had merit. Thus they did use their kings when each died in turn. So was he buried, standing, allowed to look out upon the world. And should his successor need good council he went thither and abide for a night, waiting to hear that wisdom, or to dream it. Also they were ensorceled to guard this land."

"I felt that I was weighed, yet they passed me through—"

"Because they knew the kinship of your Power. But—" Herrel's voice was troubled, "if you came that way, there are other and far worse dangers to be faced—"

I could not repress a shiver. "Yes, one of them I saw—or saw in part." And I told him of that noisome, clouded thing which passed me in the night.

"That Which Runs the Ridges—! Gillan, Gillan, you have such fortune cloaking you as I have not heard of before! That you survived even so chance a meeting as that! It cannot come into our fields, but it is death such as no living thing should ever meet."

"The rest you know—" Suddenly I was very tired. "Herrel, where is this drink you promised me? It seems an age since I had aught to even wet my lips."

"For once I may give you what you wish as you wish it." He swung the horse off the road and we came to a small shallow stream bubbling along over a pebbled bed. The very sound of that water increased my thirst, so that I wanted nothing more than to plunge head and arms into it, lap at its surface as a dog might lap. But when Herrel aided me down from the saddle I was almost too weak and tired to move.

He brought me to the water's edge and took a small horn cup from his belt pouch, filling it and lifting it to my lips.

"It would seem that I need this and food greatly," I commented when I had drunk my fill. "I am as one emptied—"

"For that also there is an answer." But I thought that he spoke too briskly and avoided my eyes.

"You said that you believed I was one who could listen to the truth, Herrel. It is more than need of food and drink which makes me thus weak, is that not so?"

"I said that time was our enemy. By now they know that I failed them. Now they draw on your life substance to feed their Gillan. They cannot slay so, but they can weaken, and so slow your searching, until it *is* too late."

I looked down at my hands. They were trembling a little, and I could not, by will or muscle, control that tremor. But—

"Fear is also a weapon they may use, my fear." I do not know whether I meant that as a question or a statement, but he answered me.

"Yes. In any way they may shake your confidence, or your spirit, by that much do they profit."

I returned then to the question I had asked earlier. "Is this an empty land through which we ride, or has it those living here who can be roused against us?"

"It is not as populated as the plains beyond the forest. There are scattered keeps and manors. As to their being set against us—had you been alone they would have mustered against you at the bidding of the Border Guard. Now that you are with me they are willing to let it be a personal thing with the Were Riders."

"But you said we ride a dangerous way—"

"The Riders will rouse what they may to front us."

"I had thought Arvon was a fair and smiling land, without peril."

Herrel smiled a wry smile. "Alas, my lady, one remembers, when one is far apart from one's beloved, only the fairness of her face, the sweetness of her words. Long were we severed from Arvon and our small memories were of her smiling face, which was what we wished most to recall. All lands hold both good and evil. In the Dales of High Hallack such good and evil is born from the deeds of men or nature. In Arvon it may be born from sorcery and learning. I told you once—we rode in exile because we were deemed disturbing factors, like to bring dissension into seeming peace. But that was not altogether so—though we were made to remember it thus. There have been struggles for power here, too—though sometimes fought with more fearsome weapons than sword blade and arrowhead or even those Alizon arms which spit killing fire. We rode in exile because we had supported lords who went down to defeat in one of those ancient battles. And then the memory that exile was of our own unworthiness was fostered upon us. As there was a treaty we were allowed our time of grace to apply at the Gate—and it was opened to us.

"That war which sent us riding into the waste is long since done and gone. There are new rulers in Arvon. But also were forces loosed then which are neither truly good nor ill, but which can be molded for the service of either. These can be commanded by the Riders working together—"

"Rulers!" I interrupted him. "Herrel, is there no law which runs in Arvon? Can one appeal to no overlord for justice?"

He shook his head. "The Riders are without the law, and you are also an outsider. We have taken no oath-service. They cannot deny us Arvon, for that is our birthright and the terms of the treaty have been fulfilled. In time the Riders will take service, with some one of the Seven Lords. Now no man can move against them as long as their targets are of their own company—me—

and you, an alien from the Dales. There is nothing for us save what lies here—" he spread out his hands, "or here." He tapped his forehead.

Out of his saddlebags Herrel brought food and we ate. For a little that revived me and I walked along the stream feeling strength and life rise in me. So I believed that Herrel could not be sure they were draining me to build their Gillan the stronger.

"Have you no kin here, Herrel?" I asked. "You could not always have been a Rider. Were you never a child with a home, mother, father, perhaps brothern?"

He had put aside the cat-crested helm, was kneeling by the brook laving his face with water in his cupped hands.

"Kin? Oh, yes, I suppose I have kin—if time and change have spared them. You have set finger on my difference, Gillan. Just as you are not Dale brood, but were fostered so, I am not wholly Were strain. My mother was of the House of Car Do Prawn—their hall lies to the north—or did. She fell under the love spell of a Rider and came to him across the hills. Her father paid sword ransom to take her back, and I do not know whether that was by her will or no. When she came to childbed her son was accepted as of her blood. Then, when I was very young—I shape-changed—perhaps I was angered, or frightened—but it made my inheritance plain to read—I was Rider rather than Redmantle. So they sent me to the Gray Towers. But still was I half blood and so not truly of the Riders either. Thus my father in time liked me as little as did those of Car Do Prawn. On this day I can claim no aid from Redmantle clans."

"But your mother—"

He shrugged and shook the water drops from his hand. "Her name I know— the Lady Eldris—and that is all. As for my father," he stood up, his face averted from me, "he was—is—among those who have set this ill upon us. It has humbled his pride that he has only a half-son."

"Herrel—" I came to him, put my hand into his. And when he would not tighten the grasp then did I, but still he kept his face turned from me, and I did not try to do more than I had done.

"Well and well," I said at last. "Since we have naught but ourselves, then that must do—" But my words were far lighter than my thoughts and did nothing to dampen my growing fear.

Herrel whistled to the stallion and the horse trotted to him. He put on saddle and bridle and then looked to me, his eyes remote, withdrawn.

"It is time to ride."

We returned to the road. Now it wound through steadily rising dale hills. At last I broke the silence between us to ask:

"You spoke of the Gray Towers. Are they the home of the Riders? Do they return there now?"

"Yes. And it is needful we reach them before they enter the Towers. In the open we have a small chance. To follow them into the Towers is hopeless folly, for there the very stones are steeped in sorcery they can draw upon for aid."

"How far?"

"We are perhaps half a day behind them. They may send on the women, wait for us—"

"Send on the women! If they send Gillan—"

"Yes!" His interruption and the tone of his voice was enough. I had put into words one of his own sharp fears.

"Herrel, can I will myself into the Gillan and so somehow delay them?"

"No! They will be watching her with great care. They would know and when they did—then they would have what they want. This time they would not drive you forth, they would bind you—to become the Gillan they wish."

There was movement behind a bush some paces ahead. I noted the horse's ears a-prick.

"Herrel!" I hardly breathed that.

"I see," his whispered answer was faint. "This may be their first move. Hold well your seat."

Though Herrel gave no signal I could detect, the horse quickened pace. We came even with the bush. There reared out of it such a creature as might have sprung from some legend. Not furred, but scaled, still also in its body shape like unto a giant wolf thing, with a kind of mane of stiffened spines across its head and down its shoulders. At the same time it reached for us, horse and riders, Herrel kicked out, striking aside its taloned paw. The thing squalled.

Scales melted into skin. Now I saw not a reptilian monster but a small brown creature a third its size raising a head which was a travesty of human with eyes in it which held no intelligence, only brute anger and ferocity. It was worse in a way than the illusion it—or others—had used to clothe it. I cried out, but I did not move in the saddle.

Herrel flailed down at the thing, using his sword flat bladed to beat, rather then edged to cut. It crouched back, slavering its rage. He shouted words which frightened it more than his blows, and it scuttled back into the bush.

"Wait." Herrel slipped from the horse. Sword in hand, he went towards the brush in which the brown thing had vanished. Just before this bolt hole he drove the sword point down into the earth and rested his two hands upon its hilt, right overlapping left as he spoke again in that other tongue, this time singsonging the words until they made the pattern of a chant. Having so done, he pulled free his sword and, using the tip as a writing tool, he drew symbols in the dust of the road behind us and along both sides for a space of several feet.

"What was it?" I asked as he returned to me.

"A wenzal. One alone is no great danger. But where one sniffs, more follow, and in a pack they are no foe to be smiled upon."

"Those marks—" I pointed to those he had traced in the dust.

"To murk our trail. That scout will seek out his kind. They will up the hunt."

"Are they of those whom you spoke—neither good nor ill, but able tool to either?"

I heard him laugh. "You listen well, my lady. No, the wenzal is wholly ill, but it is also cowardly, and it can be routed by knowing the right weapon with which to face it. Usually it comes not down from its high places. Mayhap it was intended for a guardian thing, made to be a lock upon our borders. If so, it was marred in the making, for it turns against all comers."

"Then it might be here only by chance—" I ventured.

Again I heard his laughter, but this time with less amusement in it. "This far from the border? No, the wenzal is not that great a traveler. And, as I said, it is a coward, keeping well away from Arvon's core lands. If a pack runs here now, they have been summoned."

"They must know that you have a defense against them—"

"Against one wenzal, or even five perhaps—against a full pack that is another matter. These creatures gain courage from numbers and their rage feeds in proportion to their company. When that rage reaches a certain point, then they care for nothing—save the overwhelming of the enemy. And stopping them at that moment is far beyond a single sword or any small sorcery I possess."

"There is also this," he added as he took up the reins once again. "Each small delay works to the Riders' favor." Then he fell silent. Perhaps he strove to see with the mind's eyes what new plague they could send upon us. But I had other thoughts.

As I had the day before I began to try to break the illusion, searching the ground before us. And so I was rewarded by marking a mist-walled keep backed against the dale hillside. But try as I would, I could not deepen nor darken its outlines. It would not become solid in my sight. That worried me, for I guessed that my Power was lessening. Was it true that the other Gillan grew the stronger on what she drew from me?

"Herrel," I broke the silence. "When we come to that other"—I would not allow myself to say 'if'—"then what happens? How do two become one again?"

He did not answer at once.

"How?" I demanded with more heat. "Can it ever be so? Or is that one truth you have decided to spare me?"

"It can be so, but as to the doing, that I am not sure. It may be that, once face-to-face, you will be drawn to one another as a magnet reaches for iron.

I only am sure of this, apart there is grave danger which increases every moment. And because they have *her*, you are the one under most threat."

"If I only knew more!" Once again I knew that old frustration. "To be half-witch—that is to be already half-defeated!"

"Do I not know—" he answered out of his own bitterness. "Hold this in mind—they strive to make you less than half. Had we but time we would ride to the Fane of Neave, but that is half the land away and there is not that much time left us."

"Who is this Neave that he or she has Power you may look to?"

"Neave is—no, I cannot put name, a single name, to Neave. The wind blows, the rain falls, the earth is fertile and brings forth fruit—and behind that fruitfulness stands that which is Neave. Man seeks maid and she does not deny him, bearing other fruit in turn, and Neave is there also. Neave works not against the natural order of things, but with them. The beginning of life, its natural ending, is Neave's. War sorcery, evil sorcery done for ill purposes—cannot exist in the Fane of Neave; only that which nourishes and abides. I could not enter that fane—but you could and perhaps be safe—though of that I am not sure."

"But you are not evil!"

"I am Were—and so against the true course of nature. My kind may not ride in the deep dark, but we go overshadowed through our lives. Our sun has many clouds."

"I hazard you call upon Neave—in the night—"

I could feel the sudden tension of his body through those encircling arms.

"At such times men call upon each and every Power they may know. But I am not Neave's leigeman. I would not be accepted."

So I had been led away from the question he could not answer, whether I might ever be whole again, even if I met face-to-face that Gillan Halse wooed. It was another fear I must keep at bay by thinking only of the here and now and not of that which lay yet to come.

"You have no plan, except to overtake them?"

"I have a plan, if by nightfall we reach a certain stage on this journey. But only a plan of shadow—not yet of any substance."

I did not press him. Instead I watched for more habitations in the hills and thought that, in the afternoon, I saw a second ghostly collection of walls and roofs. Only this time my second vision was even fainter.

We came to where the road split again about one of those earth mounds. This bore a single pillar at its center and Herrel drew rein beside it.

"Off with you and up." He helped me to dismount. "Swear you will remain at that pillar's foot until I come again. That is a place of safety for you."

I caught at his sleeve. "Where do you go?"

"To find that which I must have to aid us this night. But remember—at the pillar foot you are safe. These are spell encircled and only that which is harmless and of good meaning can so abide."

I obeyed, climbing to the top of that earthen platform. Again that weakness was upon me, and the effort I expended left me spent, willing to drop at the foot of the pillar. Herrel had left the road and rode along the land. Now and then he dismounted to look at what seemed to me to be the protruding roots of long-buried trees, where soil had washed away to show the gnarled wood. Perhaps this had once been a forested place, but the trees still growing were small of girth and widely scattered. These, too, he studied, but from the saddle. And at last it was under one that he set to digging with his sword. He hacked at what he had uncovered, and then gathered up a bundle of what he had unearthed and cut up. Bearing this before him, he rode back to me.

At the forefront of the mound he dumped his harvest and I could see they were indeed roots or parts of roots, crumbling with age but with yet a core of hardness. Three times he dug, hacked, and brought that ancient wood, until he had a pile of pieces which, with care, he built into a conical heap. This done, he climbed to join me, bringing the saddlebags with food and the bottle he had filled from brook water.

"What do you with that?" I gestured to the woodpile.

"That will at least reveal the nature of the peril which may creep upon us at moon rise. I think Halse will force the issue. He has never counted patience among any small store of virtues he possesses. But we do not need to watch until dark closes in. Sleep now if you can, Gillan. The night may be long and without rest for us when it comes."

XV
Herrel's Challenge

*A*fter a long space I spoke. "There is no sleep this night for me, Herrel. Tell me what you would do. To be warned by scout horn is to have shield on arm before the foes arrive."

His head turned. Though the upper part of his face was shadowed by his helm, I could see his mouth and chin. He smiled.

"Well do you speak in the terms of war and battle, Gillan. You are a shield mate and sword companion as good as any man could wish. This then is what I would do—I wait not their will, their choice of the hour and field for battle— I summon them to mine! At moonrise I shall set fire to that root heap there— and they will be drawn—"

"More sorcery?"

Now he laughed. "More sorcery. It is laid upon us that our true nature is revealed and we are drawn to flames which dance from wood as old as we.

A thousand dale years—even so long a span of time would not suffice to hold a Were from answer if you found a tree of his age. I do not think they will expect me to challenge them even this far. They will believe I shall be content to leave well enough alone—live so on some scrap of hope. For if I summon them thus, then I must be prepared to meet them with full Power and array—"

"And you believe this possible?" I could not stifle that question. I must have his reply.

"Fortune will rule the field this night, Gillan. I do not know what shape they will wear, but if I can name Halse, throw him sword challenge, then they must allow me that right. So can I bargain—"

So many chances and so little assurance that any would be the right ones. But Herrel knew the Pack and this land. He would not choose so reckless a course unless he saw no other way. I could find no protest which was right and proper for me to offer.

"Herrel, it was to me that they did this thing—have I no right of challenge in my turn?"

He had drawn his sword, and it rested across his knee. Now he ran one fingertip down the blade from hilt to point. After a long moment he raised that weapon and held it out, hilt first, to me.

"There is a custom—but it puts a heavy burden on you—"

"Tell me!"

"If you can give a shape-changer his name in the firelight, then he must take man's form again. Whereupon you may demand blood right from him and name me your champion. But if you speak the wrong name to him whom you so challenge, then you are his to claim."

"What difference might my success mean?"

"It would give *you* the right to set the stakes—that other Gillan. If I challenge there is an equal chance they could deem this Pack quarrel only, with no stakes other than life or disgrace."

"Do you think I might not name Halse? He is a bear."

"The beasts you have seen are not the only shapes we may take upon occasion, only those which are the most familiar. And at such a test as this he would not show as bear."

"But you could warn me—"

Herrel was already shaking his head. "That I could not, by word, or gesture, or even by thought! The naming would be only yours and on you the burden of its success or failure. If you stand out before them, holding this sword, then you will be the challenger."

"I have the true sight. Have I not proved that?"

"How well does it serve you now?" he countered.

I remembered the mist-halls I had seen in the afternoon and my feeling that the Power ebbed.

"This afternoon—I tried to see—" I was not really aware I had spoken that aloud, but Herrel drew the sword out of my reach.

"It is too great a risk. I shall challenge by Pack right and bargain as I can—"

He sounded decisive but still my mind played with what he had told me, and I leaned back against the pillar, running my hands along its age-pitted stone. My sight, if I could but regain that illusion-breaking sight only for the few moments needed for the naming of true names! Up and down the stone my fingers moved, around and around in my mind thoughts spun, seeking some solution. There were herbs in my simple bag which cleared the head, sharpened the senses—as well as those which cured wounds and illnesses. My bandaged arm moved now without pain. Surely there must be some way to strengthen my inner Power for as long as was necessary. If I only *knew!*

"Herrel—the healer's bag, please fetch it."

To expend even so much effort as to hunt for it would endanger what I would try.

"What—?"

"Bring it hither! How long have we before they come?"

He moved slowly, gazing at me over his shoulder as if he would have out of my mind what I planned. But he brought the bag and laid it in my lap.

"I do not know. I light the fire at moonrise—then we wait."

But that would not do—I must have a better idea of time. My fingers released the latching of the bag. I searched within for a small bottle cut and hollowed from a prism of quartz.

"What do you plan?"

I opened my fingers. Even in this shadow light the prism seemed to glow.

"Have you ever heard of moly, my lord?"

His breath caught in a half gasp. "Where got you that?"

"From an herb garden. Dame Alousan used it. Not because she would work sorcery, but because it has the power to soothe those who have come under the ill-looking of witchery. Though I do not remember that she used it save twice since witchery is not practiced in the Dales. The last time," I smiled, "was for a man-at-arms who claimed he had been ill-looked by a Were Rider, and so lay with no life in his limbs. Whether it was only an illness born of his fear, or true sorcery, I do not know. But he walked again after he had a few drops of this in his ale for three days. However, it has by legend another property. It can break illusion."

"But you do not know who will come—or which to try it on—"

"That is not needful. It is my illusions which I must break. But I dare not use it too soon. And neither do I know how long it takes these drops to work. If I choose the time wrongly I may be either clear-sighted too soon, or too late. Therefore if you can give me warning—"

"It is a great risk—"

"All we strive to do this night is by chance, good or ill. Herrel, will not this be better?"

"And if you fail?"

"To see ever the cloud and not the sun is to woefully and willingly blind oneself. But can you give me warning—?"

"This much. I can tell you that they come before I sight them. For I, too, will experience the drawing, and will know how strong it grows."

With that I must be content. But as I enfolded the prism in my sweat-dampened palm, I knew how small a warning I must depend upon.

"Herrel, till the moon rises, tell me of this Arvon of yours. Not as it threatens us now, but as it might be."

And he told me—unrolling his country before me, with its strange people, its grandeur and might, its dark places. To everyone the hills and plains of their homeland have a beauty and color beyond the rest of the world. More is this the truth when one has been in exile. But still the Arvon which came alive to me in Herrel's words was a country fair beyond the sparsely inhabited, war-torn Dales of High Hallack, and like unto a nation—time-set and sunk, that is true—yet mighty.

Though they all, those who dwelt in Arvon, shared in some use of magic and that which cannot be weighed or measured and of which only the results may be seen, yet that varied in degree and kind. There were adepts who dwelt apart, wrapt in their studies of other times and worlds which touched ours only momentarily at intervals, and who were now scarcely even of human seeming. On the other hand the people of the manors, the four clans, Redmantle, Goldmantle, Bluemantle, Silvermantle, worked sorcery very little, and, save for their very long lives, they were close akin to humankind. Between those two extremes ranged a number of alien folk—the Were Riders, those who tended the Fanes of personified Powers and Forces, a race which lived in rivers and lakes, one which chose not to be too far parted from woods and forests, and some that were wholly animal in form, yet with an intelligence which set them apart from any animal the outer world knew.

"It would appear," I said, "that there are so many marvels in this Arvon of yours one could ride forever, looking, listening, and still never come to the end of them!"

"As I have come to the end of this telling?" Herrel got to his feet and slid down the mound to the side of the piled tree roots. Then I saw that a silver moon was rising. He touched sword point into the heart of the wood and a small green spark broke from the meeting of steel and wood.

They did not leap, those flames, rather did the wood smolder contrarily, as if it had no wish to be summoned from ancient sleep, to die in ashes. Thrice did Herrel thrust with his sword, each time the point going more deeply into the pile. Then flames did crawl reluctantly to the air and there arose a smoke which thinned into a gray-white column.

I closed my hand so tightly upon the prism which held the distilled moly that the edges of the crystal cut into my flesh. Already I had loosed the stopper, but I kept my thumb upon it, making sure I would spill none.

Herrel raised his head high. His eyes were glittering green, shadows swept across his face, and vanished, only to return. But the alien shape did not take possession of him as he stood there, naked sword bright in his hand. At last he turned his head and spoke to me. His speech was no longer quite human words, but I understood.

"They are drawn—"

I stood up, away from the pillar. He did not move to aid me down from the mound, it was as if he were held prisoner there. But I came to him and held out my right hand, the left still grasping tight the prism.

"Your sword, champion."

Herrel moved stiffly, as one who fought some force, to hand me that blade. So we waited by the fire. The moon lighted the road, but nothing moved along it that I could see. After a while Herrel spoke again—sounding as if he stood afar from me and not within touching distance.

"They are coming."

How near, how far? When must I put on such armor as a few drops of golden liquid would give me? I thumbed the stopper out; held the prism to my lips.

"They are swift—"

I drank. It was acrid on my tongue, unpleasant. I swallowed quickly. The road was no longer empty. Beast and bird did not lope or fly as I had expected, in spite of Herrel's warning, but a multitude of shapes, ever changing—A mounted warrior who dropped to be a belly-crawling thing out of nightmare. A scaled dragon who rose to be a man, but one with wings upon his shoulders and the face of a demon. Ever changing—I realized I had been overconfident. How could I find Halse in all this throng mocking me with their disguises? If the moly did not aid my undersight then, indeed, were we defeated before we ever did battle. I strove to fasten upon one figure, any figure in that weaving of dissolving and reassembling forms. And then—

From the hand which gripped the hilt of Herrel's sword sprang runnels of blue fire, dripping down the blade. And I saw—

There was a web of changing forms, behind which was a company of manlike beings, concentrating upon holding the sorcery screen they had wrought.

"I challenge you!" Though I knew not the words of custom, I spoke those which came naturally.

"All or one?"

Did that buzz in my ears, formed by no man-voice? Or was it only a thought answer which came so to me?

"One, letting all rest upon that."

"And what is 'all?' "

"My other self, sorcerers!"

Grimly I held to the undersight. Halse, yes, I had found Halse—to the fore and left of where I stood.

"Do you name names, witch?"

"I name names."

"Agreed."

"Agreed in all?" I pressed.

"In all."

"Then," I pointed with the sword to Halse, "do I name among you Halse!"

There was a greater weaving of their shadow disguises, a rippling—Then it vanished and we stood facing men.

"You have named a name rightly," Hyron stood forth. "How do you challenge now?"

"Not mine this challenge. It is another's right, all resting upon it." My hand slid from hilt to blade. I passed the sword to Herrel so that his fingers could grasp the hilt and he took it from me eagerly.

"So be it!" Hyron spoke as if he pronounced a doom, and clearly he meant that doom to rest upon us and not those in his company. "Pack custom?" That he asked of Herrel.

"Pack custom."

Men moved swiftly. Hyron took the cloak from his shoulders, laid its glossy horsehide lining down upon the pavement of the road, its dun gray surface uppermost. Harl and three of the others doffed their helms, set one on each corner of the cloak, their crests facing inward.

Some feet beyond the edge of the cloak men set up four swords, points wedged well to hold them upright, and other cloaks, rolled rope fashion, were laid to connect each, forming a square.

Halse put aside his cloak and the baldric of his sword. He stepped now onto Hyron's cloak and Herrel moved to face him. Halse smiled as I had seen him do and hated him for—as one who has only to stretch out his hand to take what he wants, no one saying him nay.

"So she has more Power than we thought, Wrong-hand. But she has made her mistake now—in choosing a sword and you to wield it."

Herrel did not answer, and there was no expression on his face. Rather did he watch Hyron who had moved into the center of the cloak between the two fighters.

"This is the field. You will match swords until blood flows, or one or the other of you be driven over the battle line. By moving so only one foot, it will be deemed he who does so had fled—and full right yielded to the other." Then he turned his head and looked to me. "Should your champion lose, then you are fully subject to us. And what we wish shall be done."

I knew what he meant—they would give the remainder of my life to their false Gillan. So did he lay the greater burden of more fear on me. But I hoped that he could not read that in my face, and I tried to make my voice steady and cool as I answered:

"When your champion goes down to defeat, my lord, then you shall render freely to me what you have stolen. That is our bargain."

Though I had not made that a question, he replied: "That is our bargain. Now—" in his hand he held a scarf and this he flashed up and down in the air, leaping away from the cloak and its guardian square.

I am no warrior who knows the proper use of the blade, each nicety of thrust and parry, the art of sword mastery. And I had thought, after the brush with the Hounds, that the Riders went to war as beasts who needed no such schooling. But it would seem that though they used claw and fang, they also knew steel.

They circled, ever watching, now and then thrusting as if to try the enemy's skill or strength. And I remembered a bit of war knowledge which I had heard at the Abbey-stead table when kin of the refugee ladies came a-visiting—that it was always best to watch a man's eyes rather than his weapon—

The slow beginning erupted in a flurry of blows aimed and parried, a wild dancing to the clash of steel meeting steel. Then, retreating, they once more circled. Whether Herrel was accounting himself well, I did not know. But no blood flowed and, although he had put one foot off the cloak, he had beat his way back with speed.

For a short time was I so dazzled by that murderous play that I did not sense what else was going on. Perhaps it was the power of the moly which awakened that other acute sense in me. Halse willed his sword hand on the cloak, and so did Herrel. But outside there was a uniting of wills. Perhaps that ill wishing could not reach and weaken Herrel physically and prepare him for the finishing stroke, but it hung as a fog working for his defeat. And, if he were sensitive enough—A man's belief in himself can be delicately poised. All his life Herrel had thought himself less than whole. His anger, our need had worked upon him to refute that. But should seeds of doubt begin to grow—!

I had used my will as a tool—to see—to hold the guard in the hall, to fight the Hounds, to carry me to Arvon. Now I strove to make of it a buckler against the desire of the Pack. And because I had my own fears, this was a thing nearly beyond my doing.

My undersight was failing. Monsters ringed in that fight. I saw not two men with swords in hand, I saw a bear reared upon hind feet, reaching great furry arms to catch and crush a cat which snarled and wove about it.

"You—"

So sharp was that demand for my attention that I jerked my eyes from the fight to look at him who so hailed me. A stallion—a man—a monster stretching forth great crabclaws to my hurt.

"Hyron," I named a name and saw a man.

—You cannot win, witch, having chosen a half-one for your service—

The Captain of the Riders was turning his whip of defeat now to my beating, his thoughts thrusting at me as those swords thrust and cut on the cloak field.

—I have chosen the best among you!—Confidence, and I must feel that as well as give lip, or thought, service to it.—This is a man!—

—A man is not a Rider. He fronts those who are more than men—

—Or less—I retorted.

—You fool! Look upon your hand which had held the sword. In the moonlight my fingers were pale, thin, with an odd transparency about them. And swiftly Hyron gave me what he hoped would be the death blow to my aid for Herrel.

—You waste. Each time you use your Power now, witch, you waste. She grows the stronger! You will be shadow soon; she all substance. And what then will any victory here avail you?—

Even as he spoke I felt that draining weakness. Shadow, yes, my hand had a shadow look—

No! They were tricking me, drawing my attention away from the fighters! Herrel was being driven back, he was close, too close, to the cloak rope. If Halse could not wound him, perhaps he wished to give his enemy the greater shame of breaking the square. Herrel's face was set, he was a man still fighting dogged against some inevitable defeat.

—No!—I tried to reach him, build up the wall of strength and confidence. And now there gnawed at me the belief that Hyron had spoke the truth, that my very efforts to support Herrel were death to me. I was trembling; the ground reeled under me. I must let go—keep what I had left.

My hands—they were thinner, whiter. Do not look upon my hands! Watch Herrel, fight the fog of defeat the Pack had raised. Herrel—shadow hands— Herrel—Herrel!

It cost so much to break their united desire—and I was no longer sure I could.

—Fool, you fade—

—Herrel, you can—you can defeat the bear! Herrel!—

There was a mist between me and the men, or did cat and bear still circle on the cloak? I stood, blind, holding to what small strength I still had.

There came a shout—cries—or were those animal growls, screams of bird, neighing of a horse?

I rubbed my hands across my eyes, strove to see—A cat crouched with switching tail, fangs bared. Facing it still a bear, but one of the clawed hind paws was beyond the roping—Halse must be counted fled!

They were men again, all of them, drawing together, ranged against Herrel still. But that wave of defeat they had woven was gone as if torn away by a rising wind. Herrel raised his sword—pointed the tip to Halse.

"He is fled!" His voice rang loudly, a sharp demand in it.

"He is fled," Hyron returned somberly.

"A bargain is a bargain, we claim all—"

When Hyron did not reply, Herrel strode forward a step or two.

"We claim all!" he repeated. "Does Pack law no longer hold? I do not believe you will nay-say our right."

Still the Captain made no answer. Nor did the others. Herrel went the closer. His eyes were green fire in his face, but he was all man, not cat.

"Why do you not keep your bargain, Hyron? We spoke for all, you promised it on our winning—"

"I cannot give it to you."

Herrel was silent for a long moment, as if he could not believe he had heard aright.

"Dare you name yourself honor-broke then, Captain of Riders?" His voice was softer, but in it an ice of deadly anger, the more perilous because of the control he held over it.

"I cannot render unto you what I do not have."

"You do not have? What has become then of the Gillan you wrought through your Powers?"

"Look," Hyron inclined his head in my direction. Herrel turned his flaming eyes upon me. "The tie is broke; that which we summoned is gone."

Tie is broke—I swayed. Where was it, that cold which had led me out of the wilderness into this land? It was gone, I felt it no more—I was adrift. Then I heard laughter, low, evil, gloating—

"She has only herself to blame," Halse said. "She would use her Power. Now it has destroyed her. Nourish your bride while you yet can, Herrel. She is a shadow bride, soon to be not even shadow!"

"What have you done?" Herrel sprang then past Hyron to seize upon Halse. His hands closed about the other's throat, he bore him back to the ground. While I watched as one in a dream, far less real a dream than those they had pushed me into, the men struggled.

They dragged Herrel from his enemy, and held him in spite of his efforts to come at Halse, who lay gasping on the ground. Then Hyron spoke:

"We have played as true as we can. But the tie is broke, that other one is gone—"

"Where?"

"Where we cannot follow. She was wrought in another world, she returned there when the tie holding her here was broke."

"You brought her to life. Upon you lies the burden of returning her—or go honor-broke." Herrel shook off their hold. He spoke to Hyron but he came to me. "I asked all, Gillan asked all and you gave oath on that. Now, redeem your oath! Gillan!" He reached me, his arms were about me but I could not feel his touch. I strove to raise my hands—they were thin, transparent. No tie—I was tired, so tired, and empty—never to be filled now—never—

XVI
The Ashen World

*A*nother world—" Herrel repeated. "So be it! You have the key to its gate, Hyron. Turn it now or take the name of oath-breaker on you." He swung around, giving eye to all of them. "Oath-breakers—all of you!"

"You do not know what for you ask," the Pack Captain said.

"I know very well what I ask—that you make good the bargain. You send us—"

"Us?" repeated Hyron. "She perhaps," he nodded to me, "since she has been there before, has survived what lies there. But for you—you have not the Power—"

As a cat might stalk, Herrel moved upon his leader. I could not see his face, but his whole body displayed his determination of purpose.

"I am beginning to know that I am more than you allowed me to be, Hyron. And the need is now more than life. You shall send us both and—No, I will not ask of you for myself. That I have never done. But this I demand for Gillan: you shall sustain her to the limit of that much vaunted Power of yours. Since yours was this ill-doing, so must you aid in the undoing."

Hyron stared back at him, almost as if he could not believe he had heard aright. There was a stir and murmur among the other Riders, but Herrel spared them no glance. His attention was only for their leader.

"We cannot do it here and now," Hyron answered.

"Then where and when?" Herrel demanded.

"At the Towers—"

"The Towers!" Herrel was plainly unbelieving. "You wrought this deed in a wilderness which was far from the Towers, why now must you have them about you to undo it—at least to open the other world to the twain of us?"

"You have asked for our full aid for her after she passes through—I am not even sure we can give that. But we must have our own anchorage—or mayhap we be all swallowed up and lost."

"It is a long ride yet to the Towers. Look upon her. Do you think that time is any friend to her? It is rather her enemy."

To me that argument was a dim, far-off thing which had no meaning save words poured into my ears. I was so tired. Why would they not ride away, leave me to sleep? Yes—how good was sleep—to melt into the dark and know nothing—

"Gillan!" I must have gone a little way into that dark, for Herrel was again holding me, and somehow the force of his arms about me was a barrier against my drifting into the waiting dark. Also warning stirred in me.

"Herrel?"

"Gillan, look—think—We must ride, and you must hold to life—this life—hold!"

Hold? To life? A cord—but the cord had snapped, was gone from me. To rest . . . let me rest . . . I was so tired, so very tired.

"Gillan! See—look about you!"

Sunlight? But it had been night and there lay a cloak where two men—or beasts—had fought. A vial was pressed against my lips, a voice urged me to swallow. Feebly I obeyed and then for a short time the mists were gone. We were riding, I held in Herrel's arms, at a pace which was close to a full gallop. Cloaks streamed out from the shoulders of those about us. And it was day.

"Hold—" Herrel gazed on me as if by his eyes, the mind behind them, he could bring me under obedience to that order, "Hold!"

And that will of his coupled with the cordial he had made me drink, did keep me awake. But I saw all about me as if I passed through a dream which concerned me not. Herrel talked, as if by his voice he could hold me. I heard his words but they made no pictures in my mind.

"—Towers and then they shall send us forth and we shall quest for that other. In that world where she was made, perhaps you shall find her soon and your uniting will be the easier—"

Other? What other? But questions only confused one, better not to think of them. I lay passive, watching rising hills about us, green-gold-green. There was a melting, every changing aspect to this land which I dimly remembered—or its like. Once there had been green walls or broken walls which had flowed, trembled, formed and re-formed in a like manner. Nothing was stable, though I could feel those arms, steady as mountain-rooted stone about me.

The sunlight was gone—gray—all the world was now gray. And that flowing of landscape was performed by shadows melting one into another. Once I thought I heard shouting, and those who rode about us were gone for a space, though Herrel's horse never faltered in that ground-eating stride.

"Gillan!"

It was all a dream—a soft dream.

I was no longer on horseback, I lay on a bed or couch. No, I stood apart and looked down upon one who lay upon a couch, one who was very pale and thin and wasted seeming. And beside her lay another, straight and lithe, well muscled, for his mail and leather had been taken from him. But he was not wasted, nor did he sleep, and the words he spoke reached me as the thin whispers of wind teased leaves.

"Do as you will for our swift passing."

Smoke arose about that bed place, whirling, whirling, whirling, billowing out and the smoke touched me, wreathed about me, caught me into it so I, too, whirled, drifted, and was a part of it.

A wind within the smoke, impelling me ahead of it as if I had no more weight or substance than a leaf or petal—driving me onward through this unseeingness—this place of specters—

Specters? My mind, if I still possessed a mind, clung to that word—specter.

Shadows in the smoke, things which were rooted, for I passed them, they did not float with me. And they became darker, more real—a gnarled trunk, crooked branches up flung against a hidden sky. Uneasiness grew—sometime—sometime, long ago—I had seen their like and they carried a threat of danger—evil. What danger? What evil?

I willed, I reached, I caught at one of those branches, and so stayed my flight within the smoke-mist. Under my fingers that wood, if wood it could be, had a dry, dusty feel, as if dead and falling into rot.

Still the smoke drifted by and I could see only what I held to. There was no sound at all. For a space I held to my anchorage. Then I loosed my grip, was once more pulled forward in the mist, passing other branches, other trees, seeing no purpose in lingering by them.

There was—there was something I must find. It was not a tree, nor anchorage. But I must find it—yes, yes, I must find it! A raging need for that filled me, as if I had drunk it out of a cup—was a fever in me.

What did I seek, and where? Please, I must know—I *must* find out!

I—I must find Gillan. And who was Gillan? Witch, a whisper in the fog? Maid—bride—Gillan—I tried to open my lips and call that name, but no voice was granted me. Suddenly the fog about me thinned, the charred dead trees stood out of it, to ring me in a forest glade.

Gillan—

There was gray-white ash on the ground and it was trackless. There were no guides to turn me this way or that. Where did one seek Gillan in this alien world?

White-gray skeleton leaves upon the trees, and silence—a brooding silence. Yet still I listened, eagerly—or fearfully—I was not certain which.

—Gillan—My will sent that call questing out, though my lips did not shape the name.—Gillan, where?—

No answer, but I began to walk forward, down that aisle of trees, always the same.

—Gillan!—

On and on. To this always-the-same forest there was no end. On and on and on—no end—no answer. Nor was there any change in the wan light, no rising nor setting sun, or moon, no darkening, no lighting—always the same. So I might not have walked forward but stood in the same place. Still move I did, through those endless rows of trees.

—Gillan?—

Now that hunger which drove me was fed by uneasiness. What lay behind? I turned now and again to look back. All I saw was the silent forest, no movement. But—no longer was I alone among those trees—something had been attracted by the mere stir of my passing, was awake, padding to see what disturbed its world. And with it came fear.

I wanted to run, but I knew that running would bring it the quicker on my trail. So I must walk as always, hunting that to which there was no clue, while behind came something hunting—*me!*

—Gillan?—

I had grown so used to the unanswering silence that I was startled when this time there came an answer—or was it but a troubling of the atmosphere, a stirring? But to me it was an answer—and it lay to my right, so I turned aside from the way I had been going. But as I hurried, I knew that same troubling had alerted that which followed me. Now it was more than curious. It was aroused to a hunter's hunger and cunning.

The trees were growing taller, thicker of girth, as if now I headed into the heart of this forest. As they towered so the light was less, I walked in gloom wherein each darker shadow could hold that which was prudent to fear.

—Gillan?—

Again that answer. This time I could not mistake that it was an answer and that she I sought was somewhere ahead of me.

Now I must round trees whose trunks were like small towers of men's building, and among them were other growths, tall plumes of ashy gray, like skeletons of ferns. These fell into thick powder when one brushed against them, leaving on the air a faint trace of the odor of very ancient corruption.

But long dead as this world seemed to me, it had its own life, was home to creatures which were not of my species. I saw a many-legged thing of dull yellow flash into a fern bed. And there was something so malignant in even that small glimpse I had, that I detoured well around the spot where it had vanished, and thereafter watched the forest floor with care.

That which hunted—it was no longer alone! Others of its kind had joined it. I tried to control the panic which wished to rush me on at a blundering run through the forest, unheeding of my going. As yet, though, it seemed content to keep its distance.

—Gillan?—

The answer far sharper, clearer! Close—she must be very close. If only I did not have to weave in and out among these monstrous trees—

Among the brittle ferns began to appear great fan-shaped growths which gave forth a yellowish glow as if they were carved of phosphorescent putrescence—for they had the look of rottenness frozen before it lapsed into slime. These were so unclean in seeming I tried to keep well away from any contact with them.

Finally there were no more ferns, only the stinking fans, as the odor, faint at first, grew stronger with their numbers. And it was very hard to find a path among them. Some grew horizontally from the trunks of trees, vast ledges of corruption.

—Gillan?—

Surely by the answer she was just ahead! I picked my way along a corridor between noisome, shoulder-high barriers of the fans and came out abruptly on the border of a lake. Or was water ever so black and still? Still? A bubble arose, broke on its surface and I swayed as the fetid gas it had released stung my nostrils, choked me.

—Gillan?—

Had I only thought I had had an answer? I stood on the border of the lake, could see around its rim—the fans, the dark trunks of more trees—but there was no one there. And my last call brought only silence. A trick—a trap? I tried to listen with that sense which was not the hearing of the normal world, but here served in its stead—listening for what slunk behind. It was there—no closer—perhaps it had also halted for a space.

Again the water was troubled, but this time twin bubbles arose, an even space between them. Those were no bubbles, but eyes!—eyes regarding me, drawing—drawing—

No!

I trembled, drawn forward by the willing of those eyes, rooted by my own sense of preservation. I must not be swallowed up in that mere, go to meet the death behind those eyes. There was Gillan—I must find Gillan! And the thought of her snapped the spell those eyes had thrown upon me, so I could move, not into the water as they willed, but along the shore.

For a time those eyes paralleled me and I could feel the grasp and pull of the will behind them, tearing at my resolve, trying to force me to turn, look into them—obey—until at last I made each step with the effort of one climbing a mountain cliff, but I made it.

How long did it take me to round the end of the lake, dogged by the eyes? There was no time in this land, only purpose, need and hunger and my own hunger gave me strength to pull away, I turned my back upon the turgid waters and went on into the wood once more. Had that monstrous lake dweller picked up my call and used it to draw me?

—Gillan?—

—Here!—

Another deception, trap baiting? I could not be sure, nor could I not answer. Through the patches of fans, under trees once more—on and on—Those others, the hunters, they came too, still well behind, but coming.

—Gillan?—

—Here—

Fans gave way to ferns, trees grew smaller in girth—was I coming to the other side of the forest? A winged thing planed down, squatting in my way, looking up at me. Bird? How could one equate that name for a warm, feathered, singing thing with this small horror of loose, leathery skin, naked wattled head, a head three-quarters rapacious beak?

It continued to squat there though I walked towards it, turning its huge beaked head from side to side as if to better view me one eye at a time. Then it flapped its wings, ran to meet me in a rapid scuttle. I started back against a tree trunk, and it paused as if startled and perplexed by my action. For a long moment we were so, confronting one another.

—Gillan!—

I stared at that grotesque parody of a bird. That name had come from this monster of the specter forest. Now its clawed feet moved in the dust; it sidled towards me. I flung out a hand to ward the horror off. Trap—this creature, others—they could pick up my call—use it to confuse and entrap me. There was no Gillan—not here—never to be found—never!

Now I ran from the bird, from that place where the truth had faced me. And behind the lurkers at last made up their minds, they fastened to the chase, began to track me in earnest.

The bird did not leave me—if flapped over my head, would alight ahead to wait, each time beaming into my whirling mind its false call:

—Gillan!

Once it strove to get between my feet, as if to trip me, but a last sidewise leap saved me. I waited for it to fly at my head—perhaps strike at my eyes. But at least I was spared that. Only it did not leave me, any more than those padding hunters strayed from my back trail.

There was more space between the trees now, wider areas in which were twisted clumps of grass edged with small sawteeth. And beyond, an open country completely covered because here hung again a smoky mist, and that closed about me as I left the forest, so, glancing back a little later, I could no longer see trees, only a wall of smoke-fog.

Though I was out of the forest, I was not free of the bird. It no longer tried to impede me on the ground, but circled over my head. And once more my control grew stronger, the full force of fear ebbed.

Gillan—who was Gillan? Why—*I* was Gillan! I halted in the sea of grass. I hunted Gillan, yet also was I Gillan. How could that be? Memory, very faint and far away, stirred. Once there had been one Gillan, and then two. Now I must search for the second, that two might be one again. The bird named me Gillan and Gillan I was. Therefore in so much the bird had been true and not false.

I looked up at the circling winged thing. Painfully I shaped a question in my mind.

"Who—are—you?"

It flapped those wings vigorously, circled me more swiftly.

—Come—Come!—

Was it trying to draw me on for its own desires as that thing in the lake had toiled to bring me to its maw? I hesitated—the grass plain was an ocean of unknown ways. I might wander in its mist-curtained hold a long time. Perhaps any guide who would take me through it was to be followed. Another trap—maybe—but I had no stir of uneasiness when I looked again to the bird.

I did not form my acquiescence into any real reply, but the bird now winged away, into the mist. Yet back it came into sight each time I thought it lost. And so we went across that endless plain. Nothing broke the eternal grass, and we saw no other moving things.

—Gillan?—

Once or twice I sent out my silent call to that other who was also me. But now came no answer. Nor did the bird speak again in my mind.

Coming from the forest had not deterred those hunters at my back. I believe that they did hesitate for a space before they ventured out into the open, away from the territory which was their native ground. But that hunger, which was as strong within them as mine was within me, brought them out. And it was when I sensed that that the bird returned to circle my head.

—Hurry—hurry!—

The mist was an envelope which appeared to move as I moved, setting up a barrier against my sight some small distance away, yet never enclosing me. For there was always a clear space about my body and I was ever able to see the path I followed for several good lengths ahead. The bird flew in and out of that fog, always coming back.

It seemed to me that the ground now sloped down, on a slant from the first level of the plain. The grass still grew high, but not as thickly as it had earlier, thinning now and again to patches of open bare ground. And this was not firm, but more like mud underfoot. The bird lit on the edge of one such place, pacing back and forth there as I approached. When I would have passed, it barred my way—standing to its full height, beating its wings as a man might wave off a fellow from some danger.

—Why?—I asked of it.

—Danger!—

It did not take to the air again, but waddled in an ungainly fashion to my left, making passage from one stand of grass to the next in fluttering hops, waiting and watching while I trod in its wake. The patches of ground it so laboriously avoided were smooth surfaced and larger. My foot dislodged a rough clod with grass ends and struck it into one of those patches. It was sucked down as if puckered lips of earth had inhaled it in a breath.

Our pace was now a crawl as the bird was slow and heavy in its earthbound advance. Behind the chase was up, no more loitering along the way for the pleasure of the hunt itself. Those who coursed me were anxious to have the chase finished, to make their kill and return to their specter wood.

—They come!—

I tried to reach what mind or intelligence lay in the flapping creature leading me from one precarious foothold to the next in this treacherous land.

It fluttered faster, made a last leap, springing into the air with beating wings. Before me was a wide stretch of the too-smooth ground, and then a grass-grown strip promising safety. Still, without wings, I doubted my own ability to cross that trap.

A snuffling—the first real sound I had heard in this nightmare world, from behind me. I must leap that stretch ahead—there was no going back—The bird circled, its urging ringing in my head.

—You must!—

Must? How? How did one perform the impossible? To desire a thing! no matter how strongly—to desire a thing! Will—desire—potent, very potent. Potent enough to bring me to safety now? I had no other help or defense except what might lie within myself.

I tensed, drew upon will—any reserve of will which my body might hold. I forgot the other Gillan, narrowed the whole world to that patch of ground and the necessity of reaching its far side. Then I jumped.

A sprawling fall, my hands grabbing at grass. But about one ankle a sharp closing, a grinding pain as if great teeth gnawed at flesh and attempted to reach hidden bone. I pulled against that hold, straining with not only physical strength, but that of will. There was a reluctant loosing. I pulled, fought, lay at last on the grass, free of that which had held me. When I looked at my foot I saw a pallid ring, very pale to show against my white flesh, and the foot below that was gray, very cold and clammy to the touch. I could stand, but there was little feeling in it and I went forward at a hobble.

—On!—

My winged guide did not need to urge that. But if my spirit was ready to fly at a speed matching its, my body needs must go slower. Luckily we appeared to have reached a place of solid footing, free of more sucker pools.

—Gillan?—

I clung to a tough strand of the grass, weaving my fingers into it for support. An answer! Not from the bird overhead—not this time. From ahead—To be believed?

Yes! In me a leaping, a straining forward, such as I had not known before— a pull so much a part of me that now I could not turn from that trail, even if I had so wished.

—Gillan!—

I stumbled away from my grasses, wavered on. And it was some time before I realized that I was now alone, that the bird which had brought me out of the forest no longer held its position as my traveling companion. But there was no need—I had now a surer, stronger guide—

The hunters padded behind. Again I caught uncertainty, hesitation from them. Then in my mind and not my hearing—a shriek—a death cry of something which had known life—at least as much as those of this world knew it. And following that a burst of such hate as was like a fire flame licking out to sear and destroy.

I began to run, my numb foot unsteady under me—but still I ran—grass about me, mist beyond. Somewhere Gillan waited and behind me a pack of hunters raged. Once more the ground began to rise from the bottom which held the pools of sucking earth. I stumbled so often that I had, at last, to grasp at the grass, pull myself up and on by those holds.

So intent was I on holding my speed that I must have been running for some time between those blocks before I knew that my path was narrowing and walled. In, in. Higher the walls, more shadowed the way. Behind came death, and before me was what I sought—and now that hungered seeking was greater in me than the fear of what loped behind.

XVII
Who Is Gillan?

J came to a place which was walled, yet open to the sky. It was filled with a pale yellowish light which acted to conceal rather than reveal what might walk there. And just within the entrance I halted to peer ahead.

"Gillan?" For the first time my lips moved, my throat produced sound.

And the sound there, in that place, was shattering, breaking some age-old bond. So I needs must set my hands over my ears in protest against the echoes

I awakened. For that name came back to me distorted, made into an alien thing which was not mine.

They came in answer, moving through the light, one, two—more of them until they stood in an unending line, stretching back into obscurity. A hundred mirrors, repeating a reflection a hundred times—and each entirely like its companions.

A slender body, white of skin, bearing above her ribs the faint mark of the Hound sword, on her arm the sign of beast fangs, both healing or healed. Dark hair sweeping from an upheld head—I saw myself, but not just once—again and again and again!

And they all made answer, speaking in myriad voices, but still the one and same:

"I am here."

I had been two, now it would seem I was a troop! That which made Gillan had splintered, broken, been cast to the winds, never to be united again. So I stood, watching that company, the hunger in me raging unsatisfied. For I did not know any spell or sorcery which would draw that oft-splintered Gillan back to me.

It seemed to me that they watched me at first blankly, as bodies which moved without souls or minds. And then there grew in those eyes a cold hostility to me. I had no guide, the words which came to me were unthought—a protest—

"We are one!"

"We are many," they denied me.

"We are one!" I held to that, as if with that very statement I could make it fact.

The line stirred, their heads turned from me, they were beginning to return into the light—they were going! I moved forward, seized upon the nearest Gillan, held her fast with what strength I had in me. It was as if I had fastened my fingers about polished stone, cold, lifeless, inimical to the flesh which touched it. She looked at me then, that Gillan I held, standing without attempting to throw off my hold, but as if she were a dumb thing obedient to aught which would force its will upon her.

I do not know what I expected then—that she might flow into me, be a small answer to my hunger. Nothing happened, save that she alone of that company stood fast.

"That is not Gillan."

Words, again shattering the air of that enclosure. I loosed my grip in my surprise, looked around to he who spoke.

A shadow? No, that figure had more substance than shadow. However, it was dark, visible only in that darkness and in the two sparks of green which were near its top—eyes? The silhouette it made against the wall flowed and changed as I watched. Sometimes a man stood there, again it was beast or monster.

"There are but two real Gillans," it spoke in a hissing whisper, "you and she whom you seek. And that is the one you must find."

"But—" I looked back to the company. She whom I had held was still to be seen, fading back into the light in wake of those who had gone before.

"She is hidden, one among the many," the shadow told me.

"And how will I know her—the right one?"

"By the Power in you, if you use it aright."

"How."

"That is your own mystery, Gillan. But time grows short. If you linger here, you will be lost, just one more among the many—"

I could not depend upon that tie, that hunger which had led me here. It was as if it fastened me only to this place and not to any of the Gillans. But now— I swung once more to the shadow by the Gate and the Gate—for the hunters were here! Those which had trailed me from the forest had come.

And the shadow knew that. I saw the turn of his head, the sparks of his eyes vanished. The silhouette changed, was now that of a crouching cat—a cat?

Through the gate scuttled a many-legged thing—part spider, part something out of no world any human knew, larger than a mountain hound. It drew its legs in under it as if crouching to spring. But the cat shadow struck out at it with a large paw and the thing moved with surprising speed to avoid that blow.

"Find—Gillan. I will hold the Gate—" came the whisper from the shadow and the echoing sibilance appeared to daunt the spider foe, surprising it.

So I went on into the light, leaving the shadow embattled at the Gate, in search of one who was hidden among many, yet not knowing what would be the result of such a finding, if I were able to do so.

I closed my eyes against the dazzle of the light, tried to open instead my mind, to sharpen and hone the desire that was in me to assuage my hunger. My Power, the shadow had said. Well enough, this was the only way I had yet learned to use it—as a weapon and a defense. So would I employ it now, a weapon against puzzlement, a defense against my emptiness.

Thus did I stand unmoving, spinning out my Power in quest, hunting, searching for a spark of truth among the false. It meant that I must shut out all else, my fear of the hunters, the sounds of battle from behind, my own failing strength—all but the quest for Gillan.

I was no longer a body walking on two legs, swinging two arms, reaching two hands for grasping of what I would take. I was only desire, disembodied, a wraith—I did not see, nor feel, nor think—

Then—I was Gillan! The other Gillan. Curled into her, filling her emptiness! But—my triumph was a quick dying spark—I was not whole. I had found my Gillan true enough among the company wandering in that wilderness of light, now I must return her to the Gillan from which I had fled.

Once more I moved through the confusing radiance. Muted sounds—the fighting by the Gate. The Gillan who had been me had stood near there—I must use sound to guide me. But this body obeyed me clumsily. It needed vast effort to set one foot before the other, as if now I inhabited a semblance of Gillan which could be moved only by concentration on each and every muscle in turn. Thus I stumped back towards the sound.

My awkwardly moved foot touched against something on the ground. I tottered and fell—to lie beside Gillan. She was not cold stone under my fumbling fingers, but flesh, chill flesh. Her eyes were open, but there was no sight in them, no breath filled her lungs. She was—dead!

I think I cried out then as I clumsily gathered the other into my stiffly moving arms so we lay together as might lovers, the dead and that which should never have been wrought at all.

So they had won in the end, had the Were Riders. My mind stirred with memories. There was only one of me, the one who was biddable to their plans, But—that was not true! This was me—the real me! They had not won—yet—

I stared down into that dead face. Now I was in exile. I would never be complete until I returned to my proper dwelling which was this body I held in my arms. But how? Witch they had named me—a witch who knew not her craft.

Gillan! For the first time the two Gillans were together, locked body to body. How had this begun—with one Gillan left behind, struck by an arrow, lying under a tree in this world, and the other taken away by the beasts. Beasts! That promise Herrel had wrung from Hyron—that the Riders must aid me—

If they would fulfill it now!

In my mind I summoned a picture of Hyron—as a man, not as a raging stallion which was his shape-change. And upon that man I concentrated my pleading.

Was it Hyron's thoughts reaching mind—or some scrap of witch lore answering my need? Death and life—they were the opposite in this world, Gillan had died here afore time, to give birth to Gillan—this Gillan in whom I now dwelt. Therefore, this Gillan must die so that that other could live again. But how? I had no weapon to hand—did not know whether I would have the courage to use it if I did—for what I guessed might not be the truth.

—Hyron—give me death.—

There came no answer. But there was death in this place. And it did not only lie in my arms. It was like a creeping, seeping tide, spreading from the

Gateway. No longer did I hear the muted sounds of attack and defense from there. That shadow which had stood to bar the Gate and win me time—the shadow with green eyes, and a cat shape for battle—

—Herrel?—

My thought reached out. As it had to find the other Gillan, so now did I try to touch the defender.

—Herrel?—

A reply, faint. But—Herrel could grant me that death which was life. I began to crawl to the Gate, dragging with me that other Gillan. It was a journey of exhausting trial, for my new body was so stiff and clumsy, reacted so poorly to my will that the burden was doubly hard to carry.

—Herrel?—

This time even more faint the answer. I crawled out of the thick of the light into the space before the gate. The spider things lay there, one still kicking convulsively. And the shadow who had fought to buy me time was huddled against the wall, drawn in upon itself as if to nurse a gaping wound, while ringing it were other shadows and these I knew—the masters of the spider hounds—those twittering things which haunted the ashen forest.

I kneeled by the body which I had brought forth from the light. Herrel had slain the hounds he still held their masters at bay, but he was hurt. I gazed upon that scene, and remembered, and in me grew an anger such as I had never known before, I who had schooled my emotion through inborn need for control. Had I had the Power with which all credited me I would have loosed it in that instant to cleanse the ground of this foul crew.

Anger could strengthen, could rid the mind of shadows and doubts—or so I found it at that instant. I opened myself to anger, held no barriers against it. Then I was out among that Pack tormenting what they dared not face in open battle. I do not know whether I struck them with my fists, beat upon them—or whether that great and glorious rage made of me a torch of force, which withered them as they stood. But they reeled from my path, and I drove them before me out of the Gate as one might drive timid woodland things by the mere force of one's steps upon a forest path.

Surprise was my ally, but they might return. And Herrel—the other Gillan—time indeed had threaded sand too far through the glass for us. United—did I have a chance to serve us both better?

But when I came back against the wall, green eyes upon me.

"You—are—not—she—" his whisper was very faint.

"I am the other one—" I began.

He winced.

"You are hurt—" I would have gone to him but he waved me off with a sharp gesture.

"Where is she?"

"There—" I pointed to the body I had brought out of the light.

He wavered away from the wall, his form unstable, now a man falling on his knees beside that silent form, now an animal on all fours.

"She is dead!" His whisper was harsher, louder.

"For a space. Listen, Herrel, to make this Gillan I now wear they slew me—in this world. Therefore, should I be now slain, it must follow that I live again—in that body—"

I do not think that he understood or even heard me. So I came to stand above that body and then he raised his head, his eyes blazing—and in them a rage like unto that which had made of me a force only moments earlier. He was not a cat now, but man, still there was a beast's unminding ferocity in his eyes. He struck up and out at me, shadow sword in shadow hand.

Pain through me—such pain as was an agony to tear me apart—

Golden light, and in that light I must find Gillan—that other Gillan—but I had found her! was in her—or was I? I sat up from lying on cold ground. A body—white—but it was fading away like mist! Their Gillan—the false one! Then I was whole again—myself!

I hugged my arms across my breasts, holding in what was me. Then I ran my hands down the length of my body, knowing it to be real. No longer was I empty but filled! Filled with all they had stolen from me.

Herrel! I looked around. The shadow whose sword thrust had set me free— No shadow here, no sign it had ever been, save those dead monsters at the Gate.

"Herrel!"

The echoing of my own cry rang deafeningly in my ears. Had he made answer then I would not have heard it. I walked between the dead spider hounds to the gate. If their masters lurked without I did not see them.

—Herrel?—As I had done when I sought the other Gillan, I used the inner calling. But to it came no reply.

Yet I was aware, just as I had been on my first awaking in the ashen forest, that I was, in a manner, still tied to this ghost world. And that which tied me so was Herrel. Must I go seeking him as I had my other self?

I had not closed my eyes, nor sought for any inner vision at that moment. But before me was a shadow horse. He struck out with a forefoot, not at me, but as if to part some curtain for a clearer meeting.

—Come—

The word was an imperative command. But I did not obey it.

—Herrel?—I made that both question and refusal.

The maned head tossed high in impatience. But he gave me no answer and I demanded in turn:

—Where is he?—

—Fled.—

—Fled? That I did not believe. He who had held the Gate against the monster, who had bought me time to his own hurt, and who had swordbought my deliverance. Why should he flee?

Hyron must have read my thought for he answered it.

—He flees from that deed he did here.—

—But he freed me! He could have served me no better—

—Who is Gillan?—The question seemed meaningless.

—I am Gillan!—Of that I had no doubts.

—To him Gillan lies dead, by his hand.—

—No!—So plain was it all to me that I could not readily believe Herrel had not also seen the truth.

—Yes. Come, we cannot long hold open the way between the worlds.—

—And Herrel?—

Again the stallion tossed his head.—He chose to tread this road, knowing well the danger. Upon him be his own fate—

"No!" This time I spoke aloud, sending echoes buzzing. "No, and no, and no! Herrel comes forth."

—You also choose your path, witch—

—You are oath-bound to aid us.—

—There comes an end to all oaths. You have now your other self, as Herrel won it for you. Even our united strength cannot hold this opening long. Come back to life, or go into nothingness in time and space.—

He had given me the choice. *I* was not oath-bound to any course. Save that I knew this, in this moment I could not take the steps which would win me safety, that there was that in me which refused what I could not share. I eyed the shadowy Hyron as I answered:

—Hold as you can. Mayhap I will also find that which is another part of Gillan, or her life, as I did not know it until now.—

Now the shadow horse stood still, and those golden eyes which were the most alive part of him studied me.

—Your choice, witch. Do not ask for a second one.—

—Knowing you, I do not—I retorted, and in me again stirred that anger which had sent me at the sulking things.

Hyron's shadow form flickered, was gone. I stood where I was. With that other Gillan I had had a bond, so deep a bond, to guide me. With Herrel— what did link me to Herrel? A sense of gratitude, of shared danger, of dependence (as much as I had ever depended upon another)? None of those were deep enough to form a leading tie.

Hyron had asked me—who is Gillan? And I had answered him out of triumph, pride and knowledge—*I* am Gillan. But only because Herrel's sword had made it so could I say that.

Now I must ask myself—who is Herrel—what is he—to me?

I thought of our first meeting in the bridal dell when he had come to me in the mist because I had chosen his cloak out of those lying on the velvet sward. Taller than I, very slender, a boy's smooth face, holding eyes as old as the hills of High Hallack—that was the first Herrel. Then the feline, lying in relaxed slumber on a moonlit bed, awaking to the peril of sorcery as a net spread about us both—the second Herrel. Again the cat, crouched, eager for battle, sliding down and away to hunt those of Alizon—and he who had returned in man-form from that fight to stand with me against the anger of the Were Riders.

Another Herrel who had wooed me, to whom I did not yield, and a Herrel who had sprung at me in blood-lust. The Herrel I had seen appealing to forces and powers for my healing while the Werefires blazed about me and I lay covered with a blanket of flowers. A Herrel who had ridden with me through the day, who had waited for moonrise, telling me of his land and his loneliness—

A Herrel who was shadow fighting embodied evil to win me time—and who thought he had slain a shadow because reality lay dead—

Who is Herrel—all these and more. That was the truth stripped of all illusion, that of his people, that of my own pride. Who is Herrel? He is another part of me, as Gillan was a part. And without him, do I go bereft and lacking all my days!

Thus—as I sought Gillan—yes! This was the right way, the only way! As I sought the Gillan sorcery had made, so must I seek the Herrel which had made himself a thing which could walk this land. Again I put forth my quest call—

I came out from the Gate of that place of yellow light. Must I return to the ghost-wood? Or plunge farther into this world without sun or moon, change in time?

—Herrel?—

No answer, but a sense of drawing, of that I was sure. Not back to the wood, forward, bending on it all my powers of concentration.

Something scuttled in the rocks before me. A master with more spider hounds baying on Herrel's trail? That trail, so faint for me, might be plain for their sniffing. Still it must be mine also, if I would win to my desire.

If this world did not have a night and day according to the pattern I had always known, it would seem it had changes in weather of a sort. There was a wind rising about me, but, I noted, it blew neither hot nor cold, merely as a wind which brushed my body, tugged at my hair. And I stopped to pull that to the back of my head, fastened it there with a length of grass plucked from a tussock. That mist which had dogged my path across the bog-valley and the plain withdrew, or else the wind tattered it into nothingness.

I was on a hillside, and ahead climbed other hills, up to massive mountains which were a threatening purple against a sky never plain to see. Around the heads of the mountains crackled swords and spears of lightning fire and there was a rumbling—to be felt rather than heard.

The storm, if storm this was, had not yet hit the hills about me. I climbed among the rocks, which were broken and twisted, taking on all manner of evil shapes, suggesting they hid greater horrors, lurking to spring, rend and tear. I reached the top of the rise. Still that thread, thin as any spider's weaving, led me on. I looked down into a dusky dip. There was a trickle of liquid running there and from it arose hazy smoke, while it was as dull red as dying coals.

Along its bank a figure moved. It did not walk straight, but wove a staggering path from side to side, sometimes falling, but ever pulling up again to struggle on.

"Herrel!" Hunters to be roused or no, I cried that aloud, throwing myself at the down slope.

The stumbling one halted, but he did not turn. Then he went on at a hobbling run, reaching out to grab at holds to pull himself along. I lost my footing and fell, rolling down to come up against an earth-embedded rock. I put my hand to my spinning head, blinked at stones and earth which were no longer steady.

"Sssssss—"

The thing had scrambled to the top of a boulder facing me, hunkered there, slavering so that the spittle dripped thickly from its almost lipless mouth. Lipless that mouth might be, but it was well equipped with pointed fangs. Above was a slit which must serve it for nose, and then very large eyes, lacking pupils, flat and dull. But that they could well see me I did not doubt.

Its skull was round and hairless, the ears slits like unto its nose. But the worse was its monstrous resemblance to man—though no man could be as this horror. With skeleton fingers to its mouth it produced a kind of whistling, very high and shrill, hurting my ears. And it was answered. I was hemmed in by the hunters I had driven from Herrel. But that they would flee a second time from anger—that was too much to hope. Nor could I summon that superhuman rage to serve me.

"Herrel!" The moment that cry left my lips I repented it. What magic could he summon to our salvation? I would merely draw him back into the worst of traps.

The thing on the rock turned its head from side to side. It sat on all fours like an animal, raising one hand now and then to its mouth. Slowly I got to my feet, waiting for it to spring. Another round head came into view, a third, a fourth—How soon would they pull me down? I stopped and caught up a stone. They carried no weapons I could see, and perhaps I could give some account of myself. At the same time all that was sane in me, all the heritage of my own world, shuddered at the thought of any close contact with these nightmare things. The first of the creatures lifted its head high, opened wide its jaws and squalled.

Pride is a great deceiver. We who choose to walk apart from our fellows wear it, not as a cloak, but as an enshelling armor. I who had asked nothing from my fellows—or thought I asked nothing—in that moment I was stripped of a pride which broke and fell from me, leaving me naked and alone. I faced not death as I knew it, as I had felt it in this world, but something infinitely beyond human death, which we have been told is in reality a beginning. From this there would be no issue save a blackness it is not given my kind to face with a mind untouched by madness.

Perhaps madness did possess me now. I think I shrieked, that I called upon gods whose names had no power here, that I cried aloud for any help which might be given me. I do not know this for truth, but I think it is so.

And help came then, stumbling, weaving, but still on his feet, sword ready. Even as I struck with that stone which was my only weapon, so did Herrel come, shadow still, but alive, able to answer my plea.

Of that fighting in the rocky, stream cut valley I remember but little. I do not want to remember parts of it. But the end—that I shall always hold in memory—he who stood between two rocks, pushing me into safety behind him. His sword was a live thing, and from that blade those things flinched and cringed. Though they strove, they could not pull him down. Until at last the survivors fled and left us.

"Who are you?" Herrel held to the rock as if he dared not trust his own strength to stand erect. "Who are you?" He held up his hand, from his wrist dangled his sword by a cord. His fingers moved, slowly, painfully as if this were some effort almost past his making, and in the air he drew a symbol.

Fire, blue, so bright that my eyes were dazzled. But I called out trying to put the truth that was into my voice:

"I am Gillan. Truly, Herrel, I am Gillan!"

XVIII
The Last Gate of All

*H*e did not come to me, rather he sank to his knees, one arm thrown across a rock to support him. But his green eyes were on me, though his face was still more shadow than true substance.

"I slew—"

"You united!" I threw myself down beside him. "That other Gillan, she had to die that we might be whole again—whole! By your sword I am!"

Herrel bowed his head upon his outflung arm and I could no longer see those eyes which were the most living part of him. I put forth my hand and touched that which was not firm flesh—rather a yielding, changing stuff.

"Herrel!" I saw him as a shadow, but I had expected to touch a man. And this struck new fear into me.

Now he did raise his head again, look at me.

"I am—far spread—Go—back—Hyron—" The words came with long pauses between them.

"No! Herrel—!"

But his head had fallen forward again and he did not answer my call. In me stirred again that anger, and with it my will. I got to my feet and this time I did not plead in my summoning, I demanded:

"Hyron!"

The rolling echoes of that name boomed about the walls of that unknown valley, appeared to join with the vibrations set off by the mountain storm. But could it reach from one world to another?

"Hyron!" For the second time I voiced that demand.

A shimmering—a change in the air—behind it shadows moved—

—Come!—Very faint.

"Herrel!" I stopped, strove to draw up that collapsed shadow. But it was as if I scooped running sand in my two hands, there was nothing substantial in him for my fingers to grip upon. "Herrel!"

I glanced up. That troubling in the air, it was already subsiding—perhaps we had only seconds.

"Herrel!" Once more I tried to arouse him—to no purpose.

And when I looked again—that shimmering which marked the Gate between the worlds was gone. I covered my face with my hands, dull despair warring with my will, Hyron had warned me that they could not hold the Gate—or was it rather would not—for long. Now they had let it close—we were trapped in this nightmare other existence.

Once more I knelt beside Herrel. Was he dead or dying as this world knew those terms, or sore hurt where I could give him no real tending? Why did he wear this shadow form when my body was real and solid? Or did it merely seem so to me, and he saw *me* as a shadow? If so—then to himself he was real also—A fleeting scrap of memory touched me—that bed on which we twain had lain when we were sent on this perilous venture—had our bodies continued to lie there while we had put on other forms in this alien country?

—Herrel?—I could not touch him, bandage his hurts, give him any small comfort.

Or could I?

I had found that other Gillan, sent out that which had entered into her. But that had been because she was a part of me. I could not enter so into Herrel.

Maybe not myself, my mind worked on, but could a portion of my will, a desire for life, be so shared with another? It was so small a hope, but now my only one.

I leaned my head on the arms I had folded across my knees. In my mind I fastened upon Herrel—as I had seen him—not on our first meeting, or on other occasion, but at what I knew was a moment when some Power had touched us both, when he had stood at the moonlit, silvered pillar and called upon forces known to him in my behalf. And that Herrel I held in my mind—intent on seeing him and not the shadow man beside me.

This was like feeling one's way along a dark corridor where a danger one could not see stalked, and there were many sideways in which one could be lost. I tried to make of my will a visible thing, of substance—to reach, touch, be one with the Herrel I held in mind, blotting out all else.

He stood there, his bared shoulders silvered as the pillar was silvered. I could smell the sweet scent of the flowers—I could hear his voice chanting in the tongue I did not know, uttering words that I did—he called upon Neave—

Neave! I made of that name an anchor point for my will. Neave—Herrel—and I concentrated the force of my desire on the man who had stood in the moonlight.

—Gillan?—

Perhaps that had been several times repeated before it reached me, locked in concentration as I was.

—Gillan?—

I turned the head still pillowed on my arms, opened my eyes, the shadow beside me had also raised his head, the green eyes were open, watching me.

—Herrel! You are alive?—

—After a fashion, but what do you here? The Gate—He sat up straight.— They could not hold the Gate so long.—

—So Hyron said—I answered without thinking.

Again those sparks of eyes swung to mine.—Hyron! He told you, but then, why have you not gone?—

I did not answer. A shadow hand balled into a shadow fist, struck down on the surface of a rock.

—Why did you not go? Leave you me no pride at all, Gillan?—

I was startled, and then saw that his way might not be my way after all. That I had delivered hurt where I meant healing. And I made the only answer I had left me:

—Matters being in all ways reversed, would you have done so?—

A shadow face shows no expression for reading, and I could see no feeling in his eyes. There was a period of silence between us until I dared to break it:

—This gate being closed, where is one we may open?—Not that I expected he could name me any such, but that I might turn his thoughts from within to without himself.

—I know of none. Hyron misled you if he suggested that such might be.—

—Hyron gave me nothing but warnings. But this is the third time I have walked this land. The other two times I believed that I dreamed. And from dreams there is waking.—

—Dreams?—Again he moved and this time with more vigor. His hand went to his middle as if exploring some hurt with caution.—Gillan—I—my wound, I no longer bleed! I can move—He pulled to his feet, stood away from the rock which had been his support.—I am whole again! What sorcery have you worked, my lady witch?—

—I do not know, truly, I do not. This only—And I told him of my try with will and Power.

—Neave! You called upon Neave, and now you speak of dreams. Dreams—

He reached down his hand as if to draw me up beside him. I felt a wisp of mist wreath about me, but with no force. Herrel recoiled.

"What is this?" he whispered aloud.

"To me you are shadow," I told him hastily.

He held his hand up before his eyes as if to reassure himself. "But this is solid! Flesh—bone—"

"To me you are a shadow," I repeated.

"Dreams!" Once more he struck the rock surface with his fist. "If we now share a dreamworld—"

"Then how do we wake?"

"Yes, the waking—"

His tenuous form swung around, he stared about him as if to locate in the valley some means for shaking us out of nightmare slumber.

"What do you remember of this world, tell me all of it!"

Why he wished me to retrace in memory I did not know, but I obeyed his order, spoke of the forest, the coming of the bird—

"Bird?" Herrel halted me at that point, demanded a description of the bird. And then said:

"So in that much they kept their oath. That was a guide sent by the Pack. Where did this bird lead you?"

I told him of the passage through the bog, the coming to the place of light where I had found him and the company of Gillans.

"Yes, that was where I awoke, in that place of light, seeing them pass back and forth through it, and knowing that only one was the right one, and only you could find her. But none of this gives us any clue to the Gate or our awakening—"

"Do we have a key left us?" The muttering of the storm in those mountains grew louder. There was a kind of menace building up about us which broke through my concentration, as if the alien world was gathering its forces to deal with what we represented, an irritation foreign to it.

"I do not know. But while we can move—and think—then perhaps we still have a chance. I wonder—" I saw his head turn again as he surveyed that narrow valley. "That place of light is undoubtedly a place of power. And so might well be where we could find answers—"

"The times I awoke here were in the woods—" I suggested. Though to cross the bog land without a guide was a journey I did not relish.

"Then you dreamed under their command, awoke by it," Herrel's husky whisper continued. "If we are to go forth from there now it will be by *our* wills, united. And I believe that Power, no matter from what source, can be drawn upon in times of need—"

"But what if the Power is evil, a danger to our kind?"

"I do not think that the place of light is either good or evil. We entered therein, the creatures of this world hunting us entered. It took no part in our battle, either for one side or the other. We were apart from it, left to our own concerns. Tell me, how did you drive the hound masters forth—that I did not understand—"

"By my anger—I think," I made answer, but I was considering what he had said. That force of anger, so strong, carrying all before it—never before in my life had I been so possessed. Had that emotion been fired, fuel fed, by some Power within the enclosure? Could Herrel be right in his guess that what abided there could be tapped to aid us?

I had said there was no change from day to night in this haunted world. But around us now it grew darker. Either the storm was reaching out from the mountains, or else there was a night coming I had not seen before. We made our way dimly back up the slope to the higher land where stood the enclosure.

Within the light still swirled and around the Gate lay small white heaps. Herrel stirred one with the point of his dusky sword, cleaned bones collapsed and rolled, remains of the hounds. But of that which had feasted on the losers, or of its nature, we had no clue.

We had come here, but what must we do now? I turned to Herrel with that question, and it seemed to me that his shadow self was even thinner.

"What do we?"

"It becomes a matter of walking an unknown road, trailing across never-charted mountains, my lady witch. In my mind it is that we two still lie in the Gray Towers, that we dream there—so stand within these walls. Unless we can wake, we are lost forever. For the deeper the dream, the less able will our bodies be to escape it. As for how to wake—well, we must try different ways—"

"What ways?" His confidence seemed overly bright to me who had no trace of plan moving within my mind.

"What brought you to that other Gillan, then led you to me?" He counterquestioned. "What led you to summon me from what was death in this world?"

"I thought, I centered my will—on Gillan—on you—"

Herrel looked into the light. "If we *do* have bodies left in our own world and time, then they anchor us in part there. Perhaps if we strive to be reunited with those bodies, we shall find them. I see no other path for us."

"But—I have no clear picture to fasten upon—" And I did not—that glimpse of Herrel lying in the room which might have been in the Gray Towers—that was too fleeting a thing to serve me.

"I have!" He seemed possessed now by a rising belief in himself, as if, instead of being daunted by our plight, he was stimulated to greater efforts.

"Now listen—" He laid his hand on my arm, and I felt his touch only as I might the passing of a feather across my flesh. "This is as I saw it last—before I came here—"

He told me in detail of that tower room, of the divan on which we had lain side by side, of small things which had been imprinted in his memory in such vivid pictures that he must have rested there with greatly heightened senses before he had gone forth on this strange journey. And such was his telling that he made me see it, too, bit by bit, piece by piece, as if before my very eyes he was setting up figures and furnishings.

"Do you see, Gillan?" For the first time a note of anxiety crept into his whispers.

"You have made me see."

"If I have only done so aright!"

"And now?"

"And now we do what you have done before, we fasten our wills on this—" he paused. "I am counted but a half-man among them, since my Power does not always serve me as I will. So, mayhap I put now to the test a flawed blade. But that I cannot know until I use it. Let us go!"

I closed my eyes upon the light, upon Herrel. For this time him, too, I must shut away. He had his battle and I had mine, to the same end, yet we must fight it singly. I brought to mind that room Herrel had pictured for me—there were the windows—two—one looking north, one south, between them walls covered with tapestries so old their patterns had long since been lost, save for a hint of face here, a trace of a beast's gleaming eyes there. Braziers and from them smoke, aromatic smoke. And in the center of that chamber the divan. On it lay Gillan, Gillan whose face had shown a hundred times, a thousand times from mirrors when I looked therein, Gillan who bore the scars of wounds which had pained me. That was Gillan, the Gillan I must seek and find.

And I centered upon that Gillan, not only the body which slept, but the nature of that which wandered afar from it in dreams. Who is Gillan? No, rather what is Gillan? She is this and this, and she is also that. Some parts of her could I welcome, others I would shun if I could. For this was a measuring and an inner seeing of Gillan such as I had never known and it made me writhe for a nakedness beyond all stripping I have believed could exist. Almost did I wish to escape the awakening of that Gillan who had such small meannesses, such ill within her.

Who is Gillan? I am Gillan, in this way was I fashioned, by nature, by the will of others, by my own desires. And with this Gillan am I united for good or ill, therefore I must pick up the burden of being Gillan and—awake!

But did I wake? I was afraid to open my eyes, lest I see again the light of the alien world. Until at last I had to force myself—

I looked up at gray stone, very old. I turned my head and saw tapestries also faded by the years. I was awake!

Herrel! Swiftly I turned my head in the other direction to see him who must share his couch with me. Empty!

I sat up, reached forth my hand to that emptiness, to prove to myself that my eyes were the deceivers, not that he was gone. And then I saw the hand I put forth and I was stricken motionless.

The people of Arvon in that village—they had been shimmers of light in my eyes, so now was this hand of mine. Swiftly I pressed it down upon the fabric covering of the divan—fingers—palm—my full weight—But there was no impression!

From my hand I looked to my body. No body—merely a mist through which I could see the surface whereon I rested. Then Herrel had been wrong—we had not had bodies to focus upon left here—to draw us back to our right world!

There was a shimmer—No, I had not moved—it formed beyond me, at the other side of the divan—Herrel?

I tried to call his name. There was no answer from my throat and lips. Why should there be—I no longer possessed throat or lips! I was not Gillan for all my willing.

That shimmer which lay in Herrel's place moved. He must be sitting up.

—Herrel?—I tried to reach him by that other way as we had sometimes spoken together in the specter world.—What has happened?—

The bar of light stood upright by the divan.

—I think—I think—Slowly, painfully words came to me (and what *was* me?)—that they believed us dead. Our bodies have been moved elsewhere.—

Had I had then the power I would have shrieked aloud. If he spoke the truth what would now become of us?

—Come—

—Where?—

He had already moved to the door, that light which was now Herrel and no man.

—To find what we seek.—

We were back in the familiar world where there was night and day and, suitable to our state as wraiths, it was now night. These Gray Towers must be very old, old and steeped in a life afar from the Dales. It was in all I looked upon—that age and difference.

Along a short hall, and then down a stair which wound and wound about the skin of the Tower, Herrel led and I followed. I heard no sound, saw no one move. Slumber must have claimed those who abided here. And for a fleeting moment I thought of Kildas, of Solfinna, and that company among whom I had once ridden. Did they look upon these ancient walls as now I did, as a shell which held nothing of warmth or welcome? Or would they abide ever under the spells their Were mates wove, seeing only that which would make them happy and content?

We came out at last in a hallway which was paved and walled with stone. At set intervals on the walls were the carved representations of beasts. It seemed that their eyes measured and surveyed us as we passed, even as I had once been measured and studied by those long-dead kings set up as Guardians on the frontier of Arvon. But of their findings concerning me I could not guess.

On we went into a space which was shadow hidden as to its width or length. At the far end light burned and towards that Herrel sped, I ever behind. Green was that light and it came from the Were flames I had seen before, those which had burned about me on the mound in the road's parting. Here, too, they burned about two who slept on one bed.

Once more I looked upon Gillan, and this was a Gillan in more splendor than I had ever seen her, or arrayed her with my own hands. She wore a robe of pleasant green overworked with silver, and among the twists of that silver 'broidery were set small milky gems, which a net of the same jewels confined her hair. Her hands were crossed on her breast, and she had, I thought, a beauty which had never been hers in life. For now that I looked down upon this sleeper it no longer seemed true that I was Gillan and this was the envelope of flesh and bone fashioned by birth to hold me.

Beside her was Herrel, his helm by his head so that his face was plainly to be seen. He wore mail and between his clasped hands rested the hilt of a bared sword.

—They do me full honor—He who stood beside me spoke soundlessly.— That honor they never granted me—awake.—

—But these, they are dead!—

—Are we? I say nay to that!—

He was so very sure. Yet when I looked upon her lying so, I thought the truth was as I said. And there was not reason to doubt it.

—Gillan!—Sharp as any warning given when an enemy creeps upon a comrade-in-arms who sees him not.—You are she. Think not otherwise or you are lost. Now!—

The shimmer moved up to those who lay there. By what feat of sorcery he wrought the next I never knew. But those upright flames nearest him bent horizontally and over them he swept me with him.

What is death? Twice in the specter land I had tasted it, perhaps in my world this third time. But still I cannot put into words what it is. If I were dead indeed when we so returned to the Towers that night, then death itself was rent asunder by what brought us there.

Gillan was again Gillan, I did not need to open my eyes to know that at long last I was whole. But I did, I raised hands across a firm body finely clad, saw the small moon radiance of the gems I wore as they glistened with my movements.

"Herrel?"

"Yes—"

He put aside his sword to hold out his hands to me, draw me close. So for a moment we were breast to breast, and I met his eager lips with a need as great as his. Then he held me off a little, his eyes searching, but his lips smiling.

"It would seem, my dearest lady, that we comrade together very well in war; now let us try that state in peace."

I laughed softly. "Right willing shall you find me for such purpose, my valiant lord!"

He slipped from the couch and then raised me to stand beside him. The long folds of the fine robe they had put on me fell heavily about my limbs, hampering my feet. I pulled at the cloth impatiently with my left hand, my right being prisoned in his.

"I go very fine," I commented. "Too fine—"

"Beauty deserves beauty." Herrel did not say that lightly and I think my hand trembled a little for his pressure about it tightened.

"Mayhap, but I would go freer!" For suddenly those weightly robes tied me to the past, and that should be gone. I withdrew my hand from his, my fingers sought clasps and ties, and I shed that dragging magnificence, tossing back upon the empty couch its gemmed skirts, standing in the shorter under-robe.

"Shall we go?" His hand once more sought mine.

"Where, my lord?"

He was smiling again. "Now, that I cannot answer you, for in truth I do not know. Save we shall ride away from these Towers and this company to seek our own fortune. Do you nay-say that?"

"No. Choose you a road, my dear lord, and it shall be mine. But you do not take your helm, your sword—"

"Nor this—" one-handedly he unbuckled his belt, tossed to lie with my discarded robe. By the empty pillow still rested his cat-crested helm. "Those I shall not use again." And there was such a note in his voice that I did not question him.

As two who would join some formal dance, Herrel led me by the hand down that long chamber until we came forth by another door into a courtyard where we strode under the stars and the moon. Seven great towers were about us. But nothing there moved as Herrel brought me to a stable wherein were those dun-coated, shadow-spotted horses of the Pack. My mare he brought out and saddled, and his own stallion, and leading them we came once more into the open. Before us was a Gate.

"When we ride out, my lady, we go into the unknown—"

"Have we not traveled other unknowns, dear lord?"

"Just so!" He laughed. "So be it."

"Who goes?"

From the dusky overhang of the gate came one who wore a rearing stallion on his helm, and the moon was bright on the drawn sword in his hand.

"Yes," answered my husband, "who goes, Hyron? Give us names if you know us."

The Captain of the Were Riders looked upon us. If I had expected a sign of amaze or wonder from him, I was to be disappointed.

"So you found the way to return—" he said.

"We found it. And now we pass through another Gate—" Herrel pointed to the portal behind Hyron.

"You are Were blood, these towers are your home."

Herrel shook his head. "I do not know now what I am, for we have been a journey like to change any living thing. But of these towers I am not, nor is Gillan. So we shall go to seek that which we are—for that we must learn."

Hyron was silent for a moment, and then he said in a troubled voice. "You are one of us—"

"No," for the second time Herrel repudiated his half blood.

"You will go to your mother?"

"Do you fear that? You who have chosen not to be my father?" Herrel retorted. "I tell you, I will have none of you, dame or sire. Do you think to hold the Gate against us?"

Hyron stepped aside. "The choice is yours." His tone was now as emotionless as his face. He did not speak again, nor did Herrel as we rode forth. And we did not look back, but Herrel said:

"That, lady wife, was the last Gate between the past and the future. And who we are, what we have now, is but Gillan and Herrel—"

"Which is enough," I made him answer, and so it was.

About the Author

One of the best-loved and most famous science fiction and fantasy authors of all time, Andre Norton was named Grand Master by the Science Fiction Writers of America and was awarded a Life Achievement Award by the World Fantasy Convention. She has written over a hundred novels which have sold millions of copies worldwide, including her Beast Master, Solar Queen, and Time Traders series, among others. She lives in Murfreesboro, Tennessee, where she presides over High Hallack, a writer's resource and retreat. More can be learned at www.andre-norton.org.